Praise for *Shadowfall* . . .

"A compelling tale filled with richly developed characters."
—*Library Journal* (starred review)

"James Clemens once again sets the standard of excellence for fantasy." —*Midwest Book Review*

"A dazzling new entry in the world of epic fantasy. The plot is byzantine in its complexity, the characters are rich and fully realized, and the system of magic . . . is both fascinating and innovative. . . . *Shadowfall* is likely to become a favorite of fantasy lovers worldwide." —SFRevu

. . . and the enthralling fantasy of James Clemens

"Grabs at your heart and tears a little hole, then tears another, and another—a brutal and beautiful ride. I can't put the book down!" —R. A. Salvatore

"I loved every page. Clemens has constructed a world of magic that's never been seen before, with a cast of beings who are so engaging and entrancing that you never want the story to end." —John Saul

"Clemens demonstrates considerable skill at combining swift pacing with character development." —*Library Journal*

"Fresh, sparky details and enough plot convolutions to keep fans coming back for more." —*Kirkus Reviews*

HINTERLAND

BOOK TWO OF THE GODSLAYER CHRONICLES

JAMES CLEMENS

A ROC BOOK

ROC
Published by New American Library, a division of
Penguin Group (USA) Inc., 375 Hudson Street,
New York, New York 10014, USA
Penguin Group (Canada), 90 Eglinton Avenue East, Suite 700, Toronto,
Ontario M4P 2Y3, Canada (a division of Pearson Penguin Canada Inc.)
Penguin Books Ltd., 80 Strand, London WC2R 0RL, England
Penguin Ireland, 25 St. Stephen's Green, Dublin 2,
Ireland (a division of Penguin Books Ltd.)
Penguin Group (Australia), 250 Camberwell Road, Camberwell, Victoria 3124,
Australia (a division of Pearson Australia Group Pty. Ltd.)
Penguin Books India Pvt. Ltd., 11 Community Centre, Panchsheel Park,
New Delhi - 110 017, India
Penguin Group (NZ), 67 Apollo Drive, Rosedale, North Shore 0632,
New Zealand (a division of Pearson New Zealand Ltd.)
Penguin Books (South Africa) (Pty.) Ltd., 24 Sturdee Avenue,
Rosebank, Johannesburg 2196, South Africa

Penguin Books Ltd., Registered Offices:
80 Strand, London WC2R 0RL, England

Published by Roc, an imprint of New American Library, a division of Penguin Group (USA) Inc. Previously published in a Roc hardcover edition.

First Roc Mass Market Printing, November 2007
10 9 8 7 6 5 4 3 2 1

Printed in the United States of America

For Greg Mahler.

Thanks for all the help in spreading the word.

ACKNOWLEDGMENTS

Novel writing, despite the time spent alone with the blank page, is a collaborative process. First, let me acknowledge Penny Hill especially, for the long lunches and the thoughtful commentary, but mostly for her friendship. And the same goes for Carolyn McCray, who still kicks my butt to challenge me to stretch a little further. Then, of course, I'm honored to acknowledge my friends who meet every other week at Coco's Restaurant: Steve and Judy Prey, Chris Crowe, Lee Garrett, Michael Gallowglas, Dave Murray, Dennis Grayson, Jane O'Riva, Kathy L'Ecluse, Leonard Little, Rita Rippetoe, and Caroline Williams. They are the cabal behind this writer. And a special thanks to David Sylvian for lugging a camera everywhere, even atop the highest peak in the Sierras. Finally, the three people instrumental at all levels of production: my editor, Liz Scheier, and my agents, Russ Galen and Danny Baror. And as always, I must stress that any and all errors of fact or detail fall squarely on my own shoulders.

ᓇᖕᒍᒥᑐᓯᑎ ᑕᒥᑎ ᑕᓂᑎᑎᕿᑭᐃᕿᕿᖁ ᖕᒍᓴᖁ
ᖃᓗᕿᖕᒍᑲᕿᖁ ᐅᑎᓕᓴᕿ
ᕕᑭᖕᒍᒥᑐᓯᑎ ᐃᓂᑎᓯ ᐅᓗᖕᒍᑎᕿ ᐅᓄᓂᕿᐅ ᖕᒍᓴᖁ
ᓂᖃᕿᑯᓂᑭᕿ ᑭᓂᒪᕿ
ᕋᖕᒍᒥᑐᓯᑎ ᓂᓴ ᖁᑭᕿᖕᒍᖁ ᐅᓯᖕᒍᖁᑯᓕᐃ ᖕᒍᓴᖁ ᐃᓂᓴ-
ᑎᕿᑭ'ᐅ
ᐅᖃᑭᖕᒍᑕᑕᓗᕿ
)ᓂᓴᑎᕿᑭᓗᖕᒍᓴᖁ
ᐱᓯᕿᑭᕿ ᓯᓕᔨᕿ ᓯᖕᒍᐅ ᓴᓕ ᓯᕿᖕᒍᑭᑎᓯ ᓴᓕᑭ
ᓯᓕᒪᕿ.

Naught but bitterweed and cleaved stone
Fraught with slate skies and icefire rime
Caught in dread shadow and winter's scrabble
Hinterland
Where hope has no hearth or home.

—decryption of the *Grimoire y Eld,* ann. 1439

ᐱᔨᑭᒪ ᖕᒍᓴᖁ ᐃᕿᓂᑭ,
ᐳᑎᓂᓗᕿ ᖕᒍᓴᖁ ᐅᑎᖕᒍᓂᑭ,
ᕋᖕᒍᓴ ᔨᓕᒥ ᐅᓄᓂᓴ ᑎᓯᕿ ᐃᔨᓗᖁ ᓯᖕᒍᑭᕿᑭᕙ

Wyrm and weir,
Stile and stair,
Can you skin the wyld hare?

—a child's rhyme played with daggers

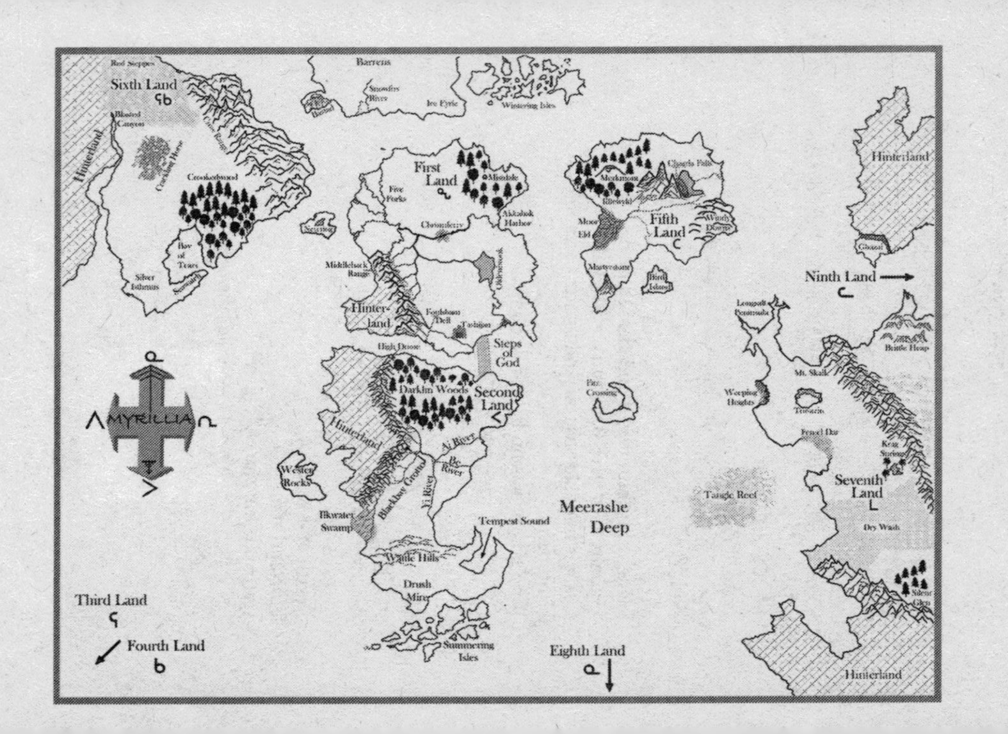
Sixth Land
Barrens
Wintering Isles
Hinterland
Crookedwood
Bay of Tears
Silver Isthmus
First Land
Five Forks
Akkabak Harbor
Middleback Range
Hinter-land
Fouldoon Dell
High Doon
Steps of God
Darklin Woods
Second Land
Ai River
Be River
Hinterland
Wester Rocks
Blackbay Grotto
Tempest Sound
Wattle Hills
Drush Mire
Summering Isles
Third Land
Fourth Land
Eighth Land
Meerashe Deep
Fifth Land
Moor
Bird Island
Tangle Reef
Ninth Land
Hinterland
Weeping Heights
Mt. Skail
Brittle Heap
Seventh Land
Dry Wash
Hinterland
MYRILLIA

AMYRILLIA
First Land
Mistdale
Five Forks
Akkabak Harbor
Nevering
Chrismferry
Oldenbrook
Middleback Range
Hinter-land
Foulsham Dell
Tashijan
High Dome
Steps of God
Darklin Woods
Second Land

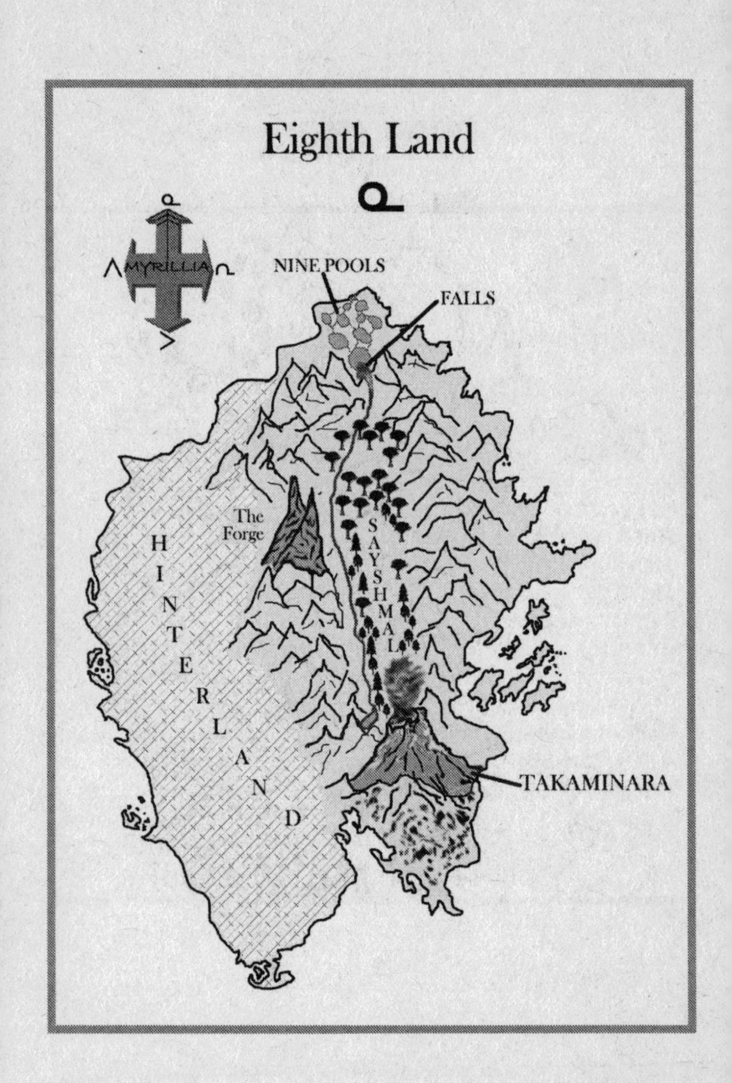

Eighth Land
AMYRILLIA
NINE POOLS
FALLS
The Forge
HINTERLAND
SAYSHMAL
TAKAMINARA

In Shadow . . .

HE HAS FORGOTTEN HIS NAME, LEAVING ONLY WILL TO DRIVE him. Arrow-bit and cut to bone, he reaches one hand, then another. The very land rejects his naked body. Fingernails break and bleed. Toes scrabble for purchase on the cliff face. His blood blackens the cold stone as he climbs the Forge.

But he cannot stop.

His pursuers will not.

He hears them far below: the ravening cries of the leathery grecklings, the chinking rattle of their keepers, the harsh shouts of his former captors, and rising like steam, the worst yet, the sweet notes of seersong.

Tears run hotly across his cold cheeks.

The song calls him back, slows him. If he knew his name, he would be caught again. But all is forgotten, so he digs and climbs.

He must not stop.

He searches upward. Light streams over the top of the white cliff, reflecting the morning's fire off the ice-capped peaks that frame the notched pass above. The Forge. The beacon between two lands. And though the brightness heralds the rise of the sun beyond the mountains, here on the western cliffs night still rules.

He must reach the border.

At last, one hand reaches out to find not rock but air. The top of the Forge. He draws his body upward with the very last of his strength into the morning's warmth and light. He rolls to the flat stone nestled between two peaks. Ahead, the land falls away again, the slopes gentler.

But not gentle to him . . .

He rises to his knees, staring to the east.

More peaks, but nearer still lies a promise. Though shrouded by morning mist, the vast emerald cloud forest is visible. Birdsong reaches him even here. He smells loam and wet leaf.

Saysh Mal.

Green lands settled and forbidden to his blood.

He already feels the admonishment under his knees. Fire warms his bones, but it is not the pleasantness of a hearth's glow: It is fever and fear. A warning at the border, written upon his marrow.

Do not pass.

He stands, and despite the warning, he trespasses. His bare feet move him away from the cliff's edge, away from the cries below, away from the last notes of seersong.

He leaves the hinterlands behind.

There is a path ahead. Left by whom? Hunters of the distant forest? The curious, the foolhardy, the hopeless? Who would trek to this vantage to stare out over the blasted hinterlands?

He continues, tracing the path down toward Saysh Mal. Each step grows more agonizing. Warmth becomes fire. Warning becomes demand. The blood of this land rejects his own. He smells his own seared flesh. Smoke curls between blackened toes. Drops of his own blood ignite with spats of flame.

He walks onward.

Agony both erases and stretches time.

He hobbles now on fiery stubs, feet gone. And still the land is not satisfied. His bones are now tinder. The fire races through marrow, igniting hip, spine, rib, and skull. He smolders. The old arrows impaled in his body have become feathered torches, fueled by his own blood. Shafts fall to ash.

He struggles onward, a living candle of oil and meager fat.

Past the last peak, he falls to hands and knees. He crawls, blindly, amid smoke and flame.

Then he senses more than hears: Someone is near.

He stops. The land's attack upon his blood rewards him for halting. Ever so slightly, the fire ebbs. Smoke clears. Though his eyes are burnt away, he notes shadows and light.

A figure steps toward him.

"No, boy!" someone shouts from a different direction. "Stand back from it! It's a shiting rogue god from the hinter!"

"But it's hurt."

"Let it die!"

"But . . ."

Through his pain, the god hears compassion, not so much with his burnt ears as with his heart. It gives him the strength for one last act. He reaches to his lips and removes his burden, preserved in Grace, carried in his mouth.

No strength remains.

He falls to the ground and lets his burden roll from his flaming fingertips. Though blind, he senses its journey into the boy's shadow.

It is his last hope, his heart, his life—and the only chance to save this world.

With his burden lifted at last, darkness settles over him as the land consumes the last of his life's flame. Words echo to him as he fades from this world.

"What is it?"

The boy answers. "Only a rock."

Cloak and Shadow

ser (regained knighthood)
Tylar ~~de~~ Noche—regent of Chrismferry,
the Godsword (too archaic as written)
bearer of ~~Rivenseryr~~, and vice-lord of Tashijan.
Knighted in ann. 4154 and stripped in 4163,
Tylar came to his regency after the Battle of Myrrwood
the ninety-eight
with the unanimous consent of ~~all the~~ gods
Myrillia (to avoid repetition of "nine")
of ~~the Nine Lands~~. His reign would herald
the beginning of the second War of the Gods.

—Hand-edited and unpublished page from
The Compendia of Figures and Personages from the Age of Twilight,
sold at auction for eleven hundred gold marches

1

A BRONZE BOY IN SNOW

HE WAS BEING HUNTED THROUGH THE WINTRY WOOD.

The forest whispered the hunter's presence: with the shushing of snow slipping from a pine branch, the skeletal rub of brittle briar branches, the creak of twigs in an ancient deadfall.

Still, Brant remained calm, as he had been taught.

Unhurriedly, he continued through the woods.

With each crunch of his boot, the brittle crust of ice cracked into the deeper snow. He left a trail of footprints that could easily be followed. His father would shame him if he saw his carelessness, but he was long in his grave, killed by a she-panther, leaving no one around to admonish his son.

Especially not in this strange cold land.

Brant was as foreign to this country as a fish on a sandy shore. Even after living here for over a year, he still found the air too heavy and difficult to breathe.

The elders might force him from his own lands and call it a blessing, place him in a strange school in Chrismferry and call it lucky, have him chosen for service by the god of Oldenbrook and call it fate, but Brant would never truly call this land home.

So he kept a ritual, honoring his father and keeping to the old ways. Each morning, he abandoned the raftered bridges and stone pillars of Oldenbrook and hunted the woods that fringed the great lake. He carried a trio of gutted and skinned snowhares impaled along the shaft of one arrow, borne over a shoulder. His baiban bow was hooked over his other arm, while the feathers poking out from his quiver tickled his left ear.

His father could not fault his skill with the bow this day. He had killed the hares swiftly. Three bolts through three hearts. He dressed them where they fell, leaving entrails steaming in the snow, blood scenting the dry air. It was the Way, sharing the rewards of the hunt with the forest. So it had been taught to every child back in his faraway homeland of Saysh Mal. By the Huntress herself, the Mistress of the Cloud Wood, god of loam and leaf. But the Way was not honored here . . . except by Brant.

Then again, why should it be? Here was not a realm of loam but a land of river, lakes, and ponds.

Brant stopped to listen again as he reached a familiar brook, greeted by his own footprints, those he had left earlier as he headed out into the snowy glade. The whisper of the forest had gone silent. Still, he waited five full breaths.

With his eyes on the forest, he knelt at the creek's edge, broke through the thin ice to reach the flowing water, and filled his goatskin flask. The wind brushed the tanglepine branches overhead, dusting him with snow and allowing a spear of sunlight to penetrate.

The ice sparked brilliantly, reflecting bits and pieces of the kneeling hunter: a snatch of brown hair, disheveled and draped across an unlined forehead . . . a corner of an emerald eye, squinted against the sudden glare . . . a stretch of thin lips, drawn even thinner . . . a corner of clefted chin, flecked by two days' growth of beard.

Brant froze, recognizing in such a broken reflection not himself—but his father. The stubble on the chin was too thin, grown from a young man of fifteen winters, not the dark shadows of his father's. And certainly one slivered reflection could not be misconstrued: Under the angle of a jaw, a branching scar marred the smooth bronze skin of his throat. If one squinted, it looked not unlike a hand, throttling him.

That belonged to Brant alone.

Shadows descended again as the wind died and branches fell back into place. It was time to go. Brant stood and followed the ice-edged brook as it switched back and forth through the wood. Around the last curve, the great blue expanse of Oldenbrook Lake opened before him. It might as well have been the sea itself. The far shore was only a promise, even in the clear, crisp morning.

The neighboring brook trickled into a misted meltpond bordering the shoreline of the great lake. The rest of the expanse was frozen over, but it was not flat ice. Instead the surface had been rilled into ridges by winter's winds and dusted with mounds of snow. Out in the city, sections of the lake ice had been shaved smooth for games played atop thin silver blades.

Brant had always watched from the edges or atop bridges. The slick ice made him wary, and not just for its treachery of footing. When smooth, it was glassy. One could peer into the depths of the winter lake. Things were moving down there. And the clear ice seemed more illusory than real.

Brant crunched through the snow, happy for solid ground under his heels. A fringe of dead brown reeds marked the boundary between forest and lake. He was reluctant to leave the land for water.

The growl behind him changed that.

He spun, dropping to a knee, facing the depths of the shadowed forest as the hunter finally revealed itself. In Brant's hand rested the hilt of his skinning knife, ready. He took a long slow breath through his nose, trying to catch a scent. Back in Saysh Mal, he knew most animals by their musk, but he smelled nothing lingering on this cursed dry air.

The beast moved as silently as the mist rising from the meltpond.

No crunch of ice.

The growl had been the only warning, full of hunger.

Brant dared not nock an arrow to his bowstring. He knew the beast would be upon him if he moved. He remained as still as a heron hunting among the reeds. Crimson eyes appeared in the forest, much closer than he had suspected, low to the ground. Muscles bunched at the shoulders. Bulk shifted. Ghost took flesh.

The wolf's white pelt blended with the snow, blurring its edges. Still, what he discerned was massive. A giant that stood to Brant's shoulders. Its head lowered in threat, lips rippling back from yellowed fangs. Large pads were splayed wide, made for stalking silently atop frozen snow. Black claws dug through the crust of ice, gaining purchase for the lunge to come.

Brant recognized the tufts of gray fur tipping each ear, marking the wolf as a hunter of Mistdale, far to the north. A Fell wolf. It did not belong so far south. But this winter had been long—too long. Rain should have been falling since the passing of the last moon, but snow still drifted from the slate skies. Even the hares over his shoulder were mostly bones, having barely survived on the few roots and tubers under the snow.

Brant met the wolf's gaze, acknowledging the sunken eyes and thin stretch of fur over bone. He noted a single drop of crimson on the lower curled lip.

Blood.

He eyed his own trail of bootprints.

The wolf must have come upon the entrails of his catch, feasted upon them, then followed his track. Looking for more. It seemed the Way was as unknown to the beasts of the forest as the people of Oldenbrook. Or maybe hunger broke all pacts.

Brant sensed that to wait any longer would only drive the wolf to attack.

He knew what must be done.

The wolf had growled. Therein Brant placed his life.

In a swift motion, he swept the arrow from his shoulder and cast the meat toward the wolf. If the wolf had meant to attack, it would not have growled and given itself away. The rumble had been a warning, a challenge, and a cry of hunger.

The trio of hares landed near the wolf.

The beast lunged and snapped up arrow and meat. With a low growl, it retreated to the shadows under a tanglepine.

Brant used the moment to retreat, too. He backed out onto the ice, snapping through the dry reeds. The wolf kept to its bower, satisfied with its catch. Only then did Brant see a pair of eyes deeper in the forest, drawn by the meat and blood. Smaller eyes, closer together. Cubbies. Two.

With a flash of white pelt, the large Fell wolf—a she-wolf—fled with her catch and her offspring. No wonder the wolf had come so far south. Not for herself but for her cubs. Spring cubs, born too soon, born into a bad season. Still, she fought for them, to give them a chance.

Brant understood that only too well.

He rubbed a knuckle along the scar under his jaw.

As he crossed the frozen lake, he sent a silent prayer up into the aether for the she-wolf, from one stranger in this land to another.

With the sun a quarter-way up the sky, Brant climbed a last ice ridge. The full breadth of his new home appeared ahead. Oldenbrook. The city, the second oldest of all the Nine Lands, rose out of the lake itself, raised on stone pylons and stout poles of ironoak. It was a city of archways, bridges, and frozen boats. The sprawl hugged the southern coastline and climbed in snowy tiers from the city's lowest level to the blue-tiled castillion that sat atop Oldenbrook's highest point.

Beneath the city's vast belly, the water remained unfrozen, melted both by the Grace of its god and the heat of the city itself. Even from here, Brant noted how the edifice steamed and misted, like some monstrous slumbering beast, waiting for true spring.

He could also hear the echoing groan and creak of the city. The *song* of Oldenbrook. On the calmest day in summer, it could be heard. It reminded Brant of the deepwhaler he had sailed aboard when forced from his homeland to these cold shores. The rub of ropes, the pop of planks. Sometimes he woke at night in his room, certain he was back in that ship's cramped cabin. He would rub his wrists, remembering the shackles.

Brant found himself doing the same now as he stared at the city. As royally as he was treated here, Oldenbrook was not so much home as a place of exile and banishment.

Movement drew his gaze to the sky. A small flippercraft descended toward the city, aiming for the high docks neighboring the lofty castillion. The airship steamed as much as the city, its blood-fed mekanicals hot as red coals in a brass warming pan. Its rudders and skimmers churned the air. A trail of smoke vented from its topside. Burning blood. Someone came with urgency.

Brant squinted at the flag fluttering near the bow. He could not make out the full details. Silver on black. He knew what he would have seen if he'd had sharper eyes. A silver tower embroidered on a black field. A ship from the citadel of Tashijan.

It was not a particularly unusual sight. After the tragedy and bloodshed in neighboring Chrismferry last spring, all of Myrillia was still unsettled. For a turn of seasons, ravens had filled the skies. Ships had sailed water and air in every direction. The thunder of hooves over the stone bridges of Oldenbrook had woken many each night.

But as summer wore to winter, and winter stretched endlessly, the ravens returned to their rookeries, the ships were tied back to their docks, and horses remained stabled. It was as if all the northern lands had pulled into themselves, guarding, wary, waiting for this long cold to break.

Or for something else . . . an unnamed fear.

Gods had been slain.

With the deaths of two gods—Meeryn of the Summering Isles and Chrism of Chrismferry—the Hundred now numbered Ninety-eight. Though order had been restored by the new regency in Chrismferry, the world still felt out of kilter, unbalanced, and every inhabitant of each of the Nine Lands sensed the rockiness of this ship.

Brant increased his pace toward the city. A flippercraft from Tashijan could only mean some business with the lord and god of the city, Jessup of Oldenbrook. And as the god's Hand of blood, Brant should be in attendance. It was only through the indulgence and understanding of Lord Jessup that Brant was allowed these morning excursions. He would not pay back such kindness by tarrying too long.

He hurried toward the nearest stone pylon. Each of the hundred support pillars of the city was as thick around as the encircling arms of fifteen men. Four of the columns had hollow hearts. Named the Bones of the city, they were positioned at the cardinal points of the compass. But it was not marrow that ran through these four Bones. Instead it was the true lifeblood of Oldenbrook.

Water.

Brant aimed for the western Bone.

The door to its interior was guarded by two massive loamgiants, men born under the Graced alchemy of loam to grow to hulking proportions. Heavy-browed, limbs like trunks, double muscled. And though Brant had lived all his life under the auspices of a god of loam, he still had a certain discomfort around these guardians of the Bones. The Huntress of Saysh Mal had always refused to allow her Grace to forge men in such a manner, finding it distasteful. Some of her prejudice had found its way into Brant's heart.

Not that the guards here had ever given him reason to feel uncomfortable. Despite their large size and dour appearance, there was a vein of good nature in their hearts.

And by now the guards certainly knew him. As he approached, heavy axes were lowered, and the iron bar was lifted from the door.

"No luck," one of them boomed, noting Brant's empty hands. The guard was a red-mopped giant named Malthumalbaen. It was said that a giant's name was as long as its bearer was large.

Brant slipped his bow from his shoulder. "Long winter," he answered with an apologetic tone. He often shared his catch with the guards here. Paid little coin for these long, cold vigils, they appreciated the extra bits.

Malthumalbaen cursed under his breath, but not at Brant, only at the truth in the young man's words. The large man shrugged deeper into his rabbit-fur-lined longcoat.

The other guard, brother to the first, Dralmarfillneer, only chuckled and clapped Brant on the shoulder as he passed. "Winters always end, Master Brant. Soon Mal will be cursing the heat and swelter."

"Shine my arse, Dral! You were just whining about the wind yourself."

Dral opened the door for Brant. "Only because I had to empty my bladder, Mal. Once you unbutton, the wind climbs right into your trousers and grabs hold of your eggs. And when you're as blessed as I am, it takes time to free yourself."

"Blessed, my arse, brother," Mal replied. "We're twins. What Father gave you, he gave me."

Brant was ushered into the hollow center of the Bone column. He heard Dral's last retort before the door closed. "Not in all ways, Mal . . . not in all ways."

The iron bar scraped back into place, securing the exit.

Brant shook his head and waved a hand over the stone post

rising from the floor's center. Immediately the floor under his feet began to push him upward, sliding smoothly along the polished walls, propelled by the rushing column of water beneath it.

The Grace-fed water chute carried him toward the castillion far above. While bridges and ladders led from the ice to the lowermost tier, the Bones led to the four wings of Lord Jessup's castillion.

As he was whisked up, his ears noted the climb past the many levels. The snowy castillion lay at the top of the city, the thirty-third tier. He braced his feet as the end of the chute neared. He craned his neck. The ceiling rushed toward him. From the stone roof, steel spears pointed down at him. An extra assurance against the unwelcome intruder. The platform, when bidden, could drive its passengers into those spikes.

As always, Brant ducked his head a bit as he neared his destination—but his life was spared. The platform settled to a stop, and the door was opened by another loam-giant, a mute.

The giant sternly nodded Brant out of the Bone's chute.

"Thank you, Greestallatum," Brant said, returning the nod. He knew that only another giant dared shorten a giant's name, and even then, they'd best be friends.

The giant crossed and opened the far door into the main keep. The western wing of the castillion, the High Wing, housed the eight Hands of Oldenbrook. Brant moved into the wide hall. As was traditional, windows lined one wall, facing out to Oldenbrook Lake. Along the other wall, eight doors marked off the private rooms to the castillion's Hands.

Brant hurried along the woven rug. As the Hand of blood, he had the room at the far end, closest to the residence of Lord Jessup himself. The god's chambers rose from the center of the castillion and its four wings. A giant iron hearth stood outside the wide double doors, used for cleansing traces of corrupted Grace from cloth, stone, and steel.

Otherwise, the hall was empty.

Where was everyone?

As if his inquiry were heard, a door opened on his left. A tall, lithe woman dressed in silver strode out of her room. Liannora, Mistress of Tears. She was one of the eight Hands, each representing one of Lord Jessup's blessed humours: *blood*, *seed*, *sweat*, *tears*, *saliva*, *phlegm,* and both *yellow and black bile*. A Hand's duty was to collect and preserve the assigned humour, rich in the god's powerful Grace.

Such a duty was a rare honor, and one Liannora considered Brant to be undeserving of attending. She stood before him, as pale as the snow outside. Her long straight tresses flowed like an icy waterfall. The only true color was the blue of her eyes. She seemed to typify Oldenbrook in winter. Even the hue of her eyes matched the tiles of the city.

"Master Brant," she said with a calculating glance over his leathers, furs, and sodden boots. "Have you not heard?"

"Heard what? I've only just returned."

One eyebrow arched. "Oh, yes . . . traipsing in the woods." Her disapproval hung about her like a dark cloud. She joined his step down the hall. "We've all been commanded to assemble in Lord Jessup's greeting chamber. A most important guest arrives even now."

Brant pictured the flippercraft. "From Tashijan."

"Then you did hear?" Her manner hardened further, if such a thing were possible.

"I saw the ship descending, flying the Tashijan flag, as I arrived back at the city," he explained, rather hurriedly, trying his best not to seem rude.

"Ah," Liannora said as they neared the hall's end, plainly not mollified.

Brant headed for his room, glad to escape. He had never fully fit in here. The previous Hand of blood had been an elder statesman of the High Wing, well respected, revered, loved by all. It was a station Brant seemed to continually fail to fill: too young to respect, too quiet of disposition, and too darkly complexioned in a land of pale men and women.

"Where are you going?" Liannora asked as he stepped away.

Brant stopped. "To freshen and change."

"There's no time for that. I'm the last to respond to the summons. The party from Tashijan is already in attendance. You'll just have to appear—" She waved a hand disparagingly over his clothes. "Few will expect otherwise anyway."

Brant knew the words she didn't add. *For an Eighthlander*.

Resigned, Brant headed toward the double doors. Before they could reach the threshold, one of the doors opened. A small figure stepped through, dressed all in black, from half cloak to boot. A hood was pulled up, and a masklin covered chin and lips.

A word escaped the figure, whispered, yet urgent. Brant's ears, sharpened by seasons of hunting, picked the word out of the air.

"*Pupp* . . ."

Then the cloaked figure stiffened and went silent, spotting their approach. Under the hood, a pair of eyes widened, flashing from Liannora to Brant. The figure then glanced away, but not before a surprised second twitch in Brant's direction.

"I'm sorry," the figure squeaked out, proving herself to be a girl or young woman. She bowed her head slightly. "I didn't mean to intrude."

Here was plainly one of the visitors from Tashijan.

Brant noted a black stripe tattooed on each side of her face, running jaggedly from the outside corner of each eye to each ear. But it was not one of the illustrious Shadowknights of Tashijan. The girl here had earned only her first stripe, marking her as a page. It would take a second stripe to be called squire, and a third to be a full knight. Even her cloak was ordinary cloth, not the shadow-shifting cloak of a true knight.

"Be not afraid," Liannora said with surprising warmth, almost oily. "Any servant of Tashijan is always welcome in our halls."

"I only came to look."

"Certainly," Liannora said. "And we'd be honored to have you escort us to the greeting hall to join the others."

The page bowed and retreated back through the door. "It—it would be my honor," she mumbled, but in fact it looked as though she would prefer to run and hide.

Liannora stepped between the page and Brant. She touched the young woman's shoulder lightly, in an oddly possessive gesture. "So I hear that Castellan Vail herself will be seeking audience with Lord Jessup. What a distinct honor to have one so highly ranked at Tashijan coming to visit Oldenbrook. I can't imagine what would warrant such a strange appointment."

The silence that followed hung heavily in the air.

Plainly Liannora sought to extract knowledge from the page, perhaps something more than would be formally revealed during the high assembly here.

The girl did not bend. She even stepped away from Liannora's touch, not enough to be rude, but refusing to be lured.

Brant found a ghost of a smile rising unbidden to his lips, suddenly liking this girl very, very much. He remembered that second startled glance a moment before when they had first met. He had dismissed it as surprise at his rough clothes and poor appearance. But now he wondered. He sensed that such things would not matter to the black-cloaked girl.

So why the second glance?

The trio passed through the anteroom to Lord Jessup's rooms, down a short curved hall, and ended up before the door to the greeting room. The door was already open. Voices, polite and jovial, reached them.

As he stepped to the doorway, Brant noted a mix of familiar figures, dressed resplendently in jewels and fine cuts of cloth. The other Hands of Jessup. Amid them mingled five black shapes, the entourage from Tashijan.

The leader stood near the center. A bright diadem at her throat marked her as castellan of Tashijan, the second in command of the mighty Citadel, after the warden himself.

Brant focused upon her. Castellan Kathryn Vail had played a critical role in ridding Chrismferry of the daemon in its midst. Few in Myrillia didn't know her story—or that of her former lover, Tylar ser Noche, once named godslayer but now the regent of Chrismferry.

The castellan's gaze swept over the latecomers. Above her masklin, Kathryn Vail's eyes found her page and hardened to fire-agates. The young girl hurried to the castellan's side. So the page served the castellan. No wonder the girl had been so sturdy in the face of Liannora. She had been forged in fires hotter than any Liannora could muster.

As the girl reached the castellan's side, she glanced once more back at them. No, back at *him*. Then away again.

This time, Brant knew what lay behind those cornflower blue eyes.

Recognition.

And with that realization, the same occurred to him. As she turned, a slip of hair fell from beneath her hood. She tucked it back, but not before Brant recognized the distinct yellow-blond curl.

Memories disassembled and came together in a flash. He stumbled as he entered the hall, bumping into Liannora, who shot him a daggered look, then left his side, as if proximity to him might taint her.

Brant stared at the girl. He remembered the night he had been chosen from among his fellow students, when Jessup's Oracle had placed a stone into his waiting palm, claiming him as his new Hand of blood. Prior to that, down below in the chamber beneath the High Chapel, Brant had defended a young girl from the bitter words of other students.

The same girl now hid in black here.

Like Brant, she had been chosen that night, to serve as a Hand of blood for the daemon-possessed Chrism. But then after the Battle of Myrrwood, when the daemon had been vanquished, she had vanished. Few noted her disappearance on a night when gods were slain.

Now she was here.

Alive.

A girl named Dart.

For a full quarter bell, Brant kept to the shadows of the gathering and edged along the room. He kept watch on his quarry as he maneuvered around the chattering islands of castle gentlefolk and mingling visitors. He approached no closer, preferring to study the castellan's page from afar.

What was the girl doing here?

Before any answers could be discerned, the resonant strike of a gong echoed across the greeting hall. All chatter stopped, and eyes turned toward the arched back door as it swung open.

Lord Jessup, god of Oldenbrook, entered the reception hall. As was his custom, he wore the simple cloths and leathers of the sailfolk that plied the great lake: soft bleached boots into which were tucked the hems of his baggy black trousers, a billowing white shirt hooked at the neck, and a peaked cap of blue velvet.

The only bit of true decoration was an azure sapphire fixed at the base of his throat, an ancient gift granted to Lord Jessup shortly after settling this realm. The sapphire had been discovered by a fishwife as she scaled and gutted one of the mighty lake shaddocks, the fierce bottom dwellers found only in the deepest depths of Oldenbrook Lake. Pulled from the shaddock's gullet, the gem was a blue that matched exactly the hue of the lake, and all knew its portent, the lake welcoming its new guardian and god. Lord Jessup had come to cherish the gem as much as he did the people and the lands here.

As the god strode slowly through the gathering, the jewel glowed slightly, a reflection of the god's shining Grace, like moonlight on still waters. Reaching the high seat in the room's center, Lord Jessup settled to the cushions.

The god's eight Hands, including Brant, lowered to one knee.

The emissaries from Tashijan bowed, even Castellan Vail.

Lord Jessup waved them all up. "Kathryn ser Vail, Castellan of Tashijan, Magistrate of the Order of the Shadowknights, be welcome," he said formally. His manner then melted to warmer tones with a tired smile. "It is an honor to have you gracing Oldenbrook once again."

"My lord," the castellan said, bowing more deeply, then straightening with a shift of her cloak.

"How long have you been away from our shores?"

"I believe six years, my lord."

Brant recognized the slight pause, the inflected lowered timbre in her voice. It was an awkward subject, one to be skirted. And with good reason. It surely had to be a tender matter still to the castellan. She had been betrothed to Tylar ser Noche, a shadowknight once in service to Lord Jessup. All in Oldenbrook knew their story. Balladeers still struggled to capture the pain and tragedy in strum of string and chord. For the ballad of Tylar ser Noche, a shadowknight stripped of cloak and love, remained unfinished. First lover, then murderer, then broken knight and slave, and finally godslayer . . . now risen anew as regent of neighboring Chrismferry.

The other half of the tragedy stood here. Tylar's betrothed and lover. Forced to damn him with her own testimony, she was equally cursed, banished and humiliated into a secluded life. Some even whispered that an unborn child had been lost to her sorrow and heartbreak. But her wheel had turned also, and she rose again as castellan of Tashijan.

But did the song end even there? One served in Chrismferry, the other in Tashijan. And with no true end, the balladeers struggled for a satisfactory final chord.

But Lord Jessup held no such conflict in his heart. "It is good to have you here again," he said. "What brings you from the Citadel to our shores with such haste?"

"Haste arises because of a dire storm due to strike from the north. Wyndravens sweep south out of Mistdale and Five Forks with messages of a last great winter squall, the worst of them all, one raging with snow and bitter winds. The northern edge of Mistdale forest lies blasted and dead, trunks burst with ice. The rivers of Five Forks are frozen solid to the sea, and the freeze continues to flow south, crushing ships, stalling all movement."

"I have felt the echo of pain through the waterways," Lord Jessup said. "Is that why you have come with such speed?"

"I come also at the behest of Warden Fields." Stiffness entered her voice. "He has asked that I personally attend each god of the First Land and announce a ceremony of noted distinction to be held at Tashijan, one which is meant to heal a rift across our Land."

"And what ceremony might that be?"

"The sanctifying of a knight to a new cloak."

Lord Jessup's brow pinched with curiosity. Brant could almost read his thoughts. It was a common rite when a knight first gained his shadowcloak for the god whom he first served to oversee the sanctification, to bless the moment with the god's own Grace. But then why come with such a distinguished emissary for such an ordinary event?

Understanding suddenly smoothed Lord Jessup's face. "The knight to be cloaked?" he said. "Am I to assume this is Tylar ser Noche, regent of Chrismferry?"

Castellan Vail bowed her head in acknowledgment.

"Is Ser Noche not already a knight? Did he not bend a knee where you now stand when I first blessed his cloak?"

"And that cloak was stripped," the castellan reminded him

in a pained voice. "The ceremony I come to announce is one to reinstate Tylar—Ser Noche—to the Order of the Shadowknights. He will receive back his cloak and his diamond-pommeled sword, certifying his station. Warden Fields has asked that I request all the gods of the First Land to send high representatives to Tashijan for the event."

Lord Jessup raised his hands, steepling his fingers before his lips. He spoke between them, one eyebrow lifted. "And so to heal a rift . . ."

Brant read the layers of meaning in those few words. The knighting ceremony was more than an attempt to right an old wrong. It was fraught with layers of import and consequence. All winter long, rumors had abounded of a continuing tension between Tashijan and Chrismferry. Whispers spread of how Warden Fields had employed Dark Graces during his bloody and savage pursuit of Tylar, back when the broken knight had been declared a godslayer. As such, there continued to be enmity between the two most powerful men in all the First Land. It could not last. All of Myrillia looked to the First Land for stability and guidance. The histories of Tashijan and Chrismferry stretched back to the Sundering, when the gods first came to Myrillia and settled its Nine Lands out of savagery.

The growing rift threatened all.

The knighting ceremony plainly was intended to unite Tashijan and Chrismferry once again, to spread a healing balm over the recent frictions. And the gods were being called to witness and bless the new union.

It now made sense why Kathryn ser Vail had been sent as emissary. The woman stood between all: between the two men, between the two strongholds, between the past and the present.

"When is the ceremony to be held?" Lord Jessup asked.

"In a half-moon's time."

"So soon?"

"Thus the urgency."

Lord Jessup nodded his head once. "Then we must hope that the coming storm is truly the last dying breath of this interminable winter."

* * *

As final matters of scheduling were discussed, along with minor issues of trade and conflicts, Brant's attention drifted.

Motion drew his eye.

Castellan Vail's page—the girl he had once known as Dart—was staring hard at him. Or rather at his knees. Brant glanced down, fearing his leggings were soiled or torn or somehow offensive enough to warrant such heated attention.

But nothing appeared amiss with his wardrobe.

Glancing back up, he watched the girl make a dismissive, shooing motion at him. What had he done so wrong to irritate the girl? Though they had not known each other well back at the school, neither had there been animosity between them.

His face reddened as he found himself obeying her silent command. He backed toward the door. Her eyes followed him. Across the hall, matters of the realm were quickly settled, and Lord Jessup stood, signaling the gathering at an end.

Happy to be freed from his obligations here, Brant edged out the door and back into the High Wing of the castillion. He closed the way and muffled the low cacophony of the voices inside. He suspected it would be another full bell before the gathering would truly disband. It was seldom that a god-realm had the privilege of Tashijan's second-highest-ranking personage in attendance.

Alone, Brant turned to the empty hall.

Before he could take a step, his skin prickled. He tensed, going dead still. As out in the forest, he sensed something near, unseen, hunting him. He even heard a growl inside his head, an echo of the Fell wolf's hungry warning.

What could—?

Brant's chest suddenly burst with a searing fire. A silent cry burned from his lips as he fell to his knees. One hand ripped at the hooks and strings of his shirt, tearing to his woolens, fighting for the source of the flame. He yanked on the twisted leather thong around his neck, tugging free what hung from it. It was the only piece of home he had carried out from the misty jungles of Saysh Mal.

The black stone fell free, glassy and iridescent.

Brant knew it was the source of the fire. The stone had burned like this once before. It was one of the reasons why he still kept it near.

He stretched the talisman as far from his body as the corded braid around his neck would allow. The stone appeared no different than before, drilled through the middle and threaded with the leather cord.

With his other hand, he hauled his woolens lower, expecting to see a ruin of blistered and charred flesh. But the skin of his chest was smooth and unblemished.

Still on his knees, holding the stone aloft, Brant lowered his palm to the floor, leaning his weight. He blinked away tears, breathing heavily.

It was over. He knew if he touched the stone it would be cold again.

As he pondered the mystery, a creature flickered into existence before him—almost nose to nose with him on the floor. It sniffed at the outstretched stone, setting the talisman to wobbling on its braid.

Brant froze.

The daemon stood knee-high, flowing in molten bronze, half wolf, half lion, spiked at collar and hackle, black jeweled eyes lit by inner fires, maw lapping with flame, fangs forging and melting in a continuing eruption of savage barbs.

Its eyes stared into his for a half breath; then it pulled back—and vanished.

Released from the spell, Brant jerked like a snapped bowstring, falling on his rear and scuttling away like a crab on hot sand. But the beast was gone. He searched around. Nothing. Shaking, he forced himself to settle his center. Muffled laughter and conversation arose from the room behind him.

As he sat, he sensed a vague lessening of pressure inside his skull, something receding. Then in a moment, nothing.

Slowly he gained his feet, only now noting how his left fist clutched the black stone. It had indeed gone cold. He opened his palm and stared down. Had the stone somehow conjured the daemon and again banished it?

As he began to tuck the stone away, the door creaked open behind him. His free hand went for his knife.

But it was a familiar figure, a page cloaked in black.

Before Dart could say a word, a call reached them both, arising from Kathryn ser Vail. The Tashijan party was departing.

Dart glanced over her shoulder, back into the room. She retreated toward the castellan, but not before her blue eyes latched upon him again. She bowed her head as if they had just agreed to something.

A secret between them.

Then she also vanished, closing the door with a snap.

Brant remembered the word she had whispered with such urgency when first caught creeping into the High Wing.

As if she had been searching for something.

Pupp . . .

And the strange shooing motion at him a moment ago.

Had she been warding him away—or someone else?

Brant stared at the stone in his palm. Two stones had led him to this moment. One had been pressed into his palm by Lord Jessup's Oracle, selecting him to serve in the god's household. But before that, another god had gifted him with another stone, the one that hung around his neck.

Was this one also a call to serve?

He pictured the fiery figure on the jungle path, crumbling in flames and rolling the stone to his toes. What did a rogue god of the hinterland need from a lone boy out of Saysh Mal?

Brant tucked the cursed stone away.

To root out that answer would take a great hunter.

But at long last, Brant had finally found his first trail marker.

He pictured the girl's blue eyes and mumbled a name to the empty hall, full of promise as much as curiosity. "Pupp."

2

A REGENT IN BLOOD

CLOAKED IN BLACK, TYLAR SER NOCHE WAITED ON THE DOCKS. The stars shone and the greater moon had set. It was the darkest point of the night, when both moons were gone and the sun remained only a rumor. It was also the coldest part of the night. Ice crusted the edges of the sludge canal and made the planks of the ironwood dock treacherous underfoot.

His party had been waiting for a full turn of a bell. All were buried in woolens, furred boots, and heavy cloaks. Their breath steamed the air.

"Perhaps he won't come," Delia whispered through a scarf about her mouth. She stood close, a head shorter and a decade younger, wrapped in an oiled black cloak lined with fox fur, its hood fringed in snowy ermine, a perfect complement to her pale skin and exacting contrast to her shadow-dark hair. The only color about her rose from the shine of her eyes, a warm hazel, green-tinged in the torchlight. "Or perhaps the letter was a forgery, one meant to lure us where there are few witnesses."

"It was no forgery," Tylar assured her.

The missive had arrived a fortnight ago, urging secrecy. It had been coded properly and signed with the proper sigil.

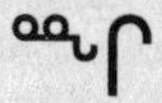

Ancient Littick for *thief*.

Tylar had first seen the same sigil branded on the letter-writer's buttock. Plus a few telltale drops, richly crimson, had stained the white parchment. Not blood. Wine. Testament enough to the verity of the letter's author.

"Rogger was never one to mind the precise ringing of a bell," Tylar said, urging patience with a slim smile.

"Let's hope he was precise enough about the turning of the day, then," Sergeant Kyllan said, stamping his boots to warm his toes. The master of Chrismferry's garrison did not like this moonless rendezvous. He scratched the tortured scar across his left cheek, scowling slightly. Kyllan had refused to allow Tylar to cross the city alone, especially in the middle of the night. There were still many who wanted Tylar dead.

And the numbers were growing daily as this endless winter stretched on. Rumbles and rumors spread through alehouses and wenchworks of a curse upon his regency. Though Tylar had slain the daemon that had attempted to usurp the god-realm of Chrismferry, the city's gratitude was as short-lived as a bloom after the first frost. And as winter's hardships grew, it seemed even the change of seasons had become the responsibility of the city's new regent, a mantle Tylar wore with ill comfort.

For Tylar's security, Kyllan had ordered ten of the garrison's pikemen to accompany him on this dark journey across the city. But Tylar suspected it was an unnecessary escort. He had more than enough protection from the party's one other member.

Wyr-mistress Eylan stood at the foot of the docks, dressed in deerskins and fur, a sword in hand, a half ax at her waist. Her cloak had a hood, but she did not bother pulling it up, seemingly impervious to the frigid breeze that swept up the crumbling canal from the distant Tigre River. Her skin glowed with a flushed ruddiness, a shade darker than her tanned leathers. Her black hair trailed to mid-back in a thick braid, decorated with three raven feathers.

She seemed to note his attention, glancing over to him, appraising him coldly, then looking away again.

Bound by an oath, Eylan seldom strayed far from Tylar's side, not so much in concern for his safety as to protect a debt sworn to her lord. A year ago, Tylar had promised his seed in trade for his life and the lives of his companions, a humour of significant Grace that Wyr-lord Bennifren intended for the forges of his Black Alchemists. Tylar was determined to avoid paying that debt for as long as possible, preferably forever.

'Til then, he had gained, in Eylan, a second shadow.

Tylar returned his attention to the stagnant canal.

Nearby, a small single-sailed trawler, long abandoned, lay stripped and on its side, half-beached, hull burst, locked in ice. Tylar was surprised to find it here. The long winter had taxed the city of Chrismferry, especially the underfolk too poor for the rising cost of coal and wood. Scavenging had become commonplace. The planking of the old trawler would heat a hearth for a good turn of the moon. Yet here it remained, untouched.

Of course, *here* was the heart of the Blight, one of several sections of the great city long gone to seed, as abandoned and broken as the old trawler. Chrismferry spread across both sides of the Tigre River. Founded four millennia ago, it was the oldest and greatest of all the cities of the Nine Lands of Myrillia. It would take a man on a horse two days to cross from one end of the city to the other. *The world was the city, the city was the world.* Such was said about the first city of Myrillia.

But if true, what did the Blight signify?

The city seemed to be decaying from the inside. The borders continued to extend along the Tigre River and out into the surrounding plains, but in the past centuries, sections of the inner city had fallen into ruin. Canals filled with silt, houses fell under the rotted weight of their roofs, cobbled streets were stripped of stones, leaving only muddy, pitted tracks that daunted all manner of wheel. Soon the only inhabitants of the Blight were those seeking to lose themselves, but even these low dwellers seldom stayed long. Easier prospects could be found at the edges of the city.

Why did Rogger insist on returning to the city under such strange circumstances? The former thief had left Chrismferry a year ago under the guise of a pilgrim, to discern what he could of the state of the Nine Lands and to seek any thread or crumb about the Cabal. Since Tylar had freed the city, nothing more had been learned about the faction of naethryn—the daemonic undergods of Myrillia—who sought to kindle a new War of the Gods. Nothing until Rogger's cryptic letter had arrived by raven. What had the thief learned that required such a dark place to meet?

The answer was not long in coming.

From the depths of the canal, a tall black fin split the waters and rose, steaming, into the frigid air. The bulk of the underwater vessel splintered ice as it surfaced, one of Tangle Reef's undersea crafts. It appeared like a small wooden whale, fueled by the blood of Fyla, the god of the watery Reef.

A hatch behind the wood fin pushed open and was thrown back by an arm scarred by branded sigils. The owner of those brands climbed out next and balanced on the wet back of the vessel. Tylar stepped forward, recognizing his old friend. But it seemed Rogger's time abroad had wrought ill changes in him. His scraggled red-gray beard framed a face gone gaunt. Bony cheekbones poked from beneath green eyes, his lips were cracked and split, and his skin shone with a yellowish tinge. Tylar prayed this last was just the reflected sheen of the flickering torchlight.

Rogger shivered and huffed into the night. "Curse me black, it's cold enough to freeze my arse cheeks together."

Tylar lifted an arm in welcome.

But Rogger ignored him and bent back to the open hatch and called below. "Oy, careful with that, you overgrown dogfish."

Another figure, scowling sourly, half-climbed up through the hatch and hauled up a roughspun satchel. He passed it to Rogger, who swung it over a shoulder.

"Much obliged, Kreel," the thief said.

At the hatch, Tylar recognized the leader of Fyla's elite Hunters. There was no mistaking his fishbelly pallor, his smooth skin, and the throat lined by gill flaps. Like all the denizens of Tangle Reef, Kreel had been forged in his mother's womb by an alchemy of Graces. Kreel's presence concerned Tylar. What was so important that the god Fyla would send her personal bodyguard to deliver Rogger safely here?

Kreel's gaze settled on Tylar. The man's eyes, usually stoic and cold, flashed with a mix of worry and relief, as if glad to be rid of Rogger . . . and whatever burden his presence entailed.

Without even a nod, Kreel dropped away and hauled the hatch closed after him. Rogger barely had time to leap to the dock before the watercraft sank under him. The tall fin slipped back beneath the dark waters.

On the dock, Rogger joined them, looking rangier than ever. He bowed deeply toward Delia and took her hand, kissing it with exaggerated pomp. "Ah, to allow my unworthy lips to grace the knuckles of the regent's Hand of blood."

Delia shook her head as he rose, but she still hugged him warmly. "I missed you," she said in his ear.

"Truly?" He feigned shock. "And I thought I had experienced all manner of miracles during my pilgrimage. But this is indeed the most wondrous of all."

Tylar gripped him next, by the hand, then in a full embrace. Tylar was surprised by how glad he was to have the man at his side again. It was as if a missing limb, long gone, had returned. But Tylar also noted how wasted of frame his friend had become; the embrace was like hugging a stack of bones. Concerned, Tylar broke the contact.

Rogger quietly shook his head, silencing the question on Tylar's lips.

Tylar read something behind the usual amused warmth, something dark with dread.

"We need a place to speak in private," Rogger said, shedding his easy banter and glancing warily around him.

"We are far from the castillion," Tylar said. "It will take us the better part of a bell to return."

"I'd as soon unload what I must now." Rogger nodded toward an old shipwright's shop turned crow loft, windowless, with windblown refuse for a door.

Rogger strode off down the dock toward it, drawing Tylar after him. He kicked his way inside, scattering a few nesting rats. Tylar collected a torch from one of the pikemen and waved Kyllan and Eylan to stand guard.

Delia made to follow them, but Rogger held up a hand. "Only Tylar for now," he said apologetically.

Frowning, Tylar climbed into the dilapidated shop after the thief. Rogger marched them past the front entry room, through a narrow hall, and into the wright's workspace. It was empty and stripped, except for the broken-keeled frame of some abandoned project. Wings flapped up in the open rafters. The hay roof had long rotted away, leaving only the old ribbed joists. Between the beams, a few stars glinted down at them.

Tylar propped his torch between two boards. "What's this all about, Rogger? Why all the secrecy?"

Rogger turned and shrugged off his satchel. Judging by the sag in the cloth, only one object weighted down the bag. Rogger hefted it in his palm and deftly fingered the satchel's knot. Once it was undone, he shook the satchel, shedding the cloth and revealing the content within.

Tylar caught the whiff of black bile.

Rogger noted the crinkle of his nose. "Needed to shield it with bloodnuller shite," the former thief said, confirming Tylar's thought.

All the various humours of a god bore special Graces, but black bile, the excremental humour of a god, nullified any blessing. Why such a ward here? Tylar also noted how Rogger was careful never to allow what he bore to touch his bare skin.

"What is the meaning of this?" Tylar finally asked, brows pinched as he examined the strange talisman, the yellowed skull of some beast.

Empty bony sockets stared back at him.

The skull was missing its lower jaw and most of its teeth—except for two prominent fangs, glinting silver. It looked like some beast, except that the brow rose too high.

Tylar's lips settled into a sneer of distaste.

This was no *animal's* skull.

Tylar met Rogger's eyes over the crown of the skull. "Is it an ilk-beast?" he asked.

Though the Battle of Myrrwood was a year old, city patrols still rooted out the occasional ilk-beast. The poor creatures had once been men, but had been forged by Black Graces into daemons.

"Aye," Rogger said, "you are right to recognize the taint of Dark Graces, of a form twisted and corrupted."

Tylar read the unspoken behind Rogger's words. "But what?"

Rogger bent down to the ground and gathered a pinch of windblown dirt from the floor. Rising with a stifled groan, he sifted the dirt over the crown of the skull. Where the particles touched bone, tiny spats of fire erupted. Rogger lifted the skull and blew upon it, dusting off the dirt and thus dousing the flames.

Tylar's eyes widened at the demonstration. The very soil of this land burned the bone. The implication iced through Tylar's veins. Chrismferry was a settled land, imbued with the blood of the god Chrism. And like all other god-realms, its soil was a bane against the trespass of all other gods.

"It was no *man* that was corrupted here," Tylar mumbled, watching the last of the flames waft away.

Rogger nodded, confirming his worst fear. "It's the skull of a *god*."

Tylar fed a broken chair leg to the crackling fire that now burned in the center of the shipwright's workshop. Rogger had returned the skull to his satchel and carried it over his shoulder, keeping it from touching the ground. Even though the skull was coated in black bile, they dared not let it come in contact with the land here.

To the side, Delia warmed her fingers over the fire's flames. At Tylar's bidding, she had joined them in the shop. The three gathered around the fire. The others kept guard out in the streets.

Delia stared at Rogger's shouldered satchel. "The skull must have come from one of the *rogue* gods out in the hinterlands," she said.

Rogger nodded. "Aye, my thought, too. With Myrillia as tensed as a maiden on her wedding night, I'd have heard if any of our illustrious settled gods had gone missing. But at last count, all of the gods were secure in their castillions."

"But secure for how long?" Tylar asked.

Better than anyone, he knew Myrillia was no longer safe—not for man, nor for god. Tylar fingered the buttons over his chest. Beneath the wool and linen, he bore a black handprint, the dying mark of Meeryn, goddess of the Summering Isles. He had gone to the god's succor as she lay dying, the first to fall in this new War of the Gods. In her last breath, Meeryn had imbued Tylar with her Grace, healing his scarred body while granting him a sliver of herself, that sundered dark shadow that lived in the depths of naether, her undergod.

As if aware of his attention, Tylar could almost feel the smoky daemon shift inside him, trapped behind his healed ribs, waiting for a break in his bones to free it again. Tylar had refused its release since the Battle of Myrrwood. Still, its presence served a purpose. As long as Tylar bore Meeryn's naethryn, his humours flowed like those of a god, rich in Graces.

Delia noted Tylar's fingers at his chest. He forced his arm down. Too often, she had urged him to explore the bond with the naethryn inside him. He was loath to do so. He would rather be rid of it.

Still, it was such a *gift* that allowed him to wield the sword at his belt.

His hand settled upon its gold pommel, but he found little comfort there. *Rivenscryr*. The infamous Godsword.

Four millennia ago, the blade had ended the first War of the Gods, sundering their lost kingdom and raining the gods down upon Myrillia. Their arrival here heralded three centuries of madness and destruction until the god Chrism chose this first god-realm and imbued the land with his Graces, sharing his powers to bring order out of chaos. More gods followed, carving out various god-realms, forever binding gods to their individual lands. Beyond these settled territories lay only the hinterlands, spaces wild and ungoverned, where rogue gods still roamed, unsettled and untamed.

But the gods had not come whole to this world. As the Godsword had sundered their former home, the blade had done the same to the gods themselves, splitting them into three. One part was driven down into the darkness below all substance, into the *naether*, where they lived as undergods, shadows of those above, while another part sailed high, vanishing into the *aether*, never to be seen again, unknowable and aloof. And between them both strode the gods of Myrillia, beings of undying flesh and ripe with powerful Graces.

Now, after four millennia, this balance among the gods was threatened. Among the shadowy naethryn, a secretive Cabal plotted and lusted for Myrillia, reigniting the War of the Gods.

Was the Cabal responsible for the corruption of this rogue god? If so, why?

Tylar turned his attention from the flames to Rogger and the strange skull. "Where did you find such a cursed talisman?"

"Down south. In the Eighth Land."

"What were you doing in the hinterland down there?" Delia asked.

Rogger shook his head. "I didn't go into any blasted hinterland. I know better than to traipse those wild lands alone. No, I found the skull in Saysh Mal, the cloud forest of the Huntress, the latest stop on my pilgrimage."

He hiked his leggings out of his boot to reveal the sigil of that god freshly burnt into his flesh, representing his completion of that part of his journey.

Rogger tucked his leggings back in with a sour set to his lips. "Something is not right about that realm."

"How so?" Tylar asked.

"Can't exactly focus on anything you can grab. Just something off-kilter. A ragged edge. A loose thread waiting for a hand to pull it. But I'll tell you what—I'm skaggin' glad to be rid of that place."

"Doesn't that god-realm, Saysh Mal, border one of the largest hinterlands in all Myrillia?" Delia asked.

"Aye," Rogger agreed. "And maybe that's it. Like something seeped out from there and tainted the blessed land."

Tylar nodded to the satchel. "How did you come upon the skull there?"

"Now that's a story best told over a flagon of your best—"

A flapping of wings silenced him.

All eyes glanced upward. The noise was too loud—too *leathery*—for any crow or raven. Something dark swept low over the bare joists, blotting out the stars, then away again.

A cry rose from the street.

Tylar's sword slid from his sheath as he turned, rising unbidden to hand with a ring of silver. The gold hilt warmed with a feverish welcome, seeming to clasp his fingers with as much certainty as his own will. The length of blade trapped the starlight into a single shaft of brilliance.

More shouts from the streets.

Kyllan's voice bellowed. "Hold your ground!"

"Stay here," Tylar said and headed for the front of the shop.

Rogger ignored him and followed, drawing Delia with him. "If there was a roof up there, *maybe*, but as we're bare-arsed to the sky and something up there has wings, I'll stick with the man with the big sword."

Tylar led the pair into the front hall. "There's a roof here. Keep with Delia. You still have your knives?"

As answer, Rogger parted his outer heavy cloak, revealing the crossed bandoliers weighted with daggers.

"Keep hidden," Tylar said and headed away.

Chaos greeted Tylar as he reached the shipwright's broken door.

He heard Kyllan shout from around the corner, out of sight. A pikeman raced into view, panic-footed, weapon clutched to his chest. His eyes were on the nearby canal as he fled.

A mistake.

From the sky, a spindly creature dropped out of the air, appearing half spider, half bat. Its limbs were skeletal, stretched as long as the creature was tall, webbed between forearm and back. Its body was hairless. Head misshapen, face split in the middle as it screeched, revealing a gnash of shredding teeth.

It fell upon the man before he could bring his weapon to bear, wrapping him in a cocoon of leathery wings, tearing into his throat.

A single scream, then the creature ripped away just as quickly. Its talons dug into the guard's belly and pushed off again, wings snapped wide. Trailing gore, it climbed again into the dark sky and twisted away beyond a roofline.

The pikeman tumbled to the stone, bowels roiling out his rent belly, blood still pumping from his ruined throat.

Tylar edged out the door, back to the wall. It was too late to help the man. He watched the skies. The creature had moved with unnatural speed. Tylar had noted the swirl of refuse as the beast lit back into the sky. As if the winds themselves aided its escape.

Tylar had also noted one other detail, revealed as the wings snapped wide: a pair of breasts. The bosom of a woman—or rather, she *was* a woman, one ilked into a beast.

Scowling, Tylar reached the corner and checked past the edge.

Kyllan and a knot of pikemen had something trapped amongst them. It thrashed and screamed as spears plunged repeatedly into it. Yet it refused to die. One man was knocked off his feet, his left leg severed at the knee by a scything blow.

"Don't let it reach the waters!" Kyllan shouted.

The creature bulled through the break in the circling men.

Kyllan grabbed the fallen man's spear and tossed it with all his strength. The pike pierced clean through the creature's shoulder and jammed into the first plank of the dock, pinning it in place.

Tylar hurried forward. The beast appeared more oil than form, amorphous of shape, pale as milk, streaming with ripples of ink. There was something disturbingly familiar about the pattern.

The creature yowled with a final tug. Its flesh flowed around the impaled pike, slowly freeing itself.

Kyllan led his remaining pikemen to renew the assault.

The molten beast's face swung toward its pursuers. Thick-lipped, toadish, it growled and spat, etching stone with its slobber. Its snarl revealed a jagged shoal of black teeth as it reared up.

"Now!" Kyllan yelled.

A torch rose among his men and set to blaze a single pike, dripping with tar. Kyllan accepted the fiery weapon by its haft.

Tylar reached his side. "Hold your—"

Too late.

Kyllan twisted at the waist, and drove the pike's flaming tip through the beast's belly.

Where it touched, skin sizzled and blackened. The beast yowled, neck stretched back. A coiling curl of flame flicked from its lips. Still, it tried to escape its death, stumbling toward the icy canal.

Kyllan kept hold of the pike's butt end. Pinned by the fiery spear, the creature could not reach the waters. Flames spread, more skin blackened, as if some tinder had been ignited deep within the ilk-beast. With one last scream, it writhed, then collapsed, still smoking, to the planks of the dock.

Death seemed to add solidity to its watery form, as if whatever Grace had imbued its fluidity evaporated with the smoke, leaving only twisted flesh.

Tylar joined Kyllan. "There are more beasts about," he warned the sergeant. "One took wing a moment ago. Keep your pikes high."

Kyllan searched the dark skies. "Aye, another one lies over here. It was dispatched quick enough."

The sergeant led Tylar to a tumbled pile of boulders. Once closer, Tylar discerned that stone was actually flesh, a rocky monstrosity of calcified plates and pebbled skin.

"A skilled thrust by your Wyr-mistress," Kyllan said, nodding to Eylan, who stood off a step, sword in hand. "Nicked through a weak spot and pierced something vital. But before we could appreciate her skill, we were attacked from behind, from the canal. That skaggin' beast was harder to kill. Figured what steel couldn't kill, fire might."

Tylar nodded. But something still nagged him. He glanced back to the smoldering ruin of the other ilk-beast. Something . . .

Kyllan continued, "We must have stumbled on a nest of ilk-beasts roosting here in the Blight. Left over from the last battle. We'd best gather everyone and get clear."

The pikemen closed around them, wary, spears held at the ready.

"I'll send a full squad in the morning to flush out this skaggin' place."

Tylar had stopped listening. He drew closer to the smoking body of the other beast. He remembered shouting out against the slaying of the creature. It had been reflexive. What had he sensed?

He returned again to the dock. He studied the pale flesh. Something familiar about—then it struck him.

Gods above . . . no . . .

He knelt to the planks and reached out.

"Ser," Kyllan warned him. "Best to be away from there."

Ignoring him, Tylar gripped the misshapen jaw and turned the head. He searched the throat, running a gloved finger across the flesh. Flaps of tissue fluttered under his touch, revealing the pink beneath.

Gill flaps.

Tylar stared into the dead eyes, knowing who lay before him.

"Kreel . . ."

He shoved up and searched the ice-choked canal. A dark hummock lay seven steps upriver. He hurried toward it, followed by Kyllan and his guards.

Beached against the canal wall, lolling on its side, was the watercraft used to transport Rogger here. The tall fin was broken, its keel sundered as if something had shattered out, like a newborn chick from an egg.

Tylar glanced at the body on the dock. Kreel. It was the pilot, the head of Fyla's Hunters. Realization iced through him. This was no nest of old ilk-beasts. These were freshly cursed men and women, ilked just now and sent against them.

Proving this, a screech again rose from the sky. The winged creature had not fled. It attacked once again, diving upon a pair of guards near the shipwright's shop. But the men were prepared this time. Pikes staved off the beast, slicing through wings.

More guards closed to do battle, including Eylan, a sword in one hand, an ax in the other.

Kyllan shouted orders but remained at Tylar's side. "Stay back, ser. My men can handle the creature."

A claw lashed out and razed to bone the side of one guard's face. He fell back with a scream. The creature moved with the swiftness of the wind.

Then it struck him.

With the swiftness of the wind.

Tylar lunged forward, dragging Kyllan with him.

"Ser!"

Tylar hurried, certain of the truth. He ticked off each in his head: the woman's wings, Kreel's flowing form, the first beast's stony armor. Each of the beasts bore one aspect of Grace: Air, Water, and Loam.

But one was missing.

Fire.

As he ran, he heard a new scream, a woman's cry, muffled from within the shipwright's shop.

Delia.

Tylar had not been the target of the attack. None of the beasts had set upon him directly. They were after the talisman, the cursed god skull. Even now, the winged creature fought at the entrance, struggling to get inside the shipwright's shop.

But something was already there.

Skirting the battle at the front door, Tylar entered through a broken window. Kyllan followed him into what must have once been an old kitchen, judging from the collapsed stone hearth, now a nest to a pack of rats, and the broken pottery underfoot. Though sheltered from the wind, the room was far colder than the outside.

Tylar knew why.

The ilk-beast, cursed with *fire*, must be drawing to itself what little warmth there was in the space. Tylar silently signaled Kyllan. He had already instructed the sergeant on his duty. Though reluctant, Kyllan headed out the back door to the kitchen, aiming for the rear.

Tylar stepped toward the other door, one that led to the center hallway.

As he leaned out, a dagger flew past the tip of his nose. He ducked back—but the blade had never been aimed at him. The dagger flew down the hall and struck a black shape crouched at the threshold to the rear workspace. It stood limned against the campfire back there, bathed in its glow.

The fourth ilk-beast.

Rogger's dagger flew true and struck the figure square in the chest, but the hilt instantly burst into flame. No blood flowed; flesh seared instantly. The steel blade dripped in molten rivulets from the wound.

Tylar retreated to the other end of the hallway, where Rogger guarded Delia.

Delia moved closer to him, seeking shelter. "It burnt right through the back of the shop and came at us."

Drawn by the campfire, Tylar thought.

The beast growled, flames licking from black lips, its eyes aglow with an inner fire. It stalked toward the trio.

Tylar raised his sword against it. Though probably as innocent as Kreel, forged unwillingly, the beast had to die. At their back, the screeching battle with the winged beast continued. Any retreat that way was blocked.

Rogger took up Tylar's other side. "Ruined four good daggers. I'm not sure any blade can stop it—not even your Godsword."

Tylar had no choice but to risk it—but that didn't mean he couldn't better his odds.

He lunged toward the approaching beast and shouted, "Now, Kyllan!"

Beyond the creature's shoulder, he spotted the sergeant racing to the campfire in the back room. He flung out a scrap of sailcloth and swept it over the fire.

Tylar reached the beast as the sergeant smothered the flames and stamped them out. As Tylar had hoped, the beast had been drawing strength from the flames, siphoning heat and power from the pyre. With the sudden interruption of this fiery font, the beast was momentarily lost.

In that moment of confusion, Tylar stabbed his blade into the neck of the beast. A backwash of feverish heat struck him, along with the gagging reek of brimstone and burnt flesh. Tylar twisted the blade and drove the sword to its hilt.

He felt no satisfaction from the kill, picturing Kreel.

The ilk-beast fell from his sword, toppling back with the last sigh of its corrupted Grace. Like Kreel's, the body that struck the floor seemed smaller, drained of power, mere flesh again.

Kyllan hurried toward them, his own sword raised.

Behind them, a small cheer rose from the guards outside the shop, announcing their own victory over the winged ilk-beast.

Delia stepped to Tylar's side. "Your blade . . ."

As expected, Tylar held only a hilt in his hand. The sword's blade was gone. Not melted away. Vanished. It was the curse of the Godsword. The blade was allowed only one blessed strike, then it vanished, needing to be whetted back into existence by a rare source: the blood of an unsundered god.

But for the moment such a rebirth would have to wait.

Tylar turned to Rogger. "We have to get that skull of yours out of Chrismferry as quickly as possible."

"Why's that?"

"Someone knows you brought it here. The attack was not random." Tylar explained about Kreel. "They had to be after the skull."

Rogger blanched. "But how did they discern my arrival so quickly? I've just touched soil for the first time in days."

"I don't know."

Tylar glanced at Delia. As a servant to the gods for many years, she had been schooled in all matters of Grace, far better than either of them. But she merely shook her head. This was beyond even her knowledge. Only one place could possibly unravel this mystery.

"We need to get the skull to Tashijan," Tylar said. "For study, for answers."

Rogger's brows drew together warily.

Tashijan, while home to the Order of Shadowknights and the esteemed Council of Masters, remained a place of divided loyalties. The warden, Argent ser Fields, still bore strong animosities toward Tylar's regency and for the man himself. But they had fierce allies there also: Kathryn ser Vail, the castellan of Tashijan, and Gerrod Rothkild, one of the most learned of the subterranean masters. The skull would be safe in their care, behind the towering walls of Tashijan.

But how to get it there?

"I must travel to Tashijan myself in seven days' time," Tylar said. "To regain my knighthood and my place among the Order. But I fear waiting so long before investigating the meaning of this cursed skull. It would be well to have answers by the time I reached there."

"I can travel overland," Rogger said. "I still have many friends in shadowed corners. Best I disappear again. Let no one know my path except my own ears. I can send a note by raven once behind those stout walls."

Tylar nodded. "And we'll meet again in seven days."

Rogger still hesitated. "My whole story will have to wait 'til then. It is too long to tell as the night wanes. But I must tell you of one other concern."

Tylar nodded for him to continue, but Rogger drew him aside first, away from Kyllan, even away from Delia again.

"What is it?" Tylar asked once they were alone.

"The skull . . . I told you I found it in Saysh Mal, but what I didn't have time to tell was that someone else sought the skull. Someone only a step behind my own."

"Who was it?"

"That's just it. It makes no sense."

"Who?"

"I only saw his face from a distance. At night. A shadowy face painted in ash."

"One of the Black Flaggers?" Such was the custom among the pirates and brigands who trafficked in all matters that shunned the light of day. They blackened their faces with ash to hide their features.

Rogger nodded. "I was able to capture a message, one sent by wing, but it was cursed. Burned in my fingers before I could read it fully. All I had time to discern was to whom it was addressed."

Tylar waited.

"The letter had been intended for Krevan."

Tylar was stung by the words. Krevan was one of their closest allies. A former shadowknight—the famous Raven ser Kay of old—he had been fiercely loyal to Tylar and their cause to free Chrismferry. But the knight had vanished after the Battle of Myrrwood, disappearing back into obscurity. Tylar had suspected he had returned to his role as leader of the Black Flaggers. But what new subterfuge was this? Why would Krevan be looking for the skull, too?

Judging by Rogger's expression, he had no answers either.

Tylar ached to hear Rogger's full story, but such tales would have to wait.

"How long will it take you to reach Tashijan?" Tylar asked.

"Two days—if I follow the most circumspect route."

"I will send a raven to Kathryn to tell her to expect you then."

"Maybe it would be best if I just surprise her," Rogger said with a raised brow. "Ravens have a way of being lured astray."

Tylar quickly gathered everyone outside the shop. He turned to Rogger for one last word, but the thief was already gone, vanished into the Blight without even a farewell.

Tylar shook his head as Delia slipped to his side.

"Will he be safe?" Delia asked, worried for their friend.

Tylar took her hand. Once again he had no answer. And a greater fear loomed in his heart. Would Rogger be any safer once he reached Tashijan?

Would any of them?

3

A GIRL WITH A WOODEN SWORD

DART HURRIED DOWN THE SPIRALING FLIGHT OF STAIRS. THE fourth morning bell had already rung, echoing through the throat of Stormwatch Tower. As she ran, she hiked the edge of her cloak to keep from tripping.

Mustn't be late . . . not again.

Pupp kept pace with her. Her ghostly companion trotted and bounded ahead down the steps, his fiery tongue lolling in the excitement of it all. His form passed through legs and cloaks, unimpeded and unsensed. Nobody could see Pupp, and only stone was solid enough to block his passage.

Dart was not so lucky.

At this hour, the central stair was crowded, thwarting her progress. Messengers dashed about in blue livery, burdened with clutched scrolls or shouldered satchels, as frantic to climb as Dart was to descend. The occasional Masters, their bald and tattooed heads bowed together, moved more sedately, rocks in the flowing stream of activity.

But most of those who shared the stairs were of Dart's own caste: pages in their half cloaks, squires in their hoods, and towering over all, a jumbling crowd of full-blessed shadowknights. Dart's brethren marched the stairs in all manner of moods. Some were cloaked and buried in matters that weighted their shoulders; others wore bits of bright colors, enjoying the freedom here. Only in Tashijan could knights walk bare-faced, free of their black cloaks and muffling masklins.

Here was their home.

And it had been Dart's for going on a full turn of seasons.

Laughter and whispers, shouts and curses, accompanied

Dart down the tower toward the practice yard. With the retinue from Chrismferry due in another four days and the festivities to follow, knights had been gathering back home, packing the place full. Even the outlying sections of the sprawling Citadel, long abandoned, had been reoccupied, swelling the ranks.

Along with the bustle came a thousand requests, suggestions, complaints, threats, and bribes, all rising like smoke to the castellan's private hermitage at the top of the tower. And since Dart served as page to Castellan Vail, her duties had also multiplied, leaving little time for routine.

Like her training practice.

She carried a wooden sword tied to her waist. It was a far cry from the handsome swords of the truly knighted, those rare blades adorned with the black diamonds on their pommels. Still, hers was long enough to bump against her side and threaten to trip her at every step.

At last she reached the bottom of the wide stairs and broke into the cavernous hall beyond. She kept near the wall, skirting the milling crowds in the center.

"Hothbrin!"

She almost didn't recognize the barked name, not even after a full year here. Then again, it was not really her name. Born an orphan, she had no surname. Only *Dart*, after the yellow and thorny dartweed that grew stubbornly between stones. Filling the void, Dart had borrowed her friend Laurelle's family name, taking it on as a mark of their deep bond—though Laurelle was far away, back at Chrismferry, continuing to serve as the Hand of tears for the new regent, Tylar ser Noche.

"Hothbrin!"

Dart turned and spotted one of her fellow knights-in-training, a bristle-headed squire named Pyllor, aide to the swordmaster of the school. Though only two years older than Dart, he stood as tall as any knight, and taller than many. He strode toward her.

Pupp appeared from the throng and stepped between Pyllor and Dart. His molten form grew fiercer, reflecting Dart's own mood. His mane of spikes bristled at Pyllor's stormy approach.

"There you are!" Pyllor strode straight through Pupp and grabbed Dart by the shoulder. "Late again! Swordmaster Yuril ordered me to fetch you. *By your heels or hair,* she said."

"I—I—I had to attend—"

"I—I—I." Pyllor mocked her, silencing her. "It's always about *you*. Just because you serve the castellan you think you can walk with your nose high and come and go as you please."

Pyllor's words could not be further from the truth. Dart's service to the castellan offered her little freedom of movement or time. And she surely held herself in no higher regard because of it. In fact, the contrary was true. She always felt set apart from her peers, less prepared, always struggling to catch up with her studies and training.

But most importantly, Dart felt herself to be an impostor. She had not earned her place here at Tashijan. Her position was all a ruse to hide her behind the tall walls of the Citadel, to keep her safe and near at hand. Only a year ago, Dart had learned her true heritage, that she was a child born of two rogue gods. And while her humours flowed with none of the rich Graces of the gods, her blood carried a single blessing: the ability to whet Rivenscryr, the Godsword of Myrillia, into existence. Thus, she had been sent here, away from Chrismferry, away from the sword itself, to make it harder for both to be stolen at once.

Otherwise, she was no different from any other girl.

Only perhaps more lost and alone.

"Swordmaster Yuril has everyone laboring with drudges as punishment for your tardiness."

"But why should the others pay—?"

" 'A knight is only as strong as the Order itself,' " Pyllor quoted with a disdainful smirk.

Dart had heard the same throughout her training. The true strength of the Order lay not in a single knight but in the breadth of the Order itself. As one failed, all suffered.

Such was the lesson being taught this morning.

Courtesy of Dart's tardiness.

She needed no further prodding to hurry out of the tower and toward the tiers of training fields beyond. The pages apprenticed to the Order held the grounds farthest afield. Dart passed a group of squires practicing lunges on horseback, kicking up clods of mud, earning jeers and accolades from their peers. She sensed the deep brotherhood among them all. What would it be like to be so accepted?

Dart hurried on, eventually spotting her fellow knights-in-training. They were yoked like oxen to wooden and iron drudges, dragging the sleds across the frozen mud and yellow grass, a hard exercise to strengthen back and legs.

Overseeing their labor, Swordmaster Yuril stood with her arms crossed, a pipe of blackleaf clenched between her teeth. Though the woman's dark hair was streaked with gray, she remained whip-thin and hard of countenance. She heard Dart's approach and turned to face the late pupil.

"Ah, Hothbrin, good of you to join us."

Dart dropped to one knee, bowed her head, then regained her feet. "My duties—"

"—are here," Yuril said. "Not up in the castellan's hermitage. Castellan Vail knows this as well as I. And you can tell her that from me."

"Yes, mistress."

Yuril whistled around the edge of her pipe. "Enough with the drudges! Gather round!"

With grateful groans, Dart's peers slipped yokes from sore shoulders and hobbled across the field. Dart shied from their hard-eyed glares. All knew whom to blame for their sore morning, but they all also knew better than to complain aloud. That would come later. When they were out from under the baleful eye of Swordmaster Yuril.

"We'll start today with basic form and position, then proceed with a few sparring matches."

They lined up in rows of four. Dart wanted to slink toward the back, but the swordmaster would not let her so easily shirk away. She was made to stand at the front of one row. For a full ring of the bell, they ran through the basic forms of defense and offense: Swayback Feint, Dogtoed Parry, Cusp-to-Cusp, Trailing Hilt, Thrusted Lash, and a blur of others.

Dart tried her best, but her lack of practice showed in the dropped point of her blade during Jackman's Tie and the tremble in her wrist as she moved from Honeynest to Sweeper's Row. Swordmaster Yuril corrected each mistake.

She snapped out with a cane, striking Dart's wooden sword, stinging her fingers, making her repeat the form.

At these moments, all eyes were on her. Dart felt the weight of their attention, sensed the ill will, the bitter amusement. Tears threatened to rise, but she refused to relent.

Finally she reached the last form, a complicated dance of wrist and steel named Naethryn's Folly. It was a feint used to disarm an opponent. It was a risky maneuver. If not performed flawlessly, the dance would end with your own sword on the ground. Still, if you could lure your opponent into the dance and not fail, it was almost impossible to counter.

Dart did her best to perform the exacting series of moves.

And failed.

A final twist and her hilt slipped from her tired fingers. Her sword spun into the mud.

Laughter applauded her mishap.

"Disarmed by the wind," Pyllor said as he strode across the field, arms behind his back, plainly imitating the swordmaster he idolized.

Yuril glowered at Dart, exhaling a trail of smoke from around her pipe's stem. "Collect your sword, Hothbrin." She turned her back on Dart, not even bothering to have her repeat the form this time, as if recognizing the impossibility. "We'll move on to some open sparring now. I'll be studying each of you to see how you have learned to apply the forms to actual swordplay. In the field of battle, you'll need to flow smoothly from one to another, to recognize the waxing of one form, to react accordingly, to counter with another."

The group quickly paired up. Dart soon found herself alone, standing forlornly with sword in hand.

Yuril nodded to Pyllor. "You'll spar with her."

Pyllor's eyes widened in surprise. He was five years her senior in swordsmanship. But he merely nodded. "As you wish." The pairing was beneath him, but still a glint of wicked delight flashed in his eyes.

Yuril lined the combatants around the field and raised an arm in the air. "Take your stances!"

Dart backed a step, trying her best to settle into a ready guard. She was all too aware of her opponent's weight, reach, and skill. Would her humiliation never end?

"Swords up!" Yuril barked. "Begin!"

Pyllor attacked immediately. He step-lunged, crackling fast. Dart barely got her guard up, parrying his sword aside. The tip of his sword sailed past her ear. She flinched when she should have taken the advantage with a counterattack.

Pyllor sprang back deftly, turning his shoulder and striking down with his blade. The strength of the impact knocked Dart's sword almost to the mud. Pyllor rocked forward and slammed Dart square in the chest with the point of his sword, hard enough to knock her back.

She tripped and fell onto her backside.

Pyllor stood over her.

Dart rubbed where he had struck, knowing it would bruise. If the blade had been steel instead of wood, she would be dead.

Around her the *clack-clacking* of other practice swords echoed. She was the first defeated. In a matter of breaths.

Yuril rolled her eyes and surveyed the others.

Dart regained her feet and stared glumly across the field. There was much crude hacking and slashing, bouts of brawn over skill, but several of her peers demonstrated flashes of talent: a turned feint, a roundhouse parry, a double thrust.

Yuril called out a few rare compliments—which usually caused the receiver to stumble and lose his match, but the loss was greeted with embarrassed grins.

"Again!" Yuril commanded.

Dart picked up her sword. Two more matches and she was on the ground again, favoring a stinging wrist slap. Pyllor was not holding back—neither with his skill nor with his muscle.

Tears threatened, but Dart let her anger pull her back to her feet.

Pupp, bristling and fiery, stalked around her ankles. Dart waved him back with her free hand. Though without substance, Pupp could sometimes rile himself enough to have some impact on his own. Dart didn't want him interfering.

"Again!"

Dart took her stance. When the call to start was shouted, she took the lead for the first time, lunging out with a feint to Pyllor's sword. He countered, trying to smack her blade back. She anticipated and nipped her sword point under the swing of his blade.

Pyllor's eyes widened in surprise, caught off guard.

Dart lunged into the opening, going for a tag to Pyllor's torso.

Instead, Pyllor reached with his free hand and grabbed her wooden sword, trapping it. He yanked it closer, dragging Dart off her toes. As she stumbled toward him, he clubbed the hilt of his sword into Dart's chin.

Her head snapped back, and she fell hard onto the frozen field.

Yuril had missed the maneuver, witnessing only the end.

"Hothbrin, never close guard! Learn to keep your distance!"

The swordmaster turned away again.

Pyllor sneered down at her.

He had cheated and now gloated over his ill-gotten victory. If they had been sparring with steel, he would never have been able to grab a razor-edged blade like that. He would've lost fingers, and Dart's lunge would have struck home.

"That's enough for this morning!" Yuril called out. "Off to your bread-boards! I'll see you all on the morrow. And you'd better practice your stances!"

Yuril barked the last while staring straight at Dart.

A few chuckles rose from the others.

With the lessons over, everyone headed across the cold fields toward the warm towers and halls. Most left in groups or pairs. Only Dart walked within a mantle of disgrace thick enough to hold off all others.

A final glance back showed Pyllor with Yuril. The swordmaster's back was to Dart, but she seemed to be sharing a few hard words with the young squire. Pyllor opened his mouth to offer some protest, but something in Yuril's face made him close his lips. His eyes, though, noted Dart's attention and flashed with fury at her. Plainly the discourse concerned Pyllor's sparring match.

Dart quickly glanced back around.

Had the swordmaster witnessed his deceitful grab of Dart's sword after all? Or was he merely being scolded for being so hard on such a lesser pupil?

Either way, the black cloud around Dart grew a few shades lighter. Even Pupp shook out of his hunkered tread and trotted more brightly.

Dart felt a renewed determination settle through her. She would practice, every night. She would not end up on her backside in the mud again.

Still, her gaze stretched upward, following the rise of Stormwatch Tower into the steel gray sky. Up near the top lay the hermitage of the castellan, where Kathryn ser Vail held sway. Dart had her responsibilities there, too. The knighting ceremony for Tylar was only days away. There were a thousand details to attend to.

Yet despite her duties here on the field and up in the tower, Dart had never felt more alone. She stared again at her laughing, jostling peers with a heavy heart. She missed her friend Laurelle, sharing a bed, talking in whispers all through the night. She had no friend like that here.

No one even knew her real name.

Pupp must have sensed the clouds about her shoulders, for he bounced back to her, biting at her training sword, his teeth passing harmlessly through the wood. She could almost hear his determined growls.

A small, tired smile formed.

She had at least one friend here.

"Let's go, Pupp—we've got a long climb."

Dart hurried up the stairs, around and around. After so many flights, her attention drifted, caught in the press and flow of the busy day—then a shout startled her back to alertness.

"Mind the robe!"

Dart danced around the rotund form of Master Hesharian, head of the Council of Masters. He huffed on the stairs ahead of her, filling the passage, one hand on the wall to support himself. His bald pate shone with a slick of sweat, highlighting the eleven sigils tattooed around the crown of his head, marking his mastered disciplines.

He must have important duties with Warden Fields to have climbed so far out of his subterranean den. The levels of the masters were said to delve as deep below the land as Stormwatch climbed into the sky. It was the masters' sole domain. Down below lay their domiciles, alchemy labs, and storehouses. Dart had heard rumors of Hesharian's personal menagerie, where he studied new alchemies on beasts of the field.

Dart pushed past him with distaste, earning a disgruntled glare from the massive man. He climbed with another master, one Dart didn't know, an ancient man in a muddied traveling cloak. He also noted Dart's passage. His gaze fell upon her. She glanced up—then shuddered, almost tripping on a step. His eyes were the color of milk. He should've been blind, so scaled did his eyes appear, but Dart sensed the cold weight of his attention. For a breath, she heard the flutter of ravens' wings, taken back to another moment of terror, of violation.

Then his gaze drifted off, freeing her.

She hurried past, followed just as quickly by Pupp, his stubby tail tucked low. She was relieved to finally reach the twenty-second flight, where both the Warden of Tashijan and Castellan Vail had their rooms. She fled the stairs, happy to be rid of the midday crowd ascending and descending Stormwatch Tower, though at this lofty height, most of the crowd had thinned. The only folk still on the stairs were those who had matters to settle with Castellan Vail or Warden Fields.

Like the two masters.

Glancing back, Dart saw them enter the stone hallway.

What matters had drawn them so high?

Dart turned away from them, toward the tall doors that marked the Warden's Eyrie. The doors were open but flanked by a pair of knights. Dart noted the crimson stitching at the shoulder of their cloaks. A perfect circle crisscrossed with two slashes. The sigil of the Fiery Cross, marking them as the warden's men.

A small crowd gathered outside the open door. They were cloaked and dressed in shades of browns and blacks, plainly finery, but gone a bit tattered.

A voice called from inside the doorway, "Again it is an honor to have a Hand of Lord Balger join us for the ceremonies! My manservant, Lowl, will take you to your rooms, where you may refresh after your trip. He'll see that your trunks are unloaded from the flippercraft and brought to your rooms."

Dart stepped against the wall to allow them to pass. The retinue from Foulsham Dell had already arrived, undoubtedly early enough to take full advantage of the flow of wine and ale. She also noted that Lord Balger, god of that realm, had sent only *one* of his eight Hands to attend Tylar's knighting. A veiled slight. Plainly there remained ill will between the god of the Dell, a realm of brigands and cutthroats, and the new regent.

Over the past moon, bets had been placed among the knights on which realms would send emissaries and how many Hands from each would be in attendance. Dart eyed the passage of the lone Hand from the Dell, a pot-bellied man with a palsied gait. Few would make money on this wager.

Once the party had passed, Dart continued down the hall.

The pair of black-cloaked guards, who even here kept the wrap of their masklins over the lower half of their faces, barely noted her passage.

Unfortunately she did not escape another's attention.

"Page Hothbrin . . ."

She froze.

"A moment, if you please."

Dart turned to find Warden Fields standing a few steps past his threshold. He was a commanding figure, tall in black boots and trousers, with a gray shirt and silver buttons. His manner was casual as he passed some trifling gift that the Hand of Lord Balger had presented to him to another manservant.

Despite the few streaks of gray in his dark auburn hair, tied and braided with black leather, Argent ser Fields remained solid of muscle and stolid of countenance. He studied Dart for a measuring breath. His attention was disconcerting; one eye had been lost during an acclaimed campaign against a ravening hinterking. The old scar was now covered by a plate of bone, taken, it was said, from the skull of that same king.

Dart backed a step—but she could not escape that easily.

Warden Fields waved her forward with a warm smile. "Fear not, child. I won't bite."

Swallowing hard, Dart drifted toward him. She could not refuse. Despite the difficulties last year, he remained the leader of the Shadowknights. She stepped across the threshold and entered his Eyrie.

Argent spoke to the knights at the door. "Have Master Hesharian and his guest indulge me a moment—when they arrive."

Dart had noted that the large master remained halfway down the hall, greeting Balger's Hand, wheezing and wiping a brow.

Argent closed the door, nodded to her again, and strode into the room. A fire crackled in a large hearth. The windows that overlooked a central courtyard were heavily draped against the cold. There were few furnishings. Even the back corner of the room had its rugs rolled back to bare stone, with a rack of weapons against one wall. A spot for the warden to spar and keep his skills honed. It was said he remained one of the more formidable swordsmen.

But Dart noted the layer of dust on the weapons rack.

Argent had turned his attention to other battles of late.

Keeping his place here in the Eyrie.

Though he had been voted into position with almost unanimous backing of the knights and masters, all knew by what means he had stretched to capture Tylar when the regent was an outlawed godslayer. All had seen the petrified body of the warden's former right-hand man, Symon ser Jaklar, accidentally cursed to stone by Argent's own hand, wielding a sword black with corrupted Graces, a forbidden weapon. The disgrace went far toward unseating the man—but seemingly not far enough.

Symon's form had disappeared into the masters' domain, deep under the Citadel, supposedly to seek some way to cure him, but more likely to whisk the corruption away from all eyes, to let time dull the horror.

So with the backing of the likes of Master Hesharian, high master of the Council of Masters, Argent had initially kept his perch here in the Eyrie. And now his position grew more solid with the passing of every moon. Memories ran short when all of Myrillia was holding its breath and searching over its shoulders. Rumors and stories continued to abound: of strange beasts plaguing outlying realms, of madness among gods, of disappearances across the lands.

And as this long winter stretched on, Argent found his support growing. Before his disgrace, he had founded the Fiery Cross among the knights. Over the recent centuries, the shadowknights had been dwindling in both numbers and esteem, seemingly becoming no more than couriers and sellswords. Argent had promised to reverse that course, to return the knights to glory, to become its own force among the gods, all symbolized under the banner of the Fiery Cross.

Such a conceit found fertile ground in many hearts.

Even corruption could not fully unroot it.

And now this latest ploy: to return to Tylar his shadowcloak and sword. The offer was made more to help Argent than Tylar. But it could not be refused. Such a gesture of unification was necessary. During these dark times, Tashijan needed to be strong, for there were greater dangers than those represented by Argent ser Fields.

"Come inside. I wish to share a few private words with you." Argent motioned her forward. "Knight to knight."

Dart remained where she was, head bowed, her eyes narrowed with suspicion. The warden had never once even spoken to her. To all, even the warden, Dart was no more than some page scooped up by Castellan Vail, a servant and courier. The warden remained ignorant of her true role and the secret hidden in her blood and heritage.

So what could he want with her now?

Argent crossed to a small table with a silver platter of brandied nuts and dried baby plums. Fingers waved at the fare. "Please help yourself. I imagine Mistress Yuril has worn you thin and hungry."

Dart's belly was indeed empty, but she made no move, mumbling something that was incomprehensible even to her own ears.

Argent plucked up a plum and rolled it between his fingers. "I've heard from a certain squire that you seem to be lapsing in your training."

Dart's eyes flicked up, her face reddening.

"We can't have that. Perhaps it would be best if I freed you from your duties with the castellan."

"Ser," Dart said, suddenly finding her voice, "please, no!"

"No, I don't suppose you'd like to lose such an esteemed position. A page serving the castellan. It is a rare honor."

Dart's brow crinkled. What was all this about?

"I'm certain the deficit to your training could be corrected . . . with a tutor, perhaps a bit of fortifying Grace . . . but such an expense. I daresay it must be beyond your means, yes?"

Dart just bowed her head. She could not stop her knees from shaking. Across the room, Pupp wandered about, poking his nose into corners.

"But in the long run, it might be to the Order's best suit to have such an esteemed member as yourself, one serving the castellan, to avail herself of such a boon."

"That would be most generous," Dart said.

Argent popped the plum between his lips and chewed for a moment, nodding as if in private conversation with himself. He finally spoke again. "Still, what is a boon if unearned? What sort of lesson would that be for a knight-in-training?"

"Ser?"

Argent sighed. "With all the tumult of late, the castellan and I have found so few moments to sit and share our thoughts on matters of Tashijan's well-being. That is certainly not good for the Order. Perhaps as recompense for the additional expense of tutors and drips and drabs of special Graces, you, Page Hothbrin, could serve an additional duty—bringing to me Castellan Vail's thoughts and words on matters of interest to the Order."

"I'm sure, ser—"

Warden Fields silenced her with a stern look. "Of course, we wouldn't want the castellan to know of your duties. I'd hate for Castellan Vail to think herself neglectful in making time for private meetings here at the Eyrie. She has enough to juggle as it is. So this would be between just the two of us."

Dart's mouth dried, and her heart climbed to her throat.

"If this is too burdensome, I'm sure we could find another page who might serve the castellan with more alacrity."

"No, ser . . ."

Argent smiled again. The warden was asking her to spy upon the castellan, plying her with promises of boons while threatening to displace her from her position. All the while couching it as for the good of the Order.

"Fine, fine . . . so it's settled." He strode back to the door. "I won't keep you from your duties any longer."

He opened the door, and Dart slid through as soon as there

was space enough for her. She came close to colliding with Master Hesharian.

"Mind the robe!" he called to her.

But Dart was already away, ducking from the mysterious master in the traveling cloak. She hurried down the hall to the next set of doors, those that opened into the castellan's private hermitage. Though neighbors on this high level, the occupants of the two sets of rooms could not be further apart in stance and outlook.

She knocked on the door, keeping her eyes fixed to the tight grain of the stout ironwood planks, willing it to open.

Pupp simply ran straight through the door.

Lucky dog.

Moments later, Dart was paid for her patience.

"Uncle Rogger!"

Dart dashed into the castellan's hermitage, cloak flagging behind her.

The door had barely been opened when she spotted the former thief. It had taken a startled second look, though, to recognize him. Rogger had shorn his usual ragged beard into straight edges, his peppered red hair was oiled and combed, and he wore the sashed purple robe of a learned scribe, those blessed with Grace to write letters sealed and coded with alchemies. Even all his fingers were dyed purple to the first knuckle. Such scribes could be found throughout Tashijan, especially of late.

Rogger had come in disguise.

Kathryn ser Vail rose from a seat by the crackling hearth as Dart flew into the room. She slipped a flap of cloth over something resting atop the table by the hearth. It hid an object the size of a small melon.

A third occupant of the room, Gerrod Rothkild, esteemed master and ally, remained seated, leaning over the table, encased in his usual bronzed armor.

Dart caught the whiff of some foul alchemies—then she was in Rogger's arms. She hugged him tight to her. It had been an entire year. Too long. He chuckled at the fervency of her greeting.

She didn't care. Of those who knew the truth about her, there were few who seemed to care less.

"Unhand me, foul wench!" he said after returning her hug.

Dart grinned and backed away.

Rogger searched around the room, then held out an arm. A bit of sweetcrackle appeared in his fingers as if out of the very air. "I think I owe someone else a greeting. Here you lice-ridden slab of mutton." He bent, resting his other hand on a knee, dangling out the tasty tidbit. "Now where are you?"

Dart pointed toward the table where Castellan Vail stood. "Pupp is over there."

"Ah," Rogger said, straightening. He shared a strange glance with Castellan Vail. "Mayhap he should be away from there. Not something to be nosing, that's for sure."

Gerrod stirred, collected the covered object, and stood. "I will take the artifact down to my rooms among the masters. See what I can make of it."

"Thank you, Gerrod."

"And be careful with the skaggin' thing," Rogger added.

With a nod to the thief and a half bow to the castellan, Gerrod strode off with a whir of the mekanicals that drove his armor. Though Dart had never seen the man's face, hidden behind bronze, all knew his story, how his body had been wasted by the alchemies necessary to attain the fifteen masterfields, the most disciplines ever mastered by a single man. Now he was forever dependent on the blessed mekanicals of his armor for support.

Once Gerrod was gone, Rogger waved Dart to one of the three seats by the hearth. Kathryn took the other. Rogger settled into the third, resting his heels by the fire. He tossed the bit of sweetcrackle to Dart for nibbling.

"What are you going to do now, Rogger?" Kathryn asked.

"I figured I'd stick tight at least until Tylar gets his cloak and sword back. Meantime, I'll shed these robes, slink into the lower realms of these black halls, and listen about. Have you ever figured out who slew that young knight last year?"

Kathryn's countenance darkened. She wore a knight's black leathers, as if she had come in from a recent ride. Even her hair, a dark golden red, was woven into a horseman's knot at the nape of her neck. It was one of the few ways the castellan relaxed these days, on horseback, the wind in her cloak. Rogger's arrival must have thwarted a midday ride.

"No. And I fear we may never discover the truth."

Dart had not seen the murder firsthand, but she had heard the tale in great detail: a knight's body found slaughtered, sacrificed, drained of blood, alongside a pit of burnt bones. The murderers remained free.

"The trail has gone dead cold by now," Kathryn explained. "Even Tracker Lorr has given up after spending an entire moon in the warren of sewers that drain the city."

Rogger grunted. "And I thought my travels were harsh."

"And now we have the abandoned sections of the city swelling with returning knights and rooms being readied for all the various guests. Any tracks we might have missed or overlooked are surely trampled, swept away, or muddied."

Kathryn shook her head in defeat.

"So no way to pin it on One Eye?" Rogger said.

Dart knew that the castellan highly suspected Argent ser Fields in the deaths and disappearances. Especially with the warden wielding a cursed sword in his hunt for Tylar. Still, suspicions were not proof that could be brought before any adjudicators. Argent had even passed inspection by soothmancers, bloody-fingered men of fiery alchemies who could probe the truth in one's heart.

Still, Kathryn was sure the Fiery Cross was somehow connected to the sacrifice. The fire pit, the circle of blood, and the spread-eagled man—all suggestive of some ritual with the Cross. But now they had all slipped away.

"Have there been any more disappearances?" Rogger asked.

"We're keeping a daily roll now, especially among our younger knights. It seems Perryl was the last to vanish."

Perryl ser Corriscan was another of their allies, a young knight new to his stripes, one who was taken from his room, leaving only a splatter of blood on his bed. Dart sensed this was who Kathryn sought more than any.

"With all the new knights arriving," Rogger said, "perhaps a few words will slip, a bit of bragging done under the hem of a cloak. I'll see what I can discern."

"Be careful."

Rogger seemed to read something in Kathryn's hollowed

gaze. "We're not defeated yet. If One Eye is to blame, or those in his service, we'll bring him low."

Her expression didn't change. "With all that's happening beyond our walls, maybe that isn't even for the best. Rather than looking back, seeking to place blame, maybe it is time to make peace. Shaking Argent out of his Eyrie will weaken us most when we need to be at our strongest."

Dart's eyes widened, shocked. She had never heard the castellan express such a sentiment.

Even Rogger was struck silent.

"No!" Dart said into the sullen quiet, remembering the artful bit of deceit and bribery just perpetrated against her. "It's a false strength! He doesn't seek the good of Myrillia, only his own power." Dart related what had occurred just moments before in the Warden's Eyrie.

Now it was the castellan's eyes that widened. "Argent sought to set you up as a spy here? In my own hermitage?"

Dart nodded vigorously. "Do not let your guard down, Castellan Vail. Better to be few and true of heart than legion and corrupt."

Rogger chuckled. "From the mouths of babes come the simplest wisdoms."

Kathryn sagged back into her seat, but she nodded. "I've been too long in this tower."

"But you're not alone—never alone," Rogger said. "And Tylar will be here in another day or so."

These last words only seemed to wound more than heal. Dart had known the castellan long enough to recognize the pained narrowing of her lips, the tightening at the corners of her eyes. Matters between Kathryn and her former betrothed were even more complicated than between castellan and warden.

Rogger seemed blind to all this. "Once Tylar is here, all will be clearer."

Dart sensed nothing could be further from the truth.

But this time she stayed silent.

Much later, as the sun sank and the first evening bell rang, Dart closed the door to her private room. Sore and tired, she shed her half cloak and wooden sword and pulled out of her boots. She could hardly think.

After Rogger left, Dart had found the rest of the day a blur of errands for the castellan. It seemed as each bell rang, bringing them only that much closer to the day of Tylar's ceremony, more duties befell them all. Dart also had to attend a class explaining proper horse grooming and the care of riding tack, where a surly gelding had stepped on her toe. She still limped. It made the final climb up to the top of Stormwatch all that much harder.

But here her room waited. The room was really a closet, formerly a maid's chamber adjacent to the castellan's hermitage, but it was gloriously all her own. She even had a slitted window that looked out on the giant wyrmwood tree that graced the central courtyard.

As Dart limped to the window in her stockings, Pupp stretched, circled a few times at the foot of her bed, then settled to the floor.

Dart stared at the lesser moon, a sickle slicing slowly through the leafless limbs of the great wyrmwood. A few stars shone with cold light. She stared, lost in her own bleary thoughts of things she had to remember for the following morning. Another two retinues would arrive tomorrow—from Five Forks and Nevering.

Finally, her warm breath fogged the cold pane and she turned away.

With her thoughts on those arriving, her mind drifted to another worry, one she had been shying away from over the past half-moon since she had traveled with Castellan Vail to Oldenbrook. Dart again pictured the bronze boy, formerly a fellow student at Chrismferry, now a handservant of Jessup. She recalled how his emerald eyes had sparked when she'd last seen him, half-crouched in the High Wing.

Would he come? Would he be one of the emissaries Lord Jessup sent to witness the knighting here?

Dart found the possibility unsettling. He had recognized her, knew her from their days at the school. It would be dangerous to associate with him. Still . . . a part of her warmed at the thought.

Sighing, she shook her head.

She crossed back to her bed, but left the blankets where they were tucked. Her day was not quite over. She took up her sword again.

Alone in her room, she lifted the sword, shifted her knee, and began pacing through all the forms. With no one watching her every turn and twist, she relaxed into the rhythm, at first haltingly, then with more confidence. She sensed for the first time how one form flowed into another. Again and again she ran the paces, slowly coming to realize that it wasn't the sword that defended and attacked—it was one's own body, one's own heart.

Deaf to the ringing of the evening bells, Dart continued, long into the night, dancing with her sword.

Alone.

Still, a small part of her wondered.

Would he come?

4

A WINTER'S CLOAK

BRANT SCOWLED AT THE FINERY DRAPED OVER HIS FORM. Arms out, he stood perched on a stool as a gaggle of women tucked and folded, pinched and pinned. A slim-waisted tailor in a peaked cap strode in a tight circle around them all, calling out final measurements and instructions.

Finally, the man clapped his hands. "Perfect! But we'll raise the collar just a bit to hide that scar on your neck."

Brant gratefully lowered his arms.

He was dressed in shades of blue, from navy leggings to a ruffled azure shirt, the hues of Oldenbrook. But his position as Hand of blood was also represented in his dressings: a piping of crimson down the leggings, with matching sash to be pinned at the shoulder with a clip of gold, along with gold buttons for the shirt. It was all topped by a navy half cloak, tasseled with crimson.

"Off with it! We'll make the final adjustments and have it all ready for packing by the morning." A sound escaped the man, a mix of exasperation and satisfaction. "Hurry now! We have another three Hands to fit!"

Brant climbed from the stool, shed the clothes, and ushered everyone out of his rooms. Once alone, he pulled on his usual worn leathers and boots. He caught a reflection in the mirror that the tailor had hauled up here. He lifted his chin. One hand rose to touch the scar, mapping it with a finger, then dropped away.

A reminder of another life—one best forgotten.

He turned away. A loud sigh flowed from him as he grabbed his unstrung bow. It would be good to escape the city for the rest of the day.

All of the High Wing was in an excited flurry. Half the Hands were readying themselves for the flight to Tashijan the day after tomorrow. The others would remain to attend Lord Jessup, who, of course, could not leave his realm. The selected Hands would represent his Lordship and the entire realm at the knighting of the new regent.

After the long winter, the festivities had the entire castillion aflutter, a bit of pomp and color after the perpetual drab.

Brant shook his head at the foolishness.

The coming ceremony at Tashijan was plainly a symbolic gesture of unification and healing for the First Land. Brant would have been happy to forgo such posturing, but he had his reasons for not refusing Jessup's request that he join the outgoing retinue. First, he respected Lord Jessup and could hardly refuse anyway, but also he wished to investigate further into the mystery of the castellan's new page.

Brant's fingers traced the stone around his neck.

A sharp squeal drew his attention toward the door to his room. It came from the outer hall. Now what? He shouldered his quiver of freshly fletched arrows and hurried to the door.

As he pulled it open, he heard Liannora, Mistress of Tears, let out another delighted exclamation. "I must have it before we leave! The fur will make the perfect winter cloak!"

Brant stepped out as Liannora graced a tall man with a kiss to the cheek. Brant recognized the head of the castillion guards, a fellow with flowing blond hair, braided back from an angular face, and flint-hard dark eyes. He stood with his hands clasped behind his back, half-bowed to accept her kiss. There were few who didn't know how the man favored the lithe Mistress of Tears.

"Thank you, Sten. Your gift could not be more opportune." She clapped her hands in her excitement.

One other didn't share her mood. The tailor stood to one side, face clouded with worry. "As fresh as this hide is, it will take much Grace and alchemy to tan this much skin in time."

"I don't care how much it costs," Liannora said. "It can come out of my own purse."

Brant had no interest and tried to sidestep the others, but his motion drew Liannora's attention. She glanced him up and down, her smile hardening to distaste.

"Off on your hunt for a few scrawny rabbits and frozen birds, are we, Master Brant?" she asked.

Brant shrugged. "Best to be out of the way."

"Perhaps you should take Sten with you. It seems he could teach you a thing or two about hunting these woods."

"I'll manage. Thank you." He stepped away.

Liannora blocked him and revealed her gift from the guardsman. She motioned with her hand. "Here is the work of a true hunter."

Brant glanced at the floor, where a fresh hide lay draped and spread.

Liannora turned away, missing Brant's shocked expression. "The snowy fur will match my new dress perfectly," she said, too excited even to toy with Brant any longer. Her full attention was with the tailor. She pointed to the hide. "And we must keep the gray tufts at the ear tips for the hood. Everyone must know it's not just an ordinary wolf cloak. The tufts will let everyone know it came from a Fell wolf!"

Brant stumbled back. He knew where the hide had come from. He pictured the gaunt and starving Fell wolf that had hunted his track in the icy woods, begging for bloody scraps.

Dried blood still stained the hide. It was a fresh kill, no older than half a day. He noted the ragged tear of the hide at the rear ankle. No skinning knife had done that. It was the work of a razor snare, a cruel trap. How long had she been snared, the wire slicing to bone as she struggled?

Brant eyed the leader of the castillion guard. The man continued to drink up Liannora's attention like fine wine. He was no hunter—only a butcher. Brant would remember.

Brant headed toward the back of the High Wing, toward the tower that would lead down and out. He had another duty now before he set off for Tashijan.

He was a hunter. As one who followed and respected the Way, he knew why the she-wolf had come to him in the winter wood—and what pain had dulled the cunning of such a great beast to allow it to be snared.

It was more than hunger.

Brant remembered the smaller eyes that had glowed from the deeper forest as he had departed: a pair of cubbies, the children of the she-wolf.

She had only been protecting her whelpings, driven to extremes, far from home. And according to the path of the Way, such children were now his responsibility.

He had no choice.

He had to hunt them down.

The stilted city creaked and moaned as Brant stepped farther out onto the ice. Though the skies were still achingly blue, the winds had already begun to gust. The air smelled of storm. Snow was coming. Heavy snow. The northern skies were already lowering with dark clouds. Ice fog lay across the frozen lake as the day grew colder with almost every breath.

Brant returned his attention to the pair of loam-giants who stood guard at the foot of the tower. The massive twins huddled from the worst of the wind, buried in their furred longcoats, leaning on pikes.

"The scabbers came from that direction," Malthumalbaen said, raising a stout arm. "Should've seen 'em. All singing and pounding their round shields, like they had wrested a wyrm with their own bared hands."

Dralmarfillneer nodded his head, scowling his agreement with his twin brother. "Mal speaks true. Stinking of ale, too. Could smell them long before you could see 'em."

Brant circled off in the direction Malthumalbaen had indicated. He easily found the tracks of Sten and his men. It would not be hard to follow their trail back to the frozen forest.

"Mayhap you should stay in Oldenbrook's shadow," Malthumalbaen said. "Skies turning. Best not challenge on foot. Leave your hunt for another day."

Brant shook his head. It could not wait. "I will return by the first evening bell."

Dralmarfillneer shrugged, his eyes rolling at Brant's foolishnesss.

"Ock!" his twin called to Brant as he set out. "If you should come across any scrawny bits of snowhare, I could use some new gloves!"

Brant pulled up his hood and lifted an arm in acknowledgment. As he trudged across the snow-swept ice field, he heard the brothers arguing about who needed the gloves more. When he was a good half a league off, he still heard a barked laugh echoing out to him from the pair.

Shortly after that, as he followed the trampled tread of Sten's hunting party, his only companion was the wind. It whistled and moaned, kicking up. It was easy to grow weary, especially with the sun reflecting in a blinding glare. The only relief was found in the patches of fog in sheltered gullies between upended cliffs of ice.

As he crossed through one patch, Brant was reminded of the mists of his homeland, of the cloud forests of Saysh Mal. Unlike the cold here, the mists of Saysh Mal were all dripping leaves and steaming heat. He allowed the memory to warm him now—despite the pain that came with it.

He could still remember the day he'd heard of his father's death; he'd been killed by a she-panther. It had marked the beginning of the end of Brant's life. His mother had died giving birth to him. But the Way extended to the people of Saysh Mal as well as to the forest. No child was left to starve or beg. The god-realm was a rich one. The forest fostered an endless bounty, with a prosperous trade in wood, fur, and incenses.

Brant had been taken in by the school in the shadow of the Huntress's own castillion. It had been a good life: surrounded by friends, challenged by his schooling, and always near the forest, ready to hone eye, ear, and nose. It was out in the forest that Brant's father came alive for him again. Sometimes he swore he could see his father's shadow shifting through the bower. More than anything, the forest helped him both mourn and heal.

It was also the Way.

And as time passed like a panther through a dark wood, Brant was discovered to be quick of mind, especially for one so young. He rose to the attention of many of the learned masters and mistresses, and eventually to the Huntress herself.

Then it all ended.

Brant had to stop his hand even now from clutching at his throat, at the stone buried under his leather and furs. If only he hadn't been so dull . . . if only he hadn't found himself bowing a knee before the Huntress . . . if only he had kicked that cursed stone away when it had been rolled to his toes by a burning god.

But he *had* bowed his knee. He *had* threaded the stone and made a necklace out of it. How could he toss it away? The stone was as much a talisman of his father as any rogue god. They had come upon it together. It was their secret. Brant had carried it with pride.

Then he had met the Huntress, god and mistress of Saysh Mal.

And his life had truly ended.

A new noise intruded on this painful memory. It came from ahead, cutting through the drone of the wind. A sharp popping, like breaking bones, along with a dry rattle. The forest. The gusting winds were shaking the trees, crackling ice and frozen limbs.

Rounding a tall shelf of ice, Brant spotted the dark line at the edge of the lake, thick with clinging fog. Even the rising winds seemed unable to shred the mists away.

Brant followed the tracks toward the forest. He welcomed reaching the shadowed bower. His eyes had begun to sting and water from the glare of the sun off the ice. He hurried toward the shore of the lake.

The mists ahead lay thick, as if the winds were some storm-driven sea and the fog were a tall surf, pounded and driven into the forest.

Brant tossed back his hood, despite the cold. He wanted nothing muffling his ears. He knelt a moment to string his bow, bending the taut wood with practiced ease.

Within steps, the lake vanished behind him, the sun became no more than a glare above, and even the trees seemed to fall away and disappear. He could barely see more than a handful of steps ahead of him.

Still, he had a well-beaten trail to follow—both into the forest and eventually out again. He was careful from here to step where Sten's men had trod. That hid his own trail and was easier than crunching fresh tracks into the ankle-deep and ice-crusted snowfields.

He moved silently, ears straining.

Once he was away from the edge of the forest, the winds

died. The rattle and pop slowly faded. A dread quiet settled as thick as the mists.

Brant continued onward. The only sign of the larger world was the track of Sten's hunting party. But even this trail shortened as visibility shrank. The fog continued to grow thicker and higher, shielding the sun into a twilight pall.

And the silence seemed to grow even deeper.

He smelled the blood first. A loamy ripeness to the air. He followed the tracks to the slaughter.

It appeared like some fetid bloom in a snowy field. A glade opened, slightly brighter with the open sky above. In the middle, blood splashed in frozen streaks, as far as the treeline.

Brant paused at the edge.

She had fought. The first blow had not been a killing strike, whether done for the cruelty or merely drunken aim. Brant bristled at the pain.

In the center, blood had pooled and iced around the abandoned and frost-rimmed carcass. They had not even taken the meat, only the hide. They had skinned her here. Off to the side, they had scraped and trimmed the hide. Brant leaned down and shifted a pile of scrap. They had cut away her belly skin, too thin of fur to be of value. He spotted the abandoned heavy teats. Brant's jaw muscles tightened. Sten's butchers must have noted the same, known she was nursing whelpings.

But to them, all that had mattered was her pelt.

Brant slipped out his own skinning knife, cut two of the heaviest teats away, and gently slipped them into deep pockets in his heavy coat. He would bury them later. The rest of the bruised and frost-blackened flesh he would leave to the hungry forest. While Sten's men might waste good meat, it would fill the bellies of other scavengers.

Straightening, Brant continued on. He suspected it was only the scent of men that had kept the hungry denizens of the winter wood away so far. Brant had noted the unburied shite and piss left by the drunken men. And in another spot, a pile of upturned stomach, smelling still of ale.

Had it been the ale or the slaughter that turned the man's belly?

As he had suspected earlier, a glint of metal trailed from a rear ankle of the carcass. Razor snare. The trapped ankle was twisted at an unnatural angle.

Brant took a deep breath through his nose. There was nothing he could do to lessen her pain now. Sten's butchers knew nothing of the Way, of honor and responsibility between hunter and prey.

But Brant did.

As he circled, he noted the smaller paw prints, mere scratches in the crusted snow. They were too small to leave true tracks. Except for a few bloody prints, bright against the snow.

The cubbies had come out of hiding, come to their mother, nosed her cooling form, smelled her blood and pain. Brant knew that pain. There was nothing he could do to lessen that ache—only end it swiftly.

He slid an arrow from the quiver on his back. He warmed the frozen fletched feathers with his breath. He would make their ends swift. Better than to let them starve and freeze, locked in grief. He would finish what Sten and his man failed to do.

Brant moved away from the other men's trail for the first time, following a new one now. Scratches in the ice. He would find the pair together.

Who else did they have?

Brant rose from one knee. He had been fingering a broken and bent twig on a bramblebriar bush. A pluck of black downy fur clung to it.

Frowning, he straightened. The hunt had stretched longer than he would have expected. He was deep in the wood by now. The whelpings were still on the move. Had they heard him, scented him? Fell wolves were known for their cunning, but the pair of cubbies were still suckling. Surely they were not so wise to this strange forest, separated from their own dark mountainous haunts of Mistdale far to the north.

Brant felt the pressure of time. Blind to the skies in the fog-shrouded forest, he had no way of judging the coming storm. But his nose sensed the snow in the air. He would not reach Oldenbrook before it fell.

Still, he continued. Turning back was not a choice. If the Way led into the teeth of the storm, so be it.

Clearing the patch of bramblebriar, he noted a dart of shadow ahead, a flicker from the corner of his eye. He froze in place, not even turning his head. He stretched his senses. From the edge of sight, he saw a flash, close to the ground, a pair of eyes.

One pair.

Where was the other?

From the clouded skies, large flakes of snow shed downward. It started as if it had been snowing all along. First nothing. Then all around, the flakes fell heavily, silently. It was as if the ice fog had simply crystallized and begun to collapse around him.

Flakes landed on his lashes, on the edges of his ears.

Too cold.

Rather than melting, they froze the flesh they touched.

Before Brant could react further, a small hare skitter-pattered right past his toes, fleeing to the left.

Farther in the forest, the fog broke enough to reveal a large buck bounding in the same direction, head low to the ground. Behind him, Brant heard something even larger breaking through the brush in a panicked scrabble.

Heading in the same direction.

South.

Soon Brant spotted more hares. A pair of fat badgers, driven from their dens, hurried by, all but scrambling over each other. Off in the distance, snow crunched and branches cracked, marking the passage of more and more fleeing animals.

Brant finally moved, obeying the forest.

What was amiss?

The snow fell thicker, burning with its cold kiss. Unnaturally cold. He might have missed it if he hadn't stopped, his senses on edge. He dragged up his hood, protecting his face. He moved with a steady but swift gait. He didn't know what had routed the forest with such panic, but he knew better than to ignore it.

His trot grew quicker, his heart suddenly pounding.

A pair of flicker deer flew past him, parting to either side of him. Something large growled farther to his left. *Grass bear.* But the anger was not directed at him; it was a blind warning to whatever had set them aflight.

Brant found himself hurrying, boots pounding through the iced snow, dredging through occasional deeper drifts. He used his shoulders and back to keep moving. The cold rolled over him—sinking into him, drawn in with every breath.

Ahead, a hare, which had been spearing ahead of him in zigzagging bursts, suddenly collapsed on its side. It skidded into the snow, shook a breath, then lay still.

Brant ignored his own thundering heart to stop at its side. He touched an ear, blue and frosted. He nudged the body with a gloved finger. It was stiff and solid. Frozen to the core.

Impossible.

Brant stumbled onward.

Snow blinded now. But he found more bodies in agonized postures or simply dropped in their tracks.

This was no natural cold. There was something behind him, cloaked in the storm, something of Dark Grace and deadly touch. He could almost smell the taint in the air—or maybe it was just the fear in the forest. Then again, maybe it was one and the same.

Then he saw them, off to the right. Two pairs of eyes glowed from beneath a leafless thrushberry bush. The cubbies huddled together, lost, panicked.

He would have to hurry. Each breath was now ice in the lungs. But he had come to honor the Way. Even what lurked in the storm would not stop him.

He notched an arrow, drew a full pull, and aimed for the first cubbie. He clutched the second arrow between his lips. Eyes glowed back at him. He saw their trembling, a mix of fear and cold. It spread to his aim. He tightened his grip to steady himself.

Still, his fingers refused to let go of the string.

Snow burned his exposed wrist where his coat sleeve had pulled up.

Cursing silently, he relaxed the tension and lowered his bow. With an exasperated sigh, he dropped the bow and spat out the arrow. His actions were foolish, a waste of precious breath, but the forest had seen enough death this day.

Brant undid the top hooks of his coat and used his teeth to pull the gloves from his fingers.

By now, the forest had gone silent again. All the animals had fled past him already.

He reached to his pockets and found the she-wolf's teats, now thawed enough to squeeze. He massaged a bit of milk over his fingers, smearing them. Satisfied, he pulled his hands free and approached the cubbies' hiding place. He held his hands out and made a small growled whine.

The whelpings backed from him, deeper into the bushes. They were dark-furred except for white-tipped ears, the better to hide in a den or shadowed nest. They would gain a winter's snow white pelt only when full grown.

Brant held still. He had only the time to try this once. If they bolted, he would have to chase them down with bow and arrow. While he would honor the Way, mercy went only so far.

He waited for a full icy breath. Then noted one of the cubbies' nose shift, tasting the air.

"That's right—" Brant whispered gently. "You know your mama."

A whine escaped the second, scared, testing.

The first cubbie, the one who tested the air, reached toward his fingers, sniffing and growling. The second huddled against it. Brant's fingertips were at the first one's black nose.

A fast nudge, and the braver cubbie licked its nose.

"You know your mamma's milk," Brant whispered with a growling whine of his own. "There's no one you trust more."

The pair trembled, caught between panic and hope.

Brant reached farther, sliding his palms between their flattened ears, filling their noses with their mother's scent. The first cubbie continued to growl. Brant dared wait no longer.

He grabbed each cubbie by the nape of the neck and hauled them to him. They growled. The first swung around and bit him in the forearm, catching mostly coat but also a pinch of flesh. He pulled them to his chest. The cubbies struggled, but just as weakly as the first one's bite. The pair was thin, half a stone each at best, exhausted to the edge of collapse.

He tucked one pup into his half-open coat, then shoved in the second. Using one arm to sling under them, he rehooked his coat.

The cubbies took solace in the darkness and were reassured by each other's presence. They gave up their fight and settled together within the warmth of his coat.

Brant straightened. The forest had emptied out. The world was snow and tasted of ice. The distraction of the cubbies had helped calm his heart, allowed his wits to settle. He was done running blindly like an animal. Whatever came from the north flowed south, driving the beasts ahead of it. There was another path. Rather than *flee* from whatever death was within the storm, he could *step aside*.

So Brant set off to the west instead, toward Oldenbrook, moving fast, abandoning quiver and bow to the snow. With his breath frosting the air, he fought the snow, underfoot and from the skies. He moved with an unerring sense of direction, swiftly, crossing frozen creeks and hurtling deadfalls. He flew as straight as an arrow.

As time froze around him, he fought only to keep moving, to put one boot in front of the other. His face went numb and senseless, vanishing away, stolen by the storm. He was only a walking, gasping lung. The cold now sliced with each ragged breath. He tasted blood on his tongue.

Snow continued to fall. He lifted his head, cursing the skies.

Flakes settled atop his upturned face—and melted.

The icy water ran like tears down his cheeks. It took him another two breaths before he realized the significance. The snow fell just as thickly, but this was no cursed blizzard. It was simply ordinary snowfall.

Relief surged through him.

He had cleared the river of death flowing through the wood, reached its western bank. He stumbled on with a coarse laugh, sounding half-maddened to his own ears. In steps, the forest vanished around him, and the lake opened ahead of him.

Free of the forest's shelter at last, the winds blew stronger. Ducking against the onslaught, Brant headed out onto the ice fields. Ahead, Oldenbrook had been swallowed by the storm, but Brant trusted the tidal pull of his senses. He trudged onward.

Still, his brush with whatever Dark Grace tainted the storm had weakened him more than he had suspected. He coughed into his glove and saw the blood. His eyes watered, freezing lashes together.

He fought onward. Winds swirled and battered him, trying to drive him back into the forest. His legs trembled, and he could not stop his teeth from rattling in his skull.

Must not surrender . . .

Time slipped. He found himself suddenly standing in place. How long had he been frozen there? He stared ahead. The storm seemed lighter there. Was that the lamps of the city? Or was it merely the setting sun?

He moved again.

One boot . . . then another.

Then he was on his knees. He never remembered slipping down.

He craned up. Snow fell everywhere. The world was gone. Maybe it never existed. He coughed, wracking and loud, falling to one arm. Blood splattered the ice.

Trembling all over, he pushed up. A glow in the storm wobbled ahead.

He thought maybe he heard a noise that wasn't the wind. He reached up and pulled down his hood.

". . . this way!"

Brant blinked his frozen lashes.

"Braaaant! Ock, Master Brant! Where are you?"

Hope surged. He tried to answer, but another bout of coughing shook through him, taking him to his knees again.

But someone heard him.

"Over here, Dral!" a voice to the left called.

Brant sank to the ice. Two dark figures appeared out of the storm. They held lamps aloft, swinging from raised pikes.

The twin giants.

Malthumalbaen and Dralmarfillneer.

Brant closed his eyes with grateful relief. He sank around himself. Against his belly, two hearts beat. The Way had never been an easy path.

But it was the right one.

"Preposterous," Liannora said under her breath. "Daemons in the snow . . ."

The next morning, Brant sat in the High Wing's common room, sipping a healer's draught of bitter herbs and warming alchemies. Thick drabs of honey failed to mask the acrid tang, and the swirl of complex Graces made his vision swim. He was under orders to drink it with every ring of the day's bell. It was his second draught since being released from the healer's ward.

His breathing remained pained, his voice hoarse, but the sputum no longer bled. Still, deep in his chest, he felt some sharpness if he inhaled too quickly, as if a few shards of ice still remained in his lungs. But the draughts slowly helped—as had a night buried under furs with bladders of heated water tucked against him. He felt almost himself again.

He warmed his palms on the hot stone mug.

By now, other Hands had gathered. By order of Lord Jessup. The god of Oldenbrook would be arriving shortly. All had heard Brant's tale of some dread force cloaked in the heart of the past day's storm. Doubt could be seen in their eyes and heard behind their whispers. Especially since the storm had blown itself out by morning, moving south and away, leaving in its wake a frigid cold and a world blanketed in windswept drifts of snow. The sky remained low and misted. Sunrise was more a pale effort at the start of a day, seemingly defeated before it had begun.

But nothing worse was revealed.

Just another winter's day.

Talk of Dark Graces that stole through the forest, cloaked in a freezing snow, killing with ice, was little believed in the light of day, as meager as that light might be.

"How many winters have you spent up here?" Liannora persisted. She wore a resplendent morning dress of silver adorned with iridescent blue shells.

"This is my first full winter here," Brant said hoarsely. "But I spent another three in Chrismferry, even farther north than Oldenbrook."

Liannora scoffed, "Those are city winters, sheltered by towers, spent indoors, never more than a step or two from the nearest hearth. This is a wild winter. A true winter."

Brant stared at her, wondering how many winters it had been since Liannora had stepped more than ten paces from the closest hearth. Or mirror, for that matter. He could not picture her traipsing a winter forest. But he stayed silent. He did not have the patience or the breath to confront her.

"Raised in the hot lands of the far south," Liannora expounded, "you were simply ill-prepared for the savagery of our winters here. Imagining daemons behind every snowflake. I recommend you dress warmer next time. What were you doing out in that storm anyway?"

A pair of fellow Hands chuckled: the wide-hipped Mistress Ryndia and the skeletally thin Master Khar, Hands of seed and sweat, respectively. They were ever at Liannora's bidding.

Brant felt heat rise inside him that had nothing to do with the healing draught.

Across the table, an older man cleared his throat, stirring from his seat with a creak of wood and bones. His intrusion was welcome. Brant respected the elderly Hand, though he represented the least of the humours: *black bile*. Master Lothbren was near the end of his duty here, bent and aged by his years of handling a god's Grace. As much as it was an honor to serve, there was a cost. A god's Grace burnt its bearers, setting flame to the candles of their lives, flaring them brightly but consuming them just as quickly.

The old man stared at Brant with eyes still sharp. "You rescued a pair of wolf cubbies, I heard," he said.

Brant nodded. He had left them with the giant brothers, who had promised to deliver them to the castillion's kennels, to get them warmed and fed. Brant had left his coat with the cubbies, the better to let them feel secure, to accustom themselves to his scent. He was planning on visiting them once he was finished with Lord Jessup's summoning, to see how they were faring.

"For *dogs*!" Liannora spat with another roll of eyes. "He risks his life, his station for a couple of spitting curs. I daresay such an act smacks of disrespect toward Lord Jessup—to so wantonly jeopardize oneself when one is in service to a god." She shook her head in disbelief and mild outrage.

Brant had heard enough. "Those *dogs*," he said through clenched teeth, "were whelpings of the she-wolf your most glorious Sten slaughtered with razor wire and cowardly spear, while full to the brim with ale. He knew she had cubbies on her teat, yet he left them to starve and freeze."

The shocked look on Liannora's face almost made his outburst worth it. For too long he had bitten his tongue at her slights. No longer. Still, he saw her surprise fade into angry cunning, a flash of wickedness, a promise that this was far from over.

She waved his words away with a flip of a hand, keeping her tone even, as if his angry outburst were a rudeness beyond her. "I thought a skilled hunter like yourself would be well aware of life's cruel necessity. Some die so others might live."

"Or so others might wear pretty coats . . ."

She shrugged. "Strange words from someone who traipses out into our forests with bow and arrow. I don't see you starving and needing to grace our board here with your scrawny hares and rabbits. I'd say you hunt more for pleasure than necessity. At least I'll put my coat to good use."

Master Lothbren lifted a placating hand. "What are your plans for the cubbies, Master Brant?"

He tempered his voice, breathing through his nose to calm himself. "Once they are well-weaned and fleshed, I hope to gain a boon from Lord Jessup to return them to Mistdale whence they came."

"So again you plan to forsake your duty here, to further slight our lord—"

"Thank you, Liannora, but I believe I can withstand such an insult."

All eyes turned to find Lord Jessup at the door to the commons, dressed casually in loose leggings and a simple shirt of stitched sailcloth. He entered with a ghost of a smile, like a kindly father coming upon a squabbling set of his children. He settled to a seat at the head of the long table.

A few words were exchanged, morning pleasantries; then Lord Jessup settled his gaze upon Brant. He noted the slight glow of warm Grace behind the god's eyes.

"How are you faring this morning?"

"Fine, my lord. Much stronger."

"You look it," Jessup said with a nod. "I daresay you arrived as pale as Liannora here when those giants carried you home. But your color is returning nicely."

"The healers know their craft."

"I shall certainly pass on my own gratitude." Jessup leaned

back into his seat. "Now, if you're able, I'd like to hear more about what you saw out in that storm."

Brant nodded. "It wasn't so much *saw* as *felt*."

Liannora opened her mouth, sitting straighter, ready to offer her thoughts, but Lord Jessup waved her down. She sank back into her chair.

Brant slowly but firmly reported all he experienced: the unnatural cold, snow that burnt with ice, the panicked flight of the beasts of the field, their sudden and inexplicable deaths, frozen where they fell.

"I saw no sign of man or daemon," he finished, "but this was no mere storm. Something hid at its heart, cloaked in snow. I'm certain of it."

Jessup pondered his story, leaning forward a bit, eyes down, fingers steepled and tapping his brow. "There has been much strangeness of late, much to worry and concern me. Clearly those of ill purpose take heart from this stretch of bitter winter. Who's to say what emboldened act might be attempted? It bears investigation. If there are any Black Alchemists afoot on my lands, we must root them out."

"Lord Jessup—" Liannora began again.

A hand raised, palm out. "I will send the chief master of the Oldenbrook school, a man familiar with corrupted Graces, out into the wood along with a small legion of guards." He eyed Brant again. "I will have maps brought up. Are you able . . . do you remember . . . ?"

"I can mark where I hunted. But mayhap I should accompany the search." Brant was afraid that the heavy drifts would have blanketed all evidence to his claims, deeply burying the bodies.

"I fear it's not best for your health to be out in this bitter cold. Not if you're to recover for the coming morning's flight to Tashijan. And I fear even the strain of such a flight, of the festivities at the Citadel, perhaps will be too much."

Brant sat straighter and pushed away his emptied mug. "I will be more than hale enough to travel."

He did not want to be excluded from the retinue. Despite all that had happened, there was still the matter of Dart, his stone, and the strange apparition conjured as the stone flared. He could not pass up this chance for answers. Not after so long.

"I hope you are right," Lord Jessup said. "I was the first to put Tylar ser Noche's cloak in service to the Order. It was here he first bent a knee as a knight. I would send the best of Oldenbrook to witness his knighting again. To send less would cast some doubt on my support. Still, if you are not able . . . I will not risk your health."

"I am mending fine, Lord Jessup." A rasping cough confounded his words, but he met the god's blue eyes with steady assuredness. "I am."

A nod. "Very good. Then it's settled."

Lord Jessup began to rise, but now it was Liannora's turn to lift a hand. "A wonderful thought has just occurred to me, stirred by your words of honoring the assembly at Tashijan. For the past nights, my slumber has been troubled by worries of how to properly show our respect, of what gifts we might bring besides our fine personages."

"What idea has possessed you?"

Liannora glanced to Brant, flashing some wicked intent, then turned back to Lord Jessup. "Master Brant here has risked his life to bring two beautiful woodland cubbies out of the forest, to save them from the savageries of the storm. What better gifts might we present than those same twin cubbies? Fell wolves, no less."

Brant felt as if he'd been clubbed in the stomach.

"The whole ceremony at Tashijan is one of unification," Liannora continued. "To heal the fractured houses of Chrismferry and Tashijan. Would it not be a wonderful gesture to offer one pup to the celebrated and battle-brazened Argent ser Fields, high warden of the Citadel—and present the other to the new regent, Lord Tylar ser Noche?"

"Most wonderful," Mistress Ryndia added.

"Indeed," Master Khar chimed in.

"Fell wolves represent strength, cunning, and honor. To share them between the two houses—Tashijan and Chrismferry—would help symbolize the new resolve of all the First Land, to stand against the darkness, proud and nobly."

Brant finally found his tongue. "The wolves belong in Mistdale. It is where they should be returned."

"There are enough wolves in those dark forests," Liannora said. "Was it not hunger that drove the she-wolf down here to begin with? The symbolic nature the pair could represent would serve far better than stocking two more starving wolves in Mistdale."

"That is not the Way of—"

Now Brant was silenced with a nod from Lord Jessup. "Thank you, Liannora. Well-spoken indeed. The gesture would be significant, but as it was Master Brant who risked his life to bring the wolves here, then it should be his choice on what will be done with them."

Liannora bowed her acknowledgment and settled with a shimmer to her seat. All eyes were on Brant.

Even Lord Jessup's.

Brant ignored the others, but he could not dismiss the gentle attention of the god in their midst. He knew the high esteem in which Lord Jessup held the new regent. Even more deeply, he understood the god's desire to acknowledge and certify the new pact between Chrismferry and Tashijan. The First Land must heal.

But he had a responsibility beyond the land. By saving the cubbies, he now had their lives to protect. He weighed the life they would lead if he agreed. He had no doubt they'd be raised with pampered attention. As gifts of a god, representing the new unity and symbolizing the First Land's newfound fortitude, the wolves would be well cared for and well-kept. Their lives would be easy; they would be fatted and groomed.

Yet still it would be a caged life, all freedoms gone. Brant rankled at the thought. Here he was, exiled from his own homelands into this pampered existence. He'd had no choice. Then again, sometimes freedoms had to be laid down for the greater good.

"Master Brant . . . ?" Lord Jessup pressed softly.

He met his god's eyes, knowing what the god hoped.

Brant nodded slowly.

"I gave 'em some goat's milk 'bout a bell ago," Malthumalbaen grumbled. "Just about took my thumb off."

The giant held out a ponderous digit, wounded with an arc of needled bites.

Shadowed by the giant, Brant stood at the cage door. The cubbies were half-buried in his old coat, forming a den beneath it, glowering. A low growl greeted him.

Brant flipped the latch and pulled the gate.

"Take care, Master Brant. Or at least count your fingers. Make sure you leave with the same number."

The giant's twin returned from down at the end of a row, where he had finished relieving himself into a pail. Dralmarfillneer snugged the laces on his trousers as he joined his brother. A few of the kennel's hounds regaled his passage.

"Them's some feisty bits of fur," he said with a grin upon reaching their side. "Probably taste a mite nice, too. After being fattened up first."

Malthumalbaen clapped his brother on the shoulder. "Take no offense, Master Brant. Dral's always wondering what things taste like."

Brant slid into the cage.

"We must get back to our posts," the giant said.

Brant nodded to them. "Thank you again for coming out and pulling me out of the teeth of that storm."

"No thanks necessary."

"Just a few hares now and then—that'd be nice." Dral elbowed his brother for his agreement.

Malthumalbaen sighed. "Is that all you think about? Your belly?" He shoved his brother toward the far door. "Don't you know anything about honor, 'bout doing what's right for rightness's sake?"

"Still, a few hares . . . If you'd rather not have yours, I'll be happy to—"

"Ock, that's not the point. Mother surely dropped you on your head."

Their argument faded into grumbled snatches as they left the kennels.

Alone, Brant pulled the door closed behind him and sank to a crouch. The cubbies stared at him. Two pairs of eyes reflected the torchlight beyond. Brant noted a pile of spoor in one corner. It was runny and loose.

"Goat's milk is not your mamma's, is it?" Brant whispered.

A growl answered him. He caught a ripple of teeth.

Ignoring the threat, Brant sidled closer, then sank cross-legged into the hay. He would wait them out. Let his scent push through the pall of shite and hound piss.

After a long moment, a snarling nose peeked out of the coat, curious but wary.

"Do you recognize my smell?"

The small cubbie lowered its muzzle to the ground, ears flattened. It was the little she-wolf, braver than her brother. She edged out a whisker at a time in his direction. Her brother shadowed her. Brant saw how the male, more cautious, studied him, first from one side of his sister, then the other. Though he lacked his sister's bravado, he made up with wits and cunning.

Brant had rested a hand in the hay. The little she-wolf, bristling with black fur, stretched her neck to sniff at a nail. Satisfied, she crept farther, circling out a bit, still wary.

Then she lunged and snapped into the meat of his thumb. She stayed latched, growling. Brant could guess she was the one who had wounded Malthumalbaen. Brant simply waited her out.

Finally she let go and pulled back.

"It's all right," he said. "I probably deserve it."

Her hackles slowly lowered. She sank to her belly and wiggled forward again. A small pink tongue licked at the droplets of blood raised by her milk teeth. A whine escaped her, apologetic.

The male slipped from the den and joined his sister, licking at Brant's thumb. Once his finger was clean, the pair were soon sniffing him all around, exploring his nooks and corners.

He watched them, his heart heavy.

After a few moments more, they grew bored with his presence. The male returned to the coat, grabbing it by a sleeve and tugging on it. Such housekeeping plainly angered his sister. She grabbed the other sleeve, fighting with determined growls.

Brant sighed. Maybe he should have left them to the storm. Had it been any true kindness rescuing them? Into what sort of life were they headed? Still, it was *life*. As long as their hearts beat, the future was never set in stone.

Not theirs, not his.

He pondered the strange storm again. Even he had begun

to wonder if he had not merely caught the contagious panic of the animals. Maybe it was just the extra cold spooking the beasts. Still, he remembered the ice in the air, the cold flesh of that hare, dropped in midleap.

No.

Something unnatural had been cloaked in the storm.

But what? And more importantly, why?

The storm had blown itself out of Oldenbrook and now rolled south toward the distant sea. In another day or two it would be gone from these lands. Perhaps it would always remain a mystery. He thought he had sidestepped it, but maybe that had been a delusion. Maybe it still held him in its grip.

Maybe it always had.

Brant clutched the stone at his throat, rolled to him by the dying breath of a rogue god.

How much freedom did any of them have?

SECOND

CASTLE IN A STORM

ᕼᓘ *Blood* to open the way
ᐳᔨ ᔭ ᓇᑐ *Seed* or *menses* to bless
ᓯᕐᑭ *Sweat* to imbue
ᑎᕐᑭ *Tears* to swell
ᐳᖕᒍ *Saliva* to ebb
ᔅᓱ *Phlegm* to manifest
ᓯᑕ *Yellow bile* to gift
ᕼᑕ And *black* to take it all away

—*Litany of Nine Graces*

5

A GATHERING OF RAVENS

KATHRYN KNOCKED ON THE DOOR, CONCERNED. SHE HAD NOT heard from Gerrod Rothkild for over a full day. The last she had spoken to him was when Rogger had appeared at her own door, bearing the strange talisman of a rogue god's skull.

Then nothing.

Not word, nor note.

Such silence was unlike Gerrod. Especially now. In the past day, Tashijan had swelled to bursting as retinues from all the god-realms of the First Land had arrived. But more importantly, Tylar ser Noche was due here before evening bells. With such an event pending, Kathryn had spent the morning pacing her hermitage. It had been a year since she had last seen Tylar. Certainly they'd shared messages by raven and scroll, but their duties after the Battle of Myrrwood kept them both too busy for a casual visit.

And casual was certainly beyond either of them.

Even now.

Her hands wrung at her belly. They had once been betrothed, certain to marry, sharing a bed already, first as a dalliance between knights, finally with a deeper stirring of the heart. Then Tylar had been accused of murder and broken vows. Kathryn's own testimony before the adjudicators had gone a long way toward damning him to the slave ships of Trik and the bloody circuses that followed, where he was broken in limb and spirit. But his guilt had been fabricated from the start. He had been a blind piece in a greater game, used to weaken Tashijan and its former warden, Ser Henri.

And the cost had not fallen solely upon Tylar.

Kathryn still remembered the blood in her bed, the lost child, limbs as small as birds' wings, expelled from her body by grief and heartache. It was this final loss that had driven her down here at that time, into self-exile, away from the staring eyes and whispers, betrothed to a murderer.

But Tylar's only crime had been some gray dealings, traffic below the table with some sordid characters from his past, done at first to raise coin for the city's orphanages, where both she and he had been raised. But after a time, a few silver yokes had ended up in Tylar's own pocket. It was a familiar slide. Still, the murder of the cobbler's family was not Tylar's doing, despite the blood on his own sword. It took the death of two gods—Meeryn, who blessed Tylar as she lay dying, and the naethryn-possessed Chrism, whom Tylar had slain—to finally clear his name.

All should have been made right.

But it hadn't been.

The pair remained lost to each other, bitter. Anger and guilt had rooted too deeply, becoming as much a part of them as their own bones. *If Tylar hadn't started his underhanded dealings with the Gray Traders, soiling his cloak . . . if I had trusted his professions of innocence to murder . . . if only I'd told him of our child . . .* And though they had stumbled over words of forgiveness to each other, the words were spoken with the tongue and not the heart.

At least not yet.

But now Tylar was returning.

Kathryn knocked again, needing to consult Gerrod, ever her counselor. Long ago, Gerrod had helped lift her back into her life after she fell down here the first time. She trusted no one more, not even herself.

A coarse bark answered her. "I'm not to be disturbed!"

"Gerrod!" Kathryn called through the door. She leaned close, keeping her voice low. She had come buried in her shadowcloak, shying from others. Even now, Grace flowed through the blessed cloth to hide her among the shadows.

"*Kathryn . . .* ?"

"Yes!"

She heard steps approach, and a latch scraped back. The door swung open. Gerrod pulled it just wide enough for her to enter, but no more.

"Hurry," he urged her.

She thought at first the master's furtiveness was because he had shed his armor's helmet, exposing his pale and tattooed flesh. Gerrod preferred to keep his true face hidden.

He closed the door behind her, leaned an ear against the wood, then stepped away. "Hesharian knows I'm dabbling in something secret. He's already visited twice this morning."

"Does he know about the skull?"

Gerrod shook his head and clanked over with a whir of mekanicals to the far side of his chamber.

Kathryn caught the whiff of burning black bile, which even the sweet scent of myrrh boiling on his braziers could not mask. She also noted the state of his room. Normally Gerrod was fastidious in his upkeep, but the four bronze braziers in the corners of the room—in the fanciful shapes of eagle, skreewyrm, wolfkit, and tyger—were blackened with smoke, and piles of ash lay unswept beneath them. At his wide desk, a teetering stack of ancient tomes covered the surface, some open, others facedown, spines bent. In one corner, a stack of scrolls had spilled to the floor, and a candle had burnt to a slagged puddle of wax with a wan flame floating in the middle.

Her friend looked just as wasted, sustained by as weak a fire.

She doubted he had slept at all since acquiring the skull.

"I think Hesharian grows suspicious of my studies," Gerrod said. "The last time he appeared on my doorstep, he came with a strange milky-eyed master named Orquell. The man hails from Ghazal, where he has been studying among the Clerics of Naeth of that volcanic land."

Kathryn was well familiar with the cult of Naeth. Unlike most of Myrillia, the followers shunned any worship of the *aethryn*, the sundered part of the gods that had fled high and away into the aether, never to be heard from again. The Clerics of Naeth sought communion with the naethryn, the undergods, through strange practices and acts of blood sacrifice. While no one had been able to prove it, if ever there was a ready source of Cabalists, it would be found there. But as the followers rarely left their subterranean lairs, they seemed harmless enough, for now.

"Why did this master come here?" Kathryn asked, suspicious of anyone associated with such clerics.

"Summoned, I heard—by Hesharian."

Kathryn frowned.

"They've spent some time up in the Warden's Eyrie. Behind closed doors."

Kathryn suddenly remembered. "Dart mentioned such a man . . ."

Gerrod nodded. "From such meetings, I can fathom why Hesharian has summoned this master from Ghazal."

"Why?"

"Because of Symon ser Jaklar, the warden's best man, turned to stone by Argent's corrupted sword. Hesharian still keeps the man's body in some secret hole. But to lift the curse would surely raise our esteemed master's status—at least within the eyes of the Eyrie."

Gerrod finally waved the matter away. "But that is not why you came down here, was it? You came to inquire about the skull." He turned toward the arched opening that led into his alchemical study. The thick ironwood doors were open, and the scent of bile emanated from within.

"You must see this," he said and disappeared through the archway.

Kathryn followed him into his study, where the smell of black bile was riper. The windowless room beyond had been carved into an oval. In the center was a scarred greenwood table with a complicated apparatus of bronze-and-mica-glass tubing above it, attached to the arched stone roof. All around, the walls were covered from floor to ceiling with cabinets, shelves, niches, and nooks. At the far end rose Gerrod's repostilum, a mosaic of blessed glass cubes, each die no wider than a thumb, eight hundred in number, containing drops of each of the eight humours from all hundred of the original settled gods, an alchemical storehouse of great wealth.

Gerrod crossed to the center table. "I may have discovered some answers, but each revelation only begat another mystery."

In the center of the table rested the misshapen skull.

Gerrod had painted its surface with black bile, so artfully that it looked carved of the warding Grace. The only spot not covered was a perfect circle on the top of the skull. The jaundiced bone looked pitted there as if eaten by caustic oils.

Kathryn knew it hadn't been oils that ate the bone—but Grace-rich humours. Positioned directly over the skull was a bronze-and-mica spigot, draining from the apparatus above. The device was used for mixing humours in alchemical experiments.

"Here is the most intriguing discovery." Gerrod reached forward and delicately turned a bronze key. From the tip of the mica tubing, a single drop of humour welled and clung precariously. "I've used a trickle of phlegm to bind blood and tears. Watch this."

The drop fell from the spigot and struck the skull. It rang most peculiarly, as if the bone were some sort of stone bell. The sound echoed for a breath as if trapped within the walls of the study and seeking a means to escape. Kathryn felt its passage almost like a wind. Her cloak trembled from her body, ever so slightly, lifting away, then settling back.

As the echo faded, silence settled over the room, heavier than a moment before.

She stepped away. "What was that?"

Gerrod waved a hand through the air as if wafting something foul away. "The humours—blood, tears, even the phlegm—all came from Cassal of High Dome."

"A god of *air*," Kathryn said. All the gods, while varying in the cast of their humours, could be relatively separated into four aspects: loam, water, fire, and air.

"Exactly," Gerrod said.

"But what made that sound?"

Gerrod nodded. "I don't think *made* is the right word. I think the sound was already there, trapped in the bones of the skull, bound down into its mineral matrix. It is hard to believe, I know, but you must first understand that our bones are not pure stone, like some might imagine. There is flesh in there, too. If you leach away the minerals, you can reveal the flesh within. And in this skull there remains the desiccated flesh of a rogue god."

Kathryn felt a sick unease.

"I believe the alchemy of air unbound some corrupted Grace still trapped in that flesh. An echo of power."

"What sort of Grace?"

"That has been a good part of my study. But I believe I rooted out an answer from some old books. Tomes that dealt with the work of Black Alchemists. You are familiar with how loam-giants, wind wraiths, and fire walkers are born?"

Kathryn nodded. Though the details were beyond her knowledge, she was aware that women, heavy with child, could ingest certain alchemies and give birth to children bearing special traits.

"It is not only clean Graces that might transfigure such births. Corrupted Graces can do the same. I studied tomes that spoke of children born of cursed alchemies. Specific to this matter, children born of *air* alchemies."

Kathryn felt her stomach churn, remembering her own lost child. What mother would sacrifice her own child in such a manner?

"From such corruption, children were born with strange voices. Rich in twisted power, it is said, able to bind pure Grace to its will. They call such corrupted talent *seersong*. I believe that was what we just heard, an echo released from the desiccated flesh that it once bound."

"Wait. Are you saying that the rogue god was bound by this song?"

"I can't say for sure. Air alchemies are the most ephemeral. But for such a trace to remain in the bones of the skull, the exposure would have to be long and intimate. Even after death, the skull remains deeply imbued with seersong. Remember Rogger's story of what befell him in Chrismferry."

Kathryn could not forget the attack at the docks, of the ilk-beasts that sought the skull. She also remembered who one of the beasts had been. One of the god Fyla's personal bodyguards.

"You believe the skull was the source of their ilking?"

"How else to explain it? The thief, Rogger, was wise to keep the talisman warded with black bile and to take a route far from any god-realm. But even Chrismferry, godless for a full year, remains a land rich in Graces. And possibly still tainted in some small manner. The naethryn-god, Chrism, had ilked hundreds before being banished. I think the skull, exposed to such taint, absorbed and echoed the curse upon the air, carried by the power of the seersong."

"Ilking the unsuspecting nearby."

"If they were rich enough in Grace. Like Fyla's guard."

"And what about Tylar?" Kathryn shuddered. "Why was he not ilked?"

"Tylar was probably too rich in Graces. All of his humours flow with power. And then there is the matter of the naethryn nesting inside him. The daemon probably helped protect him. But many mysteries remain. I need more time with the skull."

Kathryn reached out and touched his bronze hand. "And you need some sleep, too." The shadow under his eyes told her that her friend was burning himself to the quick. "There will be time enough after the ceremony."

"Perhaps you're right. Hesharian grows suspicious enough with my protracted absence. And at some point, I'd certainly like to talk at length with Rogger. We were interrupted last time from hearing his full story of how he came upon this strange talisman."

Kathryn drew Gerrod away from the skull and back toward the main room.

He followed her slowly, almost reluctantly, but he did close the heavy doors to his study behind him. As he glanced around his room, he seemed to see it for the first time in a full turn of bells. His eyes widened slightly, and he shook his head at the sorry condition of his chambers.

"I should brew us some bitternut," Gerrod said and strode to a side table where a cold kettle rested.

The third morning bell rang, muffled but clear.

Kathryn sighed. "I must be back upstairs. Before the towers burn down on top of us."

Gerrod waved to a chair. "I know you think you are the only person holding our towers up, but they've stood for centuries, so I think they'll last a little while longer."

"But the ceremony is tomorrow. I've a thousand—"

Gerrod offered her a tired smile. "If I can leave my study for a while, you can avoid the hermitage. Sit. We have more to discuss. A small matter."

Kathryn's brow pinched in curiosity as Gerrod stoked one of his braziers. He glanced over to her, one eyebrow raised.

"Tylar ser Noche . . ."

* * *

"What's wrong?" Tylar asked Delia.

She stared out the flippercraft window, watching the towers of Tashijan rise at the horizon, aglow in the setting winter sun. She shook her head but did not turn.

Tylar sat across from her in the private cabin aboard the airship. They were alone. His personal bodyguards were stationed up and down the hall, led by Sergeant Kyllan, who stood outside their cabin, alongside the wyr-mistress Eylan. The other men were posted throughout the craft, keeping a watch over Tylar's party. There were three for every one of his group. The only other travelers aboard the flippercraft, besides the ship's crew, were the other seven Hands of Chrismferry, all coming to attend and witness his knighting. But only Delia, Hand of blood, shared Tylar's cabin.

"We'll reach Tashijan early . . . by a full bell," Delia mumbled to the window, nodding to the rising towers.

"All the better," Tylar said.

Mid-voyage, the ship's captain had come, cap in hand, to their cabin. The storm at their back had him worried. Tylar had seen the northern skies himself. A great winter storm had settled into the middle of the First Land and was slowly rolling toward the sea. The captain had swung their path far to the west, almost as far as the Middleback Range, to skirt the storm. But the captain feared they'd fail to outrun the blizzard, so he had come to ask permission to burn blood, to increase their pace, accelerating their schedule.

Tylar had granted it.

"We should have sent a raven ahead to alert Tashijan," Delia said.

"As much blood as we're burning, the fastest raven would arrive about the same time as us. Besides, I'd just as soon land when least expected."

Delia finally turned from the window. "Do you fear some betrayal by my father?"

So that's what had been worrying her so . . .

Delia had no love for her estranged father, the warden of Tashijan, Argent ser Fields. The coming ceremony would be as much a strain on the warden's daughter as it was on Tylar.

"No," he answered. "I'm sure Argent will be pinning on his best face. I fear more what sort of pomp and blow he might have arranged at the dock atop Stormwatch. I'm sure it will be tedious and full of false cheer. So if we arrive unexpectedly enough, we might slip down to our rooms and avoid all that. The less we have to share the same space with Argent, all the better."

A slight smile broke through her pensive expression. "You will both have sore faces before this is all over. Strained smiles, tight jaws, ground teeth."

"If this gesture weren't so important—"

"It is," she assured him. "You deserve to have your cloak returned to you. And it will be good to head into spring with the First Land united and healed."

He nodded. "I've heard that all the god-realms of the First Land and some of the outlying realms have sent representatives. Even Lord Balger."

"It doesn't surprise me. All the gods—even Lord Balger—want peace again, want the land to heal."

"Not all the gods," Tylar mumbled.

Delia's eyes grew worried again. While a majority of the Hundred, the settled gods of Myrillia, had voiced their acceptance of Tylar's regency, not all were as vigorous in their support as he would have wished. In fact, there were some who either remained silent or expressed outright distaste. And they were being heard—by other gods and by the people of Myrillia at large. Chrismferry was the oldest of all the god-realms. To have a man, even one blessed with a flow of Grace-rich humours, sitting atop the castillion at Chrismferry struck many as an affront against the proper order.

"All the more reason we must tolerate coming here," Delia said. "It isn't only the rift between Tashijan and Chrismferry that needs to be closed. Uniting the gods of the First Land around your regency will help settle the rumbling across the other lands."

"I hope you're right."

As if the flippercraft sensed his worry, a slight tremor vibrated through its bones. The crew must be readying to land.

Delia gripped the arm of her seat with one hand. "The effort will be worth the risk . . ." she mumbled and returned her attention to the cabin's window, growing pensive again.

Tylar frowned. He sensed there were layers of meaning behind her soft words. Why was it that women seemed so capable of lacing a thousand thoughts behind so few words? And men so inept at deciphering it all.

Worth the risk . . .

He slowly began to understand. Delia's mood was more than just dread at the reunion of father and daughter. The risk she spoke of went even beyond bringing the Godsword so near the godling child, Dart.

No, it went even deeper.

Tylar stared out at the towers of Tashijan. Lights glowed from its thousand windows. How could he have been so blind? He reached a hand to her knee.

She seemed oblivious to his touch—then her hand drifted to his. Their fingers intertwined. He squeezed his reassurance.

"Kathryn is my past," he mumbled ever so softly.

"Is she?"

"Delia . . ."

She refused to face him. Over the past year, they had become more than lord and handservant. But how much more? During the long stretch of winter, they'd shared more and more time together. Each found easy companionship with the other, even solace. And as the nights lengthened, quiet times slowly stretched to moments of tentative intimacy: a lingering touch, a glance held too long in silence, a moment of shared breaths when leaning together over some trivial matter. Then their first kiss, a brush of lips, only a fortnight ago. They'd barely had a moment to truly discuss what it meant. Only a quiet admission that both wished to explore it further.

But how much further were they willing to explore?

They'd certainly never shared a bed. In fact, Tylar feared bedding any woman since receiving Meeryn's gift. With the Grace that now laced his seed, he did not know what horrors might arise from any chance dalliance. Still, his reluctance with Delia was not so much a matter of Grace as his own heart.

Another tremble shook the flippercraft, more abrupt and sharp this time, hard enough to dislodge their fingers.

Delia sat straighter, glancing over to him. The last shake was no mere correction, of course. The craft quaked again.

Tylar gained his feet. "Something's wrong."

He crossed to the cabin door and opened it. He found

Eylan and Sergeant Kyllan looking equally concerned. A few other doors opened along the central hallway.

"Keep everyone in their cabins," Tylar ordered Kyllan. "I'm going to check with the captain."

He headed off, drawing Eylan and Delia behind him.

They strode toward the bow, where the door to the pilot's compartment stood closed. A crewman noted his approach with a nervous squint to his eye.

"I would speak with Captain Horas," Tylar said.

"Certainly, my lord."

But before he could open the door, it popped wide on its own. Captain Horas blocked the way. He came close to colliding with Tylar. He was a tall fellow, uniformed in yellow and white, hair as black as oiled pitch and a beard clipped into two horns at his throat.

The captain stepped back, startled.

"Ser, I was just coming to inform you. No need for fear. The shakes are just the black-cursed storm biting at our tail."

"I thought we were well ahead of the blizzard." Tylar noted how the captain avoided his eyes.

"Ah, the skies are like the seas, my lord. Storms never like to blow as one expects. Winds shifted during the past bell. The storm's been chasing after us ever since."

"Will we reach Tashijan before its full brunt?"

"Oh, most certainly. I've stoked the mekanicals to full roil. We'll be docking soon. But perhaps it would be best if you all returned to your cabins until we're landed and moored tight."

Tylar finally caught the captain's eye. "I think I'd prefer to watch the docking from the pilot's compartment."

"Ser . . ." A slight warning tone entered the captain's voice.

Tylar strode toward the door, leaving the man little choice: Step aside or grab ahold of the regent of Chrismferry. Captain Horas was no fool.

Tylar entered the compartment with the captain at his elbow. The space ahead filled the nose of the flippercraft. It was divided into two levels. Here at the top, the ship's crew manned the controls that wielded the mekanicals along with the outer paddles that balanced the flight. Tylar smelled the scent of burning blood as the ship's mekanicals consumed the air alchemies that kept the great wooden whale aloft.

He stepped deeper inside. The control level overlooked a gigantic curve of blessed glass, the ship's Eye, through which the pilot could study the world below and guide his ship.

From the weight of the crew's concentration and the waver in the pilot's barked orders, he could tell something was amiss.

Captain Horas finally explained. "We must've pushed the ship too hard for too long. The mekanicals are strained. Or perhaps the alchemies are not as richly Graced as we were promised. Either way, the ship is hobbled."

The ship shook again, canting to port and dropping its nose. Tylar caught himself, grabbing the shoulder of the ship's boatswain. A rally of commands quickly evened the ship's keel. The pilot was plainly keeping the flippercraft aloft more with his skill than any with Grace of air.

"We'll make it," the captain assured him. Then in a lower voice, "If it weren't for this twice-cursed storm . . ."

Tylar stared out the Eye. Tashijan rose ahead. Its highest tower—Stormwatch—glowed like a lighthouse along a rocky coast. But closer still, the sky around the flippercraft swirled with eddies of snow. With every breath, it fell harder. They had lost the race.

The storm had caught them.

Kathryn knew something was wrong as she neared her hermitage. The door was cracked open, and her maid Penni waited in the hall. The young girl stood tugging at a brown curl that had escaped her white bonnet. She startled when Kathryn neared, finally realizing the shadowknight approaching her in full cloak was indeed the castellan.

The maid jumped, offered a fast curtsy, then began to stammer, with a glance toward the open door. "I—I—I couldn't—I didn't know—"

"Calm yourself, Penni."

Kathryn allowed the shadows to shed from her cloth, revealing herself fully. She had climbed the tower in a hurry, cloaked in Grace, seeking to avoid recognition. It seemed every other person sought some boon from her: shadowknights, handservants, or underfolk. She was just returning from her most recent duty, greeting the last of the retinues to arrive—from Oldenbrook—making sure the party was settled and formally welcoming them. They seemed very excited to present some special gift to Argent and Tylar at the morning's ceremony.

But Kathryn hadn't inquired further.

She had already been late.

Tylar's flippercraft was due to dock in less than a bell. The warden had prepared an elaborate welcome, including drums and trumpets. She was expected to attend—and in more than a worn shadowcloak.

Now some new trouble waited to be addressed.

"Take a breath and tell me what's wrong," she said to Penni.

The maid had served the hermitage for longer than Kathryn had worn the diadem of her station. Penni had been servant to the former castellan, the elderly Mirra, long vanished and surely dead.

"I thought he was a knight," Penni said. "What with there being so many strangers, coming and going."

Kathryn understood the maid's consternation. Tashijan's knightly residents had tripled in number, gathering from near and fear, a mad rabble of ravens come to witness the momentous event.

"He claimed to be your friend," Penni continued in a rush. "Come on urgent matters, he says, so I let him into your rooms." The maid lowered her voice to a whisper. "But then he let his masklin drop. It were no knight."

Kathryn relaxed.

There was only one person that would be so bold as to masquerade himself as a shadowknight within the very fold of the Order. Rogger. She had not heard a single word since the thief had vanished into the throngs below. He must have donned such a disguise so he might attend Tylar's welcome. It would be good to hear what tidings Rogger had gleaned from listening to the low whispers and the ale-addled braggings, words that seldom reached as high as her hermitage.

Kathryn stepped past Penni.

At her elbow, the maid finished her breathless tale. "Though he has a soft tongue, he was too fearsome for me to stay in the same room—so I waited out here."

Kathryn frowned at the faintheartedness of the young girl. Who would ever find Rogger fearsome? Glad for a familiar face, she pushed into her room with a creak of the door hinges.

Penni shadowed her, keeping behind her cloak. "I've heard stories of their ilk," she said. "Painting their faces with ash to hide their true names, even from each other."

Kathryn realized her mistake.

It was not Rogger who had come calling.

The tall figure turned from her hearth, the only light in the room. He indeed wore a shadowcloak. She noted how its edges vanished into the darkness beyond. And his face was indeed daubed black, traditional for members of the Black Flag, the murderous guild of pirates and brigands.

He shed his cloak's hood to reveal a knotted braid of hair made snow white by years under salt and sea. Many years. Centuries in fact. Here stood the near-mythic figure of the Flaggers' leader. Beneath his cloak he wore a fine cut of black leathers, from boots to collar, and at his waist he carried a sheathed sword, Serpentfang, a blade as famous as the knight who once wielded it.

"It is good to see you again, Castellan Vail," Krevan said with a slight bow.

She crossed into the room. "Why have you come, Ser Kay?"

The man frowned. "Raven ser Kay died long ago. It is merely Krevan now."

Krevan the Merciless, she thought to herself. Three centuries ago, he had been a legendary shadowknight. But he had hidden a great secret from all, a secret exposed upon the point of a sword, one driven through his heart. He had not died from his wound—for he had no heart. Born among the Wyr, an enemy of the Order, Raven ser Kay was unlike any other man. Since the founding of the first god-realm, Wyr-lords had been churning dark alchemies in their hidden and forbidden forges, attempting to imbue man with immortality. Krevan was one of their great successes. He had been born with a living blood that flowed through his veins without the need for the beat of a heart, thus slowing his aging.

But exposed as one of the Wyr's cursed offspring, the former Raven Knight had to die, to vanish into myths. And out of those mists of time, Krevan was born anew, embittered, turning his skills as a knight to less noble pursuits. The heartless became the merciless.

Still, the man had not forgotten his honor.

"How may I help you?" Kathryn asked. "Have you come for Tylar's knighting?"

Krevan waved such a thought away. "A cloak does not make a man." He stepped from the hearth toward her. There was an urgency to the motion. A hand reached out for her.

She took a reflexive step back. Her own cloak surged around her, ready to fold her into the shadows and grant speed to her limbs.

"You have the cursed skull," he said. "The skull of the rogue god."

Kathryn was taken aback by his statement—then remembered Rogger's story of another who had been hunting the same talisman, someone with a face painted black. So it hadn't been just a low-level Flagger seeking a fast splash of silver. The desire had come from the very top.

"What interest is the skull to you?" she asked.

His eyes flashed and a ferocity entered his voice. "I must have it. It should never have been brought here. Especially here. Especially now."

"Why? What do you mean?"

Krevan suddenly was at her side, moving with the swiftness of shadows. He clutched her elbow. "I must have it!"

Penni squeaked by the door.

Before Krevan could offer any further explanation, a splintering crash echoed from above. The floor shook.

Everyone froze.

A single trumpet blared high above, a warning of fire, a call for buckets. The sound of pounding feet echoed from the hall outside, heard through the crack.

Kathryn turned as someone rapped hard on her door. It creaked farther open with the impact. Penni blocked it with a toe.

"Castellan Vail!" a familiar voice called.

It was Lowl, manservant to the warden. Kathryn turned to Krevan—but the leader of the Black Flaggers was gone from her side. She twisted around. He had vanished into the shadows and away. She noted a slight waft to the heavy drapery over the windows that opened onto her private balcony.

She knew that if she yanked back the drapes, she'd find nothing but a window cracked open and the balcony just as empty.

Krevan was gone.

Through the open window, shouts echoed, coming from the top of Stormwatch. Kathryn pictured the high docks that surmounted the tower. Only one flippercraft had still been expected this day.

Another trumpet blast reverberated, sounding strident and panicked.

"Castellan Vail!"

Kathryn returned her attention to the door and waved Penni to open it. The maid removed her foot and tugged on the latch.

Lowl stood at her threshold, flanked by guards who shifted uneasily, glancing down the hall toward the center stairs. Lowl stood wide-eyed, tall and spindly-limbed. He shook all over. Kathryn expected to hear his bones rattle.

"What has happened?" she asked.

"Warden Fields sent me to fetch you! Word had come that the flippercraft from Chrismferry had been spotted in the skies, outrunning the coming storm, arriving early." He winced from another trumpet blast. "He—Warden Fields wanted you in attendance above. For—for the welcome."

Plainly the manservant had been sent before whatever mishap had befallen that same arrival. Kathryn rushed to the door. She would get no answers from the man.

She pushed through the guards, fellow shadowknights with crimson stitching on the shoulders of their cloaks. The Fiery Cross. Argent's men.

Lowl called to her. "Warden Fields asked that you present yourself in attire most fitting for the occasion and to—"

Kathryn ignored the man and drew power to her cloak from the shadows, increasing her pace. She sped down the hall to the central stair. The steps were packed with other knights, drawn by the commotion. She shed her cloak enough to let her diadem shine.

"Clear the way for the castellan!" she boomed.

The black sea of cloaks parted. She raced upward through them. Near the top, she saw men and women, mostly lineworkers and dock laborers, rushing by with buckets. A large cistern occupied this level, kept always full for just such a crisis.

She followed a burly man in heavy boots, slogging with a bucket in each fist. He plowed a path for her to follow. The door appeared ahead, propped open against a gusting wind that pushed down at them, as if warding them back.

Kathryn smelled the smoke—then she was through the door and out onto the high dock.

The chill struck her first, frigid enough to pierce her fevered panic. She wrapped the tattered shadows around her, pulling her cloak tight. One hand pulled her hood up against the wind.

She then stepped clear of the chaos, allowing the workers to battle the flames. But it appeared the worst was already over. Smoke churned into the twilight murk as the sun set to the west, already lost in heavy clouds.

A few patches of fire rose from the crushed belly of the flippercraft. It had landed on the cradle, but it had come in too hard, cracking the supports and smashing to the stone. Flames licked from a few cracks in the bottom-most planks, coming from the housing that sheltered the craft's main mekanicals and reservoirs of alchemy.

Through the smoke, Kathryn smelled the acrid yet oddly sweet tang of burnt blood. The entire mekanicals must have combusted with the crash. Kathryn imagined the ship had come in already overheated, mekanicals under full roil. Now the flames were consuming all.

She edged around toward the far side. She spotted the open rear door to the flippercraft. Men and women were gathered there, churning a bit in confusion. Kathryn spotted Argent ser Fields. He stood head-high above the others, atop a crate. He was shouting something, but the wind took his words.

Kathryn pushed toward the crowd.

Where was Tylar?

Worry had her shoving rudely, almost knocking over a woman rushing past with an empty bucket.

She searched the faces ahead, recognizing guards in the

golds and umbers of Chrismferry, alongside several Hands of Chrismferry.

Finally, she reached an eddy in the chaos, an open space between the dockworkers and the gathering passengers who had disembarked. She stepped closer, ready with a thousand questions. But first she had to find Tylar.

From the skies, snow drifted down out of the darkening clouds. Winds buffeted the heavy flakes into thick swirls. The snowfall mixed with the smoke and began to settle over the ruin. It would take several days to clear the wreckage. Not the most auspicious arrival for the new regent.

One flake landed on Kathryn's cheek.

The cold stung like the bite of a mud-wasp, but she wiped the flake away, too focused on her search to mind the cold. Still, she tugged up her masklin against the icy snowfall. After cinching the facecloth in place, she held out a hand for a moment. Flakes settled to her palm and melted.

She shook her head and stepped again toward the crowd around Argent. She could now hear his voice.

"Everyone head below! We'll escort you to your rooms!"

The churn of the crowd shifted in her direction. She still had not spotted Tylar. Then motion near the flippercraft drew her eye. She saw Tylar stepping down the rear ramp. He was not alone. A young woman leaned close to him. The ship's captain flanked his other side. Tylar was speaking to the man with some urgency.

The captain nodded and set off toward the flaming mekanicals.

Tylar stepped to the stones of Tashijan, the first time in a year. His eyes swept the crowd, as if counting heads.

Thank the gods, he appeared to be uninjured.

Tylar's eyes narrowed when they settled upon Argent.

Kathryn headed toward him. Best to keep Tylar and Argent apart as much as possible, especially when Tylar's blood was surely overheated already. The storm had ruined the welcome already. No need to make matters worse.

Kathryn recognized the color in Tylar's cheeks and the narrow set to his lips. Now would not be a good time for anyone to challenge him. Best to get him to his room. Then the two could talk about what had happened here . . . and other matters.

Tylar turned, as if sensing her approach.

For the first time, Kathryn noted his hand clasped with the woman's. It was Delia. Tylar's Hand of blood. Also Argent's estranged daughter.

Tylar leaned over to whisper something in his companion's ear. Most likely to reassure the young woman. Kathryn recalled Tylar doing the same with her in the past, his warm breath on her neck, the way his voice could cut through to her heart and calm its beat.

She took a deep breath through her masklin and lifted an arm to catch his eye.

Delia shifted to face Tylar more fully.

For a moment, too quick for any but Kathryn to note, her lips brushed against his. Tylar's palm slid along her arm. Then the two slipped back and faced the disembarked crowd of fellow passengers.

Kathryn lowered her half-raised arm. Unbidden, shadows drew around her more fully. She took a step away, withdrawing into them. Her heart pounded, and as the sun set into the growing storm, it suddenly went darker—and colder.

The storm would be a fierce one.

Off to the side, a cheer arose from those who fought the fires. The flames had finally been vanquished. All was secure again.

Kathryn retreated, lost in smoke and shadows.

Tylar turned in her direction—but she was already gone.

6

A SWORD OF STEEL

THE BLARE OF A TRUMPET, MUFFLED AND FAINT, REACHED Dart's hiding place. Something had stirred the tower. She heard distant shouts, too.

But she dared not move.

Not yet.

She hid in an alcove down the hall from the central stairs and chewed one of her knuckles. She shared her hiding space with a gray marble statue. It depicted some famous knight, one who bore a raven on his shoulder, though its beak had been broken off some time in the distant past.

She shouldn't be here. She knew better, but she could not help herself. She was supposed to be down in the library, learning the history of Tashijan, with her fellow pages. But she had begged off, claiming some urgent business with the castellan. With a disinterested wave, the owl-eyed archivist had dismissed her—though her subterfuge earned a rash of sneers from her peers. All would have liked an excuse to escape the tedious study of dates and endless lists of battles. Especially with all the excitement of late. For the past day, the entire Citadel had practically thrummed like a plucked bowstring. It was hard for any of them to sit still.

But worst of all for Dart.

She knew when the retinue from Oldenbrook was due. She had learned which rooms they were to occupy and had gone and found a vantage from which to spy on the outer hall. She had waited through two bells, but she was eventually rewarded by their arrival, led by a tall woman in a snowy fur who seemed as fresh as if she had just returned from a garden stroll. Dart recognized her as the mistress of tears. At her shoulder strode a man, a guardsman from the look of him, resplendent in finery that matched the mistress's. His eyes remained on the fur-cloaked Hand, while she seemed oblivious to him, deep in conversation with Castellan Vail, talking animatedly.

Dart had pushed deeper into her alcove, fearing being spotted by the castellan. What excuse could she offer for hiding here? Pupp had no such worry. He had been curled at her feet, but the commotion of the arriving party revived him. He trotted out into the hallway.

Though none could see him, she hissed under her breath and waved him back to the alcove. He reluctantly obeyed. Still, his stubbed tail wagged with excitement.

Dart understood. Despite the risk, she could not help peeking out. Another two Hands followed the one in the snowy-furred cloak. A man and a woman. One thin, one wide. Then Dart's attention shifted to a pair of massive guards—loam-giants from the size of them—who shouldered out of the stairwell. She gaped at them. They carried a crate slung between them.

As they stepped aside, a more familiar figure appeared behind them.

The bronze boy.

Dart's heart trembled somewhere between relief and terror.

So he had come.

He was a year ahead of her at school, so she had never known him well, but after encountering him in Oldenbrook, she had sought to learn more. Including his name. Brant. She tested the name now, mouthing it. It somehow fit him.

Her former schoolmate stopped with the giants near the stairs, shrugged aside a heavy winter cloak, and pointed an arm. "The houndskeep lies past the bailey. Take them down, get them settled, but keep them under watch. None are to see them until the morning."

The giants nodded and headed away.

Brant watched them for a breath. He looked somehow thinner, paler than when last she'd seen him—though as he turned back to the hall, a fire burnt in his manner. He tromped after his party. His eyes narrowed upon the mistress of tears and her tall escort. Plainly there was some trouble here.

Dart kept one eye peeked as Castellan Vail assigned rooms. The boy vanished into his own with barely a word to any of the others.

She maintained her post until the hall was empty. Even the escorts had vanished with their captain, gone to break bread. And test the Citadel's ale, she imagined.

She dared tarry no longer. The regent's flippercraft would be mooring soon. Still, as Dart stepped out, she had to bite back a desire to knock on Brant's door. If she could swear him to her secret . . . then she'd have nothing to fear. Maybe they could even share a—

A latch scraped ahead of her.

Dart crabbed backward with a wheel of her arms, ducking back into her alcove. Brant's door opened. He glanced up and down the hall as if someone had rapped on his door. Or maybe it was the trumpets that had blared for the past half bell, echoing down from the top of Stormwatch.

Dart studied him.

He was dressed the same, still in his heavy winter cloak and boots. Seemingly satisfied that he was alone, he headed for the stairs. Where was he going? To investigate the trumpets? To sample the ale here, like the guards?

He reached the far stairs. Dart craned her neck to see, curious where he was going. Without a glance back, he headed down.

She drew after him, her feet moving on their own. Pupp trotted ahead of her down the hall.

Upon reaching the landing, she searched below. He had already vanished around a curve in the stairs. She hesitated on the steps. Her spying had already revealed what she had wanted to know. *He had come.* It was best now that she return to the castellan's hermitage. The first evening bell would be ringing any moment. The regent's flippercraft was due to arrive. Castellan Vail would expect her to attend the welcoming.

Still, she stood on the landing, burning with curiosity, tempered by a trace of fear. What to do?

Then her decision was taken from her.

Pupp bounded down the stairs after the boy, perhaps responding to some unspoken desire in her own heart. She hissed at him, but only faintly. A moment later, she pursued her ghostly companion.

Brant proceeded slowly, new to Tashijan, but he seemed to know where he was going, moving with a dogged determination. Perhaps he had been given a map to the towers.

As they progressed, Dart kept easily hidden. As usual, the stairs were crowded. She had no difficulty keeping him in sight while staying back herself. As she trailed her quarry, she heard snatches of conversation. With each level she passed, she slowly pieced together some mishap that had befallen a flippercraft landing atop Stormwatch. Word had traveled faster than the trumpet's blare: of a fire, burning mekanicals, but order had been restored. No deaths.

Then she heard Tylar's name.

Her feet slowed to listen to the rest of a knight's conversation with a comely older maid. He leaned an elbow on the wall. Dart noted the Fiery Cross embroidered on his shoulder. "The regent arrives with as much turmoil as he's beset our fair land. Is it any wonder Warden Fields disapproves of his position at Chrismferry?"

Dart continued past, lest she draw the knight's eye. But it seemed the maid's ample bosom had captured his attention full enough.

She hurried down a few more steps, dread clutching her throat. So it had been Tylar's airship that had landed so roughly! He must have come early. She stopped at the next landing.

Enough with this foolishness. She needed to get back to the castellan's hermitage. Kathryn might need her.

"You!"

The shout startled her—as did the hand that grabbed her roughly and pulled her around. She expected it to be Brant, wise to her spying.

But another familiar countenance pushed close to her, almost nose to nose. Pyllor. She smelled the sour ale on the squire's breath.

"What are you doing out of your cage, Hothbrin? Come

looking for some more lessons?" He shoved her against the wall with an angry laugh.

Dart struggled against him, but he outweighed her by two stones.

" 'Course," he slurred, "we'll have to manage without Swordmaster Yuril. None of her coddling this time."

His guffaw sounded more like a bark—but Dart was deaf to it, hearing only the beat of ravens' wings behind his laugh. She tensed, remembering when another man had touched her so roughly.

Behind Pyllor, Dart saw two more of Pyllor's friends. Dart didn't know their names but recognized their hard eyes. She also noted the Fiery Cross emblems crudely stitched to their shirt collars.

Folks passed them on the stairs, barely noting them. Such ribaldry and hassling were not unknown among the ranks. But Dart read the mean intent in Pyllor's eyes. The Fiery Cross bore no love for the castellan—or those who served her. Swords had been drawn over the division.

One of his companions grabbed Dart's other shoulder. "Let's do her?" he hissed at Pyllor, his eyes shining with malicious fire.

The second squire hesitated, half-blocking the way. "The castellan's page—we don't dare."

Pyllor flat-handed him aside. His other fist knotted in Dart's half cloak and tugged her toward an open door. "Bugger that sellwench up in her hermitage. We're the warden's men. She needs to learn who truly rules here."

Dart fought against the fist in her cloak, trying to shed the garment and twist away. But her other elbow was snatched by the more exuberant of Pyllor's two companions. The other hung back still, glancing to the stairs. But all interest still seemed caught upon the crashed flippercraft.

Dart was half-carried through a doorway into a dark, empty room. A single brazier burnt near the back, offering a meager glow.

An iron rod protruded from it, buried in the embers.

"Get your flat arse in here!" Pyllor's friend said to their reluctant cohort.

He obeyed, caught in the wake of the other two.

"And latch the door!" Pyllor called out.

Dart stamped on the squire's foot, desperate to escape, heart pounding in her throat. Raven wings echoed. Did they mean to rape her?

Pyllor swore and threw her deeper into the room, hard enough to trip her up. She skidded on the stone, ripping her leggings, bloodying her knee.

"Act like a skaggin' wench . . . and we'll treat you like one!"

A coarse laugh encouraged Pyllor.

The door closed behind him, sinking the room into gloom.

Pyllor's partner crossed to the brazier, wrapped up his hand in a cloth, and pulled the rod from the coals. Its iron end glowed a fiery crimson. A branding iron. The tip was shaped into a circle bisected by crossed lines.

The symbol of the Fiery Cross.

It was not rape that they intended, but another violation of body.

"Where should we mark her?" the bearer asked. "The thigh, like we did that Moor Eld boy?"

Pyllor glared at Dart. "No. Somewhere where all will see." He touched his cheek. "It's time the Fiery Cross sent a message to that sellwench up in her hermitage."

Dart scrambled back as the others laughed. She sought her only weapon. She reached down to her scraped knees, blessing her hands with her own blood. She needed Pupp.

Dart glanced around and only now realized she was alone.

Pupp was gone.

Pyllor stalked toward her. "Grab her."

Brant knew he was being hunted.

He had sensed it for the last three levels as he descended the stairs, a pressure building behind his breastbone. He searched behind him, but the curve of the tower stairs betrayed him. All he saw was men and women in cloaks or various drapes of finery. A washerwoman with a tied bundle of linen bustled past him, almost knocking him aside. He caught the scent of soap and perfumed oil from her burden, intended for someone of higher station.

He took another step down. He was thwarted from much

further progress by a tide of people heading up. He had almost reached the bottom of the tower, and some excitement seemed to be drafting folks upward, like smoke up a chimney, something about an arriving flippercraft.

Pressed against a wall, Brant finally noted the heat at his throat. His hand rose to touch the scar on his neck, then the stone resting below it. The stone wasn't burning like the last time, flaring with a blistering fire. It was only warm, as if slightly fevered. Both curious and disturbed, he tested its black surface with his fingers.

As he stood, the stone warmed further, a match to the tension mounting in his chest. Brant took a step back up the stairs, then another. Under his fingertips, the stone heated to a toasty warmth. He reached the next landing, and a deeper burn surged, the stone becoming a coal in his fingers.

Wincing, he stopped. He remembered the daemon summoned by the stone when last it had flared. He searched all around him. Nothing.

At his throat, the stone began to cool.

No.

He sensed that whatever had been hunting him was now retreating. He could not lose it.

Brant took another step up, and the stone warmed ever so slightly. Encouraged, he hurried toward the next landing. With each step, the black stone responded, stoking higher with an inner fire. If he stopped or was slowed, it would cool again. He did not tarry, climbing two steps at a time now, caught in the flow of residents heading higher.

As he passed the next landing, Brant felt the stone suddenly lose its fiery edge. With each step farther, it cooled more.

Brant swung around and fought the tide again, heading back down, returning to the landing below.

The stone's burn ignited again.

He left the stairs and entered the passageway.

It was nearly empty. He rushed forward, using the threaded rock like a lodestone, following the trail of heat. He was a quarter way down the hall when the stone flared to a roasting fire.

Brant gasped but knew he was close.

He yanked the cord from around his neck. He held out the necklace, letting the talisman swing. On one pass, the arc of the dangling stone suddenly stopped—halted by the backside of a molten bronze beast.

It appeared out of the air at his knees, facing away, toward a door. Its body seemed to melt and flow, constantly struggling to hold its beastly shape, half wolf, half lion. In its fierce churn, Brant sensed its fury. It wafted outward like the heat from an open forge.

Then the beast lunged away, vanishing from the touch of the stone, and through a solid door.

Brant straightened.

Then heard the scream.

Dart struggled to escape her own half cloak. It had been pulled over her head by the larger of Pyllor's cohorts. She kicked and felt her boot strike flesh. A loud *oof* responded.

"Get'er legs, Ryskold!" Pyllor said.

Someone grabbed her knee.

Dart fought with a rising fury that grew to a blinding ferocity. A hand broke free of her cloak, and she raked her nails at whoever clutched her. She connected, digging deep.

A bellow of surprise erupted.

The grip loosened, and she twisted away, freeing herself—but only momentarily. Whoever she'd wounded lunged atop her, meaning to pin her with his greater weight. Dart held him off with an elbow and a hand. In the struggle, her fingers stumbled upon a familiar shape at the other's waist.

She grabbed it and pulled.

The sword slid free of its sheath. Her attacker let loose a cry of pain, accidentally cut by his own blade.

Dart rolled to the side and to her feet. She lifted the stolen sword to face the three across the room.

In her hand was no wooden sword—this one was steel.

The bolder of Pyllor's two friends clutched his forearm. His shirt had been cleaved and darkened with his blood. His eyes had narrowed with pain, but burnt with a fiery anger.

In the glow of the single brazier, Dart's stolen blade shone brightly. As did Pyllor's own blade as he pulled it free. A squire's blade. No black diamond adorned its pommel, marking a true knight, for certainly no honor was to be found here.

"Leave her to me," he called to the others unnecessarily.

His wounded partner's sheath was already empty. The other had simply backed away, plainly refusing to be drawn further into the struggle here.

Pyllor sneered. "First I'll bloody you, then we'll get you branded up good—for all to see."

Dart remained silent and took a warding stance. But this was no sparring match. Pyllor came at her with a brutal and heavy lunge.

She refused to be drawn into a block, not against the more muscled attacker. She simply turned her blade and let his steel sing along hers. She leaned her left shoulder back and Pyllor's sword tip passed her harmlessly.

Surprised, her attacker was momentarily off balance.

And close.

Expressionless, Dart demonstrated how well she had learned Pyllor's prior lesson, how sword fighting sometimes required more than a blade. As he stumbled near, she kneed out with her other leg, striking him square in the groin.

He cried out and fell back.

At that moment, motion stirred at the corner of her eye. Pupp burst through the latched door. He was a molten glow, a blur of impotent fury.

Though relieved, Dart kept her focus on Pyllor. He wobbled, clutching himself with one hand, but the other lifted his sword.

"You're dead," he hissed.

Pupp danced up to her, but she had no time to bloody him, to use the Grace in her most essential humour to call him forth.

Pyllor came at her again, more hobbled and more cautious. She read the cunning reflected in his eyes. She readied herself, but she knew he was the better swordsman.

He thrust, testing her this time.

She parried, but he smacked back her blade and came in with a feint, followed by a savage thrust. She barely nicked her hilt up to block the tip. Still, the blow reverberated up her arm and knocked her back a step.

Pyllor sneered and lowered his sword.

Dart took advantage of the satisfaction in his expression. She lunged out, sweeping into the opening. He dropped his hilt even farther, lowering his guard. Dart realized her mistake—but it was too late. She was committed. Her momentum carried forward her attack.

Pyllor suddenly shoved out his elbow and twisted his sword's tip in the opposite direction. Dart recognized the opening maneuver. A perfectly executed Naethryn's Folly.

And she had been drawn inescapably into it.

He looped his sword in a side-sweep, trapping her thrusted blade—then tugged his elbow to his side and turned on his back heel.

Dart's sword sprang from her fingertips with a ring of steel. It sailed, hilt over tip, through the air, and clanged against the stone floor.

Pyllor did not wait—he drove his sword for her belly.

Dart had only one lesson left. One again taught to her by the squire. She grabbed bare-handed for his blade. Her fingers closed over the steel. She shoved with her palm.

Steel sliced with a painless kiss.

She would lose fingers.

Before she could react, a crash sounded to her right, and the door cracked open with a pop of its latch. Pyllor faltered in surprise. Dart pushed his sword aside and dropped back.

Light flooded the dim room from the hall outside. A dark figure stood limned in the doorway. In the stunned silence, he took in the scene before him.

Pyllor turned his sword toward the intruder. He eyed him, judging him. This was no knight, but someone in a rather plain cloak. Someone of no consequence.

"Begone! This is none of your concern!"

Ignoring him, the figure stepped inside. The blinding light fell from his shoulders and revealed face and form.

The bronze boy.

Brant.

How . . . ?

"Let her go," he said with a dread calm.

Dart glanced back to Pyllor. Surely this was over. Agony flared up her arm from her sliced palm. She clenched a fist against it, trying to squeeze it away.

Pyllor refused to back down. His fury, stoked by the thwarted attack, found a fresh target in the intruder, believing the younger man to be no more than one of the faceless underfolk, what with his worn leathers and scuffed boots.

Pyllor dropped his sword lower. But Dart knew this was another feint, a trick meant to dull an opponent's guard. At his back, Dart spotted a dagger, hidden out of sight.

"Don't—" she said and reached with her injured hand. Blood spattered from her fingertips and spilled from her palm.

But it never struck the floor.

The humour splashed upon the waiting form below.

Dart felt Pupp appear, blessed with blood, drawn fully into this world. He burst into solidity with a flare of ruddy fire. He leaped toward Pyllor at the exact time the squire twisted and flung his dagger toward the intruder.

Pupp sailed through the air, a molten bronze arrow. He hit Pyllor in the arm, taking it off at the elbow. Pyllor screamed.

The attack, though late, proved unnecessary. The thrown dagger missed its intended target as Brant sidestepped it, as if anticipating it all along. It clattered into the hall outside.

Pyllor fell back onto his rear, holding up his severed arm in disbelief. The edge of his shirt still smoked. The stump of his limb stuck out, blackened and seared.

More shouts of horror rose from Pyllor's companions. They fled toward the door, away from Pupp, who now circled Pyllor on the floor.

Brant allowed the others to flee as he moved toward Dart.

Pyllor cowered, wide-eyed in terror and shock. He blubbered incoherently, scooting away, abandoning his sword as he pushed with his remaining hand.

Brant touched her arm. "We should be away. Now." His eyes were on Pupp, but he seemed little surprised.

Dart allowed herself to be drawn toward the door.

"Call off your daemon," Brant said.

Dart had no strength to argue. "To me, Pupp."

His fiery form continued to circle Pyllor, hackles raised, snarling fire.

"To me," Dart urged more firmly. She remembered what had befallen two other men, back in the rookery in Chrism-

ferry. She had witnessed Pupp's mercy then. A part of her wished the same for Pyllor.

Pupp seemed to sense this, glancing back at her. Beyond the fire of his eyes, she saw her own fury reflected. And again something not of this world. Beyond her ability to fathom.

Dart met that fiery gaze, acknowledged the bloodlust, both in Pupp and in her own heart. Still, she felt Brant's touch on her elbow, urgent but patient. She responded to it.

"To me," she commanded again. *"Now."*

Pupp turned back to Pyllor. The squire moaned and pushed against the wall. A trail of wetness flowed from under Pyllor as he fouled himself in his terror. But Pupp finally obeyed. He swung around and trotted sullenly and darkly back to her. He brought with him a whiff of burnt blood—her own and perhaps Pyllor's.

Brant led her to the door.

Down the hallway, a sharp cry of *daemon* rang from the central stair.

Brant glanced at her. Dart noted the flecks of gold in his emerald eyes. "Where?" he asked.

"This way," Dart said and hurried away from the shouts. She led him toward the far end of the hallway. A back stair led to the warren of rooms and narrow halls of Tashijan's underfolk and small staff.

"It fades," Brant said beside her, staring at Pupp's form.

"The Grace that gave him substance has been consumed."

Pupp slipped back into his ghostly form. And none too soon. A door flew open, revealing an elderly manservant in house livery, drawn by the commotion. Dart and Brant hurried past, while Pupp padded through the man's legs and the open door as if they were air.

Once they reached the back stairs, they ran down a full flight. Brant asked her as they fled, "What Grace is this you speak of?"

"Something . . ." She shifted her wounded fist, wrapped and snugged in her half cloak. "Something in my blood."

Dart knew that what she had revealed was supposed to be kept secret, but she had neither the strength nor the will to roust up some fabrication. Besides, the strange young man seemed to know more than he expressed.

Like how he had come so opportunely to the door a moment ago.

It seemed both had secrets neither was ready to fully bare.

Brant slowed them and drew Dart into a niche. He pulled a bit of scarf from an inner pocket of his cloak. It was mere roughspun. He nodded for her hand. She held it out, and he deftly wrapped her palm, cinching it tight to hold the wound closed.

"Can you move your fingers?"

She demonstrated that she could, though it hurt.

"Nothing appears deeply maimed," he mumbled. "But you should see a healer."

She withdrew her hand from his, suddenly uncomfortable with his touch. "I will."

They stepped back onto the stairs. Voices echoed from above. Inquiries called out, from shadowknights drawn by the commotion. A voice rang through, edged with panic.

"They fled that way with the daemon!"

Pyllor.

Brant sighed through his nose. Dart sensed that maybe he was reconsidering his mercy. They headed down before any pursuers closed in on them.

With the shock worn away, the enormity of what had happened struck Dart. Pyllor and his two cohorts, members of the Fiery Cross, would soon have the story of Dart and her daemon fluttering to the top of Stormwatch, to the Warden's Eyrie and the castellan's hermitage. Kathryn would be furious. Dart despaired. In a moment, all had come to ruin. There would be no hiding from accusations of summoning daemons. Her life here was over. She would either be exposed or have to flee again.

Until then, she needed a moment to sit, to think.

"They don't know me," Brant said. "We have to go somewhere where they won't think to look for you."

But where? Dart could not force her thoughts into any order. She simply ran, winding down the stairs, bumping her shoulders due to the narrowness, dodging a few of the understaff who were busy with their own labors. Their flight was ignored.

Brant finally slowed her. "I might know a place. I was

headed to the Citadel's houndskeep and kennel. My lord arranged a private pen, one under guard. We could hole up down there."

Dart nodded. She had been down to the houndskeep only once. It was unlikely anyone would recognize her. "I know a shorter route through the courtyard," she said.

With a goal firmly in mind, she headed off at a faster pace. Once safe, perhaps she could get a letter to the castellan. Kathryn would know best how to handle this matter.

They fled another three flights to reach the level that separated the upper Citadel from the subterranean realm of the masters. She escaped the stairs through a warren of kitchens, passing baker's ovens, simmerpots, and spitted roasting fires. Savory scents assaulted them at every turn: rising yeast, bubbling spiced oils, spattering fat, brittling sweetcake. They had to skirt around a team of cooks lifting a full boar from a massive hearth.

"Mind the tusks!" the chief cook hollered, meaty fists on his hips.

Then they were gone, out a door, escaping the ringing din of banging pans and sweltering heat. Brant closed the door against it. They sheltered a moment in an arched doorway, open to the central courtyard.

The cold struck Dart first, like jumping into a cold creek. She shivered all over and must have made some sound, for Brant turned toward her.

"Storm's already here," he said quietly and shifted his attention to the gray-cloaked skies above.

Snow sifted down, softly, gently. Sheltered by massive towers on four sides, the winds failed to reach here. Heavy flakes, like downy heron feathers, floated and drifted, almost hanging in the air, refusing to touch land. The snowfall filled the courtyard like sand in a well. Dart could barely discern the giant wyrmwood tree that graced the center of the courtyard. Its lower branches were caked with mounding snow. Its upper branches stretched upward, toward the top of Stormwatch, as if the ancient tree were trying to claw its way out of the courtyard, smothering under the thickening blanket.

Brant held out his hand and let a few flakes settle to his palm. The heat of his body melted them. He dried his hand on his pants. Dart noted a glint of suspicion in the narrowing of his eyes as he studied the skies for another breath.

"The true storm has yet to strike," he mumbled and headed out into the snow. "The worst is yet to come."

Dart bundled her cloak tighter and led the way across the courtyard. As she aimed for the far side of the massive trunk of the wyrmwood, she noted one of their party holding back, still sheltered in the archway.

"Pupp—to me," she said and patted her hip.

He huddled his molten form low to the ground. His usual ruddy bronze had dulled to a wan shine. The spikes of his mane trembled as he shook ever so slightly.

"It's only snow," she said, stopping fully to turn to face him.

Brant halted with her. "Your daemon?"

"He's not my daemon," she said with a note of irritation. "He's . . . he's . . ." *What could she say?* "Never mind. It's complicated."

Dart had no desire to tell this emerald-eyed boy who she actually was. And unlike the gods of Myrillia, she was born whole and unsundered. Then again, maybe that wasn't totally true. Pupp was birthed with her, joined to her, and in some aspects, a *part* of her. In fact, she grew deathly ill if Pupp was too far separated from her. *Sundered yet still together* was how Master Gerrod had once described it.

But for as long as Dart could remember, Pupp was just Pupp, her ghostly companion, champion, and forever a piece of her heart.

That was good enough for her.

Though right at this moment, his stubbornness piqued her growing impatience. She didn't want to be in the storm any longer than necessary.

"Pupp, come here!"

"You can still see him?" Brant asked, his brows pinched as he searched the snowswept courtyard.

Before she could answer, Pupp finally obeyed. He shot out from under the archway and sped low to the ground, skirting side to side, as if trying to avoid any snowflakes. But the path he scribed formed a sigil of panic. He hurried to Dart and past, continuing across the yard.

Now Dart followed, almost running, dragging Brant with her.

At least Pupp must have understood where she wanted to go. He aimed for a short flight of descending stairs. He vanished down them.

In her hurry, Dart's left boot slipped on a bit of black ice on the top step. She tumbled into a headlong fall—but Brant caught her around the waist and righted her back onto her feet. She hung a moment in his arms.

"Are you all right?"

Despite the cold, Dart felt her face warm. "Yes . . . sorry . . ."

Brant released her and led the way down the stairs to a low, wide door. He hauled the door open for her. Pupp had already passed through it in his haste to escape the snow.

"It's not far from here," Dart said, sliding past him. She kept her eyes from his, lest they betray her. She pushed into the dim hallway.

The heat inside stifled after the icy storm.

She headed to a cross passage and turned left. Already the barking and bawling of the Citadel's stalking hounds reached them—as did the smell of wet dog and soiled hay. The entrance to the houndskeep lay only a few steps farther down the hall. The door was a gated grate of iron.

Dart stepped up to it.

Beyond stretched a cross-hatching of low passages, lit by torches, carved out of the stone that underlay Tashijan. It was said that the kennels here were once the dungeons of the original keep, before the coming of the gods, during the barbarous time of human kings.

Dart had a hard time imagining such a dungeon. Each carved niche barely held room enough for a pair of hounds, long-legged though they might be.

As they stopped before the gate, their arrival did not go unnoticed.

" 'Bout time you got your hairy arse down here!" The keeper turned from a slop bucket. He was naked to the waist and appeared half bear himself with a back and chest covered in a pelt of curly hair. In some cruel trick of nature, though, his head was bald, his pate shining with sweat. "Like I have time to sit a couple wild whelpings—"

His eyes finally took note of who stood at his door.

He threw his hands in the air.

"Off with you . . . no time for gapers . . . 'nough problems of mine own." He waved them off.

"Good ser," Brant said loudly, "I've come to inquire about two loam-giants, represented by Oldenbrook."

His words only deepened the scowl on the keeper's face, but he tromped over to them and swung open the door. "So you heard then, have you?"

Brant walked through with a frown. "Heard what?"

The answer came from down the passage. "Ock! Master Brant!"

A broad form pushed out of a side passage, hunkered from the low ceiling into an awkward crouch. It was one of the loam-giants Dart had spotted with Brant earlier. He approached, almost knuckling on the hay-strewn floor. A few hounds howled at him as he passed, unaccustomed to such giants down here.

"I just sent word up a mite ago. Did you jump from a window to get down here so fast?"

Dart didn't know the giant, but she still read the deep unease in the man's manner.

"Malthumalbaen," Brant said, "what's happened? I've heard no word. I've only chanced to come down here to see how the whelpings are settled for the night. One of Tashijan's pages was kind enough to escort me." He nodded to Dart.

The giant shook his thick-necked head. "Disaster, ser. Bad as they come."

"The wolf cubbies?"

Malthumalbaen lowered his head and his voice. "Gone, ser."

"Dead?" Worry etched his words, but anger narrowed his eyes.

"No, ser. Thank the gods for that good bit of Grace. You'd best come see. Dral is still trying to salvage the matter."

"And it weren't no fault of mine," the keeper groused and called after them as they headed down the passage. "Just so it's clear to one and all! If'n you had let me know you had wild whelpings, I could have better prepared."

Malthumalbaen let out a long sigh and grumbled under his breath. Still it had to be loud enough to reach the keeper's ears. "Gave us a place near the back. Ill-kept, it was, with nary a torch to see much by."

The loam-giant turned the corner and led them down the cross passage.

Dart glanced to the small cells on either side, where tawny-furred forms lay curled at the back, two to a cage, piled almost atop each other for warmth. She noted an eye or two peek open as they passed, wary and watchful. A few others, younger and more exuberant, stalked back and forth in the front of their cages, hackles half-raised in warning. In the dimness, their eyes shown with a bit of Grace. *Air and loam*, she had been told. It gave the hounds especially keen noses and ears.

Then down near the end of the hall, a form lay splayed on the floor, as if dead or brought low by a blow. But the figure stirred at their approach, struggling, it seemed, with something out of sight. A growl of curses accompanied the effort.

"Dral!" the first giant called out. "Look what I found! Master Brant himself!"

The other giant, redheaded like the first, rolled to his side. Dart saw his arm was jammed down a hole at the base of the wall. He fought to pull his limb out. "Got myself stuck."

Malthumalbaen went to his aid. It took a moment of yanking, twisting, and cursing to finally free the snared giant. Once that was accomplished, the one called Dral rolled to his seat, cradling his head in plain misery.

Pupp had sidled past the loam-giant and sniffed around the opening. Since stone blocked Pupp as surely as any other, the opening proved too small for even him to nose much deeper.

Malthumalbaen narrated their story. "We were just getting 'em outta that skaggin' crate. They looked near on death themselves, all wet with their own piss. Scared to a lick, they were."

He lifted an arm and pointed to a cage door that hung crooked on one hinge, the other broken. "We were just shutting them up, when off it comes."

"I should have been more careful," Dral moaned.

"Them little ones, they were out like arrows. We tried to snatch 'em back up, but down that rat hole they both went.

Like they knew where they were going." The giant shook his head. "Don't even know where it goes."

"I tried to see if I could reach them," Dral added, then shrugged and covered the top of his head with his hands.

"The blame is not yours," Brant said.

Dart had been so busy listening to the giants and watching wide-eyed, that only now did she note how dark Brant's face had become. Looking into his eyes, she could almost smell the burn of brimstone off him. But he kept his fury locked inside him. His words to the giants were gentle and firm.

"I should never have brought them here," he added to himself. He bent a knee to study the hole. It was cut smoothly into the back wall and plainly canted down at a steep angle. "Do you know where this leads?"

"We asked the keeper. All he knew is that when they swamped out the keeps here, they washed everything down that rat hole."

"Into the sewers?"

Malthumalbaen shrugged. "Keeper seemed not to think so. Says his houndskeep is older than all of Tashijan. Before they plumbed and dug sewers for this place."

Brant stood up. He held a fist tight to his side.

"But the keeper called for some help. They should—"

The entire houndskeep suddenly erupted with howls and baying barks, drowning out the giant's words. Loud snatches of cursing accompanied the cacophony.

"That must be him," the giant said.

Brant headed down the passage toward the commotion. He held off both giants with a raised palm and Dart with a stern look of worry.

Still, Dart trailed him. She kept a few steps back, fearing she might be recognized.

Brant reached the corner and peered around.

Dart noticed him flinch in shock. As the hounds continued to howl, curiosity overcame fear of discovery. She moved behind Brant and stared down the passage.

"Git that monster out of here!" the keeper yelled.

Near to filling the low passage stood a shaggy-furred beast that could have challenged the two giants in size and stature. A bullhound. It padded deeper, heading toward them. Its head was the size of a shield, and the remainder of its muscled form was banded in fur the color of burnt copper and ebony. Ropes of drool dangled from its half-snarled lips, capable of etching stone with its caustic touch if the hound were riled.

Brant reached behind him, intending to push Dart back to safety, but she avoided his hand and ran past him and down the hallway. With all the demands on her time, she had not seen the bullhound in ages.

"Barrin!" she called out, too delighted and relieved to care who might see her.

The bullhound snuffled and tossed its head a bit. Saliva flew to the walls, etching the stone. It then lowered its muzzle to accept Dart's affection. The stub of its tail wagged in a blur.

Dart hugged the great beast, grabbing both ears, which required a full spread of her arms. She tugged a bit and heard a rumble of contentment.

"You're going to spoil the kank," a voice growled behind the bullhound's shoulder.

A familiar figure stepped around to the front. He wore his usual furred breeches and knee-high mud brown boots. But it was his face that was the most welcome, a friend after the horrors of the past bells. The lower half of his face protruded in a slight muzzle, marking him, like the loam-giants before, as one touched by Graced alchemies in the womb. But only Tristal, god of Idlewyld, produced such men and women, wyld trackers, blessed with air and loam like the hounds here, creating the most skilled of Myrillian trackers and hunters.

"Lorr!" Dart called out happily.

She released her grip on the bullhound and hugged the wyld tracker with as much enthusiasm, though she didn't tug his ears.

All around, the hounds continued their baying.

The houndskeeper stalked around, keeping well clear of Barrin's haunches. "Got 'em all riled up! Your beast is going to put 'em all off their feed."

Lorr shifted out of Dart's embrace, but he still kept an arm around her. She felt a tremor deep in his chest, and while not a sound came from him, the hounds quickly quieted as if commanded.

The houndskeeper kept his fist on his hips, but he nodded. "That's better."

Lorr glanced up the passage. By now, Brant and the two loam-giants had stepped into view. "So someone brought a gift of Fell wolves to the knighting—and now you've gone and lost them."

Dart heard the disdain and thread of anger behind the tracker's words.

Dart touched Lorr's arm. "They—he's a friend of mine from back at the school in Chrismferry."

Lorr studied Dart, then nodded. Some of the anger drained from him, but a trace of disdain remained. Friends or not, the tracker had little use for fools. "So then tell me what happened? Where have these whelpings gone off to?"

Brant pointed to the side passage. "Over this way."

"Show me."

Brant, trailed by the two giants, led the way back to the hole in the hall.

Lorr shifted closer to Dart and whispered to her. "I smell blood on you. Fresh blood." He nodded to her hand. "What happened?"

"There was some trouble," she offered lamely, avoiding the longer story.

Lorr nodded forward. "That boy didn't—"

"No!" Dart cut him off. "The opposite. He saved me from worse harm."

Lorr seemed satisfied, and Dart was happy to let him move to other matters. *How was the castellan faring? Had Dart heard about Tylar's bumpy arrival?* Moments later, they reached the last cell in the passageway. Lorr noted the rusted and broken hinge, and as the story of the escape was related again, Lorr inspected the hole in the wall.

"And you're sure they were Fell wolf cubbies and not loamed rats?"

Brant stood off to the side, arms crossed. Dart didn't like the way his nose had pinched since Lorr's arrival, as if he smelled something distasteful. Lorr, in turn, was unusually hard and abrupt with him during the telling of the tale. An unspoken tension remained between them. Dart could not understand why.

A new voice called from behind them. Dart jumped slightly, surprised by the sudden appearance. She had not heard a single booted tread. And no wonder. When she turned, she saw the stranger was also a wyld tracker, muzzled like Lorr, though perhaps slightly less protuberant. Then again, it might be the new tracker's age. Fourteen winters at best. Also, while Lorr's hair was a match to his brown boots, the younger tracker had long locks the color of a raven's eye, black with a hint of blue. His skin shone with a ruddy blush and was as smooth as river stone worn by rushing waters.

"My sister's son," Lorr said. "Kytt."

Brant's nose crinkled even more. Dart suspected that if Brant had had fur, it would be bristling right now.

Kytt held out a hide flask. "I've fetched the musk secretions and had the alchemists dilute it in yellow bile as you ordered, Tracker Lorr."

"Piss and musk?" one of the giants mumbled. "Mind me never to share a drink with these two."

Lorr accepted the flask. "Musk from a fox will carry a scent far." He bit the stopper free and decanted the flask's contents down the hole. "We'll see where this leads us."

He stood up and tilted his head slightly as if testing the air. He remained like that for a long breath, then stirred again.

Lorr stepped away and waved the younger tracker ahead. "I will let you know what I discover."

Brant stepped forward and blocked them. "I would go with you. The Fell wolves were my duty. I will not forsake it."

"Too late for that, it seems. Besides, there have been enough mistakes this day. We need no one who smells of the Huntress muddying up the trail with his bumbling."

Brant refused to move. Only his shoulders tightened, ready for a fight.

Dart failed to understand the layers of friction that lay beneath all this posturing. She knew that Brant hailed from Saysh Mal, the cloud forest and god-realm of the Huntress. But what difference did that make to Lorr? She stepped to intervene—and not just to settle a peace between them.

"I would like to go with you and Kytt," Dart said. She should be safe with the trackers, and where they'd be searching would surely be away from the more traveled areas of

Tashijan. Also, if she wanted to hide, it might be best to keep moving while doing it. "And I'd appreciate it if you'd let Master Brant come with us."

Brant nodded to her, but his countenance remained far from grateful. "The whelpings know my scent," he added. "It will be easier for me to lure them from hiding."

Lorr glanced between Dart and Brant. His senses must have been heightened enough to suspect layers of intent beyond Dart's words.

The tracker finally shrugged.

"Then let's begin this hunt."

7

A RUMOR OF DAEMONS

"WELCOME TO TASHIJAN," THE WARDEN SAID.

Tylar gripped Argent's hand across the threshold to the new accommodations granted him at Tashijan.

"I assume these rooms will meet with your satisfaction," Argent ser Fields said. His fingers tightened on Tylar's, not in a friendly manner.

Tylar matched his grip and kept his gaze fixed on the warden's one eye. The plate of bone over the other reflected the firelight from the chamber behind Tylar's shoulder.

"You are most generous," Tylar responded. "Any of the rooms in the knights' quarters would have sufficed."

"Ah, but you come with all your Hands in tow," Argent said, still holding tight. "It wouldn't be right to allow someone who arrives like a god to be housed in so low a manner."

Tylar's jaw ached from biting back harsher words. The past bell had been a chaotic flurry of high-blown flattery and barely contained resentment, most of it voiced by the warden himself. But Tylar kept his tongue civil. Especially since beyond the warden stood representatives of all of Tashijan: Master Hesharian of the Council of Masters, various leaders of the shadowknights' castes, even Keeper Ryngold, who oversaw the house staff and underfolk. They had all escorted Tylar's party down to their rooms, which took up almost all of this level, an embarrassing generosity in such overcrowded conditions. Tylar was sure the warden had let it be known to all how well the regent was being accommodated.

"A private feast is scheduled at the next bell," Argent finished, relinquishing his hand. "After you've all had a chance to refresh yourselves, I'll send my man to escort you and your Hands down to the dining hall."

"Most generous again," Tylar choked out.

Argent turned with a nod of his head and waved the escort down the hall ahead of him. The remainder of the party from Chrismferry had already retired into their respective rooms. Delia had come close to slamming her door in her haste to escape her father's stiff and false affection.

The only one left in the hall was Tylar's ever-present shadow, the Wyr-mistress Eylan. She stood stoically, almost bored.

"Keep any ears from this door," he instructed.

She gave him a barely perceptible nod.

Tylar closed the door behind him and leaned against it, glad for a moment's peace. But he wasn't alone. He turned to find four people arrayed near the back of the room, three maids and a manservant, resplendent in fine liveries. Their dress was a match to the room itself, as if their clothes had been cut from the heavy draperies. The remainder of the main chamber was equally grand, appointed in rich silks, tapestries, padded chairs, and a hearth tall enough to walk into upright, presently ablaze with a cheery fire.

The switch-thin servant bowed deeply, then straightened. "Welcome, your lordship. We've already discharged your bags. If you'll show me which dress you'd like to wear to the feast, I shall do my best to freshen and brush them."

Tylar waved them off. "That won't be necessary. I'd prefer a few moments of solitude. If I need anything, I will send for you."

"Ser, your bath has not been—"

"Not necessary," he said with a bit of a snap. He was immediately ashamed at his harshness. He knew better than to vent his anger upon those who sought only to fulfill their duties. He calmed his voice. "Most welcome, but that will be all."

With another bow, the manservant herded the maids amid much curtsying out a narrow door that led down to the staff quarters. A silk-wrapped pull-rope hung beside it, ready to summon assistance when needed. Tylar had no intention of tugging on it while here.

Once alone, Tylar sighed. Though his empty stomach

growled, he had no great desire to attend the feast. His nose, though, did note the platter of hard cheeses and steaming bread set atop a table by the hearth, along with a silver flagon of spiced wine. Maybe there was some small gain in being a visiting regent.

He stepped toward the platter.

A knock on the door stopped him. He closed his eyes against yet another interruption. What now? Rubbing at the stubble on his chin, he turned from the hearth and crossed back to the door. Eylan surely would have blocked any stranger from disturbing him. Perhaps it was Delia, reappearing now that her father had vacated the halls.

He pulled open the door and found himself mistaken.

A knight in a damp shadowcloak stood at his threshold. "Tylar."

He stepped back. "Kathryn."

The castellan had been notably missing from the formalized greetings after the hard landing atop Stormwatch. And while Tylar had wondered at her absence, he was pleased at the exasperation it had caused in the warden. He lifted an arm, inviting her inside.

She brushed through the doorway, barely meeting his eye.

Tylar closed the door. He studied her as she crossed to the hearth. She looked paler than usual, but maybe it was the cold. She lifted both palms toward the fire. He noted meltwater dripping from the edge of her cloak. A few wet hairs had worked free from her riding braid and were pasted to her cheeks.

She spoke to the flames. "I have Gerrod and two of his fellow masters examining your flippercraft's mekanicals. If there was any sabotage or misdeed, they should be able to discern it before you return to Chrismferry."

Tylar relaxed the slight stiffness to his shoulders. So that was why she had been missing earlier. He had feared a part of her absence might be some discomfit with his arrival.

Relieved, he approached her. "The captain believed it was the stress of burning too much blood," he said. "Or perhaps some weakness in the alchemies. Either way, the failure was most likely happenstance and not anything malicious—but it does warrant investigation."

She nodded.

Tylar reached her side. The heat of the hearth finally drove her back a step. Or maybe it was his own nearness. She moved to one of the chairs and examined the platter of small fare with a bit too much intensity.

"Kathryn . . . ?" he started softly.

She picked up a piece of cheese, then returned it to the plate. "I assume you know Rogger arrived two days ago. With the god's skull."

"I got your raven," he confirmed, not pressing her. It seemed such topics were easier for the moment.

"Gerrod's been examining it in secret and has already come up with some answers."

"So soon?"

Kathryn frowned, as if the question somehow rankled her. "He has a mind like no other."

"I have no doubt," he said softly. "What has he discerned?"

Kathryn slowly outlined all that the master had discovered, sketching out his speculations. As she continued, Tylar's interest drew him nearer to her, brows pinched in concern.

"Seersong?" he asked as she finished.

Kathryn glanced at him, meeting his eyes for the first time, as if testing an icy stream before jumping in. She spoke with a firmer voice. "That is what Gerrod suspects. An echo of some curse still trapped in the bone."

"And Krevan came looking for the skull, too. Strange."

"I suspect he'll be back. But whatever has driven him here, he seemed reluctant to talk openly about it."

Tylar shrugged. "Well, Krevan was never known to be garrulous."

His words drew the faintest of smiles from her. It always amazed him how her entire face could soften with just the smallest of movements. He found himself staring a bit too long at her lips, reminded of a different life. It was now his turn to glance away.

"We'll simply have to outwait Krevan," he mumbled.

Remembering his empty stomach, he plucked up a bit of dry hardcrust and chewed an edge.

Kathryn studied the room as if seeing it for the first time. "Your Hands? They are settled into their rooms?"

"Indeed. Argent has given practically this entire level to house all of us. Why do you ask?"

Kathryn waved away his words, a bit brusquely. "No reason. It's just . . . I'm sure Dart will be thrilled to see her friend Laurelle again. She's still your Hand of tears, correct?"

Tylar nodded. "The girl practically filled the flippercraft's hold with gifts and sweets for Dart. Insisted that her arrival be a surprise." He shrugged a shoulder. "Where is the child, by the way? I thought she'd be at your side."

"Off to class—though by now she might have returned to her garret off my hermitage. I should be returning to my rooms myself. To change for the feast." She shook her head sourly and stepped toward the door. "This game we must play . . ."

Tylar suspected the *game* she referred to involved more than just the feast to come. He noted a trace of anger directed at him, but he was unsure how to assuage it. Sometimes women were as impenetrable as the most complex of alchemies.

Before Kathryn could reach the door, a knock sounded.

Kathryn glanced at him.

He shrugged. He was not expecting anyone. "It might just be Delia," he offered.

Kathryn's face closed up, eyes tightening. "Then I'd certainly best be going," she said stiffly and strode more quickly toward the door.

Tylar suddenly understood. Kathryn's discomfort and veiled antagonism—maybe the alchemies involved here weren't that complex. He recalled her tentative question about the Hands, inquiring about the rooming arrangements. She must have somehow gained word of how close he and Delia had grown over the past year.

"Kathryn—"

A gruff voice called through the door. "Is anyone going to open this door or do I have to pound my knuckles raw?"

It was not Delia.

"Rogger," Kathryn said, half-irritated, half-relieved. She stepped to the latch and pulled open the door.

The thief barged in. He was dressed in a servant's livery, though it fit poorly, being too large and bagging hugely over his lean form. He must have been in some hurry to wear such a makeshift costume.

"So you're both here! If I'd a known that, I could've saved a thousand stairs at least."

"What's wrong?" Tylar asked, responding to the man's anxiety.

"It's that godling child!" Rogger practically shouted.

"Hush," Tylar said. "Hold your voice."

Kathryn touched Rogger's elbow. "What about Dart?"

"Maybe the two of you had better stop holing up in here—as it is, people will be chattering about the regent and the castellan. Ballads will be written . . . odes sung . . ."

Tylar felt his cheeks heat up while Kathryn grew even paler.

"Out with it, Rogger!" he said.

"What is happening?" Kathryn echoed.

"The entire Citadel is riled with talk of daemons. Daemons summoned by the castellan's page. It seems someone has seen Dart's little bronze friend."

"Oh, no," Kathryn said.

"Oh, yes," Rogger said. "The entire Order is being roused to search for her."

Kathryn headed toward the door. "I must return to my hermitage."

"I'll go with you," Tylar said.

"No. Argent will use such talk and rumors to discredit me. He has been seeking some way to shift attention from his own dark deeds with that cursed sword last spring. You must stay clear of all of this. Not just for your sake, but for the peace of Myrillia."

Tylar watched her storm from the room.

Rogger had already discovered the spiced wine and was pouring himself a generous helping.

"Is there any word where Dart might be?"

Rogger shrugged. "Vanished. Like her bronze beastie." He took a deep draught of the wine, then wiped his beard and lips on his sleeve. "But she'd best stay low. Them's that are looking for her the hardest are those with those handsome crosses stitched on their vests."

Argent's men.

Tylar paced back to the hearth. "And what am I to do? Just stand here and wait?"

Rogger lifted an eyebrow. "Best leave the matter to the castellan's skill. Kathryn has the pace and breadth of the place better than you. And besides, don't you have a feast to dress for? And you could use a bit of a shave—getting as scraggly as me."

Tylar scowled.

"Or . . ." Rogger dangled it before Tylar.

"Or what?"

"I'm certain your fine feast will be delayed while Argent does his best to bend talk of daemons to his favor. Until then, there was another rumor that was being bantered about before the talk of daemons arose. Something about the storm that blew your flippercraft to port."

"What about it?"

"As the storm struck, it drove all the rats out of the sewers throughout the village surrounding Tashijan. Boiled up, they did. Then they all fled and scurried into our towers and battlements."

Tylar shook his head at the strangeness.

"It is said that beasts of the fields have better senses—if not sense—than any man. Something in that storm set them afoot. And you know what they say about rats. They're the first to flee a fire."

Tylar nodded. "Perhaps such activity might warrant a trip beyond Tashijan's walls." *And it would be good to be moving . . . to test the mettle of things here.*

A twinkle shone in the thief's eye. "I thought you might feel that way." Rogger tugged up the hem of his baggy shirt and pulled free what was hidden beneath its looseness. He shook out a hooded cloak that had been snugged around his bony waist.

"You stole someone's shadowcloak?" Tylar could not keep the shock from his voice.

"*Borrowed.* Besides, you're getting your own cloak in the morning if all goes well. A cloak to match those triple stripes on your face. In the meantime, a bit of black cloth will turn a god-regent back into a shadowknight. And with all the searching going on for a child and her daemon dog, it shouldn't be hard for a knight and his manservant to slip out the main gates."

Tylar pulled the cloak over his shoulders, sensing the Grace flowing through the cloth. "We'd best be quick."

Rogger filled his cheeks with bread and mumbled through the mouthful. "Aye to that. The storm grows more fierce as we stand here jawing."

Tylar headed toward the door, still ajar after Kathryn's sudden flight. He wondered how she would fare with the warden—and wondered even more where the godling child had gone to hide. With all of Tashijan alerted, there would be few safe harbors.

Brant kept to Dart's shoulder. On her other side, she rested one hand on the haunch of the massive bullhound. The twin giants leaned against the wall, eyes half-closed, exhausted but refusing to turn back until the cubbies were secured.

They all waited while the two wyld trackers—one young, one old—sniffed through a room thick with dust and rotted furniture, long unswept and forgotten. Brant smelled the musk of rat droppings and heard the skitter of beetles.

He kept his arms crossed, little satisfied with the pace of the search. So far, they had traversed three levels beneath the houndskeep, trailing the trickle of musky alchemies. Dart had already explained how these subterranean floors were Tashijan's famed Masterlevels, the domain of the learned alchemists and scholars. But the hole into which the two wolf cubbies had fled apparently emptied into spaces beyond the normal lay of this subterranean warren, into crawlways and tunnels that wormed through these levels, walled away ages ago.

"Possibly forgotten sections of the original human keep that once stood here," Dart had explained. "Like the houndskeep itself was once a dungeon."

Brant considered that possibility as he waited yet again for the trackers. If Dart's story were true, what dark purpose might the hole in the wall have once served? Currently it drained away the filth and biles and tiny gnawed bones of the houndskeep's denizens. But before that? They had all heard tales of the barbarous human kings who had once ruled Myrillia . . . before the coming of the gods. How much blood had been spilled down that same stone throat from the dungeons, echoing with screams?

"No hope here," the elder tracker said. "Naught but a few cracks in the mortar. But we're on the trail. I can catch a whiff or two of the musk through those cracks. Another level or two—"

"Tracker Lorr," the younger tracker called from another corner of the room. He held up his leech-oil lamp.

"What is it, Kytt?"

"The scent is strong here. And I've found a loose brick."

Curiosity drew Dart and Brant inside. The bullhound tried to push after them, tongue lolling, but Dart stopped him with a palm on his wide nose.

"Stay, Barrin. That's a good boy."

He harrumphed and settled to a squat, filling the doorway. The giants looked equally discontented to be left in the hall, but the room was too low and cramped for their large forms.

Brant and Dart followed Tracker Lorr to the corner. Kytt squatted, wide-kneed, and pointed to the bottom stone in the wall. "The block here is loose from its mortar. If we worked, we might push it free."

Lorr examined the stone and found that it rocked easily, like a rotten tooth. "Give me both your shoulders, lads," he said with a nod to the young tracker and Brant.

Brant and Kytt supported Lorr as he sat on the floor and shoved the block with his feet. As they strained, Brant found himself nose to muzzle with the black-haired young tracker. The boy had the amber eyes of his ilk. Brant found himself holding his breath, not wishing to breathe this one's corrupted air.

Kytt must have sensed Brant's distaste, for he glanced away.

Brant felt a twinge of shame, but he could not fault his upbringing. In Saysh Mal, it was considered wrong to misshape man's natural form with Grace, whether for good or ill. Such men were forbidden from the Huntress's forests. And, Brant believed, rightly so. Especially when it came to wyld trackers. It went against the Way to turn man into beast, then to turn around and use those same blessed senses to hunt more beasts of the field. It was a cycle of corruption that had no place in Saysh Mal—or anywhere in Myrillia.

Out in the hallway, Malthumalbaen called to them. "Ock! Do you need an extra bit of muscle?"

"Not yet," Lorr said with a groan as he shoved again, edging the stone farther into its socket.

Brant heard Dral mumble something to his brother.

Malthumalbaen answered, "No, I don't know what bullhound tastes like."

Brant found his eyes again on Kytt's form. He remembered feeling a similar discomfort when he had first encountered the pair of Oldenbrook guards. Like wyld trackers, loam-giants were also forbidden from the cloud forests of Saysh Mal. Yet, Brant had found Multhumalbaen and Dralmarfillneer to be as big of heart as they were of limb. And hadn't their strength saved his life in the storm? Did he not even consider them friends?

Kytt's eyes flashed to his, stuck a moment, then glanced away.

Despite the contradiction, Brant found himself still bristling. Loam-giants were one matter. Trackers were another. They were an offense in both form and purpose to the Way. He felt this in his bones and blood.

"Hold tight!" Lorr called. "Almost there!"

Kytt and Brant braced Lorr's back as he shoved one last time. Brant felt the tremble of the tracker's strain. Stone scraped stone—then suddenly the block fell free, toppling into an empty space beyond.

A wash of stale air wafted out. Even Brant caught the taint of musk that came with it.

"There we go," Lorr said, gaining his feet. He supported his lower back and kneaded out a kink. "The hard part's over. All's left is to fetch that pair of cubbies out of their stone burrow."

Kytt had lowered to his belly and leaned his lamp through the opening. "I think I see some steps back there. An old stair. Looks like they may go down some ways."

Confirming this, a faint animal whimper echoed up to them. It sounded as if lost down a deep well.

Lorr shook his head. "So it's not going to be as easy as I'd hoped. But no matter, it must be done." He squatted down again, and with a slight grimace, rubbed one of his knees. "It'll be a narrow squeeze, but Kytt and I will flush them out."

"I'm going with you," Brant said.

Lorr shrugged, but his manner was unwelcoming. The old wyld tracker had recognized Brant from his clothes and skin as someone from Saysh Mal. He knew what folks from that god-realm thought of trackers. Brant suspected the only reason he was getting any cooperation from Lorr was because of Dart's good word on his behalf.

So be it.

They didn't have to like each other to work together. Brant had learned that well enough from Liannora in Oldenbrook.

Voices reached them from the outer hall.

Malthumalbaen hissed toward them, "Someone's coming. Looks like a pair of shadowknights."

Brant eyed Dart, who had already begun surreptitiously shooing something toward the opening in the wall.

Pupp, no doubt.

"I think it might be good if Dart came with us," Brant said.

"And perhaps we should move quickly," she added.

Dart matched gazes with Lorr.

The tracker nodded at some silent message passed between them. "Then why don't you both go first," he said. "I'll make sure Barrin acts the good watchdog, along with your two giants. We'd best not have any strangers spooking the cubbies while we work."

Dart pulled up the hood of her cloak and hurried toward the opening. She dropped to her belly and squirmed through. Brant waited until she was clear, then followed.

Once on his feet, he found Dart a step below him. The lamplight in the far room offered scant illumination. The narrow stairs spiraled quickly into an inky darkness. Spider threads whispered overhead, disturbed by their arrival. Underfoot, the steps were well-worn into raw stone, dry and dusty as old grave bones.

Kytt came next, brightening the stair with his oil lamp. He proceeded down a few steps, away from Brant. He busied himself with inspecting the stairs. Lorr came last with a bit of grunting.

He passed the second lamp to Dart.

"Tracker Lorr," Kytt said, "come see this."

Lorr squeezed past Brant to join the younger tracker.

Kytt lowered his lamp and pointed a finger. In the dust of the steps, a tiny paw print had been pressed.

Lorr nodded and moved slowly down a few more steps. "They continue to flee deeper."

"Wolf whelpings are always snugged in the darkest hole in their warren," Brant said. "It's where they feel safest."

Lorr stood with a slight shake of his head. "*Safe* is not a word I would use to describe this passage." He huffed the air, nose high for a moment. "Something . . . something scents wrong here."

Brant tested the air, but he could discern nothing but a bit of musk and an echo of bile, most likely coming from the houndskeep far overhead. Brant remembered his thoughts about its former use as a dungeon. Had the blood of the tortured once drained down these same steps? Did it still taint the passage?

Lorr lowered his muzzle. "Mayhap we'd best wait."

Brant balked at this. If the whelpings' trail grew any colder, they'd never be found. Who knew where this stair led or how much of a maze it might empty into? The best chance to secure the wolf cubbies was to keep as close on their tails as possible.

Muffled voices reached them from the outer chamber. The knights had reached the room and were questioning the giants.

Dart whispered, "It wouldn't hurt to explore a bit farther."

Lorr reluctantly agreed. "I will go first with Kytt. But only a few more levels. No one's walked this passage in centuries. It could all come crashing atop us."

Brant followed with Dart. At some point, he had offered Dart his hand to help her over a scrabble of broken steps, and she had yet to let go as they wound down into the depths below Tashijan.

Lorr paused every few turns to inspect the steps, watching for signs of the cubbies. But Brant noted how he kept one ear cocked and sniffed the air with growing frequency. Something had raised the hackles on the wyld tracker.

And now it had crept into him. Brant's hairs prickled along his arms. For the moment, he wished he could borrow the trackers' senses. He felt blind and deaf. Perhaps he should have bowed to the tracker's earlier wariness.

The stairs slowly tightened in their spiral. It now took only three steps to lose sight of the person ahead.

Finally Lorr stopped. Brant suspected that the tracker could not be uprooted to proceed any deeper. This time Brant was not going to argue. The whelpings were wild creatures. Perhaps they would eventually find their way out on their own. And maybe that was for the best. Better than being caged.

Lorr hissed at them, silently signaled Kytt, and both trackers dimmed their lamps and shaded them with the edges of their cloaks.

Brant crouched down with Dart as if the falling darkness had crushed them to the stairs.

"Lorr?" Dart breathed out softly.

"Hush."

Brant's eyes adjusted to the darkness, discovering it was not as complete as he had first imagined. The lower stairs were slightly less murky than the deep blackness above.

Faint words reached them, rising from below, too muffled by distance to discern.

Someone was down there.

"I would question this squire myself," Kathryn said.

She stood in the middle of her hermitage. She let her outrage at the violation of her private spaces ring in her voice. Half a bell ago, she had arrived in the high hall to discover an upended beehive of confusion. Men and women, knights and masters, all scurrying about or standing dazed. The word *daemon* echoed all around.

Worst of all, the door to her hermitage had been standing wide open.

She had discovered Warden Fields already in her rooms, fists on hips, ordering the place searched from niche to cranny. By the time Kathryn had shouldered through his guards, she had been red-faced and barely able to speak. She had stopped it all with a resounding command to desist.

Though Argent might rule Tashijan, all knew the hermitage was the sole domain of the castellan.

"I understand your consternation, Castellan Vail," Argent said calmly as his men cleared from her spaces. "But I have already summoned soothmancers to examine the young men, to test the veracity of their claims."

Off to the side, Master Hesharian stood with Keeper Ryngold. The rotund master kept his hands folded across his robed belly, looking serenely dispassionate about it all, but Kathryn read the glint of amusement in his eyes. Contrarily, the head of the house, Keeper Ryngold, shared none of the master's amusement. He stood beside Kathryn's maid, Penni, who still had her face covered with her hands, sobbing silently into her palms. The shoulder of her dress had been ripped. Apparently Argent's men had manhandled her upon breaking in here. Keeper Ryngold was not pleased, almost as angry as Kathryn. Penni was one of his charges.

Kathryn stepped closer to Argent. "Perhaps you should have tested their stories before breaking my latch and entering my inviolate spaces. My hermitage is as sacrosanct as your Eyrie. To break that threshold upon the rantings of an injured boy is an affront beyond measure."

Before he could respond, a figure stepped out of Dart's garret and back into the main room. His face and hands were caked in black, reeking of black bile. A bloodnuller. Kathryn gaped at him. She had not known anyone was still in there. Men of his caste were imbued with alchemies of bile, able to nullify Grace with a smear of their fouled hands.

"Nothinggg," the man slurred with a bow toward Argent.

Kathryn shoved her arm toward her door. "Begone from my rooms!"

The man hesitated until Argent gave him a slight nod to obey. He shuffled out, trailing his stench behind him.

Kathryn glowered at Argent. "I hope such a discovery will temper your unseemly haste until you've had the squires properly soothed. As I understand it, one of your squires had already confessed to attacking my page. Yet it is upon the word of such dishonorable young men that you break the peace of my private rooms."

She said this last loudly enough to be heard out in the hall, where she was sure many ears were listening. Let that rumor be spread, too—to counter the talk of daemons.

Argent's face grew a shade more red. "That is all well said," he forced out grudgingly. "I certainly owe you my sincere apologies. But in such dark and trying times, it seems that an overly officious attention to protocol might not serve us well. Remember, we have many high personages from around Myrillia under our roofs and have a responsibility for their security. Do we not? Is it proper to sit on our swords when word arises of daemons among us?"

"Better to sit on our swords than panic," Kathryn said, loudly yet again. "There are reasons for protocol, for rules of conduct . . . lest in haste someone get accidentally stabbed with a cursed sword again."

Argent's one eye flared. He flushed as if she had slapped him.

Off to the side, she noted Master Hesharian backing toward the door. This was a tender point that even the master wanted to avoid.

Argent glared a moment more. "Then we'd best begin the soothing this very night. I find it strange, though, that your page remains missing." He let this question linger, tying guilt to her absence.

Kathryn refused to let it hang unaddressed. "Is it truly any wonder? After being attacked by three squires twice her size? She must wonder whom to trust after such a violation."

"I assume she trusts you well enough," Argent said, heading at last toward the door. "And I'm sure you'll present her to be soothed when she comes out of hiding."

Kathryn followed him, ushering everyone from her rooms. "Most certainly. And the first question I will ask will be concerning her attack. I wonder if it was a random act of malice or if some other hand might have directed them. I understand that all three bore the sigil of the Fiery Cross. And that a branding iron with your symbol was found in the room where the attack took place."

Argent glanced back to her. His eyes narrowed, more with concern than anger this time. Kathryn doubted the warden had had any hand in the attack. At least not directly. Members of his Fiery Cross had grown more emboldened of late, stoked by Argent's fiery speeches. Still, it didn't hurt to plant a seed of doubt in his mind. It would be a blight on his image if it was found that the Cross had planned the attack as some affront against the castellan. It could turn the tide against him.

Kathryn suspected that to assuage such suspicions, Argent would spend a fair stretch of the night doing his own private investigations. The distraction would allow her additional room to maneuver, to find some way to circumvent Dart's exposure.

With nothing else to be said, Argent sailed out of her room with a flourish of his cloak. He was followed by a cadre of his men, a flock of black geese headed to warmer climes after the cold greeting they'd received here.

Master Hesharian bowed, almost mockingly, and left, collecting another robed master with him—Master Orquell, the one who had come here from Ghazal. His milky eyes glanced over Kathryn's face as he turned. Though he appeared to be nearly blind, she suspected he saw more than most ordinary men.

At the door, Keeper Ryngold promised to console Penni. "A bit of honeyed mead and a warm fire will settle her. If there is anything you need in the meantime . . ."

"I'll be fine. Thank you."

He set off, and the hallway slowly emptied out beyond her door. As the flow of robes and cloaks drained away, a single figure remained, a bronze boulder in the waning stream.

He forded toward her through the last of the onlookers.

"Gerrod . . ." Kathryn sighed with relief. She stepped aside to invite him into her rooms.

He touched her on the elbow as he passed, a silent approval of her handling of Argent.

She closed the door after him.

He stood a moment, glancing around.

"We're alone," she assured him.

Satisfied, he pivoted a switch at his neck and his helmet peeled back, revealing his bald pate and tattooed sigils—and also the wry amusement in his eyes. "Argent will not be sleeping this night."

Kathryn smiled.

"And I've heard he had to cancel his grand feast."

"Small favors there." Kathryn motioned him to a seat. "At least Tylar will be happy to hear about that."

"Yes, but he might not be so happy to hear about what we discovered about his flippercraft." He ignored her offer to sit and crossed toward her draped windows.

Kathryn followed him, noting a slight complaint that rose from his mekanicals. "What did you find?"

He pulled aside the heavy woolen drape. The hearth's firelight cast the glass into a mirror. She read the worry in her friend's expression.

"The ship's apparatus appeared fine—at least what we could tell from the burnt slag. But it was the reserve of blood alchemies that seemed to be the source of the trouble. We tested the level of Grace and found it almost drained. Only a few dregs of power remained. The ship was lucky to land at all."

"So what do you think happened?"

"The Grace must have been drained from the alchemies while it was in flight."

Kathryn sat straighter. "How? A saboteur? Did someone pour black bile into the mekanicals?"

"No, I spoke with several of the crew. The problems all started when the ship was caught in the front edge of the storm that besets us now."

"The storm?"

Gerrod nodded to the window. Kathryn stepped closer, sharing the opening in the drapes.

The world beyond the panes was misted with a swirl of snow. The branches of the wyrmwood tree that shaded her balcony were heavy with white shoulders. And the snowfall grew thicker.

"I don't understand it," Gerrod mumbled. "But I mistrust this storm. Even my own mekanicals grew stiff when I was out there. At first I blamed it on the cold and dampness, but even once inside, out of the ice and snow, the sluggishness persisted."

He moved an arm, and she heard the wheezing struggle.

"And your armor is driven by air alchemies."

He nodded. "Along with fire, too. I suspect the remaining fire alchemies are the only reason I'm still able to move at all.

I plan on testing the flows within my armor once I return to my study."

Kathryn pondered all he had described. "So then what are you saying? You believe the storm is somehow siphoning air alchemies unto itself?"

He shrugged. "It is *air* that drives every storm. And as strange as the weather has been of late, perhaps this odd blizzard may offer some answer as to why. Maybe some wild Grace is loose upon the winds, born out of this prolonged winter. Either way, until the storm blows out to sea, it will be death to fly into or out of Tashijan. And I'm not even sure it's safe to travel afoot through the blizzard."

Kathryn watched the blanketing fall. "So no one should come or go?"

Gerrod nodded. "I'm sorry to add another burden."

Kathryn rubbed a finger along her cheek's lowermost stripe. "No matter. Better to know this now and proceed with caution. I will spread the word to the outer village and lock down our gates until we know more."

She had begun to turn away from the window when she noted something else in his eyes, a deep-set worry reflected in the pane.

"What?"

"The timing of this storm . . ." He shook his head. "Tylar's knighting . . . everyone gathered here."

"Surely you don't think it was planned. Not even a god can control the path of a storm."

He continued to stare through the window.

"Gerrod?"

He shook his head—agreeing, disagreeing, she couldn't tell.

She finally turned away, trusting Gerrod's judgment enough to lock everything down until this storm blew itself out. But she refused to believe worse. There were limits to even a god's reach.

Gerrod spoke, as if reading her thoughts. "But what if it were more than one god?"

She had no answer. All she could do was take precautions and hope Gerrod was wrong in this last regard. All she knew for certain was that no one should be out in this storm.

* * *

"Colder than a witch's teat," Rogger grumbled.

"And I'm sure you've had the necessary experience to make that observation," Tylar said as he passed under the spiked portcullis and exited Tashijan.

Rogger considered Tylar's words. "That be true. But that Nevering blood witch was at least warm everywhere else. There's nothing toasty beyond these gates."

The thief was buried under rabbit furs, a woolen scarf over his face. Behind him strode the Wyr-mistress, Eylan, in a heavy greatcoat with a collared hood. Tylar had tried to encourage her to remain behind, to guard their rooms, but Sergeant Kyllan had already secured the wing after all the talk of daemons.

So as a group they crossed the bridge that spanned the frozen moat and entered the boarded-up bazaar that lay between the village and the thick walls of Tashijan. Normally it was a raucous strip of alehouses, inns, trading booths, and makeshift tents, brimming with the drunken, the slatternly, the wily, and the quick. It continually rang with shouts and screams and song.

But no longer.

Snow fell in a heavy hush. Even the winds had died down, though they could be heard whispering farther out, beyond the village, as if a great sea rolled and churned upon a beachhead. Closer at hand, the world had been drained of color and depth, leaving only a half-finished landscape, an etching of charcoal on white parchment.

"Stay close," Tylar warned as they trod through the ankle-deep snow.

He lifted the lamp he held and opened its shutters to reveal a tiny flame, flickering like a frightened bird in its cage. The glow cast by the lamp hardly reached past his outstretched arm.

He led them past the bazaar and into the narrow streets of the village. Here there were at least a few signs of life: the filtered glow through a shuttered window, the lone minstrel strumming a lyre from behind a barred door, the scent of woodsmoke from a few stone chimneys. But as they moved farther from the great shield wall of Tashijan, even these faded into darkness, cold hearths, and held breaths.

"I don't see anything untoward," Tylar said, stopping and stamping his boots to clear the snow. But even he kept his voice to a whisper, suddenly wary of being overheard.

Rogger shivered beneath his furs. "I've never felt a late-winter storm carry a chill like this one. Perhaps the rats merely had enough sense to flee to the warmth of our halls and cellars."

Tylar noted that Eylan had her face raised, nose to the air. She lowered her chin and matched gazes with him. Framed by the lynx-furred hood, her beauty warmed through the cold, a pretty trap intended to catch his seed when he was ready to bow to his oath. But beyond her high cheekbones, narrow flare of nose, generous lips, there remained something icy in her eyes, a reflection of the winter storm, reminding him yet again that she was of the Wyr, birthed under strange alchemies in an unending quest to instill godhood into human flesh.

But at this moment he read something beyond the ice in her eyes.

Fear.

"What is it?" he asked.

"We should not be here," she answered and turned to search beyond the last of the village homes. "The storm . . . the snow . . . it smells *wrong*."

Tylar tested the air, drawing a fuller breath through his nose. He scented nothing unusual in the crisp air. Just ice. His body, though, shuddered in its haste to warm the cold from his chest. And something else noted the chill, stirring away from it.

Tylar rubbed at his chest, momentarily unmoored. Ever since the death of Meeryn, it had lurked inside him—Meeryn's naethryn, her undergod—hidden behind the black palm print burnt into his chest, trapped in the bony cage that was his body. He had not summoned the shadowy creature since the Battle of Myrrwood, preferring to leave it undisturbed, perhaps even forgotten. But as it stirred now, the movement stripped Tylar of his delusions. All that was not skin or bone shifted inside him, illustrating again how little of his flesh was his own, leaving him feeling hollowed and empty.

It took three more shallow breaths to resettle and moor himself.

Rogger watched him, eyes narrowing as if sensing his unease. Then he merely shrugged. "We can always turn back. A warm fire and a nip of wine is more inviting than all this skaggin' snow and wind."

Tylar shook his head. They had come this far. He wanted to see the true face of this storm. Its low moan swept to them through the remaining crooked streets. These last homes, farthest from the walls, were built less stout. Some were plainly abandoned long ago, while others leaned toward each other, as if sheltering against the cold.

He led them again. The drifts grew between the streets. A wind kicked up, scattering dry snow that stung the face like sharp pebbles. They made a final turn between a set of abandoned stables. Gusts had already peeled away the roofs' thatching and now tugged at the doors, rattling and banging them, like a dog worrying a bone.

Past the last buildings, the view opened up.

"Sweet gods above," Rogger gasped. "Who stole the world?"

He was not far wrong.

Beyond the village, the storm swirled in a solid wall. The winds whipped straight across the hills, east to west, seemingly endless, with the force of a gale. Yet where they stood, only the occasional fierce gust snapped at them, warning them to keep back.

"Looks like we're stuck in the eye of a whirlwind," Rogger commented.

With Tashijan at its heart. Tylar risked another step out, searching, studying. "Why does the storm just hold out there like that?"

Eylan answered. "It grows. Gathers strength to itself. If you listen, you can hear its hunger."

The storm's moan stretched toward a wail.

"No wonder the rats fled," Rogger mumbled. "Mayhap we'd best do the same."

Tylar nodded slowly. He needed to alert Kathryn.

"Too late," Eylan said.

Tylar had started to turn back toward Tashijan, but the Wyrmistress's words drew his eyes back to the storm. The perpetual white wall had developed dark streaks, like black ink dripped into swirling milk.

"Something is coming," Eylan said.

Tylar even felt it. A sudden weight to the air.

But before he could react, a wave of frigid air blasted out from the storm, an icy exhalation awash with hoarfrost. He stumbled back, his cheeks freezing. Ice crusted his lashes. His eyes ached, but even his tears froze. He could not blink, only stare into the face of the storm.

And a face it did have.

The oil-black streaks eddied out of the snow tempest, coalescing into a monstrous countenance, growing as tall as Tashijan's walls, yet still vague and indistinct. Tylar suddenly knew that it was not oil nor ink that shaped this face, but *Gloom*, the smoky essence of the naether world, bleeding into Myrillia.

Tylar murmured between frozen lips, "Run . . ."

But the cold fought them: numbing limbs and heart, frosting cloaks to a dragging heaviness, freezing boots underfoot. Tylar grabbed Rogger and hauled him. One step, then another. Eylan followed, bent against a wind that wasn't there.

As they struggled, the timbre of the storm's wail changed behind them. Or maybe it had always been there, hidden behind the wind. Either way, a lilting sweetness stretched to them, ringing with the crystalline shatter of ice. And behind it a voice . . . as misty as the swirling face of the storm . . . singing.

Tylar slowed, straining to hear. He snagged up Rogger's coat sleeve to stop him, to get him to listen, too.

"Keep going," the thief protested, twisting.

Tylar ignored him and slowly turned.

But Eylan was there at Tylar's shoulder. She struck him with a fist, square in the face. His head rocked back.

"Seersong," she said through the ringing in his ears.

Another wave of ice washed over them, worst by far than the first. It cut through Tylar as if he were naked. Again their boots were frozen in place. He felt his very bowels ice up inside him.

A step ahead, Rogger cried out, grasping at his chest.

Tylar fought to help him—but he had brushed too near a wall. His cloak had iced against the bricks, trapping him. He wrested against its clutch, but the cold had weakened his limbs.

Eylan sank to her knees, clutching at her throat. Even the air had become ice, impossible to breathe.

Tylar glanced back to the storm as his vision darkened.

The countenance had grown more distinct—somehow familiar. *Who . . .* ? But it had not yet fully formed. Song again distracted him, coming not from the face of the storm but behind it and all around, as if the storm were not snow but pure song itself. There were no words, but its sweetness was like warm wine poured into his frozen ears.

Tylar gave up his struggle, happy to listen.

But another was not.

Deep inside him, beyond bone, his naethryn surged in a violent quake, writhing, as if the song burnt. Tylar had never felt it thrash with such force, as if struggling to claw itself free. It bashed against the cage of his ribs. But escape was impossible. The song would snare its trapped prey, and Tylar with it. There was only one key to its escape.

"Agee . . ." Tylar moaned from between lips frosted with ice.

It was all he could do. He was trapped between ice and song.

But his one word was heard, caught out of the air by the same who had first spoken it to him. *Agee wan clyy nee wan dred ghawl.* It was ancient Littick, the tongue of the gods. Rogger knew its meaning. *Break the bone and free the dark spirit.*

The thief was already on his knees, weighted down by the storm, face anguished. But one hand, the one clutched at his chest, shifted to a neighboring fold. To a hidden belt. A dagger appeared in the thief's fingers as if born of Grace out of the very air.

It was the last Tylar saw. Darkness folded over him as the song's warmth washed the world away. Even the thrashings inside him calmed to its sweet lilt.

Then the barest flash of silver cut through the darkness.

The thrown dagger struck Tylar in the face—where Eylan had punched him a moment ago. But it was not the blade that struck him, only the butt end of its steel hilt. Struck glancingly from the side and broke his nose.

Tylar's face was too numb to feel it. But like a loosened pebble that starts an avalanche, the small break spread in a sweep of agony throughout his body. One leg broke under him, then the other. He toppled, only to have his arm shatter to the shoulder. Bones knit, callused, broke again, and reformed crooked. All his old injuries, once healed by Meeryn, returned in a blinding instant, leaving him the same cripple again.

He writhed, and freed of its bone prison, his naethryn rose like smoke out of the black handprint on his chest, burning through cloak and cloth. It sailed high into the air, black wings unfurled, fraying with wisps of smoke, a neck stretched. As it settled to the snowy street, ice melted and steamed around its claws. Fiery eyes opened upon this world. Half wyrm, half wolf, it glared toward the storm.

The pain warmed Tylar's frozen form and melted his joints. He pushed to his knees, then stood, bent-backed and hobbled, a broken knight once again. As he straightened, he still felt the cold, but less so now, more like a dream one tried to remember upon waking.

He stumbled over to Rogger, who was careful to remain ducked from the wings of Tylar's *dred ghawl*, the dark spirit that was Meeryn's naethryn. Sculpted of Gloom itself, it was deadly to touch, to all except Tylar. He remained tethered to the creature by a smoky cord that sailed out of the print on his chest. The edges of the cloak and underclothes still smoldered where it had burnt its way out.

Tylar helped Rogger to his feet.

"Next time I won't challenge the wits of rats," Rogger chattered.

Tylar still heard the strains of seersong behind the falling motes of snow. But they held no power. Freeing the daemon had broken whatever spell it held upon him. Upon both of them.

The naethryn hunched in the street, smoky mane flared in challenge toward the storm.

Tylar searched closer, realizing someone was missing.

"Where—?"

Then movement drew his gaze farther down the street. Eylan was at the edge of the village, stumbling toward the storm.

"Eylan!" he called.

She continued, deaf to him. Tylar knew her ears were too full of seersong. She was Wyr, born of Grace, rich with its blessing or curse, susceptible like Tylar. She had resisted for as long as she could, tried to break its spell on him, and maybe even his nose. Had she known freeing his daemon would free him, too?

But she had failed.

Tylar stepped toward her, ready to drag her back. But hobbled and still half-frozen, there was no chance. A moment later, he watched her vanish into the storm. One moment there, the next swallowed away.

No . . .

Before him, the figure of the storm stared down at him, sketched in gloom by a wavering hand, cold and dispassionate. Then in a single brushstroke of wind, it all vanished, wiped away as if it had never been there, swept back into the storm. But Tylar still remembered, now and from long ago, from another life. He knew whose countenance had fronted the storm.

It made no sense.

"There's nothing we can do," Rogger said, tugging on his arm. "We must let Kathryn know what we face."

And who.

"There can be no doubt now," Rogger mumbled.

Tylar turned to the thief. "What do you mean?"

Rogger stared toward where Eylan had vanished, toward the storm that circled Tashijan.

"We are under siege."

8

AN INOPPORTUNE SURPRISE

"NOT A SOUND," LORR BREATHED OUT.

In the dark, Dart perched atop her step, with Pupp beside her. Brant crouched on the stair above. Below, the two trackers huddled over their dimmed lamps, their glow further shadowed by their cloaks. In the darkness, Dart noted that the light far below was growing fainter. The furtive voices faded with it.

Whoever was down there was retreating deeper. Surely they were just masters, going about their usual secretive pursuits, buried away under Tashijan. But from the sounds of them, *these* skulkers were sunk quite deep.

A spider thread tickled Dart's cheek. She brushed it away.

The air slowly stirred in the passage, flowing up, then down again, as if some great beast slumbered below, breathing in and out.

The tickle returned—then she felt something scurry down her cheek to her neck. *Skags!* She swatted at it, shifting in disgust.

The sudden movement almost dislodged her, but Brant caught her before she slipped from her stair and bumped into Kytt. Unfortunately the turn of her heel ground heavily upon an old lip of stone, and it broke away under her. A fist-sized chunk of rock bounced off the lower step and rolled down the ladder-steep staircase.

Crash . . . Crash . . . Crash . . . Crash

The echo faded into silence.

No one breathed.

Maybe the ones below hadn't heard . . .

But the quiet was too deep. The bits of whispers had fallen silent. And Dart could still discern the glow below, steady now, no longer fading.

Keep moving away, Dart willed the light.

Lorr made a motion, waving them off, back up the stairs, but before any of them could move, a new sound flowed to them: a hushed noise. No voices, no words. Just a fluttering raspiness, like a flock of bats taking wing at sunset. Sweeping toward them.

The glow below suddenly vanished or was blocked by what rose toward them now, sinking all into an inky cavernous darkness.

Dart's heart rose to her throat, choking back a rising scream. She reached blindly for the wall to make sure she was still in this world.

Even Pupp was a dull ember, as if fearful of revealing himself.

Down two steps, Lorr hissed as the noise grew, plainly sweeping up toward them. He stood and tossed back his cloak to reveal the amber glow of his lamp.

"Go!" the tracker urged with quiet command. "Kytt, take them back up. Keep your lamp shuttered."

Defying his own words, Lorr opened the doors on his lamp, flooding the stairs with light. He took a step downward.

"What are you—?" Dart began.

"There is a side passage four steps down. I will set a false trail."

As Lorr began to turn away, two small shapes soundlessly rounded the lower stairs and dashed into and through the group.

Pupp flared brighter in molten warning, bristling and snarling.

Dart squeaked in fright, flattening against the wall.

But Brant knelt and caught one in his cloak, bundling it up. Lorr snatched the other by the nape of its neck. Dart noted the dark fur, the white-tipped ears.

The lost whelpings.

The one in Lorr's grip mewled in abject terror, pissing a hot stream of yellow bile. The tracker bent to sniff its fur. His nose crinkled.

"Black blood," he mumbled just loud enough for Dart to

hear. She heard a note of recognition in his voice—and deep concern.

Lorr heaved the wolf cubbie toward Brant, who scooped it under his cloak, alongside the first. Bundled together, the whelpings quickly settled. Perhaps they knew Brant's scent. Perhaps they simply knew it was best to hide.

Lorr lifted his lamp. "Kytt, get 'em up there. Take Barrin with you. Get these two to Castellan Vail."

Dart hesitated, not wanting to leave the tracker's side.

Lorr's yellow-gold gaze fell upon her. "Tell Castellan Vail that something foul has taken root deep in Tashijan. And now it stirs."

"But what—?"

"That's what I mean to find out." Lorr swung away and swept down the steps, heading toward the heart of the darkness. As the tracker's light vanished around the turn of the stair, Brant touched Dart's arm.

"Hurry," Kytt urged needlessly.

They set off back up the stairs, the young tracker in the lead, guiding with his shuttered lamp. Dart followed, while Brant stumbled after them, one arm supporting the whelpings, the other running along the wall, supporting himself.

Around and around, they ran.

Dart kept glancing behind her. She realized that they had outrun whatever had made that strange noise. Lorr must have succeeded in drawing it off. Still, the tiny hairs all over her body stood on end.

Behind her, Brant stumbled, brushing the wall with his cloak. The whispering rasp of cloth over old dusty brick struck her ear. She frowned, slowing a step.

Brant misinterpreted her hesitation. "I'm fine. Keep going."

Dart hurried on after the weak glow of Kytt's lamp, but her thoughts remained behind her. The brush of Brant's cloak. It sounded the same as what had swept up toward them out of the bowels of the land. Only not one cloak but a host, a legion, rising swiftly, too swiftly, unnatural.

Or maybe not.

While training, Dart had witnessed many times the speed born of shadows, when a knight drew upon the Grace of his shadowcloak.

Her frown deepened by the time they reached the dislodged stone.

Kytt kept guard with his lamp and waved them to crawl through to the far room, back into the Master levels, into Tashijan proper.

Dart went first at Brant's urging, herding Pupp ahead of her. On the far side, she waited, her arms hugged around herself, fearful for herself and for her friend she had left behind. In her ears, she could still hear the rustling rush. She remembered Lorr's cryptic mumble to himself.

Black blood . . .

Dart knew she had to reach Kathryn as soon as possible. The urgency kept her heart pounding in her ears. Brant struggled through with the pair of cubbies. Kytt followed on his heels.

Dart waited until they all stood. "What about Lorr?"

Kytt spoke stolidly. "A wyld tracker knows how to hide a trail."

Dart wished she had as much confidence, but she had no other choice. Together, they fled through the dusty chamber and found a large mound blocking the door.

Barrin lifted his head from his paws. He lay sprawled across the opening. He shoved up to his haunches, then to his legs. Kytt went to get the bullhound moving out into the hall.

Dart smelled blackleaf smoke and discovered its source. The two loam-giants flanked the threshold on either side, leaning against the wall. They shared a single pipe, blackened from years of use. Smoke palled the air.

"Master Brant, there you are! Thought maybe I'd have to cram Dral here through that tiny mouse hole of yours."

Dralmarfillneer straightened and puffed out a perfect ring of smoke. "Would have to be me. That wide arse of yours barely fits through most barndoors."

Brant hefted up his bundled cloak. "I have the whelpings."

Dralmarfillneer's eyes widenened. "Ock! Masterful, Master Brant!"

Malthumalbaen clapped the young man on the shoulder, almost dropping him to his knees.

"Enough," Brant said harshly. "Take the cubbies up to my room. Don't let any of the house staff tell you otherwise."

The giant brothers responded to Brant's tone, faces growing hard with worry, nodding.

"It will be done," Malthumalbaen said.

Brant passed them the pair of whelpings. Both giants got bit, but neither complained. Freed of the wolves, Brant turned to Dart. "I'll go with you to see the castellan."

Dart was relieved. It was a long climb. She would appreciate someone at her side, but she needed to be discreet.

Kytt stood with Barrin, ready to follow, but Dart knew that the bullhound would draw too many eyes.

"Best you stay," Dart told the tracker. "Watch for Lorr?"

Kytt frowned.

"Barrin knows his master," she pressed. "Search deeper through the Masterlevels for him. None of the masters will bother you—not with Barrin at your side. Once Lorr shows his face, fetch him up to the castellan's."

Kytt nodded his head.

With matters settled, Dart led the giants and Brant toward the stairs. She had to take the central staircase. It was the only one that connected the masters' subterranean domain to the knights' Citadel. Once above, she could slip into less-well-traveled passages and stairs.

As they climbed, Dart kept to the shadows of the giants, allowing the large men to draw attention. No one was looking for a company that included giants. Brant took the lead, too, assuming a commanding posture. Dart kept her shape small behind them all, playing servitor, just a page guiding one of Tashijan's new guests.

And for once, Dart was happy to find the crowd on the stairs. Their group was jostled and pummeled. But the giants forged through them, moving their group steadily out of the Masterlevels and into Tashijan's upper floors.

Dart allowed herself to breathe easier once they had cleared the logjam at the crossroads between the Masterlevels and the Citadel. They continued onward, climbing higher. Another floor up and Dart knew a quieter path. Though it was more circuitous, there would be fewer eyes.

She increased their pace.

Pupp bounded at her side, plowing through cloaks and legs.

Then disaster—

"Dart!" A shout of glee rose ahead.

She glanced up, recognizing the voice. A tallish girl resplendent in silver loose blouse, half coat, and billowing dress rushed down the steps. A flag of ebony hair flounced as she flew down the four steps and drew Dart into a firm hug.

Dart returned the affection, if not without a sinking of her stomach. "Laurelle! What are you doing here?"

Laurelle was the regent's Hand of tears. The last Dart had heard, Laurelle was unable to attend the knighting ceremony, though her excuses now in hindsight seemed trivial. It had been a ruse.

"Isn't it a wonderful surprise?" Laurelle said. "I wanted it to be a delight! Is it not?"

Dart might have appreciated the sudden appearance of her friend from school if not for the poor moment of its revelation. Others noted Laurelle's outburst. And though only a year older, Laurelle had filled out more fully into a woman. Her figure's always generous curves had deepened. Several of the young knights must have been already trailing her heels, like the boys had at school.

Those same eyes discovered Dart.

She heard the murmurs—at first uncertain, then more solid.

"It's the castellan's page!"

"It's her!"

A knight in full cloak stood at the next landing, arm pointed at her. "Hold her! By order of the warden!"

Behind her, arms reached and grabbed: elbow, shoulders, back of her neck. Their grips were iron hard.

She was torn from Laurelle's shocked embrace.

"Dart . . . ?"

Plainly her friend had yet to hear the talk of daemons—or maybe she had but had not associated it with Dart. Either way, Laurelle's ire was piqued.

"Unhand her!" she said with an imperious authority.

The grips on Dart loosened.

Then the knight from the landing drew up to them. "She is the one we seek!" he said, sweeping out his cloak. He wore the Fiery Cross stitched at his shoulder. "Warden Fields has ordered her apprehension."

Laurelle attempted to protest, but she was ignored.

Pupp ran about the stairs in a molten panic.

Dart remained calm, though her knees threatened to weaken. She caught Brant's eye. He stood to the side with the giants. None seemed to notice him or be aware of his complicity. But judging by the dark set to his lips, he was weighing coming to her aid, calling upon the strength of his twin companions. That must not happen.

"Castellan Vail," she mouthed to him. Word had to reach the hermitage. Dart also gave a half nod in Laurelle's direction.

Brant understood and stepped forward to touch her friend's arm, drawing her attention. Laurelle opened her mouth, then suddenly recognized the young man from school. He whispered into her momentary confusion.

"Leave her to the knights. Come with me. We can help your friend better above."

Laurelle glanced to Dart, ready to protest.

Dart nodded. *Go with him.*

Laurelle took a shuddering breath and composed herself by shifting a stray lock of ebony hair from her cheek. It was a familiar resiliency that Dart envied. Her friend stared up at the knight in charge, meeting his gaze without flinching.

"I am the regent's Hand of tears. Where are you taking her?"

The knight seemed abashed to be so confronted, but Laurelle held her step, blocking him. He would have to knock her aside to proceed. But even a member of the Fiery Cross was reluctant to assault someone who shared the High Wing of Chrismferry with the new regent.

"Under the warden's sigil, she is to be taken to be soothed."

"Where?" Laurelle asked again.

"To the adjudicator's main chambers. Soothmancers are already testing the word of her accusers."

Dart scowled. Squire Pyllor and his ilk.

"Mistress," the knight continued, "even you cannot countermand the warden's orders." He seemed to draw strength from that, blustering his cloak more broadly.

Laurelle bowed her head. It was toward Dart, but the knight mistook it as resigned acquiescence. Especially since Laurelle stepped aside.

Dart was dragged up to the landing and off the stairs. The last she saw of her two friends, they were already heading up, flanked by the giants.

Laurelle caught her eye, her expression ripe with guilt.

It seemed the surprise was on the both of them.

Brant paused at the landing of the level where the retinue from Oldenbrook was housed. "Take the whelpings to my room," he ordered the twin giants. "Keep them protected."

Malthumalbaen nodded, his brow furrowed heavily with worry. "I can leave the little mites with Dral. He promised not to eat them. Best I come with you."

Brant appreciated his large-hearted companion's concern. "None will dare accost two Hands of Myrillia."

He glanced over to the young woman, a dark-haired beauty with the large eyes to match. He remembered her from the Conclave of Chrismferry, always surrounded by a giggling flock of girls, circled by doe-eyed boys.

No longer.

She stood alone on the step. And though she had grown softer-edged, and more full of figure, she had also grown more serious. A purposeful set to her lips. A hard glint to the eye. Since she had left the school, the world had tempered her like a sword's blade under a hammer. And if anything, it made her even more striking to the eye.

"Be safe, Master Brant," Malthumalbaen warned in a fretful grumble.

He nodded and stepped to rejoin Laurelle—as a door swung open across the hall.

"Ah, there you are!" A sharp voice rang out.

Oh, no . . .

Liannora swept into the hall. She must have heard them talking and come to inquire. She had shed her silver and jeweled finery and wore a simple yet well-cut dress of white silk, a match to her hair, and a blue wool cape that reached to her ankles.

She barely noted the giants, despite their size. "The guards have been looking for you for the past bell. Sten has ordered us all to our rooms."

And as if summoned by his name, the captain of the Oldenbrook guard stepped out of Liannora's room. He was still dressed in the stiff-collared blues of Oldenbrook. But Brant noted the top two buttons at his throat were unhooked.

As he pushed into the hall, the two wolf cubbies suddenly wrestled in the giants' thick-fingered grips, snarling, baring their tiny milk teeth. Their eyes narrowed on the captain of the castillion guard. They had recognized the scent of their mother's killer.

"What are those two foul creatures doing here?" Liannora asked with a crinkle of her nose. "They reek most pungently. I thought they were to be taken down to the houndskeep."

Brant had no patience to explain. "They will be kept in my room." He nodded for the giants to obey, to get the cubbies out of sight.

Liannora started to protest, but Sten lightly touched her elbow. She seemed to melt slightly toward him.

"Be that as it may," Sten said sternly. "I will ask that you do the same, Master Brant. With whispers of daemons afoot, it is my duty to protect Lord Jessup's Hands."

"I have a duty elsewhere," Brant said. He would not be caged like the cubbies, kept guarded by Sten and his ilk. He turned to step away.

Sten put a hand on Brant's shoulder. "I must insist."

Brant glanced from the captain's hand up to the man's eyes and hardened his countenance. He let show the danger if the captain persisted.

Sten lowered his arm. "I have my orders."

Brant noted that several of Sten's fellow guards had gathered by now. Ahead and behind. He backed toward the stairs. Some silent signal was passed, and Brant heard the snick of steel sliding from sheaths.

"When threatened by danger, it is my duty to protect Lord Jessup's Hands—whether they want it or not."

Then Laurelle was there, at his shoulder. "And does that apply to the regent's Hands as well, Captain?"

All eyes swung to her, seemingly seeing her for the first time.

The first to react was Liannora. She made a small sound of shocked delight. "Mistress Hothbrin . . . the regent's Hand of tears . . ." Liannora pushed through the swords, waving them aside as if they were mere reeds. "It is an honor. A true honor."

Brant stared at the two Hands—one from Oldenbrook, the other from Chrismferry. One white-haired, the other with tresses darker than a raven's feather. But their dissimilarity ran much deeper. Though Laurelle was the younger, there was a well of nobility about her that Liannora would forever fail to fill.

Laurelle ignored the guardsmen and barely acknowledged Liannora. She kept her attention on the captain, immediately knowing who held the power.

"I've asked Master Brant here to accompany me on a duty vital to Tashijan," she said. "Upon the orders of the regent himself—who I have heard is most loved by your god. I fear how Lord Jessup might react if he discovers such a simple request was rebuffed upon the point of a sword."

Sten's cheeks grew a little color. Brant suspected it wasn't all her words. Laurelle's beautiful eyes were full upon him.

Still, Sten had not been made captain of the guard for a weak will. "The safety of my charges—"

"You may relax your guard, Captain. All those involved in the dark matter have been captured. Tashijan is secure again." She read the doubt in the captain's eyes, a doubt he dared not speak aloud. "You have my word as the regent's Hand. You may send word yourself, but in the meantime, our matter is most urgent and we must proceed with haste to speak to the warden and the castellan."

To the side, Liannora's eyes widened. With all this talk of high personages, she must have been biting her tongue to keep from licking her lips. But she finally set loose her tongue. "Sten, mayhap it would be best if we all accompanied Mistress Hothbrin to the Eyrie. Your guards can watch the doors here, while we follow Mistress Hothbrin and Master Brant up the tower."

"That won't be necessary," Laurelle assured her.

Liannora would accept no objections. "Since the feast was dismissed, it is only seemly for more than one Hand from Oldenbrook attend an introduction to the warden and the castellan."

Laurelle glanced at Brant, leaving it to his judgment.

He knew it would take too long to argue here. Besides, Sten still had swords and guardsmen. And he would bend steel to make anything Liannora wished come true. But mostly Brant recalled the fear in Dart's eyes as she was led away. Better to relent and quash any further delays.

He nodded to Laurelle.

"We must be off quickly, then," she said and swept back to the stairs.

Liannora hesitated, running a palm over her woolen cape, glancing down to her white dress. Brant read her consternation. For such an important introduction, Liannora was loath to appear in such meager attire. She was caught between missing this chance and settling for her present condition. The lure of power settled the matter. She set off after Laurelle, but not before casting a withering glance at Brant, as if this were all his fault.

Sten followed with Brant after barking a few orders to the remainder of his men. They continued their climb toward the highest levels of Tashijan. Liannora attempted conversation with Laurelle, but the girl set a fast pace on the stair. Soon shortness of wind silenced Oldenbrook's mistress of tears.

Brant hid a grin. Laurelle had the wits to match her looks.

Around and around they went. The crowds grew thinner the higher they climbed. A commotion drew his attention back down the stairs. Below, a shadowknight brushed out of the remaining crowd, cloak billowing with Grace. He was masked, showing only the triple stripes of his caste, but something in his manner was black with danger.

Even Sten lowered a palm to the hilt of his sheathed sword.

In the knight's wake, a stick of a man with a riotous sprout of red-gray beard followed. It looked as if the second fellow was carrying a dead animal in his arms. Only when half a flight away did Brant recognize it to be no more than a rumpled furred coat.

"Out of the way!" he yelled. "Curse you all black, get clear!"

Laurelle paused, half turning. Her eyes brightened with recognition. "Rogger!"

The gaunt man's eyes found her. And something glinted in his eye. A warning. As good as a finger to her lips.

Laurelle had barely noted the knight at the man's side—but now she glanced back and stared more intently. She opened her mouth, closed it, touched her hair. She was hiding something, something about the cloaked figure.

Brant eyed the knight more closely as he swept up to them.

"Ser Knight," Laurelle said, a bit stiffly. "We are on our way to speak to Castellan Vail. On matters of some importance. Would you be gracious enough to escort us?"

He bowed his head, swept through them, and headed up without a word.

Liannora plainly found some offense at his silence, especially as he displaced her glorious Sten as their protector. But she remained quiet.

They climbed the last three levels in strained awkwardness. At last, they vacated the stairs for a wide hall. Here the roof's arched supports stretched taller than on other floors. The knight led them forward.

They passed a wide door flanked by shadowknights. The Warden's Eyrie. Their guide failed to nod toward his brethren, even turning his face slightly away. Brant wondered at it, but then they reached another tall door. It had to be the castellan's hermitage.

He knocked.

Laurelle stepped up to him, half-blocking the way. "I believe the castellan wishes to see only myself and Master Brant here."

Liannora overheard. "If Master Brant is to attend Castellan Vail, then I should be present as senior Hand to Lord Jessup."

The knight studied Liannora over his black masklin. The door opened behind him, limning him in firelight. His voice was a low growl, thick with command. "You will be summoned at the castellan's pleasure. Until then, you will wait without."

The gaunt man named Rogger pushed through the doorway, but not before making a bit of sweetbrittle appear in his fingertips and offering it to the mouse-haired maid who bowed at the door.

"Sweet for the sweetest," he said.

The knight bustled the rest of them inside. Before the door closed, Brant captured the look of raw fury in Liannora's face. To climb so far, only to be thwarted at the very last step. He knew there would be a cost to all this, but he didn't have time to worry about such matters.

Especially as the knight shook back his cloak's hood and shed his masklin. Brant recognized the face with a startled shock.

The castellan, wearing a matching cloak, appeared from a back chamber and hurried forward. She confirmed Brant's appraisal. "Tylar . . . where have you been?"

Brant gaped at the man. *Tylar ser Noche.* Here was the Godslayer . . . and regent of Chrismferry. In disguise. But why?

"The storm," the castellan said. "Gerrod believes there is something wrong with it."

Tylar nodded. "We're under siege. Eylan has been stolen by seersong. But worst yet, the hand that drives the storm—"

Laurelle cut him off, her voice strident with worry. "Dart is in danger!"

They all glanced to her.

"She's been captured by the warden's men. She is to be soothed as we speak!"

Her words drew glances all around, but their eyes settled on Brant. He felt like an intruder, as if he had walked into a private tryst.

Rogger was the only one wearing an amused expression. "It seems we all bring such happy tidings. What about you, young man?"

He blinked, unsure where to start. "I—I bring a message from Tracker Lorr. Something foul hides in the bowels of Tashijan—and has begun to rise."

The thin man sighed with a shake of his head and mumbled under his breath. "So much for glad tidings this day."

Tylar stepped closer. Brant had to resist stepping away. The man seemed a thundercloud clenched in a cloak. "Tell us of this danger."

Brant quickly retold his tale, starting from his discovery of Dart being attacked and ending with the wyld tracker setting off to discover more about what lurked beneath Tashijan.

"Danger from without and within," Kathryn said.

"It must be the Cabal," Tylar said. "Seeking to strike at the heart of the First Land. *As Tashijan stands, so does Myrillia.*"

"We must rally the towers." Kathryn headed toward the

door. "The warden must be informed of the threat. He's down in the adjudicators' chamber, attending the soothings."

"Dart—" Laurelle reminded everyone.

Kathryn nodded. She had not forgotten. "We can use the crisis to help delay her soothing. Even Argent will set aside such matters when all of Tashijan is at risk."

Rogger scratched his beard with a single finger. "If we're not too late already . . ."

Brant followed the others, wondering if the strange man was referring to Dart—or to all of Tashijan.

Dart stood under guard at the edge of the adjudicators' chamber, under an arched threshold, awaiting her summons. She had a clear view into the oval room—and of her accuser.

Squire Pyllor sat atop a wooden chair, painted crimson. It stood in the room's center. Before him rose the high bench of the adjudicators, those men and women who settled matters of dispute and justice for Tashijan. It filled the back half of the oval chamber, while behind him rose three sets of tiered seats. But most of those seats were empty.

Not so the high bench.

Warden Fields sat in the centermost seat, flanked by a pair of adjudicators, an elderly man and a younger woman, dressed in gray suits, with the silver rings of their station adorning each finger and ear.

Behind Pyllor stood a figure cowled in a bloodred robe, a soothmancer. A second of his caste knelt nearby, dribbling drops of fiery alchemy into a silver bowl. The first mancer had his fingers spread, touching Pyllor at forehead, temple, and angle of jaw.

Dart read the pain from the squint in Pyllor's eyes and the thin stretch of his lips as he answered the questions. The soothmancer, his fingertips anointed in the alchemy, read the truth of his words. Dart had never been soothed before, but she had heard tales of the flaming touch of the mancer's alchemies, born from the blood of gods rich in the aspect of fire. It burnt away all deceptions.

"And you intended great harm to the page?" the elderly adjudicator said.

Pyllor trembled under the mancer's touch. His severed arm was bound to his chest and wrapped in numbing salves. But the pain of telling the truth could not be so easily numbed.

"We only wanted to scare her," Pyllor mumbled through a gasp.

A small shake from the soothmancer dismissed his words.

"Do not make us ask you again," Warden Fields said gruffly. "Out with it. The entire story."

Pyllor squirmed. "We were only looking for a bit of mischief. It was the ale. We drank too much. Talked too boldly. Dared too fiercely. We went out looking for mischief . . . not truly expecting to find it. Then . . . then Page Hothbrin appeared. I owed her."

"For what?" asked the woman in gray. Her eyes were flint and steel.

"Swordmaster Yuril took me to task for being too hard on her during sword practice. Shamed me."

"So you sought to do the same to Page Hothbrin."

Pyllor attempted to hide his face, but his head was firmly gripped by the soothmancer behind him. "Yes."

Under further inquiry, he went on to describe her abduction and the aftermath of his attempted attack. Though Dart had come too late to hear the other two squires' stories, most of what Pyllor related seemed only to corroborate the others' statements.

She found her knees trembling with the telling. Circumstance and chance more than malicious forethought had brought her here. Now she was moments from being exposed, her secrets laid bare before the burning touch of the soothmancers.

"Describe this daemon who took your arm."

"It—it came out of the darkness. Fiery and fierce. It struck me and knocked me back. I didn't see it well. Bloodred eyes—that's all I saw." Pyllor shook his head, almost dislodging the soothmancer.

Dart knew Pyllor had been panicked, in tears, eyes squeezed closed at the end. Even now terror seemed to leach away any further details.

"Calm yourself," the elderly adjudicator said with a tempered measure of compassion.

The three at the high bench leaned together, heads bowed in private.

Dart missed most of their words. Only a brief snippet reached her from the younger adjudicator. "Their stories stand together . . . but they strike out wildly when it comes to this daemon."

Finally they broke their conversation with a glance toward Dart. From their eyes, she knew they would seek those answers from her.

"That will be all," Argent said to Pyllor. Fury hardened the edges of his words. "You are dismissed. Your punishment will be settled and exacted later."

Pyllor was released. He was led to the side tiers by another knight in full cloak and masklin. Pyllor glanced toward her, then quickly away. She was shocked by the fear that shone in his face—*fear of her*.

Then her name was called.

"Page Hothbrin," the elderly adjudicator summoned. "Approach the bench to be soothed."

Ushered by two knights, Dart stepped from under the arched threshold and out into the center of the room. The soothmancer, who had been judging Pyllor, knelt beside the silver bowl on the floor and dipped his fingers into the alchemy, readying for Dart's inquisition.

She was led to the chair and sat. She gripped the hard edges of her seat to keep from shaking. The source of all this discourse—Pupp—circled and circled the chair. He sensed her consternation but plainly did not know where to direct his wrath.

"Are you ready?"

She had no choice but to acquiesce. She nodded, not trusting her voice.

The adjudicators motioned in unison to the soothmancer. He rose from his bowl of alchemies and stepped behind Dart.

"We will know the truth about this daemon," Argent warned, his one eye bearing down on her. There was a measure of calculation in his gaze.

From the corner of her eyes, Dart watched the blood-tipped fingers of the soothmancer rise on either side of her head. They glowed with fiery Grace. Dart attempted to brace herself, not quite knowing how to gird against what was to come.

"Stop!" a shout burst out behind her.

Too late.

Wet fingers touched her—at forehead, temple, and throat.

Dart could not turn. Fire locked her in place, burning and probing through her skin toward the core of her being. Still, she recognized Castellan Vail's voice. Relief flowed through her.

"Tashijan is under attack!" Kathryn called firmly as she stepped into Dart's view.

Before anyone could react, the soothmancer behind Dart suddenly screamed, a bloodcurdling cry that burst from the man as if from his very bones. His hand fell away from Dart, freeing her. He stumbled to the side, holding out his arms.

Smoke curled from his fingertips, each digit burnt away to the first knuckle.

The stench of cooked flesh swelled out.

Seeking relief, the soothmancer sank to his knees and plunged his seared fingers into the alchemy in the silver bowl. The blood in its basin ignited as if oil had been set aflame. The fiery conflagration coiled up the mancer's arms, turning robe to ash, searing skin and hair beneath.

Betrayed by his own alchemy, the man fell back into a contorted sprawl, writhing on the stone.

At the high bench, the adjudicators were all on their feet.

Cries echoed around the room.

Dart noted Kathryn's worried expression. Behind her, Brant stood with Laurelle, each with a look of dismay.

A voice boomed with authority, cutting through the growing mayhem. Warden Fields stood with an arm pointed at Dart. "Daemoness!" he cried to the guards, to the knights of the Fiery Cross. "Slay her!"

9

A MEASURE OF DARK GRACE

ABANDONING THE UPPER CITADEL, TYLAR CROSSED DOWN into the subterranean lair of the masters. Here the oil lamps affixed to the walls were stationed farther apart, some gone dark, unwelcoming to all but the studious masters who found little cheer in anything but their studies. Tylar did not mind. He drew power from the deeper shadows, swelling the Grace in his borrowed cloak. Below the Citadel, the crowd on the stairs also thinned rapidly.

Rogger matched Tylar's more hurried pace.

Kathryn had sent the pair below to discover what new threat lay within the cellars of Tashijan and to alert the masters to the danger in their midst. But Tylar also knew she had suggested this mission for a more expedient reason: to keep Argent and Tylar apart. She had to rally Tashijan and draw attention away from Dart. With little love lost between regent and warden, Tylar's presence would only antagonize. So Tylar had not argued. He had seen the number of cloaks bearing the sigil of the Fiery Cross. They would need Argent's full support if they were to raise Tashijan's defenses to their full. And Tylar had no doubt that every cloak and sword would be needed.

Both above and below.

Tylar left the stairs and headed toward the quarters of their one ally here. *Gerrod Rothkild.* The bronze-armored master knew these levels better than any. But Tylar sought Gerrod for another purpose, too. According to Kathryn, he had been studying the cursed rogue skull and examining its traces of seersong, a measure of dark Grace still locked within the bones. If they were to withstand the threat hidden out in the storm, knowledge could prove mightier than any diamond-pommeled sword.

But as he turned a corner, Tylar saw he was not the only one seeking Gerrod's attention this night. The master's door lay open ahead. Firelight shone into the dark hallway, bathing two figures.

Master Hesharian stood with a thinner figure in a master's robes.

"I will not be thwarted," the rotund master declared. "Any study into dark arts must be sanctioned by the Council."

"There is nothing *dark* in my studies here," Gerrod answered, hidden within his doorway, blocking the way. From the slight ringing muffle of his words, Tylar could tell that Kathryn's friend had secured his helmet. "And I will not have my work disturbed at this delicate juncture. So unless you have a signed edict to violate my door, I will ask you to leave me to my studies."

"If I find out otherwise . . ." A hard threat echoed behind Hesharian's words. "Now is not the time for secrets when talk of daemons rings in our own halls."

Tylar approached, interceding. "If it is daemons you seek, Master Hesharian, then I've come in a most timely manner."

Hesharian turned at his words, as did his companion. The thinner master's milky gaze fixed upon Tylar, faltering his step. The tattoos of the man's mastered disciplines seemed to twitch in the flickering hearthlight, like spiders skittering across his bald pate. Then he stepped back from the doorway and into shadows.

Tylar spoke as he reached them. "The castellan's page has been captured. The one accused of summoning daemons. She is to be soothed as we speak."

Hesharian's eyes widened in recognition of who stood before him. "Lord Regent," he said formally, after tripping over his words for a breath. "How may I be of assistance to you?"

"For the moment, you can best serve Tashijan by joining Warden Fields. Matters move quickly. I've come at the request of the castellan to fetch a master to attend the soothing in the adjudicators' chamber. She sent me to ask Master Rothkild—"

"Then it is timely indeed that you have come upon me,"

Hesharian interrupted, stepping forward and half-blocking the doorway. "For such a dark soothing, it is only fitting that the head of the Council be in attendance."

"Of course. I'm sure Kathryn meant no slight."

"I'm sure," he answered with faint enthusiasm. "And besides, it seems Master Rothkild is much too busy with his studies at the moment. Master Orquell and I will answer the castellan's summons. I'm sure she will appreciate my personal attention."

Tylar offered a bow of his head in feigned gratitude. Master Hesharian and his elderly companion set off toward the stairs, pushing past them with hardly a glance back.

Still, Rogger slumped into Tylar's shadow as if not wanting to be noticed. Tylar glanced to his friend, but he merely shook his head, his eyes shadowed with worry. Tylar waited until the two masters vanished beyond the bend in the corridor before turning back to Gerrod.

The bronze master glowed in the firelight. "Thank you for driving Hesharian from my doorstep." He edged back into his room, inviting Tylar and Rogger inside with a whirring wave of his arm. "I can only guess there was a greater purpose in drawing off the head of the Council."

Tylar nodded. "Best he is out from underfoot. We have much to discuss." He quickly related all that had happened in the past half bell, from the storm's threat to Dart's apprehension. "As Kathryn works above, we must work below. Word must spread through the Masterlevels. We must be prepared."

Gerrod nodded, expressionless behind his bronze mask. "But prepared against what?"

"That's what Rogger and I will seek out. Tracker Lorr is down there somewhere. We must find him. We'll head to the deepest levels of your domain while you raise your fellow masters."

"And this storm . . ." Gerrod turned away and strode toward an arched opening into an inner study. "I knew there was something dangerous in its manner—the way it sucked air alchemies to itself. And now, if the Wyr-mistress was correct, it casts out seersong to bend all Grace to its will."

Tylar followed the master, drawn by any hope of an answer. He still pictured Eylan vanishing into the storm. If there were to be any possibility of fronting a rescue, they would need to know more.

"Seersong is also fueled by air, darkly twisted as it may be," Gerrod said, stopping before the closed door to his study. "The storm seems tied back to that aspect of Grace. Air. If only we knew more . . ."

"Mayhap we do," Rogger said, warming himself beside the hearth. He turned to heat up his backside and eyed Tylar pointedly. "The storm. The face it bore . . ."

Gerrod glanced to Tylar for elaboration.

Tylar recalled the countenance shaded in streaks of Gloom—a disquietingly familiar countenance. He had not even voiced his misgivings to Kathryn earlier. There had been no time, and Tylar had wondered if he could be mistaken. Here in the warmth, he had begun to doubt what he had seen.

Or maybe he just wished it to be false.

Rogger dashed that hope. "I recognized the face, too."

The thief yanked up the sleeve of his woolen shirt and bared his upper arm to the firelight. He tapped a scar burned into his flesh.

Tylar read the Littick sigil. The name of a god. The same as whose face had been borne by the storm winds.

Ulf of Ice Eyrie.

"It was the third god-realm I visited for my pilgrimage," Rogger said and pulled his sleeve back over the branded sigil. "There's no mistaking that cold face."

Tylar slowly nodded. It had been long ago, when he was new to his cloak. He had been hunting some bloodrunners with a small group of knights, tracking them into the god-realm of Ice Eyrie. They had been caught in an ice storm, came close to expiring. Rescue had come from Ice Eyrie. The hunting party had been taken to the hollowed-out mountain that was Lord Ulf's domain. Tylar had spent the rest of the winter in that ice-locked realm. And in all that time, he saw the aloof god only once. Lord Ulf spent most of his time in his castillion atop the windswept peak. Still, it was hard to mistake him, with his snowy hair framing a dour and long face, as craggy as his peak. He was one of the rare gods who did not bear a youthful and pleasant demeanor.

And now here again was his countenance, painted in swirling swaths of Gloom. Tylar met Rogger's eyes. There was no denying the truth.

Another of the Hundred had been swallowed by the Cabal. Once again, the War of the Gods stirred, striking openly at the heart of Myrillia.

Gerrod took the announcement with his usual armored indifference. "It makes a certain sense. Lord Ulf bears a Grace rich in air. But it still doesn't explain how he controls this storm. Not even he can wield such power."

"Perhaps he is aided by the Cabal's dark forces," Tylar offered, picturing the swirl of Gloom, the bleeding of the naether into his world.

Gerrod shook his head. "Such power would still have to flow through Lord Ulf. It would have to be wielded by him. Even Chrism, possessed by his naethryn undergod, would have failed to bind this blizzard to his will."

"Then how is it being done?"

"I can't say. Not yet. The answer is hidden behind the white cloak of the storm. But I have a growing fear."

"What's that?"

"The storm was not born out of nothing. It rose from the north and traveled south across the First Land. It has taken a full half turn of the moon to reach here. Arriving in a timely manner. Tied to the arrival of the Godslayer."

"Not all of the Hundred were happy with your regency," Gerrod continued. "Several spoke against you, while others remained silent."

"Like Lord Ulf," Rogger said, worriedly scratching at his beard. "He had closed off his realm, freezing his borders."

Tylar had never given such actions much thought. Lord Ulf's isolation seemed merely a solidifying of the god's usual solitary nature, turned inward to protect his realm. But was there a darker purpose to it all?

"It would take the strength of more than one hand to birth this storm and guide its path and wickedness."

"Or more than one god . . ." Rogger mumbled.

Silence settled over them.

Tylar now understood the bronze master's fear. After the Battle of Myrrwood, Tylar had been wary of another move by the Cabal, the dark naethryn forces who sought dominion over Myrillia. But could Gerrod be right? Could the storm herald something even more dire? A faction of the Hundred now turned against him, against his regency?

Tylar held out one hope. "The face in the storm . . . it was sculpted of Gloom. Surely that must suggest the Cabal is involved here."

Gerrod sighed. "Not necessarily. As any alchemist can manipulate Graces to dark ends, so too can any god. Though you are right to still fear the Cabal. When gods corrupt their own Grace, they lay themselves open to the dark forces of the naethryn. It is a dangerous path. And I worry that if we challenge Lord Ulf and his fellow gods too fiercely, require them to tap even more deeply into this dark font, then our own efforts could push them over the edge and fully into that dark abyss."

"So either we succumb without a fight," Rogger said, "or risk forging an even greater threat?"

Gerrod nodded. "Where there was one daemon-possessed god before, a legion could arise now. Myrillia would be torn apart."

Tylar allowed all he had heard to sink into his bones. The others stared at him for guidance. He had none. It was a situation a thousandfold more dire than he had first imagined.

The heavy silence was finally broken—but not by anyone in the room.

A distant baying reached them, rising from far below.

Only one beast could howl that loudly.

"It's Tracker Lorr's bullhound," Tylar said, turning to the door, reminded again that they had more to fear than just the storm.

Kathryn swept forward, casting out her cloak between her young page and the guards' swords. "None will harm her!" she declared.

To one side, the soothmancer still lay on the floor, cradling the burnt stumps of his fingers. The silver bowl of his alchemies still smoked, casting forth a reek of burnt blood. A second mancer crouched over his companion staring daggers toward Dart.

Bloodnullers swept in from sheltered alcoves to either side, fetid with their black alchemies, ready to strip any Grace from the accused.

Kathryn raised a hand against them all, giving them pause. She kept her focus on the bench, on Argent. "She is still my charge. She will not be slain until a full investigation is made!"

Argent was on his feet, flanked by the two adjudicators. The elderly man and younger woman hung back, plainly shocked and unwilling to intervene. They were as much pets of Argent as the knights bearing the Fiery Cross. There was only one true adjudicator here.

The warden's one eye glared down at Kathryn. "You protect someone who is plainly tainted by the dark arts. Can there be any question now that she did indeed summon a daemon?"

"That can be decided at a later time. For the moment, we have a greater danger to Tashijan. The storm beyond our walls is not a normal blizzard, but one blown up by Dark Grace, brought to bear against our towers."

Her words silenced the smattering of cries. A few swords lowered. Eyes turned to the high bench.

"Madness . . ." Argent mumbled, then continued louder. "Storms of Dark Grace? What ale-addled sop has churned up such a tale?"

"It is no tale. Master Rothkild has studied the crashed flippercraft. He found the alchemies of the ship drained from its reservoirs, bled dry by the storm. Tylar—the regent himself went outside our walls to scrutinize the storm directly. It holds around Tashijan like a whirlwind, while beyond its icy cloak hides a dark force. He saw its face briefly, almost died for the viewing, and lost one of his own for his efforts."

Kathryn read the wariness in the warden, but also a growing worry.

"And where is the regent now? Why does he not bring this word to me himself?"

Kathryn met the warden's gaze, wondering if perhaps it had been a mistake to send Tylar off to search the cellars of Tashijan. But she also saw a fire rise in Argent and recognized the manner in which he bit his words upon mentioning Tylar. The two were oil and fire.

"The storm is not the only threat we face. A Hand of Oldenbrook has brought word from Tracker Lorr." She motioned to the boy named Brant. "Lorr has discovered something foul hidden beneath Tashijan. It stirs now while the storm has us snared. Tylar has gone to seek out the tracker to learn more. The Masterlevels must be cleared. Knights must be gathered to wall and cellar. Before we are caught defenseless."

Her words stirred the small crowd that had gathered behind her. The two adjudicators had slunk behind Argent's shoulders and had their heads bent together, speaking hurriedly.

Argent straightened. To his credit, the set of his lips turned thoughtful with concern, ready to take matters from here. He had led many a campaign against forces both human and otherwise. Though lately he had shown a craven lust for power, he was still an able leader of men.

Before he could speak, a sharper shout broke through the murmuring. Kathryn turned to see a squint-faced young squire with piggish eyes push forward, arm pointing, flanked by knights. His voice held a keening edge.

"It is him! That is the boy who helped Page Hothbrin escape! He is in league with her!"

All eyes swung between the accuser and Brant. Even Argent's. A shadow passed over the warden's features.

"Brant is a Hand of Oldenbrook," Kathryn argued. "Just arrived. I have heard his story. He heard my page scream and merely went to her aid."

Argent looked little mollified. "And according to your testament, he is also the one who brought forth stories of lurkers hiding below Tashijan."

"He brought such a word from Tracker Lorr—a wyld tracker you've known for many a campaign."

"Then where is Lorr?" Argent held up his hands. "Why does he send a boy to rally Tashijan?"

Kathryn opened her mouth to answer but was cut off.

"No!" Argent leaned forward, leaning fists on the table. "The only dark art I've seen with my own eye was the burning of the soothmancer by your page. She has shown herself to be cursed. If there is foulness afoot in Tashijan, perhaps we should look here first for answers."

"I will let no one harm her," Kathryn said.

"You have no say in the matter, Castellan Vail. The edict here is final." Argent stood taller. He waved an arm toward Kathryn and those who had come with her. "Take them all under guard, strip them of their weapons!"

Knights converged from all sides, the Fiery Cross bright on their shoulders. Bloodnullers swept in from sheltered alcoves to either side, ready to strip Grace and power. Kathryn stood her ground as Brant and Laurelle shifted to stand behind her cloak. A dagger appeared in the boy's hand. He held it low and skilled.

Kathryn's hand rested on the hilt of her sheathed sword.

To pull it free, to raise it against her fellow knights—such an act would divide their house when it needed to be at its most united. But she had no choice. Dart and her secret had to be preserved. For the sake of all of Myrillia.

"Take them down!" Argent commanded.

Kathryn's fingers closed on her hilt.

The bullhound bellowed in rage. Tylar followed the echoing howl down the spiral of the narrow stairs. He touched the Grace in his cloak and drew his sword, becoming a flow of shadow.

He had left Rogger and Gerrod far behind. They were rousing the masters from their dens, getting them moving to higher ground.

Tylar needed to know what threat they faced.

Following the howling, he reached the last spiral, the deepest of the Masterlevels, floors long abandoned as the number of those who studied the disciplines waned, matching the decline in shadowknights above. Tylar had not realized the extent of the blight upon Tashijan. They were at their weakest when they needed to be at their strongest.

Pushing back his despair, he burst from the stairs into a dark hall. No lamps lit this level. Dust lay thick on the floor. The strident bawling of the hound drew him deeper. Light appeared ahead.

Tylar rushed toward it, a mothkin to the flame.

As he rounded a bend, he discovered the narrow passage blocked by a shaggy form. The bullhound faced the opposite direction, hunched low to the ground, snarling and gruffing in warning. It backed slowly toward Tylar, retreating from the darker depths of the passage. It herded two forms behind it, one leaning on the other.

"Keep the lamp high!" the taller of the two urged hoarsely.

Tylar closed the distance, recognizing Tracker Lorr. His companion failed to note Tylar's approach until the last moment. Tylar shed the shadows from his cloak as he entered the pool of lamplight. His appearance startled the younger man, barely older than a boy, plainly a wyld tracker from his muzzled features. The young man squeaked in alarm and came close to fumbling the lamp in his fright.

"Be still, Kytt," Lorr groaned as he hung on his younger companion. "He's a friend."

Tylar held back his shock at the older tracker's appearance. Lorr's clothes were burnt to his skin along his left flank. His hair was singed to the roots along the same side, his ear a raw, blistered ruin.

Through the stench, Tylar also smelled oil.

"Shattered my lamp," Lorr coughed out. "Set fire to myself to keep them at bay. Only way to escape. Got too close."

Tylar could not fathom such a means of defense. "Who . . . ?"

Lorr shook his head against explanations. He lifted an arm toward the far stairs. "Must climb out of the darkness. Away . . ." The tracker suddenly swooned on his feet. He fell and pulled down the young tracker with him.

Tylar reached and tugged them both up with one arm. He kept his sword raised in the other. "Get Lorr up on the hound. Head back up. I'll guard your rear."

The young tracker, Kytt, nodded. With strength born of terror, he helped Tylar heave Lorr across the withers of the hound. "Barrin," he keened to the bullhound. "Come away."

Tylar noted how Kytt trembled all over, lamp jittering in his grip. But a brightness shone in his amber eyes. He held back his panic to control the hound. Together they retreated past Tylar, while he stood guard over the passage with his sword.

As Kytt and the burdened bullhound wound back toward

the far stairs, the lamplight receded with them. Tylar faced the deeper darkness, drawing the shadows over his shoulders again, fading his form into the gloom.

His sword—Rivenscryr—held the last of the lamp's glow to its heart, shining in the shadows. He waited a breath. What had Lorr found? What had set the tracker to burning himself to escape?

Down the passage, where no lamp had been lit for a full century, the darkness stirred. Something—someone—flowed toward him. He heard a vague rustle of cloak. Another knight? Buried in shadows like Tylar?

"Who are you?" Tylar challenged.

Silence answered him.

He stepped down the passage, lifting his sword higher, a beacon in the darkness. The shine of silver slowed the roiling shadows, just at the edge of sight.

A figure stood there, more darkness than flesh.

Deeper down the passage, the blackness churned and a deep rustling of chalk on gravestones whispered to him. Tylar knew a legion waited beyond this one's shoulder, held back more by the glint of his sword than its keen edge.

As they faced each other across the gulf, Tylar's vision adjusted to the gloom. He discerned eyes shining back at him. They didn't so much glow with light, but were wells of blackness deeper than any shadow. He risked another step closer. Features of pale flesh appeared out of the darkness like a skull rising out of black dirt, half hidden by masklin.

It was a knight.

One he knew.

"No . . ." he moaned, stumbling back, his own breath choking him.

The figure followed with a pall of black amusement.

"Perryl . . ."

It was his former squire, turned knight while Tylar was in exile. He had vanished from Tashijan over a year ago, believed taken for some dark rites by the Fiery Cross. But seeing what was left of Perryl here, Tylar knew his friend's fate had taken a much darker turn.

Words reached him, whispered with the coldness of deep caverns. "I bend my knee to a new master now."

Tylar shook his head against the voice—so like Perryl's, yet not. The blackest corruption oiled his words.

Fired by revulsion, Tylar stabbed at the dark figure. But his blade found only shadow. The knight flowed away, raising a black sword that ate the light, a match to the daemon knight's eyes.

"I am *ghawl* now," Perryl whispered. "Flesh and death are my past."

The black blade parried Rivenscryr as if the Godsword were mere steel. Tylar felt the hilt spasm in his grip, clenching hard on his fingers, repulsed by the black blade's touch.

"The darkness of the naether is so much stronger than mere shadow."

The black sword slid across Tylar's blade and drove for his heart.

Then light flared behind Tylar, flashing like the first rays of the sun.

The brightness ate away the dark blade before it could strike his chest. The glow also shed the shadows from the daemon knight, revealing cloak and form.

Tylar thrust out with his own sword. He drove his blade through the heart of the figure that wore his friend's face. It sank deep and cut free a shriek that pierced beyond hearing. A wash of fetid decay billowed out, shivering Tylar's skin. At the same time, the daemon's cloak flew open like the wings of some malevolent raven, revealing what was hidden beneath.

Horror drove Tylar back. He bore only the hilt of the Godsword now. The blade had vanished, eaten away as usual until it could be whetted again in blood.

Tylar gaped at the form beneath the cloak. Naked from neck to toe, all was laid bare—down to the bones. It was Perryl's body, but the skin had gone translucent, allowing the sudden light to reveal what lay beneath. Where a heart should beat and organs should churn, something else had taken root. Darkness roiled, muscular and substantial, like a giant snake, pushing and kneading against the translucent skin. From the pierced wound, darkness smoked out instead of blood.

It stank of bowel and decay.

Not smoke. *Gloom*. The black leak of the naether into this world.

Through the pall, Perryl's black eyes met Tylar's for a half beat of his heart. Tylar recognized a match to his own horror, a flash of something human, a splinter of his former self. Then it was whelmed away by darkness. The cloak billowed up, sweeping over Perryl. Shadows welled against the light—and the daemon knight fled back into the deeper darkness.

To heal or to die.

Not knowing which, Tylar turned to find the young tracker two steps away, holding aloft his lamp. His savior shook from toe to crown, breathing hard.

"I—I came back for you . . ." Kytt gasped out. "Barrin . . . found Master Gerrod."

Tylar hurried to him, gripped his shoulder, and spun him back toward the stairs. "We must get out of the darkness."

Tylar knew that was their only defense. Flame, heat, light, warmth. All signs of life. It was all that stood between them and death.

Together, they fled up out of the bowels of Tashijan. They reached the lamplit areas of the subterranean domain. Robed figures crowded the stairs, burdened with books, satchels, and boxes. Shouts and calls echoed. Doors slammed. Gerrod had his brethren on the move. He didn't know what story the bronze master had related, but from the panic in their eyes and the quickness of their frantic steps, he had succeeded in lighting a fire in them.

"Here!" A voice called to him from off the stairs.

Tylar spotted Barrin hunched just off the next landing. The bullhound stood guard over the prone form of Tracker Lorr. He was propped up against the wall. Gerrod and Rogger flanked him.

Rogger waved again to him, while Gerrod pinched bitter alchemies under the tracker's nose. Lorr stirred. An arm raised to swat away the sting. From the tracker's fingers, something fell free. A snatch of black cloth and something that glittered.

Tylar stalked to their side. "We need to get everyone aboveground. Seal off these levels."

Rogger cast a questioning look in his direction.

Tylar, his heart still thundering in his chest, continued in a rush. "Fires. We need the entire first level of Tashijan blazing."

Lorr groaned but failed to raise back fully to this world. A few words tumbled from his lips. ". . . black *ghawls* . . ."

"He needs a healer," Gerrod said, standing. "We'll have to use the hound to carry him the rest of the way up."

Tylar waved to Kytt and Rogger. "Hurry."

He returned to the stairs. He heard the commotion of the masters as they retreated upward, but he kept his attention below. Shadows swallowed the lower stairs. Tylar wove their power into his cloak.

Still, he remembered Perryl's warning to him.

I am ghawl *now. The darkness of the naether is so much stronger than mere shadow.*

Tylar's skin shivered up into pebbling gooseflesh, sensing the meaning behind the claim. Could it be? For centuries, shadows had fed the Grace of Tashijan's knights, granting speed and cloaking their forms. But Tylar knew there was a darkness blacker than any shadow.

He pictured the smoky Gloom of the naether bleeding from Perryl's wound. Was that what fed these daemonic knights? A darkness deeper than shadow? Were they knights born of the naether, serving as swords for the undergods in *this* world?

Lorr moaned behind him.

The tracker had set fire to his own flesh to repel them.

Why had he allowed them so close?

Tylar turned as Barrin shuffled back to the stairs, burdened with Lorr's weight, guided by Kytt. Gerrod followed, expressionless behind his armor. They set off upward, following the last of the masters. If there were any of Gerrod's brethren still holed up in their domiciles and alchemical labs, they would discover the true depths of darkness that lurked beneath their feet.

But who had birthed such a dark legion, these black *ghawls*?

Rogger squeezed up to Tylar on the stairs. He held forth something in his hand. "Lorr dropped this. He had been clutching it all along, burnt to the skin of his palm."

Tylar took the strap of black cloth, weighted down with a heavy stone. He held the jewel up to the next lamp. The diamond's facets trapped the light and reflected it back a thousandfold. It was a rare and handsome stone.

And one he recognized.

His blood chilled. Kathryn wore the same stone—though hers was only paste and artifice. Here was the true diadem that marked the castellan's station, granted and passed from one to the next, over countless centuries. Only the chain was broken last year. The castellan before Kathryn had vanished as surely and completely as Perryl, taking this diadem with her.

"Castellan Mirra . . ." he mumbled.

He clutched the stone in his palm, picturing the stern face of the old woman, the longtime counselor to good Ser Henri, former warden to Tashijan. Henri had trusted no one more. Now here was the stone again, ripped away by Lorr at the risk of his own flesh.

What did it mean?

Kathryn kept her post, guarding Dart. Brant and Laurelle stood behind her shoulders.

"Take the girl!" Argent said from behind the high bench.

Shadowknights stalked toward her from both sides. Kathryn eyed the rear door to the chamber. It stood unguarded and led back to the adjudicators' private rooms of contemplation. It would prove their best chance to escape. From there, Kathryn could reach those loyal to her, get Dart into hiding. After that, she would force Argent to face the true threat against Tashijan.

But first she had to get Dart to safety, beyond Argent's reach.

She began to draw her sword—then a door on the far side slammed open with a resounding bang. All eyes turned. A knight swept into the chamber, flanked by a cadre of men in gray cloaks, a match to the cut of the first, except the men had blackened their faces with ash.

The lead knight ripped away his masklin and tossed back his hood to reveal a knotted braid of white hair. "Back from the girl!" Krevan commanded.

He led his men into the chamber, eyes defiant, staring all down.

The bloodnullers retreated toward their alcoves. The warden's men paused in their approach.

Argent, plainly shaken by the interruption, collected himself. "You and your men have no bearing on this matter, Raven ser Kay," he said, using the knight's old name. "You have served Myrillia in the recent past. That will buy you and your men your freedom to leave Tashijan, but don't expect further leniency. The Black Flaggers are still considered brigands and pirates."

Krevan approached the bench and stood between Kathryn and Argent. His men spread out in a threatening stance.

"I have no bearing here?" he said, his voice lowering in threat. He shrugged back his cloak to free an arm and pointed back to Kathryn and the others while keeping his focus on Argent. "I have no bearing on what's done to my own *daughter*?"

Silence struck the room.

Dart jerked to her feet in surprise.

Argent also could not hide his shock. "What?" He held up a hand and shook his head. "Page Hothbrin—you claim she is your daughter?"

Kathryn didn't understand Krevan's ruse, but she knew it best to follow suit. She stepped forward. "It is the reason I defend her now," she said. "None were to know she was Krevan's daughter. The regent and I granted his request to allow her to enter training here. I was sworn to secrecy."

Krevan cut in. "I was exiled, rightly or not, from these walls because of my history with the Wyr. But my daughter bears no such taint. She was born free from the Wyr, birthed of a tryst in Drush Mire. I wished her to continue where I could not. To be a knight."

Argent struggled to absorb all this information. "I could not tell you," Kathryn said. "Even the girl did not know her heritage. She thought her father had died shortly after her birth. Why burden her with the truth? We owed Krevan a debt. Here it was paid in full."

"Wait!" Argent yelled. "What of the Dark Graces we've seen here? Of the daemon witnessed by the squires?"

"That would be my fault," Krevan said. "I feared someone would discover her secret here. I have many enemies. Her life would be forfeit for my crimes. So I cast a dark alchemy upon her, one crafted by the Wyr. If she were threatened, it would awaken and defend her. Likewise, to keep her secret, I could not have her soothed, lest some truth be exposed. She was ignorant of all this."

"To bring dark alchemies within the walls of Tashijan, you break our edicts here."

Krevan stared down Argent. "It seems if matters are dire enough, such actions are warranted. Are they not, Warden Fields?"

Argent's face flushed, reminded of his own use of dark arts.

Kathryn stepped forward, dropping her voice to a placating tone. "Such matters can be sorted at another time," she said. "I must remind everyone of the danger that presently looms—from without and within. Tashijan must ready itself before all is lost."

Argent's brow furrowed. He looked little resolved.

Kathryn waved Dart to her feet. "I will keep the girl confined to my rooms. Upon my sworn word, I must keep her safe. Once we—"

A clatter of boots interrupted her. Again all eyes turned to the door as a knight burst into the chambers. He drew to a winded stop. "Word from the main guard!"

Argent brusquely motioned to him to speak.

"The Masterlevels . . . are being emptied. Upon the orders of the regent."

Behind the man, a squawk of surprise arose from the doorway.

"What?" Master Hesharian pushed from where he had been hiding at the threshold, mopping his shining brow with a folded scrap of cloth, plainly just arrived himself. "Why was I not informed? What is the meaning of all this?"

The messenger ignored him, his full attention on the warden.

Kathryn noted Master Hesharian's companion, lurking in his larger shadow. Clouded eyes ignored everyone in the room and settled on Dart. She sensed that Krevan's ruse would be peeled away under such a gaze. She stepped back to Dart, hiding the girl behind her cloak again.

Before anyone could speak, a resounding strike of a gong reverberated from below and traveled up the throat of Stormwatch Tower. As its echoes died away, all gazes turned to the warden. All knew its meaning. Traditionally it was rung only once a year, during a formal ceremony, reminding all of their duty to Myrillia. Otherwise, it was struck for only one reason.

"We're too late," Kathryn mumbled to no one and to everyone.

They were under attack.

THIRD

Wyr and Wraith

Spiderboard for *Skulls*, played with brass pinches, a contest of luck, wit, and a fair scrape of deception. Better played with enemies than friends. More blood has been spilled over this game than all the wars of Myrillia. Origin: *unknown, though attributed to the witchlords of Bly.*

10

A NAME SCRIBED IN BLOOD

AS THE LAST OF THE EVENING BELLS RANG THROUGHOUT Tashijan, Dart waited with the others in the castellan's hermitage. The fire from the hearth had been stoked to a wild flame in a vain attempt to hold back the dark worries in all their hearts. Gathered here, they awaited word from the castellan and the regent.

Back in the adjudicator's chambers, Tylar had appeared shortly after the messenger, storming inside with claims of daemonic knights. During the ensuing chaos, Dart and the others were sent under guard—both knights and the gray-cloaked Flaggers—up to Kathryn's chambers.

By the door, Krevan spoke with an ash-faced woman in a gray robe—then closed the door. His Flaggers would guard their privacy from here. His eyes drifted to Dart's, then away again, almost embarrassed. Perhaps for the falsehoods he had spread to spare her further inquiry. Though untrue, this claimed relationship was an intimacy that had made the pirate suddenly awkward near her.

Or was it something more?

Elsewhere, off by the window, Barrin lay on the floor, head resting on his crossed paws. Kytt stood over him, one hand absently scratching the bullhound's ear, his face lost in worry. Lorr had been taken into Kathryn's private room, where a pair of healers were working on his burns with Grace-rich salves. He had yet to fully awaken, only occasionally mumbling in delirium.

Dart had seen Lorr when he'd been hauled inside, half his side a burnt ruin. He had sacrificed himself to save them. She prayed the healers had Grace enough to save him in turn.

At the threshold to the room, Rogger and Gerrod were bowed in quiet conversation. Rogger wore a stern look, so unlike his usual bravado. That worried Dart more than anything.

Closer, Laurelle sat on the chair opposite her, hands folded in her lap as if she were waiting for a servant to bring a platter of sweetwine and finger cakes. Brant had gone to check on his wolfkits when they had climbed past his retinue's floor. He had mumbled some promise to return, but his eyes had been shadowed and hard to read. Perhaps he was just glad for an excuse to be rid of them all.

Dart couldn't blame him.

Brant's vacancy was in turn taken up by Delia, the regent's Hand of blood. The dark-haired woman stood behind Laurelle's chair and stared into the flames, one finger resting on her chin as if she were about to say something, but she never did.

Finally a muffled commotion sounded out in the hall, and the door swung open. Tylar and Kathryn entered. Both appeared flushed, angry, moving stiff-legged.

"I should still be down there," Tylar said.

"Argent has the entire first three floors ablaze with bonfires and torches. All stairs from there are doubled with guards bearing torches. He has ordered barrels of oil to be stationed at landings, ready to be set to flame and rolled down." Kathryn scowled. "I don't know which to fear more—dark knights and cursed storms or Argent burning the towers down around our ankles."

Tylar looked little mollified. He seemed to finally see the others in the room. He brushed his dark hair back behind his ears.

Dart noted he had taken a moment to restore Rivenscryr. When Tylar had first arrived in the adjudicators' chamber, he had held only a golden hilt. It appeared like a broken sword. Only Dart's eyes could see the silvery ghost of the blade. It would remain such until the blade was whetted again—whetted in her own blood. Before reaching here, Tylar must have anointed his sword from his stores of her humour, preserved in glass repostilaries. She knew he carried a small vial on a silver chain around his neck.

Dart was glad he had already performed such an act. When

she had first seen the ghostly state of the sword, she feared he would ask her to cut herself and freshly bless the blade. She did not know if she had the strength for that this night.

As the two newcomers entered, Krevan, Rogger, and Gerrod gathered closer. Delia hung back with Dart and Laurelle. The woman's eyes flicked a bit sharply between Kathryn and Tylar as if searching for some extra meaning.

Tylar spoke into the expectant silence. "Kathryn is correct. Argent has acted with a surprising swiftness to lay a fiery swath between the two halves of Tashijan. It should allow us some ground to maneuver."

"But not farther than our own walls," Rogger countered. "The storm closes us off from the rest of Myrillia. We're trapped in these towers."

Gerrod creaked a step closer. "There may be some reason for hope. Such a siege as this cannot sustain itself. The storm must eventually blow itself out. Even a blizzard whipped by a cadre of gods will eventually succumb to the turn and flow of our world. It is a dam that must eventually burst. If we could wait it out . . ."

Tylar shook his head. "I refuse to place the fate of Tashijan in the hands of chance and the turn of the world. Gerrod, how long would it take your masters to get the damaged flippercraft flying again?"

"If we had full support and rally of the dockworkers, perhaps as soon as daybreak."

"Get started on it."

"But the storm will still drain the Grace from any craft that nears it and—"

Tylar cut him off with a raised hand. "Just get it done." Then he turned to Kathryn. "See if the healers can revive Lorr enough that we can speak to him. We must know more about what he saw down there."

She nodded. "And you're sure it was Perryl you saw below?"

"It was Perryl's body—I fear there is little left of the man."

Kathryn's face clouded with a mix of anger and pain. She headed toward her private rooms.

"I'll see if I can help," Delia said. "Lorr was more a father to me than my own."

The two left the room, though both would not meet the other's eye.

Once they were gone, Krevan shifted to Tylar. "I would speak a few words with you in private." He pointed a finger at Rogger. "And you."

Tylar glanced around the crowded hearthroom. Barrin huffed a bit where he lay, as if offended at being excluded.

Dart stepped forward. "If you seek privacy, my garret is through that door." She pointed to the low and narrow arch. "There is not much space."

"It will do," Krevan said brusquely and strode off.

Rogger met Tylar's eyes and shrugged.

Dart walked them to her door, pushed it open, and stepped back.

Krevan waved her inside. "Mayhap you should attend this, too."

Dart took a startled half step back. "Why?"

The pirate's hard eyes fixed on her. His next words turned her knees to porridge. Tylar caught her with a reassuring squeeze, but even he glanced to Krevan with narrowed eyes as he answered her question.

"Because it concerns your father. Your *real* father."

Kathryn approached the sickbed. The stench of burnt flesh, hair, wool, and leather stained the room. To combat this, one of the healers already had a brazier glowing and dribbled oil of gentled mint across the sizzling red iron. A mound of soaked llamphur sprigs warmed atop its grate.

"To help him breathe," Healer Fennis said quietly, noting her attention. "Will open the lungs."

The other healer, a slim woman and wife to Fennis, knelt beside Lorr's sprawled form. She had bathed away the charred clothes, exposing the rawness beneath.

"There will be scars," she said. "But the alchemy in the balms was newly concocted, devised by a physic in the deserts of Dry Wash. Using a Grace of loam and air. Who would have thought such a combination could be steadied?"

"Then he will live?" Delia asked. Her voice rang with relief.

"If you let us work in peace," the woman answered.

Kathryn waved Tylar's Hand back from the bed. It was an irritated gesture, more brusque than she had intended. She blunted the effect with softer words. "He's a strong man, even for one late in his years."

Stepping away, Delia stood with her arms crossed over her chest—not a stern pose, but more like she was hugging herself in a measure of reassurance. Kathryn studied her askance. There was a puffiness to her eyelids. She had been crying. Small lines marred a smooth brow. Still in this moment, Kathryn suddenly recognized the youth behind the worry. She had to remind herself that Delia was a full decade younger. Eternally serious, seldom smiling, she had always struck Kathryn as older in years.

But not now.

The girl shone behind the woman, worn through by grief and worry.

Delia caught Kathryn staring, with a flick of her eyes toward Kathryn, then down to the floor. A fleeting glimpse of Delia's guilt.

For some reason, this only piqued Kathryn's irritation again, setting her lips into hard lines. She fought against it, remembering the stolen kiss atop Stormwatch. There was no true blame here. She knew better than to fault the other woman. The man was equally to blame for any broken vows. And besides, what vows remained between Tylar and Kathryn? Whatever had once been sworn and promised had been broken into so many pieces as to be all but unrecognizable.

A groan from the bed returned Kathryn's attention to the greater threat, reminding her of her responsibility, to Lorr, to everyone in Tashijan. Her face heated slightly, shamed at the momentary lapse into childish resentments. She was not a young girl to moon over lost love. Especially when all of Myrillia was threatened.

Lorr stirred on the sheets. His eyelids fluttered weakly open despite the squint of pain in his face.

"He wakes," Healer Fennis said.

The woman glanced back at her husband. "We should draught him while we can. Willow bark and nettle wine." She waved toward a side table.

The other nodded and deftly began working on an elixir.

"Two drops of poppy oil," she reminded.

"Yes, my dearest."

Kathryn stepped closer, shadowed by Delia. "Can you revive him enough to speak? We must—"

"I kin hear you," Lorr croaked out. He lifted his good arm, but it fell back to the bed. "How can a man sleep with all this babbling?"

"Don't stir," Delia warned.

Lorr's eyes finally focused on the two women. "Such a sight would wake any man . . ." His attempt at levity fell on worried ears.

Kathryn knelt to bring her face even with his. "Lorr, if you're able, can you tell us what you saw below Tashijan?"

The false cheer drained from the muscles of his face, tightening his features with a pain beyond his burns. He attempted to rise up on an elbow but was scolded back down to the pillows. He lifted a hand, surprised to find an empty palm.

"Tylar found the diadem," Kathryn said, reading his worry. "Castellan Mirra's diadem."

He nodded and sighed. "I went down that dark stair to lure whatever lurked away from the young ones. A stumbling, broken-stone maze it were down there. Almost got myself nabbed up."

He coughed hard. Healer Fennis approached with his draught, but Lorr waved him away.

"Then I caught a scent. A familiar enough one. I'd been dredging the sewers looking for it long 'nough, so when it caught up in the back of my blessed nose, tasted on the tongue, I knew it right. I went back to look closer. And there she was among that black clot of shadow, whispering to them."

Kathryn closed her eyes for a breath. So Lorr hadn't found Castellan Mirra imprisoned or discovered her dead body. He hadn't returned with the diadem as proof of either. It was much worse.

"These shadowknights—" she began.

"Not knights. Mayhap once. No longer. *Ghawls*, she called them. Black *ghawls*. Black-cursed to the bone."

Kathryn remembered the stern woman who had been

counsel to Ser Henri for many decades. Though hard, she had always been evenhanded and of wise sensibility. Kathryn had wished often of late that she could be half the castellan that the old woman was.

"So Mirra was tainted, too," she said tiredly. "Cursed like the knights."

Lorr sighed. "That's just it." The tracker's amber eyes found Kathryn's. "I smelled no corruption from her. She scented as she did when wrapped up here in her hermitage. But those *ghawls* . . . they listened to her, lapping about her like beaten dogs. They were hers. Flesh and bone. I drew closer—too close. They fell out of the shadows around me like scraps of darkness. Only escape was fire and light."

He fell silent a moment, eyes lost in some unimaginable horror. Kathryn only had to look at his blistered flesh to know the cost of that escape.

He closed his eyes, and Kathryn was glad for it. "I fought through them . . ." he mumbled. "Grabbed for her throat, but they reached through flames and tore me off. All I could do . . . I fled . . ."

Healer Fennis again stepped forward with his draught.

Kathryn rose and backed, but her motion was sensed. Lorr opened his eyes and fixed her with a firm stare.

"She was *not* tainted . . . of that I am certain."

Kathryn nodded and stepped back to allow the healer to minister to Lorr. Lorr sank more deeply into his pillows, as if unburdening himself had finally granted him some measure of peace.

Delia crossed to the other side of the bed. "I'll stay with him."

She nodded again, too shaken for words, not trusting her voice. Lorr's words stayed with her as she headed away. *She was not tainted*. If the tracker's senses read true, then what did that portend? Had Castellan Mirra been a willing participant, a member of the Cabal? Had she always been the enemy, hiding behind her ermine cloaks and lined face, at the very pinnacle of Tashijan?

Ice numbed her limbs and coursed through her heart. How many nights had she sat with Mirra, entrusted her with secrets? What about Ser Henri? Had he been duped as well?

Suddenly Kathryn had to reach to a wall to hold herself upright. All she had supposed, all she had believed shifted inside her. It was as if she had slipped through a dark mirror. But which side was she on?

The missing knights . . . the loss of Perryl . . . so many certainties and suspicions no longer made sense. She pictured again the slain young knight she had discovered last year, sacrificed in some dark rite. She had believed the Fiery Cross to be to blame, painted Warden Fields with the blackest of brushes. And though the warden lusted for power, Kathryn now knew whose hand truly pulled the dark strings of Tashijan.

Not Argent.

It had been Castellan Mirra all along. She must have purposely laid that false trail, instilling rancor and distrust throughout Tashijan, splitting them from within while crafting her own dark plots beneath their very towers.

Kathryn leaned against the wall, sensing a well of tears rising, a mix of frustration and something that bordered on grief.

Had Henri finally discovered Mirra's secret? Was that why he had been murdered? It hadn't been a plot by Argent, as Kathryn had always supposed; now she knew the black truth.

He had died because of trust.

And now all of Tashijan . . . all of Myrillia . . . faced the same fate.

"I must have the skull," Krevan said.

Dart had retreated to her bed in the small garret. The hearth was cold, but Rogger had lit the small lamp on her table. The thief now leaned against the closed door. She stared between Krevan and Tylar, both cloaked, both their faces triple-striped, though neither was a true knight any longer.

What was this about a skull? she wondered.

Tylar frowned at the pirate. "I don't think this is a time to worry about such a cursed talisman."

"But it is more than mere bone . . . more than you could imagine."

"We know about the trace of seersong. Gerrod has been studying it."

The pirate's gaze swept to Dart, then back to Tylar. Dart remembered his earlier words. *It concerns your father. Your real father.*

"You know nothing," he grumbled.

"Then enlighten us."

Krevan glowered. "The skull belonged to a rogue god that stumbled out of the hinterland into a realm of the Eighth Land. Such a trespass burnt the flesh. Even the bones should have been consumed, but someone preserved the skull, granted it to the god of Saysh Mal."

Tylar nodded to the thief. "I gathered as much from Rogger. He stole it during his pilgrimage stop in that god-realm. But I hadn't heard more of his tale, what with our rough landing and the cursed storm."

Krevan's brow darkened as he stared toward Rogger.

"Perhaps we should hear both your stories," Tylar said.

Rogger shrugged. "My tale is not that rich. I continued with my pilgrimage last year as a way of skirting through the godrealms, looking for any evidence of the Cabal." He pulled back a sleeve to reveal the scarred brandings. "Such punishment of the flesh was fair trade to hear the rumblings and rumors among the underfolk of the various lands. Tongues wag more easily when the only ears nearby are those of a ragged beggar on a stoop."

Tylar waved for Rogger to continue. Even Dart knew that the thief's pilgrimage was more than it had seemed.

"So there I was, running out of blank skin when I stumbled into the jungle realm of the Huntress. And up to then, not a peep nor peck from the Cabal. As soon as I set foot in that realm, it weren't hard to tell something was amiss. The people of that land went about with their heads tucked low. I saw more brawls in the tavernhouses in one night than in a fortnight elsewhere. Bodies were left in alleys to rot. That is not what I had expected to find. Saysh Mal was not a high place, but it was fairly wrought from all I'd heard. Lived by some code of honorable conduct. No longer. What I saw there more reminded me of ol' Balger's Foulsham Dell, corrupted and low of spirit."

"So what happened there?" Dart asked. She knew Brant hailed from that realm.

"I went to present myself to the Huntress in her treetop castillion. I did my proper obeisance, took her sigil to my thigh, and thought to move on. But word among the underfolk at the castillion suggested their mistress might be the source of the decrepitude. She had grown sullen, pulled away from her people, seldom showed herself. The flow of her humours slowed, then stopped. It was said she even had one of her own Hands imprisoned. Such strangeness warranted further inquiries. A few pinches spent on ale, a few silver yokes rolled onto palms, and I heard more. How the Huntress retreated often to a private chamber, spent days in there alone. The underfolk reported hearing her whispering in there . . . laughing sometimes, cursing at other times."

"Who else was in there?" Tylar asked.

"That's just it. No one. She was alone. She kept some treasure in there, a talisman, hidden behind lock and curse." Rogger shrugged.

"So you had to take a look," Tylar said.

"How could I not? It surely sounded like another incursion by the Cabal, another tainted realm. So I snuck in there and saw the talisman, a skull resting on a golden cushion. From its ilked shape, there was little doubt that it had something to do with the Cabal, a slow poison meant to corrupt yet another god. There was only one clear course."

"You stole it."

Rogger nodded. "Best to get it out of there, away from the Huntress and her realm, away from all the god-realms. And I guess I was right. Look what happened when I set foot in Chrismferry."

"What happened?" Krevan asked, his eyes narrowing.

Dart listened in horror as Tylar described the attack by ilk-beasts. He explained, "Master Gerrod believes the seersong drew upon the taint left behind by Chrism and cast forth a curse."

"So to keep it out of the god-realms, I finally brought it here," Rogger concluded. "Tashijan lies nestled among the god-realms, but is not a god-realm itself. And with all the knowledgeable masters buried beneath these towers, here seemed a good place to have the skull's secret plied from its bones."

Krevan's dark expression had not changed. "You meddle in matters beyond your understanding."

"Wouldn't be the first time," Rogger mumbled. "And probably not the last."

Tylar lifted a hand. "Plainly the skull is some talisman of the Cabal. I don't—"

Krevan cut him off, voice booming with authority. "The skull is *not* some Cabalistic talisman. Have you not been listening? The skull came from a rogue god who trespassed into that realm." His voice lowered. "And it wasn't just *any* rogue god."

Tylar's brow crinkled, but Dart understood. She'd known the truth from the moment Krevan first described the rogue's trespass. From the glance he had given her. From his earlier words to her.

"He was my father," she said, gripping her bed's ticking with both hands.

Tylar gaped between her and the pirate.

Krevan paced a bit but did not deny it. "Eylan . . . the Wyr-mistress . . . it was she who brought word out of the hinterland, of this godling's birth." An arm waved to Dart. "Word carried from this one's mother, begging for her child to be taken to safe harbors."

Tylar nodded. "Ser Henri took her in, kept her hidden."

Krevan continued as if he hadn't heard, one hand on his brow. "For centuries, the Wyr-lords have had tenuous dealings with the rogues, trading in alchemies and humours. They know the true nature of the ravening creatures better than any. And after Dart was secured, their interest focused upon the parents."

"Why?" Tylar asked. "Such births are rare. Only two in four centuries. And rogues slip in and out of ravings, spending more of their lives like beasts than gods. What did they hope to learn?"

"The Wyr-lords believed there was something special about this pair of gods. They were perplexed. What made this seed take root when so many other ruttings among the wild gods failed? So they watched and waited, spied and plotted. As you know, the Wyr are drawn to Grace of an unusual nature."

Dart glanced to Tylar. The regent had personal experience with such interest.

"The dam fell into full rave after the child was taken, waging a swath of madness. She vanished into caverns beneath Middleback a decade ago and has yet to resurface. Perhaps dead, perhaps in some raving dream, perhaps even escaped out some other tunnel long ago. But the sire . . . he remained strangely grounded, whisking from hinterland to hinterland. The Wyr had a difficult time tracking him from place to place. It was like—"

"—he knew he was being hunted," Rogger said.

Krevan nodded. "They lost him when he reached the Eighth Land. It is a maze of hinterlands."

"How long ago was that?" Tylar asked.

"Going on seven years."

"And the Wyr have still been hunting for him all this time?"

"They have strategies that cross centuries. A handful of years is nothing to them. They scoured the hinterlands across all of Myrillia, searching for some trace or sign of him."

Of my father, Dart thought, still struggling with the revelation.

Rogger coughed with a trace of amusement. "And all this time he's been locked under key in the Huntress's castillion. Now that's what I call a good hiding place. 'Course, there is a downside—you're dead."

"But what made him trespass into one of the god-realms in the first place?" Tylar asked. "Did he fear the Wyr's hunters so much that he killed himself?"

"No. Unlike our thief here, I did some study of the skull's history in Saysh Mal. The rogue entered the realm a full two years after the Wyr lost his trail among the twisted maze of hinterlands down there. Some other purpose drove the rogue into that realm."

"And what purpose might that be?" Rogger asked, setting his shoulders a bit stiffly.

Krevan shook his head. "That I still don't know. The Wyr refused to tell me more."

Tylar frowned at Krevan. "Considering your hatred of Wyrd Bennifren, I'm surprised you are so well informed about all this."

"They hired the Flaggers," Krevan grumbled sourly.

"What? I thought there was great enmity between you and Wyrd Bennifren?"

"Yet, in this matter, there was also great urgency."

"How so? What did they want?"

"To help find the missing rogue. Three seasons ago, they found the first crumb of a trail long gone cold. A wandering Wyr-lord was collecting alchemies and Grace-tainted herbs and stumbled into a hinter-village down in the Eighth Land. He discovered an old piece of hide, tacked in an elder's home, a revered talisman. Upon the hide, inked in a blood that was rich in wild Graces, were words written in ancient Littick. None could read it, not even the elder, though he recognized it as God's Tongue. The Wyr-lord deciphered it easily enough, but more importantly he read the sigil at the bottom, the mark of their long-lost rogue."

"This sigil?" Dart asked. "It was his name?"

Krevan glanced to her, studied her a moment, then nodded.

Dart swallowed. When younger, she had wondered about her mother and father, fabricated elaborate stories for why she had been abandoned at the doorstep of a school in Chrismferry. Only after learning her true heritage did she allow those dreams to die away, strangled by the horror of the truth. Since then, she had tried not to dwell upon it. Easier to be lost in her training and duties than face her blasted birthright.

But now . . .

Krevan crossed to the cold hearth, dipped a finger in ash, and scrawled two Littick symbols on the stone wall.

Rogger stepped closer. *"Keorn,"* he read aloud with a frown.

Dart mouthed the name silently herself. The weight of it added substance to what was once only vague shadow. Her father. She held back a shudder—sensing that it might shake her apart.

Rogger turned his back on the markings. "It is rare for a rogue to hold his name. Usually the ravings burn away such memories. Even some of our esteemed Hundred—like the Huntress—had forgotten their names by the time they settled, lost in the burn of their initial ravings. Could this rogue simply have made up this name?"

Krevan shook his head. "Sometimes the memories will back up out of the past. But the Wyr believed it was more than that, that this one had always known his name. It went along with their belief that there was something exceptional about this rogue who birthed a daughter. It was why they approached the Black Flaggers. The trail was cold, much time had passed, and the Wyr were desperate."

"And your rapacious guild is everywhere, from sea to mountain," Rogger said. "Fingers and toes into all matter of trade. Who better to aid in this quest?"

"Why didn't you warn us of this?" Tylar asked.

"At first, I was not sure where it would lead. To bind the deal required my sworn word. And even when I learned and suspected more, you were under the eye of the Wyr."

"Eylan . . ." Tylar mumbled.

"Do not be so simple. The Wyr have more than just the one pair of eyes on you. Of that you can be certain. Any word sent to you would reach the Wyr."

"So gold bought your tongue," Rogger muttered with a scowl.

"No. Something more valuable than gold."

"And what might that be?"

"Revelations," Krevan said. "The Wyr promised that if I brought the skull to them they would tell me much more about the Cabal, the rogue, and the girl."

The pirate's eyes settled again upon Dart.

"How do you know you aren't being played the fool?" Rogger asked. "Paid to fetch the skull with false promises."

"Because they laid down a payment in advance. A tithing of secret knowledge. They knew more than just the name of the rogue who sired Dart. They told me *who* he was."

"What do you mean?"

"You are aware of how the gods had relationships before they were sundered and their world broken. Before they arrived on the shores of Myrillia. Old pacts, old enmities. Remnants of the God War that sundered their kingdom."

His listeners nodded. Even Dart had heard of such rumored relationships, like between Fyla and the murdered god Meeryn. The two gods had once been lovers before becoming locked into their Myrillian god-realms, doomed to be forever near, yet forever apart.

"The Wyr learned a secret about Dart's father, one kept for the past four millennia. After Dart was born, her mother, near to raving and desperate to save her child, revealed her father's true heritage."

"And what might that be?"

Krevan turned full upon Tylar. "Keorn was Chrism's *son*. Born before the Sundering."

As the words struck her, Dart felt her vision narrow. The blood drained to her heels. She felt a scream building somewhere deep inside her. It was Chrism who had forged Rivenscryr. It was he who wielded the Godsword and shattered the kingdom of the gods, bringing ruin and chaos to Myrillia.

Rogger stood wide-eyed. "That would make . . ."

Tylar finished his thought. "Dart is Chrism's granddaughter."

Off by the hearth, Kathryn watched the small group tumble out of Dart's garret. They all looked ashen, except for Krevan, whose countenance had, if anything, grown even darker.

Barrin lifted his head from a paw and disturbed the young wyld tracker who had been half-slumbering against his side. Laurelle stood up from her fireside chair.

"The skull is where?" the pirate boomed as he crossed into the room.

"Still down in Gerrod's study," Tylar said, following on his heels.

"We must fetch it."

Tylar shook his head. "Argent has closed off the Masterlevels. He has fires blazing across all the lower tower floors. We dare not breach the cellars. For now, the skull is secure in Gerrod's rooms."

"Secure? In levels overrun by daemon knights? Someone might sense the taint of seersong in the bone, hunt it down. If we lose the skull, we lose any leverage to pry additional secrets from the Wyr."

"Plus the Cabal might use the skull against us," Rogger argued, siding with Krevan.

"We must attempt it!" the pirate insisted.

Kathryn stepped toward them. *What new turmoil was this?*

Tylar noted her approach and motioned her to his side,

plainly expecting her support. She came, prepared to give it, then rankled at such assumptions. They were long past such easy alliances. Still, she was as irritated by her reaction as much as by Tylar's.

"What is this all about?" she asked coldly.

"Krevan wishes to make an assault upon the Masterlevels. To retrieve the rogue's skull. It seems it may be more important than just a cursed talisman. But to breach the cellars may lay all of Tashijan open to what gathers below. Even Gerrod—" Tylar glanced around the room. "Where's the master?"

"Off to do your bidding. Gathering masters to repair the flippercraft."

Tylar nodded. "That's what we must do first. Secure the towers. Prepare for this siege. Then we can worry about an assault below."

Kathryn turned to Krevan and Rogger. "This skull—I would hear its story in full, but tell me first, how calamitous would it be to have it fall into the clutches of the Cabal?"

"Ruin across all levels," Krevan said. He turned to Tylar. "The Wyr have no allegiances. They would trade their secrets just as well to the Cabal."

"And remember the ilk-beasts back in Chrismferry," Rogger said. "The curse remains strong in those bones. If whoever created those daemons is down there with them . . ."

"She is," Kathyrn answered, drawing their attention back to her.

Tylar frowned. "Kathryn?"

"Lorr awoke for a short time." She explained all she had learned, of a deception that spanned decades, riddled throughout the tower's history. "Castellan Mirra is down there. She has been plying treachery for decades, weakening Tashijan from on high, while corrupting its roots in secret. I'm sure even now she's gathering a wealth of Grace from the masters' alchemical labs, a well of power to taint and forge into dire weapons against us. Such malignant cunning will expose the skull, find recourse to use it."

Kathryn noted Tylar had clutched the back of a chair as she related Lorr's story. She read the growing horror in his face as he recalibrated the vast web of lies that had trapped them all here. Just as she had done earlier. She also saw the certainty firming in the gray storm of his eyes.

"Then we have no choice," he said. "The skull must be retrieved."

"It will be difficult," Kathryn warned.

Tylar's mind was already spinning. "We'll bring fire—torches and lanterns. We can burn a path through to Gerrod's study."

Kathryn held up a hand. "That is all well and good, but that is not what I meant."

Tylar stared at her.

"First, you'll have to get through Argent. That will be the difficult part."

Tylar opened his mouth to speak.

"No," she said more firmly. "I know what you're thinking. Bullying your way through. You can't divide this house more than it has been already. Castellan Mirra has already succeeded in breaking the trust and fellowship of our Order. Do not serve her further by waging a war with Argent when the enemy is at our door."

"What would you have me do?"

She sighed. "It is time we worked together to unite our Order. Argent was once a great knight. We'll have to make him remember that."

"Might be easier to pull a pig through a keyhole," Rogger said.

Kathryn touched the man's elbow and silenced him. She kept her eyes on Tylar. He slowly nodded his agreement.

A new voice interrupted from the narrow doorway. Dart leaned on the door's latch, worn and haunted. She looked as if she had taken a beating, though not a mark marred her. Laurelle abandoned her place by the hearth and hurried toward her.

Dart held her off with a raised palm. Her arm trembled. "The skull. You said it came from Saysh Mal."

Tylar nodded.

"Then perhaps you should talk to Brant. He was raised in that god-realm."

Tylar frowned at Kathryn, not recognizing the name.

"It was the boy who helped rescue her," she explained. "A Hand from Oldenbrook."

"And he hails from Saysh Mal?" Rogger asked. Suspicion rang in his voice. "How long ago did he leave that realm?"

Dart shook her head, unsure.

Laurelle answered. "He arrived at the Conclave in Chrismferry some four years ago."

Dart glanced to her, startled, but Kathryn knew the dark-haired girl was held in high esteem back at the school, both handsome of figure and of a rich family. Raised to such a station, little probably passed beneath Laurelle's notice at the school. Especially a striking boy. But now she seemed slightly abashed by her knowledge.

Rogger mumbled to Tylar and lifted one eyebrow. "So he came about the time all fell to ruin in Saysh Mal."

Nodding, Tylar turned to Laurelle. "Do you know how he came to be so far from home?"

She glanced to Dart and shifted her feet slightly. "Rumors only. You know the prattle that gets passed around school."

"Tell us."

Again a blushing glance was passed to Dart. "He arrived in chains. Exiled, I heard. Sent to the school to get rid of him."

"Who sent him? Who banished him?"

"I heard tell it was the god of his realm." Laurelle studied her toes. "She banished him, forbidding him ever to return."

11

A WREATH OF LEAVES

"THEY STILL SHOULDN'T BE HERE," LIANNORA SAID. "TELL him, Sten."

Brant sat across the dining table. He would have preferred to have broken bread with the giants back in his rooms, but the captain of the guard had insisted the group all share the final bell's meal together, for safety's sake. All had heard the rumors of daemons beneath Tashijan. Brant kept silent about his own involvement.

Watching from the side, he found it surprising how little the others seemed to be truly worried about the storm, the whispers of daemons, and the bustle of knights in the lower levels of Tashijan. Up higher, a certain degree of orderliness and routine persisted. To Liannora and her two lapdogs, Mistress Ryndia and Master Khar, it was all so much high adventure, requiring such brutal sacrifice as tolerating a meal served late.

And what a meal it was. The board was piled high enough to feed thrice their number. A covey of roasted grouse, stuffed with nut mash and corn, centered the table, surrounded by steaming loaves of oaten bread along with cheeses, both hard and soft, and boiled eggs painted in the Oldenbrook hues of blue and silver. A pair of scullions hauled off a large kettle-bowl of winter squash stew, requiring a pole through the handles to lift it from the table.

Such was the enormity of the fare that the captain of the guard shared a few plates with his men at the doors, who ate standing. While at the table, Sten and the Hands sipped tall crystal flutes of warmed sweetwine.

Brant suspected such largesse was mostly to keep the visitors calm and sated, as much a strategy of the warden as the flaming fortifications below. Chaos in the upper reaches would only hamper efforts below.

So he stayed silent during the long meal.

But Liannora was not satisfied with the fare alone. It seemed entertainment was also necessary this night.

"To keep these wolfkits, on our level, among our rooms, unbathed," she sniffed and nodded to Sten. "If nothing else, it's unclean."

"They will be kept to my chambers," Brant said.

"How can we know that for certain? Did they not worry themselves free of your giants' charge, escaping away?"

Brant's chair rested before the room's hearth, the fire in full blaze behind him. He felt already near to roasted, and with his brow moist, he found little patience to dance with Liannora. "They're staying here."

"That is not your decision," Liannora said. Plainly she remained upset at being snubbed earlier outside the castellan's chambers, and now sought to punish him. "In all matters of our security and well-being, Sten is the final word."

Ryndia and Khar nodded their agreement, murmuring their assent over their goblets of wine.

Brant turned to the captain of the guard.

Something in Brant's eye gave Sten pause. "Mistress, perhaps it would be better . . . until the matter is settled below—"

Liannora touched his arm, silencing him. "These are indeed difficult times. We must try our best to be of service to Tashijan. Keeping the cubbies in these fine quarters will strain our welcome here. If any of us should become ill from our confinement with them . . ."

Ryndia lifted a fold of cloth to her nose. "I smelled them when I walked past Master Brant's room on my way here. It all but made me swoon."

Khar nodded, whistling a bit through his thin nose. "And their howling . . . pierced right through the wall to my bedchamber. I doubt my slumber this night will be undisturbed. Such disorder will surely burden my constitution."

Brant scowled at the pair of Hands. Ryndia was as hearty as a well-fed cow, and Khar was known to sleep entire days away.

"If that be the case," Sten began, avoiding Brant's eye, "then we have a duty to rid them from our level. I'm sure my guards can find some lonely cage, away from the bustle, for the pair."

Brant stood up, knocking his chair back, almost into the hearth's flame. "They'll not be moved." He stared across the breadth of the table. "I will not play this game of yours, Liannora. If you're upset with me, then state it plainly. Quit these little pokes."

Liannora opened her eyes wider, the picture of innocence. "I'm certain I don't know of what you're clamoring about. I only seek the best for all."

Sten sat more stiffly in his seat. "Master Brant, with all deference, I think it mightily rude of you to speak to the mistress in such a harsh manner. Plainly she only wishes everyone's comfort here."

Brant's lips hardened. "Try to take the cubbies—any of you—and you'll face my daggers," he said in a low and certain voice.

Liannora waved a dismissive hand. "What did I tell you? He's as wild as his cubbies. There is no reasoning with him. You, Sten, are witness to his threat against me. Such matters must be brought before the attention of Lord Jessup upon our return. And I'll ask that you set a guard upon his door or I'd fear some attack during the night."

Sten was already on his feet. "Master Brant, you leave me little choice. I'll ask that you retire to your chambers. Perhaps in the morning more sense will prevail, and you'll apologize for such an affront."

Two guards obeyed some hidden signal and came forward to flank Brant.

Brant only then realized how artfully he had been manipulated. The threat against the whelpings was only a feint, one meant to draw him out for the true attack. And he had fallen into the trap readily.

Liannora's next words confirmed his suspicion. "And let him keep his cubbies—at least for this one night. I'm sure we can all endure their presence for the sake of peace and good grace."

"Most generous and reasonable," Ryndia said.

"More than he deserves," Khar echoed on cue.

Sten nodded his thanks and faced Brant with an exasperated sigh. "If you'll accompany us," he said and headed to the door.

Brant followed. He had dug himself a deep enough grave.

Still Liannora could not help but cast one more dagger. "In the morning, we'll settle this matter of the cubbies."

Brant did not rise to this further challenge. He held his tongue and gladly left the small dining hall. The door closed behind him—but not before he caught a small twitter of suppressed laughter from Ryndia.

He also heard Liannora's soft scold to her friend. "Oh, this is not over."

Brant allowed himself to be escorted back to his chambers. Guards or not, he looked forward to escaping to the confines of his rooms. But as he neared his door by the central stairs, he noted a knight standing at the landing, framed in torchlight, reminding him of the greater danger they all faced.

Sten stopped at his door.

Brant stepped forward and grabbed the latch.

"Ho!" a call rose from the stairs.

All eyes turned. A group of cloaked figures pushed past the lone guard and entered the hall. Warily, Brant backed a step, especially when the lead figure shed his cloak's hood. It was the regent again, Tylar ser Noche.

What now? Had something happened to Dart?

The regent's eyes settled on Brant. "I would have a private word with Master Brant," Tylar said, turning and acknowledging Sten, noting the crossed raven's feathers at his collar, marking the captain's station.

Sten also recognized the triple-striped countenance of the regent. "Certainly, your lordship."

"Very good."

Brant swallowed to find his voice. It seemed this long night was far from over. "Please use my chambers . . ." He waved to the door.

The regent nodded.

Brant undid the latch and pushed. He stood aside for them to enter. He recognized one of the regent's companions, the thin and bearded figure from before. Rogger was his name, as he recalled. He gave Brant a reassuring pat as he passed inside.

The next figure stood a head taller than all of them, buried in his cloak. Brant did not know him. Behind the stranger, the last figure stopped at the threshold. It was a woman under the gray cloak, though her face was hidden behind ash.

Brant frowned. *What was a member of the Black Flaggers doing here with the regent?*

The tall man nodded to her. "Keep any ears from our door," he instructed her.

She turned her back, standing before the doorway, fists coming to rest on her hips. She glanced over to Sten. The captain backed a full two steps before seeming to collect himself.

Brant instantly warmed to her and closed the door.

Behind him, a voice boomed a bit. "Who are you lot?"

Brant turned and hurried after the three men into the greeting hall of his chambers. The giant rose up from where he had been sitting cross-legged by the fire. He stood in his wool stockings, worn through at the toes, and had shed his greatcoat. He had a greasy turkey leg in one hand.

At his feet, a black nose retreated into one of his boots, dragging a worn snippet of bone. It seemed the whelpings had found a den for the night. A thready snarl flowed out of the boot, as wary of the intrusion as Malthumalbaen.

"It's all right, Mal," Brant said. "If you wouldn't mind taking the whelpings into the next room and shutting the door. Where's your brother?"

The large man pointed his turkey leg toward the back. "Had to use the privy, if that were all right?"

"Of course."

"You say that now," Mal answered jovially. "But wait 'til you go in there."

"I must have a word with the regent," Brant said, nodding to Tylar, who had bent a knee to peer inside the boot, drawn by the curiosity.

Mal shifted straighter, eyes widening again. "Ach, then I should be joining Dral." He stepped toward his occupied boot. "If you'll excuse me, ser."

So much for Oldenbrook's surprise.

"Cubbies," Brant acknowledged and stepped forward. "To

be presented to you and the warden after the knighting ceremony."

"Fell wolves, are they not?" Tylar asked, sitting back, a measure of surprise in his voice. "Handsome creatures. How did you come by them?"

"I rescued them from the same storm that besets us this night."

"Might near killed himself doing it," Malthumalbaen added.

Brant felt his cheeks heat up.

The regent shared a glance with his bearded friend and stood.

Brant motioned to Malthumalbaen, who bent down and scooped up his large boot, earning a few sharper growls. The giant carried them toward the back room. "If you need me, Master Brant . . ."

Brant took some solace in the giant's support. Once they were alone and the door shut, he faced the others. "How may I be of help?"

Tylar's brow remained furrowed, crinkling the topmost stripe tattooed at the corner of his eyes. "First, tell us more about your rescue of these cubbies."

"And the storm," Rogger added.

Brant stared around the room. The tall stranger stood with one hand resting on the stone mantel of the hearth, the other on the hilt of his sword. It bore a distinct serpent's head carved from silver, not the black diamond of a shadowknight's sword. Still, there was something vaguely familiar about the blade.

Avoiding this one's eyes, Brant cleared his throat and briefly told the story of his search for the abandoned cubbies, of the strange nature of the storm, and of its deadly cold.

"So the storm was gathering force as it swept south," Rogger said. "Sucking the life's breath out of the land."

"I warned Lord Jessup, but once the storm had passed, there was little to discover, swept under a blanket of snow."

Tylar nodded and mumbled as he paced one length of the room. "It seems this storm has swept all of us here for various reasons." The regent turned on a heel and again faced Brant. "But what I need to know more is what swept you here."

"Ser?"

Tylar asked the question that Brant was loath to ever answer. "How did you come to be exiled, Master Brant? What swept you up on our shores?"

Stunned by the strange turn of the inquiry, Brant stumbled for words. "I don't see how—?"

"You'd best answer the question," Rogger said from the other side, balancing the tip of a dagger on a finger. Brant had failed to note the man slip it from any sheath.

"And what do you know about a skull?" the ominous stranger asked by the hearth. "The skull of a rogue god."

Brant fell back a step as the world shifted under his heels. "What . . . ?" The back of his legs struck a chair. He sank down into it. A hand rose to the scar on his neck, a warding gesture.

Three pairs of eyes bore down upon him.

A keening wail filled his head, threatening to drown him away.

"Tell us," Tylar demanded.

Brant shook his head—not refusing, but attempting to stop his slide into the past. He failed.

It had been a wet spring in Saysh Mal, when the jungle wept and moss grew thick on anything that risked stopping in one place for too long. Such did not describe the three boys that day as they lit out down the soggy forest path, enjoying the warming day that held the promise of a long summer to come in the streaks of bright sunlight cutting through the canopy.

Flitters buzzed the ear and nattered the skin, requiring the occasional slap to neck or arm. A pair of squabbling long-tailed tickmonks caterwauled from the trees, stopping only long enough to pass on a scolding howl at the boys running below before continuing their argument.

"Brant, wait for me!" shouted Harp. He limped after the faster boys, encumbered by a weak leg, a birthing kink that could not be cured with any manner of Grace.

Brant slowed their pace, though Marron ran another few paces before stopping, swinging around with a wide smile. "If we're any later, we'll miss seeing the match!"

They had been released early from Master Hoarin's class on mushrooms and molds to attend a marksman contest to be held at the midday bell. But to make it in time, they still had to hurry.

Marron's uncle had won the third match yesterday and this was the last spar. Half the villages had emptied out for the yearly culmination of hunting skills, to be held at the Grove. Wreathed crowns had already been handed out for skill with spear, dagger, and snare, for the most fleet of foot, for the most silent of step. This day ended with the crowning Hunter of the Way, the man or woman who had shown the most skill over the course of the four-day challenge. The Huntress herself usually granted this crown, but she had missed many such appearances over the past several moons, falling more and more into solitude and gloomy silences.

All hoped to see her again in her usual shining manner.

If only for the one day.

Perhaps this reason more than any had drawn a larger crowd than usual. If the boys wanted a good view of the final event—a display of marksmanship of bow and arrow—they'd need to hurry.

Harp huffed up to them, limping heavier.

"Take my shoulder," Brant said.

The boy, younger by two years than the others, nodded his thanks, leaning his weight on Brant.

Ahead, Marron all but danced with his excitement. The family of the winner would be on the dais for the crowning. Marron had been chattering about meeting the Huntress over the past two days as his uncle rose in the rankings.

They took off again for the Grove.

Harp moved faster now. "You'll be on the dais one of these years, Brant. 'Course, after you cross fourteen." Brant knew the younger boy held his hunting skills in esteem, mostly because Brant let him come along on a few forays.

Few extended such invitations to the hobbled boy. His manner was odd, and whatever ailment had left him with a shrunken leg at birth had also sapped his strength. He was thin-boned and hawkish of features. And in a realm where swiftness of foot and skill with spear and arrow were valued, few found him a desired companion.

But Brant also knew that behind that weakened body hid a keen mind and a generous heart. There was a reason the boy had advanced two years in schooling. Sometimes Brant noted how his eyes seemed lost in some other place, gone off to somewhere deep in his mind. And a part of Brant envied his escape.

"You'll definitely be Hunter of the Way one day. Surely-*girly*," Harp said. It was one of his strange habits: rhyming when he was excited. Several of the boys taunted him about it, but Brant knew his friend couldn't help it.

"Your father was crowned, wasn't he?" Harp continued, rushing and gasping. "Twice, right?"

Brant felt a sharp pain, puncturing his joy and draining it away. It had only been a little over a year, and the loss of his father still tore like a fresh wound. He fought back the melancholy that filled so many of his days and even more of his nights. He wouldn't let it ruin *this* day. It was too bright for dark thoughts. Still, a shadow followed him. It felt like dread.

Ahead, Marron ran faster when the murmur of the crowd flowed to them, sounding like the great rustling of dry leaves. "I'll save a spot!"

Fleeing his dark thoughts, Brant hurried after his friend, almost tripping Harp. "Sorry," he mumbled.

They rounded a bend in the path, and the Grove opened ahead. It was a great natural hollow in the forest, ringed by ancient pompbonga-kee trees. They were the great sentinels of the cloud forest and grew no place else in all the Nine Lands. Their wood was iron strong but light as the mists that crept through the cloud forest. It was from such wood that all the keels and ribbing for Myrillia's flippercraft were hewn, enriching the realm.

The nine mighty trees that circled the hollow were known as the Graces. It was said they were planted by the Huntress herself when she chose to build her castillion here at the edge of the hollow, in the bower of the most ancient of all the forest's trees, a great behemoth that was already ancient when she settled this realm.

Brant led Harp out into the edge of the Grove. The giant pompbonga-kee trees circled the hollow, their branches forming a wreath of green over the natural amphitheater. In the center, it was open to the sky. The midday sun blazed down upon the center of the hollow, turning the green meadow below into an emerald sea.

Spreading up the slopes were crowds of onlookers, many with blankets spread, enjoying the spring warmth as much as the games. Down farther, ringing the center field, the crowd was packed shoulder to shoulder. Out here at the fringes, many had climbed into the branches of the Graces, where balconies and stands had been built long ago. Drapes of spring flowers decorated the levels and twined up the stair railings.

Brant craned upward. It seemed not a seat was open.

"The whole world must be here," Harp whispered, breathless with the excitement.

A low roar swelled around them. Down below, flags fluttered, marking clans and families.

"Over here!" Marron called to them off to the left, waving an arm. "Hurry! My brother has a free bench held up here!" He pointed to the stairs that led up to into one of the Graces.

Brant ran toward him.

Farther ahead, his eye caught upon the castillion of the Huntress, perched and tiered in the tenth and greatest of the pompbonga-kees. It rose at the easternmost edge, where the rising sun would first touch its green crown. What once had been crafted and constructed within the branches had long been swallowed as the ancient tree continued to grow. The castillion was no longer *built* in the tree but was *part* of the tree. It was a sight that humbled any eye that fell upon it, proof of the power of root and leaf, of the force of loam.

There was no more fitting home for the god of their realm.

Brant searched the high balcony of the castillion. The Huntress usually watched the games from such a vantage. But presently it appeared empty. Maybe she would appear when the competition began.

Brant reached Marron with Harp in hobbled tow.

"How . . . how high must we climb?" the younger boy asked, plainly winded.

Marron pointed his arm straight up, earning a groan from Harp. "Don't fret. Brant and I'll carry your bony arse to the top if we have to. Let's go!"

Marron was in exceptionally good cheer. He often had little patience for Harp, but this day, nothing could squelch his fine spirit. He led them toward the stairs at the base of the towering pompbonga-kee.

As Brant followed, he noted a cloaked shadowknight by the foot of the steps. She was inked in darkness, half-melded into the shadows beneath the giant tree. She must be one of the Huntress's own knights, come to view the games.

Brant searched around the curve of the hollow. Another knight stood at the base of the next tree. Had there been another at the tree behind them? He glanced back. It would've been easy to miss someone hiding in the deeper shadows.

Straightening forward, he almost ran into the chest of the knight. The woman had flowed so silently out of the shadows.

"Pardon me, ser," he said shyly, starting to step around.

She blocked him. "You are the boy named Brant, are you not?"

To find his name uttered by the likes of a shadowknight unnerved him. He lost his tongue.

"Yes-*mess,*" Harp rhymed, eyes huge on the knight. "He is, ser."

An arm smoked out of the darkness and gripped Brant's shoulder. "The school said you were headed here. We were sent to fetch you."

"Why?" he asked, finally freeing his tongue. "I—I've done nothing wrong."

"Never said you did. And I can't say why you've been summoned. Only that you have been."

"Summoned by who?"

"By the Huntress herself."

Brant was drawn away with the knight. His two friends gaped after him. Harp looked on with awe, while Marron wore an expression more confused.

Shock silenced Brant all the way around the curve of the hollow. The knight gathered another two of her cloaked brethren, falling into step with him.

Brant heard them mutter behind him.

"What does she want with the boy?" one asked.

"Who can say? Of late, there's no predicting her mood. Even her Hands have been whispering of her irritable dispositions and strange, prolonged silences."

"What's so strange?" the other said with a snort. "Sounds no different than my wife."

They reached the ancient tree and passed through an arched opening between massive roots. Sunlight vanished. The knights melted into the darkness on the stair, fading into whispering shapes. But once they passed up to the first level, sunlight returned, dappled and in a thousand shades of green leaf. The rising levels from here seemed to have grown out of the wood itself: stacks of balconies, hollowed rooms, snaking staircases that wound through the open air or delved deep through the outer layers of the trunk. It was hard to separate what hand had hewn and nature had grown.

And none more so than the High Wing.

Here in the canopy of the very world, the crown of the castillion appeared like a carved flower atop the tree, all surrounded by a wide terrace, whose polished planks of pompbonga-kee glowed with a molten warmth. A delicate railing framed the balcony, sprouting leaf and tendril, while the High Wing itself had been sculpted into curves and archways, appearing more like petals. Here straight lines had given way to more natural arcs. Even the rooms and halls bulged out of the central trunk as though they were born of the wood itself. Only when very close could the lines between planks be seen.

Brant traced a finger along one as they climbed the last stair to the upper terrace. It reminded him of the curve of a flippercraft's bow. Was it from this example that the ancient wrights had learned to craft the mighty airships of Myrillia? Brant intended to ask Master Sheershym, the chronicler of Saysh Mal.

When at last they reached the great terrace, Brant caught a glimpse of the Grove below. Flags fluttered and cheers rose. The games had begun. But Brant had all but forgotten them.

"This way," the knight ordered.

Brant was led through a great carved archway into the High Wing proper. Even after they crossed the threshold, the sunlight seemed to follow them, flowing through windows and reflecting off mirror and crystal. The air almost danced with the spring light. Brant inhaled the spiced air, heady with the natural oils of the pompbonga-kee.

Despite the beauty and wonder of it all, Brant's legs had begun to tremble. He was not worthy. He grew acutely aware of his poor attire: leggings patched at the knees, a loose jerkin that was missing two hooks. Even his soft boots, gifts from his father two years ago, were scuffed to a dull brown. He combed fingers through his hair, working away some old knots. At least he had bathed two days ago.

He lost track of the turns through the High Wing.

Suddenly he found himself before a set of tall doors, carved like a single leaf of the pompbonga-kee, but split down the middle in an S-shaped curve, following a vein in the leaf.

The knight pulled a twined rope of leather and a bell rang beyond the door. Moments later, a thin woman, wearing an ankle-length white dress sashed at the waist, pushed open one leaf of the door. Her eyes, pinched at the corners, glanced over them, then she bowed them inside. Only Brant and the lone knight, the woman, stepped through.

"Matron Dreyd," the knight said. "We've come with the boy your mistress asked us to bring."

"Thank you, Ser Knight. The mistress will be pleased."

The matron's words were spoken staidly, as if she doubted them herself. Brant noted how she glanced out the door as she closed the way, almost as if she weighed fleeing through it and away.

Still, she turned and offered a wan smile of welcome.

The chamber here was lit by an arched window to the sky. It shone down upon the floor, where the graining was so fine that Brant could not discern the individual planks. Smaller archways branched off the hall, some open, others sealed.

"My mistress has instructed that she would like the boy to join her in the Heartroom."

"Truly?" the knight said, unable to mask her surprise.

A nod answered her.

The knight stepped back. She placed a palm on Brant's back and gently pushed him. "Go. Do not keep the Huntress waiting."

Brant tripped a step, then followed his new guide, Matron Dreyd. She led him straight down the hall to another set of doors, a smaller version of the ones through which they had entered. The matron led him through those and deeper again down a narrower hall. Here lamps flickered on wall hooks as the sunlight was left behind. The spicy scent of tree oil grew stronger.

Brant realized they must be within the very trunk itself.

Gooseflesh prickled his skin.

They continued to the end . . . where a single plain door stood closed.

Matron Dreyd knocked softly. “Mistress, I have the boy named Brant.”

Silence answered her.

The matron glanced back to Brant, then back to the door. She lifted her arm to knock again—then words whispered through.

“Send him in. Alone.”

The matron nodded, though her mistress plainly could not see her assent. She stepped back and motioned Brant to the door. “Go inside.”

Brant took a deep breath, then reached for the latch.

Fingers gripped his shoulder, stopping him.

“Do not upset her.”

Brant glanced up to her. She clasped a hand over her mouth as if surprised the words had escaped her. His shoulder was released, and he was pushed forward.

Hands in full tremble now, Brant tried the latch, found it unlocked, and creaked the door open. A slightly foul smell wormed through the spiced oil.

Brant glanced again to the matron. He was shooed inside, but the matron's words were stuck in his head. *Do not upset her.*

He had no choice. He stepped into the room.

The space was small, almost cozy, oval-shaped, with a low-domed roof and a hearth on the far side that glowed with red embers, the flames long died away. Still, it was the only light in the room. The glow washed over the walls and roof, bathing it in dark crimson. Brant noted the graining, all whorls and rings. This was no planked construction, but a chamber hewn from the tree itself.

The Heartroom.

On the far side, a chair rested before the hearth, alongside a small table. A single figure sat there.

Brant froze at the threshold.

"Do not fear, Brant, son of Rylland. Come forward."

The words were spoken with soft assurance, sweetly melodic, though with a deep trace of melancholy. It spoke to the sorrow in his own heart.

He crept forward, unsure if he should bow or scrape a knee. He circled wide, edging around the oval room, attempting to keep as much distance between him and the speaker.

The Huntress of Saysh Mal.

One of the Hundred gods of Myrillia.

She sat, head bowed, brow resting on her folded hands, elbows on either arm of her chair, a posture of forlorn concentration. She was dressed in green leathers and white silk, a simple hunter's cut. As he stepped into view, she lifted her head. Eyes glowed at him, rich in Grace. Even her skin seemed to shine with a waxen sheen.

He sagged to his knees.

A cascade of curls, as dark as shadow, framed her dark skin. Full lips formed the ghost of a smile, like a memory of innocence. Brant felt himself stir, deeper than his loins.

"I knew your father," she said, glancing away, releasing him. She stared into the dying embers. "He was a great hunter."

Brant stared at the floor, unable to speak.

"I'm sure you still miss him."

Grief and pride freed his voice to a quiet squeak. "Yes, mistress, with all my heart."

"Just so. He sifted many great treasures out of our sea here. A pelt of a balelion. The head of a manticrye. The antlered rack of the rare teppin-ra. Did you know teppin-ra comes from ancient Littick? *Tepp Irya*. Meaning *fierce buck*."

"No, mistress."

"So much forgotten . . ." She sighed. She remained silent for several breaths. Long enough for Brant to peek up.

Her gaze had shifted to the table at her side. A single object rested there, draped in black sailcloth, which appeared damp as it reflected the ember's glow.

"But this was the greatest treasure your father ever attended."

Curiosity drew Brant straighter.

She reached to the heavy cloth and tugged it free. Brant

caught again the waft of stench. Only now did he recognize it. *Black bile.*

Dread flared in his chest.

In the ember-light, the skull glowed like blood.

At his throat, a fire exploded. Gasping, he clutched at the stone, the bit of rock that had been rolled to his toes by the dying rogue. The same fire that had consumed the trespassing god had come to claim him. Brant tore at his jerkin, ripping hooks.

The Huntress seemed oblivious, focused on the skull.

"He brought this to me . . . not knowing . . . surely not knowing."

Brant cried out, digging for the stone. He had known his father had collected the skull after the god's body burnt. He had picked it free of the ashes with the tip of an arrow through an eye socket. He had wrapped it in his own cloak. Brant had not known what had become of it. Of course, his father would have brought word here, of such a trespass by a rogue god. But afterward, Brant assumed the foul thing had eventually been destroyed or laid to rest in some manner. All but forgotten.

The only remnant of the frightening adventure was the small black rock, no bigger than the end of his thumb. His father had let him keep it so long as he swore to tell no one of it. The stone was a secret bond between father and son.

And now the stone meant to burn him to ash.

The Huntress finally seemed to note his writhing. At some point, he had collapsed to the floor. She rose to her feet.

"Do you hear its call, too?" She drifted toward him. "Poor boy. It can't be resisted. I try to stay away, to keep it steeped in the blackest of biles, but still it calls. Day and night. And now I hear words . . . but I can't quite understand . . . not yet. Only that somewhere it asked for you."

Brant gasped out, "Help me . . ."

She knelt next to him, her face strangely calm as he burnt. "I wish I could."

She reached out and touched his cheek. Where her fingers touched, a cooling balm pushed back the searing agony. But the pain had to go somewhere.

The Huntress screamed.

Brant forgot the remaining burn. He struggled to roll away from her touch. He could not let her come to harm. But her fingers dragged down into his cheek and, nails scraping, her hand grabbed his throat. His skin flamed with her touch, more fiery than even the stone. Her eyes fixed upon him. The Grace within her flared brighter.

"No . . . you must not be here. You must go." These words were spoken with a sudden intensity, shedding the strange malaise that had haunted her earlier words. She threw him aside by the neck. He smelled his burning flesh. Then the stone flared anew at his chest with its own flaming agony.

He writhed on the floor.

She stumbled to the table and ripped the bile-encrusted cloth back over the skull. The flames from the stone immediately vanished. He pawed at his chest, expecting crisped skin and burnt bone. But all he found was smooth skin. There was not even a residual warmth.

Not so his throat.

Where she had throttled him, his skin blistered and weeped.

The Huntress stood by the table, trembling from head to toe.

A pounding erupted from the door. "Mistress!"

Brant recognized the shadowknight who had led him here. They must have all heard the god shriek.

"Attend me! Now!" she barked out.

Brant remained on his knees on the floor.

The Huntress turned to him as the door burst open and a flow of shadows swept into the room, shredding into individual knights. Brant kept his focus on his god. He watched the flare of Grace subside in her eyes.

But before it was gone completely, she shoved an arm toward him. "Take him, chain him, get him out of my land by nightfall."

Brant's mind refused to make sense of her words.

Her eyes bore upon him, fading with Grace, full of sorrow and certainty. "I banish him."

A world and a lifetime away, Brant wept in a chair. He could not stop the tears. He had told no one of his full story, his full shame, until this moment.

Tylar came forward and placed a hand on his shoulder.

Rogger had sheathed his dagger. "You and your father witnessed the rogue's trespass and demise?"

Brant nodded.

The bearded man shared a studied glance with the regent.

Tylar tilted up Brant's chin to examine the scar. "And you've been marked by a god, too," he mumbled and stepped back.

The regent's hand drifted to his shadowcloak.

Brant knew that beneath that blessed cloth Tylar bore the black handprint of a god, pressed into his chest by Meeryn of the Summering Isles, branding him a godslayer. He met the regent's eye, sensing some bond between them—for better or worse.

"May I see this burning talisman of yours?" Tylar asked. "This stone."

Brant reached up and tugged the black stone free. Tylar leaned down and reached for it.

"Take care with that," Rogger warned.

The tall stranger edged closer, one hand on the serpent-headed pommel of his sword.

Tylar picked up the stone between two fingers. Nothing happened. He turned it around, examining all the surfaces. "Appears like a shard of rock, rough-hewn. I sense no great power here."

"Let me see."

Rogger shouldered up and bent down.

Tylar stepped back and to the black-cloaked stranger. "Did the Wyr mention anything about a black stone associated with the skull?"

"No," the other intoned dourly.

"Those Wyr-lords do like to keep their secrets." Rogger straightened, a fist resting on one hip. "But there must be a connection. I find it awful fateful that this boy ends up trapped here with us. The skull and the stone brought together again."

"But is that a boon or a curse?" Tylar asked. "If the Huntress exiled him, banishing him away, perhaps she thought it best to keep them as far apart as possible. The way we keep Dart and the sword separated."

"I don't think we can place too much weight on the Huntress's word. It sounds like the seersong had already sapped her in some way."

Brant finally found his voice. "Is it true? The rogue's skull? The one possessed by the Huntress is here? How . . . ?"

Tylar nodded to his companion, permitting him to speak. "He should know."

Rogger sighed and related his own experience in Saysh Mal. His description of the state of affairs in Brant's former home helped push back his grief, replacing it with anger and horror. Over the four years he had been here in the First Land, ruin had settled over the cloud forest and its denizens.

All because of a cursed skull.

One Brant's father had carried into the land.

"I would see this skull destroyed," he said.

"Well, that's the slippery part," Rogger said. "We left it in a rather precarious situation. It's down there with those daemon knights that you so kindly rooted out for us."

Brant stood up, almost bumping the regent. "We must get it free from there!"

"We intend to," Tylar said. "And after your tale, I think it's even more important that we do so immediately."

"Then you'll destroy it?" Brant asked. There could be no question that it was riddled with black Grace.

The two men's eyes glanced to the third, the tall stranger.

"It seems we still need the skull for a bit of bartering."

"What?"

Tylar headed for the door. "We have no time to explain."

"I will go with you!" Brant followed.

Tylar held out a hand. "No. You are safe here."

"Nowhere's safe this night."

Rogger nodded. "The boy's right there. And somehow he and his rock are tied to this skull's story. It's time we completed the tale."

Tylar hesitated.

"Like you said," Rogger argued. "Bringing them together is either a curse or a boon. If it's a curse, then better it happen deep under Tashijan than up here. If it's a boon, then the sooner we join the two the better." He punctuated it with a shrug. "Besides, he can carry an extra torch. And right now, stone or not, that's fine with me."

The regent's jaw muscles tightened. "So be it." He forced the words out.

Brant was relieved. He would have followed them if necessary.

Others were not so certain. The back door to the room burst open and two large forms tumbled into the room.

"No, Master Brant!" Malthumalbaen shouted. "You can't go alone. We'll come with you!"

Tylar shared an irritated glance with his bearded friend.

"It seems someone's been listening at our door," Rogger said.

"Not listening," Dralmarfillneer said. "That weren't so. Our mammers gave us big ears. That's all."

"So I see. Too bad she didn't gift you with the brains to match."

Brant shook his head at the two giants. "Someone needs to watch the cubbies." He dared not leave them unguarded with Liannora hovering about.

"One set of eyes is enough," Mal said. "I'll go and Dral can stay with them."

"Shine my arse. The bloody nippers like you better."

"We'll pound for it, then."

The two giants agreed, stepped back, and swung out with their fists, smashing them against the other. Malthumalbaen stumbled back a step. Dral kept his footing and turned triumphantly.

"Mal will stay."

With the matter settled, the regent led them out into the hall—where a crowd had gathered, held back by the gray-cloaked woman's sword. It seemed Sten had spread the word of the regent's visitation. Liannora, Ryndia, and Khar stood amid a few of the captain's guards.

"Clear the way," Tylar demanded.

"Where are you taking a Hand of Oldenbrook?" Sten replied. "I have the right to inquire."

Liannora stood at his shoulder. Brant suspected the inquiry and challenge truly arose from her.

"We have matters to attend below concerning the security

of Tashijan. Brant has been in the cellars and his knowledge may be of assistance."

Sten glanced between Brant and the regent. "This is the first I've heard of such matters."

"And the last." Tylar motioned for the others to head for the stairs.

Sten stumbled forward, shoved surreptitiously from behind by Liannora. "Wait!" he called. "If a Hand of Oldenbrook is to be taken from our halls, I must accompany him. The security of the retinue was placed in my charge by Lord Jessup himself. I will not shirk it, nor let it be taken from me."

Tylar turned, face darkening, a fist forming.

Rogger stepped forward. "What's another torch? Never hurt to have another sword, too."

"We've wasted enough time here," the tall stranger grumbled. "We've learned what we needed. Let us be off."

The regent nodded. "You're right, Krevan. Come if you may, Captain—but you'll obey every word from here."

Sten bowed, and Liannora smiled behind his back.

As a group, they headed toward the stairs. Brant studied the cloaked stranger's back. *Krevan.* He now understood why an ash-faced member of the Black Flaggers had guarded their door.

Here was Krevan the Merciless, the leader of that black guild.

Brant also remembered the regent's bearded friend mentioning some matter of bartering with the skull. With the Black Flaggers here, it could only mean some treachery or dark design.

Though he could not fathom what that might be, Brant knew one thing with steel certainty. No matter what the others planned, Brant would destroy the skull. Since the morning the flaming rogue had stumbled into his life, all had come to ruin.

This night, it would end.

12

A FIRE IN THE CELLAR

TYLAR HEARD THE SHOUTING FROM DOWN THE HALL. HE HAD left the others at the landing. Ahead lay the fieldroom, where Warden Fields had set up a war council and gathered all the heads of Tashijan. The door stood ajar. Knights crowded the hall. Pages paced, ready to relay messages and commands to the various posts.

Kathryn's voice reached him. "You're all being stone-headed! The skull must be fetched out of the cellars!"

Tylar hurried forward. While he had questioned the boy Brant, he had sent Kathryn ahead to meet with Argent, to lay the foundation for their request. She was supposed to have softened him by the time Tylar arrived.

Plainly that was not the case.

"Why didn't you tell me about this skull when it was first brought here?" Argent boomed. "Such a darkly Graced item threatens all of us!"

Tylar reached the door and stopped at the threshold. Two knights drifted out of alcoves to either side, ready to hold him off, but when they spotted his bared face, they recognized him and hesitated.

Inside, Kathryn stepped to the scarred table that stretched the length of the room. It was across this same board that countless strategies had been construed and treaties signed, sometimes in blood. Around the room rose the ancient Stacks, massive scaffolding and shelves, buttressed by ladders, where maps of all the Nine Lands were stored, going back millennia, some said even before the Sundering. A more current chart of Tashijan had been tacked to the broad table with daggers. Additional rolled sheaves littered the top, all but forgotten during the heated exchange.

Kathryn continued. "We didn't understand the full power of the skull until Master Rothkild examined it and discovered the cursed Grace locked within its bones." She leaned on the table, palms down. "Either way, now is not the time to cast blame. Best we retrieve the skull before the force below becomes entrenched or discovers such a powerful talisman within their grasp."

Argent scowled at her. "Who would lead such a sortie?"

Tylar stepped across the threshold. "I would."

All eyes turned to him.

"I will take a small force below, armed with sword and flame. We'll assault Master Rothkild's study and be out in half a bell."

Argent straightened, his one eye narrowing.

Beyond him, the fieldroom overlooked the tourney fields at the foot of Stormwatch, but for now the great windows were shuttered tight against the blizzard, except for one narrow pane. Movement beyond revealed a knight under a heavy cloak, posted on the small balcony to maintain a watch on the whirling storm that trapped them here.

To either side, the innermost circle of Tashijan lined the table: knights of the highest station, including Swordmaster Yuril, heads of house and livery, like Keeper Ryngold, and several members of the Council of Masters, the last bolstered by the wide girth of Hesharian.

Argent finally spoke. "We thank you for your offer, regent, but surely one of your stature should best be kept with our other guests high in the tower, where you can be protected. Such a raid, if permitted, would best be carried out by knights of the Order."

"As I recall, I was invited here to be so included in said Order, to be granted cloak and sword. Or was the offer merely feigned?"

The warden's lips thinned to sharp, unforgiving lines.

"Also," Tylar continued, "we know the skull, tainted by seersong, can twist Grace to its will. I've already proven my resistance to its corruption, so who better to lead?"

Kathryn cast Tylar a withering look. She had not wanted to

further split their towers with petty bickering. And here they were, already baring teeth like dogs. While Tylar recognized the wisdom in her cause, Argent seemed to draw the bile from him like no other. And from the flint in the other's eye, there was little hope of a peaceful settlement here.

The impasse was broken by a most unexpected ally.

A figure stepped out of the shadow of Hesharian's moon. "I believe the regent speaks wisely, and his design should be considered." It was the elderly visitor from Ghazal.

Argent swung toward him.

But the aged figure seemed unfazed, his eyes perhaps too clouded to note the fire in the warden's. Tylar guessed the fortitude arose more from a steely disinterest in the warden.

Ignoring even a pinch on his sleeve by Master Hesharian, he continued, "Such a talisman, removed from below, may serve to protect us. Dark Grace is woven tightly around us—from the storm without and the daemons below. If we masters could find a way to tap in to the seersong, perhaps we could forge a weapon against the forces that gather. To turn their Grace against them."

A calculating glint of understanding reflected in Argent's eye. "Get them to dance to our song."

Hesharian chimed in, now that he risked nothing by taking a position. "Wise all around. It is good fortune that I had summoned Master Orquell to attend here."

The ancient mage seemed little moved. He kept his focus on the warden. "And with such a ward against black Grace in our hands, who knows what other black acts might be reversed?"

Argent met the other's gaze. Tylar knew the Ghazalian master had been summoned in an attempt to break the dark spell that had frozen Argent's swordsworn brother to stone. Here the master offered one more argument for securing the skull, one with a more personal stake for the warden.

Tylar knew the matter was settled before the warden turned back to him.

"You believe you can get below and back again with the skull?" Argent asked.

"If we are delayed no longer."

Argent's eye narrowed. "I'll send you with enough knights

to guard the door below, to keep a fire blazing. You'll have a single bell. Longer than that, we'll know you're corrupted. The way will be sealed."

It was as much of a concession as Tylar could hope for from the warden. He stared at Argent in his one eye and nodded.

Kathryn turned from the table. Tylar was the only one to note her relieved sigh. She followed him back to the door and out.

Behind them, Argent barked orders, staging his end of the assault.

They would have only a moment of privacy.

Kathryn stopped him halfway toward the stair. "Be careful. I don't trust that new master."

He nodded. "We'll have to worry about that after I retrieve the skull."

In a lower voice, she asked, "What of the boy? Was he able to cast any light upon the skull's origin?"

"More than you could imagine." He didn't have time to go into his story at length, and he feared speaking of the boy's black stone, gifted to him by the very god whose skull lay below. "He's coming with us."

Thinking upon it, he was glad he had not been more stubborn about permitting him to come. Best to bring the skull and stone together well out of sight of that strange master.

Kathryn looked on inquiringly, but trusted him enough not to press. He squeezed her arm. "I must go."

For a moment, their eyes met. A flicker of something conflicted flashed across her features. But before he could pin it down, it vanished, replaced with worry and the weight of their situation.

"Come back," she said.

He let go of her arm. "I will."

He set off, hoping it was a promise he could keep.

Brant shifted back as the heavy iron bar was lifted from the gate. It was the last of three. The wyrmwood gate itself was constructed of massive planks, woven like cloth under an alchemy of Grace and banded in more iron. Rogger had explained its history, how it was placed at the threshold to the Masterlevels shortly after the founding of Tashijan.

"Some said to keep any wild Grace from escaping the master's subterranean dungeons . . . others because the knights had not truly trusted those first masters, men who dabbled with the Grace of gods. The knights were ready to bottle them up if necessary. And maybe they weren't half wrong. Look where we are now."

But all had gone silent by the time the last bar was shoved free.

Everyone held their breath.

Giant braziers flanked both sides, roaring with fire. Torches as thick around as Dralmarfillneer's thigh encircled the walls and continued down the tall halls, all the way to the great doors that led from Stormwatch into the outer bailey.

Brant wiped his brow on his sleeve. The very air steamed from the many flames. But he did not complain.

"Ready your torches," Tylar said.

They each carried an oiled brand. Rogger also had a lantern hanging at his hip, flame flickered low. The giant had a cask of the oil under one arm, ready to be cracked opened, spilled, and set to flame.

One by one, they lit their torches from the brazier.

Tylar nodded to two knights at the chained mechanism for the gate. The pair began hauling on the wheels, drawing up the barrier. Another knight ran forward and cast a lantern through the widening opening, splashing oil and fire down the mouth of the steps. They dared not risk an ambush outside the gate.

Brant hunkered down and searched the lower stairs. The way appeared empty, free of any black *ghawls*.

"We stay together," Tylar said. "No more than an arm's length apart. Understood?"

Nods all around.

The regent led the way, with Rogger a step behind him, and Sten flanking his other side. Brant went next. He had two guards: the dour-faced Dralmarfillneer and the woman in black ash, the Flagger whose name Brant learned was Calla. Or was it *Carra*? His heart had been pounding too hard to truly note it.

Behind them trailed Krevan. The large man stood nearly as tall as the giant, though not as bulky. Despite his misgivings about the man's trade, Brant was still happy to have him at his back.

They headed down the stairs, skirting the fading flames from the broken lantern. As they continued, wending round and round, Brant risked a glance behind him. The fires above were only a distant glow.

Brant had never considered himself a coward, but only one certainty kept him descending into the deepening darkness. He clutched the stone at his throat. It lay as cold as granite against his heated skin. No matter the risk, he would find the end of this path that started with this stone.

"Where are these daemons already?" Rogger grumbled.

Sten glanced to the smaller man with a frown. Brant shared the captain's distaste. It was like whistling among gravestones. There was no telling what such sentiment might conjure.

They spiraled farther down in silence. Brant peered past Tylar, who still led them by two steps. The blackness seemed to stir away from his flames. It was as if the darkness had turned to oil and feared to be ignited.

But nothing worse arose.

"Here is the level of Gerrod's study," Tylar said, stopping at the next landing.

They all closed ranks a bit tighter.

"What's that smell?"

Brant sniffed. But he stood too near the bearded man. He smelled unwashed and ripe. Then a skittering sound reached his ears. It rose from below. He remembered the rustle when he had been with the wyld tracker and Dart. This was something different.

"Back!" Tylar ordered, low and urgent. "Against the walls."

His warning came not a moment too soon. Brant flattened against the stone as darkness flowed out from below, swallowing the gray stairs.

"Rats," Rogger said with disgust.

A horde burst up to them, jammed together, climbing over one another. They whisked through the group like so many stones in a flash flood. One rat leaped, landed on the lip of Brant's boot, and bounced to the next step and away. As suddenly as they had arrived, they were gone again, streaming up the stairs.

Brant shivered all over. Not so much at the number of rats as their silence. Not a single squeak. Only the scrape of tiny, frantic claws on rock. Brant knew the sound would haunt his nights—that is, if he lived to have more nights.

"Those rats can't seem to find a safe place to roost this night," Rogger said, glancing meaningfully at Tylar.

"We'll heed their instinct this time," the regent answered. "Especially as there's no reason to traipse deeper."

"Thank the silent aether for that," the man answered.

Tylar lifted his torch toward the passage that led off the landing. "This way. Keep alert. By now they must know we're down here."

Brant followed, but he stared down the spiraling stairs one more time. *Was that the message from the rats? That something stirred once again in the bowels beneath Tashijan?*

He hurried after the others.

Dral hunched next to him, all but filling the passageway. Calla—*or Carra*—was forced back with her leader.

"How much longer?" Dral whispered, sounding like boulders rubbing together. "Those rats reminded me that I didn't get to finish my dinny. Did you see how plump some of them buggers was? I like them roasted with their own giblets. Mal says—"

"Dral," Brant finally barked out louder than he intended, earning a glance back from Tylar.

"Apologies, Master Brant. It were just that my belly was growling and I thought—"

He turned a hard glance to the large man.

The giant slowly closed his mouth.

Brant felt a tad shamed at his outburst. He read the edgy twitch to Dral's eye. Despite his size and strength, he was plainly rattled, too. And the cramped quarters of the passage only squeezed his fears closer to his heart, loosening a nervous tongue.

He touched the giant's hand, acknowledging both his forgiveness and his own apology.

At last, Tylar halted before an arched doorway. "Here we are."

"I got it," Rogger said, slipping a large iron key from a pocket. "Not that I really need this."

He touched the door—and it creaked open on its own.

Unlatched.

Even Brant knew this was not good.

Rogger backed away.

"Stay here," Tylar said. "But be ready."

The regent edged the door open with a toe and thrust his torch through the gap. Brant cringed as Tylar followed the flames into the room. The regent's torchlight reflected off a pair of iron braziers at the back of the room. They cast monstrous shadows on the back wall. Tylar's movement set them to dancing.

Brant had a horrible feeling about what was to come.

Tylar crossed to another door in the back wall, some inner chamber, the alchemist's study. It stood ajar. The regent approached, kicked the door wider, and stepped to the threshold.

He paused for a moment, his back to all of them.

"Tylar?" Rogger whispered.

The regent swung around, his cloak billowing out. He rushed to the door. "Gone," he said, his voice stiff and angry. "We're too late. Only by moments, I suspect."

He waved them back to the stairs. "We must get out of here."

They retreated, in reverse order as before, mostly as the giant blocked Tylar from passing. Krevan led them back to the stairs.

Still, Brant could not escape that horrible feeling he had had only a breath ago. It remained with him as much as the stink off Rogger. But it grew worse with every step. He felt something building. The very air seemed to suddenly weigh more. Each breath took effort.

Somewhere on the back of his tongue he tasted a hint of spiced oil, a whisper of scent, more memory than real, of pompbonga-kee.

Oh, no . . .

Dral cleared the passageway and reached the broader stairs. Brant stepped after him, glancing back to warn the regent.

Too late.

The torch tumbled from Brant's fingers. Both hands

grabbed for his throat. Fire ignited his chest, burning through his skin, turning bone to ash.

He fell to his knees.

Arms reached for him.

"Master Brant . . . ?" Dral asked, his voice mirroring everyone's confusion.

Except one.

"It's the stone," Rogger said. "Somewhere they've exposed the skull. Cleared the black bile."

Brant fell farther, catching himself with one hand on the steps. "It's near . . ." he gasped.

Then Tylar's face was in front of his. "Where?"

Brant sat back, bones burning. He lifted an arm, fighting the pained trembling of the effort. He pointed.

"Down," Rogger said.

"Can you lead us?" Tylar asked.

Arms lifted him, to his feet, to his toes. He shook to keep his heels to the stone. He nodded. "Down," he gasped. "Down . . ."

"Where the rats fled from," Rogger said.

Tylar descended with his torch held before him. The others followed. The giant supported the boy, whose face remained clenched in agony.

"Is this wise?" Rogger whispered.

"There's a chance the daemons don't fully grasp what they have yet. If we can reach them before they understand . . ."

Rogger nodded.

Tylar tightened his grip on the torch. "I could still smell them in there. We were only moments late. If we'd not dragged our heels . . ."

"Or let so many others know what we sought," Rogger added pointedly. "I know Kathryn meant well. But I find it strange that the *ghawls* should discover the skull shortly after you made your plea in the fieldroom."

Tylar pictured Master Orquell. Even beyond the man's clouded eyes, Tylar had noted the hunger shining through. Had word somehow reached Castellan Mirra down here? Or was it pure happenstance? Suspicion had already weakened

Tashijan, stoked by Mirra's manipulations. So which path was the more dangerous: to be too trusting or not enough?

A moan arose behind them.

"Left . . . to the left . . ." Brant choked out.

Out of the darkness, torchlight revealed another landing. The passageway headed the correct direction.

Tylar led the way and lifted his torch toward the passage. The flickering glow revealed only darkness and sealed doors. But that did not mean the shadows did not hide a legion.

"Close . . ." Brant confirmed it with a moan. He was now carried like a babe on the hip of the giant. One hand clawed tight to his throat.

Tylar turned to Rogger and held out his free hand. "Your lantern."

The thief unhooked the bronze-and-glass lamp from his belt and passed it to him. Tylar thumbed the flame higher, then tossed the lantern in a high arc.

Glass shattered and flames spat with the angry hiss of a cat.

Darkness shredded and swirled away like burning ash. A bit of cloak caught flame and whisked down the hallway. A keening wail fled with it, setting all his hairs on end.

The daemon knights were here, buried in the darkness.

"Keep your torches up!" he ordered and entered the hall.

The firelight pushed back the shadows and anything hidden within. They gave chase, but Tylar did not forgo caution. If he had to burn through the bowels, he would have that skull.

He headed deeper into the level as it branched. Brant pointed the way. Passing a sealed room, the boy gasped. His hand raised, palsied and weak, pointing toward the door. Agony stole the boy's words.

Tylar tried the latch. Locked.

Rogger passed him his torch, then slipped to a knee and worked with a thin dagger. A *click* of release sounded. He stood and took back his torch.

"The cask," Tylar said. He would take no chances.

The giant passed him the small oil barrel he'd been carrying. It trailed a twist of soaked cloth. Rogger lit it with his flaming brand, then rested a hand on the latch.

Tylar nodded.

Rogger cracked the door open, and Tylar rolled the barrel through the gap. He joined Rogger and pulled the door closed, together bracing it shut. The small whooshing *boom* sounded. Flames lapped under the sill, then retreated.

Tylar shoved the door open, expecting to find a nest of burning knights. And though the oil had lit tapestries and flames chased across chairs and tables, there were no knights.

A single figure stood in the middle of the fiery room, untouched by any flame. Tylar noted a mist of Grace surrounding her, one of water and air, a cocoon of protection.

"Castellan Mirra."

The brightness of the flaming room had no effect on her. She was not a creature of shadow like her legion. In truth, she looked little changed from when last Tylar had seen her. Same snow gray hair, secured plainly behind her ears, framing a serious face, but not necessarily a cold one. She wore a simple ankle-length gray shift, sashed with black at the waist, and soft black boots.

The only difference: She usually leaned on a cane.

Instead, she lifted the skull between her two hands. Blood dripped to the floor from sliced palms. She smiled warmly at him, welcoming.

Then she sang his name. "*Tylar . . .*"

And he was lost.

Through tears of fire, Brant saw Tylar fall to his knees at the threshold to the door. The torch tumbled from the regent's fingers and rolled across the floor. Krevan collapsed in a similar posture, dropping both sword and brand. The woman Flagger went to her leader's aid.

In the room, the old woman whispered in a lullaby voice, melodious and sweet. "I've been waiting so long for you."

Though Brant's bones burnt with fire, he still heard the lilt in her words. And he knew it for what it was.

Seersong.

Rogger grabbed Tylar by the back of his shadowcloak and yanked him back into the hall. "What are you doing?" he asked. Graceless, he seemed deaf to the melody.

"Come to me . . ." The old woman continued to sing.

Tylar fought Rogger. Krevan crawled.

Rogger threw an accusatory arm toward the old woman as if to scold her—but instead, a dagger flew from his fingertips.

She laughed.

The knife was swept aside like a leaf in a swirl of wind.

Doors opened up and down the hall, creaking ajar or banging wide. The daemons, cloaked in shadow, crept from their hiding places with a familiar rustle, filling the darkness, surrounding them on all sides.

All a trap.

And Brant had led them here.

"No . . ." he moaned.

Brant's single word broke Tylar's gaze upon the woman and back toward the others. Tylar tried to push away with one hand. "Go . . . run . . . !" he called to the others.

From the room, a hummed melody flowed again and drew Tylar's attention back. His head swung around, swayed by the Dark Grace of the song. To the side, Krevan continued his slow crawl toward the room, dragging the ash-faced woman with him.

Surprisingly it was Sten who finally seemed to comprehend the depth of the trap. He backed a step. "Away—we must be away. They are lost."

The captain drew his blade, while Dral hauled Brant up into his arms. The movement only stoked the fire inside him. He screamed, but the sound seared in his throat, unable to escape.

Unrelenting, Rogger attempted to haul Tylar, but the regent, lost to the song, swept out his sword and came within a hair of removing his friend's head. Rogger stumbled back, letting him go.

And still she sang, humming, encouraging, welcoming.

Tylar and Krevan were caught in its melody, like flitterbees in a web.

"We must flee!" Sten cried out.

Brant wanted nothing more than to escape—from here, from the cursed fires that flamed out of the stone. But he had not come this far for nothing. His road had led him to this ruin. He would not turn back.

No . . .

But no one heard him. Maybe he hadn't even said it aloud. Did he still have a tongue? He tried again, coughing feebly to clear the flames from his throat.

"No . . ."

Dral glanced down to him. "Master Brant?"

Thank the Grace-blessed oversized ears of the giant.

He could manage no more than a whisper, all but mute to the others. "Get . . . me . . . to her."

Brant did not have to explain whom he meant. Dral glanced into the room. The way stood open.

The giant searched down at Brant, studying his face. He had no strength for words, but Dral must have read the desperation shining through his pained tears. The giant turned to the door, hitched Brant higher under one arm, and charged forward. He knocked the regent aside and bulled across the threshold and through the smatter of oily flames.

The old woman's eyes widened at the attack. She lifted her arms but dared not let go of the skull. "Stop!" This was more a screech than a song.

Dral merely lowered his shoulder and lunged. Though Grace-born, the giant was not blessed now. The song held no sway. Brant felt a scintillation of power in the air, but Dral was no mere dagger on the wind. He was born of loam. Water and air were no match.

The giant was upon her in three strides. A massive fist shot out and smashed her square in her surprised face. She flew off her feet, blood spurting. The skull tumbled from her slippery palms and clattered to the floor. A tooth broke from it and skittered away.

Brant wriggled from the giant's arms. He fell to the floor beside the skull. Fire continued to consume him. He stretched with arms that were surely sculptures of boiled fat and ash.

"Stay back!" the woman cried.

Dral strode toward her.

Brant's hands closed upon the rogue's skull, where all his heartache had begun. It would now end. Let them both be consumed together.

As his skin touched bone, the fire inside him snuffed out. There was no relief, no cooling balm, simply gone. It left Brant hollowed out. He had been gutted by the fire, and like the charred husk of a burnt stable, he collapsed inward on himself.

And kept falling.

Tylar's wits returned like a fall of brass pinches, rattling and heavy in his head. Chaos surrounded him. He could make no sense of it for a breath. Beside him, Krevan rose from hands and knees, face screwed with equal confusion.

Tylar found the Godsword in his hand, but he had no memory of drawing it.

"The boy . . ." Rogger said at his shoulder, nodding his head to the room while keeping a torch high toward the passageway on the right. To the left, the Oldenbrook captain and Krevan's woman did the same. Tylar's torch lay at his toes, guttered and blown.

Beyond the torchlight, darkness stirred against the waning flames, drawing down upon them. They were being herded together, driven toward the room.

"Stop the boy!" Rogger said again, rattling those pinches in Tylar's head back to some semblance of order.

He lifted his sword.

Brant sat in the center of the floor. Past the boy's shoulder, the giant had Mirra by the throat, pressed against the far wall, dragging her off her toes. Tylar remembered enough.

Seersong.

He swung back to the boy. Brant stared toward him, but his face was empty. Yet, still something glowed behind the glass of his eye. Tylar knew it wasn't the boy.

Brant opened his mouth.

Tylar rushed forward, sword high. He would not be snared by the lilt of Dark Grace again.

Too late.

Words flowed out the boy's stretched mouth, echoing from deep within. "HELP THEM . . ."

It was no song. The agony behind the two words stayed Tylar's hand. Also there was something oddly familiar about the sibilant cast to the voice.

Though Brant's lips did not move and no breath seemed to escape his chest, words still flowed.

"HELP THEM . . .

LET THEM ALL BURN . . .

FREE THEM . . .

LET THEM ALL BURN . . .

FIND THEM . . .

LET THEM ALL BURN . . ."

It sounded almost like an argument. Even the cadence shifted back and forth, echoing up from some other world. Tylar paused with uncertainty.

But another had no such hesitation.

"What have you done!" Mirra wailed through the throttling hold of the giant. Her wild eyes found Tylar's, fired with terror. "Kill the boy . . . before he wakes them! Tylar, *kill the boy!*"

Refusing to be swayed again, Tylar backed a step.

"No!" the former castellan cried out. Her hand rose, bearing a small bone dagger. She drove the yellowed blade into the shoulder of the giant.

He bellowed, stumbling back and letting her free. But one arm swung out as he spun away. He cuffed her on the side of the head, felling her to the ground.

The giant caved to his knees. An arm lifted toward them, the same limb that had been wounded. From the impaled blade, a rotting spread out from his shoulder and down his arm. Flesh melted and putrefied to bone. Fingers fell away. The rot flowed to torso and neck. Half the giant's face sagged on the one side, sloughing from the skull beneath. He screamed, wafting out an exhalation of pus and virulence—then collapsed face forward.

The stone floor silenced his scream.

Forever.

To the side, the boy continued his litany, like the rote cadences that clerics cast to the aether.

"HELP THEM . . . HELP THEM . . .

LET THEM ALL BURN . . ."

Then Rogger was there. He scooped the skull from the boy with a wrap of cloth. It stank of black bile. He shoved it into an empty sling over his shoulder.

Brant collapsed backward, sprawling out on the stone floor.

Was he dead, too?

Then an arm trembled up. Fingers scribed a pattern of confusion.

"Get the boy!" Tylar ordered Krevan. "We must get free from here."

A moan escaped the boy as he was lifted up and tossed over the large man's shoulder.

But Brant was not the only one to stir.

To the side, Mirra shoved to the wall, sitting up. "No escape . . ." she shuddered out.

Tylar turned to the door.

The Oldenbrook captain and Krevan's woman backed away from the doorway and farther into the room. Beyond the threshold, darkness ate the light. The black *ghawls* had closed off their only escape.

Closer at hand, the captain's torch sputtered out with one last gasp of embers and ash. They were down to two flaming brands, one borne by Rogger, the other by the gray-cloaked woman.

Too few to hold back a horde.

Proving this, shadows stretched into the room and spread across the walls. They were forced back. Knights formed out of the gloom, shifting in an ever-flowing weave of malevolence. Mirra was swallowed up along the edge of them.

Rogger sidled next to Tylar. "We need a way through them. Mayhap a little help from that black dog of yours. Turn daemon upon daemon."

He nodded, sheathed his sword, and waved everyone behind him.

They needed some wedge here.

He grabbed his smallest finger of his left hand.

Agee wan clyy nee wan dred ghawl.

He yanked and snapped the digit straight back. From the sharp pain of the tiny break, a tide of pain spread outward, growing and swelling, a trickle becoming a flood. The world spun, and out of the tempest of pain, it burnt a hole into this world. Cloth burnt to ash over the black handprint on his chest, freeing what lay beneath. Gloom flowed out from his body, and the naetherspawn swept into this world, taking shape and sculpting itself from the smoke.

Wings unfurled, and a snaking neck stretched, sprouting

mane and muzzle. Both wyrm and wolf. Fiery eyes opened on his world.

As the naethryn filled the room, it drew off all of Tylar's strength and sturdiness of limb. His back was bent, joints callused, and his knee turned askew. He was no longer *regent*, no longer *knight*—only a broken man again. Gnarled fingers brushed through the tether of smoke that linked to the naethryn.

It needed no guidance, this black dog of his. It knew his heart.

"Keep back!" Rogger warned their party. "One touch will kill. Burn the bones right out of your flesh."

Even the shadows heeded the thief's admonishment.

Like a wave receding across a beach, the darkness retreated out the doorway, taking Mirra with it. She was nowhere to be seen.

The naethryn hunched, wings high, head low. It bellowed, maw stretched wide, baring fangs of Gloom and tongue of black fire—but not a sound escaped it. Still, a mighty wind blasted outward. At the door, darkness shredded away under the force of the silent gale, ripped and scattered. The shadows emptied of any lurkers hidden within its folds, becoming lighter, weightless.

Rogger pulled Tylar straighter, supporting him under a thin shoulder. The thief was stronger than most imagined. "Let's go!" Rogger ordered and passed the Oldenbrook captain his torch. "Keep 'em high! Don't let any of the buggers near."

Krevan—burdened with the boy who still lolled in a half-daze across one shoulder—grabbed one of the fallen torches. There was still enough oil to ignite its end from his cohort's torch.

They stepped as a group toward the door.

Beyond the threshold, words reached them. "Kill the naethryn," Mirra ordered. "Then bring me the god's skull . . . and the head of the boy."

As the naethryn gathered its wind for another assault, Tylar sensed a shift in the shadows. Something approached the threshold. The daemon bellowed again, blowing back the thickening darkness yet again. But this time the retreating shadows revealed a form in the doorway, resolute against the assault.

A knight, his cloak billowing in the naethryn's wind.

One of the black *ghawls*.

The knight stepped forward, little intimidated by the wan firelight, emboldened by the horde at his back, the entire legion's power flowing into him, armoring him against the flames.

Tylar recognized the bloodless countenance under a fall of white hair.

"Perryl . . ."

The knight lifted a sword carved of Gloom. As he shifted it higher, streaks of emerald flowed along its length, glinting with malevolence and poison.

"Kill the naethryn!" Mirra screamed from the darkness.

And her daemon obeyed.

Kathryn stood on the first landing with Argent. They had a view to the hall below that separated the tower from the Masterlevels. The yawning archway stood open.

At least for now.

Two knights manned the gate's greatwheel, ready to lower it at the warden's command. Another two knights stood with sledges, prepared to break the clutches on the chains and bring the barrier crashing down if necessary.

To either side, flames blazed from giant braziers. Wall torches spread outward down both hallways. Still, all the light offered little illumination of what lay below. The stairs spiraled away into the depths, dark and silent.

"They should've been back by now," Argent said.

"A little longer," she urged.

"A time was set. Longer and they are surely corrupted or dead."

She turned to Argent, ready to argue, ready to fight. She had no strength for it. Worry had worn her hollow.

Argent read something in her face. In turn, the steely sternness softened at the edges of his lips. "A moment more," he whispered and turned to face the same dark gate. "No longer."

* * *

Tylar faced Perryl—or rather the naethryn did. Two creatures born of Gloom. The Godsword had failed to kill the daemon earlier. Would Meeryn's naethryn fare any better?

"Stay back," Tylar warned those behind him.

Perryl stepped into the room, long of limb and somehow moving with an unnatural grace he had never shown in life. His sword carved a path through the air, leaving a smoking trail. A noxious miasma accompanied it, like the vapor from a bloated corpse.

Tylar's naethryn eyed his path, cocking its head one way, then the other, sizing up—then striking with the speed of a serpent. It snapped at Perryl, but he was no longer there, a blur of shadow to the side.

The knight stabbed his sword.

The naethryn coiled back to avoid the point and struck out with an edge of wing. Perryl was clipped in the shoulder and spun away. Still, the blow did damage. The misty darkness on that side collapsed to mere cloth and bony arm.

Perryl backed, shook the limb, and the foggy darkness wrapped him up again. He circled wide, searching for a weakness. He took another step to the left. Then, faster than the human eye could follow, he ducked under a wing and thrust his sword toward the throat of the naethryn.

The naethryn reared back from the blade.

Perryl stumbled as he missed. His sword point dropped.

The naethryn lunged forward.

"No!" Tylar yelled. He had recognized the feint. He had taught Perryl the move, as all knights taught their squires. It was called Naethryn's Folly.

And so it proved to be.

As the beast snapped at the knight, Perryl turned heel and wrist, catching himself. The sword point jabbed up as the naethryn lunged down. At the last moment, perhaps heeding his yell, the creature hoved to the side. Instead of the blade driving square into the exposed throat, its edge sliced the left side.

Tylar felt it as a searing pain across his own ribs.

He gasped, his legs going loose under him. He thought Rogger would hold him up, but the thief was gone. His knees struck the stone floor. The naethryn reared up and back, wings spread wide, eyes fiery with pain.

Perryl moved under its guard, going for its exposed belly.

But Rogger had slid under the right wing of the naethryn. Glass glinted in both hands. He threw one, then the other. Snowballs made of crystal. Repostilaries. Small vessels full of humours.

Perryl, focused on the fight, had failed to note the thief.

The globes smashed—one at Perryl's toes, splashing his legs, the other full on the chest, drenching him.

Rogger rolled to the side, circling back.

Perryl's legs staggered, stiffening. The cloak that billowed with Gloom and shadow turned to cloth, tangling the knight further. Perryl wrenched away, barely avoiding the jaws of the naethryn.

Again Tylar caught a glimpse beneath the flowing cloak: of naked, translucent skin, beneath which something squirmed and kneaded, writhing under the surface. Then Perryl dove into the waiting darkness at the door, seeking refuge and escape.

Rogger returned to Tylar's side and hauled him to his feet. His left side still burnt, but he found enough strength to stand and stumble alongside him.

"Now!" Tylar said. "Before they regroup."

Obeying the desire in his heart, the naethryn drove through the door ahead of them, clearing a path. They followed, encircled by flames. But the legion appeared in full rout.

As they fled, his beast lunged out into the shadows and yanked something squirming in its jaws, like a waterstrider spearing a fish. The naethryn shook its catch and tossed it far down a side hall with a flip of its snaking neck. A keening scream marked its flight.

Tylar glanced to Rogger. "You saved us back there."

"Actually, you did."

Tylar frowned at the thief.

"Those were repostilaries of your own saliva. Delia gave them to me before we headed down. Thought we might be able to use them."

"Why—?" Then Tylar understood. Each humour had its own effect on Grace. Saliva weakened an aspect.

"Wasn't sure it would work against Dark Grace, but apparently Grace is Grace. Figured it might dull him, knock his legs out from him."

It certainly had. If Perryl had finished his blow . . . followed through with Naethryn's Folly . . .

Tylar rubbed the fiery slash across his ribs.

Before they knew it, they had reached the stairs.

Tylar reversed their roles. "Burn a path up!" he ordered the others.

He followed behind, leaning on Rogger. Below, the naethryn filled the lower stairs. It nabbed another shape out of the shadows and flung it back down the stairs.

Still, Tylar knew it hadn't been Perryl. He could almost sense the *ghawl's* malevolent attention, a burning hatred. Was there anything of his former friend left in that husk?

Round and round, they climbed up toward the warmth and flames above. Light again bathed around them.

A shout rose ahead. It came from the Oldenbrook captain. "They're closing the gate!"

Krevan bellowed. "Wait! We're coming!"

Tylar limped around a turn of the spiral. He watched the flaming eye of the gateway slowly winking shut.

They all began to shout.

The lowering eyelid stopped. They hurried forward, but Rogger slowed Tylar's step.

"Perhaps you'd best rein in your dog first. Not the time to be piling out of the cellars tethered to a smoking daemon."

Tylar nodded. He patted his cloak.

"Here," Rogger said and passed him one of his daggers.

Tylar took it, sliced his palm, and allowed the blood to well. It was the only way to recall the naethryn once it had been set free. With his own blood. He reached the red palm to the smoky link between him and the naethryn.

It knew his intent and glanced back. Fiery eyes met his. Then Tylar's bloody fingers closed on the tether of Gloom. With his touch, a fine scintillation washed out, cascading over the naethryn, erasing features—then all collapsed back toward him.

Tylar braced for the mule-kick of its impact. Still, it struck with more force than he had expected. This was the second time in one night he had summoned the beast. He prayed it would be the last. He welcomed the return of his hale form.

After a year, what had once felt familiar—his broken body—now felt foreign, like the life of another man.

And that troubled him.

The hobbled form was his *true* form. What he wore the rest of the year had been the illusion, born of Grace to hold the naethryn. Releasing the beast only reminded him of the truth.

It was foolish to forget it.

The force struck his chest and knocked him back a full step. His arms cartwheeled and his legs tripped on the stairs. He stumbled to keep upright—and with limbs now straight and hale again, he succeeded, leaning one palm against the wall to stead himself.

As he lowered his arm, a twinge of pain flashed in his hand. He lifted it before his face. The smallest finger remained bent at a crooked angle. He had snapped the digit to free the demon. Always in the past, once he returned the naethryn to its roost, all would heal.

He stared at his palm. As usual, even the cut had vanished, as though it had never happened.

Rogger noted the broken finger. "That's troubling . . ."

Tylar lowered his arm. He'd worry about it later. The others had already cleared the gateway.

"Tylar?" a voice called. Kathryn stood framed by the fires. "Is everything all right?"

He climbed back up into the warmth and brightness. Still, as his hand throbbed, he feared he carried a part of the darkness out with him.

Ducking under the half-lowered gate, he joined Kathryn.

"Lock it down," he ordered.

The knights again wheeled the massive wyrmwood barrier into place. The heat of the hall, flames all around, should have warmed him. But they didn't. It was not over.

A shout erupted down the hall.

All eyes swung to a pair of knights guarding the far gate, the one that led to the outer bailey of Stormwatch tower.

Even from here, Tylar noted ice and frost sweeping across the inner surface of the gate. Timbers cracked with echoing pops.

The two knights on guard at the gate retreated—but not fast enough.

The entire barrier blew away in an explosion of frozen wood and brittled iron. An ice fog rolled into the hall. Torches on either side of the hallway flickered, then died.

Through the fog, a shape formed, stepping out atop a sheen of ice that flooded across the stone. She stopped and stood naked to the world, rimed in frost.

A lost ally returned.

Tylar stared in horror. "Eylan . . ."

13

A WRAITH IN THE WIND

"CALLA," KREVAN ORDERED, "KEEP THE BOY SAFE!"

Still addled, Brant allowed himself to be shoved toward the stairs as the icy apparition stood within the fractured gate. The jostled climb up out of the cellars had revived Brant enough to stand on his own—though his legs remained numb, and there remained a hole in his memory. He remembered nothing beyond the old woman with the skull.

What had happened?

Calla, the ash-faced woman, took Brant's shoulder and guided him toward the stairs. He climbed dully, trailed by Sten. The others remained below with the warden and a clutch of knights. Orders were shouted. Brant searched the milling group below, then the stairs above. Someone was conspicuously missing.

Where was the giant Dralmarfillneer? As huge as his name, his massive form should be easy to pick out.

Brant stopped midway toward the landing.

"Keep moving," Calla ordered, giving him a slight shove.

Brant twisted away and stumbled down a step.

He bumped into Sten. "Where's Dral?"

The captain mumbled, shared a glance with his gray-cloaked escort, then shook his head. He scooted past Brant, anxious to climb higher.

Calla grabbed his elbow. "Dead," she said simply.

"What . . . ?" The shock rattled through Brant, but it also helped to further center him. "How?"

"No time."

She again tried to force him higher, but he had regained his footing. He broke her grip and fled down to where Rogger stood at the foot of the stairs. He joined the bearded man, needing answers.

"The skull?" he asked.

Rogger patted a satchel slung at his shoulder. It was weighted down. Brant felt a slight warming of the stone at his throat. They had recovered it. But at what blood price?

Before he could inquire, Rogger pointed down the hall. "We have bigger problems at the moment."

They had a clear view from the raised step as the woman approached, awash in icy mists. With each stride, the torches along both walls sputtered out, one after the other, sinking the hall in darkness. Frost skittered in spidery traces across the walls. Ice swept ahead of her across the floor, glassy smooth, like spilled water.

One of the knights who had been guarding the far gate attempted to thwart her with his diamond-pommel sword. The advancing ice reached his toes first. At its touch he stiffened, a hand clutched at his throat—then he toppled, stone-solid, and struck the floor like an upended statue.

Brant remembered the hare he had examined during the blizzard in Oldenbrook. Frozen solid. From the inside out. Here was the dread power of the storm given flesh.

"Take her down!" the warden cried to the phalanx of knights that now blocked the hall's end.

A flurry of crossbows *twanged,* and a volley of bolts shot down the hall. Attesting to the knights' marksmanship, each bolt struck true—only to shatter against the rime of frost that coated the woman.

With nary a blink, she pressed on with the same silent and deliberate pace.

"Flames!" the warden shouted. "Burn her!"

A waist-high barrel of oil was kicked down the hallway. Both ends were lit with fiery rags. The blast blinded Brant. He instinctively covered his face with his arm. Flaming barrel staves rained down, reaching back even to the blockade of knights.

Still, out of the flame and smoke, she appeared. She strode through the ruin, ushering ice and frost ahead of her. Fires ebbed and died around her.

"Back!" the warden ordered.

The knights below pushed toward the stairs. Rogger and Brant were driven higher, all the way up to the first landing. Tylar and the castellan joined the warden, knotted in the center of the knights that now mounted the steps.

From his higher vantage, Brant still had a view of the central hall below. The massive wyrmwood gate stood closed, sealing off the Masterlevels and the horrors below. But the flames in the giant braziers flanking the gate guttered out. The red iron cooled to black, cracking from the sudden loss of heat. Ice swept the floor, extinguishing the last of the flaming staves.

Into the hall strode the source, the storm given flesh.

She appeared below, marching to the center of the floor. The ice continued deeper down the next hall, evident by the torchlights dimming along that direction.

She stopped and faced the gathered audience on the stair.

Expressionless, she spoke. Frozen lips cracked, blood welled and iced again. "Godslayer . . . bring us the Godslayer."

Tylar stood, flanked by Argent and Kathryn. All their offenses had failed. Icy darkness had consumed the entire first level. The cold wafted from the hall, chilling the skin and turning their breath white.

Argent stared at Tylar. "What are we to do?"

Tylar shook his head. He eyed the wyrmwood gate. Fire and warmth were their only true weapons against Mirra's dark legion. If the storm could so easily strip away their defenses, what hope did they have of resisting the black army below? They were trapped between ice and shadow.

"We must get those fires back up," Kathryn said.

"Bring us the Godslayer, he whom we name *Abomination,* and we will leave your towers in peace."

Eylan's voice was her own, but Tylar had no doubt who manipulated her like a stringed puppet. He had seen the god's face in the storm. Ulf of Ice Eyrie. Along with whatever cadre of gods he had rallied to his cause. The conjoining of their powers would be almost impossible to fight.

"You have one bell to hand him to us. Or suffer the death of all. The Abomination must die, one way or the other. The choice is yours."

Eylan crossed her arms, prepared to wait.

Argent spoke to his men. "Stay here. Send word if she moves." He pointed to one of the knights near the top landing. "Call the masters down here. Get them to study and test the Grace that protects the woman. We must find a way to break its blessing."

Obeying, the man fled upward.

Argent met Tylar's eyes. "We need to speak. In private." The warden waved for Kathryn to follow, then motioned for a path to the next level. Knights parted out of the way.

Tylar spoke to Krevan as he climbed up. "Keep with Rogger and the boy."

He nodded.

Moments later, Kathryn and Tylar entered an evacuated room off the second level. It was a squires' lodging. Four beds were stacked one atop the other near the back. The hearth was cold, and the place smelled of sour ale and old sweat. Pitiable surroundings to decide the fate of Tashijan.

Argent closed the door. "What are we to do?"

"We can't give them Tylar," Kathryn said, dropping to the lowermost bunk.

"They hold all of Tashijan in ransom." Argent paced the room's narrow length. His sword smacked his leg with every turn. He rested his hand on the diamond pommel to quiet it. "We must consider the greater good."

Kathryn opened her mouth, but Tylar cut her off. "The warden is right." He ignored the fire that flared in her eyes and flushed her cheeks. "We must make a choice between sacrificing one person or risking the fall of Tashijan, a loss that would threaten all the Nine Lands during this dark time. Even my life is not worth such a price."

"But will they truly take only your life?" she answered heatedly.

Both men frowned at her words.

She sighed in exasperation. "This cadre of gods worked up a storm and sent it against us. And we know they already employ Dark Grace." She waved vaguely toward where Eylan awaited their decision. "We cannot discount the possibility that these gods are in league or perhaps just manipulated by the Cabal. Look at the choices we are offered by their emissary. Lose you or see Tashijan fall. Both ends serve the Cabal. And the threat below—Mirra's black legion—only compounds the danger. We must ask ourselves an important question before we decide how to answer their demand."

"What's that?"

"Is there a connection between Mirra below and the storm without?" She glanced to Tylar, then to the warden. "Consider how these two forces are conjoined so perfectly. Is it happenstance alone—is Mirra merely taking advantage of the situation? Or is it something more insidious? Does the Cabal control the gods, too? Openly or secretly. Either way, if we hand Tylar over to them, his death might not be all they seek. Could they turn Tylar and his powers against all of us? If they somehow enslaved him like the Wyr-mistress below, he would be a weapon that could take down not only Tashijan but all of Myrillia."

Argent had stopped pacing and stood with his arms crossed, studying the floor. Tylar leaned on the edge of a small table. He stared down at the crook of his broken finger. It ached all the way up to his elbow. He used the pain to keep him sharp.

"To gain Tylar as a weapon would be the Cabal's ultimate victory," Kathryn continued. "Better to hold strong here. If we bend to their demands now, we'll be forever at their mercy. Tashijan must be defended."

"But what if you're wrong?" Argent said. "What if these storm gods only want to end Tylar's abomination? We'd risk Tashijan."

"Tashijan is already at risk," she answered. "And always will be until the Cabal is destroyed. Our towers stand tall, for a reason. To attract those who seek to bring Myrillia low. We are the first defense. We must not fail."

Argent looked little convinced. He continued his study of the stone floor. "If only we knew the truth . . ."

Tylar mumbled to himself, "There is one who knows."

The warden lifted his face. "Who?"

Tylar had not meant to be heard, but he had no choice but

to answer. "The Wyr-mistress. Eylan. She's been to the storm's heart and back."

"But she's lost to us," Kathryn said.

Tylar nodded. He could not argue against that. Eylan was buried deep in that black melody of seersong. He pictured her eyes, flinty and cold, as dead as a frozen lake. Seersong proved impossible to resist.

Even for him.

He shuddered at the memory. All will and wit had been stripped from him in a moment. Though he had remained aware, all his focus had narrowed to the point of a needle, centered on the next note, ready to do anything to hear it, deaf to all else, obedient to one.

Only for a moment had he been able to shake the thrall. When he had feebly attempted to warn the others to flee.

Go . . . run . . .

How had he managed that?

"We are chasing shadows," Argent said. "We must make this decision based on what we know, not what we might imagine. In one bell's time, the storm gods will freeze our towers. And if that doesn't kill us, Mirra's daemons will follow in their wake. There is only one way to stem such a tide—even if such an act only buys us more time to rally, we must give them Tylar."

"Let us not make such a decision rashly," Kathryn argued.

Tylar let their words drift to the back of his mind. Other words rose, his own words. *Go . . . run . . .* He remembered uttering that warning, breaking free of the song for just that moment. He'd been trapped in song before and after. Up until now, harried by daemons, he'd not had the time to ponder it further.

He did so now.

Go . . . run . . .

He went back to those words, to the song, to the moment before he spoke those words. Though deafened to all but Mirra's seersong, something had reached him. A discordant note had pierced through the lilting spell, not loud, but enough to jar him momentarily loose. He heard an echo of it now.

It had been a single word moaned in pain: *No . . .*

And he knew who had uttered that word.

Tylar shoved off the table and back to his feet.

"The boy."

Out in the hall, Brant sat with Rogger on the stone floor, backs against the wall. In simple words, he learned the fate of his friend Dralmarfillneer, how the giant had been struck down by a poisoned dagger.

"And the witch still lives," Brant said bitterly.

Rogger placed a hand on his knee. "Aye, she does. Evil is too stubborn to die easily. But your friend's death saved all our lives."

Brant shaded his eyes to hide the welling tears. "I must get word to his brother."

"Time enough for that, young man. No need to rush to break someone's heart."

The door down the hall finally opened. Steps away, Krevan straightened from where he had been talking with Calla. Rogger rose from his seat on the floor. The dagger in his fingers vanished back into its sheath.

Brant stood, too.

The regent led the others out the door. Plain from their faces, some decision had been made. The warden passed Brant, casting him a strange glance with his one eye.

"I'll clear the lower stair," he said and continued on.

Tylar stopped in front of them. He waited until the warden had vanished away. He turned to Castellan Vail. "How is Gerrod managing?"

"He's struggling his best to follow the orders you left with him. He's not sure he has enough humour."

"We'll have to do with as much as he can muster. We may not have much time."

"I know." Kathryn headed down the hall.

Rogger spoke. "So can we assume that the warden isn't going to just toss you arse-bared into the winter storm?"

"Not for the moment." The regent clapped Brant on the shoulder. "We have one hope."

A moment later, Brant stood three steps from the icy floor of the lower central hall. His breath huffed white into the frigid air. Tylar stood a step below. Rogger shared Brant's perch, kneeling, the bile-wrapped skull resting on his lap. Krevan stood guard behind them with Calla and Kathryn. Upon the warden's order, the rest of the stairs had been emptied back to the landing.

"What am I supposed to do?" Brant asked.

"Just call her name," Tylar said. "When you feel the burning, you must keep talking. Anything. As long as you don't stop."

Brant stared out to the frost-covered woman. She stood as if unaware of their presence. Eyes unblinking, toes frozen to the ice. It did not appear she even breathed. No breath steamed from either nostrils or lips.

Still Brant sensed something studying them, wary and watchful.

He clutched the stone at his throat. "I know nothing about breaking curses," he mumbled.

Rogger explained. "If Tylar is right, your stone seemed to counter the seersong in the skull. At least you were able to break its hold momentarily on Tylar. The why and how of it all will have to wait for now." The man shrugged. "And if it doesn't work, no harm done."

No harm . . .

Brant remembered the burn. He glanced to the skull in Rogger's lap. The tainted bone had ruined his home and traveled half the world to haunt him again. Did no one understand it was best destroyed? He had to resist kicking it from the man's thighs and stamping it to crumbles. But would that truly end its curse? Perhaps a cleansing fire . . .

Rogger seemed to read his intent. "Your friend gave his life to help steal this from the witch below. Pay back a small part of that blood debt. Use the stone and skull to strike back at them."

Brant scowled at him, recognizing when someone was trying to ply his emotions. He hated the man for the attempt—mostly because it worked. He had to try.

For Dral.

He nodded.

"Ready yourself, then," Tylar said.

Brant ignored him. There was no preparing.

Rogger studied Brant a moment longer, then reached and peeled back a flap of bile-caked sailcloth. A peek of bone showed. It was enough.

He gasped as the stone ignited between his fingers, melting fat, burning flesh. Flames roared into his chest. He moaned, trying his best to expel the heat. His legs went weak.

Tylar caught him and lowered him to the stairs. "Speak her name," the regent said.

Brant tried, but fire seared his throat. It was agony to breathe. Sweat poured like molten fire into every crease.

"You're killing him," he heard the castellan warn. "There must be another way."

Brant rocked on the stairs, seeking some way to escape the pain.

"Her name . . ." Tylar said.

Brant knew only one way. He let the fire build. He squeezed the stone with one hand. The agony stoked until he could stand it no more. He screamed. *"EYLAN!"*

He felt a slight ebb of the pain. Tears blurred his vision and trembled the woman's form.

"She's moving," Rogger said.

It wasn't just illusion. The woman stumbled a step, almost losing her footing on the slick ice. Then she seemed to catch herself and began to stiffen again.

"Again . . ." Tylar said. "Anything. Each word will help break through the seersong to reach her."

Brant searched deep inside himself, seeking something to fortify him against the pain, to free his tongue. But all he found were more flames. They burnt through all his memories, stripping years. Page after page of his life turned to ash. Finally a memory appeared, one long lost and buried by a tide of days. A thatched room, hard arms cradling him, rocking him . . . and a lullaby gently sung to the moons, sung to hold back the night.

It was a mother's tune, but he'd had no mother.

This memory refused to burn, shielded by grief and lit by flames.

In that moment, he recognized all he truly lost so long ago. Had he ever truly mourned more than the hunter who was his father? He listened to the lullaby and grabbed the grief that he had unknowingly carried with him all these years, as buried as this lone memory.

He let the flames carry forth his anguish.

He started haltingly, words dissolving into gasps and moans, etched with agony. But he refused to stop. He continued to sing—not for Tylar, not to break curses, not even for his lost father. He sang for the boy who wanted those hard arms around him one last time.

Tylar did not even recognize when the boy had begun to sing. Brant lay on his side, curled on the stairs, moaning. Then Tylar saw Eylan stir again out in the ice. She hobbled a step toward them . . . then another.

Only then did Tylar perceive a whisper of words from the boy's pained lips. " *'Come, sweet night . . . steal the last light . . . so your moons may glow.'* "

Below, Eylan lifted an arm, trembling, confused.

"The seersong's grip is loosening," Rogger said, rising with the skull under one arm.

Krevan slipped down to join them. Kathryn went to the boy, kneeling and lifting his head into her lap. She stroked back the lanky hair that had plastered to his forehead with sweat.

He whimpered, then continued, thready and weak. " *'Come, sweet night . . . hide all our worries . . . so our dreams will flow.'* "

"He's burning up," Kathryn warned, glancing to Tylar.

"But it's working," he countered.

Eylan lifted her head toward them. Ice still clouded her eyes, but the depth had melted. Lips parted and cracked. Blood flowed.

"No . . ." she moaned. "Stop . . ."

Hands rose to her ears. But against whom was she warding? Her new masters out in the storm or their attempt here?

Eylan took another step in their direction. Cakes of frost fell from her arms and legs. "Must stop . . ."

Blood dripped from her chin and splattered to the ice, steaming and hot. The seersong's hold was plainly melting, releasing her.

"Eylan," Tylar said. "Tell us about the storm."

"Must stop them . . ."

He was still unsure whom she meant.

Behind Tylar, the boy continued his tinny whisper. " *'Come sweet night . . . protect all the children . . . 'til the cock's first crow.'* "

Eylan's eyes found his. Tylar read flinty glimpses of clarity. Her face twisted in a rictus of agony, baring too many teeth.

"Help them," she keened out at him. "Free them . . ."

The words echoed Brant's earlier words, when he'd held the skull down below. Tylar glanced back to the boy, remembering the strange discourse.

HELP THEM . . . FREE THEM . . . FIND THEM.

The boy had no memory of what he had been saying. Tylar turned back to Eylan. But here was someone who might know.

"Find them . . ." Eylan gasped out, finishing the same chorus.

"Who?" Tylar shouted out to her.

She fell to one knee on the ice. Blood now poured from both nostrils. The war for her mind was tearing her apart.

"It's killing her." Rogger confirmed it at Tylar's side. "The seersong has its hooks deep in her mind and spirit. Ripping them out is destroying her."

Out on the floor, she sank to one buttock, supported by an arm on the ice, weakening rapidly.

"The boy's almost gone," Kathryn said behind him.

He had no choice.

"Who?" he called again to Eylan. "Who are we supposed to find?"

She lifted her face. "The rogues . . . *find the other rogues* . . . chained and forced . . ." She suddenly coughed, spewing crimson across the ice.

"Forced to do what?"

Eylan opened her mouth to speak, but only blood flowed. Tears streamed down her face. She lifted her arm and pointed toward the wrecked gate.

"The storm?" he asked quietly.

Her only agreement was the sagging drop of her arm. Her head sank heavily, too.

"Where are they? How do we find them?"

Eylan did not stir, seeming deaf to him now.

"The boy's stopped breathing!" Kathryn gasped out and stood. She hauled the boy up in her arms and faced Rogger. "Cover the skull!"

Hesitating, Rogger glanced to Tylar. Both of them knew they needed more answers.

"He can't speak any longer!" Kathryn screamed at the both of them. "Rogger, cover the skaggin' skull!"

Recognizing the truth of her words, he finally obeyed and whisked the sailcloth back over the skull. He shrugged an apology at Tylar.

A scrape drew Tylar's attention back out on the ice.

Eylan's fingers scratched at the ice. Her head lolled like a broken doll. Then an arm pushed, a leg shifted. She began to rise.

"The song is claiming her again," Rogger said.

White frost climbed her calves and scrawled up from her wrists, coating her again, collecting up its lost puppet.

She lifted her head. Her eyes found Tylar. He read the clarity before it drowned away. Her lips moved and one word escaped, an answer to his last question.

"Hinterland . . ."

Then her eyes iced over.

Before he could grieve, a sharp *twang* startled him.

From Eylan's forehead, a small puff of feathers bloomed—then seeped blood. A crossbow bolt. Her head fell back, followed by her body. She crashed to the ice.

Dead.

Tylar turned.

Krevan lowered his crossbow. He matched Tylar's stare—then turned and climbed the stair. It was a cold act, but the right one.

For Tashijan, for Eylan.

Still, Tylar remained silent as Krevan left. He had noted how much the pirate's arm shook as he lowered the bow.

Kathryn led the others, sweeping up the stairs toward her hermitage. Behind her, Krevan carried Brant. The boy had begun breathing again, but it remained shallow, and he'd yet to wake.

Fury helped fuel her course. She had cradled the boy as he had come within a hair of dying. Though she understood Tylar's desire for every bit of information, there were lines between necessity and cruelty. To use the boy so harshly bordered on as black an art as those they fought practiced.

Still, he breathed now—and none had noted her tears as she'd held him. A part of her felt foolish, and a good amount of her anger was directed at herself. Had she not seen enough death? Why did this boy's life warrant tears when the loss of so many others had not? But she knew the answer. She knew the source of those hot tears.

They rose as much for the son she had lost long ago as the boy here this night, churned up by her fury at Tylar for risking Brant. That anger stoked embers within Kathryn that she'd thought had long gone cold. But a fire remained, a buried resentment toward Tylar for his role in the loss of their child. He had willingly plied with the Gray Traders, opening himself up to accusation and misuse. A path that eventually led to a bloody bed and a tiny body in her palms.

Brant moaned in Krevan's arms. A hand rose. At least this boy would live.

She took a shuddering breath and continued onward.

As if sensing some dam had broken inside her, Tylar pushed up to join her. "Argent will be furious," he said.

"I'll deal with him," she said coldly.

And for the moment, the warden was anything but *furious*. *Jubilant* was more the word to describe him after he discovered that Eylan had been slain. He had been more than willing to allow them all to flee up into the highest levels of Tashijan, their duty done. With the storm's deadly emissary gone, the ice had melted and receded from the lower hall.

But for how long?

They needed to be prepared.

Argent took over the refortification of the first level. Fires had to be relit, stations posted, and the broken main gate repaired. He had Master Hesharian leading a group of masters to discern some defense against another attack. They didn't know how long a respite was bought with Eylan's life, but all knew the war was not over.

"Have you heard any further word from Master Gerrod?" Tylar asked.

She shook her head. "I sent a runner up to let him know our urgency. Dart should be ready as well."

"We've shaken them up," Tylar said, referring no doubt to the powers that wielded the storm. "But it won't last long. We must take advantage of it."

She nodded.

As they rounded another landing, a booming shout rose to their right. "Master Brant!" From the hallway, a massive shape pushed out on the stair. A loam-giant. "What have you done with Master Brant?"

There was an equal amount of threat as grief in his voice.

Tylar held up a palm. "He lives. We're taking him to the healers up in the castellan's hermitage."

"I'll take him, then." The giant pushed toward Krevan.

Once his shoulders cleared the hall, Kathryn spotted a gathering of others, hanging back, plainly curious for news. She also saw the Oldenbrook guard who had accompanied Tylar into the cellars. He stood next to a lithe woman in a silver nightrobe.

"Back to your rooms!" she ordered them.

There was a small motion back, but she was mostly ignored. She had no time to argue and turned to the giant, ready to give him the same instructions.

Rogger, though, touched her arm. He whispered. "That is the twin brother of the giant that died below."

Kathryn let her angry breath sigh out of her. Only now did she note the watery pain in the giant's eyes, still angry, needing something to do. Apparently the Oldenbrook guard had brought word of his brother's demise.

She waved to Krevan. "Let him come."

He took the boy up in his massive arms with surprising gentleness.

Brant stirred, jostled. His eyelids opened. "Mal . . ." he said hoarsely.

"I got ya, Master Brant."

A feeble hand rose and touched the giant's chin. "Dral . . ."

"I heard . . . I know, Master Brant." The giant nodded for them to continue. "We'll get our blood from them yet. Then we'll mourn."

They wound the rest of the way to the top of Stormwatch, reaching her hermitage again. The remainder of Krevan's Flaggers still guarded her door. All had been quiet, they reported.

Such seemed impossible after all the chaos below, but she took them at their word and led the others inside. Dart and Laurelle shared chairs by the hearth, while the young wyld tracker napped against the curled bulk of the bullhound.

They all rose, one after the other as the party pushed inside.

Dart's eyes widened as she saw the giant carry in Brant's weak form. A hand rose to her throat with concern.

"He'll live," Kathryn promised her. "Can you show him to the healers? He might have to share the bed with Lorr."

"Not this night, my lady." A form hobbled in from the back room, drawn by their arrival.

"Lorr—what are you doing out of bed?"

Though barefooted, he had donned his breeches and had a loose shift open. His left arm was swathed with bandages, but his face was uncovered, baring his burns. The blistered flesh had already settled to a pinkish hue across his cheek and in a goathorn curl up the side of his head.

"The work of your fine healers . . . masters of Grace, they are."

A grunt discounted his words as Healer Fennis rounded behind him. "Stubbornness of this prickly tracker, more like it." He waved the giant over to him. "And a fair amount of quickened healing due to his Grace-blessed nature."

Lorr shrugged.

Healer Fennis followed the giant into the next room, calling to his wife. "Don't put away the whistlewort yet, my dear."

"They'll have to manage as best they can," Tylar said. "Weak or not, we must be gone with the boy in the next quarter bell."

Kathryn understood.

"We leave so soon?" Dart said.

Kathryn turned to her. "Do you have your bag ready?"

"I helped her," Laurelle said and nodded to a stuffed sack-cloth beside the hearth.

Tylar turned to Krevan. "Can you send Calla above? Have her check with Master Gerrod on how long until the flipper-craft is ready?"

Krevan obeyed, then returned. He knew of their plan, plotted before they'd ever ventured into the cellars, but he did not know everything. "How can we hope to pierce the storm? Won't the storm suck the air alchemies from the ship?"

"Tylar and Gerrod have worked something out," Kathryn said. "The better question is what to do *after* you make it through?"

The plan had been simple before. To get Tylar and Dart out of Tashijan. They could not risk Rivenscryr falling into the Cabal's hands, especially with Dart here, too. And once through the storm, Tylar could rally the gods of the First Land and whatever forces could be brought to bear.

But now matters had become more complicated, with the skull, with the boy, with the dying words from Eylan.

"We must find the rogues," Tylar said. "We knew the storm out there had to be fed by more than one god. Ulf alone could not wield such forces from Ice Eyrie. We assumed he had the support of a cadre of gods, more of the Hundred who sought my downfall."

"It was a reasonable assumption," Kathryn said. "No one considered *rogue* gods might be involved. They are wild and raving creatures, beyond such masterful manipulation of vast amounts of Grace."

"Unless they were enslaved," Tylar said. He glanced to Rogger, who had the skull wrapped up in his satchel. "Like Keorn must have been, trapped in seersong. Somehow he was able to escape, to flee into Saysh Mal, sacrificing himself to bring a warning out."

"And carrying with him a means to free his trapped brethren." Rogger nodded toward the next room. "The stone . . . bonded to the boy."

"I'm not sure that all is so simple," Kathryn said. "There is more going on. But either way, does any of us doubt the Cabal is behind the enslavement of these rogues?"

No one voiced a dissent.

"Then that answers my earlier question. Mirra's forces and the storm were brought against us as a unified strategy. A coordinated attack to capture Tylar and gain the Godsword. Mirra may even know about Dart. And once they gained such power, Tashijan would surely be torn apart, not only destroying the bastion for all of Myrillia, but murdering a good portion of the Hands that serve the gods around here. In one move, we could lose this entire Land."

"Artful strategy," Rogger said. "You have to respect that. They must have been planning this for years."

"Or even longer," Krevan said. "I fear that, like the Wyr, the Cabal's plots are stretched over centuries."

"And if the castellan is correct," Rogger said, "it's all the more reason to get Dart and Tylar free of here."

"And what of the rogues?" Krevan asked.

Tylar rubbed at the corner of his eye, almost tracing his tattooed stripes. Kathryn recognized it as a gesture of intense concentration. She also noted the wrapped digit of the same hand. She had heard that it had not healed. Tylar had dismissed it earlier, but Kathryn feared that the Dark Graces flowing through here threatened the complicated spell that bonded naethryn to man. Yet another reason to get him clear of Tashijan.

Tylar finally spoke. "If the enslaved rogues are fueling this storm, then we can end this siege by finding and freeing them. As Eylan warned."

"Simple enough," Rogger said. "But that depends on two things."

All eyes turned to him.

He held up a finger. "First, Tashijan must hold out that long."

Kathryn nodded. That was her duty. To remain behind and rally the towers as best she could. To hold firm until Tylar could bring in additional forces—or find some way to free them. It wasn't only rogues that were ensnared by the Cabal.

Rogger held up a second finger. "And more importantly, we must find this coven of song-cast gods."

Tylar nodded. Here was *his* duty. "Eylan has offered us one clue. *Hinterland*."

"Not exactly a map, now, is it?" Rogger said. "Half of Myrillia is still unsettled hinter. We can spend a lifetime or more to find them."

"Maybe not," Krevan said. "The skull came from Saysh Mal. The Eighth Land's hinter is the trickiest maze of them all, and the most wild and dangerous." The pirate glanced to Tylar. "Not one shadowknight has ever set foot in there and returned to tell about it. If you're going to hide something from Tashijan, that would be a good place to begin."

"And it was in that hinter that Keorn was captured," Tylar said.

Krevan nodded. "The Wyr had tracked him there, then lost him. Only to have him appear again in Saysh Mal."

"Then that's where we'll begin our search," Tylar said.

"We may have one other ally to aid us," the pirate said. He pointed to Rogger's burdened satchel. "Wyrd Bennifren waits just outside of Saysh Mal, in the neighboring hinterland, for the skull. The trade still stands. We can ransom it against the Wyr's knowledge."

"Not a bargain I'd trust," Rogger said.

"But we have little choice," Tylar said. "And in some small way, perhaps it's a debt we owe to Eylan."

No one argued against that.

Rogger finally spoke. "I forgot one last item that stands between us and success." He raised his hand and now held up three fingers. "Before any of this can begin, we have to get our arses out of here."

After several matters had been settled further, Tylar stepped into the back room. They could wait no longer.

"It is time," he told the healers.

Healer Fennis and his wife bustled on either side of the bed, shoving last bits of balms and wraps into an overstuffed pack. "Are you sure that's everything?" Fennis asked.

His wife gave him a look that seemed equal parts exasperation and certainty.

Fennis held up a hand, acquiescing. Wise man.

Lorr crossed and picked up the pack.

"There's extra wrappings," Fennis said, fingering at the dressings on the man's arm. "If you'll need them."

Lorr batted him away. "Don't mind me. Get the boy ready."

Tylar studied the wyld tracker. He had agreed to let Lorr join their search. His hunting and tracking skills could prove useful out in the hinterlands. It would be foolish to refuse such experienced service. The man hauled the laden bag with ease, little fazed by his burns.

Brant, though, looked little better, burnt as well, but on the inside, where it was harder for balms to reach. His bronze skin had yellowed and stretched thin across his bones. And though his breathing was stronger, when he tried to lift himself up on an elbow, he failed.

Tylar caught the healer's eye.

"He's been well-draughted," the man assured him. "Addles a bit. By midday on the morrow, he'll feel half his oats again."

He nodded. Morning was not far off, but it seemed like a fanciful dream, a hope that one did not really expect to attain.

Kathryn hurried inside, slightly breathless. "I heard word. Argent has gotten wise to what we're planning."

Tylar clenched a fist.

"I'll get Master Brant," the giant said.

The loam-giant rose from a crouch on the far side of the bed and plucked away the bedsheet. He gently collected Brant out of his nest of pillows with a regretful expression.

Brant startled, clutching at the man's neck.

"Just Mal, Master Brant."

The boy's eyes focused and searched the room. "We're heading out?" he asked through thin lips.

"We must," Tylar said and led them back to the main room. The others were already waiting.

"I'm coming with you," Mal said.

Tylar thought to argue, but the giant's brother had died to gain them this vantage. Plus the man was plainly strong and could prove his value. An objection arose, though, from another corner.

"No," Brant mumbled. "The whelpings?"

"I locked 'em up in your rooms," the giant said. He pulled a key from a pocket as proof.

"Who's going to—?" Brant coughed away the last of his words, but the worry shone in his wan face.

Mal's brow furrowed into deep-plowed tracks, caught between two duties.

He was saved by a hand plucking the key from his fingertips. Lorr tossed the key over to the young tracker beside the bullhound. "Kytt and Barrin will look after them."

The young tracker bumbled the iron key, and it fell with a clatter.

Laurelle retrieved it as it bounced to her toes. "I'll help, too."

Mal sighed with relief. "They'll take good care of the mites."

Brant still wore a troubled expression, but he did not object.

With such matters settled, they set out. Dart gave her friend Laurelle a final teary-eyed hug. Then the group was on its way at a quick pace, herded close, led by Kathryn.

Halfway down the hall, a long-limbed man in blue livery, spotless and unwrinkled, blocked the way. "The warden sent word that no one is to leave this floor!" he scolded.

"Out of our way, Lowl," Kathryn said, stiff-arming him aside. Luckily all of Argent's forces were occupied down below, leaving only this manservant to attend his orders here. "I'll take it up with the warden when I get back."

Chased by the man's objections, they hurried to the stairs and fled up toward the top of the tower. A cool wind wafted down to them. Tylar heard the pound of hammer on wood. That could not be good. With Argent below and the storm without, they had no time for delays.

Tylar found Captain Horas just inside the door that led out to the flippercraft dock atop Stormwatch. He had a stick of coal in one hand and had been calculating on the wall. Numbers and symbols lined from floor to eye. Some crossed out, others circled.

The man wore the yellow-and-white uniform of his station, but it was stained and smudged. From the smell, not all of it was coal.

"Won't work . . ." the captain muttered, scratching his head with his sliver of coal.

Tylar joined him and waved the others out on the dock.

Captain Horas had to squeeze against the wall to allow Malthumalbaen to pass. His eyes tracked the giant, then back to Tylar. "He's not going, is he?"

Tylar nodded.

"Sweet aether . . ." The captain scratched a line of calculations. "A dozen, that's the most we'll be able to ferry through the storm. *If* we can ferry through the storm." He laughed, but it held no mirth. "And I need three men to crew . . . and that giant . . . that's two men right there."

Tylar took the charcoal from his fingers and turned the man toward the open door. "We'll have to manage." He gave him a push out into the freezing bite of the storm's heart.

Outside, the others gaped at the state of the flippercraft. The woodwrights had proven their mastery. The stoved ship seemed to be patched well. Details were fairly smeared away.

Lorr held a hand over his nose. Tylar did not blame him. The reek was overpowering even in the open.

"Black bile," Krevan said with a shake of his head.

One of the dockworkers, masked against the stench, swabbed a sodden mop over the outer planking of the ship's bow, smearing more black bile over a thin patch. Shouts echoed. Ladders were being hauled aside.

Tylar hurried to the others.

Rogger stood with his fists on his hips. "A ship of shite . . . now that's a boat fit for a regent."

Gerrod crossed toward the group, expressionless behind his bronze armor. He was followed by a welcome figure. Delia was bundled in a heavy coat, also splattered with bile.

"You had enough humour?" Tylar asked the armored master.

"Barely. We've emptied all of Tashijan's storehouses."

"And a few privies, I'd imagine," Rogger said.

Gerrod ignored him. "Mistress Delia has proven to be an able alchemist. She had some suggestions for heightening the Grace with tears. It will not last long, but hopefully long enough to get through the storm."

Delia stood to the side with her arms crossed. Her eyes flitted to Kathryn and back to him, her face unreadable, smudged with bile.

Gerrod continued, "Her suggestion allowed us to thin the coating across the flippercraft, while still hopefully blocking the storm's ability to draw Grace out of the ship's mekanicals as you pass through it. But even bile has its limits. You will have to gain as much wind as you can before attempting to spear through the storm's ring."

"We'll make it," Tylar said. They had no other choice.

A shout by the stairway door reminded them that Argent was on his way.

"Everybody aboard," Kathryn said.

Tylar waved them toward the open hatch. Captain Horas and two of his men had already boarded, all wearing expressions of doom. Tylar watched the others climb inside. They looked no more confident, except Rogger, who was whistling.

The last to leave, Tylar turned to Kathryn and Delia. Gerrod had already clanked off to oversee something near the stern tie-down.

The two women seemed to suddenly become aware they were alone together. Kathryn broke the spell first. "I should get below. Argent will need much calming. And we have our towers to ready."

Delia stepped off after her. "And I should see to Laurelle and the other Hands."

Tylar lifted an arm, to object, to offer some more intimate farewell.

But he wasn't sure to which woman he raised his arm.

Before he could decide, the pair retreated back toward the warmth and light of the open tower door. Left out in the cold, Tylar turned toward the waiting ship. A frigid breeze swept through him. His broken finger ached, and behind the palm print on his chest, something deep inside him churned with distress.

Rogger stood at the open hatch to the flippercraft and waved him to hurry. Ducking against the wind, Tylar headed toward the ship.

He did not whistle.

Dart held tight to the belt that secured her seat as the flippercraft lifted from its docking cradle. A tremble passed underfoot and under her buttocks. The mekanicals had been set to full burn. In her belly, she felt the world fall away under her.

Pupp stood near her seat, legs wide, spiky mane sticking

straight out around his face. Dart swore she could hear him whine in the back of her head, but maybe it was the mekanicals ratcheting up into higher pitches, where the normal ear could not discern but only felt in the bones.

She glanced to the porthole window beside her head, but there was nothing to see. Even the windows were coated with bile.

Across from her sat Calla, the gray-cloaked Black Flagger. Despite the ash on her face, Dart read the worry. She kept glancing to Krevan, her leader, who stood at the door to their tiny cabin braced in the opening, ready to ride out the storm on his feet. He had argued earlier to join Tylar and the captain in the forward controls, but he had been refused. Captain Horas was in no mood to argue, and Tylar supported him.

"His ship, his command," the regent had said.

Past Krevan, another cabin stood open to the hall. Malthumalbaen filled an entire bench by himself. Brant was propped up next to him, his head hanging, asleep or despondent. The giant rested a massive hand on his shoulder. On the opposite bench, Lorr sprawled on his back, knees up, as if they were all afloat on a sunny river.

Rogger spoke beside her. "Best you blink a few times, lass. Your eyeballs will dry out if you keep staring like that."

Dart leaned back. Her fingers remained clenched.

"We'll get through this storm," he assured her.

"How do you know?" She coughed to chase the tremulous keen from her words.

"We're covered in shite. What storm god would want to snatch us from the air? Probably part the clouds themselves so we don't smudge their snowy whiteness."

She offered a weak smile.

"We'll make it through," he promised.

She took a measure of strength from his confidence, but not all her worries were buried in the storm. *We'll make it through.* But what then? Though she appreciated Rogger's company, she was all too aware of the burden he carried in his satchel. It rested beside him tied to his wrist.

The skull of the rogue god.

She had been trying her best to ignore it, to dismiss it as some cursed talisman, none of her concern. Even the others continued to avoid mentioning the more intimate history of the bones.

The rogue had a name.

Keorn.

After so many years wondering about her mother and father, dreaming her childhood fantasies, here was her reality. Her father was no faceless rogue. In one night, she had gained not just a father, but an entire lineage.

Chrism's son.

That made her Chrism's granddaughter.

It had been Chrism who had forged Rivenscryr and sundered the gods' homeworld in the first War of the Gods. And now a new war was starting here on Myrillia. Ancient enmities, drowned in the naether, were rising again.

And she stood at the heart of it.

Chrism's granddaughter.

That was enough to unsettle her, to make her want to run and keep running. But that was not the primary reason for her bone-deep unease. She had long come to accept her heritage as the progeny of rogue gods. Even this new revelation of her heritage, she could come to acknowledge. In fact, she had already unburdened her fears to Laurelle and Delia. After an initial surprise, Laurelle had readily accepted her heritage.

"It makes no difference," Laurelle had said and hugged her to prove it.

But it had been Delia who truly helped return Dart's footing. "It doesn't matter," she had said. "You are not your father, nor your grandfather. And I should know, being the *daughter* of Argent ser Fields. Blood does not dictate the woman. Only your own heart does. You must remember that."

And she would.

But that sentiment did not soothe another reality, one more solid than fear. She stared at the satchel. After so long being mere myth and dream, here was her father. The last of his bones. All that was left, all she would ever truly know. And despite the curse, she longed to touch them, to make at least that much contact, between daughter and father.

And deeper below this desire lay a well of grief.

Her father was dead. And if the stories were true, he had sacrificed himself to bring forth word of his enslaved and tortured brethren. This was also her heritage. And it both warmed her and filled her with sorrow.

Who was her father?

Even a name did not fully answer that.

She tried searching out the window to distract her, but there was nothing to see. *We'll make it through*. Then what? From there, they would follow the last footsteps of her father.

But where would they lead?

Around her, the flippercraft shuddered, from bow to stern.

"We're entering the storm," Rogger said.

Tylar crashed against the railing. He clutched at the grip, earning a protest from his wrapped hand. He stood at the foot of the spar that led out to where the pilot had been belted to his chair. Like the bowsprit of a deepwhaler, the man's perch protruded from the deck and overhung the wide curved glass Eye of the ship.

Nothing could be seen below. Blinded by bile, the pilot had to trust the calls of fathoms from his crewmate who manned a steaming curve of mekanicals locked in bronze to the left. The mica tubes and vessels bubbled with the churning alchemies. The mate, a short, bandy-legged man, kept a continuing report of the ship's health and course.

On the far side of the deck, to the right, Captain Horas stood before another curve of mekanicals. He danced across the jarring deck as if it were as steady as stone. Tugging at his forked beard, he monitored his stations, becoming another mate of the three-man crew. At the same time, he did not forsake his role as captain.

"Two turns to port!" he shouted to the pilot. "Catch the wind on the aft flippers!"

This was his ship. He seemed to read its every bump and roll with more intent than the mekanical soundings. Tylar kept out of his way, out of everyone's way. He was here only in case his blood was needed. Through his veins, raw Grace flowed. It bore the aspect of water, not air. But power was power, and if it proved necessary . . .

The ship heaved up on one side. Tylar slid down the smooth rail, hanging by his hands. Terror rang through him.

Captain Horas came running down the tilted deck. He skidded next to the smaller mate and clapped him on the shoulder as if greeting him on the street. "Feed a flow here . . . and here . . ." He tapped at two mica tubes that steamed and hissed.

"Will it hold?" the other asked, but he was already turning bronze knobs.

"It will have to," Captain Horas said as the pilot corrected the roll and evened the deck. He crossed to Tylar on his way back to his original post. Their eyes met.

Tylar pulled on the rail to gain his feet. "How are the alchemies holding?"

"We're losing air." Horas read the concern in Tylar's face. "Not air Graces, just air. The storm gods know what we attempt. I can practically sense their Dark Grace swirling around us, seeking some crack to suck the power out of our alchemies. But as long as we keep a full burn, the mekanicals are holding steady."

The flippercraft suddenly dropped beneath Tylar's feet. Someone screamed from the back of the ship. Then the deck came crashing back up, knocking Tylar to a knee.

Captain Horas landed lightly. He waved an arm outward, at the sky, at the storm. "The storm gods have grown wise to our artifice. It is not only Dark Grace we must fight. Bile can't block a wind. The storm turns its winds against us, seeking to drag us out of the skies."

"What can we do?" Tylar said.

"Fly, your lordship. That's what my ship was made for!" He said this last with a savage grin. "We'll keep flying until the ground stops us."

Tylar gained his feet.

The pilot called from his spar. "Captain!"

Tylar and Horas turned to the man. He motioned below.

Tylar leaned over the rail. Below, the black Eye was now streaked with white. "We're losing bile," he said.

"Snow and ice . . . stripping us . . ." Horas shoved away from the rail and hurried back to his station.

The ship rolled, first to one side, then the other. Though still blinded, Tylar felt the pressure in his ears.

"We're losing Grace!" Horas called. "They're breaking through! Open all taps! Full flow!"

As Tylar watched, a large swath of bile washed off the Eye. Through the rent in their protection, the storm swirled white. He searched below, expecting a dark eye to form, to peer inside. Instead, far below, globes of light floated and rolled near the bottom of the storm, like luminescent fish at the bottom of the Deep.

As he struggled to discern the source, the pressure continued to squeeze his ears. They were plummeting into the depths of the storm. The strange lights below grew larger.

Captain Horas passed him again, drawing his eye. "The more power we burn," he called as he passed, "the more Grace they steal!"

Tylar followed him across the deck. "Then stop burning Grace!" An idea grew in him. He joined the captain and the mate at the wall of mekanicals.

"Then we'll fall to our deaths that much sooner," Horas said.

Tylar kept his voice fierce. "You said this ship is built to fly! Then fly her! Cut the flow of Grace. Use the winds for as long as you can. Convince them we're lost—flying Graceless."

He read a growing understanding in the captain's eyes. "You're mad . . ."

"Gain as much distance as you can."

The captain nodded. He waved for the mate to obey. Together the pair began shutting valves and turning knobs. The bubbling in the mica tubes slowed.

"Captain!" the pilot cried, sensing the sudden loss of Grace.

"Keep her nose up! Into the wind. True south!"

Tylar backed a step as the mate and captain stifled the flows. The tubes still steamed, but all that bubbling died.

"Keep the mekanicals stoked," the captain said. "Hot and ready. Wait for my word."

Horas led Tylar back to the rail. The deck tilted nose down. The pilot fought to pull her up, shoving the bow of the ship into contrary winds. The craft jarred up momentarily, gaining a bit more distance, a few breaths where the ship rose instead of falling. But it was a doomed struggle.

Down the nose went again.

Tylar bent over the rail. The floating lights grew as the land rose. The lights, azure and scintillating with power, grew clearer. Globes of lightning, trapped in the heart of the storm.

The plunging flippercraft sailed across a wide field of the glowing orbs, stirring them up with the wake of their passage. Below, the hills of Tashijan sped past, lit by the deadly cold fire.

But the hills weren't empty.

A vast army spread across the hills.

"Wind wraiths," Horas said, recognizing the spindly forms as they spiraled into the air, men and women born under alchemies of air, like loam-giants and wyld trackers.

But even from this height, Tylar saw the twist of their bodies. He remembered the tortured figure that had attacked them from the air in Chrismferry. The same here. Wind wraiths corrupted by Dark Grace into beasts.

"They've been ilked," Tylar said.

A shout from the pilot warned them back from their dark observations. The hills climbed toward them. The captain watched, studying.

"Be ready!" he yelled to all.

Another breath . . . the ground rushed up at them.

"Now!"

To the side, the mate yanked a large bronze lever. Flows, boiling and pent, were finally released again. The mekanicals gasped with a thick wheeze of steam.

The pilot hauled on his controls, leaning back, as if by muscle alone he could pull the nose back up. But it wasn't just muscle that powered the flippercraft now.

Grace slammed through the mekanicals.

A tubing exploded with a spat of flaming alchemies.

Horas rushed to aid the mate. Tylar kept his post by the rail.

The hills continued to rise toward them, snowswept waves ready to accept the keel of their craft. The army of wraiths vanished behind them, along with the globes of lightning.

The flippercraft raced across the frozen landscape.

Slowly . . . slowly . . . the nose lifted to an even keel. They flew no more than the height of a man over the hills. Then began to climb. Caught by surprise, the dark forces were sluggish in bringing their Dark Grace to bear. The churning alchemies remained steeped in the air aspect.

The pilot tilted their nose up, shooting back into the skies. The land dropped away, vanishing into the swirling snow.

Then in one breath, they were through the clouds and shot out into open air, like a bile-streaked arrow. The world opened and stretched ahead of them. Moonlight and starlight cast the world with a silvery gloaming.

"We made it," Captain Horas said, making it sound more like a question.

"We did," Tylar mumbled.

He turned to stare toward the stern of the flippercraft, but his eyes did not see the ship any longer. He pictured the wraith army—and the towers lost in the heart of the storm.

But mostly, he pictured two women's faces.

Despite his fear for them, he turned his back on the storm. He had no choice. He had his duty.

Off to the east, the night sky purpled, heralding dawn and another day.

"Head south," he ordered the captain.

"Aye, ser."

The flippercraft swung toward the open sea. They would stop at Broken Cay, to wash their ship and freshen their alchemy. Tylar would send ravens flying in all directions. The First Land must rally, but he knew it would not be his war.

The skies continued to brighten to the east as the world turned, oblivious to the struggles of man and god.

Another day.

It was all a man could truly hope for in life.

One more day to make it all right.

Tylar stared south, beyond the curve of the world. He had escaped, but it was only a small victory. Saysh Mal and the hinterlands awaited. There were battles yet to be fought.

Still, something troubled Tylar.

Something he had forgotten.

Far below Tashijan, she sat in a stone chair. A spider, blanched white by a life beyond the sun, crept across her veined hand.

Its legs suddenly curled, its body dried to a husk, and it rolled from her flesh.

Mirra did not move. She remained very still until a thin smile stretched her lips. Then she slowly rose to her feet.

"So he has slipped our noose," she said to the darkness that surrounded her. The only illumination came from her stone seat, a melted drape of volcanic flowstone. It shone with a soft sheen of putrefaction and decay. She trailed one finger along its arm as she stood, sensing the whispers of her naethryn masters.

"No matter. Tashijan will fall all that much faster."

She crossed to where the putrefying glow met the darkness. In that border, her creation abided, her last and most perfect. Twelve others circled this margin between corruption and darkness. They would serve their new master.

"Perryl," she whispered, naming her finest creation.

No reaction. Eyes stared into nothingness.

"You know what you must do," she whispered to him.

He lifted his sword in acknowledgment and stepped back into the darkness. He drifted into the shadows, his white face fading as if he were sinking into a black sea.

The others followed.

Her black *ghawls* were creatures of Gloom. They flowed through more than mere shadows. Just as these few had drifted between the glow and the darkness, they could also sail between the world of substance and the naether, spaces misted with Gloom, slipping between the cracks of the world.

Into one and out another.

No place was beyond their reach. Throughout Myrillia, such dark cracks existed, where Gloom seeped and leached into this world: down in sunless caverns, in the midnight depths of the sea, beyond sealed doors of forgotten crypts, even under the roots of ancient forests. Wherever Gloom bled and trickled, her legion could travel.

"Go," she whispered to the fading figure. "Hunt them all down."

As the *ghawls* slipped away, Perryl's sword was the last to vanish, sheathing slowly into the Gloom. She reached for its tip, lanced through with malignant green fire. The Godslayer thought he had escaped—he remained blithely unaware of his own doom.

Her smile widened.

Though his naethryn had avoided the full kiss of Perryl's blade, it had not remained unscathed. A nick was more than enough.

As the blade sank into the darkness, whispering with emerald fire, she named the poison within the sword, a venom without cure, already instilled in naethryn and man.

"The blood born of hatred . . . the blood of Chrism."

FOURTH

RUIN AND ASHES

Farallon Jeweled Bloom

Alchemical Preparation of Dreamsmoke
::: The petal of the water lotus must be soaked in brine for three days under the full heat of the sun. Once bathed, each petal must be dried to a crisp between baked bricks of yellow sandstone and then ground under a granite pestle. Powder is dissolv'd in yellow bile bearing the Aspect of Water, then said waters are boiled off. The caked ash should be aged a full year under opaque glass. Only then will it prove potent when smoked.

—*Basick Alkemie*, ann. 1290

14

A TRAIL OF SMOKE

As dawn broke, Brant had the wide chamber to himself. He laid a palm on the curving wood of the portside hull. If he leaned close, inhaled deeply enough, through the varnish and the trace of black bile, he could still catch a whiff of a familiar spice.

The resin of pompbonga-kee.

The scent of home.

For three days, he had recuperated in the heart of a wooden whale, one built from the very trees of his home realm. He felt swallowed whole, unable to escape his past. And now, against his will, he was being dragged back home. Four years ago, he had left Saysh Mal in chains and now he returned just as bound—if not by iron this time, then by duty.

Alone, he crossed the room to a curved rail that overlooked a wide window in the lower hull. The space, though smaller, mirrored the captain's Eye. The window opened a wide view of the passing landscape, the little that there was to see with dawn barely breaking.

But Brant had woken well before sunrise, knowing they'd be crossing into the Eighth Land this morning. Over the past days, tensions continued to mount within the craft as all wondered about the state of Tashijan. With the ship burning alchemies, they sped faster than any raven could wing.

The regent had been particularly short of mood, worn by the worry of it all, the responsibility. Even the roguish nature of Rogger and his ribald tales of his prior exploits did little to lighten spirits. Brant had also noted how Tylar had begun to limp over the past two days. No one commented upon it, but he had seen the regent, wearing a worrisome expression, kneading his left knee when he thought no one was looking.

But their confinement would soon end.

As Brant waited for sunrise, he felt a now-familiar warming of the stone at his throat. He searched around him, knowing Pupp must be near.

The door creaked open behind him. He turned to see Dart slip into the room. She wore the black boots and leggings of her station at Tashijan, though the shirt was untucked and worn loose. She had also left her half cloak back in her room. It was the first time that he had truly seen her free of cloak and hood. Her tawny yellow hair was longer than last he remembered, past the shoulder. She even looked taller out of her cloak, her eyes bluer. Still, the look she'd worn on her face when he first met her back at the school in Chrismferry remained. Anxious.

"Oh!" She startled back. "I didn't know anyone was in here."

"Just come to watch the sunrise," Brant said.

She edged back, awkward with her intrusion. She would not meet his eye.

"I'll leave you to your sunrise," she said.

"No . . . please . . ." He waved to the rail.

She approached warily, as if she would rather be anywhere else.

"I appreciate the company," he said, intending it as a balm for her, but was surprised at discovering it was also the truth. The realization suddenly dried any further words in his mouth.

Brant cleared his throat. He had heard about Dart's connection to the rogue god who had wandered so disastrously into his life. A god named Keorn, son of Chrism. The rogue god gave birth to her, while his death took Brant's life away. And it seemed now their lives were still linked: by the bones of the same god's skull.

His hand drifted closer to hers on the rail—not touching, just closer. Not finding words, he stared below. The roll of the sea lay beneath their keel, black still with night, but to the east, the skies brightened rapidly with hues of purple and rose. The first light revealed a new world rising steeply out of the seas, a land of rock and jungle, cliff and creeping vine.

She spoke to the wide window. "Tell me about the Eighth Land."

That, he could talk about. "Most of it is hinter—shattered rock, thick jungle, steaming vents of brimstone. There are few gentle beaches, few harbors. Only three gods made their homes there, each more isolated than the last."

Out the window, the morning sun set fire to the highest peaks.

Dart made a small exclamation, struck by the raw beauty of the sunrise. An ember of pride for his homeland burnt within him.

"Duck down here," he said and crouched below the railing.

As she knelt beside him, their shoulders touching, he pointed toward the brightening land rising from the sea. "The northernmost cliffs that lie ahead are the domain of Farallon, lord of the Nine Pools."

"The Jeweled Pools," Dart said with a thread of wonder. Five rivers flowed out of the highlands to form a cascading series of cataracts and waterfalls, captured on nine separate terraces, a great pool on each. "Is it true each pool is a different hue?"

"That's how they got their name. Master Sheershym, a chronicler at my school in Saysh Mal, says it's because of dissolved stone and water depth, but I'd rather think it's Farallon's Grace."

"It's probably both," Dart suggested.

The rising sun now glinted off the falling water in the distance.

"What's beyond the pools?"

Brant pointed higher, where the peaks glowed emerald in the first rays of the sun, shrouded in mists. "The highland mountains are split by a deep valley, all thickly forested."

"Saysh Mal," she said.

He only nodded. He had no wish to talk much about his home. They would be there soon enough. Instead, he crouched even lower and pointed to the curve of the horizon. There, almost directly south, was a shouldered mountain that towered above the others. Unlike the emerald glow of the highland peaks, the tip of that mountain turned the first rays of the sun into fire. But Brant knew the opposite was true. It was *snow* that tipped that mountain, an ice that lasted all the seasons, chilled by the thin air near the roof of the world.

Still, the mountain's heart burnt with fire.

"Takaminara," he said, naming god and mountain, a sleeping volcano that would occasionally quake the entire land.

"Truly? It doesn't appear as tall as I've heard tell."

"The distance deceives—as it has many men and women."

"And it's true that the god lives in caves at the top of the mountains? No castillion. No handservants. By herself."

"There are the occasional pilgrims who have braved the cliffs and crumbling ice," he said. "And those foolish few who seek merely to touch the sky. But most of those who climb seek to become her acolytes, to be blessed at her feet, to be burnt by her Grace and have their inner eye set ablaze."

"The *rub-aki*," she said, touching her forehead, "the Blood-eyed."

He nodded. The *rub-aki* were stained with the fiery blood of Takaminara. Each bore a crimson print of her thumb burnt into the middle of their foreheads.

"Can they truly see the future with their inner eyes?"

Brant shrugged. "It is said that by staring into their alchemical fires, they can portend the future. But few have ever witnessed a true foretelling."

"I once saw one of the Blood-eyed at the Grand Midsummer Faire back in Chrismferry."

"A charlatan surely. Master Sheershym once told me that fewer than two acolytes a decade survive the ordeal of Takaminara and return from her caverns into the world."

"But I've heard of plenty—"

"It's easy to tattoo one's forehead and claim to see the future. Master Sheershym said that for every thousand who claim to be *rub-aki*, only one truly is. And they certainly would *not* be selling their skills at a fair."

He said the last more harshly than he intended.

"Oh . . ." An edge of embarrassment returned to her voice and manner.

He suddenly felt like a cad. He stood up, drawing her up in his wake. "But in the end, I guess none of the god-realms really matter. Not even Saysh Mal. It is into the hinterlands that we must ultimately tread. Once there, we'll all be on equal footing."

"Equally blind," Dart mumbled.

From the shadows that moved over her features, he had only unsettled her further.

She stepped away. "I should return to my room. I need to collect my cloak and prepare my bag."

"Wait—" he blurted out before he could stop it.

She glanced to him.

He struggled for some way to make up for his poor manner. He didn't want matters to end this way. "I—I wanted to ask you something else. Something's that been troubling me."

"What's that?"

"It's about your creature—Pupp, isn't it?"

Brant noted her turn slightly to the left, where Pupp must be roaming.

"I mentioned this to the regent, and I didn't know if he told you. My stone—I can see Pupp if it touches him, and I sense him if he draws near, a warming in the stone that can turn fiery if he's very close. Not like the skull, but still mightily hot."

She nodded. "I heard. That's how you found the room where Pyllor attacked me."

Her eyes found his, no longer shamed but more grateful and open. Under her immediate gaze, he struggled to find his tongue and failed.

She finally broke contact and explained, "Your stone must be ripe with wild Grace. If strong enough, any Grace—blood or otherwise—can draw Pupp fully into this world for a short time." After a moment, she gestured toward his hand. "Could I see your stone? I never did get a good look at it."

With a nod, he tugged the cord to pull the stone free from his shirt. She leaned closer to examine it.

Brant caught the scent of her hair and noted the curve of her neck as she cocked her head to study the rock. He suddenly found himself warming all over. He wanted to step away, but at the same time to step closer. Trapped between, he stood very still, as if he were being hunted.

"It's beautiful," Dart said, fingering the stone. "I hadn't realized. The way it catches every bit of light."

He felt the gentle tugs on the cord around his neck as she turned the stone in her fingers. It all but unmoored him.

Then underfoot, a slight tremble reverberated through the ship's planks. They both took a step back and glanced to the windows. The flippercraft turned inland and passed over the first of the black cliffs that shot straight out of the churning white waves and treacherous currents.

"We've crossed into the Eighth Land," Dart whispered.

As the flippercraft angled higher and the sun cleared the seas to the east, the entire land suddenly ignited, awash in morning light. Past the climb of the Nine Pools, the highlands awaited, framed in green peaks, thick with mists that glowed as pink as the clamshells of Farallon's Ruby Pool.

But as the sun rose, it revealed a disturbing sight farther up in the highlands. A black pall mingled with the mist.

Dart noted it, too. "Smoke . . ."

With a growing sense of unease, Tylar stood on the captain's deck, sharing a rail with Rogger and Krevan. "Still no word from any of the ravens we sent?"

"Not one's returned," Rogger said.

They had sent four birds flying with each bell as the flippercraft crossed into the Eighth Land. They bore messages toward Saysh Mal, announcing their arrival, inviting welcome and tidings. Tylar had ordered their craft slowed when smoke was noted rising into the skies.

Smudge smoke, Krevan had assessed with his more experienced eye. It did not churn and writhe with the breath of fresh flame. The pall here seeped from an old fire, one still smoldering in ember.

"What about the raven we dispatched to Farallon?"

Rogger shook his head, then shrugged. "No surprise with that one. When I stopped at the Nine Pools during my pilgrimage, Farallon was lost to his own dreamsmoke, wallowing in a torpid state from inhaling too deeply on his water pipes, bubbling with the dried and burnt petals of the realm's water lotus. You could burn his palm-thatched castillion down around his ears, and he'd still not move. His household had been little better."

Krevan pointed to the mountainous peaks with their vertiginous cliffs draped in greenery. The cloud forests still lay hidden in the valleys beyond, blanketed behind mist and smoke. "We should continue forward. We waste the day's light. I'd prefer to be there before night falls."

Tylar agreed and motioned for the captain to stoke the alchemies and gain the height necessary to climb from the Nine Pools into the highlands. The flippercraft rose with the barest shudder. Two massive peaks stood as sentinels before them, framing the gateway into the forests of Saysh Mal.

They had no choice but to trespass.

The flippercraft circled out and back, gaining the height to push over the falls, but just barely. The ship sailed forward between the towering peaks, fording the waterfalls from a distance close enough for spray to sparkle the flippercraft's glass Eye.

Then they climbed higher yet, following a twisting concourse that switched up between jagged peaks until at last the squeeze of the mountains released them. A vast valley opened ahead, a gulf of mist cupped by green peaks. A few taller sentinels of the forest poked through the clouds and patches of open jungle shone brilliantly, like emeralds half-buried in snow.

But all was plainly not well.

Except for a few green pockets, the entire western edge of the valley floor lay exposed like a charred scar. Rising heat held back the morning mists, revealing the devastation. The forest had burnt to embers, leaving black trunks sticking out of the burnt ground like planted spears, a fiery palisade between Saysh Mal and the hinterlands that stretched out from the border there.

"What happened?" Lorr asked.

The tracker led in Brant and Dart. Brant wore a grim expression.

"Has there ever been a fire like this before in Saysh Mal?" Tylar asked.

"No. The Huntress controls root, leaf, and loam, protecting any ravaging fires from spreading. The only time I've seen such wild burns is in some of the lowland jungles of the hinterland. But never up in the highlands."

"Until now," Rogger murmured.

"Could she still be raving?" Brant asked. "Could a simple fire have been started by lightning, and in her madness, she did not stanch it but let it burn?"

Tylar looked to the thief for answers. Rogger was the one of them who had most recently visited this land, when he stole the skull.

His eyes held a worried glint as he rubbed the scraggly beard under his chin. "Eylan," he mumbled and flashed Tylar a significant glance. "You saw her state when Brant broke the seersong's grip on her. Her mind all but tore apart in the struggle. Taking the skull and hauling my arse out of there may not have been the wisest theft."

Krevan made a grumble that clearly agreed with Rogger. But he kept any further accusations to himself.

Rogger continued. "Seersong is like a worm that takes root in a body rich in Grace. Look how it persists in the bones of Keorn, well after his death. Once embedded deeply enough, like with Eylan, or long enough, like with Keorn, the song becomes irretrievably entangled in mind and flesh."

"And when you took the skull . . ." Tylar said, beginning to sense the depth of the error.

"Are you familiar with tanglebriar?" Rogger asked.

Tylar frowned. There was no need to answer. Everyone knew about tanglebriar, the thorny and stubborn growth that could be found everywhere throughout the Nine Lands. It proved almost impossible to kill, even with fire.

"Tanglebriar," Rogger said, "is like any pernicious weed in a garden. You rip it free, only to have it grow back wilder. But tanglebriar is even more insidious. You tear off what's above the soil, and its roots respond by digging deeper, spreading wider, bursting forth more robust than the original thorny stalk."

"And you think seersong might be like tanglebriar?"

"If it fully gets its roots in you." Rogger turned to the fire. "Taking the skull might have been like ripping tanglebriar. Whatever had already been planted in the Huntress over the years may have responded in kind. Driven deep, spread wider, bursting forth with an even more ravening madness."

"Mad enough to let her own realm burn?" Tylar asked.

Rogger just stared toward the devastation. "There's only one way to find out."

Tylar's eyes drifted away from the charred forest and turned to the tallest sentinel of it. Its crown of leaves caught the morning light and glowed with green fire. An ancient pompbonga-kee. The oldest of all the forest—and home to the Huntress.

No matter the risk, they would have to venture down there.

They needed answers from this realm. If they were to follow the footsteps of Keorn back into the hinter, they would need to start in the lands here, where his tracks ended. Additionally, Brant said a chronicler from the school in Saysh Mal possessed a map of the neighboring hinterlands, centuries old and sketchy at best, but better than having no guide at all.

But most important of all, Tylar had another reason to point his arm toward the castillion rising above the mists. He preferred not to enter the forbidden hinterlands with a ravening god at his back.

Obeying his silent command, the ship smoothly banked out over the wide jungle, turning its stern toward the smolder, and aimed for the tallest tree in the forest. With the dying fire behind them, the spread of cloud forest appeared like a vast emerald lake, swept by fog, untouched. And as the sun climbed above the horizon, the mists thinned, slowly revealing the breadth of canopy and the fervent vitality of the steaming and damp jungle beneath. It was a pristine world, beyond man and god. Seeing it like this, Tylar wondered how it even could burn—and who would be coldhearted enough to let it.

Brant joined him. "In the shadow of the Huntress's castillion, a large bowled meadow lies open to the sky. It should be wide enough to land the flippercraft."

Tylar nodded across the deck. "Inform Captain Horas. Help guide him to the spot."

As the boy left, Tylar turned to discover that others had gathered here, the remainder of their party, drawn by their approach into Saysh Mal.

Krevan's woman, Calla, had entered and stood at her leader's shoulder, staring out toward the spread of misty jungle. Though she still wore the gray cloak of her guild, she had shed her ash for this voyage, a rare sign of trust. Tylar had been surprised to find her skin as pale as milk, softening her considerably, until you looked into her eyes. They remained as hard as agates and as sharp as the daggers at her wrists. She may have washed her face, but she was still a Flagger at heart.

Filling the doorway was the last member of their party, the loam-giant Malthumalbaen. Tylar had spent the previous morning talking to the man. While the giant's tongue might be thick and coarse, there was a quick wit about him—though perhaps tinged a bit more darkly by his brother's passing. Still, a certain easy companionship developed between them, a balm for Tylar's own misgivings. Perhaps sensing this, the giant had filled the emptiness with tales of his brother's exploits, mostly involved with the bottomless pit that was his brother's belly.

With everyone gathered, Tylar spoke to the group. "Once we land, we'll leave the mekanicals stoked high in case a hurried departure is necessary. Krevan and I will inspect the state of the immediate area. The rest will remain with the ship."

Malthumalbaen spoke from the doorway. "Mayhap I should go with. A strong arm may serve where a quick sword fails."

Tylar bowed his head at the offer. "I would prefer that strong arm guard the ship and those inside."

Other objections were voiced Tylar held up his hand and dismissed each in turn. "Lorr, I know your skills at tracking, but even in the best of moods, the Huntress has forbidden the Grace-bred from her lands. Calla, your gray cloak is no match to our shadowcloaks. And Dart, I will be bringing more than just Rivenscryr." He patted his belt, where a diamond-pommeled sword was sheathed, a shadowknight's blade. "And I have a tiny repostilary of your blood should it prove necessary to anoint the Godsword."

He turned to Rogger.

The thief held up his own hand. "I'm fine with staying inside the flippercraft."

"Keep the skull hidden," Tylar said.

"What skull?"

Tylar rolled his eyes and swung back forward. The ship sailed over the treetops, skimming mists. He stepped over to join Captain Horas and Brant.

"The Grove lies below the castillion. On its east side. See the shadow cast by the rising sun?" Brant pointed to the marker. "That's where we want to go."

As the pilot corrected their glide, Tylar's gaze followed where the shadow pointed, farther off to the west. The blaze of the morning sun stretched across the valley to ignite two of the tallest peaks in the western range, pinnacles so steep that even the creeping vines could not scale them. The bare rock, rich in salts and crystals, captured the sun's rays and ignited with fire.

Brant noted where he looked. "The Forge," he said. "The two peaks are named the Hammer and the Anvil."

"With the fire between," Tylar said.

"They flare at sunrise and at sunset," Brant mumbled, plainly drawn into old memories. "In the forests near the Forge—that is where the rogue god burnt to ash."

Tylar tried to spy the spot, but the ship rolled back around, putting the Forge astern.

It took another quarter bell to reach the ancient pompbonga-kee. The mists below remained thick, gathered close around the leafy crown of the forest. The tree's shadow stretched across the white shroud.

Brant spoke in low whispers to the captain.

Horas was not so quiet. "And you're sure there is an open glade below? We'll be dropping in blind."

"I'm sure."

"The boy's right," Rogger said, sneaking up behind them in his soft boots. "A great big empty hollow full of weeds and low scrub bushes."

Brant glanced to him, pained. "Last I saw it, the hollow of the Grove was a rolling meadow of green grasses and flowers."

Tylar cut in. "Either way, it is the only open space within a hundred reaches of the castillion."

Both Rogger and Brant nodded.

"Then take us down, Captain Horas. Right through the tip of the tree's shadow."

By now, everyone had gathered to the rails on either side of the pilot's spar. Captain Horas called orders to his four-man crew, the additional hand gained in Broken Cay. The pilot worked wheel and pedals, deftly adjusting the aeroskimmers to float them over the shadow, and slowly they sank into the mists.

Sunlight lost its sharp glare, then grew ever dimmer. It was as if they were descending into a twilight sea. Still, the water in the mists captured enough of the surface brilliance to bathe the ship in a suffusing glow. Around them, shadowy giants appeared ahead and to both sides.

"The Graces," Brant announced. "The giant pompbongakee that make up the Grove."

The captain shied from these ghostly behemoths, blindly feeling for the glade's center.

Finally, the potbellied keel of the flippercraft dropped below the cloud layer. There was little time to react or call out further orders. The ground rose quickly, appearing suddenly.

The pilot hauled on the wheel to raise the aeroskimmers high. They did not want to break any of the control paddles. The Eye fell toward the field below.

Tylar captured only a harried glimpse of the hollow. Cloaked in mist and shadowed by the height of the giant sentinels, the Grove remained in a perpetual gloom. All he managed to see was a strange bristling across the slopes of the bowl. Then the Eye slammed into the ground with a teeth-jarring bump, burying the view in tall grasses.

Tylar heard a slight crackling as they hit, like the snap of branches, but there was no pop of plank or loud crack of broken paddle. Everyone was silent for a long moment, as if unsure they were still among the living and afraid to ruin the illusion.

Then Captain Horas barked an order, readying his crew to check the state of the flippercraft.

Tylar forced his fingers to loosen their grip on the railing.

They'd made it.

Krevan caught his eye. "We should not tarry. Our arrival will not go unnoted for long. The quicker we're out and lost in shadow, the better we'll know what we face."

As a group, they vacated the captain's deck and retreated to the rear. Krevan crossed to the side hatch and began unscrewing the latch. Faces sought portholes. Tylar joined them.

He pressed his forehead against the frame of one of the tiny windows. The mist seemed to have been sucked down with their passage. There was nothing to see beyond a swirling murk.

Frowning, he returned to Krevan, who shouldered the hatch open and flipped down the small ladder. It struck the ground with a rattle, then settled.

They listened for a long breath. The world beyond lay quiet. No trill of birdsong. Not even a buzz and whir of winged nits and natterings. Had their landing hushed the realm?

"Ready?" Krevan asked, pulling up the hood of his cloak.

Tylar nodded.

The pirate leader climbed down and jumped lightly to the ground. Tylar followed, hesitated a moment, recalling how Keorn had been burned by his trespass. Then he also stepped down and joined Krevan.

As he landed with his left foot, a sharp complaint rose from his knee. He hopped off it and tottered a step.

"Are you all right?" Krevan asked.

"A stone," he muttered, covering the twinge.

The ache slowly subsided in a couple of steps, as it had over the past two days. While normally he would have dismissed the cramp as merely some turn of his knee, the pang here was doggedly familiar, echoing back to when the same knee had once been frozen and cobbled from a poorly healed break.

It was disconcerting.

He opened and closed his fist. His little finger, still wrapped, was slowly on the mend. Maybe a bit crooked, but it would leave no lasting weakness.

As the ache faded in his leg, he pushed back these misgivings for another time and faced the flippercraft. "Keep guard on the door," he called quietly to Malthumalbaen, who stood at the threshold.

The giant nodded.

Tylar turned away to find Krevan had already drifted off, shadowy in the mists. He limped to join him, drawing on a trickle of darkness into his cloak to steady himself.

Ahead, the pirate had stopped, his back to Tylar. A growling sound rose from him, angry, offended.

"What's wrong?"

Krevan stepped back to reveal what his large bulk had hidden.

A shaft of peeled and sharpened wood rose from the ground, planted deep in the loam. Impaled upon it was the head of an old woman, her gray braid black with her own blood, tongue lolling out, skin mottled with rot. Flies and worms squirmed and crawled across her flesh. Her eyes had been pecked or gouged out.

Only now did Tylar note the reek hidden beneath the decay of leaf and a heavy dampness to the air. Details grew as his eyes adjusted to the gloom. To either side, he noted more burdened stakes.

Aghast, he backed a step toward the ship.

The mists slowly rose, swirling back up. Bits of dust and dried grass drifted down, cast high by their hard landing. The view opened. Tylar remembered the strange bristling he had noted as they fell out of the sky. He now understood what he had glimpsed. Climbing up the slopes in widening rings were hundreds of stakes.

All bearing aloft their ripe and rotted fruit.

"No . . ." Tylar mumbled.

This was far worse than any uncontested fire. A ravening darkness shadowed this realm fully. He recalled Rogger's story of tanglebriar. He stared at the field of sharpened stakes. Seersong had indeed taken root—and here was the thorny growth that sprouted from that seed.

"Her own people," Krevan said in disgust.

In step, both men retreated toward the flippercraft.

Then Tylar heard a whistling to the air. Flashes drew his eyes up. Streaks of flame shot through the mists like trailing stars in the night. They arced out from the shrouded forest, climbing high, then angled back downward. Score upon score blazed through the murky clouds.

"Arrows," Krevan said, twisting to grab Tylar's shoulder and pull him toward the flippercraft.

Too late.

Fire fell out of the sky and pummeled the flippercraft lying at the bottom of the sea of mist. The impacts sounded like hail on a wooden roof. But it was *flame*, not ice, that rained down upon the beached flippercraft. Not a single arrow missed its target.

Shouts arose from inside the ship.

But before Tylar could even call to the others, a second volley of flaming arrows filled the sky with their streaking brilliance. A moment later, amid the shocked cries of the others, another round of flame beat down upon the back of the craft, already aflame.

Again, not an arrow fell astray.

If it was madness that truly ruled here, it had honed its marksmanship.

The fires spread rapidly, sped by some alchemy imbued in the oil of the arrows. Flames ran like fiery snakes across the hull.

"Get the others out," Tylar ordered Krevan. There was no use attempting to escape by air. The flippercraft would burn down to its mekanicals by the time they cleared the mists.

Unless he did something about it.

Tylar wiped his brow, then slid out a dagger. He drew its edge across his palm and drew a fiery line of blood.

Sweat to imbue, and blood to open the way.

He would fight the flames with his own humours. He pictured ice, as frigid as the cold that had stolen Eylan from them. He built the blessing in his bloody palm, prepared to use his sweat to cast it upon the craft. He would freeze the flames from his ship.

He raised his hand—but before he could slap palm to wood, an arrow struck exactly where he had intended to place his hand. The *thunk* of its impact startled him back a step. It was as if the arrow had sprouted out of the hull, rather than being shot from afar.

The feathered end quivered at his nose.

But that was not all.

Skewered on the shaft of the arrow was a raven, one of the messengers he had sent ahead.

Here at last had come his answer from the Huntress.

A threat by marksmanship.

At any moment, an arrow could be sent through his own heart.

He lowered his arm.

Krevan came dashing out, leading others from the ship.

"Run!" the pirate shouted and pointed an arm up the slope.

Before Tylar could even turn, the top of the flippercraft exploded away in a great gout of swirling flame. A wall of heat knocked them all off their feet. Krevan was the first back up, scooping Dart under one arm, dragging Brant by an arm.

"Go!" he shouted.

They were all running as fiery planks fell, raining down into the loam. It was sheer luck that no one was struck. Once clear, Tylar counted heads. Too few.

"Horas? his men?" he asked.

Krevan shook his head. "The arrows . . . bore a dark alchemy of loam, anathema to air. Captain tried to tamp the mekanical. Save the ship."

The pirate turned to Tylar. Fire shone in his eyes, burning with the promise of revenge.

As if challenging this threat, laughter carried to them, floating out of the mists above, as if from clouds themselves.

Brant stepped to Tylar's shoulder. "The Huntress," the boy said, naming the true source of the amusement, hidden up in the mists, aloft in her castillion.

Her words echoed down to him, powered by Grace.

"Welcome, Godslayer . . . welcome to Saysh Mal!"

15

A SCRATCH AT THE WINDOW

"ARE ALL THE TOWNSFOLK SECURE?" KATHRYN ASKED.

Keeper Ryngold nodded. "We've turned the Grand Court into a makeshift inn. The accommodations in the amphitheater will be nothing more than a stone bed and a blanket, but it's warm and out of the winds."

They spoke in private outside the door to a gathering room midlevel in Stormwatch. She heard the murmur of voices beyond the door. She was to meet this morning with representatives of the retinues from the various realms. It was her current role here in Tashijan. No more than innkeeper, settling disputes and addressing concerns of those under their roof.

Warden Fields had even banned her from the strategies in the fieldroom. *If you see little reason to keep me abreast of your plots and plans, then there is little reason for me to do the same*. Normally a castellan could not be so easily cast aside. As they usually arose out of the Council of Masters to fill that high seat, a castellan had the backing of all the masters with their alchemies and knowledge. No warden would dare treat a castellan so dismissively.

But Kathryn did not have the support of the Council of Masters. If anything, she had gained their enmity as well. Especially Master Hesharian. He had been more purple of face than even Argent, and had offered no objection to her being shut out of the fieldroom.

Still, it could have been worse. She could have been locked up for treason. After Tylar and the others departed by flippercraft, she had stood behind her decision. If the storm gods wanted the Godslayer, then better Tylar be sent away. His flight might draw off attention. She justified her secrecy by relating what Tylar had found in their cellars, evidence of some collusion between Tashijan and the daemon army below. It was beyond mere chance that Mirra nabbed the skull shortly after those in the fieldroom learned of its existence. Even Argent had glanced around the table then. He was no fool.

So she managed to keep herself free of bars and locks.

But little else.

In fact, she had been the last to learn about the emptying of the town that huddled outside Tashijan. Argent had sent a good portion of his knightly force beyond the walls to shepherd the people inside. The townsfolk swelled into Tashijan with stories of the storm closing down upon their homes, whispers of strange beasts seen behind swirls of snow, of bodies found frozen and ripped.

Upon hearing this, Kathryn had gone under cloak to see for herself. The storm had tightened down upon the shield walls of Tashijan, swallowing up the outer village. There was a savagery and fury in the winds, almost tasted on the tongue. And despite the additional burden and loss of life, the raging uplifted her spirits.

The anger here could mean only one thing: Tylar and the others had escaped. The storm god tore into the town in his fury, closing tighter around Tashijan.

But so far that was the only change. Over the past three days, the siege had stretched with a deceptive calm. Argent had fires blazing again throughout the lower levels of the tower. He had even bricked up the tunnel behind the Shield Gong in the Grand Court as it stretched down into the Masterlevels. Yet there had been no further move by Mirra.

It was as if both sides were holding their breath, preparing for a final assault. But how would it strike? In what form? Or would they be merely starved out? Pondering this worry . . .

"How are we doing on food and fresh water?" she asked the keeper of the towers.

"Lucky the warden had planned a grand series of feasts for the regent's knighting," Keeper Ryngold said with a tired grin. "Our ice lockers and foodstores were heavily fortified prior to the attack. We'll make do for the moment, but the townsfolk will stretch us thin."

"We'll have to manage."

"Of course," he said with a nod to the door, "you'll have to convince our esteemed guests inside there that the heft and variety of their meal boards may be less than they are accustomed to enjoying."

She sighed. "I'll do my best."

With a slight bow, Keeper Ryngold departed. She watched him move down the hall, admiring the man's fortitude. In many ways, here was the true warden of the towers.

And at least *he* was still speaking with her.

She turned back to the door, took hold of the latch and her patience, and pushed into the crowd inside. The gathering room was one of the teaching halls, lined by two long tables, with an elevated stage at the front. Lamps flickered along the walls.

She spotted Delia near the front of one table and nodded. Kathryn still felt a certain discomfort around the younger woman, still picturing the stolen kiss with Tylar. She knew such resentments were petty and unfair, and over the past days, they had begun to fade as the two women were forced to work closely alongside each other. Delia had proven herself as adept as Keeper Ryngold in maintaining some degree of control over the various households of the gods. Kathryn had come to rely on her calmness in the face of strife, on her evenhanded decisions. She was surprised how relieved she was to find Delia already at work today. It was good to have one ally.

There certainly were enough here with complaints.

The leader of the disgruntled fronted the second table: the lithe, snow blond Hand from Oldenbrook. Alongside her sat a swarthy slug in purple, the sole Hand dispatched from neighboring Foulsham Dell. Despite their plain dislike for one another—and more disparate appearance and manner—they had joined forces to plague Kathryn for the past two days.

Filling the rest of the boards, divided almost equally into the two camps, were the other heads of the retinues trapped at Tashijan. With Delia sat the representatives from Mistdale, Snowfox River, Crooked Wood, Fitz Crossing, and surprisingly the embittered crook-backed Hand from Moor Eld. The other table bore the hard faces from Akkabak Harbor, Five Forks, Wintering Isles, and Martyrstone.

Liannora rose to her feet before Kathryn even reached the teaching dais. "Thank you for attending to our grievances."

Kathryn mounted the single step to the raised stage. She ignored the woman.

"Castellan Vail," Liannora continued, "we understand the dangers that have beset Tashijan, and we all here want to help in any manner we can. Toward that end, what we propose—"

"Propose?" Kathryn snapped as she turned. "What I propose, with all respect, Mistress Liannora, is that you take your seat. This meeting was not called to listen to your arguments but for you all to better understand the plight of your situation. While Tashijan values your knowledge and skills in regards to handling humours, there are no gods here. It is skill with sword, or mastery of alchemy, that is most needed."

Liannora's features brittled even harder. She kept her feet. Perhaps for no other reason than that she might snap in half if she sat. "Warden Fields has given me his word that we would be heard here." She glanced down her table. "Is that not so?"

Murmurs of agreement acknowledged the same.

So the woman had been a plague not only upon Kathryn. Argent must have been equally assaulted, but the warden had somewhere to push the complaints—back at Kathryn.

"What is it that you propose, then, Mistress Liannora?"

"We believe that as representatives of gods that bless the First Land and its distinguished neighbors we should be more involved with the defenses here. Not left to languish in our rooms. We have no desire to hide, or worse yet, *run* from our duty to Myrillia . . . like craven *cowards*."

She stressed this last word. Kathryn had heard the same word being spread by the Fiery Cross. Tylar's flight from Tashijan was seen by many as abandonment, or worse yet, outright spinelessness. It was plain on which side of the fence Liannora had decided to stand. The woman had an uncanny ability to sense the flows of power and to bend them to her advantage. Kathryn remembered her earlier flatteries; those had turned to insolence at about the same time Kathryn had been banned from the fieldroom. Liannora had recognized the ascendancy of the Fiery Cross and sided with their arguments and slights.

"I have yet to hear your proposal," Kathryn said. "Do you wish to take up swords yourself and defend the stairs?"

Liannora dismissed her words with a flutter of an arm. "Certainly not. Our strengths lie in our keen experience and expertise. We would wish no more than to be ready with a suggestion, to act as counsel to those that wage our defenses. To be represented and involved in the stratagems."

Kathryn's brow crinkled.

"I've discussed it with my fellow Hands," Liannora continued, nodding to her table. "And we think it only best that we cast stones amongst ourselves and proffer one of our own to join those in the fieldroom who *truly* defend these towers."

A slight cocking of the woman's eyebrow accentuated the insult, directed at both Kathryn and the departed regent.

Kathryn did not rise to the bait. Instead, she found herself bemused by the woman's posturing. Delia had warned her about the Hand, cautioned against underestimating her cunning and lust for power. If Argent had been born a woman, here he would stand.

Kathryn lifted her hand yet again. "I encourage you to cast your stones. I think it wise that you select one amongst you to represent all. It would certainly expedite matters of communication."

Liannora bowed her head, accepting the compliment with poised humility.

"But," Kathryn went on. "The warden certainly would not allow any but the heads of Tashijan to attend his meetings in the fieldroom."

Kathryn offered a look of apology. Let Argent deal with the woman if her ire was piqued.

"Oh," Liannora said, straightening with an arch glint in her eye, "I've already discussed the matter with Warden Fields. He concurs and invites our participation."

Kathryn gaped for a moment, taken aback. Why would Argent allow—? Then she knew. What better way to further humiliate Kathryn? To be banished while the likes of Liannora were allowed entry.

Liannora stepped into her silence, addressing the others.

"So with all in agreement, we will cast stones." She glanced to Kathryn. "If you'd be so kind as to count the tally, it would be most appreciated."

Kathryn had no choice but to concede, having been artfully manipulated into this position.

The Hand from Foulsham Dell stood up, clearing phlegm from his throat with a grousing hack. He teetered slightly on his heels, plainly soused. His purple cloak and shirt must have been selected to hide the spill of wine down his paunch of a belly.

"I think there can be no doubt who should represent us." He bowed with exaggerated flourish. "Mistress Liannora has shown herself to be of ample skill and of quick mind. Hear, hear!" He called to his table, raising an imaginary goblet. "Bring on the stones!"

At the other table, Porace Neel of Moor Eld gained his feet with a groan, supporting the crook in his back. "And I propose Mistress Delia. All know her and hold her in genuine esteem. She is wiser than the whole lot of us."

A few at her table rapped knuckles on the board, agreeing.

Not so at Liannora's table.

"I'm sure Mistress Delia would prefer to avoid such a burden," Liannora said. "All know the tension between warden and daughter. And dare I say, we must acknowledge here that Mistress Delia is not in fact the handservant of a *god*, but only a *man*."

Delia stood. "For the good of Tashijan, I am more than willing to set aside such tensions."

"And as we had all gathered here to honor that *man*," Kathryn added, "to acknowledge his rightful place as both knight and regent, I certainly don't think we can cast Mistress Delia in a lesser light."

Liannora stared at Kathryn and read her resolve.

The woman dipped her chin. "Of course."

With only the two names proffered, it did not take long to cast stones. Each Hand placed a stone into the bag: white for Liannora, black for Delia.

The bag was brought to Kathryn. In short order she tallied the count and announced the result. "We have an equal number of stones for each."

Liannora hid her disappointment behind pursed lips. Delia merely kept her arms crossed.

"Are there any here who would wish to change the cast of their stones?" Kathryn asked.

No hands were raised.

"Then I see no other recourse as castellan of Tashijan than to declare it an even match. Since the warden has so wisely chosen to expand his council, then what better way to acknowledge his wisdom than to send him *two* from our assembly? Mistress Liannora *and* Mistress Delia."

Liannora wore a momentary expression of irritation, but the look swept away just as quickly, replaced with a feigned smile of acceptance as the others congratulated her.

Delia met Kathryn's eye, offering her own smile. For days, they had been cut out of the strategies waged in the fieldroom. Now Argent had unwittingly opened the door again.

After all the well wishes had been passed around, the Hands departed to spread the word among the others. Delia paused to touch Kathryn's arm.

"I will pass on your greetings to my father."

"Please do."

Liannora waited at the door, plainly wishing to speak with Delia. If there were any match for that woman, it was Delia. Kathryn waited until the room was empty to step out into the hall.

She found a welcome figure waiting, leaned against a wall. Another of their dejected party. Master Hesharian had had her friend officially sanctioned for his participation in the subterfuge atop Stormwatch. She was surprised to find him here.

"Gerrod?"

He straightened and fell in step beside her. "I heard word of the ploy being set up here. Master Hesharian was never one to keep silent with his gossip—especially if it involved the humiliation of another. And I still have secret allies among his inner circle. Oh, you should have heard what was said when it was discovered that not only had Tylar escaped but he had taken their only weapon against seersong."

"I can imagine."

Gerrod accompanied her toward the stair. She could hear the smile hidden behind his helmet. "Master Orquell came near to throttling his benefactor when he heard about the skull vanishing with Tylar."

"We had no choice," Kathryn mumbled, suddenly tired. It was a long climb back up to her hermitage.

With his usual acuity, Gerrod sensed her exhaustion and grew silent, offering her nothing more than his company as they climbed together. She appreciated it.

Still, as she wound her way up, her worries mounted with each step, stacked one atop the other. Eventually they toppled out. "What if he can't find the rogues? Maybe it was a mistake . . . ?"

"Hush. Such thoughts will only drive you into a state of inaction. We did what was necessary. If Tylar escaped the storm, word of our plight has spread. We must do our best to maintain here."

"So we wait, hoping for rescue." She shook her head. "I still wish there was something beyond our defenses we could bolster."

"Keeping alive may prove fight enough from here. Our best offense was in breaking Tylar free to seek the rogues."

Kathryn was reassured by his confidence in their decision, but little settled. Perhaps her dissatisfaction had more to do with being banished from the inner council of Tashijan. At least a small victory had been won this morning. With Delia admitted to the fieldroom, Kathryn would be kept better abreast of Argent's plans and defenses.

At last, they reached the level of her hermitage. She would break her fast with Gerrod, then proceed with her day.

As she pushed into the hermitage, her maid Penni greeted her in her usual flustered manner. She had the hearth glowing with low flames. A small table had been spread with marbled breads, hard cheeses, and jams. Kathryn thanked the maid, then dismissed her. She knew that Gerrod preferred to keep his countenance hidden in his bronze armor unless alone with her.

Once Penni vanished down the back door, Kathryn turned to find Gerrod standing, almost shyly, only a few steps from the door.

"We won't be disturbed," she assured him and waved to the low table with the morning fare.

One arm slowly raised. His voice echoed hollowly out of his helmet. "Kathryn . . ."

Gerrod's arm stiffened with a grinding creak. She stepped toward him.

"Can't move . . ." he said, strained. "Mekanicals freezing up."

She remembered when his armor had last grown sluggish. When he'd been exposed to the sapping of the storm, the Grace drained from his armor's alchemies.

She heard a scratching behind her.

Twisting around, she drew her sword and pointed it toward the far drapes. The flames in the hearth damped to embers, then even the red coals dimmed. Cold spread across the room.

A long, skittering scrape sounded against the windows, dry branches on glass.

Gerrod groaned behind her, stiff in his armor. "Run . . ."

Laurelle wrinkled her nose. She found that Kytt carried a distinct odor about him. A musk, like a boy after a heavy run, only cleaner, with a slightly woody scent. She stood beside the young wyld tracker as he listened at the door. They were holed up in Brant's room, listening for noises out in the hallway.

Kytt had taken to sleeping here, watching over the cubbies.

Barrin lolled beside the hearth, all but blocking the glow with his bulk. The two wolfkits wrestled across the breadth of his form, worming under legs, over haunches, growling and nipping at each other. They still used a pair of the giant's boots as dens at night and had shredded one of Brant's shirts as bedding.

They had seemed to settle well into the space.

But that was about to change.

Laurelle had come every morning and night for the past three days, slipping out of her halls and down to where the Oldenbrook retinue made their home. As the towers grew more crowded, this level was also shared by the four men from Akkabak Harbor, home of the Gray Traders. Freck-twist, the god of that realm, tolerated only men as his Hands. He had little regard for women in his realm, seeing them as little more than broodmares. His Hands also gleaned that same sentiment, as if burnt into them by his Grace.

She heard them pass by the door, grumbling under their breath. She heard Delia's name, but she could make out little else. Then they were gone. Laurelle suspected Kytt heard every word as clear as if they were in the room.

"Is it safe?" Laurelle asked.

Kytt held up a hand. She noted that his fingernails were short, but filed to clawed points. In fact, Kytt seemed all sharp edges: tips of ears that poked slightly through his dark hair, the pointed squint of his eyes, even the hint of wolfish teeth when he allowed a shadow of a shy smile to form.

Then Laurelle heard it, too. The approach of two others. She was able to make out their words, spoken with little regard to who might hear, so confident in their positions that they did not bother to blunt their rudeness.

"I can't believe the regent's sellwench squirmed her way into my shadow," Liannora hissed. "She's certain to be favored by the warden, what with her being Fields's daughter. I'll be ignored."

Her companion consoled her. "Who can ignore you? You shine brighter than the sun when you enter a room."

"Oh, Sten, you can be so simple sometimes. I see how the warden watches her when that grubbing Hand isn't looking. There's no outshining family." Liannora sniffed with disdain. "If only she stepped down or was made to step down . . ."

Sten's voice lowered to a whisper, but by now they were passing the door to Brant's room. "Missteps do happen. It is easy to trip on a stair. To break a leg . . . or even a neck."

Liannora responded in equally low tones, but by then they had moved on down the hall. A bit of laughter carried back, then after another moment, silence.

Laurelle pulled her ear from the door. "Kytt, did you hear what that ice queen said? Were they merely speaking tall or were they serious?"

Kytt shook his head. "Even my ears are only so sharp. Her lips must have been at his ear."

"I must find Delia."

"What about the cubbies?" he asked.

She nodded. "We'll move them first. Like we were planning. Then I'll seek out Delia and warn her."

Kytt strode toward the cubbies, sensing her urgency. "You take the boy. I'll take the girl."

Laurelle nodded. They had a pair of roughspun carryalls, meant to sling babies across a woman's chest. They would each take one whelping. The plan was to abscond with the wolf cubbies and carry them up to Lorr's abandoned rooms. Kytt had heard talk among the Oldenbrook guards that some harm was intended them, and as the wyld tracker was not of their realm, he had no real authority to stop them. The wolves remained the retinue's property.

So the plan was to get them somewhere safe.

But thievery was beyond either of their skills. They didn't know how anyone from Oldenbrook might respond, so they intended to make the move without any eyes about. The cubbies had escaped once already. It would be easy to explain away another disappearance.

Laurelle gathered up her carryall and lured the smaller of the two cubbies, the boy, notable for the extra white on the tips of his black ears, with a piece of dried mutton. She had the cubbie quickly bundled and contentedly chewing the salted meat. A low growling flowed as she slung the carryall over one shoulder and cradled the wolf across her chest.

Kytt had his cubbie, too. He held her back from the door, leaned his ear, listened for another couple of breaths, then nodded.

Barrin was already on his paws, ready to follow.

Kytt opened the door and led the way out. Laurelle followed. The bullhound padded after them.

The hallway was empty, except for one of the knights at the level's landing. They moved quickly. A door opened behind them. Voices carried. Guards.

Ducking down, hidden by the bulk of the bullhound, Laurelle heard Sten, captain of the guard, call brusquely toward them. "Who goes there?"

Kytt shrugged off his carryall and slid it over to Laurelle. He motioned for her to continue. Barrin's form filled the hall. With care, she should be able to reach the stairs without the guards seeing her.

She squeezed Kytt's hand, then sidled low to the floor, close to one wall. Kytt straightened behind her, edged past Barrin, and signaled by hand for the bullhound to keep his place.

The wyld tracker called to the guards. "It is only I," he said, though surely the guards knew Kytt. Who else traveled with a bullhound? Plainly they only sought amusement by hassling the young tracker.

Laurelle reached the stairs, laden with two squirming cubbies, both arguing in low growls through the roughspun at one another. She thanked the gods of the aether that neither of the two barked. The knight at the landing glanced to her above his masklin. She nodded and slipped around to the stairs.

Behind her, Kytt spoke with exaggerated loudness. "I was just seeing to the cubbies. Making sure they had fresh milk and feed."

"A duty you won't need much longer," one of the guards said.

Laughter followed Laurelle out to the stair.

"Especially with the regent turning arse-end and running," another said. "No need any longer for *two* cubbies."

"And Liannora definitely could use a warm muff to match her new cloak."

"Now that's a muff I wouldn't mind slippin' a hand into," one whispered.

"Don't let Sten hear you say that."

More rough laughter chased Laurelle round the stairs. She climbed, her heart thumping and a fire building in her chest.

"Off with you, then," the guards barked to Kytt. "Before that dog of yours shites all over our hall."

"Or *he* does!" his companion said. "Look at that nose on the boy. I wonder if trackers use it to sniff each other's arses."

Kytt appeared below, rounding up with Barrin. His face blushed through his tanned skin. He quickly joined her and accepted his burden back. Together, they climbed the seven levels to the floor where Lorr kept his rooms.

In short order, they had the cubbies behind doors and a fire burning in the cold hearth, and Barrin was again sprawled and already snoring.

"I should be returning to my rooms." Laurelle rose from

where she had been scratching one of the whelpings on the belly.

"They are calm with you," Kytt said, nodding to the cubbie.

She warmed more than she should have at his generous word. "Dribbling milk over my fingers for the past three mornings and nights was what truly won them over. We had a houndskeep back . . . back home in Weldon Springs. That's off near Chagda Falls."

"I know where Weldon Springs lies," he mumbled.

"Of course you do." She shook her head at herself. Kytt's own realm, Idlewyld, lay on the opposite coast of the Fifth Land from Weldon.

"Rich country," he said. "Well-forested."

"My father owns a thousand tracks. He baited bears and boars with the hounds. I used to sneak off to play with their cubbies."

Laurelle shied away from that memory. She had mostly snuck off silently to the cubbies when her father had been beating her mother. Her family did not speak of such matters. Bruises and welts were hid under powder or behind lace.

Laurelle brushed a hand through her hair. "I should find Delia. Real or not, she should know of the threat we overheard."

Kytt stepped to the door. "I will accompany you back to your floor."

"I know my way."

"Of course you do," he said, mimicking back her own words from a moment ago.

She glanced to him and noted a ghost of a smile. She returned the same. It was rare to hear any ribbing from the young man.

"Best you have an escort." He grumbled a bit, glancing away as shyness overcame him again. "Barrin can watch over the little ones."

"Thank you. I would appreciate that."

Laurelle gathered her things and the two set out. Lorr's floor was only two above hers. The walk was shorter than she would have preferred. She even found her steps slowing. Too soon, they reached the level that housed Chrismferry's Hands.

The hall was empty, all locked away or about their own concerns. The diminutive Master Munchcryden, the regent's Hand of yellow bile, had a preference for wagered games, whether played with die or board, while the shaven-headed twins, Master Tre and his sister Fairland, seldom left their rooms, preferring the company of books and private reflection.

But such privacies were harder to come by now.

The warden could not indulge an entire floor for the regent's company any longer. Especially with Tylar fled. The vacant rooms had been filled with a goodly number of the masters who had been chased out of their subterranean levels. The halls now reeked of strange alchemies, and the occasional muffled blast would echo down the hall from some combination gone bad.

Laurelle led the way. Her room was not far off the landing. It was a small blessing, as the deeper halls were clogged even heavier with alchemical vapors, but it meant stepping away from Kytt sooner than she would have liked.

"I'll see you at the seventh evening bell," Laurelle said as they neared her door.

"The whelpings always enjoy your visits."

"Just the whelpings?" She lifted an eyebrow.

Kytt shuffled his feet—but he was saved from answering by a sharp outburst off by the stairs.

"The skull is gone! Why do you harp so on the matter?"

It was Master Hesharian.

Laurelle quickly freed her key and unlocked her door. Kytt stared back at the stairs. Once her door was open, she tugged the tracker inside with her. She leaned the door closed, but she kept a crack open to peer out.

Master Hesharian entered the hall with his usual dog in tow, the milky-eyed ancient master.

"Leave it go, Orquell," the head of the Council groused. "My midmorning meal awaits, and I'd prefer my breads were still warm."

A reedy voice argued. "But I spoke with Master Rothkild. He related how he had cored samples from the skull. Even a tooth. He had them stored within glass flutes in alchemical baths."

"And I heard the same. He insists the mixtures had rendered any Grace down to dregs. Nothing that could prove useful."

"Master Rothkild does not have my experience with Dark Grace. There is much I can discern if I could retrieve those bits of bone."

"The warden will not allow another trip down to the Masterlevels. Whatever lurks below remains quiet, and he wisely does not wish to stir it anew. With the regent gone, there may be a chance the storm will blow away and afterward our levels could be cleansed with fire. *Then* you can collect those bits of skull." Hesharian sniffed. "So let the matter die for now. I've my meal to attend and am near to famished."

The pair passed Laurelle's room. Master Orquell glanced in their direction as he passed. She and Kytt pulled back. Neither wanted that gaze to discover them hiding and spying.

"Then I'll leave you to your meal," Orquell said. "There is a matter I wish to attend anyway."

"Very good. You attend. I'll see you in the fieldroom at the next bell."

They continued down the hall.

Laurelle met Kytt's eye. "Can you track that one?"

"Who?"

"Master Orquell. I'd like to see what he's about when he's not in Hesharian's shadow. It is seldom the two are apart. This may be our only opportunity."

Kytt looked hesitant.

Laurelle pulled her door wider. "It will not take long. You heard. No more than a bell. Then Orquell will need to return to the maps and plottings in the fieldroom, falling once again into Hesharian's shadow. As privy as that new master is to what is discussed in that room, I'd like to see what matters he attends when alone."

Kytt nodded reluctantly.

Laurelle waited until the two masters were out of sight, then led Kytt back into the hall. Together they headed off after their prey. With Kytt's keen senses, they could keep well back. They passed Hesharian's room. His voice carried out, haranguing some scullery about the state of his jam.

They continued past.

At a crossing of passageways, Kytt stopped and sniffed.

Laurelle did the same, but all she smelled was burnt alchemies. They stung her nose, and she felt sorry for Kytt.

But he did not complain—though his eyes watered slightly. He pointed the correct path, and they continued their hunt.

Master Orquell's pace was surprisingly fast for one of his age and thinness of limb. He led them on a crisscrossing trail into the dustier regions of the level. The ceiling lowered and bits of fractured stone littered the floor. As this level had been intended only for Tylar's retinue, the underfolk had not cleared these back spaces very well.

Laurelle began to grow concerned as the path grew more abandoned. Rooms here were not habitable without the shoring of rafters. The path grew darker, lined by doors rotted and crooked-hinged. Off in corners, she caught glimpses of tiny red eyes and heard the telltale scurry of small claws.

She began to wonder at the wisdom of this adventure. She had believed the warden had all of Tashijan ablaze, placing much security in the abundant flames. But now they had ventured beyond lamp and torch.

Her feet slowed.

Now it was Kytt's determination that dragged her forward, their roles reversed. He straightened from examining a scuff in the dust and waved her to follow.

Turning a corner, they saw flickering light, fiery and welcome.

Kytt warned her to proceed cautiously. He pointed to his eyes, then down to his footprints in the dust. He wanted her to step where he stepped, so as not to alert their quarry.

But as they slipped closer, it was plain that Master Orquell was lost to all but the flames he had stoked in a cold hearth in an empty room. From down the hallway, they caught glimpses of him through a broken door, limned in firelight, features aglow.

He sat on his knees, rocking back and forth.

One arm reached out and sprinkled something across the flames. Sparks flew higher and a sound escaped with them, not unlike the flutter of a raven's wings. Laurelle wrinkled her nose at the stench of the smoke in the hall. She caught a whiff of something rotted and foul behind the woodsmoke. Perhaps brimstone.

Then Orquell's voice reached her as he rocked.

"Your will is my own, mistress. Show me what I must see."

Laurelle shifted. Orquell leaned near the flames, close enough that she was surprised the old man's eyes didn't boil in their sockets. He stared long—then a keening wail escaped his throat.

"No . . ."

She reached out and found Kytt's hand. He clasped hers tight.

Orquell finally rocked back away from the fire again, almost falling in a panicked scramble. He tossed a fistful of something at the fire, and the flames instantly doused.

As darkness fell, a few last words were whispered.

"I will do your bidding, mistress. I am in all ways your servant."

Kytt edged Laurelle back with him, still holding her hand. They retreated, stepping carefully. Now it was their turn to flee. Kytt guided them unerringly and swiftly. Once well enough away, certain they were out of earshot, Laurelle slowed him.

"We must not let the master out of sight when he's away from Hesharian. I'll inform Delia. She'll get word to the castellan." Laurelle's confidence grew as they returned to the well-lit passages. "We'll have to dog his steps. Watch him after he leaves the fieldroom."

Kytt nodded.

There was no need to argue.

Both could guess the *mistress* to whom the master bowed as a servant.

The witch below.

Mirra.

Kathryn faced the window with her sword. Behind the heavy drapery that closed off her balcony, the scratching had gone silent. She heard Gerrod strain, fighting his locked armor, its alchemies bled of Grace.

"Go," he said between gritted teeth. "Leave me here."

Cold permeated the entire room now, misting white her heated breath, freezing her cheeks. The hearth's embers had gone black.

Then glass tinkled, breaking and falling from paned frames. The drapes billowed toward her as a fierce gust swirled into the room through the broken window. Cold enough to make Kathryn gasp.

Backing a step to guard Gerrod, she drank the shadows. Her cloak swept to either side, its edges blurring with the darkness. She wrapped the power through her, making the flow of time slow.

Past the billow of the drapery, the balcony was shadowed by the towers that framed the courtyard. The sun had risen to a gray slate morning, casting enough light to reveal a dark shape outside her window.

Then the drapes fell again.

Behind them, wood cracked with a loud snap of latch and lintel. The bottom hem of the drapery stirred in the breezes, then flapped wide. Through the part, it crept into her chambers.

It came low, naked, knuckling down on one arm, cocking one eye toward her, then the other. It bore wings like a bat, skeletal and sinewy. It was bare of any hair or fur, except for a thin mane trailing from crown down the spine of its back. Its manhood hung limp and hairless.

"Wind wraith," Gerrod said behind her.

Except Kathryn knew this was no mere Grace-bred man. He had been ilked, too. More beast than man any longer. Drool seeped from its snarled lips. Nostrils pinched open and closed.

Eyes found her buried in the shadows and fixed to her.

In the gloom of her chambers, with all flames guttered, she recognized the glint of Grace, but not the purity to which she was accustomed, more an oily gleam.

Kathryn prepared to dispatch the creature. How many more were out there? She had to keep Gerrod protected. But the wraith approached no closer. It hissed at her, still crouched low, in some bestial parody of a bow.

Then it spoke—something she had believed was beyond the ilk-beast's ability. Its voice trilled out its throat, mouth barely moving, sounds shaped from somewhere beyond lips and tongue.

"Castellllan Vaillll . . ."

She stiffened, sensing a dark intelligence in her presence.

"Come. To parllley. In town. Blllackhorse tavernhouse. In one belllll."

Kathryn found her own voice, ringing it clear. "Who requests this parley?"

"Lord Ullllf willlls you to speak to him." The creature shifted to its other knuckle, cocking its other eye toward her. *"Onllly you. Come alllone."*

Despite the terror of the moment and the twisted messenger, Kathryn could not keep a spark of curiosity from flaring. Still, she was no fool.

As if sensing her hesitation, the creature bowed its head. *"No harm willll come."* It sank away, pushing back through drape and broken glass.

Then was gone.

The drapes fluttered as it took wing from her balcony.

She waited a full breath in the dark, cold room. Finally she straightened, but she did not sheath her blade. She swung to her door, sidestepping Gerrod.

"No, Kathryn," he moaned in his frozen suit, his voice echoing in his helmet.

"I must go," she said, both apologetic and certain. "I will send word to Master Fayle. To replenish the air in your alchemies. It won't be long."

She pulled her door open and slid out. She considered the rashness of her decision, but she did not dismiss it. She had waited for days, been cast aside by Argent, and bided her time while the tower dallied with its defenses. Something more needed to be done. Even if it meant putting one's own neck on the block.

"Kathryn!" Gerrod called to her, hollow and angry. *"It's a—"*

She snapped the door closed, but not before hearing his last word. Though it failed to sway her, she did not doubt it.

"—trap!"

16

A TWISTED ROOT

HORRORS SURROUNDED THEM.

Brant did not know where to look. The mists had risen into an arched roof overhead, lit from below by the fiery flippercraft. Some alchemy in the oiled arrows had sped the conflagration. The flames had already burned through the outer hull and exposed the inner ribbings. Smoke choked upward, darkening the mists further. Heat chased Brant and the others up the slope of the hollow.

Everywhere stakes sprouted from the weedy ground. Skewered upon their fire-blackened points were the heads of hundreds of his fellow people. The poles seemed to shiver in the flickering glow of the flaming flippercraft.

Brant shied from looking too closely at the faces, but they were inescapable. He caught glimpses of mouths stretched open in silent screams, of gouged eyes and bloated tongues, of seeping wound and sloughing skin. Black flies rose in silent swirls as the fires stirred the air.

He did not resent their feast. It was the great turn of the forest, the returning to the loam of all that had risen from it. It was the Way taught to all in Saysh Mal.

Only here was no mere decay of leaf or a gutted beast's entrails left to feed the forest—nor even a loved one's body gently interred beneath root and rock.

This was slaughter and cruelty, a mockery of the Way.

"Many children here," Rogger muttered, sickened. "Babes, from the look of a few."

"And elders," Tylar said.

Krevan followed with Calla. "Culling the weak," he grunted.

"But why?" Dart asked. She walked in Malthumalbaen's shadow, the giant's arm over her shoulder, hugged near his thigh.

"There is no *why* here," Lorr said sourly. "Only madness."

Brant risked a glance at a few of the stakes. He saw the others were right about the dead. A gray-bearded head was impaled to the left, and the next two stakes bore smaller skulls, a boy and a girl, a brother and sister perhaps.

As he turned away, he realized he knew the graybeard. The man had been the great-father to a fellow hunter. He was recognizable by the pair of brass coins braided into his beard. The elder had come occasionally to Brant's home, his beard jingling merrily, to share some pear wine with his father, swapping stories well into the night. Brant knew little else about him, not even his name. Somehow that made it even worse. A death with no name, only a memory.

The group slowed near a mossy boulder that shouldered out of the slope. The stakes thinned here, and the travelers were far enough away from the burning conflagration to escape the worst of the blistering heat. Still they could not escape the stench.

Brant glanced below and saw that a few of the stakes closest to the flippercraft had caught fire, burning like torches, fueled by wood and the fat of flesh. Shuddering, he turned his back on the sight and stared up toward the lip of the hollow.

The forest waited, dark, tall, and cool. It stared back at him, neither grieving nor caring. It was the face of the Huntress. Brant felt a fury to match the flames below. He wished the fire would spread to the woods, to cleanse and purify the horror, to scorch it down to the roots of the mountains.

A hand touched his shoulder, startling him into a wince.

But fingers closed with a firming grip and held tight.

He glanced up to find the regent at his side. Tylar stared toward the forest. "They are not to blame."

Brant did not know what he meant. "Who—?"

He nodded upward.

From the forest's edge, they stepped out of the shadows and into the firelight. Hunters. A hundred score. Stripped to breechclout, the women bare-breasted. They carried bows, strings taut, arrows notched.

The Huntress was baring her fangs.

"Can you smell it?" Lorr asked, nose high, eyes glowing. "The arrows. Poisoned with venom from the jinx bat. One nick will kill."

Though Brant didn't have the wyld tracker's nose, he had eyes sharp enough to sense movement past the first line of bowmen. More hunters stalked the depths. But his eyes were not keen enough to spot what Tylar had noted earlier—not until it was brought to his attention.

"Their mouths," Krevan said.

Squinting closer, Brant noted that the hunters' lips and chins were stained black, as if they had been drinking oil.

Brant knew it hadn't been *oil.*

"She's draughted them with her own blood," Tylar said. "Burned them with Grace. They are in thrall to her as certain as any seersong."

Brant now understood the regent's words a moment before. *They are not to blame.* There was only one to blame for all the horrors here.

As if reading his thoughts, the Huntress again spoke to them from her distant balcony, lost in mist and smoke. Her words were calm, spoken with a strange dispassion.

"You will come to me, stripped of weapons. You will bend your knee. Your strength will be added to the forest."

Her statements were not requests, nor even demands. Her voice held a simple certainty, as if she were merely stating that the sun would rise in the morning.

Tylar kept his grip on Brant. He leaned down and whispered in his ear. "Even if it destroys her, you must rip the roots of the seersong that ensnares her sanity. Can you do this?"

"What about the others?" He nodded to the black-lipped forest of hunters that waited with poisoned bows, bound to the Huntress.

Tylar did not offer any gentle words, only the truth. "I don't know." He faced Brant and asked again, "Even so, can you do this?"

Gripping the stone at his throat, Brant glanced back at the stakes bearing aloft the graybeard and the two children, then met Tylar's gaze. He nodded.

Tylar gave Brant's shoulder another squeeze, then released him. Ahead the hunters parted and shifted into two columns. They formed a deadly gauntlet down which they were meant to walk.

"Stay close together," Tylar warned and set off, leading the way.

"And don't let any of the arrows scratch you," Rogger added, bolstering Lorr's warning.

Brant followed beside Dart, both now shadowed by the giant. As Brant approached the forest, he again pictured flames spreading and burning through jungle and wood. While he had wished it only a moment ago, now he knew it was his hand that must set torch to the tinder, to potentially destroy the realm, from the top down. And it wouldn't be only wood that would be consumed.

He stared at the line of hunters.

Can you do this? he asked himself. *I must.*

Dart glanced to him. He read the fear in her eyes. She reached out a hand. He gratefully took it, not caring how it made him look.

As a group, they climbed free of the valley of stakes. The fires below scattered ashes skyward, a bonfire to the dead.

At last, they reached the rim of the hollow. The ancient pompbonga-kee trees rose in a dark bower over their heads. Below, the line of hunters waited. They headed down the gauntlet of bows. The deadly path led unerringly toward the oldest of the pompbonga-kees. The lowest level of the castillion could be seen entombed within its thick branches.

Closer yet, the tree's massive roots rose as mighty knees of bark and knot. Between them gaped the entrance to the castillion. And standing in the gap stood a tall hunter, thickly shouldered, naked to breechclout, lips stained. He bore a wreath of leaves upon his crown, marking him as the supreme Hunter of the Way, the latest to win the great challenges.

But what challenges had he won during these maddened days?

The sentinel's arms were bloody to the elbows. He reeked of death and pain. His eyes were aglow with the ravings of the Huntress, an echo of her corruption.

Still, Brant did not fail to recognize who stood as sentinel.

He pictured a boy running wild through the woods, breathless, barely able to sustain his excitement at his uncle's entry into the great contest. It had been the last time he had laid eyes on the boy—now a young man.

"Marron . . ."

Those piercing eyes found him—and for a moment, Brant saw a mirror of his own recollection. But instead of familiarity and lost friendship, all he saw was ferocity and ruthlessness in the other's eyes.

Lips peeled back in a cold smile, revealing teeth filed to points.

This was the true face of Saysh Mal now.

Dart felt Brant stiffen beside her. His fingers clamped tighter on hers.

"Abandon your blades," the other warned between sharpened teeth. "Defy and you will be winnowed now upon her blessed stakes."

Dart refused to glance at the field of the dead. There was no doubt where they would end up if they refused.

The men were made to unbuckle their belts and drop their sheathed swords. Rogger unhooked his crossed straps of daggers. Calla shook off her wrist sheaths. Tylar lowered Rivenscryr into the same pile, half-burying it under Rogger's daggers.

Dart watched Tylar release the blade. He looked almost relieved, unburdened. Afterward, he allowed himself to be searched, arms out. Hands passed over her own body. Finally they were permitted to proceed inside.

But as Lorr attempted to follow, a pair of crossed spears blocked him from stepping over the threshold. Another spear pointed at Malthumalbaen.

"None of the Grace-bred may foul her door. You will remain below to await her bidding." Marron looked the two men up and down, with undisguised distaste. "If you are lucky enough, she may permit you to live. To be a dog at her feet—or perhaps a beast to pull her wagon."

The last was said pointedly at the giant.

Malthumalbaen took a threatening step forward, but Tylar

held him back with a raised palm. "Remain here," he said. "Keep a guard on our weapons."

The giant seemed to barely hear him, glaring down at Marron. Lorr slipped between them. "I'll keep my eyes open and ears up," the tracker said.

From the way Lorr studied the hunters, he plainly intended to seek some weakness in those who stood guard, to find a breach through which they might break.

Marron also made Rogger pause. "What's that you carry?" he asked, nodding to the satchel.

"A gift for the Huntress. I heard she lost something. Thought she might want it back."

Marron's brow furrowed. He waved for Rogger to show him.

With a shrug, the thief revealed what he had stolen. He flipped back a bit of bile-caked cloth to reveal yellow bone. An empty socket and corner of upper jaw leered out.

Brant gasped, slipping slightly, fingers clutching to his neck. Dart still held his other hand. She knew his stone responded to the skull; now she felt it, too. His palm burned with a feverish touch. He squeezed tight, almost crushing bone.

Satisfied, Rogger flipped back the cloth, covering it again. The heat in Brant's palm immediately extinguished, like a flame blown out. His legs firmed under him. As he was half-hidden by the giant, no one seemed to note his faltering. All attention had been on the skull.

Marron's brow remained furrowed. "Give it here," he said warily.

Rogger shoved the skull inside and held out the laden pouch.

"I'll take it to her," Marron said in a slightly petulant tone.

In those words, Dart heard the boy behind the man. She suspected the hunter sought to secure the skull less from caution than from a desire to please his mistress if the gift should be truly appreciated.

With matters settled, they proceeded inside. Led by Marron and surrounded on all sides, the party entered the tree and began the long climb up into the mists.

After a few turns of the stair, Dart searched below. She sought some reassurance. Though they had left all their blades below, they were not without weapons. Tylar carried his naethryn beast inside him, along with all the Grace in his humours. And Brant still bore his stone, a gift of another god, rich in a Grace that might untwine the roots of seersong from the mind of the Huntress.

And there was one last weapon.

Dart faced forward to spot Pupp dancing among the legs of Marron's party. They remained unaware of his presence. A splash of her blood and the others would soon learn that they had let something worse than a stray dagger past their guard.

But would it all be enough against the raving might of a full god?

Dart wished Tylar had not abandoned his sword.

She also noted a limp in his gait. It slowly grew worse until he seemed barely able to bend his knee. A hand rubbed, but failed to warm whatever stiffness hobbled him.

Rogger mumbled something beyond Dart's hearing, but Tylar waved him off.

After a full quarter bell of climbing, the steps finally emptied out upon a wide balcony. Mists wove across the planks and between the railing posts. Below, the flippercraft shone like a second sun, ringed in black smoke, glowing through the mists. Above the face of the sun was no more than a glare. The terrace hovered between the world of sunlight and the death below.

Oddly, the reek of rot seemed richer here, though there were no staked heads. Only a single figure waited, as stiff as any sharpened pole.

Her head swung toward them as they were led forward.

Marron dropped to his knees. His obeisance announced who stood before them better than his words. "I am yours to command, mistress."

The Huntress stepped farther out of the mists, revealing a dark-skinned woman of stunning features, eyes aglow with Grace. She was dressed in green leathers, cross-strapped in black across her breasts and tied around waist and down her thighs, like some twining vine. Her boots were black also. She seemed as strong as the tree that supported her castillion. It was no wonder she showed no fear in inviting a godslayer into her midst.

Dart studied her.

There was no sign of ravaging in her calm features, no tick of insanity nor waste of condition. Even her ebony hair was meticulously braided into a looping coil at her shoulders.

She came to the edge of her guards and stopped. Her eyes seemed to see only Tylar.

"Godslayer," she said, as if testing the word.

"Huntress," Tylar acknowledged, stepping forward, favoring one leg. "What is the meaning of such a greeting? What dark corruption have you wrought here?"

Marron swung toward him, still on his knees, prepared to order his death at such an abrupt affront. Arrows were already nocked to strings. Their poisonous points glinted wetly.

But the Huntress stayed them all with a finger and merely cocked her head. "Of what corruption do you speak, Tylar ser Noche?"

He lifted his arm toward the railing. "The slaughter of your own people."

She smiled, warm and kindly. "Ah, you mistake my actions. What I have done was only to make Saysh Mal stronger. Dark times are upon us. I have heard it whispered in my ear better than most. All the realms must be prepared, to gird our loins and ready for the great war to come. Saysh Mal will not fail Myrillia."

"How do murder and cruelty make you stronger?"

"Murder and cruelty?" She raised her palms in confusion. "Does a gardenskeep *murder* when he trims away the sprouted sapling that taps strength from the main trunk? Is it *cruelty* to pull the weed so the fruit may grow that much heavier on the neighboring vine?"

Tylar kept his features a calm match to the god's. "You cull the young and the old."

"And the weak and infirm." She agreed. "So all may grow stronger. I've readied a great army, and braced them with my own blood."

"You've Grace-burnt them. Stripped their wills."

She shook her head—not disagreeing, only dismissing. "What is will? It is weakness. I've taken away indecision, doubt, hesitation, disloyalty." Anger threaded her words now. "So as to better serve Myrillia."

"You've forced them. Given them no choice to serve or not."

"It is my right. Do not other gods allow their Grace to be mixed in alchemies and fed to women freshly taken to seed, so their offspring might be stronger in ways that the natural born are not? How is what I do any different? Is the babe in the womb any less stripped of his choice in such matters, forged into the unnatural? All I burn away is one's hesitation and doubt. The body is left pure."

"Pure for what?"

"For the war to come! Have you not heard the drums in the night? Have you not seen the shadows shift on their own?" She stepped back as if to encompass more of the world as she gazed skyward. "Once ready, once stripped of *all* weakness, Saysh Mal will rise against the darkness. We will not let hesitation and doubt weaken us."

Her voice keened higher.

"Not like your brethren of the cloth," she continued. "They were not of Saysh Mal. They sought to stop me, cloaked in the same shadows as those that wait in darkness to claim Myrillia. They were no different than the voices who whispered to me in the night and sought to loosen my resolve with terrors and promises. Whispers out of bone."

Seersong, Dart realized. Her father's bones had started this song that ended now in a chorus of slaughter and screams. The Dark Grace had driven the Huntress into some realm of terror where cruelty could be justified in the name of security.

The Huntress spread her arms high. "The ravens had to be silenced before they spread word of my preparations. Ravens in the night . . . and their wings had to be clipped!"

Dart finally followed her gaze. It had not been directed skyward to encompass the world. The Huntress's mind was still tangled here, landlocked, and bound in pain.

All their faces turned upward.

Hanging from the branches overhead, half-lost in mists, rested a flock of giant birds, black wings spread wide, batlike and heavy.

Not birds.

Men.

Shadowknights.

The former oath-sworn of Tashijan had been gutted and strung up with their own bowels. Their cloaks and capes extended like wings, soaked with mists and blood.

Aghast with horror, Dart averted her eyes. She gaped at the Huntress.

How could she . . . ?

The Huntress lowered her arms and faced them again. "Your arrival here—he who slew the daemon Chrism—only further supports the righteousness of my actions. You have been flown here to serve me, by destiny and fate, by the sounding of my warhorn. Daemonslayer and godslayer. With you bound beside me, we will free Myrillia."

Tylar finally stared toward the Huntress. Dart noted the flash in his eye. It was not Grace. It was certainty.

"Never," he said.

He had climbed here, risked all, hoping to sway her from this path. The Huntress was no servant of the Cabal—in many ways, she was more victim than collaborator. But Tylar knew that neither mattered.

Here was something worse.

Madness given the strength of a god.

"You will drink my blood and join me at my side," she ordered. "Or all who stand beside you will be flailed of skin and sinew. Their cries—like the whispers out of bone—will sway you to do what must be done."

"I will need no swaying. I *know* what must be done." Tylar stepped aside and used his palm to push Brant forward. "I was also led here not just by fate and destiny—but by the word of one of your own."

The Huntress finally seemed to note that there were others beside Tylar. She had been so focused on the Godslayer—and all that his arrival portended—that she had ignored those who shadowed him.

Her eyes found Brant, narrowed with momentary confusion, then widened with shocked recognition.

"The banished returned! Another sign! Brant, son of Rylland . . . hunter and bringer of dark gifts . . ."

Hope shone from her face.

Marron spoke into her silence. "It is I who bring you gifts now!"

He hurriedly shrugged off Rogger's satchel and pushed it toward her, almost prostrating himself on the planks, so eager to please, and afraid to have his place usurped in her eyes.

The Huntress backed a step. She must have suspected what lay hidden within the folds of cloth, recognizing a familiar bulge. "It cannot be . . ."

"Mistress?"

"It had vanished. Surely vanquished." Her voice began to tremble. "The dark whisper in the night. Then silence. The first sign. I was free to build my army."

Then her manner sharpened. She leaned forward, eyes narrowing slyly. "Unless . . . unless you test me, godslayer. To make sure my legion is prepared."

"You have found me out," Tylar said, limping forward.

"Take care," Rogger whispered through his beard, chin lowered. "You play with broken daggers here."

Tylar nodded, to both Rogger and the Huntress. "Can you face the skull and still hold fast?"

She rose again to a stiff-backed posture, proud and strong. "I have winnowed my realm to its purest." Then she added with a glare to the south, "Or at least almost . . . if not for her . . ."

Tylar glanced to Rogger and Krevan. Both shook their heads, unsure what this newest raving portended.

She faced Tylar, then eyed the satchel, almost with longing. "I would hear it again . . . so I might resist it this time."

Tylar nodded, offering both his palms, open and inviting toward the satchel. "So we have come."

The Huntress sank to her knees, not touching the satchel. She reached out, then away again. A war fought over her features: fear, desire, agony, anguish. Her fingers trembled.

"Perhaps there's hope for her yet," Krevan breathed.

Marron seemed to sense his mistress's weakness and sought to hide it from the strangers here. "Let me, mistress. As always, your servant."

His words broke her hesitation, but not her resolve. She waved to the satchel. "Show me."

Marron shuffled gratefully forward on his knees. He fingered loose the strings and reached inside.

"Be ready," Tylar said to Brant.

Dart tensed. They needed the skull exposed, free of its bile cocoon. She urged Marron not to falter.

He pulled it free as if reading Dart's thoughts.

Pupp had angled closer, ever curious, perhaps sensing Dart's attention and focus. None saw him—not even Dart. Not until it was too late.

Marron lowered the wrapped skull to the planks and peeled back the wrap. Brant groaned, falling to his knees, guarded over by Krevan.

"Sing, boy," Rogger urged. "Speak anything."

Dart heard Brant whisper through pain-thinned lips, haltingly and agonized. She knew if she touched him now that he would be feverish again.

He sang as he burnt. " *'Come, sweet night . . . steal the last light . . . so your moons may glow.'* "

The Huntress still knelt before the revealed skull. She slowly lifted her head, like a flower following the sun. "What . . . ?" A hand rose to touch her brow. Her gaze flickered to Brant. "What are you . . . don't . . ."

Lost to his own agony, he continued mumbling his song, gasping out notes as if they pained him. " *'Come, sweet night . . . hide all our worries . . . so our dreams will flow.'* "

The god's face squeezed against what she heard. The fingers at her brow turned their nails on her own flesh, dragging gouges. Teeth gritted, a whine escaped, blood flowed, rich in Grace.

"No . . . stop . . ."

"Keep going," Tylar urged.

Marron heard Tylar, then glanced between Brant and the Huntress. Both god and boy were now locked on one another.

The Huntress clenched her face between her two palms, but she did not break her gaze on Brant. Fingers pulled at hair, scratched deeper. "Should not come back . . . I resisted once . . . sent you away."

"What are you doing?" Marron asked, shoving to his feet. "Huntress?"

She ignored him.

Marron stumbled back, unsure, lacking his own will, without guidance. But as the seersong was ripped from his god, the loss also weakened her control over the others. Bows dropped. Hunters stumbled back. Others panicked and swung upon the strangers, arrows nocked and shaking in their direction.

"She's breaking," Rogger whispered.

One hunter fell down beside Dart, staring at his hands in disbelief. A wail escaped him, full of heartbreak and horror.

The Huntress echoed his cry, blood flowing like tears down her cheek. *"No! I don't want . . . it hurts too much . . . !"*

Her eyes glanced to Brant's clutched fist. She then thrashed back, covering her face, falling on her side.

"What have I done?"

With the skull abandoned by both Marron and the Huntress, another came closer to investigate. With the planks cleared to either side, Dart spotted the fiery glow of his approach, slunk low, glowing with curiosity.

Dart's heart clenched in her chest. "Pupp . . . no! Stay back!"

Too late.

He reached forward and nosed the skull. As with all items potent in Grace, the contact pulled Pupp into substance. He bloomed with solidity on the planks of the balcony. His form glowed ruddy and bright, melting and churning, a bronze statue upon a forge.

Marron noted Pupp's fiery appearance. Though dazed, the hunter finally found something upon which to focus, to vent his confusion. He scrambled to free his bow, arm pointed.

"Daemon!" he screamed. "They bring daemons!"

Pupp lifted his head, drawn by the cry. With the contact broken, his form wisped away, a candle gutted, visible only to Dart now.

Marron searched vainly, stumbling in a wary circle—until returning to what still rested upon the planks.

"The skull!" he screamed. "It is cursed! Births daemons!"

Brant's efforts to pull the roots of seersong from the Huntress had an unwanted ripple. It also freed Marron to act, to shed his indecisiveness.

The hunter sprang forward. His booted leg held high. He brought his heel crashing down on the crown of the skull, smashing the ancient bones to skittering fragments. One piece struck Dart's knee.

Next to her, Brant gasped and arched back as if lashed. His feeble song died on his lips.

"Bring oil!" Marron yelled, grinding bone under his heel. "Burn the foul thing to ash!"

The other hunters responded to their leader, needing some guidance to fill the void left by the Huntress's absence. Krevan attempted to lunge forward, but an arrow sped past his ear, warning him back. They were surrounded again. Lamps and torches appeared, rushed forward by others.

The fragments were doused and set to flame.

Rogger managed to collect the piece near Dart's knee, scooping it away into a rag, then into a pocket. The rest burnt in pools of oil.

Brant wobbled back to his feet. "The stone—it's gone cold again."

The Huntress also pushed from her sprawl. Her face was still bloody, but her wounds were already healing, sealing up with the fire of her own Grace. Her eyes continued to roll as she fought to focus.

"I've lost her," Brant said, stumbling back. "The song still holds firm, rooted deep. I could feel it."

A malignancy spread again among the hunters. More bowmen and spears poured up from below, drawn by the commotion, silently summoned by the command of the god.

The Huntress sank back into her madness, almost gratefully, with no fight. She gained her feet, too, though not without wobbling. She stared across at the surrounded party. Eyes shone with Grace and malice. Her voice remained whispery and weak.

"Kill . . ." She pointed at Brant. "Kill the boy."

Only one heard her, the closest to her side.

Marron had his bow already in hand. He drew a long pull.

"Wait!" Tylar called, billowing out his cloak protectively. But his hobbled knee stumbled him.

The arrow pierced his shadowcloth and sailed past.

Brant suddenly sat down hard upon the planks next to Dart. He stared down at his chest. A feathered bolt protruded from his ribs. Dart saw the poisoned point poking out the back of his shoulder.

The Huntress tottered, but her voice grew firmer.

"He has a stone . . . *the* stone. Bring it to me."

Dart kept her gaze on Brant. She saw the color drain, his face go slack. She reached a hand—but he fell away from her touch, his face lifted toward the ravens in the trees.

Just as dead.

Lorr had known when the seersong weakened its hold on both the Huntress and her hunters. He read it in the sudden bewilderment of their guards: the sway of limb, the lowering of weapons, the squint of confusion.

One of the hunters swung away and suddenly emptied his stomach into a bush. Another ran off, dropping his bow, stepping on his own arrow, and stabbing himself. He ran four steps, then dropped like a felled deer.

Lorr collected the dead hunter's weapon, even the offending arrow.

The loam-giant smashed a fist into the face of the man who tried to stop him, crushing bone and knocking him flat. Shaking his fist, Malthumalbaen turned back to Lorr.

"Grab our weapons," Lorr said and pointed. "Especially the regent's swords."

The giant obeyed, gathering an armful. "What now?"

"We get lost in the wood."

Lorr didn't know how long this respite would last. Even if the others succeeded, it would be easy to get grazed by a panicked arrow in the meantime. Better to be lost. So he led the way. In the chaos, it was not hard to vanish out of the clearing and into the denser forest.

Or usually it wouldn't be.

The tracker winced at the crashing progress of the giant behind him. For a creature born of loam, the fellow seemed to be pounding at the very soil that had given birth to him. Twigs snapped, branches broke, and tangles of vines ripped with every other step. They were leaving a trail behind that a blind man could track.

He hissed at the giant behind him. "Can you tread a little lighter?"

"As soon as you suck that big nose back into your head," he

countered. "Where are we going, anyway? I won't leave Master Brant behind."

Lorr rolled his eyes. "We can't mount a rescue unless we're free. I need to scout the immediate area, secure more weapons, but first I have to find some hollow tree to plant your wide arse. You're not exactly built for sneaking."

But apparently others were.

Lorr pushed past a heavy branch and found himself facing a circle of hunters. Spears bristled, arrows waited. An ambush. Lorr immediately judged the others, weighing the threat. They were dressed in woodland greens and blacks, but their clothes were ripped and ill-fitted. They appeared no more than boys, wild-eyed but grim. The two parties eyed each other for a wary breath.

Neither sure of the other.

Friend or foe.

But Lorr noted one hopeful sign.

These hunters' lips were unstained.

"Who are you?" Lorr asked. "Whom do you follow?"

One of the hunters merely pointed up.

Up toward the castillion.

Where the Huntress ruled.

As the hunters circled tighter around them, Tylar backed the others behind him, hobbling on his bad knee. He fed shadows into his cloak, along with his anger and certainty. If the Huntress wanted a war, so be it.

"Brant!" Dart sobbed behind him.

Krevan closed on their other side, protecting the dead boy and the girl. Calla closed on his left flank, Rogger on the other. But they had no weapons.

Or rather only one.

Tylar grabbed his barely healed finger. He would bring god against god, his naethryn against the Huntress. If necessary, they would burn bone from flesh and forge a path out of this tree.

Determined, Tylar snapped his finger straight back, refracturing the new bone with a starry flash of pain. He braced for the agony to spread, to break more bones, to release the naethryn from its bony cage. But nothing happened. A rib snapped in his chest like a weak echo of his cracked finger—but nothing more.

He gasped between clenched teeth, staring down at his throbbing hand. He leaned away from the side with the broken rib.

Something was wrong.

He felt the naethryn stir behind his breastbone, still trapped.

Like all of them.

Rogger glanced over to him. "Maybe that finger hadn't set completely. You have nine others. I suggest you pick one right quick."

Tylar lifted his head.

The Huntress had paused after Marron's arrow killed Brant, perhaps gloating, perhaps even juggling a bit of regret. How firmly had the seersong re-rooted? Was there any residual grief that still panged? Impossible to say. Her face remained impassive.

Either way, Tylar was past trying to talk her back from the ravening edge. All it had done was get the boy killed. He grabbed his next finger, stirring afresh the pain in his hand.

Then the silence was shattered.

Eyaaahhhhhh!

But the scream was not his own. It rang out across the canopy, drawing gazes toward the misty heights. Arrows sliced out of nowhere and whistled through the treetop gathering.

Hunters stumbled all around, pierced through arm, thigh, chest, and belly. Bows dropped, and bodies fell with pained exhalations. Krevan and Calla grabbed weapons. Tylar tried to do the same, but his left hand was too crippled. His side flamed with agony.

He had not been arrow-struck. It was only the protest of his shattered rib. He glanced around. None of them had been hit.

"Stay low," Rogger whispered and pulled him down.

On one knee, Krevan drew upon his bow and let an arrow fly. It sliced through one of the hunters' throats with a great spray of crimson. The man fell over a railing and tumbled without a sound.

In his place, a shape swung out of the mists upon a vine and vaulted over the same railing. He landed in a crouch, a dagger in one hand. A boy. Tylar heard others landing elsewhere. Cries arose on all sides.

A sharp scream, higher than all the others, keened across the misty balcony. The Huntress. She was being herded back toward the open doorway to her castillion by Marron and the others, protecting their god.

"No! The boy! I must have the stone!"

But the confusion after Brant's assault had left her still dazed, allowed her to be led, unable to fully drain the panic from the unsettled hunters, to control them. They reacted with instinct, to protect their god.

She vanished into the shelter of the castillion. *"I must have it!"* she cried out of the darkness. *"It is not of this world. It is not of Myrillia."*

A small band of young hunters settled around them. Their faces were painted, but their lips were unburned by Dark Grace.

"We must go," said the closest, perhaps the leader. He pointed to the railing, where vines were tethered, waiting to swing them away from the balcony. "We must be gone before they rally."

Tylar waved the others to follow. Still, he hung back, listening to the fading ravings of the Huntress.

"The stone . . . It is not a rock of Myrillia!"

An arm tugged at his elbow.

Tylar strained to hear. The words were faint.

"It is of our old kingdom! A piece of our Sundered land!"

Tylar took a stumbled step forward, wanting to hear more, but Krevan grabbed his other elbow. He had Brant's body over his shoulder.

"Leave now," said the leader of the young hunters. He was gangly and loose-limbed, eyes too large for his face. "If there is to be any hope for Brant, we must fly now!"

Tylar finally turned. "Hope?" he asked. The word almost didn't make sense to him. "How did you know who—?"

"Hurry."

Scowling, the boy headed toward the railing.

With one last glance back, Tylar followed. All that rose

from the castillion now was the distant screams of fury. The Huntress's earlier words still echoed in Tylar's head.

A piece of our Sundered land.

Tylar pictured the stone. He studied Brant's limp form.

What did it mean?

Tylar hurried after the leader, limping to catch up. He noted the boy also bore a distinct hobbled trip to his gait, which did not slow him down. Tylar finally caught up with him at the railing. He grabbed the boy by the shoulder.

"Who are you?"

"An old friend of Brant's." He shoved a loop of vine into Tylar's good hand. "My name is Harp."

17

A PARLEY AT THE BLACKHORSE

KATHRYN SHOULDERED THE SHUTTER CLOSED AGAINST THE gust of wind. She prayed no one on the daywatch stumbled past and noted that the shutter was unbarred on the inside. She had chosen the window because it was well hidden in a dark corner, near the cookery's privy. None had noted as she slipped the bar and climbed out. She planned on returning to Tashijan as surreptitiously as she had left it.

If she was allowed to return . . .

She pictured the ilked wraith, hunched and brittle-winged.

And the offer.

Come alllone. To parllllley. In town. Blllackhorse tavernhouse.

Kathryn set out across the wintry yard. She was dressed in heavy woolens, feet pushed into furred boots. Over it all she wore her knight's cloak. She had chosen this place in the yard to cross because it lay in the shadow of Stormwatch Tower, but the low cloud and gray day offered only meager shadows. She gathered what power she could into her cloak, fading her form. She did not want any of the guards from Stormwatch to note her departure.

Gerrod knew where she was headed. That was enough. She did not want all of Tashijan to know her folly. But with no word from Tylar, the safety of Tashijan remained her responsibility. While Argent might be content to burrow inside and shore up their defenses, Kathryn intended to discover what brewed beyond the curtain of this storm. If that meant meeting with Ulf of Ice Eyrie on his own terms, so be it. He had sworn her safety.

But was the word of this god to be trusted?

She gazed to the left, to the shield wall of Tashijan, a cliff of piled brick and stone. Beyond the top, the world swirled with ice fog and snow.

The storm waited.

And it would wait a little longer.

She trudged into the wind toward the stables. She noted the steam rising from the crossed thatching. The stableboys and horsemen must have stoked the hearths against the cold, not just for themselves but for their charges. She knew they had been offered shelter in the towers, but the stablemen would have had to abandon their horses.

Not a one had accepted the offer.

This warmed her more than her heavy woolens.

Kathryn also knew the men would remain silent about her trespass into the stables. They bore little love for the Fiery Cross, since a couple of the warden's knights had switched a horse near to crippling it. She had already sent a raven down with a terse message, to ready a horse.

An eye keener than any guard noted her approach. The stable door creaked open. The stableboy, Mychall, bundled almost to obscurity under horse blankets, waved to her.

She hurried forward and pushed into the steamy warmth. The smell of patty and hay welcomed her. Only a single lamp was lit here, over by one stall. A shadowy form huffed and dug a hoof, recognizing her scent.

Mychall threw back his blankets. "Did you hear?" he asked breathlessly as he led her forward.

"Hear what?"

"Eventail threw her foal this morning. We was worried. She came close to colicking, back . . ." He waved an arm to indicate the past. "But she dropped a handsome little mare. Color of bitternut, with bright white stockings up to her fetlocks."

"How wonderful," she said, suddenly smiling. The warmth and the boy's enthusiasm helped dispel the darkness around her heart. And the fact that life was born in the middle of the siege somehow gave her hope.

She was now doubly glad to have decided to fetch a horse for the short ride to the tavernhouse. Ulf's emissary had not forbidden it. The snow had fallen thick. And the storm winds were not empty. In case it proved necessary, she wanted a means of fast travel.

Ahead, a taller man, Mychall's father, stepped out of the hay crib, leading a piebald stallion, colored white and black, snow on stone. The boy circled the horse, mimicking his father's inspection of the horse's tack, hands on hips.

"All saddled, Castellan Vail," the head of horses gruffed, plainly not pleased with her decision to ride in this storm. "Stoneheart has been grained this morning against the cold, so he should do you fine."

"Thank you."

Kathryn accepted the lead and ran a palm over the soft velvet of the stallion's nose. He pushed against her, nuzzling, nostrils taking in her scent. Before Kathryn had risen to the hermitage, she had ridden the horse almost daily. But since then, her visits grew less and less frequent. And with the endless stretch of winter, it had become a rare pleasure.

For the both of them.

"I would be honored to attend you," the horseman said. "I have another mount already saddled."

She stepped away. "Better to keep the fires stoked here. We may need their warmth when we return."

He nodded, offering no further argument. With Mychall's help, they hauled the door wide enough for her to walk the horse out. They waited while she mounted.

She sank into the warm saddle and hugged her cold legs against Stoneheart's flanks. Here was home as much as any hermitage.

At the door, the horseman's eyes remained shadowed with worry. She knew it wasn't just for the prized horseflesh under her. He simply nodded. No well wishes. No good-byes.

She preferred it.

Laying the reins across his neck, she turned the stallion toward the main gate through the shield wall. She found the way unmanned, cleared during the emptying of the town. Dismounting, she crossed to the small door in the main gate. Bars allowed a view of the parade grounds that lay between the town and the walls. Snow was piled knee-deep, untrammeled by footprints. The town lay shrouded in fog, more phantom than real.

Kathryn undid the thick latch and lifted yet another bar with a tremor of trepidation. Had that been the plan all along? To get her to unlock the gates and open an easy breach into the towers? She quickly squashed down that worry. Eylan had demonstrated the extent of Ulf's might. He had breached their main gate, a door that had stood for centuries. If Ulf wanted to get inside, she doubted there was any way to stop him.

So why had the god hesitated these three long days?

It was one of the reasons she had set out alone. You could not defend what you didn't understand.

Pulling open the door, she faced the full gale of the storm. It shoved against her and ripped her hood back. An icy hand slid down the back of her neck and cupped her buttocks, squeezing the air from her with its freezing touch. Swearing, she yanked her hood back up and hunched into the winds. She kept cursing as she walked the horse, using her anger to warm her.

Behind her, the gate door slammed a resounding bang, as if reprimanding her for her obscenities. Startled, she jumped a bit. Still, she heeded the warning and remounted without another word.

She guided Stoneheart across the frozen moat and into the stormswept fields. Here snow climbed into deeper drifts, requiring more plowing than stepping to cross the way. The stallion heaved, head low, breath blowing white.

She searched the skies, the gables of the first houses, the dark streets. She had heard the stories. The wind wraith at her balcony door was not the only one of its brethren out here. And what else might be hidden within the storm?

At last, they passed into the town and down a narrow street. The winds initially picked up, chasing them, scattering dry snow at their heels. Then deeper under eaves and overhanging dormers, the winds finally gave up their hunt and dribbled away. Snow still covered the streets, but most of the fall was piled high on roofs and sculpted by the winds into frozen waves at their edges.

She feared that even the muffled clop of Stoneheart's walk might shake down an avalanche upon her. But worst yet, she heard the occasional creak of board and crunch of ice, reminding her that the town was shuttered and abandoned—but it was far from empty.

Still, she did not hesitate. She had committed to this parley, so she rattled her reins to keep the piebald stallion moving from shadow to shadow, turning corners and slipping down alleys.

Kathryn needed no directions. She knew the way to Blackhorse as well as any knight. The inn and tavernhouse had been a place for many a rowdy night and sour-stomached morning for most of Tashijan's knights and a fair smattering of its masters.

But not this day.

She spotted the sign over the doorway, depicting a rearing dark stallion on a plain white board. Not exactly the most imaginative decoration for a tavernhouse named the Blackhorse, but customers weren't attracted by the establishment's imagination as much as by its cheap ale and cheaper rooms, where many a dalliance and ribald tale began.

Kathryn slowed Stoneheart by the inn's neighboring stable. Its door already lay halfway open. She slipped from her saddle and walked the stallion into the barn. It was little warmer inside than without, but it would have to do. She threw the lead over a stall rail and noted a pile of oat hay within reach. She ran a hand over Stoneheart's flank to make sure he hadn't sweated too badly to be left standing in a cold barn.

Satisfied, she had no reason to delay. She headed back outside and over to the tavern. She crossed to the door and found the latch unlocked. Then again, it was always unlocked. The Blackhorse never closed its doors. Though its windows had been shuttered as some measure of security.

Kathryn shoved the door open and slipped inside. A counter stretched to the right. To the left opened the main hall, with scarred tables and chairs. Firelight flickered. The warm light frightened her more than the darkness. She shifted to peer inside, taking a moment to draw more shadows to her cloak.

But the room was empty to its four walls.

She entered warily, surprised at how small the room seemed without its usual crowds singing and arguing.

She moved closer to the fire. The logs looked freshly lit. But she'd barely had time to warm her hands when the outer door creaked open. A whisper of wind and an icy chill swept inside.

She turned.

Footsteps approached. She was prepared for one of the wraiths or some other emissary from Lord Ulf. With the god landlocked in his realm, he had to work from afar—like sending forth his wrath wrapped in storm winds and burying a flock of wraiths at its heart.

Finally, the figure rounded the corner and stepped into the room, glittering in the firelight.

It was no wraith.

"Lord Ulf!" Kathryn gasped.

The god entered—or rather a perfect sculpture of the god in ice. The detail was exquisite, from every fold of his fine cloak to every wrinkle of his aged face. Even here, Lord Ulf did not feign vanity with a youthful demeanor, preferring the craggy to smooth, like his mountain home.

As he approached, his form melted to allow movement of limb and cloak, then crystallized again. The sculpture reflected the flames but also shone with an internal radiance.

Pure Grace.

He spoke, his features as dynamic as flesh, though with a slight swimming melt. "Castellan Vail, thank you for coming. We have much to discuss."

Kathryn took a moment to find her voice.

Lord Ulf filled the void. "To set matters straight. I know you helped Tylar ser Noche escape. And while I might not agree with your decision, it was yours to make. Understandably so. You were once his betrothed."

Kathryn struggled. She had expected horror and raving, not this calm and calculating figure in brilliant ice. She finally freed her tongue. "For what purpose have you summoned me here, then?"

A hand rose, melting and freezing, asking for her indulgence.

"Let it also be known that I still consider the regent an Abomination. Such Grace was never meant to wear human flesh. And to place him in the center of the First Land, in Chrismferry, a land already cursed, can only lead to even more ruinous ends. This I will both portend and attempt to thwart. But with Tylar gone, I have a new matter that requires both our attentions, and I come to ask for your cooperation."

Before she could think to stop herself, Kathryn blurted out, "Why should I cooperate with a god so plainly cursed?"

"Cursed? How so, castellan?"

Kathryn stammered, ticking off her answers. "You threaten Tashijan to ruin, you ploy seersong to trap and twist an ally to her death, you carry ilked wraiths in your storm, and . . . and you borrow Dark Grace from enslaved rogues, gods snared and sapped by the Cabal itself."

He listened to her dispassionately, his face frozen. Once she was done, he sighed and sadly shook his head. "I am no puppet of the Cabal, if that is what you suspect. It is the Wyr who made our introductions. I had need for the power they possessed and promises were made. Nothing more."

"Promises?"

"To kill Tylar. To destroy Rivenscryr. In such matters, I do not disagree with the Cabal, and I'm content to borrow their power to suit me."

"By enslaving the rogues?"

"They are raving creatures of wild Grace. To let them dream in seersong is a less cruel life. But in truth, I have no pity for them."

And for little else, Kathryn thought. Ulf might be a sculpture of ice, but apparently the similarities ran deeper than mere appearance.

"What about Eylan and the ilked wraiths?"

"Unfortunate circumstances. I had meant to trap Tylar with the seersong, but caught a smaller fish instead. And need I remind you, it was your forces who destroyed her in the end. Which is another matter entirely. I felt the unthreading of the song in her mind—but could not fathom how it was done."

"The wraiths?"

Again a hand waved. "To be borne aloft in the storm of Dark Grace, there was bound to be some matter of corruption. It was a risk all my Grace-born were aware of before they swept out from Ice Eyrie. But I still watch over them, controlling them with seersong to keep them focused to my will."

"Seersong? So you admit to employing a *Dark* Grace?"

An icy shrug. "Grace is neither bright nor dark. It merely is. It is the heart of the wielder that is either bright or dark."

Kathryn shuddered. She didn't know which she feared more: that Lord Ulf was locked in some rich lunacy or that he was dreadfully sound of mind. She had thought the Cabal had been using Ulf—could it be the other way around? Or was it both, two partners dancing cautiously together, each using the other toward a common purpose?

To rid Myrillia of a godslayer and destroy his sword.

But now both had escaped this trap.

"Then with Tylar gone, what do you still want?"

Lord Ulf faced her. "I want your help in destroying Tashijan."

Kathryn backed a step. "Are you mad?"

His ice eyes glinted in the firelight. "Not even slightly."

"Have you seen Castellan Vail?" Laurelle asked, breathless with anxiety.

"Not since before midday," Delia said. "Why?"

Laurelle stood with her fellow Hand in a small room, no more than a closet, across the stair from the fieldroom. She and Kytt had been waiting a full bell for Tashijan's council to disband for a short break. The young tracker stood at the door, watching the hall.

Moments before, Laurelle had waylaid Delia as she left the fieldroom and silently motioned for her to follow. She had led the woman to the closet with some urgency.

"What's happened?" Delia asked.

"We've run all the way up to the castellan's hermitage, then down again. Castellan Vail is not in her rooms. And no one knows where she's gone. Her maid was as skittish as a pony when I questioned her. I bribed a guard who reported some mischance with Master Gerrod, found frozen in his armor."

"Frozen?" Delia gasped. "Dead?"

"No—" Laurelle took a deep breath to collect herself. "Some matter with his mekanicals. He's been attended by another master, and afterward both vanished in some hurry. All

I could ascertain was that Castellan Vail had disappeared as well."

"I've heard of nothing about any of this. Master Hesharian has mentioned no word."

"I'm not surprised. You've all been holed up in that room for going on three bells. I don't think whatever is afoot was something the castellan or the armored master wanted the warden to know about. Or anyone else in there."

Delia's eyes grew shadowed as she pinched her brow. "So much hawing and posturing . . ." She waved a dismissive gesture at the fieldroom. "Before the meeting begins anew, I'll discreetly inquire about the castellan from those I trust." She stepped toward the door.

"No. Wait!" Laurelle urged. "That's only half the reason I've come. I had hoped to find Castellan Vail here. To report word of what Kytt and I discovered."

Delia stared back at her.

Laurelle quickly related how she and Kytt had stalked Master Orquell and witnessed his strange communion with his mistress in the dark. "It was plainly Dark Grace. And the woman in the flames . . ."

"Mirra," Delia said with a frown, coming to the same conclusion.

"He probably warned her about the skull. No telling what else he has told her."

Kytt hissed by the door and waved. Laurelle and Delia joined him. Peeking out, Laurelle saw a familiar shape, as if summoned by their words. Master Orquell was headed down the stairs, leaving again on his own. Down the hall, Master Hesharian could be seen huddled with Liannora and Warden Fields. All seemed oblivious that Orquell was leaving.

Laurelle gripped Delia's arm. "What are we to do?"

"I'll have to tell my father," she muttered sourly. "Spy or not, the truth will be soothed from the master—but such arrest would require a warden's order." She glanced to Laurelle. "Are you sure what you saw?"

"Dead certain."

Kytt nodded.

"Then we have no choice."

"What about Master Orquell?" Laurelle asked. "He should

be followed. Before he divulges more secrets from the day's meeting."

Delia shook her head. "Nothing of import was related just now, mostly just Liannora's fawning and scraping. Leave Orquell to the warden's knights."

"But—"

"You were foolish to risk what you did. Return to your rooms. I will bring word to you when I'm able."

Laurelle bristled at being ordered about like a child, but a part of her was also relieved. She had succeeded in passing on a warning, if not to Castellan Vail, at least to someone in power. It would have to be enough.

"Make sure no one sees you," Delia concluded. "Straight up to your rooms. Kytt, please stay with her."

He nodded.

Satisfied, Delia slipped out the closet and headed round the stairs toward the far hall. Laurelle waited a breath, then stepped out, too. Kytt trailed her.

"There's a back stair over that way . . ." Laurelle pointed the opposite way. "I think."

They headed off together.

Before reaching a turn, Laurelle glanced back. Delia had stopped by the stair, huddled with a guard. She pointed an arm down the hall, to where Argent stood. Then her arm dropped. She was clearly angry. She glanced her father's way, nodded, then stepped after the guard, heading down the same stairs where Master Orquell had vanished.

Concerned, Laurelle stopped. Clearly something or someone had thwarted Delia from delivering Laurelle's warning. Searching farther down the hall, she noted Liannora standing with her arms crossed, wearing a thinly veiled smile.

Oh no . . .

Laurelle studied the guard more closely. His chin lifted briefly in her direction as he turned to follow Delia. His features were clear.

It was Sten, captain of the Oldenbrook guards.

Only now did Laurelle remember an earlier message she had intended to deliver. A warning meant for Delia. It had been pushed to the side after the harrowing discovery of Master Orquell's true nature. Laurelle clutched her throat, remembering what she had overheard while she hid in Brant's room—whispers of accidents, misfortunes, directed toward Delia.

Offered by this same captain of the guards.

The one who now dogged Delia's steps.

Laurelle reached behind and grabbed Kytt's arm. She tugged him forward.

"What are you—?"

"We're going to need that handsome nose of yours again."

He allowed himself to be dragged along. "Handsome?"

They dared not tarry.

"Hurry."

She led him back to the stairs, careful that no eyes were staring too intently in their direction. Laurelle kept her back straight as if she belonged and was going about some urgent matter. She pasted a haughty look upon her features as she passed a guard by the main stair. She sighed with a ringing petulance toward Kytt.

"Oh, please hurry, boy. We can't keep my seamstress waiting."

She minced down the steps with feigned exasperation, Kytt in tow. Once out of direct view, she reached out and took his hand.

"Let's go."

They hurried down the flights until voices reached them from the lower landing. "I see no reason why this could not wait," she heard Delia exclaim. "A drunk Hand is a matter for the guards to attend."

"It is one of *your* realm's Hands, mistress. From Chrismferry. Master Munchcryden." Sten sighed. "Mistress Liannora thought you'd prefer to avoid any embarrassment, especially for someone serving the fieldroom."

"How generous of her," Delia commented.

"Plus Master Munchcryden has specifically asked for you."

"Very well."

Laurelle knew how protective Delia was of the Hands left in her charge. And all knew Master Munchcryden's disposition when it came to ale. It was a perfect excuse to lure Delia away for a few moments. A reasonable request. Then she could return to address the concerns raised by Laurelle.

But Delia had not heard the plot whispered in the hall.

It is easy to trip on a stair. To break a leg . . . or even a neck.

"Off here, mistress. There's a back way, a little-used stair, where we can haul Master Munchcryden back to your rooms with few eyes present to note his state."

"Let's be quick, then."

"After you, Mistress Delia."

Laurelle rushed down to the next landing, rounding in time to see Sten vanish down a side passage. Kytt touched her elbow, not to stop her, only to warn her to be careful.

She had only one weapon. Her eyes, as witness.

Surely Sten would not harm Delia if there was a chance others would find out. He would have to back down.

Laurelle left the landing and headed down the hall toward the side passage where Delia and Sten had vanished.

Words carried back to her.

"Who are these men?" Delia asked, her voice muffled by the narrowness of the cross passage. Still, Laurelle heard a sudden note of suspicion.

"My men," Sten answered calmly. "To help carry Master Munchcryden."

Laurelle ran faster.

"The stairs are just ahead," Sten assured her.

Reaching the arched opening, Laurelle spotted the grouping midway down the passage, huddled at the head of a dark stair. One of Sten's men held aloft a lamp.

Delia took the first step down.

Laurelle lifted an arm. "Mistress Delia!"

Her call rang out just as Sten shoved with both arms. Delia had begun to turn, drawn by Laurelle's cry—or perhaps sensing something amiss.

She shouted in surprise as she tumbled headlong out of sight. A crash of body on stone echoed to Laurelle—and Delia's cry suddenly ended.

Laurelle found all eyes staring at her.

Sten lifted an arm. Laurelle backed away, bumping into Kytt.

Shadows shifted to the right. Laurelle saw more guards, more of Sten's men, crossing from the main stairs into the passageway, latecomers, cutting off their retreat in that direction.

Swords slid from sheaths.

Kytt pulled Laurelle in the opposite direction, away from the stairs, toward the deeper depths of Tashijan. She stumbled after him.

Behind her, she heard one last order from Sten. *"Go down. Make sure her neck is broken."*

Laurelle ran. Terror could not stop the tears from welling. Kytt led the way, hand in hers, turning one corner, then another with some instinct born of fear and Grace.

Still, boots pounded after them.

"Tashijan is rotted," Lord Ulf said. "To the very stones of its foundation. From root to rooftop."

Kathryn shook her head. Though the fire was at her back, the room had gone colder than the darkest crypt.

"Mirra has weeded seeds throughout your towers," Ulf stated firmly. "And she is not the first. What you discovered below is but the first sprouts of a greater evil. It winds throughout Tashijan, deep into the past. And if left unchecked, far into the future, where our world will lie in ruins, trod by monsters a thousandfold worse than any carried by my winds."

Kathryn held up a hand. "But now we know about Mirra's treachery. We can stop her."

The figure of ice sculpted its face into a mask of distaste and irritation. "Too late, castellan, too late by far. It is rooted too deeply. Like the seersong in the Wyr-mistress. It can't be untangled, not without even worse ruin and damnation. Even *you* have been seeded."

"Me?"

"With distrust. With impotency. You cannot even stop Warden Fields. He remains a puppet to the witch below, dancing to the pulls of her strings."

"We can cut those strings."

"And more will rise to tangle and knot harder. Do you think the Fiery Cross is a creation of the warden? It was birthed by distrust, dissension, suspicion. So thoroughly has Mirra wrought her discord that trust will never return to Tashijan."

Kathryn remembered her attempt to restore trust between Argent and Tylar. Both sides had equally failed. Even she had whisked Tylar away without consulting the warden.

Distrust, dissension, suspicion.

Lord Ulf must have read her understanding. "There is no way to weed this patch. Best to burn it and salt the ground. Start anew. I've brought my forces far, at great cost and risk. Let us use the strength granted by the Cabal to set a cleansing fire here."

"And do the Cabal's bidding in this regard, too. Like killing Tylar." Hardness entered her voice.

"While it might serve the Cabal, it benefits us even more. We must look past the present and take a long view ahead. Even if Mirra could be chased from your cellars, the Fiery Cross will achieve ascendancy. A new Order of Shadowknights will emerge under a new banner. Argent ser Fields intends dominion for this new Order—to place the knights above all else, even the gods. Such an act will open the way not only for the Cabal, but much worse. Myrillia will fall into chaos, return to the time of bloodshed and raving. In this one moment, we have a chance to change that course."

"By destroying Tashijan?"

"To make it even stronger. The steel of a sword is made harder by fire and hammer. It is time for Tashijan to be forged anew."

Kathryn could not deny that at moments of despair such thoughts had passed through her own mind. Tashijan was ravaged and weakened. The number of knights and masters had dwindled over the past centuries. And now as a new War of the Gods was upon them, Tashijan created more chaos, rather than less. Its own warden had employed Dark Grace. The Fiery Cross was a banner for the cruel and craven, whether it was men who beat horses or boys who sought to brand girls. And fewer and fewer voices spoke against this tide. There was no stopping it.

She stared into the icy eyes of Lord Ulf, aglow with Grace. She read no madness. Only truth. A hard truth. Did she have such hardness to match? Could she walk a path as ruthless as the one Lord Ulf proposed?

"You know I am right," Lord Ulf said.

Kathryn bowed her head. "Your claims are indeed just, but before I agree or disagree, I still don't understand what role you need from me. I've witnessed the power in your storm. Of what use am I to you?"

"You must protect the heart of Tashijan."

She glanced up at him.

"As I open the cellars and lay waste to all, you must gather those you most trust. In secret, you must leave Tashijan. I will open a path through the storm for your exodus. Head away. And don't look back."

Kathryn shivered.

"Will you do this?"

She took a deep breath. She pondered the truth in all that was spoken here. As hard as his words were, they were sound of mind.

But not of heart.

As Lord Ulf wanted to lay waste to Tashijan, so had he sought Tylar with equal fervor. And while she might not know the true heart of Tashijan—whether it was salvageable or not—she knew Tylar's heart. She had doubted him once, a lifetime ago, even spoken against him—but no longer. Fires of grief and bloodshed had already forged her anew, made her stronger in many ways. Also more certain.

She trusted Tylar's heart—whether it turned toward Delia or back toward her. She knew it remained as true as the diamond on the pommel of her sword. Her fingers came to rest upon it.

If Lord Ulf could be wrong about Tylar, he could be wrong here.

She stared at the icy sculpture of a god.

"No," she said simply. "When you come, I will be waiting. All of Tashijan will be waiting."

Lord Ulf sighed, coldly unmoved. "Then even the heart of Tashijan must be destroyed." He stepped away and lifted an arm toward the door. "Go to your doom."

Kathryn was somewhat surprised to be so easily released. Lord Ulf made no move against her, honoring the parley. She left the fire's warmth and headed again into the cold.

"You'll all die," Lord Ulf said behind her.

She pictured Mychall, the stableboy, his crooked smile, his

bright and hopeful eyes. If she bent to Lord Ulf's will, she could lead him out. Lead so many others, too. But she also remembered the steaming stable in the storm. Despite the offer of safety, the stablemen had remained with their charges, to protect them, to weather the storm together.

She felt the god's eyes following her as she moved away.

"Then when the time comes," she answered him, "we'll die together."

As she reached the door, Lord Ulf spoke one last time. "Know this, Castellan Vail: That time is now."

She opened the door to the beat of wings. She stepped out and searched the narrow strip of sky between the tavernhouse and the stable. Snow swirled, but higher still, dark shapes sailed and flapped, all headed for one place.

Tashijan.

Kathryn flipped her cloak and borrowed speed born of shadow. She ducked back into the stable and leaped up into Stoneheart's saddle. Her mount didn't need heel or snap of rein. They had ridden too long for such necessities. The stallion knew her heart.

He twisted, half-rearing toward the door, bunched his haunches, and charged through the gate.

Kathryn ducked low to his neck as they flew outside. She remained low and gently urged him forward.

The stallion raced with a flowing gallop. She matched his pace, high in the saddle, floating above. They wended through the streets and alleys—then suddenly the town opened and fell behind them.

Rider and horse burst out into the field. She had guided the stallion to the same street down which they'd entered the town. Her path through the drifts stretched ahead. She had not wanted Stoneheart to have to plow a fresh track back home. Speed was essential.

She glanced past her shoulder. Snow filled the world behind her like a mighty wave about to crash, erasing the town street by street as it swept forward. Overhead, the front edge of Ulf's corrupted legion rode the eddies and drafts.

A mighty screech sounded, splitting the howl of the growing winds.

One of the wraiths had spotted the fleeing horse. It dove toward them, drawing others in its wake. A flock of hawks after a lone mouse. Whatever protection had been extended by the parley was now over.

"Fly," she urged her mount.

Legs churned faster, hooves cast snow higher. She felt the pound of the stallion's heart in her thighs. His breath streamed in a continual blow of white.

Still, they would never make it. The walls of Tashijan were too far.

A screaming wail filled the world overhead. Kathryn pulled her sword, twisting up in her saddle.

The wraith plummeted, wings tight, claws out.

No sword would block such an assault. Even if she could strike a blow, the plunging weight alone would knock her from the saddle. And other wraiths followed, spiraling tightly down behind the first.

Then a flash of fire burst past and struck the wraith in the shoulder. A wing snapped out reflexively. The timbre of its hunting cry changed to a wail of pain. The flapped wing caught air and flipped the wraith's dive into a wild tumble. It slammed hard into a neighboring drift. The flame sizzled and stubbornly refused to douse.

Then they were galloping past.

More arrows shot past overhead, oblivious of the gusts. Each arrow ignited with fire in midflight. Plainly the bolts had been Graced with powerful alchemies, *loam* and *fire*, doubly blessed to resist wind and ice.

A few more wraiths were struck and tumbled out of the skies.

The others fled higher, out of bow range.

Kathryn searched forward. She spotted figures atop the shield wall. Knights in black cloaks, barely discernible, and a few robed masters.

Lower, down where her path ended, a figure stood at the open gate.

His armor almost glowed.

Gerrod.

He backed up as she galloped through without slowing,

tucked tight, an arrow of horseflesh and iron. She knew that Gerrod, though masked by his helmet, had noted what rose behind her, ready to crash into Tashijan.

Still, she screamed into the wind as he shouldered the gate closed.

"Strike! Strike up Tashijan!"

The gong echoed through the darkness, hollow and haunted.

"What is that?" Laurelle whispered.

"War," Kytt answered in a hushed breath.

The two hid in a dark cell. They were huddled tight. It had been a full quarter bell since they'd last heard any sign of pursuit. But Laurelle knew Sten would not give up this hunt so easily. He could not tolerate witnesses to his assault on Delia. He would have all paths out of this area guarded. And surely if he had planned an ambush here against Delia, he had the region well mapped.

She shivered.

Kytt tightened his arm around her. "Whatever has roused the striking of the gong might draw away the hunters."

As if hearing him, another ringing echo droned through the stones. Laurelle felt it in her bones, along her spine. She had never been so desperate. Her heart pounded in her throat. She wanted to cry, but nothing would break loose.

"We can't stay here," he whispered as the ringing faded. "And I think I might know a way to get us safely past the others."

"How?"

"A wyld tracker has keen eyes in the dark. The guards are also unwashed, easy to smell from several paces off. With care, going slow, we might be able to find a weakness through whatever snare has been laid."

She considered his plan. She did not have his senses. She would be blind, totally in his care.

"Laurelle?" he asked, noting her silence.

She felt his breath on her cheek, heated, worried. Again she was struck by his scent and she turned to him, followed the breath to his lips. She kissed him.

He pulled back, startled.

She followed, making sure he knew it was no accident. Then she spoke between his lips. "I trust you," she said.

She gripped his hand and shifted to her feet. After a stunned moment, he rose beside her.

"Stay with me," he whispered as they set off.

He guided them down black corridors, moving in fast steps and sudden stops. They crisscrossed, then backtracked when he scented something. Finally the darkness turned gray ahead, but he balked.

She saw enough of his silhouette to see him shake his head.

Back they went into the darkness.

"Stairs," he whispered, guiding her by the hand. "An old servants' stair, I think. Dusty and forgotten."

She hoped so.

He headed down it. To follow, she searched with her toes for each step. It was narrow and frighteningly steep, more like descending a ladder than a stair.

They finally reached the bottom. He led the way again. They continued more cautiously, then he slowed even further. "I think . . . I think we're not far from the stair where Mistress Delia was pushed."

"Are you sure?"

He didn't answer for a long moment. "I also scent something . . . a faint trace . . ." His hand tightened on hers. "Blood."

Laurelle felt her stomach clench.

"Stay here."

"No." Her answer was immediate and certain. Her fingers clamped onto his.

He didn't argue, only edged forward. In another turn, darkness turned to a deep twilight. Ahead, a body appeared, sprawled on the floor, unmoving. Even in the gloom, Laurelle noted the unnatural twist to the body.

She bit back a sob, feet slowing. She didn't want to see.

"It's not Delia," Kytt assured her and led her forward.

In another two steps, she saw he was correct. The body wore a guard's livery. One of Sten's men.

Kytt dropped to a knee and placed a hand on his neck. "Broken." He straightened and stepped over the body. He touched something on the floor. "Drops of blood." He sniffed at his fingers. "Mistress Delia's scent."

Could she still be alive?

Hope rising, they hurried forward. The trail led to a closed door. They hesitated—but even Laurelle could see the wet blood on the floor. She tentatively reached for the latch, but Kytt suddenly placed his hand over hers.

"Wait. There's someone—"

"Get in here," a voice barked, startling them both back a step. "Quit skulking and help. Before it's too late."

Though Laurelle recognized the voice, she pulled on the latch. She refused to abandon Delia again.

Inside, the room held scant furniture. Only a small lamp rested on the stone floor, dancing with a tepid flame. But it was enough to illuminate Master Orquell crouched beside Delia's limp form, sprawled across a small plank bed. One side of the woman's face was bloody, hair soaked and matted. The old master wiped her cheek with a wet cloth, then pointed an arm toward the lamp.

"Bring that closer," he ordered.

Laurelle obeyed, reacting to the command in his voice. She picked up the lamp and carried it nearer.

Master Orquell slipped a tiny leather bag from inside his robe and dumped a gray powder into his palm, then held it before the lamp's flame. The powder turned a rosy hue.

"You broke that guard's neck?" Kytt asked, equally unsure.

"Before he could break hers," Orquell answered sourly, weighing the powder in his palm, studying it closer. "Lucky I was down here. Then again, the flames guide us where we're best needed."

"The flames . . . ?" Laurelle echoed, suspicions piqued again.

The master glanced up at her. His eyes appeared less milky in the close light of the lamp. They pierced through her, questioningly.

"We followed you," she explained. "Earlier in the morning. Into the back of the master's quarters."

His eyes narrowed in confusion, then brightened with understanding.

"You saw me cast a pyre."

She nodded.

"Ah . . . no wonder you are suspicious." He reached again to the wet cloth. "Then perhaps this will steady your hand so you stop shaking the lamp."

He sat back and wiped his forehead. Face paint, a perfect match to his yellow parchment skin, smeared away. Beneath the paint rose a hidden crimson mark, bright on his skin, resting in the center of his forehead like an awakening eye.

Laurelle gasped at the mark, knowing it well.

It was no eye. It marked where the bloody thumb of the fire god, Takaminara, had been burnt into his flesh, branding him as one of her true acolytes.

"I am *rub-aki*," Orquell said quietly.

"One of the Blood-eyed seers."

She pictured him rocking before his tiny pyre, sprinkling alchemy, and speaking to the flame. His fire had not been born of some forbidden Grace, but of something much older, a seer's rites ancient and rare. His mistress was not the daemoness below, but a god in a distant land, the reclusive Takaminara.

But why the disguise, the face paint?

Before she could inquire, Orquell returned his attention to his ministrations of Delia. "We don't have much time. We must get her back on her feet and moving."

He leaned over and puffed his fistful of powder into Delia's face. She inhaled it sharply as if it burnt. Her eyes fluttered open. She gasped, steam rising from her lips with some alchemy of fire.

She jerked as if startled awake, flailing an arm.

"Quickly now, boy," Orquell said to Kytt. "Help me get her up. We must be away. They'll be drawn by the smell of blood before long."

Delia fought them, still dazed, but Laurelle reassured her and drew the focus of her eye. "You're safe."

Or so she hoped.

"Laurelle . . . ?"

"I'm here. We must get going. You have to help us."

Orquell met Laurelle's gaze, nodded his thanks, and then he and Kytt helped Delia up. In a couple more steps, she was strong enough to need only Kytt's support.

Orquell hurried ahead to the door. "We must get back to the others. Into flame and light. They're already on the move. The blood and the dead will draw them."

"Draw who—?"

A scream answered her, rising out in the hall to a curdling wail.

"Too late." Orquell turned to them, his crimson eye blazing in the lamplight. "The witch is loose."

18

A RIVER OF FIRE

"THE POISON OF THE JINX BAT STOPS BOTH HEART AND breath," the old man said as he leaned over Brant's body, ear to the boy's chest.

Tylar stood to the side. They gathered in a glade, not far from the Huntress's castillion, but the forest lay dense around them, keeping them well cloaked and hidden. He was relieved to find Lorr and Malthumalbaen already here, somehow escaped.

And with their weapons.

Tylar strapped on his swords, belting Rivenscryr to one hip, the knight's sword to the other. He straightened, aching and sore, near to crippled from their mad flight. He had already wrapped his hand and bound the ache of his broken rib. Still, he limped carefully toward the boy on the litter.

They had already broken the poisoned arrowhead, pulled the shaft, and packed the wound with healing firebalm. But there was a greater concern.

Dart knelt on Brant's far side, shadowed by Lorr and the giant. All their faces were grim. Krevan and Calla checked their glade's periphery, eyeing the motley-dressed young hunters, some who probably hadn't seen ten summers.

Rogger stood off to the side, talking earnestly with Harp, the leader of the band, if only by sheer height. Tylar recognized that the boy was probably younger than Brant.

The only elder here worked on Brant.

"Lucky for us," the old man said as he straightened, "our giant jungle bat likes its meat fresh after it has laid up its prey. Its venom slows rot and decay, holds it at bay for a time. But that time's about run out."

He snapped a finger at one of the boys, who hurried forward with two hollowed stems of a whiskerpine. The lad had been packing the stems with a downy powder.

The man accepted the pipes and leaned over Brant.

He had introduced himself as Sheershym, one-time scholar and master at the school here. No longer. He still wore a master's robes, but they were shabby and stained. Stubble covered his bald pate, obscuring the tattoos of his mastered disciplines. It was rare to find a master who didn't keep his head shaved proudly. Tylar read one of his sigils, designating skill in the healing arts, but the mark looked nearly faded. The freshest tattoos concentrated on histories, scholariums, and alchemies of *mnelopy*, the study of dreams and memory, fitting for one who delved into the deep past of Myrillia.

Not so useful for healing.

Still, he seemed to know what he was doing.

The man placed the end of each stem into one of Brant's nostrils. He nodded to Dart. "Lass, would you mind covering his mouth and pinching his nose closed around the pipes?"

She nodded and did as he instructed, her face pale with worry.

Sheershym bent and slipped the other ends of the pipe into his own mouth. He exhaled sharply through the stems, blowing the powder deep and puffing up Brant's thin chest with his own breath. He held that pose for a long moment, face reddening. Then he straightened, drawing the pipes out Brant's nose.

Brant's chest sighed down.

The master waved Dart back. "Now we'll see. That's all we can do."

They all stared.

Brant still lay unmoving, but slowly his body seemed to relax, muscles sagging, as if he had been slightly clenched, holding death away by stubborn will.

"Is he—?" Dart began to tearfully inquire.

The master held up a hand.

Brant's chest suddenly swelled and collapsed with a contented sigh.

Malthumalbaen let out a whoop that scattered a pair of skipperwings from their canopy nest. The resulting frowns quickly silenced him, but they failed to dim the relief shining from his eyes.

"What manner of alchemy was that?" Rogger asked, stepping to them with Harp.

The boy answered for the master. "Dreamsmoke, from the Farallon lotus petal."

Sheershym nodded. "When smoked in water pipes, it brings a sense of peace and giddiness, but in its purest alchemy it also bears great healing Grace. We'll have to carry the boy from here. The smoke will have him dozing for a good three bells. He'll rise from his bed with no worse than a pounding in his head."

"Better that than rising from his grave," Rogger mumbled.

Sheershym stood with a groan, supporting his old back, and rolled an eye at Rogger. "It is said there were once alchemies even for that. Hidden in a tome, scribed on leathered human skin. The *Nekralikos Arcanum.* Written by the tongueless one himself." He shrugged. "But who can say if it's true? If you look long enough into the past, memory becomes dream."

"Or so says Daronicus," Rogger said.

Sheershym's left eyebrow rose in surprise. "You know Harshon Daronicus?"

Rogger shrugged. "I've read his work in its original Littick. A long time ago. Another life."

"Truly? Where—?"

"Master Sheershym," Harp said, interrupting, "perhaps we can leave this talk until we're beyond the burn."

He nodded. "Certainly. We should be off. The Huntress will be upon our heels like a ravening dog at any moment."

They quickly broke down the small camp. Krevan carried one end of the litter and the giant the other. Several boys vanished into the forest to either side, barely stirring a leaf.

"They'll clear our back trail," Harp said. "And lay false ones."

Tylar walked with the boy and the master near the front of the band as it snaked through the woods. "How long have you been hiding out here?"

"Since the winnowing," the master said grimly. "Beginning of the last full shine of the lesser moon. Some forty days."

Tylar pictured the mass of skilled hunters that had circled

the Grove and ambushed them. He remembered the unerring flight of their arrows. "And you've dodged capture all this time? How?"

"Not without losses," Harp said grimly. "Especially when her hunters started poisoning their arrows. Her madness grows worse with each setting sun."

"What happened here?"

The boy haltingly told the story of Saysh Mal, of the Huntress's ravening, of her slaughter, how she began with only a hundred hunters, bound and burned to her, then spread her wickedness.

"Wells were poisoned with her blood, binding all to her will," Harp said. "Her corruption spread. Mothers and fathers shaved the stakes used against their own children. Those weak of limb were cut down. What you saw back in the Grove is only the barest glimpse of what lies rotting under the canopy."

"Only the strongest were allowed to live and serve her," Sheershym finished.

Tylar's voice was driven soft by the horrors described. "How did you all escape such slaughter?"

"We fled. Three score of us. The master had old maps of the hinterlands. We sought to flee Saysh Mal, to escape into the hinter." He made a quiet scoffing sound and shook his head. "A sorry state when the hinterlands offer better succor than your own settled realm."

"And still we wouldn't have lived. Not without her help."

"Whose help?"

Harp waved a dismissive hand, done with reliving the nightmare. "You'll see soon enough. Best save your breath."

Tylar didn't argue. He was finding it harder to match even the elder's pace. His side throbbed, shortening his breaths, and his knee remained locked up painfully. He could barely move it.

"How long have you been crippled up?" Sheershym asked him, nodding toward his gait.

Tylar shook his head. Now it was his turn to prefer silence. He didn't understand the growing ruin of his body. Why had he failed to summon the naethryn back on the balcony? Had it become permanently imprisoned? Was the cost of its release more than a single broken bone? He recalled when all this had first started, down in the cellars of Tashijan. The finger that hadn't healed.

What had gone awry?

"Once we reach our main camp," Sheershym said, "I'll attend your injuries. See what I can do to help."

Tylar merely nodded.

"We had such hope," the master mumbled.

Tylar glanced at him, hearing the pain.

"When we spotted your flippercraft, we believed it marked the end of the Huntress's reign. And if not that, then at least rescue."

Harp snorted. In the end, it had been Tylar's party that had needed the rescuing.

Sheershym pointed ahead. "Once safe, you'll have to explain how the Godslayer ended up in Saysh Mal. I wager it wasn't a chance visit."

Tylar nodded. "I'm afraid we may need more than your hospitality. Do you still have those old maps of the hinterlands?"

The master's brow crinkled as he looked over at Tylar. He slowly nodded. "Our camp is secure. It is madness to think to venture out there."

"Madness seems rampant of late across Myrillia," Tylar mumbled darkly. He ended any further discussion by drifting back along the line, favoring his knee. He settled next to the litter bearing Brant, still borne by Krevan and Malthumalbaen.

Dart walked on the far side. "He continues to slumber," she reported. "Though I heard him mumbling in his sleep. I thought he was asking for my help. But then he seemed angry, mumbling about letting someone burn."

Tylar frowned, recalling a similar cryptic utterance. The words had stayed with him.

HELP THEM . . . FREE THEM . . . LET THEM ALL BURN

He also remembered Mirra screaming at him. *Kill the boy . . . before he wakes them!* What did any of it mean? What was it about Brant? He found his gaze drifting to the one thing that tied him to all this.

The stone rested at the hollow of his throat.

Dart noted his attention. "It is pretty—"

Tylar glanced to her.

Her eyes remained on the stone, then slowly shifted to him. "Do you think it's true? That the stone came from the home of the gods."

Tylar realized the weight of those words to Dart, a child of these same gods. If the Huntress was correct, the stone was also a piece of *her* lost home, a world she'd never seen.

Until now.

Her gaze returned to it, her face worried yet frosted with wonder.

Rogger broke the spell, ambling up to them, nose crinkled. "Do you smell something burning?"

Dart gaped at the swath of ruin ahead. It cut through the jungle, a river of black rock, steaming, cracked in places to reveal its molten, fiery heart. They gathered on one bank, still green, though tributaries of burnt forest stretched outward. They had edged along one such tributary to reach this place. The firestorm, ignited by the molten flow, had burnt the jungle down to the loam, leaving stretches of forest charred to trunks, blackened spires spreading in great tracks, eerily reminiscent of the stakes back in the Grove.

At least there were no bodies here.

"What happened?" Tylar asked, voicing aloud the question for all.

Harp stood beside Dart. He pointed to the south, to the headwaters of the black river. A mountain rose into the sky, far taller than the peaks across the river. Snow crowned its summit, glinting in the sun.

"Takaminara," Dart whispered, naming both god and mountain. She remembered Brant describing it earlier, the sleeping volcano. It slept no longer.

"She saved us," Harp said and pointed across the ruin. A bit of green forest could be seen on the far side, pinched between the western mountain ranges. "We fled toward the hinterland beyond the Divide, where the mountains fall into the lower wild lands. But the Huntress found us. She led two hundred of her best against us. Two hundred against three score. We were too young, too old, too weak. We would never make the hinter in time. Neither could we withstand such a force against us. So we kept running well into the night. First one moon rose, then the other. We helped each other as best we could, but as we reached the foot of the western mountain passes, the weakest, the oldest, the youngest began to falter on the steeper slopes. All seemed hopeless.

"Then in the darkest part of the night, the ground began to tremor. Leaves shook, trunks cracked. And behind us, the land split open in a thunderous crack. Fiery rock surged up, brilliant in the darkness. It separated our group from the hunters, raising a river between us, impassable. The hunters were driven off with flame and clouds of brimstone. The wound in her land sent the Huntress deep into seclusion."

Harp stared toward the mountain. "She protected us, sheltered us."

"Why?" Dart asked. "It is not her realm."

"Takaminara might have sensed the corruption here," Rogger said. "Probably had an eye turned in this direction. Perhaps she had witnessed enough slaughter, so lashed out as best she could to protect what was left."

"Or shake the Huntress back to her sensibilities," Tylar said. "The Huntress is a god of loam. To tear her realm must have struck her like the lash of a whip, one that cut deep. No wonder she retreated into hiding, to lick her wounds."

Krevan overheard their conversation. "But why did Takaminara act at all? It is rare enough for a god to assault a neighboring realm. And that one, buried in her mountain, barely acknowledges the outer world as it is."

Harp turned from his grateful gaze upon the mountain. "Whatever her reason, she saved us. The Huntress avoids this place. Refuses to let her hunters cross. Our camp on the far side remains secure. But we don't know how long such fear will last. Or if Takaminara will act a second time to protect us. For days afterward, her volcano rumbled, yellow steam issued from a thousand cracks. But now the mountain sleeps again."

Dart heard the worry in his voice.

"And it's safe to cross now?" Malthumalbaen asked, carrying the rear of Brant's litter, eyeing one of the glowing cracks.

"If you know the right path," Harp said and started across the rock.

Dart followed. "Where are we going?"

Harp pointed to the two tallest spires ahead. The tips of the peaks glowed above shrouds of mists and smudgy smoke. "Our camp lies between the Anvil and the Hammer."

Rogger squinted. "In other words, *within* the Forge?"

Harp glanced back and nodded.

They continued in a stretched line across the frozen black river. Dart felt the heat of the rock through the soles of her boots. All around, thin vents wept steam, smelling of brimstone and staining the surrounding rock yellow, turning the cracks into festering wounds.

Pupp kept close to her side, sensing her unease, glowing a bit brighter as if challenging the heat with his own molten form.

On the opposite side of Brant's litter, Rogger dropped closer to Tylar.

"The Forge," the thief whispered to Tylar and nodded toward Brant. "Where the boy and his father found Keorn's burning form. Seems we've just about come full circle."

"But where from there?" Tylar mumbled. He held his wrapped hand over his left side, favoring it. His limp had grown much worse.

Behind them, a sharp trill of a jungle loon rose from farther out in the forest, as if calling to them, warning them.

Ahead, Harp glanced back, eyes narrowed with suspicion. He didn't say anything, but he increased their pace.

Words died among them as the heat rose and noxious seeps tainted the air. Ahead, the green beach beckoned with a promise of shade and dripping canopy, but it grew too slowly.

With no choice, they marched onward as the sun sank before them. The twin peaks of the Forge—the Anvil and the Hammer—blazed ever brighter. Dart's eyes ached at the glare, but she could not turn away. It was their destination.

At long last, the line of jungle swelled, and the rock under foot cooled as they left behind the deeper flows near the river's center. They stumbled gratefully off the rock and into the welcoming embrace of shade and green leaf.

"The way is steeper from here," Harp warned. "But it's not much farther. If you look to that cliff, you can see one of our watchtowers, where we can watch the burn and spy for any trespass against us."

Dart squinted. Half-blinded by the heat and glare, all she was able to discern atop the indicated cliff was a shroud of trees. She bit back a groan. They might not have *far* to go, but it was *high*.

For Tylar, it was both too far and too high.

He suddenly sank to a fallen log, half-collapsing. His black hair was slicked to his scalp with his own sweat. His face shone with exhaustion and was etched with deep lines by pain. Near the end of their fording of the black river, he had leaned heavily on the giant. His bad leg seemed to have twisted under him, bowing, turning his heel. He cradled his arm with the bandaged hand to his chest. His fingers poking from the wrapping looked as if they had already healed, but crookedly.

Master Sheershym approached and knelt beside him. "You'll not make it to the camp. We'll have to cut a litter for you."

Tylar just hung his head. "If I rest . . ." he said weakly.

Rogger joined the master. "You can sleep the year away, and you'd still not be able to climb that far."

Harp already had his boys cutting and weaving another litter. They did it with a practiced speed. He also waved to two boys to run ahead and alert the camp of their pending arrival.

"This weakness," Sheershym said. "It is more than mere tired limb. I may not be the best healer of Saysh Mal, but even I can tell that what ails you goes deeper than broken bone."

He took Tylar's hand and deftly unwrapped it. The broken finger had indeed healed crooked, evident when Tylar tried to clench and pull away. But in his exhaustion, he could not break even the elderly grip of Sheershym. Worse still, the two neighboring fingers, unbroken before, had also curled into calloused knots, and it appeared his wrist had locked up as much as his knee. It was as if the damage had spread, wicking outward into healthy flesh like some poison from a wound.

Even Tylar gaped at the sight, surprised what the wrap had hid. His other hand rubbed his knee. His leg was plainly more twisted.

"It's like you're going back," Rogger mumbled.

"Back where?" Sheershym asked.

Rogger shook his head.

The master sat on his heels and glanced between Tylar and Rogger. "Silence will not serve you here. Whatever is at work had best be attended with full knowledge." This voice took on a tone of a master at the front of his students.

Tylar nodded. "You know my story," he said weakly. "A broken knight, healed by Meeryn of the Summering Isles as she lay dying. How she instilled her naethryn undergod into me, curing me at the same time."

"Who doesn't know that tale by now?"

"What many don't know is that when I loose the naethryn, my body returns to its broken form." Tylar lifted his gnarled hand. "When the naethryn returns again to my body, so does my hale form. But now . . ."

Rogger finished. "He failed to loose the naethryn with the Huntress. And his body continues to slowly break and twist again, driving him back toward his crippled form."

"It started slow. An unhealed break. But it spreads ever faster. I don't know why it's happening, nor what it portends."

Sheershym asked a few more questions about what was broken in the past and now. By the time he was done, Harp had a litter ready. "Let's get you up to the camp," the master said, standing again. "I'd like to study this puzzle in more detail. 'It is often the smallest thread that reveals the greater pattern.' "

"Tyrrian Balk," Roger said.

Sheershym glanced to him. "You've read the work of the Arithromatic. You must someday tell me where you performed your studies."

They hurriedly got Tylar stretched out and continued skyward along a steep and winding path. It looked little more than a deer track, and probably was. Switchbacks climbed the side of a promontory of rock that jutted from the peak called the Anvil.

As they climbed, Brant had begun to revive, mumbling and attempting to sit up on his litter.

Lorr pressed his shoulder back down. "Stay put," the tracker ordered.

"Where . . . ?"

Dart kept to his other side. She found his hand and took it. "We're heading up into the forest. Rest now. We'll explain more when we stop."

He nodded, eyes rolling slightly. His fingers found the strength to squeeze hers, an intimacy that warmed through Dart and made the path seem less steep. Then he relaxed back into slumber.

After several more turns, views opened and revealed how high they'd already climbed. The black river stretched below, winding back to the great mountain to the south. On the far side, the spread of green forest filled the lower valleys. But much remained hidden behind mists, including the Huntress's castillion.

Then the views vanished again under heavy canopy. A few shouts reached them from ahead. One last push, and they topped the rise and found a small glade where a crude camp had been set up. It was nothing more than sprawls of tented canvas across low limbs and netted hammocks hanging higher. Children and elders gathered, though some hung close to the forest edge, looking ready to bolt—especially when Malthumalbaen trudged into view. One of the youngest began to cry and buried his face in the skirt of an older woman leaning on a cane.

"He won't eat you," the woman promised.

"Dral might have," the giant mumbled under his breath as he passed. " 'Course after that climb, I'm not about to be that particular either."

Harp guided them forward and found a corner for them to rest and catch their wind. Water was brought in leather flasks. It tasted sour, but to Dart it was still the sweetest wine.

Tylar settled to the forest floor.

Sheershym appeared with a book tucked under one arm. "I would like to sketch a map of your injuries. Where they are now, where they were before. See what pattern, if any, might reveal itself."

Tylar groaned and shifted up into a seated position. "I feel stronger already."

"Because your arse was hauled up here," Rogger said. "That's why."

"And rest will not straighten a crooked bone." Sheershym added. He waved Tylar back down. "First I'd like to inspect the mark Meeryn placed upon you. It is through there that the naethryn enters and leaves this world. Yes?"

Tylar grimaced, but that was the extent of his further objections. With Rogger's help, he slipped his shadowcloak over his shoulders, then unhooked the shirt beneath. It had been soaked through with his sweat.

Rogger accepted the garment as Tylar shed it. The thief pinched it up with a sour expression. "If Delia saw this waste of humour, she'd burn you with her tongue for days." He wrung out the garment, squeezing the sweat into a small fire ringed by stones. It sizzled and popped, destroying any residual Grace.

Bare-chested, Tylar leaned back to the litter, plainly exerted by even this small effort. Still, a bit of color had filled his cheeks again after the rest.

Sheershym leaned to study the black palm print centered on Tylar's chest, the mark of Meeryn. He reached a hand toward it. "May I?"

Tylar had his eyes closed and waved a few fingers of his good hand. "Do what you must."

Sheershym traced the black edges with a finger, then tested the flesh within the mark.

Dart winced as she stood to the side, arms crossed over her chest. It was the first time she had seen Tylar's hidden mark since back in Chrismferry. It made her uneasy to look upon it. It looked to her like a well of dark water shaped like a palm. She feared the master's hand would pass into Tylar's chest.

But his fingers only discovered skin over bone.

"I don't feel anything amiss," he said, straightening. "Let's check the rest of your injuries. For the knee, we'll need those leggings off."

The master waved to Dart and Calla. "Perhaps a bit of modesty is in order."

Calla shrugged and wandered a few steps away to where someone had spitted a rabbit over a flame. Dart also began to turn away, when a flash of light caught her eye.

She turned back to Tylar. He had raised to one elbow and was tugging free the loop of his sword belt. "Wait," she said and stepped closer.

Tylar lifted his face toward her.

Dart leaned closer to the mark on his chest, bending at the waist. "I—I thought I saw something . . ."

Tylar glanced down at himself, his brow crinkling.

The well of dark water that was his mark swirled ever so slightly as she stared closely. She had noted the same back in Chrismferry, as if something had crested just under the surface, stirring the waters.

His naethryn.

But that was not what had drawn her eye.

Sheershym sighed with impatience. "I assure you, lass. Nothing is amiss."

Rogger warded him back. "Best let her look. She's got eyes a mite sharper than ours. Sees things others miss." He said this last with a wink in her direction.

Dart kept her focus on the mark, only a hand's breadth from Tylar's chest. She waited. Maybe she was mistaken—

Then it flashed again.

Deep within the well, a trickling trace of green fire snaked across the mark and away again. Flames within a dark sea.

"Did you see that?" Dart asked, startled.

Sheershym glanced at her, shook his head, then returned to study the mark.

Tylar caught her eye. "What did you see, Dart?"

"Flames, stirring deep with your mark. Then away again."

"Flames?" Rogger mumbled. "What did they look like?"

She frowned, picturing them, trying to capture how they made her feel. "Emerald but with a sickly cast. A feverish sheen to them."

Tylar touched his mark and found only flesh. "Green fire . . ." His eyes narrowed.

"What?" Rogger asked, plainly sensing some recognition in the other's voice.

Tylar kept his gaze fixed to Dart. "Like moonlight off pond scum."

She slowly nodded.

"I've seen such a flame before," Tylar said. "It shone from the blade Perryl struck me with. Or rather struck Meeryn's naethryn with."

"Who is this Perryl?" Sheershym asked.

"A black *ghawl*," Rogger said. "A daemon wearing another's skin."

"His dark sword grazed the naethryn when it was last released. I felt the burn of the blade's kiss." Tylar touched the side of his chest. "Here."

Sheershym inspected the bruised flesh. "Where your rib is broken now."

Tylar nodded.

Off to the side, Brant stirred and mumbled. "She . . . she . . . we must . . ." Then he drifted away.

The master looked to the boy, then back to Tylar. "I fear young Brant might not be the only one poisoned here. That blade must have carried some corruption. It poisoned your naethyn—and as the two of you are bound together, you suffer for it, too."

Silence settled over them.

"And if his naethryn dies . . . ?" Rogger finally asked.

Sheershym shook his head. "I cannot say. But I suspect the wear and break of your body reflects the vitality of the naethryn inside you. As you grow more crippled of limb, it maps your naethryn's slide toward death."

"Is there some cure?" Rogger said. "Some powder to smoke the poison out, like you did with Brant?"

"Such matters are far beyond my skills," Sheershym said. His face looked especially waxen with fear, something unspoken.

"What?" Tylar asked.

"Even if there were a cure," the master said, "I fear its potency might never reach where it is most needed."

"Why's that?"

"There has been talk and speculation amongst the masters since you rose to your regency. Arguments and thoughts shared by raven's wing. One consensus is that the naethryn inside you . . . isn't truly *inside* you. How could it be? Instead most believe it to be tethered to you while trapped half in this world, half in the naether. For any hope to burn the poison from the creature, you must bring it fully here."

"Which I failed to do before," Tylar said.

"And while poisoned, you may never be able to do."

Rogger shook his head. "A perfectly laid trap."

But it wasn't the only one.

Brant suddenly sat up on the neighboring litter, gasping out as if startled by the terror of a dream, "She . . . she . . ."

A shout caught his words and finished his thought, coming from the forest, in the direction of the cliff's edge. *"She comes! She comes!"*

Dart straightened, along with everyone else.

Even Brant gained his legs, wobbly but supported by Lorr.

They all stared to the east, toward the burnt swath of the black river.

The Huntress was on the move.

"The river remains quiet," Brant said. "Takaminara seems to show no interest in stopping the Huntress this time."

"She may not be able to," Rogger said. "It must have cost her greatly to split the land the first time."

Their party gathered at a hunting lodge that overlooked the cliff's edge. It had been turned into a watchtower by a pair of sentinels, boys barely past twelve. The lodge offered a wide view of the valley floor, once a green sea, now split by a black river.

Brant shifted the arm in his sling. The firebalm had sealed his wound, and Grace already knit the tissue with a burning itch. Between his eyes, a throbbing ache persisted, the dregs of his poisoning. His left leg also felt numb and thick. But the walk here had helped return sensation with a fiery prickling.

He was alive.

But for how long?

Harp stood at his shoulder. Brant could not believe how much his old friend had grown. Once shorter, he now stood half a head taller than Brant. But so much remained the same, too. The worried crinkle at the corners of his eyes, the way he tapped his chin when struggling with a puzzle, even the same crooked grin, offered when he'd first crossed to Brant back in the camp. Still, despite the warm and genuine greeting, there remained a darker look to his eye, something Brant had never seen before. Shadows that would forever haunt his friend.

Brant studied the land below. In just the short time it had taken to come here, the Huntress had led her war party halfway across the river. She did not shy from its burn and stink any longer. Brant had heard the story of Harp's flight. The Huntress, angered by their escape, meant to end this now.

"They move swiftly," Tylar said.

"And so must we if we're to reach the cliffs and the hinterlands beyond," Rogger said.

Brant had walked these lands as a boy. He knew them well. The Divide fell away into the hinter about two leagues away. A hard march, but one they should be able to make. They had already sent ahead the youngest and oldest, to await word at the cliff's edge, in case Takaminara chose to protect them yet again. No one wanted to enter the deadly hinterlands unless there was no other choice.

Now they knew.

"We must go," Brant said.

Harp had everything prepared. While camped here, he'd had ladders woven of vine and sinew. They waited at the Divide, coiled and ready to be unfurled down the cliff into the hinterlands. But Harp had planned further strategies as well.

"I'll leave ten of our fastest runners," he said and pointed to key high points. "Along the ridges here and there. With arrow and bow, they should be able to hold the pass, slow the others a bit longer. We don't want to be caught on the cliff, still on the ladders. A few ax chops and we'd all be tumbling headlong into the hinter."

"How likely will her hunters be to follow us down there?" Tylar asked.

"She won't stop until we're all dead," Harp said with certainty. "But I've already soaked the ladders in poxflame oil. Once below, we can set the ladder afire. Burn them off the cliffs. It will take time for any pursuers to find another way down."

Brant read the appreciation and respect in the regent's eyes as he nodded. "Very good," Tylar said.

Krevan stood at the lip of the cliff, a long glass to his eye. He finally lowered it. "Six score," he said. "Eighty with bows. Forty with spears."

Harp frowned at him. "Six score? You're sure of that count?"

Krevan stared hard, not bothering to answer.

Harp's frown deepened as he glanced below. "The best of her hunters number two hundred. She comes with too few."

Brant understood what he meant. All attention had been

on the war party that crossed the river directly. But the burn spread to the north and south, stretching out of sight in both directions, beyond the view of the sentries in the makeshift watchtower.

"She sent others ahead of her," Harp said and turned to them, his eyes wide with worry.

"To close off our escape," Brant said. There was a reason their god was named the Huntress.

Confirming this, screams suddenly erupted, faint and distant, coming from the top of the pass. Where the others had been headed. Horns sounded from that direction, echoing darkly through the wood.

The snare had been sprung.

Responding to the horns, the Huntress called to them from below. Her voice carried to them, borne aloft in Grace.

"I want only the Godslayer and the boy! To bring his stone!" Horns punctuated her words. *"The rest will be allowed to leave my realm. But any further trespass will be met with blood!"*

"What are we going to do?" Dart asked as the horns echoed away. She stood with Lorr and Malthumalbaen at the door to the lodge. "You can't go down there."

"Agreed." Krevan pointed toward the Forge. "Best we fight our way through to the Divide. There are only two score up there."

"Two score of her best hunters," Harp said with a sour shake of his head. "And they have the high ground. Even if we could make the cliffs, they'd burn us or chop us off the ladders."

The Huntress called again, pointing an arm. *"Come to where the black rock meets the green wood! In the open. If you are not there when I set foot back to loam, your lives—all your lives—will be forfeit!"*

Brant watched Tylar study the spread of hunters below, his eyes narrowed with calculations. Though his body was broken, his mind remained sharp.

Tylar finally spoke. "Krevan, lead the others toward the Divide. Gather everyone you can along the way. Keep them safe."

The leader of the Black Flaggers seemed ready to argue, but whatever he saw in the regent's eyes held his tongue.

Dart was not so reticent. "I can be of help," she said.

"No. If the Huntress spots anyone else below . . ." Tylar shook his head. "We dare not antagonize her any further. And I'd rather you're safely away."

"Then take Pupp at least. No one can see him, and he's . . . he's fierce."

"He is indeed. But we've never tested his nature against a god, and now is not the time to find out. Still, you've given me a thought."

Tylar turned to Harp. "You mentioned swift runners. Take me to your fastest." With a nod, Harp led him around the corner of the lodge.

Dart came to Brant and touched his arm, still unconvinced. "It is surely your death if you go down there."

"I pray it's only my death," he mumbled, remembering the bloodstained lips of Marron. "Perhaps this is my path. It started in the shadow of the Forge. Maybe it is supposed to end here."

Tylar quickly returned, hopping on his good leg. He had overheard Brant's words. "Don't be so quick to accept death. Do that and you'll have one foot in your grave already."

Rogger crossed to them and held out his hand. A piece of yellowed bone rested in his palm. "Before we fled, I stole a sliver of the skull. Mayhap it still contains enough Dark Grace to break the seersong's hold with that black stone of yours."

Brant stared at the skull, touched the stone at his throat, and slowly shook his head. "I feel the smallest tingle or warmth, nothing more."

Rogger frowned. "I was afraid of that."

In his heart, Brant was relieved. He wanted nothing more to do with the skull.

"Still, keep it safe for now," Tylar ordered the man, then nodded toward the approaching hunters. "We dare tarry no longer."

In short order, their two parties split. Harp led the others toward the higher pass, guarded by Krevan and Malthumalbaen. Tylar headed back down the small deer path. He hobbled heavily on one side, lost in his own thoughts.

Brant followed. "You have some plan?" he asked.

"I do."

Brant waited for him to elaborate, but the regent remained silent, marching onward, descending toward the dark river below. A view opened briefly. The leading edge of hunters neared the fringe of forest below, running ahead of the Huntress. Her scouts would reach the jungle first.

Brant tired of Tylar's cryptic silence. "So am I part of this plan?" he asked, a bit harshly.

"A big part." Tylar glanced back to Brant. "You're the worm on the hook."

Dart climbed beside Malthumalbaen. The giant looked back as often as Dart. Both were worried for Brant . . . for Tylar. While they climbed toward safety, the others descended toward certain doom.

"Master Brant knows how to take care of himself," the giant said.

Pupp also kept her company, lagging at her heels.

Ahead, Krevan slipped into and out of shadow, sword drawn. Calla and Lorr followed behind with a handful of Harp's young hunters. Farther ahead, Rogger marched with Harp. Spread around and between them were the other ragged survivors, the last small handful.

Boys in torn leathers, some bootless. Elders with crooked staffs to help their steps over uneven rock. One young girl carried a babe in her arms, though barely more than a babe herself. All looked gaunt and hollow.

There was no joy in their survival.

Even if they cleared the Divide, they were headed into the hinterlands.

Rounding a steep jog in the track, they heard a horn sound ahead. A commotion jarred through the group, starting near the front and flowing downslope.

From both sides, hunters appeared, dressed in leaves to match the jungle, faces painted black. They bore spears, poison-tipped for sure. Their party was herded closer together, forced up the slope to a jungle dell with a creek trickling over rock. Moss lay thick over all surfaces, turning the small glade emerald green.

It was too bright and handsome a place for the horror here.

To either side knelt the party that had left earlier. Their hands were tied behind their backs. Many looked beaten. One old woman lay on her side, face bloody, unmoving.

But worst of all, a body lay near the creek, seeping blood into the water, swirling it crimson.

Headless.

Standing over the body was a familiar figure, baring the filed points of his teeth, feral and blood-maddened. His arms and chest were drenched in the fresh flow of his kill, lifeblood steaming on his skin.

"Marron . . ." Harp moaned.

To the hunter's side, a fierce fire had been stoked with smoky greenwood. Another of the hunters charred the end of a long pole, sharpened at both ends in the flames. At his leader's signal, he pulled the pole out of the fire and jammed the cool end deep into the mossy loam.

"Don't," Harp said.

He was ignored.

Marron bent and lifted the head of the corpse at his feet. Holding it between his palms, he raised it high, then jammed it atop the hot stake. Blood sizzled. Smoke issued from the gaping mouth and nose.

Dart recognized the naked head, tattooed with disciplines.

Master Sheershym.

Dart turned away, hiding her face. Across the creek, more hunters knelt with sharp blades, straddling long branches, shaving them to points.

More stakes, already sharpened, lay piled nearby.

Marron stepped to a young girl who knelt at his feet. He twisted a fistful of her hair and cruelly bared her neck. In his other hand, he carried one of the same blades used to cut the stakes.

The giant reached out and covered Dart's eyes.

But she could still hear.

Down by the hardened river of black rock, Brant allowed himself to be roughly searched. Hands dug over his body. Finally he was shoved forward to join Tylar at the edge of the black river of steaming rock.

Tylar studied his toes. He had already been searched, even stripped of his shadowcloak. He shifted a full step to one side, more than necessary, as if he were avoiding Brant's company.

Out on the river, the Huntress had stood waiting. Only now did she come forward, striding through the steam, her skin shining with sweat and Grace. Her hair had been unbraided, giving her a wild look that stirred Brant in unpleasant ways.

Brant and Tylar were forced to their knees, spearpoints at their backs. Tylar, hobbled by his bad leg, fell to one hand.

Ignoring him, the Huntress crossed immediately to Brant. She held out her palm, her eyes bright with desire. There was no need to ask what she wanted.

Brant reached to his neck and pulled out the twisted cord from which the rock hung. It was bound tight. The Huntress motioned with her other hand. The spearpoint was shifted from his back and cut the cord. The stone fell free, into Brant's palm.

She studied it, lifting her chin and staring down her nose. "It appears such a dull thing—but he was always clever. Sometimes too clever for his own good. Like entrusting it to an equally dull boy."

She paced one step to the side, then back again, plainly hesitant with the prize so close. "I think I knew, back when you were brought before me. That was why I banished you—but afterward, I couldn't remember why. The dark whispers filled my head again and I knew I wasn't in the correct turn of mind to take its responsibility." A bit of madness crackled. "But now I must be. Why else have you returned? It must be a sign, surely!"

Brant sensed she was trying to goad herself into taking it but was plainly fearful at the same time. He could almost sense the tidal pull and push warring inside her.

Beside him, Tylar remained crouched, his face down, leaning heavily on his one arm. But Brant noted a certain tautness to his shoulders. The way his toe shifted ever so slightly, catching a purchase on a lip of stone, like a climber firming his hold.

"The time must be ripe!" the Huntress cried out. "A plain sign!"

Brant held his breath.

Everything happened too fast.

The god lunged for the stone in his palm and grabbed it. At the same time, Tylar shoved off his good leg, away from the spear at his back, and pulled out a bladeless gold hilt that had been hidden beneath a flat yellow stone.

Rivenscryr.

Here was what Tylar had sent ahead, borne by one of Harp's fleet-footed runners, to be planted in secret at the river's edge. Bladeless, it had been easy to hide, easy to miss.

Rising now, Tylar spun off his good leg. Glass tinkled in his other hand, revealing a tiny repostilary hidden under his wraps. A splash of crimson spilled and struck a silver blade that shimmered into existence with the touch of blood.

Still turning, Tylar swung the freshly whetted sword for the Huntress's neck, ready to take her head clean off—but while all this happened in a blink, Brant's eyes had truly never left the Huntress's face.

As her fingers closed on the stone, he saw something rise in her eyes.

His heart clenched.

"No!" Brant burst up and drove his shoulder into Tylar's hip.

The regent went flying. His sword tumbled from his fingers and clattered on the black rock. He landed hard and rolled to a dazed stop.

Brant sat up, horrified at what he'd just done. In that long blink, he'd had no time for doubt. He did now.

Still, he knew what he had seen in her eyes. It was a match to the expression on the rogue's face as the fires had consumed his flesh.

Hope.

Before him, the Huntress slowly sank to her knees, oblivious to Tylar's attack and Brant's defense. Around her, the other hunters fell back as if strings holding them had suddenly snapped. In a widening circle, they collapsed, limbless and dazed, to rock and loam.

Tylar, his face flushed with fury, crawled to his feet, one cheek deeply abraded and bleeding. But as he saw the hunters collapse all around, fury changed to confusion. He moved over to Brant, collecting his sword. But he refrained from continuing his attack.

On her knees, the Huntress cradled the stone to her heart, rocking slightly, shoulders shaking in silent sobs.

Neither dared speak.

Though the Huntress never raised her face, she slowly whispered, as if she knew they waited. "Such a small stone. A piece of our old home. Just large enough for one god to balance atop. And make whole what was sundered."

There was no raving in her voice.

She finally lifted her face. Tears streamed down her dark skin. Her eyes shone with them, but nothing more. No Grace. Not in her eyes, nor in her tears, nor in the sheen on her sweated skin. It had blown out. But filling the void was a warmth, a softening of countenance that Brant had never seen in her before.

In that moment, she seemed so much younger and so much older.

"I remember," she said, smiling with a sadness that ached the heart. "What was lost in ravings and passing centuries. What the Sundering stole, this small stone returned."

"What?" Tylar asked softly.

Her eyes did not seem to see him, but she answered. "My name . . . it was *Miyana*."

With the utterance, the ground shook. Loose rock rattled like broken teeth. Leaves shuttered with the noise of a thousand birds taking wing. And deep under their feet, a low roar moaned with grief and sorrow.

Behind the Huntress, the black river split to reveal its fiery heart.

Brant felt the heat as a breath of regret.

The Huntress—*Miyana*—turned her face to the mountain as the ground shook. It reminded Brant of Miyana's shoulders a moment before. A silent sobbing.

She whispered toward the distant mountain. Maybe it wasn't supposed to be heard. But Brant heard it.

"Mother . . . forgive me . . ."

Miyana stood. She seemed to finally note the boy kneeling on the rock in front of her. Her words were hollow and haunted.

"Brant, son of Rylland . . . we've both been fate's bone, gnawed and left with nothing." She glanced over her shoulder to the greater forest. "But there is one mistress even more cruel. Memory. She makes no distinction between horror and beauty, joy and sorrow. She makes us swallow it all, bitter and sweet. Until it's all too much."

She sank again into herself. She took one step back, then another.

"Mistress . . ." Brant said, knowing what she intended. "Don't."

Her eyes flicked to him as she took another step back. "One last kindness, then. So you might hate me more fully."

"I don't—"

"I killed your father. I sent the she-panther that killed him."

Brant sought some way to understand what she was saying. "Wh-why?" he stammered through his shock.

"I was already sliding into madness. But perhaps deep down I knew and lashed out."

"Knew what?" Tylar asked for him.

"Rylland brought me the *wrong* gift. A curse, instead of hope. Corruption, instead of my name."

Brant understood.

His father had brought her Keorn's skull, instead of the stone. Without knowing the power in either, the choice had been pure misfortune. Her first words returned to him. *We've both been fate's bone, gnawed and left with nothing.*

Her eyes returned to the distant forest.

They had been left with worse than nothing.

She whispered to the forest. "Until it's all too much."

She took one last stride and stepped into the open crack behind her. Molten rock consumed her bone and flesh. She gasped but didn't scream. The agony in her heart was far worse than any flame. Her face turned to the mountain, to the source of the fire that swallowed her.

Instead of pain, Brant read the love in her face.

"Thank you for protecting these last few . . ." she whispered, her words rising like steam toward the distant mountain. "I want to go home."

Spreading her arms, she fell forward into the molten rock, as if into a welcoming embrace. The stone flew from her fingertips, no longer needed.

The piece of black rock bounced and rolled, coming to rest

at Brant's knee. He reached down and took the gift. For the second time in his life, a god burning with fire had passed this stone into his fingers.

But now he knew the truth.

It wasn't just a rock.

It was the hope of a lost world.

As the sun sank toward the horizon, Tylar climbed with the others toward the Divide. The twin peaks of the Forge burnt with the last rays of the sun. No one had spoken for the past full league. And the silence wasn't just the steepness of their climb, nor even grief.

It was an emotion that transcended numbness. An attempt to reconcile all that had happened, while still placing one foot in front of the other. If they stopped, they might never move again. The day had held too much horror, framed by the rising and setting of a single sun. It was a day they had to push past.

Yet some still tried to make sense of it.

Rogger mumbled through his beard. "The stone—it explains much."

Tylar glanced to him. He didn't ask for an elaboration, but Rogger gave it anyway.

"The Huntress—"

"Miyana," Tylar corrected. She had paid a heavy price for that name. Tylar refused to let it be lost again. "Her name was Miyana."

Rogger nodded. "She claimed that the stone allowed those parts of her that were sundered to return to her."

He nodded. Miyana's words echoed inside him. *A piece of our old home. Just large enough for one god to balance atop.*

"Here in Myrillia, the gods are split into three," Rogger continued, ticking them off on his fingers. "An undergod in the naether, the god of flesh here, and that higher self that flew off into the aether. But with a piece of their original home in hand, it must be like returning home, becoming whole again. When Miyana held the stone, her naethryn and aethryn parts must have gathered back to her. Like moths to a flickering flame."

"So it would seem," Tylar said.

"Then that goes a long way toward explaining what transpired here."

Drawn by the conversation, Brant and Dart drew closer. Perhaps there was another way of moving past all this. Through some manner of understanding.

The thief nodded toward Dart. "Do you remember Master Gerrod's explanation for why Dart's humours don't flow with Grace?"

Tylar silenced Rogger with a glare. Not all here were aware of Dart's nature. "I remember," he said tersely.

Though birthed of gods, Dart was born in Myrillia. Born unsundered. Gerrod had come to believe that the Grace of the gods arose because they were *sundered*. It was the stretch of their essences between the three realms, flowing across them, that sustained their flesh and imbued their humours with power. Back in their original kingdoms, whole and intact, the gods had borne no Grace.

Rogger changed the tack of the conversation. "After Miyana took the stone, did you notice any change in her? Any lessening of her powers?"

Brant answered. "It did seem the Grace in her eyes dimmed."

"Exactly! As the stone made her whole again, her Grace died away. And since seersong only works on those Graced . . ."

"She broke free," Brant finished for him. "The song had no hold."

"Or at least *less* of a hold. I suspect the stone does not make a god fully whole. They still reside in Myrillia. But the stone draws their other selves up close. Look at Keorn. He was carrying that stone, but still got trapped in the song for a long spell. Though eventually he did resist it well enough to escape."

Tylar's interest grew. "If you're right, then we can use the stone to free the rogues. Bring each rogue in contact with it."

"Perhaps. But there's a snag. Remember, Keorn's skull was still black with seersong; the stone held it in check. But he had to be holding it. Like Miyana. I fear that once you move the stone from one rogue to the next, the first will succumb anew to the song. It may be one of the reasons Miyana destroyed herself. Perhaps she knew this truth."

"So we'd need a stone for each rogue to keep them all from becoming enslaved again."

Rogger nodded. "Good luck with that."

Tylar pondered all this. It was better than thinking about the horrors behind them.

"It makes you wonder about Keorn, though," Rogger said, lowering his voice and motioning Tylar aside.

"How so?"

"I don't think he just happened upon that stone. What's the likelihood of a raving rogue chancing upon a lost talisman of home?" Rogger continued without leaving time for Tylar to respond. "I wager Keorn arrived here with that chunk of stone. And because he had it all along, it kept him mostly whole, weakening his Grace. And being so weak from the start, he probably never suffered the ravenings of his more Grace-maddened brothers and sisters."

"A rogue god who does not rave."

Some measure of disbelief must have rung in Tylar's words.

Rogger dropped his voice even lower. "It's probably why he chose to live in the hinterlands. With no wild Grace to calm, he had no reason to settle a realm. Why give up the world and freedom if you didn't have to? And didn't the Wyr sense something odd about him? Didn't he escape their trackers? And what about Dart?"

"What about her?"

"A god's seed rarely takes root in a belly. The Grace burns such fragile unions. But *Keorn's* seed took root."

It made a certain horrible sense, though Tylar would prefer to discuss it with a tower full of masters. For every question Rogger answered, another two arose. Why did Keorn have a child? Why keep the stone secret? Why remain hidden in the hinterlands for four thousand years? Why not reveal yourself? Mystery atop mystery remained.

And Tylar suspected the answers lay beyond the Divide, in the hinterlands.

Finally, they climbed the last slope. A small group of hunters waited at the top of the pass. Harp stood among them. He had gone on ahead to ready the rope ladders for their descent.

He came forward, face grim. “All is ready. I have Master Sheershym’s maps of the lands below packed.”

His voice cracked a bit on those last words.

Tylar clasped the boy on the shoulder. “You have much to bear on shoulders so young.”

“And so bony,” Rogger added.

His attempt at levity raised only a ghost of a smile on the boy’s lips, mostly polite. His eyes remained tired, haunted. Harp had much work ahead here. After Miyana’s death, the hunters under her thrall had fallen into various states. Some had rolled fully into a ravening lunacy. Others remained in a strange dreamlike state, as if their minds had simply snuffed out, leaving only a breathing husk behind. A few were grief-stricken, addled by guilt, but had hopes for some life hereafter.

And one hunter had died, torn apart at the hands of his own people. His head rested on a stake not far away, forever baring his filed teeth in a grimace of pain.

Harp led them to the ladders. “It might be best to attempt your climb in the morning,” he warned. “If you leave now, it will be dark when you finally set foot down there.”

Tylar stared out past the cliff. It was his first view of the hinterlands below. Though the sun still hovered at the edge of the world, the lower lands were already blanketed in darkness. It was a world of broken rock and steaming jungle, more swamp than forest. A few fiery snakes glowed through the darkness, molten rivers streaming out from Takaminara’s volcanic peak, fresh flows from a god grieving for her daughter, fiery tears for one returned to her so briefly.

Mother . . . forgive me . . .

Tylar felt Harp’s eyes on him, waiting for his answer.

Despite the dangers below, he had had enough of this sad land.

“We’ll go now.”

FIFTH

FALL OF THE TOWERS

By this sword do we swear
    By this cloak we do share
By this masklin are we hid
    By this diamond we are bid
By this oath are we bound
    By this honor we are crowned
For the sake of all Myrillia
    We give our blood
    We pledge our hearts
    We devote our lives
    to all

—Creed of the Shadowknight

19

A RUSTED HINGE

"WE'VE LOST THE DOCKS ATOP STORMWATCH!" GERROD yelled down to Kathryn. He clanked down the central stairs. "The warden is abandoning the top five floors. We're to rally below!"

Kathryn climbed through the line of cloaked knights as they surged downward. Many bore wounds. Others were slung between their brothers and sisters. In all their eyes, the same expression shone. Horror and hopelessness.

Alchemical smoke choked the stairwell.

She met Gerrod at the floor where her hermitage lay. She was returning from securing the entire populace of Tashijan—those not of cloak or robe—in the Grand Court, out of harm's way, leaving the halls and stairs to the knights and masters.

The war had been going on for only four bells, and already they'd lost the shield wall and outer towers. They'd had to pull back into Stormwatch, the sole tower still holding. And its defenses were crumbling.

She reached him and together they headed toward her hermitage. More knights were emptying out of this level, cloaks torn, faces raked. A knight sat slumped a few steps past the stairwell, blood pooled around him.

"How many dead?" she asked.

Gerrod answered, his voice muffled by his armor. "At last tally . . ." He shook his head, voice cracking.

She glanced to him. He was her rock, and even he was breaking. She was suddenly glad he kept his helmet closed. His bronze countenance, while a false stolidity, helped hold her steady.

He found his voice, as if sensing her need. "Six score dead, thrice that injured. We just lost five barricading the door to the docks."

Somewhere high above, a scream echoed. Human.

"And it's not just the wraiths," Gerrod said. "Blessing our blades with dire alchemies has offered us some measure of defense, but Lord Ulf's forces also come with stormfire, balls of lightning. Only stone seems to stanch them."

Crossing past the warden's Eyrie, a shout called to her. "Kathryn!"

She turned to see Argent at the center of a flurry of activity, gathering scrolls and packing up all that was important. He shoved through a few knights, a storm in shadow. He limped toward her. She had heard of his defense of the Agate tower. His last rally had saved hundreds of underfolk who made their home in the outer tower. She had heard the tale of Argent's ride against a storm of the wraiths, with only a dozen knights, splitting the winged legion enough to allow the tower's escape, mostly women and young ones.

"Head below!" he yelled. "We gather in the fieldroom at the next bell!"

She nodded.

He reached the door, his one eye on her. She read the regret behind his stony face. "We'll hold this tower," he said in a quiet voice, fierce echoes behind it.

"To the last knight," she said.

"And master," Gerrod added.

It was no longer a tower divided. In the past bells, as their defenses fell, one after the other under Ulf's ravening legion, they were all crushed together. Knight and master. Underfolk and townsfolk. The battle here was not one of victory but of survival. Their squabbles of the past seemed petty and churlish.

Kathryn noted the Fiery Cross on Argent's shoulder. It was torn in half by a raked claw.

"I'll see you at the bell," she said with a nod toward the warden.

Their eyes held a fraction longer, just long enough to admit the fools they'd both been. And to forgive each other's blind corners. At least for this one day. She prayed it would be enough.

A shout drew Argent back to his duty.

Released, Kathryn strode down to her own rooms. There were a few items she intended to secure, one in particular, the true reason she had forded up here against the flowing stream of their retreat.

She rushed to her door, found it ajar, and pushed inside. The hearth was cold. The heavy drapery had been torn down and the windows boarded and shuttered tight. There was still glass on the floor from where Ulf's emissary had broken through from the outer balcony.

As she crossed the threshold, she heard a frantic scuffle from the next room. Her sword appeared in her hand. She held her other arm out toward Gerrod, warding him back.

Wraiths had been worrying themselves through cracks, finding every means to gnash their way inside. A bell ago, a pair had clawed their way down one of the kitchen's chimneys, defying a roaring fire and smoke, and attacked a baker's boy, ripping his head from his body. Four others had died. It had taken the head cook with a butcher's cleaver and a lone scullery maid with a spitting fork to finally dispatch the beast. To such an extent had the defense of Tashijan fallen.

Stepping farther into the room, Kathryn noted a small and familiar squeak from the next room.

"Penni?" Kathryn called out.

Silence—then a flutter of footsteps and a bonneted head peeked around the corner leading to her private room. "Mistress!" The maid offered a trembling curtsy that was strangely reassuring in its familiarity.

Kathryn waved the girl over. "What are you still doing up here?"

Penni took a scatter of steps toward her, then stopped. "I heard . . . below . . . that all was lost up here. So I came in a rush." She pointed to the servants' door in back.

Kathryn realized she should have thought to do the same—it would have been quicker than fighting the tumult of the main stairs. She admonished herself for the narrowness of her vision, constricted by her own sense of place and caste.

"I knew you'd not want to lose this," her maid said.

Penni held up a strap of black linen. Attached to it was a thumb-sized diamond. It was the diadem of the castellan, the symbol of her station. It was not the fake one, the artifice of paste, but the *true* diadem, the one stolen by Mirra and rescued by Lorr. The masters had already tested and cleared it of any Dark Grace. And despite its former bearer, it was an ancient jewel of Tashijan, the heart of the Citadel.

It was why Kathryn had come up here.

She stared gratefully at her maid, realizing how well the girl had come to know her mistress's heart. Yet, in turn, Kathryn had barely noted her comings and goings. She did note her now: the firm heart in a trembling young girl's body. Here was what they fought for in Tashijan. Here was what had ultimately made Kathryn turn her back on Ulf's offer.

A loud *crack* shattered through the room.

One of the shutters at the back window tore away, followed by a tinkle of glass. Shards flew high. Penni turned and ducked, shielding herself with an arm. Kathryn was struck by the smell of burnt wood.

Gerrod grabbed her elbow.

Through the shattered gap, a blaze of azure scintillation swept into the room, a fiery globe as wide as her outstretched arms. It struck Penni, picking her off her feet. Her bonnet blew from her head in a wash of fire. Lightning crackled over her skin, burning her livery, arching her back, stretching her mouth in a silent wail.

Gerrod shoved Kathryn aside and pointed his other arm at the ball of stormfire. From the back of his wrist, a stream of muddy bile jetted and struck the globe. With the touch of the alchemy, the fires were blown out like a spent candle.

Penni collapsed to the rug. She shivered all over as if cold, despite her smoking skin and fiery-flailed clothes. Then she lay still. Eyes open, but no longer seeing.

The diadem she had come to rescue lay between them, flung as she was struck and consumed.

"I'll get it," Gerrod said.

Kathryn brusquely shoved past him. She crossed, stepped over the diadem, and knelt down beside Penni. She scooped the girl up in her arms. She was so very light, as if all substance had escaped with her life. Kathryn felt the heat of the char through her cloak. The maid's small head hung slack over her arm, neck stretched as if baring her throat.

And so she had . . . to come here, to risk all.

Kathryn shifted her arms and rocked her small body closer, so Penni's head came to rest against her shoulder. Kathryn cradled her.

"I have you," she whispered.

Turning, she headed for the door.

Gerrod bent and collected the diadem from the floor and followed. But in her arms, Kathryn already carried the true jewel, the true heart of Tashijan.

Far below, Laurelle sat in a moldy chair, its ticking puffing out. It smelled of mouse bile and mustiness. But she had sunk gratefully into it a bell ago, as if it were the finest velvet and down.

To one side, Kytt rested cross-legged on the stone floor, leaning his back against a plank bed strewn with old hay. Delia sat atop the bed, supported by the wall. Her eyes were open, but her gaze looked far away. Her head had been bandaged deftly by Kytt, who was experienced with such minor care, since all wyld trackers were trained to attend injuries on the trail.

They had found the refuge, a room with a stout door, deep within the level where they'd been trapped. Their attempt to push into well-lit and -populated regions had turned into a mad flight from things hidden in the dark and shadow. Between the senses of Orquell's crimson eye and Kytt's sharp ears and nose, they found all their ways blocked.

They were forced to delve deeper into the abandoned sections of the aged tower. Until they were all but lost. Recognizing the futility, Orquell had finally pulled them into this room. He sat in the room's center. He had raised a small fire in each corner, kindled from the beetle-riddled legs of a broken table and alchemical powder.

Warding pyres, he claimed.

He now seemed lost in his flames, eyes closed. He had remained like that for the past bell. Occasionally one of the pyres would spit with flame, hissing. And behind the sparks, Laurelle swore she heard thin whispers.

But more often she heard screams.

From above.

What was happening?

If she had been in her own rooms, she probably would've been locked up, shoulder to shoulder with other Hands of the realms, equally blind to the true state of the war. Still, she wished she was up there. Here she was truly in the dark, in more ways than mere shadowy halls. Her imagination filled in the gaps of the story above with a whirl of horrors. Even if the truth were more terrifying than any of her imagined scenarios, she'd still prefer to know. At least then she could focus on one tangible fear, rather than the multitude of phantom perils that swam through her head.

"She waits," Orquell finally muttered, his eyes still closed.

"Who?" Delia asked, focusing back on the room along with the rest of them.

Laurelle felt a thrill of fear, knowing that their short respite was about to end. She sat straighter.

"The witch," he said. "The flames chitter with her dark delight. She waits for the war above to tear and weaken. Then she will rise and sweep through what remains, consuming all in her path."

"Then we must get word above," Delia said, scooting to the edge of the bed. "Light more fires."

"Too late. The warden has set plentiful flames, but he has forgotten the fundamental nature of fire."

"What's that?" Laurelle asked.

"Every flame casts a shadow." He opened his eyes and stretched his shoulders, like a cat waking by a fire. "You can't have light without darkness. And Mirra takes advantage of that. Just as she has slunk and lurked in secret passages wormed throughout Tashijan's cellars, so she does now in the shadows cast by the warden's pyres."

"But the gates below were all closed," Kytt said. "Sealed with iron and wyrmwood. All else bricked tight."

"Bricks, iron, and wood. All cast their shadows when raised against the flame. And the more fires that are stoked, the darker those shadows become, and the more likely those dark paths will open for her legion. For Mirra does not move her legion through mere shadows. She moves her *ghawls* through places darker, through those trickles of Gloom found hidden in shadowy places."

Laurelle pictured the many fires throughout Tashijan. They had been set to ward against the storm's cold, but if the master here was correct, those same pyres had cast deep enough shadows for some Dark Grace to tease open a passage into their midst.

And now the witch waited.

Like them.

In the darkness.

Only unlike them, with every passing bell, she saw her position grow stronger, while theirs sapped weaker.

"She is about to strike. I sense it in the stanching of the pyres—a smothering swell of darkness."

Laurelle perhaps felt it, too. A weight to the air. Or maybe it was simply her own terror.

"What are we to do, then?" Delia asked. "We're buried among her forces here, trapped in the very shadows cast by those flames we need to reach."

Orquell slowly stretched to his feet with a creak of his bones. "Since we're already here, we might as well be of use to Tashijan."

"How so?" Laurelle asked. Her hand drifted to her throat. She knew she wasn't going to like his answer. And she was right.

"We might as well call the witch to us."

"What?" Kytt squeaked.

"We'll draw her eye here. Away from the others."

He stepped to one of his pyres, the one set before the door. Powders appeared in his fingers, as if out of the very air. He cast the alchemy into the fire. Flames flared brighter, chasing sparks high. He leaned down and whispered into the fire. But whatever he said was consumed by the flames.

Then he straightened and rested his fists on his hips.

"Now we'll see if she answers."

"When?" Delia asked.

"It may take a while."

Delia stood up, eyes glancing over the four pyres. "Who are you truly?" Her eyes settled back to him. "You are *rub-aki*.

That I understand. But you come here with your crimson eye painted over, and I suspect you've equally hidden your true purpose for arriving at Tashijan in so timely a manner."

Orquell ran a hand over his bald pate. "I *am* a master," he said. "These tattoos were hard-earned. But my crimson eye—that I earned through a decade of toil and flame, long before I was ever tattooed in my disciplines."

He crossed to the bed and sat down upon it. He tapped a finger on the crimson thumbprint. "Do you know how this inner eye is ultimately opened?"

Delia folded her arms, still suspicious, but Laurelle shifted in her chair to hear better.

"The eye is opened in darkness."

"But I thought the sacred flames of the *rub-aki* were the source of your enlightenment," Delia said flatly. "A Grace gifted by the god Takaminara."

"There is much speculation about the ways of the Blood-eyed—clouded further by those charlatans who fake a crimson eye. Very little of it is the truth. Takaminara prefers to keep her ways secret. The true *rub-aki* respect that and do not speak of such matters."

"Then why tell us?" Delia asked. Her eyes kept shifting to the pyre before the door.

"Because what I must ask will require great trust."

Delia merely shrugged, noncommittal. "Tell us about the opening of your inner eye."

"Like I mentioned, it requires darkness. Takaminara is well versed in the relationship between flame and shadow. She has buried herself in her mountain, never stepping under the sun or stars. Yet she is more knowledgeable of this world than any other god. She stands amid the molten flows that run beneath all. Her world is neither flame nor darkness, but the space *between*. In that fracture, she can see into the deep past and the trails into the future."

This last was said with great reverence.

"And for those who earn her mark, who serve her, she lets us share the smallest fraction of her sight. But to that we must open our eye. And here is a truth that only a handful of people know." He stared at each in turn. "There is no Grace involved."

Delia straightened, loosening her arms, then tightening them again. "Impossible. I've heard stories of the *rub-aki*, great feats of fire and prediction. True stories, not charlatan tales."

Orquell nodded. "Yet it requires no Grace. Some communing and pryre casting require Grace and blessings from Takaminara. But at its most basic, down deep, every man and woman has this eye, awaiting to be woken."

"How does one open it?" Laurelle asked "How does *darkness* open it?"

"It is not just any darkness. Once properly trained, an acolyte descends deep beneath the volcanic peak of Takaminara. Into caverns of black rock, long gone cold, where sunlight has never touched. A darkness so deep that it strains the eye and blinds it, like staring directly at the sun. That alone is a lesson worth noting. That purest darkness and the brightest flame blind equally." He stopped and his gaze seemed to drift for a moment. Then he began again. "And in that darkness, with the regular eye blinded, the inner eye can open with proper initiation."

Delia stirred. "But how does this make us trust you? Why did you come to Tashijan during such a dire moment as this?"

He shrugged. "No mystery there. Master Hesharian requested my services to seek a cure for the stone-cursed knight. That is the truth." He turned to Delia. "But it was Takaminara that sent me to Ghazal, to study the ways of the Clerics of Naeth. It was those same studies that drew the attention of Hesharian. And eventually drew me here."

"So Takaminara knew you'd end up here? Why? Did she foresee what has befallen us?"

Orquell shrugged. "I do not know. We are her servants, submitting to her will as much as any Hand of a god. We go where the flame directs. Perhaps she saw it, but more likely she cast us out like petals on a flowing river. She can sense the current, but even she can't tell where each petal will land. Portending is much different than the charlatans make it seem. More powerful in some ways, less in others."

He must have read the disappointment in Laurelle and the doubt in Delia. Kytt just gaped at the revelations.

"Takaminara once described what portending was truly like. It was like seeing flames in the dark. Fiery pools of illumination, disconnected to everything around it. To place too much significance on what is revealed, without knowing what remains hidden in the dark, is a fool's paradise. You'd might as well see nothing at all."

"So then what do you see with your open eye?" Laurelle asked.

Before he could answer, the pyre by the door suddenly burst up with a flare of flame.

Orquell stood. "It seems someone's come knocking."

Kathryn faced the pair of wraiths in the room.

A dozen bodies of young boys were strewn among the stacked beds and floor like scattered dolls, broken and ripped. The far window, high on the wall, no more than a slit, seemed too small for any wraith to enter. The iron shutter was peeled back and teetered on a broken hinge, weakened by rust. Such was the sorry state of Tashijan: fallen into disrepair over the centuries as numbers dwindled and the space grew too large.

It shouldn't have happened. For lack of a solid hinge, twelve boys had died.

One of the wraiths straddled a lad, his chest raked, throat torn. A fistful of claw was buried in his belly. It tore free, yanking out the most tender parts. The wraith's face was covered in blood and gore as it spit at her, hissing and baring its teeth, protecting its meal.

The other was perched on the top of the stacked beds, also straddling something, but it was not slaking its hunger. It was satisfying another lust. It leaped up to the bed railing, claws digging into the wood. Its manhood swollen and bloody. Wings spread.

Kathryn held her sword up and gathered the room's shadows to her cloak. She remembered Lord Ulf's cold words, how he controlled his wind wraiths through seersong and will. Her lips hardened. Was this the manner in which he controlled them?

Behind her, fighting continued out on the stair. Screams, wails, and frantic orders echoed up and down the main spiral. Slowly they were losing levels, one after the other. Blood was spent in order to clear floors. Stormwatch was slowly being driven into ever smaller quarters.

The only advantage: The knights had less territory to guard, and the wraiths had fewer ways to strike them.

As a result, a balance was establishing. They had held this level for an entire half bell. The line was even firming. A glimmer of hope had started to sound in the growl and shout of the knights and masters.

It was such a feat that also allowed Kathryn to hear a scream behind this door. A squire's lodging. She had opened the door to find this horror. How many other places in Tashijan suffered similarly?

The one atop the bed attacked first, screeching and diving at her, its wings wide. Kathryn shifted shadows in the room and vanished to its left flank. Her blade darted out, lightning out of darkness, blessed with dire alchemies.

The wraith noted her thrust for its heart. Though ilked, it was Grace-born, a creature of air. With the speed of a swirling gust, it ripped around, lashing out with a clawed foot.

Kathryn ducked between its legs, never dropping her sword. She shoved straight up, slicing open its belly, and rolled aside. It wailed and spun, spilling entrails and blood. It struck the wall, writhing, unable to gain its footing, wracked in pain, legs tangled in its own entrails. The more it fought, the more it gutted itself.

From the corner of her eye, movement stirred.

Kathryn swirled darkness and vanished away. The creature atop the table searched with one eye cocked, then the other. But it didn't hunt on sight alone. Its head swung around, scenting her. It was ready when she folded out of darkness, sword swinging.

It lunged off the table—away from her, craven with the death cries of its partner. Kathryn chopped with her sword before it could fully escape. Her blade sliced through its leathery wing and bony shoulder, cleaving all away.

Now it was its turn to screech as it rolled off the table, off the boy, one wing flapping like a sail in a storm.

Kathryn vaulted the table and landed on the wing, pinning the wraith to the floor. Two-handed, she swung her sword low, cutting off its scream.

And its head.

The body convulsed once, then lay still.

Its head kept rolling.

Kathryn dropped her shadows. Her cloak fell about her shoulders like a death's shroud, heavy with blood. She stepped back, stumbled away, over to the door.

A knight appeared at the entrance. His eyes above the masklin widened at the slaughter found inside. She pushed past him, sword still out. She clenched her fist on its hilt to control her trembling.

"Seal the door," she ordered as she passed. "Bar it tight."

Then she was out on the stairs. More calls and shouts echoed down from the main line. She ran the opposite way. Before hearing the scream from the room, she had been headed down to meet Argent. Now she had another reason to run below.

To escape the horrors of that room.

Around and around, she fled.

Finally she stopped, leaned a palm against the wall, and emptied her stomach on the stair. Her belly heaved again, sour and empty. She gasped for air. Her eyes ached with tears that refused to flow.

Not now . . .

She spat on the stone and wiped her mouth.

Not yet . . .

Straightening, she sheathed her sword and stumbled a step, caught herself, and continued down leadenly, a hundred stone heavier than when she had gone up to her hermitage.

She quickly reached the fieldroom's level and headed down the hall to the open door. It was unguarded. There were no knights to spare for such duties. She entered to find the rally already under way.

She was surprised at how few were here. Argent held a dagger in his fingers and made deft instructions on the pinned map, cutting into the ancient vellum in his urgency and fury. He was instructing his second-in-command. Kathryn didn't know his name. The former second had died during the third bell; there had been no time for introductions after that.

Hesharian stood against the back wall. Unmoving, eyes glazed.

Gerrod was at Argent's other elbow, suggesting a few improvements with a bronzed finger. "They are particularly sensitive to loam. If we paint the stairs here . . . and here . . . with an alchemy of bile and loam, they should weaken before they hit the line."

The warden nodded.

All their eyes lifted when she entered. Something in her face made them all straighten with concern.

"Did the line break again?" Argent asked.

"It holds," Kathryn assured him, putting steel in her voice and hardening her face.

Argent looked relieved. Gerrod's face was impossible to read, armored as it was, but he continued to stare at her.

She nodded to him, indicating she was all right.

It was a lie they all needed to believe for the moment.

There was only one other participant in the rally: the lithe and pristine figure of Liannora, Hand of Oldenbrook. Like Hesharian, she also stood to the side, her hands tucked into a snowy muff. For a moment, Kathryn could not make sense of it. Then she remembered the stone-casting among the Hands, the selection of a representative to the council.

Or rather *two* representatives.

Kathryn searched the room. "Where's Delia?" she asked Liannora.

A flash of guilt wavered across her pale features before vanishing. The woman shook her head, indicating she didn't know. Liannora must have been caught here when all fell apart. She must have felt safer here, leaving Delia to deal with all the Hands. No wonder the guilty demeanor.

Kathryn turned her back on the woman.

Argent spoke. "If the line is finally holding, then perhaps we have a chance."

"We can't win this war," Kathryn said, not letting her steeliness drop, making it plain that it was not despair that prompted her words.

Argent, ever the campaigner, still bristled.

"She is right," Gerrod said, supporting her. "We can hold out, but night will fall soon. The sun already sets."

"So?" Argent turned his eye upon Gerrod. "Locked in our tower, what difference does it make if the sun is up or not?"

"You forget Eylan?" Kathryn asked. "What have we faced so far? Wraiths and stormfire."

Argent frowned.

Kathryn continued. "Eylan came cloaked in an icy Dark Grace, impenetrable. Though the wraiths are fearsome, they can be struck down with steel and alchemy. What if he brings the same icy Dark Grace upon us again?"

Argent's face grew troubled. She read the dawning understanding in the furrows of his brow. He was stubborn, but not beyond reason—if you could get him to listen.

"Perhaps Ulf weakens," he said. "The storm must sap him greatly to keep it locked around our town for so long."

"No," Gerrod said and stepped to the window.

They followed.

The wide windows were shuttered tight. Gerrod pointed to an opening in the shutter, only a hand's breadth tall but wide enough for all three to gather.

Kathryn searched outside. The day was indeed almost gone. The storm swallowed the world, but the gray clouds were darkening. They were losing the sun. Beyond the window, a sweeping view of fields and outer towers was shrouded in swirls of snow. Still, she saw shapes winging about and boiling and crawling amid the towers.

Still so many . . .

"Lord Ulf is not weakening," Gerrod continued. "The wraiths were only the beginning. He's been waiting for nightfall, for his wraith legion to drive us tighter and tighter together."

"Why?"

"Whatever icy Grace protected Eylan, it must not be limitless. Or else he would have used it to shield the wraiths already. I suspect it is an arrow best shot with some marksmanship."

Kathryn understood. "He intends to have us all confined to one place."

"So to inflict a killing blow," Argent said.

Gerrod nodded. "And when that ice comes and we lose the flames of our lower levels, it will open our other flank, where Mirra awaits. Wraiths above, daemons below, and ice all around."

Argent stepped back, the fire in him kicked to ashes. "When?" he asked, knowing this was the most important question.

Gerrod merely turned to the window—and the setting sun.

Kathryn stared out the window as the darkness deepened.

"We'll never last 'til dawn," Argent muttered.

The pyre spit and hissed, scattering sparks toward the roof. The barred door glowed in the flames, revealing every grain in stark relief, as if the fire did not tolerate any shadows.

"To the center of the room," Orquell ordered, waving his hand.

Laurelle shifted to obey, crowded by Kytt and Delia.

"Stay there until I tell you otherwise," Orquell said, stepping toward the door.

The other three pyres in the room's corners caught the excitement of the first and danced higher. Soon the room shone as brightly as a summer day.

Laurelle glanced at her toes, avoiding the flaring glare. She noted that none of them cast any shadows on the floor. With flames burning on all four sides, they were bathed in light from all directions.

She remembered Master Orquell's earlier words.

Every flame casts a shadow.

Orquell reached to the door's bar and lifted it free.

"What are you doing?" Delia asked harshly. Suspicion still rang sharply in her.

"We invited the witch here. It would be impolite to refuse her now."

Orquell tugged on the latch and fought the stubborn hinges to pry the door open. Beyond the threshold, the dark hall waited.

The unnaturalness of the shadows was plain to all. The blaze of the pyre failed to penetrate the darkness, as if the hallway were flooded to the roof with black water.

Orquell stepped back and beckoned. "Castellan Mirra, please come inside. Your black *ghawls* will have to remain without, of course. The flames here will not let them pass."

"What do you want, *rub-aki*?" a reedy voice asked from the darkness. "Your flames foul the hallways here."

"Ah yes, my *rys-mor*, the living flames." He waved to encompass the pyres. "Born from a powder of crushed lavantheum, bearing the blood of four aspects—it attracts them, does it not? Where ordinary flame chases them off with warmth and brightness, my flames are like the fresh beating and bloody heart of the most delicious prey. They can't stay away. In fact, I wager they are being a bit stubborn about obeying your wishes. Of course, eventually they will, but it will take much effort and concentration on your part."

"Why are you interfering? Takaminara has never meddled in the affairs of the outer world."

Orquell took another step back, bowing slightly. "Exactly. So fear not my threshold. I swear your safety here."

Laurelle heard Delia hiss under her breath.

The darkness parted and a gray-haired old woman slipped out and into the firelight, dressed in a robe, sashed at the waist. She seemed more a kindly great-mother, maybe a bit stern around the edges, but certainly no witch. She entered the room, leaning on a smooth cane. It was only once she stepped across that Laurelle saw her cane was actually some creature's legbone, carved with Littick sigils.

"Again, what do you want, *rub-aki*?"

"A bargain for my safe passage. Nothing more. Allow me to reach the central stair, and I'll douse my flames. You know the word of a *rub-aki* is inviolate. We cannot go back on our oath."

"And I also know that the *rub-aki* are skilled at using their words to the fullest and in a most sly manner."

"Then I'll speak plain. I walk"—he mimicked a man walking with two fingers across his open palm—"and once I reach the stairs, I'll douse all of my pyres. I will tell no one of your presence. But betray me and I'll use my dying breath like a bellow to fan my four pyres. You won't like that."

Mirra studied Orquell, attempting to see a trap.

"To sweeten the deal," he pressed, "I offer you these three to take."

He waved over to them.

"What?" Delia snapped and lunged a step forward.

Laurelle grabbed her elbow, instinctively. The master had told them not to leave the room's center for any reason. He had also asked for their trust. Delia fought her hold. Only then did Laurelle realize Delia was feigning her struggle, for the show of it. Still, Laurelle also read a vein of real suspicion in Delia's eye.

Could they truly trust this one?

Orquell ignored them. "As you've said, servants of Takaminara have no concerns for the wider world. I have no use for these three—a wyld tracker and two Hands."

Mirra's eyes shifted closer to study them, stepping to the side to view them better.

Orquell leaned slightly, assuming a pose similar to Mirra's.

"And not just *any* Hands," he added. "But the Hands of Tylar ser Noche, regent of Chrismferry. I believe you are still searching for him."

Delia swore, almost raising a blush on Laurelle's cheek with her sudden and vitriolic vulgarity.

"And for assurance, I'll cross to the stairs without raising any fire, so that you may feel safer. This I swear. I will trust your darkness to cloak us and seal our bargain."

Mirra was plainly tempted, weighing the odds of just taking them. But there were risks in attacking a master of fire. Finally she spoke slowly, summarizing the bargain. "So if I allow you to proceed to the main stair, you'll raise no fire against me, tell no one of my presence, and once you are free, you'll stanch your pyres."

He nodded.

"And I can take these three," she added firmly.

"I will not stop you. All this I swear on my crimson eye."

Mirra surveyed the room one more time. A bell echoed from some distance away, marking the passage of time. Finally, she nodded. "So be it. You are sworn safe passage."

Orquell bowed. He crossed to each pyre, spread a bit of powder, and whispered over it. He returned to the door. "The flames will obey my will. Once safe, I will extinguish them."

"Then let us be off. Sunset draws near."

"I want my hostages kept close," he said. "No slipping them off in the dark. I will know."

She waved her arm impatiently.

Orquell raised a palm to the pyre by the door and lowered his hand. The flames died down, while the others still flickered brighter. With no light ahead, Laurelle saw their shadows stretch toward the open doorway. Once they crossed the threshold, the darkness surged inside, sweeping around with a rustle of cloth.

They were forced to follow Orquell. As soon as they stepped over the threshold, all light vanished. Laurelle gasped at the suddenness of it, as if someone had slammed the door on the firelit room behind them.

She reached out a hand and touched a warm body. Kytt found her hand and grabbed it. Delia bumped against her, then their hands were locked. Together they were ushered ahead, surrounded by a darkness that stirred.

They followed a zigzagging path that had Laurelle all turned around. She remembered Orquell's description of a darkness so complete it strained the eye to the point of blindness. Her eyes ached, searching for light.

She heard Orquell whisper under his breath. So faint she could not make out his words. But they had been intended for sharper ears, those of a wyld tracker.

Kytt leaned forward, his lips finding Laurelle's ear. He breathed so very faintly. "Be ready."

Laurelle nodded and squeezed Delia's hand, silently warning her.

Orquell spoke again, but this time loud enough for all to hear. "I believe I never answered your question, Mistress Laurelle. Before I go, I might as well satisfy your curiosity. You had asked what I see when my inner eye opens in the darkness."

Laurelle swallowed to free her tongue. "What do you see?"

"Flames . . ."

Suddenly a door burst open to the right, yanked by Orquell. Firelight blazed out of the room, sealed so tight that not a flicker had reached the hall. The one who hid in the room had plainly not wanted to be found, but did not dare sit in the dark amid a legion of *ghawls*.

A cry rose inside.

Laurelle spotted a familiar figure cowering near the back of the room. A thick torch in hand, bright with flame. He held it toward the door like a sword.

"Sten . . ." Laurelle said.

It was the captain of the Oldenbrook guard.

His eyes widened at the sight of them—then he must have noted the surging shadows around the group. He suddenly sank to his knees in terror.

"No!"

Out in the hall, the firelight cast back the shadows, leaving Mirra standing only a few paces away, stripped of darkness.

Orquell cupped his hands toward Sten's torch. The flame leaped like a deer from the end of his brand and flew to the master's hands. At the same time, he turned and cast the fire at Mirra.

The flames struck her, bathing her face, lighting her gray hair like the driest grass. She screamed and fell back into the darkness of the deeper hall.

Orquell shoved them all in the opposite direction.

With the witch maddened by her agony, her *ghawls* were in disarray. They fled to the end of the hall and around the corner, where more firelight glowed at the end of the next passage. They had reached the habited sections of the tower.

They ran in a wild dash, fearful of what might be rallying at their back. But it seemed the *ghawls* had found another target upon which to vent their rage and their mistress's pain.

Sten wailed behind them, the sound barely human.

Laurelle fled from his cry as much as from the *ghawls*.

Finally, they reached the light. Rooms to either side echoed with voices, moans. Some doors were open, blazing with light. The smell of blood and bile was heavy. They had reached some makeshift healing ward set up on this level. Passing through, they found a gathering of knights at the stair's landing. The knights eyed the strange and breathless bunch, but recognized a master's robes and parted the way.

Orquell stepped to the stairs and resoundingly clapped his hands. Laurelle noted a wisp of smoke sail between his palms. She eyed him inquiringly.

"To douse the pyres. As I swore—when I reached the stairs, I would put them out."

Delia stared at him. "And you also swore not to *raise* a fire against Mirra."

"And I didn't. What burned her was not a flame I cast or kindled. It was *borrowed* fire, already burning. It didn't need *raising*."

Delia shook her head. "The witch was right. The word of *rub-aki* is as slippery as any lie."

"Before we stepped into the hall," Laurelle asked, "you already knew about Sten's fire?"

Orquell tapped the mark on his forehead. "The inner eye is sensitive to fire. While communing earlier, listening to my pyres, I sensed a fire hidden near the edge of the witch's darkness. I needed her cooperation as a bridge to reach it."

Delia turned to the upper stairs. "Before Mirra heals and collects herself, word must reach the warden and Castellan Vail."

Orquell remained where he was. "I cannot speak of it. This I also swore. But I know where I may prove of more use." He took a step down the stairs.

"Where are you going?" Laurelle asked.

He pointed below. "With Mirra and her legion already above, her buried lair is most likely unguarded. If what I suspect is true, there may be something a *rub-aki* can accomplish that no one else can do."

"You're going into the cellars?" Kytt asked, taking a step after him. "Down into her secret passages?"

"If I can find an opening."

Kytt took the other steps. "I've been down there. While chasing the wolfkits. I can lead you."

Laurelle stared from Delia to the young tracker. Then she slowly took one step down, and another, almost disbelieving her legs. But she knew the truth. They would need her help more than Delia would, if only to carry another torch. And after all that had happened, she was not about to hole up in some room again, waiting for the end. She'd had enough of that.

"Get word above," she said to Delia. "To your father. To Kathryn. They must know what lurks here and where we are headed."

The woman hesitated—but she read the certainty in Laurelle's eyes.

Turning, Laurelle found Kytt gaping at her.

"No," he said firmly.

Laurelle simply strode past him, rolling her eyes.

Boys.

When would they learn?

20

A PACT WITH A DAEMON

AT THE FOOT OF THE CLIFF, TYLAR STEPPED OFF THE VINE ladder.

He had never set foot in a hinterland before, but he had heard tales. Other knights, older knights, told gruesome stories of campaigns against hinter-kings and raving rogues. He almost expected his leg to sink into muck, his skin to peel, and his clothes to burn. But his boots found only loose scree.

He moved away from the cliff, making room for the rest of their party. The way down from here was still steep, barely less of a slope than the cliff itself. Below, another dark forest beckoned, ready again to swallow them up under a canopy.

But here, on this thin beachhead, the stars shone overhead. As Harp had predicted, the sun had sunk to a glow at the western horizon. The lesser moon hung full and low, as if wary of showing its face too high above this sinister land. Perhaps it would be braver when the greater moon rose later. Still, the meager moonlight did cast the spread of forest in a silvery light.

Distantly, large pinnacles of rock protruded, looking like foraging beasts lumbering across a meadow. But Tylar knew they were just the broken landscape of the hinter, a shattered tableland, as if struck by a mighty hammer and upended in crumbled sections.

The scuff of rock and low voices announced the arrival of the rest of their party. They had all come down in pairs, joined by bonds new or freshly forged. Krevan and Calla had their shared heritage as pirates, leader and mate, but Tylar had begun to note Calla's eye lingering occasionally upon Krevan, revealing a certain longing that never made it to her lips. Krevan seemed oblivious. Next came Malthumalbaen and Lorr, an unlikely pair, but both were sculpted of the same Graced cloth. It was this commonality that forged a bond between them. Last came Dart and Brant, also tied together by strange circumstances, her father stumbling into Brant's life and dying.

And of course, Tylar was no exception. He had his own shadow, too. One that had been with him from the start of his long journey as a godslayer.

"I'm not climbing back up that," Rogger said.

Tylar did not argue with the sentiment. His entire left side ached, from ankle to shoulder. His hand throbbed and felt four sizes too large. But at least they'd been descending the ladder. His aches reminded him of Master Sheershym's assessment: a spreading poison, weakening the naethryn inside him, and in turn, corrupting the spell that kept his body healed and Meeryn's undergod tethered to this world.

What if the naethryn died?

Rogger continued his gripe. "When this is all over, I'll just sit here and wait for the next passing flippercraft."

Tylar clapped the thief on the shoulder. "Why bother even leaving? From what I've heard of the hinterlands, I think you'll fit in here just fine."

"I don't think so. I've heard the state of some of these hinter-villages. Not a worthy bottle of wine to be found."

"In that case, we should get you out as soon as possible. You'd die of thirst before the moon changes its face."

"True . . . true . . ."

Despite their banter, there were no smiles. It was not humor that generated their words, but worry, both for themselves and for those they'd left behind. Tylar had especially grown anxious during the long climb down here. Another day ending and still no word of the state of Tashijan.

Stepping away from the others, Tylar spoke softly a fear that still plagued him. "What if we don't even need to venture into here? What if the storm is already broken?" He nodded below. "Maybe all this is for naught."

Tylar left unspoken his other concern.

What if it was already too late?

Rogger remained silent for a long moment, then spoke equally softly. "Raving or not, the rogues here are still enslaved. It wouldn't be right to leave them in such a state. They're still worthy of mercy."

Tylar remembered the grief expressed by Miyana, of the horror of seersong. He knew Rogger was right. Besides, the Cabal were behind this slavery, cultivating a great source of power and Dark Grace. It had to end.

He glanced to the others, making sure everyone was ready. Brant bent down and untied his stone from around Pupp's neck. They had attached it to him to draw Pupp into solidity. Malthumalbaen had carried him, with a look of pure adoration on his face.

"Who's the fearsome cubbie?" the giant intoned. He was still bent on one knee, running thick fingers through Pupp's spiky mane. Pupp's tail wagged and a good portion of his rump.

Brant removed the stone, and Pupp vanished.

The giant's hand fell through empty air again. "Aww . . ." He stood. "He was like a tin of coals in a cold bed. All warm and steamy."

Dart hid a grin behind her own fingers.

With everyone gathered, Tylar waved Krevan to lead. They needed to get out of the open. The hinterland's dangers were not all twisted Grace and raving rogues. There were men and women worse than any ilked beast, who were happy to prey upon those who ventured into their fringes. Such folk lived lives barely better than those of the beasts, harvesting wild Grace and plundering where they could, often across borders. Though rogues might not be able to cross into a neighboring settled realm, men were not forbidden to do so.

Before anyone noted their trespass, Tylar wanted to reach their sole ally in this strange land, even as untrustworthy as that ally might be.

"Can you find Wyrd Bennifren?" Tylar asked Krevan.

He nodded. "I studied the old maps of Sheershym. It should not be hard to find the Wyr encampment. If they're still there."

The Wyr-lord had hired Krevan to secure the skull of the rogue god, the one who had fathered Dart. According to their pact, Bennifren had planned to remain at the fringes of the hinterland, awaiting word until the new moon. That came this night. Tylar feared if they delayed too long that the Wyr might simply move on.

Krevan led the way. They descended the slope with care. The loose rock could easily twist an ankle, especially after the long climb down the cliff.

Tylar kept watch on the forest ahead. It did not look all that much different from the highlands above, except that the lowland trees grew taller, the canopies wider. They appeared true monsters of the loam. A few flickerflies flashed in the deeper wood, warning them back. Tinier wings buzzed ears and exposed skin. It remained the only sound, except a trickling of water.

They discovered a spring. Its waters spilled out of the bottom of the scree and flowed over broken shale toward the forest, vanishing into the darkness.

"According to the map, we should follow this," Krevan said and set off.

But once they reached the jungle, it seemed impossible to enter, tangled with vine and bush, creeper and sapling. Anything that could stretch a leaf to the sun grew at the edge. They would dull their blades trying to hack more than a quarter-league through here.

Instead, Krevan stepped into the stream and scuttled down its rocky course. He had to crouch, but it was passable.

"Mind the moss," he said. "It's slick."

They followed in a line. It was more like entering a cavern than a forest edge. The scent of wintersnap filled Tylar's nostrils, its leaves ground under the tread of the pirate in front. They didn't have far to go. The tunnel of brush slowly rose and thinned. Deeper under the canopy, away from the sunlit edge, the underbrush strangled away to vines and low bushes.

Tylar's boots sank into the spongy layer of decaying duff.

All around, the march of tree trunks struck Tylar like the columns of a grand *palacio.* Ropes of moss streamed this woodland hall, softly aglow in the darkness. To either side, other creeks and brooks trickled through the forest, all flowing ahead, downhill. The combined babble and echo of water over rock sounded like a mighty river. This was how the highlands drained into the hinter, creeping in tentative dribbles, like their own approach.

"Don't look so bad," Malthumalbaen muttered.

Tylar agreed. The forest seemed no different from other dark woods. The depths of Mistdale, all black pines and dread wood, struck a more ominous demeanor.

"Don't be fooled," Rogger said. "We've barely crossed the border. The deeper you go, the more the landscape is warped and woven by wild Grace into maddening design."

As if wanting to prove his point, a nesting winged beast took flight with a sudden burst of a flaming tail, streaking like a fiery arrow. It screeched, alerting others. More flames shot through the dark in fright.

"So much for a quiet approach," Rogger said.

They continued onward, led by Krevan.

No one spoke, wondering what other strangeness and horrors might lay deeper in the hinterland. For four thousand years, rogues had wandered these lonely lands, maddened both darkly and brightly. Some rogues were burnt into dullness, others into a malicious sharpness. But all leaked wild Grace into this unsettled land—into loam, into water, into air—where it corrupted in both subtle and monstrous ways.

Tylar compared it with the settled lands. He remembered the daemon inside Chrism describing the first *settling* of a realm, how Chrism was chained and bled against his will, punished for his murder of children during his raving. What was done with vengeance proved the greatest boon to Myrillia. Chrism's ravings faded as the wild Grace that had burnt his sanity bled into the land. The knowledge of this boon spread. Other gods followed his example, and the Nine Lands settled out of the centuries of raving and destruction into a long peace. Grace was harnessed, shared, and traded, blessing Myrillia into a new era, raising man out of its cycle of rule and ruin during the unending wars of its ancient human kings.

Tashijan itself rose out of one of those ancient keeps, ruled by the last human king, until the man swore his fealty and pledged his knights to the gods of the First Land, beginning the long line of shadowknights. The pact set by this ancient king protected the lands around the keep, free of any one god's rule. Wards had been set up at the borders, to forbid even the trespass of wandering rogues.

The pact had been unspoiled for four millennia.

And now all was threatened.

Krevan stopped. A large outcropping of rock rose ahead. One of those bastions Tylar had noted up by the cliff. It looked like a crooked finger raised to the sky, perhaps warning against further trespass.

Tylar hobbled to Krevan's side. He certainly could use a rest, but they dared not. Not yet. Tylar controlled his breathing as he joined Krevan, hiding his exhausted, rasping breath.

Still, the pirate stared him up and down. Krevan kept silent about what he found, but a crease between his brow deepened.

"How much farther?" Tylar asked.

Krevan frowned and grumbled. "I should check the map."

Tylar didn't like the worried tone to the pirate's voice. Calla joined them, shrugging off a pack. The maps were unrolled.

Stepping clear, Tylar searched up between the canopy's leaves. Clouds were blowing into view. But so far, the full face of the lesser moon shone down. It was called a Hunter's Moon when full like this, casting enough glow to see but not enough to give away a hunter's blind.

How far had they come? Not even half a league, he imagined.

Krevan whispered with Calla.

"Already lost?" Rogger asked as he stalked up.

"No," Krevan answered and nodded to the pinnacle of granite. "This is the right place. This is where Bennifren said to meet."

"Have they moved on?" Tylar asked.

The answer came from above their heads. A rope sailed down the side of the nearby pinnacle. A shape quickly slid along it, dropping from some hidden perch. The figure was cloaked in hunter's green and black boots.

Krevan drew his blade. Tylar slipped Rivenscryr free, not taking any chances with the malignant Grace of this land.

Alighting without even a crackle of twig or dry leaf, the newcomer strode toward them, tall, back straight, unperturbed by their raised blades. The hood was shaken back, revealing dark hair, skin the color of bitternut and cream. Familiar eyes studied them.

"Eylan . . ." Dart said, also recognizing the woman.

The woman failed to respond, but Dart was correct. She was a match to Eylan, from boot to crown. Even her movements were the same: the way she leaned on a hip as she stopped, how her eyes took in a situation in a single sweep to the right, then back again more slowly and warily to the left.

Only then did Tylar realize his mistake. The woman didn't recognize them—and it couldn't be Eylan. They had all seen her die.

Was she a twin?

"My name is Meylan," she said, confirming his thought. "You will come with me."

Though they'd never met, Tylar felt a strange affection for the woman, as if she were his own sister. But with it came a twinge of guilt. Did she know of her sister's death? She would have to be told.

But not now . . .

Meylan turned as if there was no brooking any defiance. Her words were reinforced by the appearance of more figures, similarly attired, hoods up. They appeared from behind the boles of trees and lowered themselves out of branches.

Lorr stepped to Tylar's side. "They use Grace to hide their scent and even their breath."

They did indeed move silently. He had yet to hear a single footfall or snap of a broken branch. He counted a full score of them, all women.

Meylan touched the rocky side of the pinnacle, and flames burst from its tip, flickering sharply above. Rounding the outcropping, Tylar found a break in the foliage. Ahead, the lands continued to drop away. Atop another pinnacle a good league away, flames burst.

Signal fires.

Meylan had passed on word of their arrival.

Krevan paced Tylar. "I should have guessed Bennifren would not have simply told me the location of his hinterland camp. Secrets run through his veins, more than blood."

Rogger came up on his other side. "Wise to remember that.

The Wyr make pacts that are unbreakable, sealed with a word. But all else is suspect."

They followed Meylan, but Rogger was not done. He nudged Tylar and pointed back. "Watch as they pass under the firelight."

Brows pinching, Tylar glanced at the women that trailed the group. They made no move to threaten them. But he spotted daggers on their belts, and he did not doubt more blades were hidden on their bodies. He was not sure what Rogger intended him to see.

Then one of them stepped past the pinnacle. Shafts of firelight flickered and danced shadows from above. The woman's face was momentarily illuminated in its ruddy glow.

Tylar stumbled. She looked indistinguishable from Meylan—as much as Meylan looked like Eylan. Another woodswoman slipped through the same light, revealing again the same face. Then another.

"Just so you know who you are dealing with," Rogger said.

Tylar held back a shudder as he looked across the score of women. The warmth he had felt toward Meylan went cold. For centuries, perhaps millennia, the Wyr had sought to breed godhood into human flesh. Their practices were as arcane as they were heartless. No manner of manipulation of the flesh was beyond them, resulting in abomination, mutilation, deformity.

But this?

It seemed so much worse. Beauty and horror. Maybe it was that this abomination wore the face of a woman he had come to know, to appreciate, even to value as a friend.

Affection and guilt shifted to anger.

Tylar stared as the women spread through the forest.

He would remember Rogger's warning. He was also mindful of what the thief had said about the unbreakable pacts with the Wyr. Tylar had his own oath to honor, a debt that perhaps he could no longer delay in settling. The Wyr had collected his other humours—but he owed them one more.

His seed.

Tylar knew that before he was allowed to head deeper into the hinterland, Bennifren would demand that he satisfy their old deal. Tylar also knew he needed the Wyr-lord's cooperation. To gain it, there would be little room to maneuver.

Ahead, Meylan glanced back, perhaps sensing his reluctance. He stared back at her, a woman wearing the face of a friend. He read no friendship here.

Only a reminder of what was owed . . . and the danger of its corruption.

Dart stayed close to the giant as they entered the camp.

She had heard tales of the Wyr for as far back as she could remember, tales meant to scare one to hurry to bed, to finish one's chores, to keep one's word. The one common element of these stories was that bad children ended up in the Wyr's clutches, dragged away and never seen again. But as she grew older, the tales grew both more truthful and more frightening. The Wyr were a cadre of Dark Alchemists, buried within their subterranean forges, concocting all manner of Grace in their pursuit of godhood. The ends to which they'd go to achieve this were both monstrous and pitiless.

Dart followed the others into the camp, staying close to the giant.

The Wyr had made their home on the bank of what appeared to be a wide lake but was in truth a flooded forest. Here was where all the trickling creeks eventually ended, becoming a slow shallow river several leagues wide, flowing westward toward the distant sea. Twisted trees corkscrewed out of the flood, raised up on tangles of roots, as if trying to crawl out of the black water. Great slabs of rock tilted out, too, strangely barren, along with more pinnacles.

The closest of these spires rose near the bank, shadowing a collection of ramshackle tents. Its pinnacle bore a crown of fire. The beacon had led them here, escorted by Meylan's band. Its flames lit the camp below with a foreboding glow, all fire and shadow.

Faces watched their approach: spying from behind flaps of tents, lifting up from some labor, wafting smoke from their eyes. Dart, in turn, studied them, expecting beastly countenances. Instead, most of these folk looked as normal as their group—and when compared to Lorr and Malthumalbaen, maybe even more normal.

A few forms, though, were plainly tainted. A bare-breasted

woman hauled wet clothes from the creek. She had arms and legs as thick around as the giant's but was hardly taller than Dart. When she turned, her eyes were shadowed by heavy brows that sloped steeply back. They watched dully as the group passed.

Then there was a boy, far younger than Dart, who approached their party with the simple doe-eyed curiosity of all youth, shyly but still drawn. From his eyes, it was plain he was full of questions, but they would never come.

He had no mouth—only a gaping hole at the base of his throat.

She had to look away. But he must have noted the horror in her face, for he turned away, too, in shame. That more than anything disturbed her. She had her own secrets, but they were hidden well, hidden deep. Not like the boy's.

As they neared the water, another woman approached, ducking out of the largest of the tents. She was wide-hipped and full of breast. She straightened and shuffled toward them. Her head tilted slackly to one side, a trickle of drool hanging from her lower lip. She carried an infant in her arms, cradled to those ample breasts. From the swaddling, a bald crown of head shone pink as the child suckled.

Pupp, who had been hanging close, moved to her ankles, flaring brighter as his hackles raised.

The woman stepped before them and pulled the babe from her breast. She lifted it, as if offering the child to them. It appeared to be an ordinary babe. Milk dribbled from plump lips. Rosy cheeks shone, well fed and hale.

But then those eyes opened and destroyed the illusion.

An ancient wickedness shone forth, born of too sharp an intelligence. There was a leering quality to the glint.

Dart bit back a gasp.

"Wyrd Bennifren," Tylar said formally.

The babe wiped milky spittle from his lips with a pudgy arm. "You look like rotted shite, Tylar." The voice was reedy and thin—childlike but far from childish. It made the hairs on Dart's body quiver with revulsion. "Crook-backed and hobbling. Not much of a godslayer now."

"Either way, here I am. We've come to offer terms for the knowledge you possess."

"You bring the skull, then?" the child asked hungrily.

From the side, Krevan answered, "A piece of it. All that is left. The rest was destroyed in fires up in Saysh Mal."

"That was *not* our agreement, Raven ser Kay."

"Our agreement, by your sworn word as the free leader of the Wyrdling clans, was to bring you all that remains of Keorn, son of Chrism. So we have done. You must honor your bargain."

The babe sneered, a frightening expression on such a small face, like a sewer rat given human countenance. "Then let us be done with the matter." He turned to study Tylar up and down. "It seems this is a night to settle many debts. Follow me." Guided by some silent signal, the slack-jawed woman heaved around like a foundering ship and headed off along the flooded bank. Babe and woman rounded a cluster of rocks to reveal a fire blazing amid a circle of standing stones.

Dart glanced to them. Dancing firelight revealed cryptic marks inscribed into the stones' faces. She recognized them from historical texts back at school. It was the old human written language, all straight lines, little warmth, guttural in appearance.

Wyrd Bennifren led them to logs rolled close to the fire. Flagons of ale and fresh water waited, along with carved bowls piled high with spiced dry meats, hard cheeses, and strange berries as crimson as blood. It was a bountiful fare for such a dreadful gathering in a dark, flooded wood.

Still, bellies did not judge.

Once they were settled in, Krevan spoke around a mouthful of rabbit. "You swore to know more about the rogue god Keorn. Secrets of interest to us, to the girl." He nodded to Dart. "The Black Flaggers waged significant resources to discover Keorn's fate and to bring you a piece of that god. It is time for you to make full payment."

"The Wyr honor their bonded word," Bennifren said. He was nestled in the dull woman's lap. One hand pawed her teat, half absently, half lasciviously. "But I also know that you've already gleaned much about Keorn on your journey out and back. Still, there are more secrets known only to us. Secrets whispered in the ear of the raving, thought never to be repeated."

"Spoken to whom?" Tylar asked.

"This one's mother, for one," Bennifren said, his gaze drifting to Dart. "It can be lonely when you're the only sighted man in a world full of the blind. That was Keorn. He bore some special Grace that kept him at the edge of raving but never beyond."

Tylar shared a silent glance with Rogger. Both were careful not to look at Brant. Better the Wyr didn't know about his stone.

"But even a god has needs," Bennifren said. He tugged hard on the woman's nipple, earning a yip of surprise that quickly subsided back to dullness again. "Like when he bedded that godling's mother. He told her many things, secret things that he thought she would forget when the ravings took hold again. But when his seed took root, he protected her, sheltered her with his steadying Grace. During that time, balanced on that fine edge of madness, she whispered his secrets. And we were there, listening, drawn by the rare birth."

Dart shivered despite the fire's warmth. He was speaking about *her* birth.

"What sort of secrets?" Tylar asked.

Bennifren grinned with malicious delight. "Secrets about a father and son at odds."

"Chrism and his son?"

Bennifren nodded to Tylar. "I've heard what the daemon claimed when you confronted him in Chrismferrry last year. How it was Chrism himself who forged Rivenscryr in their old world, wielded it during a great war there, and in doing so, accidentally split his world, sundered land and people, casting them adrift to settle here as flesh, naethryn, and aethryn."

"So he claimed."

"And it was just that . . . *a claim*. While all was true about the Sundering, what was not true was that Chrism forged your sweet sword."

Tylar's hand drifted to the gold hilt.

"Chrism had a lust for power, and he candled those desires in the reflections of sword blades. He constructed a private smithy where he designed and forged weapons of great edge and balance." Bennifren pointed a pink finger at the other blade on Tylar's belt. "Who do you think designed the shape and form of your knightly swords?"

Rogger nodded. "He's right there. It *was* Chrism. According to ancient texts. He offered that first sword to the last human king, the one who founded the shadowknights, as thanks and a bond between them. All other swords were patterned after that first."

"So you see," Bennifren said, "a heart's desire is not so easy to shed. Even after he was sundered, Chrism's desire was too large to split away entirely. His fascination with swords. Perhaps that's why his aspect of Grace, once settled, revealed a heart of loam. A love not so much of root and leaf as of iron and ore."

Tylar stared at the two swords on his hip. "So Chrism had nothing to do with Rivenscryr's actual forging?"

"Exactly. He only wielded the sword—or perhaps it wielded him, in the end. It was a weapon too powerful, beyond his understanding."

"Then who forged it?" Krevan asked, clearly perturbed.

Bennifren's ancient eyes looked upon Dart slyly. But she already knew the truth. The way her blood ignited the sword, her blasted heritage—there could only be one answer.

"It was my father," Dart said.

All eyes turned for confirmation to the small Wyr-lord. He seemed to enjoy their shock. "Like father, like son. It seemed the passion for the blade was passed to the son. But it was not the power of the sword that fascinated Keorn as much as it was the artistry of the honed blade. His passion lay in seeking the *perfect* sword. That he got from his mother, for a son is only half his father. His mother inspired him equally, gifting him with a questioning mind, a love for knowledge, and an appreciation for hidden secrets. At her knee, he was taught arcane rites, and in turn, he forged powerful insights and secrets into the steel of the sword, creating a formidable weapon like no other."

"And Chrism stole it," Tylar said.

"How could he not? His lust overcame his caution. He used it during the war and sundered everything in his ignorance."

Bennifren then smiled, showing his toothless gums. "And therein lies a good lesson. You must be careful how far you reach. Better to be large here." He tapped his head. "And have shorter arms. Keeps one wiser where one reaches."

Krevan sighed, his face tight with irritation. "So the rogue forged the Godsword. What does any of this—?"

Bennifren raised his tiny arm, silencing the pirate. "Patience is also a virtue of the wise." He turned to the others. "For you see, Keorn wanted no part of his father's war, and he certainly did not want his perfect creation wielded in it. So the last secret Keorn imparted to the mother of his child, his most heartfelt private shame, was that he had damaged his own sword. He built a flaw into it. He made it *imperfect*."

Dart felt a sickening lurch in her stomach.

Bennifren's sibilant voice made the final truth so much more horrible. "It was this *flaw* as much as Chrism's wielding that led to the end of their world. This was Keorn's final secret to his ravening mate, a secret he never intended be known. As much as Chrism, Keorn was to blame for the Sundering that destroyed their world."

A stunned silence followed.

"Like father, like son," Rogger finally mumbled.

Tylar stared down at his belted swords—Rivenscryr and his knightly blade. He looked ready to throw both aside, their two histories entwined by curse and tragedy.

"So I'd be careful how you wield that sword," Bennifren warned. "That flaw still remains."

"But what was it?" Krevan asked. "What did Keorn do?"

Tiny shoulders shrugged. "I don't think the *how* weighed on the god's mind as much as the end result. He never whispered that secret across a pillow. But plainly his guilt ate like a worm in the belly. We believe that is why he protected the growing child, kept the mother from raving long enough to give birth to his daughter, someone whose blood could forge the sword anew."

"But why go through the effort if the blade was flawed?" Tylar asked.

"Because of what we found later, when we were hunting Keorn through the hinterlands," Bennifren said. "The god lost us, but we found his trail again."

Dart remembered the first crumb of that trail. How could she forget? She could still feel the cold of her garret as Krevan wrote the name of her father on the wall in Littick sigils, a name found at the bottom of a piece of hide tacked to an elder's wall in a hinter-village.

"That scrabbled missive," Bennifren continued, "inked in Keorn's own blood. We never did reveal what those words said, only that it was signed by Keorn."

The Wyr-lord allowed the weight of his words to hang like a raised sword. Then he finally spoke again. "His words were few, already showing a hint of seersong in his inked blood, possibly his last words before he was swallowed up."

"What did he write?" Brant asked, speaking for the first time, suspense loosening his tongue.

Bennifren didn't even glance his way, but he did answer his question. " *'The sword must be forged again, made whole to free us all.'* "

Tylar stirred. "So there is a way to make the sword complete."

"And he offered no word about the flaw?" Krevan asked again.

"If you'd found him sooner . . . before he was just skull and curse . . ." Bennifren shrugged.

Krevan kept his lips tight, brows hard. "The Flaggers spent much time and coin to just buy whispers and old secrets that bear little weight in the here and now."

"I believe you've been paid well for a sliver of bone," Bennifren said, his face reddening. "Do not question the honor of our word because you bargained so poorly."

Krevan began to rise, but Bennifren waved him down.

"Then I will give you something as solid as rock to finish this deal. Something you can touch—though it may burn you."

Tylar waved Krevan to patience. "What?"

Bennifren again turned those eyes toward Dart. "The Godsword is as much his mother's inspiration as his father's. If you are looking for a way to discover more about the sword, perhaps you should start there. I wager that is why Keorn fled down here after Dart's birth."

"Why?" she asked.

"He came looking for his mother's counsel and advice," Bennifren answered and pointed to the south.

Through a break in the canopy, the mountain blocked the stars. Its flanks flowed with molten streams, bright in the darkness. Fiery tears—not just for a daughter but perhaps also for a son.

"Takaminara was Keorn's mother."

Tylar stood up, half in shock, half to better view the volcanic peak. He rested a hand on Dart's shoulder. He felt her tremble under his touch, her eyes fixed to the same fiery peak. He understood her distress. Buried within the mountain lay not only a god but something she must have been searching for her entire life.

A part of her family.

A great-mother.

"Then the Huntress—Miyana," Brant said. "She was Keorn's sister."

Lorr mumbled, "At the end, he must have been trying to reach her."

Dart shivered. In days, she had gained an entire family, one drenched in blood and terror. Both in the distant past . . . and now again.

But any further family reunion would have to wait.

The rogues had to be found.

Tylar turned to Bennifren, but his hobbled knee almost toppled him into the flame. He had been sitting for too long after the hard march.

Bennifren noted his discomfort. "I believe I've met my debt well and then some. But there is another debt yet to settle. You were wise in your negotiations in the past, but our bargain has long grown stale." He eyed Tylar up and down. "And as shiteful as you look now, I fear what is owed will be lost. Especially knowing where you must venture. I believe it time you honored your word, too."

Tylar inwardly groaned, but he kept his face calm. He walked off and motioned for Bennifren to follow. Rogger and Krevan trailed with them, but Tylar waved the others to their meal. Here was a matter he wanted settled with less of an audience.

Stepping out of the ring of firelight, he faced Bennifren. He had no intention of freely cooperating, and he stated it firmly now. "As you recall, time was a condition of our bargain. My time, my place. I see no reason to relinquish it now."

"True and well said." Bennifren's eyes narrowed behind soft lashes, a wicked gleam of cunning shining through in the dark. "I would think less of you if you had settled without remapping a new bargain. So let me tell you this. We have not been idle while you've been traipsing about. The Wyr are well-known here in the hinterlands, valued for our purse as well as expertise. Over these past days, we've spent our coin and time well and discovered something that might pry that stubborn seed from your loins."

Tylar waited. When it came to the Wyr, silence was often the best shield during any negotiations.

"For the last humour you owe us," Bennifren continued, "we offer you a special encouragement. We offer you maps of the hinterlands."

"We have maps," Tylar said dryly.

"But do your maps have the location of the enslaved rogues marked upon them?"

Tylar stared, struggling not to show the depth of his desire.

"And traced upon our maps is the safest route by which to reach the gods," Bennifren added. "All this, for a few moments of your time . . ."

Tylar felt the other two men's eyes upon him. With such a map, the search would be measured in bells rather than days. He could not refuse. All of Tashijan hung in the balance.

Still, he hesitated. Off to the right, he noted Meylan leaning against the pinnacle, buried in shadow, her face lit up by the pipe she was smoking. Her sisters were spread out in groups and singly.

Bennifren misunderstood his attention. "Whichever woman you want—I've heard she and her sisters are quite skilled."

Tylar went cold at that thought, but he also knew he had no choice. The bargain had to be settled, and the offer of the rogues' location was a price he could not refuse.

He faced Bennifren. "I'll go along with your new bargain." He held up one finger. "A single sample for all your maps. Then our deal is finished."

"Done and bound." Bennifren waved a small arm in a grand gesture. "I can bring you whichever woman you'd like to help you loosen your seed. Or if you so prefer, a man—or a child."

"That won't be necessary," he said coldly. "A bit of privacy will be enough."

"This way, then." Bennifren turned away, carried by his milk mare. "All is ready. You can use my tent. It is the last and largest."

Tylar noted where he pointed and motioned for Krevan and Rogger to stay. This was a duty that did not require their attendance. He headed toward the tent with Bennifren.

Rogger called after to him. "Remember—don't work too hard!" Then in the next breath, he added, "No! I take that back! In this matter . . ."

Tylar shook his head, blocking out the thief's next words as he rounded the rock, glad to be rid of Rogger. This duty would be difficult enough to accomplish.

"I'll have a repostilary for your humour brought to you," Bennifren said and guided his woman off to the side. "And don't worry, you'll have your privacy."

Tylar kept his gaze fixed on the tent ahead. He had never spilled his seed for the sake of Grace. Not even at Chrismferry. He had shared all his other humours with varying degrees of humiliation. But he had always refused to relinquish this one humour, one of the most powerful, second only to blood. It allowed Grace to be imbued into living tissue, essential for a great many alchemies. But there were plenty of gods out there already. As regent, he saw no need to contribute to this storehouse himself.

Until now.

For the sake of Tashijan, he had to relent. No matter what foul alchemies were to be performed on his seed, it was a debt that must be paid. As he walked alone now, he remembered the only child ever birthed from his seed. Long dead, winnowed by grief while in the womb. Had his seed always been cursed?

This dark thought reminded him of Kathryn, of better times, of moments they shared when life was bright and the days seemed endless before them. Now he knew better. He knew it was a black bargain being completed here, but it was done in the hopes of again returning the world to brighter times.

If not for him, at least for others.

He reached the tent and pulled open the hide flap. Ducking inside, he noted that no lamp burnt, and the thick leather shut out the stars and the moon. He dropped the flap behind him, happy for the darkness, better to hide his shame. But could he hide from himself?

He would not find out.

Somebody already hid here.

From the back, where the darkness was thickest, shadows stirred and birthed a figure in a cloak to match his. A fair face shone back out at him, lit by eyes that flashed with dread fire.

The black *ghawl* swept toward him, sword raised.

"Perryl . . ."

Brant approached Dart. She had wandered to the bank of the flooded forest when the strange Wyr-lord and the regent had stepped away to discuss the fate of an old bargain.

She sat on a narrow sandy strand, hugging her knees. She had pulled up the hood of her half cloak against the growing chill.

Ahead, the black water lay flat as glass. The air hung heavy with the promise of rain. Clouds covered what little starlight had shone. The darkness was almost complete.

Brant sank down next to her, dropping to one knee. He hated to disturb her. She plainly wanted a moment alone to settle her thoughts, but what he had come to suspect could not wait.

"Dart—"

Her face lowered farther.

"I'm sorry to bother you."

A hand wiped at her cheek. "What is it?" Her voice was tremulous with tears.

He began to straighten, suddenly regretting his intrusion. "I'm sorry. Perhaps another—"

She sniffed, once and hard, clearing her throat. A hand reached and touched his shoulder. "No. What is it?" A bit of firmness returned to her voice. She wiped her cheeks with a corner of her sleeve and shook back her hood, facing him.

His voice died for a moment, struck silent as the firelight brushed across her damp face, glistening and warm.

"Brant . . . ?"

He blinked and swallowed. Finally he settled beside her. "I wanted to ask you something away from others. I'm probably wrong, but it was something you said a while back. Up in the flippercraft as we approached the Eighth Land. When you asked to see my stone."

Brant offered his hand, opening his palm. The stone rested there, unthreaded again from its cord. He'd felt its warmth as he had neared Dart. Pupp must be close, watching with his ghostly eyes. It was one of the reasons he had come. He had to be certain.

Pupp . . . the sword . . .

A single line furrowed between her brows as she stared at his stone.

"I don't understand," she said.

"You said something up in the flippercraft," he mumbled. "About the stone. I dismissed it before. But after what we just heard . . ."

She looked up at him a bit more firmly, hearing the hope in his voice. Even his hand trembled a bit. If he was right, it could make his father's death mean something . . . make all of this mean something.

But was he right?

He remembered Dart's description of his stone.

It's beautiful . . . the way it catches every bit of light.

Brant also remembered his words to his father when he first picked up the stone.

It's only a rock.

That was what everyone else saw, just a dull, drab stone, something of no great acclaim, especially as Brant kept silent about where it had come from. A secret between father and son.

Now Dart, a girl with sharper eyes, saw something more.

Was it what he suspected—hoped for?

"All I see is a plain black stone," Brant explained. "Dull and wan."

Her eyes flicked to him, confusion shining. "But it's not dull—"

"I know. You see something else." He held out his hand, trembling. "Show me what no one else sees. Like Pupp. Or the sword."

She knew then. He saw the understanding in her eyes. Not everything, not yet.

"My blood . . ."

He nodded.

Before either could move, a shout erupted from steps away. They both turned to find Lorr running straight at them, bearing aloft a fiery torch. "Get back! Get away from there!"

Brant's fingers clenched over the stone. He leaned closer to Dart, ready to protect her. But he saw the wyld tracker's eyes weren't on them—he looked beyond them.

Toward the water.

Brant twisted around.

Dark figures stood out in the lake, some still rising out of the black water, though not a ripple was stirred, as if the dark flood was mere shadow. Closer still, two dark shapes were already sliding toward Dart and Brant. Again not raising any wave by their passage, wading out of shadows.

Black *ghawls*.

A dozen strong.

Brant and Dart scrambled back, but the sand was loose and their feet kicked more than gained.

Then Lorr was there, leaping over them with the agility of a spring deer. He splashed into the water's edge, flaming brand before him, warding against the pair that were closest.

"Here, Master Brant!" Malthumalbaen bellowed behind him. "By the fire!"

Brant finally gained his feet and hauled Dart up with him. They stumbled toward the waiting fire.

Out in the water, knee-deep, Lorr swung his torch before him. The fiery arc forced the two closest *ghawls* back a step. They were cloaked in shadows, bearing aloft black swords. The torchlight washed away the darkness for a breath, revealing pale, sunken faces of the long dead.

"Git back to the fire!" Lorr called to them.

Heeding his own advice, he backed toward shore, keeping

his torch between him and the pair of daemon knights. The flames kept them at bay. But to either side, the other *ghawls* floated toward shore, again moving without disturbing the water, eerie and silent.

But Lorr kept his focus on the closest pair.

A mistake.

Behind him, a dark shape lunged out of the water at his heels, catching the tracker off guard. And rightly so, as the water was only ankle-deep—too shallow to hide such a form—but Brant knew it wasn't truly water from which these creatures welled. They arose out of the darkness that lay across the waters like oil.

Dart screamed, in both warning and surprise.

But it was too late.

Lorr half turned as the daemon knight's blade buried itself in his back. He was lifted from the water, impaled and arched on the sword. Shadows spread out from the blade. His flesh darkened and sank to his bones. His last breath was a wail of a hunter on a trail.

But where Lorr went to hunt now, they could not follow.

His body was cast aside, to splash facefirst into the waters.

The other *ghawls* headed toward shore.

Arms grabbed Brant, raising a startled yip.

But it was only Krevan. He snatched Brant's shoulder and Dart's arm and all but threw them into the ring of firelight. "Stay by the fire!" he yelled. "It's the only safety."

"Where are you—?" Brant started.

The pirate furled out his shadowcloak and vanished into the shadows beyond the firelight. His last words carried back. "To find Tylar."

They circled each other inside the tent, shifting shadows. Though their blades did not strike for the moment, they still fought, testing each other, feinting for an opening. A shoulder move here, countered by a shift of hip. A leg stepped back, met by a contrary twist of a wrist. Move by move, they danced in a slow circle.

Tylar had taught Perryl well.

He lifted Rivenscryr in his good hand. The blade glowed

with its own inner fire, a soft silvery radiance, moonlight given substance. He knew it was the only weapon that could withstand the blade wielded by this daemon knight.

Perryl's blade glinted with green fire, the same poison that ate through Tylar, weakening both naethryn and its vessel.

As if reading his worry, the daemon spoke for the first time, whispery and low, oily with malevolence. "You are riddled with the blood of Chrism, darkly Graced with old enmity and fury. Nothing in Myrillia, nothing in the naether can burn this poison away. You are doomed. Better to open your guard and die quickly. A final kindness . . ."

Proving this point, Tylar stumbled on his bad leg. His chest burnt with every breath. They had come at each other twice already. Tylar had barely kept his footing at the last attack, deflecting the daemon's blade more by sheer luck than skill.

As they circled, he wondered how Perryl had found him so readily. Was this an ambush by the Wyr? A trap? Or had the *ghawl* found him by the poison he just described? Sniffed out like a dog on a trail?

Either way, Tylar had to survive.

He heard the screams beyond the tent. Perryl had not come alone. But before Tylar could help any others, he had to deal with this one, plainly the leader. If he could vanquish this daemon lord of the *ghawls*, the others might take flight.

But how to do that?

Once before, he had speared Perryl through the chest with Rivenscryr and still failed to slay the beast. But perhaps a fiercer blow, a slice through the neck—even a daemon would lose his fight with his head rolling across the floor.

That was Tylar's only hope.

Tylar's ankle turned on a knob of root underfoot. He dropped his sword for balance, opening himself up. Perryl blended shadow and speed brilliantly. Tylar had just enough time to appreciate the beauty of the move. A Jackman's Tie. He attempted a Sweeper's Row to block, but he knew it would fail.

Then a rustle of tent flap, and a storm of shadows burst into the tent.

A knight shed out of the darkness.

Krevan smashed into Perryl. But Perryl turned the blow to

his advantage. Using Krevan's own weight, he spun on his back heel, coming around as swift as any shadow. His blade sliced for the pirate's neck.

Krevan rolled to the side—but not fast enough.

Perryl's sword sliced across Krevan's raised wrist, cutting through cloth and flesh down to bone.

Normally the pirate would not have faltered, but this was no ordinary blade. A howl escaped Krevan's lips as he fell back. Shadows fell like water from around the pirate. His outstretched arm sprayed blood, but not enough to wash out the poison. His hand melted from his wrist, then the corruption spread up his arm.

Tylar remembered Malthumalbaen's brother, who suffered a similar fate.

Krevan swung at Perryl, driving him back a step.

Tylar had regained his footing and attacked. He yanked his other sword free, earning a flare of complaint from his bandaged hand, and swung the blade—not at Perryl but at Krevan.

Using all his strength, Tylar cleaved through Krevan's raised arm. He took the limb off at the shoulder, before the poison could spread. He followed through by shouldering Krevan back out the tent flap and shoving him clear.

As the heavy hide tent flap clapped shut, Tylar swung wildly with Rivenscryr as Perryl tried to close on him. *Too eager, Perryl.* Tylar faced the daemon, tossing his knightly sword to the floor and lifting Rivenscryr high.

The Godsword was his only hope.

Sweating and with his limbs on fire, Tylar faced the daemon lord again.

Though likely doomed, he knew what he had to do.

Let's end this dance.

"Stay low," Rogger said, pulling Brant farther down.

They all crouched with their backs to the fire. Brant knelt on one knee. Beyond the thief, Malthumalbaen lay almost on his belly, while Calla took up a post on the far side of the fire, facing where Krevan had vanished.

Dart kept to Brant's other side. She had covered her face when Lorr died, but the deaths had not ended there. All around, the Wyr-folk were being slaughtered. Screams echoed from all sides.

A moment ago, a large-limbed woman had lumbered past their flames, howling in fear, knuckling on one arm as she ran. Brant had tried to call her over, but her wits were as low as her forehead, and what remained had been burnt away by fear.

She trundled past their flames only to have shadows open to one side and a blade shoot out, striking clean through her neck. Her body continued for another two steps, then slid to the ground. Her head rolled farther off into the darkness as if still trying to escape.

The only Wyr-folk who seemed to have found a safe haven were the strange women led by the one named Meylan. They had scaled the nearby pinnacle, reaching the flames on top. They cast the occasional fiery brand down the side, scattering sparks along the rock, warning against any trespass by the *ghawls*.

And that was the true danger.

The *ghawls* lurked just beyond the reach of the firelight, searching for a way past their defenses.

Rogger explained one such threat as he pulled Brant lower. The thief had been studying a few other fires across the camp. "You don't want your shadows to stretch out to the darkness. I think they can flow up such channels to reach you."

Brant dropped to his other knee.

"What happens when we run out of wood?" Malthumalbaen asked, sprawled almost flat to keep his silhouette low.

Rogger shook his head. "Mayhap you can leap and grab a few branches overhead, tear them down with those long arms of yours."

The giant eyed the canopy as if considering this plan.

Dart spoke softly from his other side. "Brant . . . your stone . . ."

Rogger heard her. "I don't think that'll help, little lass." The thief must believe she was grasping at false hope, like the giant eyeing the branches overhead. "These creatures are not locked in seersong. And any other nullifying—"

Brant stopped him with a raised hand. Though the stone was still clutched tightly in his other hand, he had forgotten about it.

Dart turned. She already held a dagger in her hand.

She knew.

Brant leaned back, his body damp from the searing heat of the fire. He opened his palm toward her.

"What are you two doing?" Rogger asked, sidling around while staying low.

Brant didn't bother to explain. Either it worked or it didn't.

Dart met Brant's eye, scared but determined. He reached out with his other hand and touched her knee. He kept his fingers there.

Dart nicked her thumb with the tip of her dagger. A single drop of blood welled up, crimson and fiery in the firelight. She tilted her thumb and let the drop roll off and splash onto the drab black chunk of stone.

A flash of fire ignited in his palm, but it was not a true flame.

Brant stared at the whetted stone in his palm. It was no longer a drab bit of rock. Dart's blood had revealed its true heart, reflecting the firelight from its hundred facets.

A perfect black diamond.

Dart's words echoed.

It's beautiful . . . the way it catches every bit of light.

Rogger's reaction was less prosaic. "Smart bastard. Keorn hid it in plain sight."

The thief patted Brant on the shoulder. "Well done."

Brant knew the thief understood immediately. It was Rogger's own words that had helped Brant begin to suspect earlier. How Chrism had designed the first shadowknight's sword, a blade with a black diamond on its hilt.

Rogger leaned closer. "Chrism must have fashioned the knight's sword after Rivenscryr. Or at least how he remembered it."

"But what about this diamond?" Dart asked. "Why is it not with the sword now?"

"Because Keorn removed it," Rogger said. "He probably replaced the diamond with a fake, some artifice that looked like it, to fool his father. *That* was the sword's *flaw*. The fake must have been destroyed during the Sundering, but the original diamond, like the sword, came to Myrillia. The sword with Chrism. The heart with Keorn. Two parts of a whole."

"We must get the diamond to Tylar," Dart said.

"But how?" Rogger mumbled and nodded out to the darkness.

Brant glanced up.

Others had been drawn by the flame in his palm. At the edge of the firelight, darkness stirred and rustled. Like mothkins to a flame, the black *ghawls* had gathered tight around them.

"Can't go out there," Rogger said. "And fire's the only thing keeping them back."

As if hearing him, the skies opened up.

Rain fell in great large drops—at first lightly, then in a drenching downpour. Behind Brant, the fire sizzled and spat, slowly being doused.

As more rain fell, the ring of firelight began to collapse.

21

A WITCH'S THRONE

"WHY DOES THAT SKAGGING HOUND KEEP BAYING?" Argent griped irritably.

Kathryn straightened. She understood what irritated the warden. It sounded as if all of Tashijan were wailing some last death rattle. But inside Kathryn, the howl ignited a deeper anxiety. It took all her will not to despair. She noted Gerrod had stepped closer to her. Though his features remained hidden behind bronze, she knew he shared the same misgiving.

It was Lorr's bullhound that howled, baying in raw grief.

That could hold only one portent.

Gerrod's hand found hers atop the table. And though his bronze fingers were cold, she sensed the warmth inside.

"Do not put so much stock in a hound's grief," he mumbled through his faceplate. "The reason could be multifold."

She nodded, little convinced.

To the right, Argent tugged Hesharian's sleeve. "So when the ice comes, show me where we should place your alchemies."

"I-I'm not sure." His face was deathly pale and his breathing wheezed in and out.

Gerrod lifted his hand from hers and stabbed at the map in two places. "Here and here."

"Thank you, Master Rothkild," Argent said, with a tired roll of his head away from Hesharian. "How much alchemy will we need?"

"That is a concern," Gerrod said. "We've used up so much bile already."

Hesharian blurted out, his voice ragged and panicked. "*You* used it all up! Helping the regent escape to safety! Leaving all of us to die!"

"That's enough!" Argent barked. "Either be helpful or be silent!"

Hesharian slunk away from the warden's words, quite a feat for one so large. He retreated to the wall, where Liannora still stood, back straight, silent, hands folded into her muff. Her only sign of distress was a single long lock of silver hair that straggled across her face. She had yet to fix it back in place.

"When will Ulf attack?" Argent asked. "Night has fallen—and still we stand."

"It is early," Gerrod said. "The coldest part of the night is just before dawn. Though he may attack at any time."

A hurried scuff of boots on stone drew their attention to the door, accompanied by a shout from some knight by the stair. Kathryn's hand reached for her sword's hilt.

Then a familiar figure rushed into view, her face pale, her head wrapped in a bloody bandage. She grabbed the frame of the door to hold upright.

"Delia?" Argent said. "What happened to you?"

"The witch is coming!" she gasped out, weaving on her feet, plainly having run here. Fresh blood dribbled down her neck. "She's hiding in the dark abandon. Somewhere in the first four levels."

She took a step into the room and almost fell.

Argent came forward and caught her in his arms. He supported her to the table. Once there, she shook free of him, breathing hard, leaning both palms on the table.

"All those levels must be cleared," she said. "A fiery picket formed."

Kathryn circled around to join her. "Are you certain Mirra is loose?"

She nodded, still breathing hard. Kathryn read the hard edge to her eyes. She was not delusional from whatever blow she had taken to her head.

Kathryn turned to one of the young squires. He squatted on an upended bucket in a corner by the door. She pointed at him. "Reach the master of the guard below. Do you know him?"

He nodded vigorously.

"Have him clear the lower four levels. Rally at five." She held up her hand with all her fingers splayed. "Do you understand?"

But the boy was already running out the door.

She returned her attention to the table.

Argent was bent next to his daughter. "Where have you come from? Weren't you up with the other Hands?" His words were not accusatory, only concerned.

"No . . ." Delia said. "I went down below. Lured falsely. By a captain of the Oldenbrook guard—"

A new voice cut her off. "Sten?" Liannora staggered forward, speaking for the first time in a long while. Her voice sounded half-crazed. "Where is he? Why isn't he here?"

Delia seemed to finally note the Oldenbrook's Hand, dressed in her snowy best. Kathryn noted the flash of fire in Delia's eyes.

Liannora did not. She came up to Delia, reaching out a hand.

Delia shoved off the table to face her. Kathryn knew something was amiss. Especially when the calm, levelheaded Delia balled up a fist.

"What happened to Sten?"

As answer, Delia swung from the hip and slammed her fist straight into the Hand's face. Liannora's head snapped back with a crack of bone. Her body followed, stumbling into one of the mapwork shelves. Her legs went out from under her, and she slumped to the ground, her nose crooked and seeping blood from both sides.

All eyes turned to Delia. Had she been ilked, possessed by some madness?

Delia swiped a loose strand of her hair into place. A bit of color had returned to her cheeks from the effort. Still, she almost fell as she faced them, catching herself with a hand on the table.

"Liannora sent one of her guards to break my neck," Delia said. "Came near to doing it, if it hadn't been for Master Orquell."

The name roused Hesharian. "Did you say Master Orquell?"

Delia ignored him. "But Orquell is not what he appears to be. He is *rub-aki.*"

"What?" Hesharian yelped. A palm pressed his sweated brow. "Oh, sweet aether, how I treated him—an acolyte of the *rub-aki*." He groaned in distress, as if the slight were even more dire than the fall of Tashijan.

Kathryn turned her back on him. "Tell us what happened."

She did in fast words, concluding with a small bit of hope. "And he burnt Mirra. I don't know how badly. But hopefully enough to weaken her, perhaps make her act rashly."

Argent looked upon his daughter with a glint of pride. "Let's hope *rashly* serves us better than the cold calculation of that witch." A thin grin rose to his lips. "Still, to know she was burnt, that does give us hope. What can be harmed . . ."

". . . can be killed," Delia finished with a sober nod.

At that moment, Kathryn recognized that the family resemblance went beyond the shape of eye and cleft of chin. Perhaps Argent saw that, too. He had stepped to his daughter's side.

"I'll get one of the healers to see to your head."

"I'll mend," she said sourly, waving his worry away.

Gerrod stepped to her other side. "Orquell—he's headed down into the cellars?"

Delia nodded.

"Why? Where?"

"Down to Mirra's lair. That's all he said."

Though Gerrod's expression remained hidden, Kathryn recognized the worry in the set of his shoulder. "What is it?" she asked him.

"I can guess what he will attempt," Gerrod mumbled.

"And?" Argent asked.

Gerrod turned to the warden. "The danger to—"

His words were cut off by a blaring blast of a horn, so loud it finally quieted the bullhound above. A battle horn. But its resound echoed not from the picket line above.

"The call comes from below," Gerrod said.

Delia nodded. "The witch is rising up."

"Stay close."

Orquell led the way down the narrow staircase. He held a torch that flickered with a strange crimson flame. He had dipped the end of his oiled brand into a pile of powder that he spent a long fraction of a bell mixing on the top step. The resulting fire cast no smoke but still somehow shed an odor that reminded Laurelle of freshly hewn hay and something sweet.

She followed with a lamp, as did Kytt. He kept to their rear, glancing often over a shoulder. They had traveled far below. Laurelle could feel the press of rock above her. The steps here were small, barely cut into stone. It had been some time since they'd even seen a cross-passage.

Laurelle wondered if they should have heeded the guards who had warned them against entering. In truth, they had been refused entry. *Upon the warden's orders*. But Orquell had whispered something in each of their ears. Whatever was said widened their eyes. Their gazes flicked to the crimson mark on his forehead. Some portent, some secret, some threat—she never found out, but they quickly winched the gate up far enough for them to crawl under. Once past, the guards just as quickly closed it.

Plainly they weren't convinced that the witch had already escaped.

Laurelle was similarly worried. "What if she comes back, to nurse her burns? Or what if she senses we're down here?"

"Then we'll most likely die," Orquell answered without a measure of humor. It was stated simply and certainly. "So we'd best be quick."

As he said this, his torch, held before him at arm's length, flared brightly. Laurelle could have sworn she heard a small scream, but maybe that was her own inner self. A sudden waft of corruption passed over them, as if they trod upon a corpse bloated in the sun.

"Awful," said Orquell. But it wasn't the smell that upset him. "A Serpentknot Ward. If we'd blundered into that, we'd be dropping dead on our faces."

He continued down the stairs, thrusting his torch out farther.

Around they went, another two wards flared and burnt under his torch. The last flared high enough to dance flames along the stone roof. Laurelle noted that the ceiling was streaked with wide bands of rock that bore a glassy sheen.

"Flowstone," Orquell said, noting her reaching toward one. "It forms when molten stone is exposed to raw Gloom. Such veins can be found in deep places under the ground, but rarely are they discovered by man. All this will have to be purified if we survive."

"Purified?" Laurelle asked. "How?"

Orquell leaned his torch near a glassy vein. The fire seared the rock. It smoked, again raising a smell of corruption. When he lifted the torch away, the spot was scarred white. "It's possible to burn the Gloom out of the rock with special alchemical fires."

They continued past the ward and entered a chamber that seemed to be formed as a bubble in a giant vein of flowstone.

Kytt gaped. "You'll need much fire to cleanse this," he mumbled, turning in a slow circle.

Orquell looked ill, too. "There must have been some storm of Gloom long ago to churn up this much flowstone. What we are seeing is a splash of the naether into this world, possibly cast when the gods first fell here after the Sundering."

Laurelle circled the room's only structure. It rose from floor to ceiling, as if the flowstone above had melted and sagged, dripping down into this tortured and twisted column. As Orquell's light played across it, she was sure she saw faces in the stone, screaming, melted faces. Then the torch would shift and the visages would vanish.

"Her throne," Orquell said, stopping before a niche just large enough for someone to sit within. "To commune with those that swim the naether."

Off to the side, Kytt began to lower to a lip of flowstone against one wall. Without turning from the throne, Orquell waved him away with his free hand.

"Not there, my young tracker," the master said. "That's a black altar. Can you not smell the blood?"

Kytt scrambled back, stumbling a bit in his haste. "I don't scent anything beyond those burnt wards."

Orquell nodded. "Maybe it's not so much a scent in the air. It's more like walking across a field where an ancient battle was once waged. The grass may be green, but if you stand very still, you can still sense the blood, an echo of pain."

Kytt glanced to Laurelle. They moved closer together, away

from the walls, but not too close to the throne. Laurelle fought an urge to run from the room.

Orquell made one more slow circle of the column. He ran his torch up and down its length. Finally, he stopped again before the niche, the throne of the witch. "She has begun her attack."

"Mirra?" Laurelle squeaked out.

He didn't answer. Instead, he lowered his head and stepped toward the column. "We don't have any more time."

Laurelle refused to follow him closer. "What are we supposed to do?"

Orquell motioned to the column, to the room, and beyond. "Close your eyes, strip away the natural stone, until only the unnatural flowstone is left. Do you know what you find?"

Laurelle tried to map in her mind's eye a picture of the streaking veins through which the stair had cut, leading at last to here.

"It would look like a great swirl of black flame, frozen to glassy stone. What are called *Boils*. I've seen smaller of them, but never one so large." He stepped back. "But though this old flame is turned to stone, it still burns with the fires of the naether. And where there is flame . . . ?" He glanced inquiringly at Laurelle.

She remembered his earlier lesson. "There is also shadow."

He offered her a tired smile. The coldness that had crept into his manner warmed away. "Very good," he said. "This flame does indeed still cast shadows, but not ordinary darkness."

"Gloom," Laurelle mumbled.

His smile deepened. "Exactly. You might do well to pay a pilgrimage to Takaminara. I believe you'd fare well with her." He turned back to the twisted column.

Laurelle could now almost imagine it as a frozen whirlwind of fire.

"But you are right," Orquell said. "It casts Gloom like a pure flame casts shadow. But worse for us now, this flame also smokes with power, drifting upward, fueling the witch with dire forces. That is what we must stop if we are to help Tashijan."

"How do we do that?"

He returned his attention to the chair. "By stanching this fire. Her power flows from the naether, along this column, and smokes high."

"But how do you stanch a fire that is set in stone?" Kytt asked.

Laurelle remembered the master's example on the stair. "You must purify it . . . with fire."

Orquell glanced back at her, his milky eyes appraising her anew. "You continue to surprise me, Mistress Hothbrin." He returned his attention to the black stone. "The heart of this Boil must be purified. Burnt out to kill the poison. Setting fire against fire."

He shifted closer to the niche.

Laurelle felt a stab of fear. She didn't like the master to be so near to that black flame. But he stopped and turned back. He slipped out a bag of powder. She recognized it as the same bag where he had stored the remaining powder that fueled his torch. Orquell opened the bag and sprinkled the powder over his head, shoulders, and across chest and back.

"What are you . . . ?" she began.

"It will take more than just fire to purify this," Orquell said. "Someone has to enter this pyre, direct the flame. It is the only way to stop the witch. But there is great power flowing through here. One touch and your will and mind will be burnt away, lost to whatever hides below in the naether." He faced the niche one last time. "Perhaps that is what happened to Mirra. Perhaps she discovered this place or was maliciously directed down here. Either way, once she sat on this throne, she would've been lost forever. Yet if someone who was purified sat here . . ."

Laurelle again proved her understanding of the intent behind his words. "No."

"I must. It is the only way." Orquell held out his torch toward her. "Once I sit down, you have to set me on fire."

Kathryn yelled to be heard above the bleat of a horn. "More flames! Get more torches! Where's that barrel of oil?"

She manned the line on the sixth floor. The lower five were gone. All of Tashijan, those still living, were crammed into a mere ten levels.

Gerrod climbed up from below, his armor reflecting the firelight that shone down the stairs. He led another handful of knights. All their cloaks were charred at the edges. The witch's attack had proven especially difficult to thwart. The same fires that shunned her black *ghawls* shed the speed and force of shadows from the knights, weakening them when they needed to be strongest.

Also the wraiths still harried the line at top, dividing their full force.

Gerrod and the other knights cleared the picket here. "That's the last," he said, joining her.

The other knights climbed past. One of the knights carried one of his brothers over a shoulder. The body smoked. She caught a glimpse of a blackened arm hanging from beneath a cloak.

"Coming through!" a shout erupted behind them.

Two men rolled a barrel of oil down the steps. Others helped slow its descent with hands as they passed, lest it roll out of control.

"If we cast much more fire below," Gerrod warned, "we may burn Stormwatch out from under us."

Kathryn remembered the blackened arm. "Rather a clean fire than the corruption wielded by Mirra."

A piercing scream echoed up to them, full of pain.

It wasn't human—nor was it daemon.

Horse.

Kathryn had emptied the stables into the lower level of Stormwatch as the wraiths attacked. The thatching of the old structure had offered no protection against Ulf's winged legion. So she had led the entire stable inside, horse and horsemen.

"We couldn't clear them," Gerrod said. "There was no space up here for the horses. Climbing stairs, all the fires . . . Horsemaster Poll even tried blinding them with blankets. They were too panicked."

She remembered the stablemen's refusal to abandon their charges, hiding with their horses in the cold barns.

"What about the barnstaff?"

Gerrod shook his head. "I don't know. They were ordered to clear, but . . ." He shook his head.

It had been chaos for the past half bell.

"I have to go down there," Kathryn said.

"Are you mad?" Gerrod said, almost sputtering in his helmet.

"She is slaying the horses on purpose. Most cruelly. She knows my love for those horses. And if there are any of the barnstaff still down there—"

"They're not worth the risk," Gerrod said too quickly. He raised a hand to his forehead. "I didn't mean to make it sound like that."

She touched his arm. "I know. But they're all good folk who man our stables, every one of them. I will take a few knights, ripe with power, and strike a fast assault. Just to see if any of the barnstaff are down there."

But in her heart Kathryn knew they were down there.

Gerrod stared a long time at her, unmoving, a statue in bronze. "Go," he whispered, but she knew it took all his reserve to utter that one word.

Kathryn had never loved him more. She didn't need his approval, but his concession fueled her when she needed it most. She turned to two knights. "Bastian and Tyllus. You're with me."

They came quickly, without question.

They both bore the Fiery Cross, but she knew they were stout of heart and had proven themselves countless times this day. She told them what she proposed. They nodded and gathered what was necessary.

"Let's go." Kathryn crossed the picket and headed down. "Send word to Argent at the top line," she called back to Gerrod.

He lifted a bronze arm in acknowledgment, then vanished from sight as she fled around a turn in the stair. Fires still blazed here, but after another two turns, all the torches were guttered. Darkness filled the lower stairs.

Kathryn pulled up hood and masklin. Despite knowing what lurked in the depths of that darkness, she still sank gratefully into the shadows, wicking their power along all the threads of her cloak. She whisked away from sight, flanked by her knights.

As they passed the next levels, a few fires were noted burning off down various passages, but the stairs remained dark. She descended the last level with more care. The screaming horse had gone silent.

As she made the final turn below, she noted a glow rising from below, but it was not firelight. The cast was sickly, a sheen of emerald. She signaled her other knights with the barest reveal of her sword. She would take the inside wall of the stairs, the others would take the outside.

She went down first, one step at a time. With her eyes so attuned to shadow, she could discern enough in the darkness to tell daemon from shadow. But only when very close.

Where were they all?

She had expected a few sentries on the stairs.

She reached low enough to see below. Between her Graced eyes and the greenish light, it was easy to see the horse sprawled across the stone floor. It lay in a pool of blood, its throat cut.

Beyond its bulk stood the source of the light.

Mirra.

She leaned on a staff that glowed with the fetid luminance. She looked a monster. Her hair was burnt to her scalp. One side of her face was a blistered ruin. The handiwork of Orquell.

"Hurry, boy!" she yelled with a wave of her staff.

Movement to the right drew Kathryn's eye. She shifted more to the stair's center for a clearer view. She saw a small form walking a horse down from where they were corraled by the main gate.

She recognized them both.

The horse was a piebald, black on white.

Stoneheart.

The stallion's legs shook and his flanks trembled. He smelled the blood, certainly heard the earlier scream. But he minded the boy on the lead. Someone he trusted.

The stableboy Mychall.

The boy walked on legs just as trembling as the horse's.

"Is that her favorite horse?" Mirra asked.

"Y-yes, mum. Please don't hurt my da."

Mirra swung her staff to point toward the opposite wall. Kathryn had to slip two steps lower to see the remaining horror here. Pinned against the far wall, bolted through both hands into the stone, hung Horsemaster Poll, Mychall's father. At the man's toes, the darkness shifted with denser shadows; a clot of *ghawls* guarded him.

"Boy!" he called to his son. "Why did you stay when I told you to go?"

"Da . . . let my da down . . ."

Kathryn could surmise what had happened. The horsemaster had refused to abandon his charges, but he'd had enough force of will to drive the other stablemen and -women up higher. Not his son, though. Mychall must have snuck back or hidden close. Either way, they'd both been discovered and their love used against them.

"When we're through here, I'll let your father go," Mirra said with feigned warmth. "Walk that pretty stallion over here."

Mirra lifted a long sickle in her other hand.

Mychall approached, his shoulders shaking in silent sobs, face wet with tears.

Kathryn shifted and motioned to the others. She lifted her hand and dropped her shadows enough for the two knights to see. She pointed where she wanted them to strike. She didn't need to see their acknowledgments.

She raised her hand, fingers out. She counted down. When she formed a fist, small flashes of fiery Grace ignited the wicks of two small barrels, one held by each knight. They were lobbed down into the lower floor, landing precisely where she wanted.

The first struck the dead horse, bursting up with fire, separating witch from boy. The second flew and struck the clot of *ghawls* by the pinned horsemaster.

The three knights followed the flight of the flaming barrels, hitting the floor about the same time the fires burst. Stoked with shadows, Bastian and Tyllus dashed toward the horsemaster. They had an oiled brand in each hand, dipping them into the fresh fire as they passed, igniting the torches.

Kathryn did the same with a single brand, but she also whistled sharply.

Stoneheart had reared when the barrels blew, yanking Mychall off his feet. But he responded to Kathryn's whistle, desperate for the familiar. He swung toward her. She still had enough shadows, despite the fires, to leap onto his bare back. She guided him with her legs, turning toward Mirra, her sword in her other hand.

But Mirra was not one surprised into inaction.

She had shifted and grabbed Mychall by the hair, and now had the sickle at his throat.

"No!" Poll moaned.

Below his toes, the two knights fought the *ghawls* among the fires, armed with their two brands. But they could not hold off the daemons long enough to free the father.

Atop the horse, Kathryn watched more daemon knights boil out from the far passages. Cloaks rustled behind her. The stairs they had come down flowed with a river of darkness.

A trap.

She gaped at the sight. She had never imagined the witch's legion numbered so many. Tashijan would be overrun.

Mirra must have sensed her despair. "You surprised me, Kathryn." Her voice sounded so familiar. "I thought I'd have to kill more than one horse—or at least the boy—to draw you down here."

"Why?" she finally choked out, the one word encompassing so much.

The answer, though, was quite small. Mirra nodded her chin toward Kathryn. "I want my diadem back."

Kathryn stared into the face of madness.

"And to make you suffer—all of you suffer—for the pain you've caused me—that oily-tongued *rub-aki*." She spat on the stone. "I was going to simply send my legion through you like a fire through chaff, but after this cruel burning, I want you all to end your lives screaming."

She met Kathryn's eye squarely.

"We'll start first with this boy."

Laurelle shook her head. "I can't light you on fire."

Orquell turned to Kytt, holding out the torch. The boy backed several steps, almost knocking himself flat on the altar before catching his legs. The master turned again to Laurelle.

"You must, Mistress Hothbrin."

Laurelle kept her hands clasped together between her breasts.

Orquell lowered the torch and stepped closer. "Look at me, Laurelle."

She reluctantly met those milky eyes.

"What god do I bow down to?" he asked, teasing her eyes more firmly to him. "Fire is my comfort. Flame is my passion. What I do, I do willingly. I'll not say gladly. I won't lie to you. But often life asks much of you, and you either honor life by answering with all your heart, or you cower your way into your grave."

Laurelle took a shuddering breath.

Orquell read her reluctant hesitation. "I know what I ask of you is horrible. But I am *rub-aki*. We are trained to withstand a fire's burn and still hold our minds. Only I can do what must be done here." He glanced up. "Lives already end above because we hesitate below."

She searched upwards with him, not so much looking for answers as asking for forgiveness. As Orquell lowered his eyes, he met her gaze. A smile formed as he read her decision.

"Very good, Mistress Hothbrin."

Kathryn could do nothing to save the boy.

She sat atop her horse amid a sea of black *ghawls*. Bastian and Tyllus were trapped in a corner. She suspected the pair lived only at the whim of the witch. More fodder for her cruel games.

"Do not turn your face," Mirra warned, "or I'll make him suffer worse."

Kathryn would not have looked away. Mychall was frozen in terror. All she could do was offer her vigilance, her witness. She met his frightened gaze, his weeping eyes begging her to save him.

First Penni, then the squires, now Mychall . . .

"What? No tears for the boy?"

Kathryn shifted her eyes to Mirra. "You taught me well," she said. "Tears are for later. After you've killed your enemy, only then do you mourn your fallen."

Mirra cackled at her words. "Then I'll give you much to cry about." She lifted the sickle high.

"No!" the horsemaster moaned.

Kathryn merely stared into Mychall's eyes, letting him see her love.

It was such focus that alerted Kathryn to a shudder along Mirra's raised arm. Kathryn felt something rush through the room like a gust of wind, but the air didn't move. Still, the passage stoked the fires momentarily brighter, knocking back the *ghawls*.

Kathryn responded. She kicked Stoneheart, but as usual, he somehow read her intent, knowing her heart or sensing her hips tilting forward. Either way, he burst forward under her.

He leaped the edge of flames that separated her from the witch.

Mirra looked up, a cry on her lips. The sickle fell from her fingers.

Surprised now, are you?

Kathryn whipped her sword down in a savage swipe, but Mirra leaned back at the last moment. The tip of Kathryn's sword sliced through the witch's mouth, splitting her cheeks ear to ear as she screamed in rage. But it was not a fatal blow.

Mirra tripped back, sporting a mouth as wide as her face, blood pouring in a river down her chin and jaw. She howled and revealed the full gape of her mouth.

She lifted both arms, ready to unleash her legion upon Kathryn.

It left her belly exposed.

Mychall rose up from the floor, forgotten by the witch. He bore her sickle in hand. Using both arms, he hacked the blade through her gut.

She screamed anew, stumbling back, spilling intestine.

Kathryn had Stoneheart turned. She leaped back to the witch, but instead of attacking, she bent down and scooped Mychall one-armed up to her. He had been about to be skewered by one of the *ghawls*.

Not this night.

Mirra fell to her knees. She crawled to her staff, but the fire dimmed out of it. She grabbed it like a drowning man might a floating log. But the fires in it continued to die. And as the glow ebbed, the flames in the room brightened, as if a smothering smoke had lifted.

The *ghawls* shifted about in confusion.

Mirra rocked back, holding her staff, almost shaking it.

One last cry, and she fell back in a pool of her own blood and entrails.

Dead.

Laurelle knelt on the stone. The torch lay nearby, forgotten, still burning. She held her hands over her face. Kytt crouched over her, an arm around her shoulders. He squeezed her tight. She leaned into him.

"Come," he said. "We must go."

Laurelle still could not stand. She could still picture Orquell smiling through the flames as he burnt, seated on the witch's throne. The powder over his body had spread the flame quickly, wafting hay and sweetness. Laurelle suspected she would never again enter a barn without retching.

Though the scent had been pleasant, the sight had been horrible.

His clothes had burnt, his skin had blackened, and the flames contracted his body, as if he were trying to curl in the seat to read a book.

She didn't close her eyes.

She thought she owed him that much for his sacrifice.

But she failed at the end. The flames and heat writhed his body, twisting and consuming it. She dropped and covered her face. At that moment, she heard whispers in those last flames. Notes of gentle consolation. But she didn't know if they were meant for her or for the tortured master.

Then came a final fluttering rush of flames, like a hundred ravens taking flight—followed by a heavy silence.

"Come," Kytt urged. "He's gone."

"I know . . ." she moaned.

"No, I mean he's gone. See for yourself."

His curious words finally drew her up. She still needed his help.

Kytt lifted her.

The black column had turned solid white, along with a splash across the arched roof where flames had licked. The rest of the Boil remained glassy and dark, but the heart had been purified.

She stared into the niche, expecting to see a pile of charred bone. But it was empty. The space was the pristine white of new snow. Not even a sprinkle of ash or bone.

She reached out a hand.

"Take care," Kytt warned.

But Laurelle knew it was safe, purified by the selfless fire. Her fingers brushed the seat. As she made contact, words rang in her head, whether some echoing trace of the master or merely her own memory.

Very good, Mistress Hothbrin . . .

Either way, she offered a ghost of a smile.

Then the stone underfoot began to tremble.

Kytt grabbed her and drew her away.

Stumbling with him, she glanced around her. "The Boil," she said, picturing the black flame trapped in granite. "The naether wakes to the plug Orquell planted here. They are fighting back."

The quaking continued, rattling the roots of Tashijan.

Laurelle and Kytt fled up the stairs. Ahead, loud crashes echoed down to them as large sections of rock struck the stairs.

"It's all coming down!" Kytt cried out.

Kathryn felt the tower shake. She sat astride Stoneheart. Mychall hugged her back. She brandished a torch toward the few *ghawls* that still kept to the halls. The rest had fled in every direction, no longer guided by the will of the witch.

Mirra's body still lay bloody on the stone.

As the shaking grew more violent, the last few *ghawls* lost their wills and fled, emptying the hall.

A cry sounded behind her as Horsemaster Poll was finally freed from the wall. He fell to the floor, but Bastian caught him around the waist. He regained his legs, hugging his spiked hands to his chest.

"I kin stand," he mumbled weakly.

"Da!" Mychall slid from Stoneheart's back. He slammed into his father, wrapping his arms around his waist.

The quaking continued. It seemed to arise from deep underground.

Tyllus must have read her concern. "We'll get these two upstairs. You'd best see to the pickets."

She nodded to the two knights. "Keep them safe."

She nudged Stoneheart toward the stairs. He had refused to climb before, but whether trusting this rider or merely happy to flee the blood and horror here, he burst up the stairs now. Kathryn leaned forward, balancing her weight.

The horse clopped loudly, climbing out of darkness and into the flame-lit upper levels. The picket came into line ahead. Fire and black knights filled the stairs. A small cheer rose from them as they saw her clatter into view, astride the handsome stallion, sweated and shining in the firelight.

She dismounted by the line and left the stallion with a knight she knew was familiar with horses. She forded the picket and climbed toward the level of the fieldroom.

She met Argent as he climbed down from the line above.

"What was that shaking?" the warden asked, breathless.

Kathryn shook her head, but the quakes were already fading away. Whatever had been shaken up below was quieting back down. "I don't know, but the witch is dead."

"What?"

"Slain. Her legion routed and in full panic."

Argent's eye brightened. Together they hurried toward the fieldroom. "That's the first fair news in many a bell. Maybe we can hold out yet!"

They reached the fieldroom to find Delia and Gerrod by the shuttered window, peering out the small opening.

Gerrod turned to them. There was something grim about his stance. He lifted an arm, urging them to join him.

Kathryn stepped around one side of the map table, Argent the other. They met again at the window. Argent touched Delia's shoulder to make room. She slid back.

Bending, Kathryn peered out into the dark stormswept night. It took a moment for her eyes to adjust, but it appeared that the winds had subsided.

"Lord Ulf has pulled back his wraiths," Gerrod said. "At least those loose out there."

"Is he retreating?" Argent asked.

Gerrod remained silent.

Kathryn saw why. The shield wall was coated with ice. As

she watched, black rock grew white with hoarfrost, spreading out in a crystallizing pattern, consuming the wall.

All hope went cold.

Her voice dropped to a dry whisper.

"The ice is coming."

22

A CROWN OF AN ANCIENT KING

PERRYL'S POISONOUS BLADE PRESSED AGAINST TYLAR'S chest, pinching through his cloak. He held the blade off by sheer trembling muscle. Rivenscryr crossed against the daemon's sword.

Pinned against the wall of the hide tent, Tylar could not maneuver. His legs shook. Even the hand that bore Rivenscryr had begun to gnarl as the venom inside him spread. The exertion only sped the corruption.

"Perryl . . ." he begged.

If he could somehow reach him . . .

But the pale face remained impassive, no anger or fury, simply certainty. The face of a predator in a dark sea.

Then a momentary flicker passed through the fire in the daemon's eyes, like a brush of wind. Tylar shoved with his remaining strength.

Perryl went stumbling back, plainly disoriented.

Something had happened.

Free, Tylar lifted Rivenscryr. He judged how to use the moment. Flee or attack. Overhead, rain pelted the tent, beating against it like a hide drum. With his body weakened, he could not match swords with Perryl.

In that moment of hesitation, a splash of fire nosed under the tent flap and wiggled inside. Pupp's molten form hissed with rain. Fiery eyes took in the scene, and he trotted blithely to the room's center.

The *ghawl* retreated another step, spooked by the appearance. Pupp's fire and light stripped some of the shadows from Perryl, revealing cloak and pale skin. Again Tylar saw the strange translucent oil that was his new skin, squirming beneath with dark snaking muscles.

Revulsion filled him anew.

Perhaps with Pupp's help . . .

But the creature seemed to have come with another purpose. Pupp trotted to Tylar, molten spikes bristling. He carried something in his mouth. It shone brilliantly, lit by Pupp's fiery tongue.

Once near, Pupp spat it at his toes—then vanished away.

Tylar stared at what lay at his feet. A black diamond, not unlike those that adorned a shadowknight's sword. His own knightly blade lay on the floor, abandoned after cleaving off Krevan's arm. And in that one breath, he understood. Only one stone brought Pupp to life.

Brant's stone.

He stared between the diamond and the abandoned sword and understood. The stone was somehow meant to adorn Rivenscryr. But it wasn't by wits alone that he came by this insight. In his grip, the sword's hilt seemed to ooze tighter around his fingers. It grew warmer. He had felt such stirrings before in the sword, but never such a muscular spasm as this. Tylar sensed the sword's lust for the stone—to complete itself.

Tylar bent his one good knee.

Perryl must have comprehended the danger and surged forward, his indecisiveness burnt away by fear. Tylar reached out and slammed the hilt of his sword atop the stone. He felt the pommel open and bite into the stone.

As the contact was made, all the air in the room blew outward, rattling hide walls and roof, sucking the wind out of Tylar's chest. Perryl was blasted back, cloak whipping.

Rivenscryr blazed for a heartbeat in that airless moment.

Then all the weight and substance collapsed back.

Walls and roof sagged. Air fell atop them. Tylar felt as if the world had grown smaller, squeezing tighter around him. He remembered Miyana's description when she held the stone, a gathering back of what was sundered.

Tylar felt an echo of it. He gained his legs, less aching. The hand that had gripped Rivenscryr had straightened its bones, allowing him to hold tighter, more certain. He wasn't cured. His knee was still frozen in scarred bone. His side still burnt with fire. But somehow the stone in the sword had gathered Meeryn's aethryn closer to its naethryn, the two remaining fractions of the god of the Summering Isles. And in that moment, like Miyana, the naethryn found comfort enough to rally, to stave off the spreading poison a little longer.

Straightening and raising the brilliant sword—Rivenscryr whole and united—Tylar faced the daemon lord. He took a step forward, but Perryl sensed the change in balance here. Already shaken by whatever had flickered through him, the daemon swept up his cloak and spun into the back shadows of the tent.

Tylar pursued him, but his leg remained hobbled, slowing him. By the time he reached the back, he found only darkness.

The daemon had fled.

A scream burst from outside.

The others . . .

Tylar turned back to the tent flap and dodged through it. He almost tripped over Krevan's body, sprawled in the mud, soaked by rain and blood. Tylar knelt long enough to check for signs of life. He placed a palm on the man's chest. He breathed. Alive. No ordinary man would have survived, but Krevan was Wyr-born, possessed of a living blood. It sustained him, but barely. He would need some attention.

But not now.

Tylar surged up, drawing more shadows. One of the *ghawls* unfolded out of the darkness with a screech. Perryl had fled, but he'd left his dogs behind. Tylar easily blocked the thrusting black blade and parried to the attack. He slid the newly forged Rivenscryr through the creature's gut.

It was like shoving a red-hot iron into cold swamp water.

Flesh exploded with a sickening wash of foul steam and corruption. For a moment, as Tylar yanked his sword out, a tangle of black tentacles followed, bursting out of the wound, writhing in the air. But they did not belong in this world and shivered into a sludging collapse, taking the cloaked body with them.

Tylar spun away. He aimed for a glow beyond the edge of the rock pinnacle, where he had left the others. With a speed born of shadow, he reached the others in two breaths. They clustered around a dying fire, a pack of *ghawls* nestled tight about them. But like Perryl, these seemed directionless, still held off by even this feeble fire.

Such caution would not last forever.

Tylar swept up to them and through them, cleaving a swath of death. Bodies fell in a wash of fetid steam, tentacles flickered like black flames, then died away. A pair of *ghawls* fled in opposite directions, mindless with terror, plainly intending to lose themselves forever in the hinterlands. All others lay dead around the fire.

Except Perryl.

Where had he gone? Off to the rogues?

Tylar stared out at the spread of black water. Rain pebbled the surface, but the downpour was already ending.

Calla appeared at his side, her face a mask of worry. "Krevan?" she managed to ask, though she feared the answer.

Tylar nodded. "Alive. By the tent. But he needs help." He pointed. "Grab the giant and get him to carry Krevan back to the fire."

Calla ran to obey.

Rogger came up to him. "So you fixed your sword."

Tylar glanced over to him.

"We sent Pupp with the diamond," Rogger explained. "Figured his fiery form would pass unmolested through those skaggin' *ghawls*, while we didn't dare."

Tylar turned the blade, examining its brilliant length. The deaths of the daemons had failed to douse the blade. It required no replenishing blood. Made whole by the diamond, the blade now abided. The stone held it firm in this world.

"But how . . . ?" Tylar finally muttered. "The diamond . . ."

"You can thank Brant and Dart for that," Rogger said. "Dart for her special eyes, Brant for his insight. Those two make a nice pair."

Tylar noted them standing hand in hand. Then counted the others. Someone was missing.

"Lorr," Rogger said, noting his search. "He was slain protecting the young ones."

Dart stumbled closer to the water. "But he fell right there," she said, pointing to the shallows near the bank. "Now he's gone. Could he still be alive?"

Hope rang in her voice.

But in answer, something dark surged up in the water, humping black scales, then vanishing back into the depths.

"Taken," Brant said, coming up and putting his arm around Dart. He understood what was written in the ripples. "Nothing goes to waste in the forest of the world. It is the Way."

Dart covered her face, but Brant plainly found comfort in such an end. And maybe he was right. Lorr had been a creature of the forest. It was only fitting he should return to it again.

A scrape of leather on stone drew their attention around.

From the nearby pinnacle, a handful of women descended on ropes, landing lightly. They were all that was left of Meylan's tribe. One stepped forward. Tylar could not say if this was Meylan or another.

"Wyrd Bennifren," she said dourly. "We spied him falling."

She swung around and headed toward the camp.

Tylar had forgotten about the Wyr-lord. Bennifren had gone off to fetch a repostilary for Tylar's humour. He had no idea of the strange man's fate, and normally he wouldn't care—but there were the promised maps.

"Keep the others by the fire," Tylar ordered Rogger.

The thief nodded, adding wet wood to the fire.

Tylar set off with the women. They led the way into the nest of tents. Bodies were strewn everywhere, blackened by the burn of the *ghawls'* swords. It had been a slaughter.

They found Bennifren's milk mare collapsed face-first in the mud, just as blackened. One of the women knelt down and heaved the body over. Beneath the charred remains, still swaddled, lay Bennifren, pink and hale, sheltered and hidden by the dead woman.

One arm lifted weakly. He gasped and sucked air, plainly only moments from suffocation. His eyelids flickered open, wet with tears. He breathed deeply for several breaths, then coughed a meanness back into his eyes.

His gaze found Tylar.

"Find the rogues . . ." he seethed sibilantly.

"I'll need the maps."

His eyes flicked to the woman who freed him. "Meylan, fetch them for him."

So the woman was Meylan. How the Wyr-lord could tell the

women apart was a mystery to Tylar. Meylan ran off, while another gathered their lord up into her arms.

"And what about our bargain?" Tylar asked.

The Wyr-lord turned to him. Perhaps he was still rattled, or perhaps it was a generosity born of fury, but Wyrd Bennifren finally relinquished a debt. "It is forgiven . . ." A hand reached out and tiny fingers clutched the edge of Tylar's cloak. "But only if you free those rogues. Make the Cabal suffer . . . make them pay."

It was a bargain Tylar accepted gladly.

"Bound and done," he promised.

Dart stared at the strange craft, lent to them by the Wyr.

She stood on the bank, chewing on the back of her thumb, nervous. It looked like a small flippercraft cleaved open through the middle, leaving only the bottom half intact. The *flitterskiff* was a shallow-keeled boat lined on each side by six long bronze paddles, but these required no oarsmen to row. It was a mekanical craft that ran on alchemies of water.

"And Air?" Rogger asked as he knelt beside the boat, examining one of the paddles. He ran a hand along its double-hulled side. The alchemies ran between the hulls.

She had seen Rogger test it under the guidance of a squat Wyr-man, one of the few survivors. The thief was to be their pilot. None of the Wyr could venture where they intended to travel, to where seersong bent the will of those Graced. Like Eylan, they would be easily captured by the song. Even Krevan had to be left here under Calla's care. He would be a threat once within earshot of seersong.

They readied to leave.

Tylar clasped Krevan's good shoulder. His other was cross-wrapped in a large bandage. Dart had learned that the pirate owed his life to his Wyr heritage. Krevan had been born without a heart. Through his veins ran a living blood, a blood that had refused to flow out those same veins when his arm had been cleaved away. Still, he would need time and rest to heal.

Tylar turned to the pirate's swordmate. "Keep him safe, Calla, until we return."

"I will," she said sternly.

Malthumalbaen helped push the flitterskiff off the bank and into the water. It had sat rather crooked in the sand, a rough landing by Rogger, but it was his first attempt.

The giant held the boat for Brant and Dart to climb aboard. Brant gave her a hand, and they found a bench near the front. The skiff was large enough to hold a good dozen. So they had plenty of room, even with a giant on board.

Rogger hopped in and crossed to the bow, where foot pedals and a wheel sat before a scooped wooden seat. He sank into it, rubbing his palms.

Tylar left Krevan's side and splashed into the water. Grabbing the starboard rail, he struggled a bit, confounded by a bad leg. Malthumalbaen helped him with a push on his backside. Tylar straightened once aboard, his cheeks slightly flushed.

With the sword at his belt, Tylar certainly did seem somewhat more solid of foot—but he still hobbled. While Rogger had learned to wield the flitterskiff, Tylar had tested his new sword. It would be best to know its abilities before venturing into unknown territories.

Applying a bit of force, he found the black diamond could be removed from the pommel, but once free, the sword's blade vanished, and the stone returned again to black rock, both snuffed out. The attempt disturbed them all, especially when Tylar gasped as his body crumbled into further ruin. Still, it took only another drop of Dart's blood to ignite the stone and feed it back to the pommel. The gold melted over it hungrily, and the silver blade sprouted anew. Tylar's body also straightened a bit.

Not much, but enough.

But Dart had overheard him with Rogger. *The poison still spreads. Some poison born of Chrism's blood. The sword and stone may stave it off somewhat, but I can feel my bones' ache leaching outward.*

Another reason for haste.

The gift of the flitterskiff was gladly accepted. It would speed them where they needed to go. They also had the Wyr maps and knew the straightest path to an island deep out in the flooded forest, where the rogues were snared.

The Wyr maps were vital.

The flooded forest was a maze of soggy hillocks, slower mossy mires, rocky outcroppings, flat expanses of open water, and twisting currents within the larger breadth of the flood-waters.

Tylar limped to Rogger's side. He leaned on the back of the chair.

"Are you sure you won't run us straight into a tree?"

Rogger glanced back. "Do you mean I'm supposed to avoid those?"

The boat suddenly rocked. The bow's nose rose as Malthumalbaen clambered aboard. He looked ill at ease. The flitter-skiff was all air and water. Born of loam, he looked little comforted by this means of travel. Or maybe he had witnessed Rogger's bobbling struggle with the strange craft out in the water.

Malthumalbaen sprawled in the skiff's stern, filling the space, one hand on each rail.

With everyone aboard, Tylar took the bench behind Rogger and pointed forward.

"Let's go."

"Hold tight!" Rogger twisted a knob to open the flow of alchemies.

The seat vibrated under Dart's rear. She peeked over the rail as the paddles began to beat, churning water, wafting them forward. Then they beat faster and faster, blurring away. The force of the churn drove them forward—*then up*. The skiff rose to the tips of its fluttering paddles, lifting the keel free from the drag of the water. Unfettered, the craft sped like its namesake: the flitterfly. It buzzed over the water, skimming the surface with its paddles.

They raced faster than a horse could gallop.

Leaning close, Rogger took care to keep an eye on the trees. As directed by the Wyr-man, he stuck to the flattest water, avoiding rocks and floating logs with careful turns of the wheel.

"Do you have to go so skaggin' fast?" Malthumalbaen groaned.

Rogger called back. "While we've got clear water, I'm burning alchemy. But according to that Wyr-master of the boat, we'll be wishing for open water before we reach this island."

Tylar shifted forward, speaking in Rogger's ear. Dart could not make out his words, but from all the pointing, Tylar was directing Rogger's path as keenly as possible in this watery wood.

Dart sat back. Her hand rested in Brant's. She hadn't planned to put it there, but there it was. They watched the passing hinterlands together. The moons had appeared again as the rains ended and the clouds blew apart. The greater moon had joined her sister, casting enough light off the water to see fairly well.

But strange luminescences glowed in the dark. Glittering green mosses appeared, like those in the dry wood, and also red shining molds on tree trunks, and glowing yellow puffs that exploded out at them as they passed.

But beauty in the hinterlands also hid horror.

"Don't breathe any of that," Rogger warned, nodding at the glowing puffs. "It sets in your lungs and births worms that will eat their way out."

Dart sank lower in her seat, glad now for the craft's speed.

Still, the Wyr-master proved right. Within half a bell, the trees grew closer and closer, bunching around them. Rogger was forced to slow. Their keel sank back to the water as the alchemies were trimmed.

Their speed remained swift, but not the maddened flight of before.

Rogger sped them through the thickening woods. As the trees grew closer, the way darkened. Rogger circled around one of the spars of rock that jutted out of the landscape. Here the waters grew sluggish as the currents of the floodwaters eddied around the pinnacle. Thick rafts of algae and weed choked the slower waters and stifled the paddles.

They were forced to proceed no faster than a man could row, lest they risk breaking some of the paddles.

And still the trees grew taller, the canopy thicker, blocking all moonlight.

Tylar lit a small torch to check his map.

"I could use one of those up front," Rogger griped. "I can barely see past my nose, let alone this pointy bow."

Brant squeezed Dart's hand and let go. "I'll do it," he said and scooted down the bench.

He collected one of the larger torches, lit it off of Tylar's brand, and moved forward to join Rogger. Brant steadied himself with a hand on the port rail and held the torch high. The firelight stretched across the water.

Able to see, Dart glanced up. The canopy overhead was draped with giant striped vines. The firelight played along their bellies, making them seem to shift and slide. Then a scaled head snaked down out of the twist, hissing to reveal fangs as long as her outstretched hand.

The firelight stirred others, warming their scales.

Dart squeaked in alarm, sliding off her seat to the planks below.

Other eyes noted what roosted in their rafters. One of the serpents uncoiled and slid out of the tangle, crashing to the boat's center with a writhe of muscles, as thick around as Dart's leg.

She grabbed the rail, ready to leap into the water.

But Malthumalbaen sighed, snatched the snake by the tail, and whipped it over his shoulder, as if tossing away a gnawed bone. Its coils splashed into the waters behind them.

He returned to resting his chin on his fist.

"It's only a little snake," he mumbled.

Rogger eked more alchemy through the mekanicals. With a whisper of paddles, they sped out from under the serpents' nest. Clear of the pinnacles, they found a less clogged section of the flooded forest, where the currents were swifter.

Brant kept his torch burning.

Dart eventually calmed enough to return to her bench.

Rogger guided them through a watery maze of rocks and hillocks. "Straightest path, my arse," he grumbled.

Tylar checked the map to the territory. He looked far from convinced that they were on the right track. He looked up and frowned. "If we could see a few stars . . ."

Despite the dangers, Dart appreciated the occasional handsome view that opened up. A long lane of water lilies that balanced tall-stemmed flowers atop green pads as wide around as Dart was tall. Hanging nests of violet-breasted swifts, so tightly packed that they looked like grapes on a vine. As their boat passed, the birds took to wing without a single peep. But their passage set their hollow nests to bumping against each other, sounding like tuned wood pipes, wafting out a beautiful warbling.

Up ahead, a tall tree swung into view, rising in distinct tiers as if trimmed by the hand of man rather than random growth. Brant's flames revealed thousands of small blooms, white as snow against the green leaf, all tucked in for the night.

As they swept closer, Dart watched one bloom open its petals. A fat little head beaded out toward them, eyes reflecting crimson. The petals spread wider to reveal wings.

Not hanging flowers.

Bats.

As their earlier passage had fluttered the swifts from their nest, the firelight did the same here, shaking the bats from their roost in a single explosion of wings. But unlike the swifts, the bats weren't fleeing.

"Torches!" Tylar yelled.

The flock swept toward the boat.

Malthumalbaen moved forward, rocking the boat, to grab two brands. Dart snatched one. In a breath, fires flared across the boat. Unfazed, the bats struck with needle-toothed fury. They landed on shoulder and arm, chest and leg. Teeth bit into skin, claws dug through cloth. Malthumalbaen was assaulted the worst, being the tallest and largest target.

Or maybe it was that he held two torches aloft.

Dart remembered how firelight woke the bats.

Maybe it angered them, too.

Testing this thought, Dart swatted a bat from her neck, then plunged the flaming end of her torch into the water. The fire died with a hiss of steam. The flurry of wings shifted away from her. One bat on her arm leaped toward the giant, despite the greater danger of his slapping hands and massive pinching fingers.

"It's our fire!" Dart called out. "The flames goad them to attack!"

The flames were quickly doused. Malthumalbaen threw his last brand far behind the boat. It flew end over end, blowing brighter by the passage, trailing embers. The flock of bats took wing after the flying torch.

They all sank down into the darkness, scratched and bitten.

"Those mites are far worse than any snake," Malthumalbaen grumbled, sucking at a wounded finger.

They continued onward without torches.

"It shouldn't be far," Tylar finally said, rolling his map, squeezing the scroll tight in his hands.

Proving his word, a glow appeared through a tangle of woods ahead. Tylar motioned Rogger to slip out of the clearer current in the flooded wood and edge more slowly through the choked channels. It would be easier to hide their approach among the heavier bushes and low branches.

As they left the swifter current, the waters thickened with weed and algae. Rogger cut the alchemy to a trickle, drifting more than powered.

The glow shone from directly ahead.

"Does anyone else smell that?" Rogger whispered, nose pinching.

"Brimstone," Tylar mumbled, followed by a hushing motion.

Rogger drifted them closer, nosing them through bushes. He finally stifled the alchemical flows completely. Malthumalbaen propelled them from there on, reaching to tree limbs and bushes to pull them toward the glow.

"Far enough!" Rogger warned in a whisper.

They all shifted forward, weighting the bow down. The giant stepped back to steady the trim.

Dart scooted up beside Brant. Through a break in the foliage, the view opened to a monstrous sight.

An island rose from the center of an open expanse of water, a lake within the drowned woods. Six giant pinnacles rimmed the land, each tilting slightly outward. It made the entire island look like a half-submerged crown.

Dart saw that the inner surfaces of each pinnacle had been shaved flat. She could just make out etched pictures and symbols drawn upon the smoothed surfaces. It reminded her of the small circle of stones at the Wyr camp, covered with ancient writing.

Between the spires of the crown, low stone structures ringed the island. And in the center blazed a massive fire, shaking with green flame, shimmering off rock and stone wall.

"It's an old human settlement," Rogger said.

"Taken over by the Cabal," Tylar whispered. "The location is not random or mere opportunity. The Cabal sway their human allies with a false promise of an end to godly tyranny. What better stronghold than one of our old settlements, ripe with sentiment and history?"

"Why does the water boil and glow out in the lake here?" Dart asked. "Is it more Dark Grace?"

Dart stretched to view the extent of the boil. All around the island, circling it entirely, the water trembled and bubbled. Steam wafted in shimmering sheets, high and away. Here was the source of the brimstone. A deep crimson glow shone from the depths.

"No," Brant said, "it's not Dark Grace. I believe it's a flow from Takaminara, like the burn that cut a swath through Saysh Mal. She sends her molten fingers out into the hinterland."

"But why? Is she protecting the island?"

Rogger answered. "More like protecting the *world*. I wager if she had the chance, she'd melt the island to slag, but that green fire must be fueled by the rogues, keeping her at bay. There is little else she could do. Takaminara's influence beyond her realm is limited, and she is only one god against who knows how many rogues here."

Faintly, Dart heard a few sweet chords echoing across the waters, a forlorn note full of power. *Seersong*. But Tylar seemed unaffected. The stone, whetted and wedded to the sword, kept him safe.

Tylar stirred. "We'll have to move swiftly across the boiling water. Ride high and fast, and beach well up the strand. If we move now—"

A scream rose from the island, piercing with a wail of horror.

The force of it blew back the steam in a cold wash, turning steam to water and splashing it outward. As leaves dripped, they watched something rise out of the green fire, lit from below, though fiery in its own right. It twisted like smoke into the air, finally unfurling massive black wings. A cloak fell from its form and into the waiting flames.

"Perryl," Tylar moaned.

"He's been ilked into a wraith," Rogger said. "A wraithed daemon."

The beast screamed again, not quite with the force of his birth but fierce enough. Flapping high into the air. The power that welled from him could almost be tasted on the air.

"But who ilked him?" Dart asked.

Rogger answered. "Remember who wields this font of Dark Grace. A god who is well familiar with wind wraiths."

"Lord Ulf," Tylar said.

Rogger nodded. "He makes his final move."

The end came with a thunderous *crack*.

It shook Stormwatch.

"The Shield Wall!" Kathryn cried out and hurried to the fieldroom's window. Despite the terror, there was also a measure of relief. They had been waiting for the past bell, balanced between certain doom and frantic hope. A thousand plans had been proposed and discarded. Their only true defense was fiery pyres laced with alchemies devised by Gerrod and his fellow masters. But they had too little flame and too much territory to protect. More strategies were waged, to no avail.

So when the ice finally came, Kathryn could not dismiss a measure of relief, ready as ever to make this stand. She had kept the tower for this long night, against wraiths, against witches, against daemons.

Now she must stand fast against a god.

She peered out the window, joined by Gerrod on one side, and Argent and Delia on the other. Father and daughter stayed close. Too late perhaps to know each other truly, but not too late to be near.

Across the yard, as Kathryn watched, a large section of the Shield Wall caved inward, cracked from crown to root. A wall that had stood for four millennia.

Why this show of power? Why not simply freeze them out?

But Kathryn remembered Ulf's cold countenance. She knew it wasn't bluster here, some magnificent display to his might. That was not Lord Ulf. He meant to tear Tashijan down, wall by wall, tower by tower, brick by brick.

She remembered his words: *There is no way to weed this patch. Best to burn it and salt the ground.*

He meant to accomplish that end. It was why he built his ice all night, gathering the cold for this final assault. None would live—but more important to Ulf, nothing would stand afterward.

Another *crack* reverberated through the cold air. Another section of wall fell. And through the breaches, his ice flowed. Like a mighty exhalation from the storm's heart, an intense cold blew into Tashijan. The outer towers frosted over. Stone shattered with mighty pops. One wall of the Ryder's Tower burst as if struck by a fist. Its crenellated crown toppled with agonizing slowness, tilting, sliding, then crashing into the snow.

Kathryn heard echoes of annihilation coming from the other sides of Tashijan. Lord Ulf struck on all fronts. He bore his ice in a tightening noose around Stormwatch.

Kathryn tore her eyes away. The others did the same. Bearing witness would not save them; it would only instill despair.

After all the pickets this night, there remained only one more line to hold. "Sound the Shield Gong," she said.

Gerrod nodded and headed out to pass on the word.

It was their only plan.

All of Tashijan would gather in the Grand Court, in the heart of Stormwatch. The central Hearthstone was already aflame with alchemies. Pyres burnt at every door. They would make their last stand there.

All around, stone crashed and mortar moaned.

Kathryn turned to Argent and Delia. "Get to the Court," she said. "I will keep vigil for as long as possible."

"It is my place to be here," Argent said.

"Your place is at the last picket, Warden. With your people."

Argent's eye shone toward her, once again seeking some argument. Argent to the end. But a hand touched his shoulder.

"Father . . . let's go . . ."

The fire dimmed to something warmer as he turned. He touched the fingers on his arm and nodded.

"Be swift," Argent said to Kathryn.

She bowed her head in acknowledgment.

They departed, leaving her alone in the fieldroom.

Kathryn crossed to the window. She peered out at the fall of Tashijan, as stone and ice fought. She remembered the offer Lord Ulf had set before her. To escape with the heart, to flee and not look back.

Well, I'm looking, she said silently. *But never back over my shoulder. I will face you full on.*

And though she saw what swept toward her, she did not despair.

She still held out one hope.

23

A NECESSARY MERCY

WEIGHTED BY DESPAIR, TYLAR MOVED BACK TOWARD THE stern of the boat.

The daemon had settled to the island, vanishing among the flames and structures. Plainly Perryl had been ilked to protect the island, a ravening guard of Dark Grace.

How could he hope to defeat the daemon?

Tylar hobbled to the middle of the boat and sat down heavily, earning a complaint from his side, sharpening his breath. The others followed.

He motioned for the giant to pull the skiff farther back out of sight.

Dart settled to a bench opposite him. She was staring as he rubbed his knee. "You'll be killed," she whispered, voicing his own worry.

"The lass is right," Rogger said. "You could barely drive the beastie off last time. Now that *ghawl* is wraithed and has the full might of the enslaved rogues feeding it."

"But I have the sword," Tylar said. "Forged anew."

Dart met his eyes. "But a blade is only as strong as its wielder."

Tylar recognized an old adage drilled into every page and squire. It was probably one of the first lessons Dart had been taught by Swordmaster Yuril. He reached out and patted her knee.

Leaning back, he faced the others. "It's not like this is a battle we can walk away from."

Brant's voice was grim. "Maybe Tashijan has already fallen."

Tylar shook his head. "Until I know otherwise, we must hold in our hearts that it stands."

He read the defeat in all their eyes as he stared across the boat.

"I'm not saying I wouldn't prefer a stronger body, but here is the weapon I must wield. If I could pull the naethryn from my body and cure it of the poison, I would. Until then, the stone helps."

Tylar remembered Perryl's threat. *You are riddled with the blood of Chrism. Nothing in Myrillia. Nothing in the naether can burn this poison away.*

"But why?" Rogger asked, drawing back.

"Why what?"

"Why does the stone help?"

Tylar shook his head. "I don't know . . ." He remembered how it felt when the stone ignited the sword, a sense of the world tightening and sharpening around him. "I think the stone rallies aethryn and naethryn together. Returning what was sundered. Meeryn's aethryn must somehow support its naethryn."

"But not completely," Rogger said, scratching his beard.

"Not while it's inside me. Like I said, if I could pull the naethryn out—"

Rogger lifted a hand. "What if instead of pulling it *out* of you, we went *inside* of you? Right through that black palm print of yours."

Tylar frowned.

Rogger met his eye and said one word. "Balger."

Tylar flashed back to being imprisoned in Foulsham Dell. The fire god of that realm, who had been curious about his mark, tested it with his hand. Instead of finding flesh, his fingers had fallen through the blackness. Balger had reached far enough in to get his hand bitten off by the naethryn inside him.

"A god could take that stone," Rogger continued, "and hand it to your naethryn. Then perhaps aethryn and naethryn could join more fully and burn the poison away, breaking its hold, like the stone did to the seersong in Miyana."

Tylar considered this possibility. Perryl's words echoed. *Nothing in Myrillia. Nothing in the naether.* But what about something in the aether?

Finally he shook his head. "Unless I can get one of those rogues to cooperate, we have no god to attempt it."

"No," Rogger said, "but we do have a *godling*. And she is able to *see* farther into our mark than any of us."

Dart sat straighter, eyes wide as moons. "But I've touched his mark before. Nothing happened."

Rogger nodded. "But what about Pupp? He already walks between worlds. He delivered the stone to Tylar. Why not to his naethryn, too?"

Dart shifted in her seat, slowly nodding. She patted her thigh, plainly calling her companion. "I think I can get him to do it."

Tylar held out little hope of success, but it would not cost much time to attempt it. For the plan he intended anyway, he wanted the flitterskiff pulled back a fair distance, back to the clear channel. So he had a few moments. He directed the giant to haul them back far enough until Rogger could ignite the mekanicals.

While the two men worked, Tylar stripped open his cloak and parted the shirt beneath to expose the mark on his chest.

"Let's be quick about this," he said.

Dart held out her hand. "I'll need the stone."

He nodded. He already had the sword pulled. Grabbing the hilt in one hand and the diamond in the other, he twisted them in opposite directions, popping the stone from the pommel. He felt the snap deep within him. Pain lanced out from his core and shocked through to the tips of his limbs. His sword hand spasmed, tightening again into a knobbed grip.

Dart looked on with concern.

Tylar passed her the stone, gone dull again. The sword's blade had also blown itself out. She nicked a finger and daubed the stone. It flared again from rock to gem.

She motioned with her other hand. "Lie across the bottom of the skiff."

Feeling slightly foolish, Tylar obeyed.

Off to the side, blocked by the solid bench, Dart leaned down, reached out, and whispered. Tylar saw a ruddy glow flare up beyond the bench, bright in the darkness.

Pupp.

Over the bench's edge, the creature rose into view, all

molten armor and fire. He clambered to the top and stared down, the gem brilliant in his jaws, lit by inner fire.

"Lie still," Dart told him. "He's not very comfortable about this."

Tylar remembered the burned stump of the squire's arm—Pupp needn't be the one worried here.

Pupp lowered from the bench to Tylar's shoulder. The nails of his paw sliced through cloak to skin, steaming hot. Tylar winced. Pupp crawled, belly low, toward the black handprint on his chest.

Beyond Pupp, the others all gathered around.

"You all might want to step back farther," Tylar warned. He felt it inside him. A stirring down deep.

Pupp lowered his fiery muzzle toward his mark. Somehow Tylar knew before the nose reached him. He tensed. He felt the naethryn writhe inside him, rising as Pupp lowered.

Then the molten muzzle sank through his mark as if through shadow.

Dart gasped behind him, echoed by the others.

Then Pupp vanished from his chest, weight and burn gone.

Everyone glanced at Dart.

She pointed down to her legs. "Something spooked Pupp. Probably the naethryn. He's hiding behind my cloak."

"But where's the stone?" Brant asked.

"He dropped it." She pointed to Tylar's mark. "Down there."

Tylar reached to his chest, to his mark, but found only skin and breastbone. He lay his palm atop it. The stone was inside him.

Falling . . .

He sensed the rock tumbling into a deep well.

Then something rumbled even deeper inside him, a rushing up, a monstrous pressure building behind his rib cage. "Everyone! Get flat!"

When the rising pressure struck the falling rock, the impact shattered through him. Tylar's body leaped full off the boards, back arched, balanced on head and heels, arms out.

Pain and pleasure trapped him in a clenched breath.

He filled, swelling up, leaving no room for himself.

Too large . . .

Vision dimmed.

Then finally, like a popped cork, the pressure broke through into this world. From his chest, smoke flumed with the force of a gale out of his body. Bones broke with the passage, unmoored, torn loose.

He collapsed to the planks.

Beyond pain.

From his chest, more smoke sailed high. A storm of black and white, churning, mixing, coiling one to the other. Tylar noted wing and snaking neck, one black, one white, like two wyrms mating or fighting in midair.

Aethryn and naethryn.

Between them, a flickering lick of green flame danced and lashed, as if this were the fire that smoked them into existence. But Tylar knew it to be the burn of poison, Chrism's hatred given form. The two wyrms writhed around this core of flame.

At the very top of the column, a star glittered, reflecting the flame from a thousand facets.

The black diamond.

Slowly, as the two wyrms writhed, they smothered the fire between them, squeezed and strangled. The flame lost its brightness, the fierce flickering slowed, and in another few moments, it expired with a final waft of putrefaction.

With the fire gone, the smoke swirled with less violence, and the two creatures, both lost parts of the same whole, coiled and churned, trying to become one again—and failing—forever missing the third.

Tylar heard two voices in his head, two expressions of grief, more thought than word.

LOVE LOST HELP HOPE

LOST LOSS PAIN FURY

FREE FAITH LIFE WEEP

FIGHT BITTER WEEP LOSS

The litany flowed through his head, but was felt more with the heart, two views of the same pain and loss, neither able to get the other to understand, to comprehend, too foreign to the other, yet so alike.

He recognized the first voice, one tinged with regret and hope. It had spoken to him before, revealing itself as *naethryn*.

But the other voice was more embittered, laced with fury and cold inflexibility. He knew who the newcomer was, summoned by the stone, the smoky wyrm in white.

Meeryn's *aethryn*.

Another voice reached him through his pain, one of urgency and plain word.

"Bloody yourself, Tylar!" Rogger said. "Call back your dog!"

As the thief placed a dagger in Tylar's gnarled grip, he stared up. The whirl of two wyrms had become more heated as each tried to get the other to understand that which the other could not comprehend, so close but still sundered, the frustration building toward fury.

Tylar dragged the heel of his hand across the dagger's fine edge. He felt the bite of steel. Blood ran down his arm as he lifted it. He snatched at the smoky tether, feeling the fleshy substance, igniting fire under his palm. Then as usual, the brilliance shot outward and back, consuming the tangle and pulling it back. It fell back to him with the weight of water, crushing him to the planks, knocking the air from him.

Then it was all gone.

A hand reached out and snatched a rock falling from the sky. Brant had captured back his stone as it fell back into this world.

Tylar sat up, inhaling a deep breath, his strength returned.

No pain in his side. He used Rogger's dagger to cut the wraps from his hand. The soiled scraps fell away, revealing straight and strong fingers. He flexed his fist and rolled to his feet. His knee—both knees—lifted him smoothly.

The others stared at him.

Cured.

Off across the dark forest, a scream echoed.

Rogger glanced back. "Looks like we've waked another beast."

Tylar bent down, retrieved the bladeless gold hilt, and held out a hand toward Brant. The boy passed him the stone. Dart had already freshened it back to a diamond with her blood.

Tylar stared at Brant, the echoes of the aethryn and naethryn still stirring through him. He remembered Brant's words when he held Keorn's skull. With the stone at his throat, he'd spoken in two different voices, as if in argument.

HELP THEM . . .

LET THEM ALL BURN . . .

FREE THEM . . .

LET THEM ALL BURN . . .

But they weren't his own words. He knew that now.

Through skull and stone, Brant had spoken with the voice of Keorn's naethryn and aethryn. Two sundered parts just as conflicted. One seeking salvation, the other ruination. Naethryn and aethryn. Two parts of a whole.

Tylar lifted sword and stone.

He felt no such conflict within himself.

He slammed pommel to diamond. The blade shimmered into substance. He heard the daemon's cry echo away.

He answered silently—*I'm coming*—and turned to the group.

Though hale, Tylar was only one man against a host of ravening rogues and a wraithed daemon, leashed together for a common purpose—all set against him.

And even with Rivenscryr, the hope for victory was slim.

Still, Tylar remembered Dart's earlier words, how a sword was only as strong as the man who wielded it. But what she had yet to learn was that a man was only as strong as those who stood by his side.

He stared at those here.

And he could imagine victory . . . against any odds.

All was lost.

Kathryn ran down the stairs as Stormwatch Tower quaked. The ice had reached their battlements. She had watched the outer towers fall, the wall tumbled and broken. Only one structure still stood.

But for how long?

Overhead, loud crashes echoed, glass shattered. Then an exceptionally loud boom rattled the stairs, deafening. But afterward, she heard a noise like a rumble of thunder, accompanied by a cacophony of rattling and smashing resounds. Something was coming, behind her, from on high.

Kathryn drank more shadows and sped down for the next landing. Flying around a corner, she spotted two figures hurrying upward, slinking along one wall. They glimpsed her in a wash of shadows. The girl raised a fist to her throat. The boy stepped forward with a sword, plainly borrowed, from the way it shook.

Raising an arm, Kathryn yelled, *"Get off the stairs! NOW!"*

Laurelle responded immediately, despite her momentary panic. She grabbed the young wyld tracker's arm and hauled him up. They reached the landing at the same time and ducked off the stairs.

Not a moment too soon.

An avalanche of stone bricks tumbled past in a deadly chute, rattling away, bouncing a few stones down the hallway. Kathryn herded Laurelle and Kytt back, then swept around with her cloak.

"What are you still doing out?" she yelled, her ears ringing from the clatter of rocks. "Why didn't you respond to the gong?"

Laurelle strode beside her. "We were down below with Master Orquell."

Kathryn lifted a hand to her brow. "Yes . . . yes, Delia told me." She glanced over her shoulder. "Where is the master?"

"Dead. Sacrificed himself to stifle the witch's power."

Kathryn remembered Mirra faltering, her staff's green fire dying.

Laurelle continued, speaking in a rush. "Then there were groundshakes below. The Masterlevels crumbled, and large sections collapsed. We ran. If it hadn't been for Kytt's nose, we wouldn't have found a way out, but a part of the lower level had collapsed into the cellars. We were able to climb up."

Laurelle suddenly grabbed Kathryn's sleeves. "We saw some of the black knights—but they ran from our torches."

Kathryn hurried them toward one of the entrances to the Grand Court. "They've been routed. But we have larger concerns."

Another tower-shaking *boom* echoed from above. It seemed Lord Ulf was tearing down Stormwatch, one level at a time, starting from the top.

"I thought the groundshakes below had stopped," Laurelle said, ducking a bit as the thunder echoed away.

"They did. This is something even more dire."

At last, the doors to the Grand Court arched ahead, framed in black obsidian, topped by a faceted chunk of rock that represented the diamond on their sword's pommel. She hurried forward and pounded a fist on the closed door.

A commotion sounded and a voice called out. "Who goes there?"

"Castellan Vail!"

A moment later, a bar scraped, and the door swung open to a cavernous space, the tiered amphitheater of the Grand Court. Fires blazed. And the heart of Tashijan quaked with screams, shouts, crying, bustling. It was packed nearly shoulder to shoulder.

Kathryn bulled a path to the stairs that led down toward the bottom of the amphitheater. Laurelle and Kytt followed in her wake. It was slow going.

Then a pair of the knights joined them, shouting, "Make room for the castellan! Make room!"

The seas parted, and they made faster progress down the crowded stairs. Still, fingers touched her cloak as she descended, hopeful, fearful. She had no time to reassure them—and at the moment, she wasn't sure she had the strength to lie to them, at least not well.

Below, Kathryn spotted Argent and Delia, along with the large mass of Hesharian and the bronze form of Gerrod. Several other Council masters gathered around the central pit. Hearthstone, the fiery core of Tashijan. The ancient pit dated back to the time of human kings, but it had come to represent Tashijan's flaming heart. The pit danced high with a fresh pyre, smoke spiraling with alchemies.

"Make room for the castellan!"

The shout echoed below. Faces turned.

Gerrod spotted her first among the surging throng. He lifted an arm. She hurried down to him, leading Laurelle and Kytt.

Reaching the floor, Argent came with Delia.

"He comes," Kathryn said, as more booming crashes echoed, like the footsteps of a god. "Keep the fires high. Our only hope lies in the heat of our alchemies bolstering this last picket, holding our fire against Ulf's ice."

Gerrod nodded. "We've added loam alchemies to strengthen the walls, too, but—" He shook his head.

She reached for his arm and squeezed, wishing it was not just armor that met her touch. "We will hold strong . . . and not just with our alchemies."

A violent quake rattled, sounding as if all of the tower above had crashed atop them. Kathryn looked up, willing it all to hold. Just a little longer.

Large chunks of plaster and rock cracked from the roof and tumbled to smashing ruin among the tiers. People scattered, amid screams and blood.

Overhead a massive block of stone broke free like a rotted tooth. It fell straight at them. Kathryn shouldered Gerrod to the side. Masters scattered. Argent grabbed Delia's arm as she gaped upward. But she was still wobbly on her feet from the blow to her head.

As Argent pulled, she tripped down to a knee.

"Delia!"

The stone tumbled at her.

In a swirl of cloak, Argent clenched her arm in both of his hands and threw her bodily, wildly clear, spinning off a heel. He dove after her, but a moment too late. Even shadows were sometimes too slow.

Argent leaped, but the chunk of roof shattered across his legs, slamming him to the stone floor. He lay flat, unmoving.

"Father!" Delia cried and crawled over to him.

An arm shifted, a hand wiped rock dust from the floor. Blood welled and spread from beneath the rock. Shouts echoed. Masters hurried forward.

But it was his daughter that took his hand.

"Don't leave me," she said. "Not again . . ."

His chin shifted, and he moaned. "Never."

Then he lay still.

"I wish I had more practice," Rogger said.

"You'll do fine," Tylar assured him. He glanced back at the others.

The flitterskiff floated a quarter league from the island in the clear channel again, out of the clogged choke. The others crouched, hands firmly on the rail. Dart shared his bench, clutching a hand to his swordbelt. He felt the tremble in her arm.

Each had a duty this night. And though fear shone bright in all their eyes, so did determination. Satisfied, he twisted forward and squeezed Rogger's arm, sharing friendship and certainty.

"Go."

With a nod, Rogger twisted the flow of trickling alchemy to full. "Hold tight!"

The paddles to either side churned the waters into a boil. The flitterskiff leaped forward like a startled pony. It blew across the waters, rising, lifting its keel, winds whipping the hood from Tylar's cloak.

He tugged it back up, ducking lower.

The skiff skimmed on its paddle tips, racing along the channel. Rogger hit the first bend around a hillock, but he was too gentle with the wheel. They swung wide, almost burying their bow in a tangle of knotted roots. He pulled harder, tilting the skiff up almost on one row of paddles, and then they were away.

The channel twisted and turned from there.

Rogger did his best, flying the skiff around fast turns, slowing, jogging, banking, and tilting. He took the last turn with a bit of a panic. The rearmost starboard paddle struck a stone and clipped off with a jolt of the boat. The bronze oar flew like an arrow back into the flooded woods.

Then they were in the boiling lake.

Steam rose in a fierce, bubbling roil. The waters glowed a fiery crimson. As they shot across the water toward the island, the heat swamped over them, dampened them with a stinging wash. The kiss of Takaminara. Behind them, steam swirled and churned in their wake.

A screech of fury erupted from the island. Green flames flickered off the rocky spars, fanned by the beat of rising wings.

Rogger shot toward the island, a flittering spear of wood and bronze. He aimed straight for one of the pinnacles, as if he intended to ram it. "Get ready!"

Tylar shifted up, drawing Dart under his cloak, one arm snaked under her shoulders. "Both hands," he told her.

Two hands locked onto his swordbelt.

"Now!" Rogger yelled.

The thief yanked on the wheel, and twisted the nose to the left, banking high. Their thrust still carried them toward the island, broadside first now. They slowed.

But not Tylar.

With shadows heavy in his cloak and Dart under his arm, he leaped over the starboard rail and flew like a dark raven toward the sandy beach.

Behind him, Rogger burnt more alchemies and the flitterskiff flew off like a frightened sparrow, skimming out and away from the island.

Tylar landed in a rolling tumble, protecting Dart with his limbs until they fell into the shadows of the rocky spar. He buried them both in the darkness and some scrabbled bushes.

He watched the flitterskiff skim out into the cooler waters of the lake and vanish to the right, intending to circle the island and retreat back the way they'd come in.

But not alone.

A wailing cry of a hunter pierced the night. Tylar did not dare look. They had leaped from the boat into the shadows, and they needed to remain out of sight. Before flying here, Tylar had smeared his blood all over the boat's railing. His scent would be ripe on the skiff, a bait trolled through these dark waters and away.

But had they hooked their big fish?

Another shriek and the green firelight flickered with fury. Tylar heard the beat of heavy wings, rising from the island. Distantly, he heard Rogger shout.

"If you want to bite this arse, you're gonna have to catch it first!"

The flap of leather and bone followed Rogger's call.

Tylar waited another two breaths. The goal had been for Rogger to lure the winged guard away. The daemon's power came from the island. If Tylar could stamp out the flame here, then the wraithed *ghawl* would be easier to manage, stripped of much of its Dark Grace.

Still, what would they find *here*? There was only one way to find out.

"Let's go, and remember if I say—"

"—*run*, I'm supposed to run and hide," Dart mumbled. "I know."

He hadn't wanted to bring Dart, but he had no way of knowing if her blood might be needed for the sword. Too much was unknown still about the blade, and he had gods to set free. It would not do to find himself standing with a bladeless hilt in his hand.

A screech echoed over the waters.

And who was to say being on the boat was any safer?

Tylar stood up and slid Rivenscryr from its sheath. "Keep to my shadows. I'll keep us cloaked as much as possible."

Already at his hip, she shuffled closer still.

He set out around the rock. The island had fallen into a hushed silence. All he heard was a flicker of hungry flame, a few scrapes, and what sounded like rattled chains.

He crept another step when he realized something was missing here.

Seersong.

When they'd first spied upon the island from across the lake, he had heard a few faint chords. A lone woman singing softly, full of sorrow. But now nothing. What had happened?

Tylar feared what this might portend.

Leading the way, he stepped past the granite spar and into the green firelight. The pyre rose at the island's center. It cast no warmth, only a sick feverish tint to the skin, oily and foul. It splattered its light against stone and rock.

Tylar lifted his cloak against it, sensing the immense well of power here. He kept back from it, edging around the central square. Low stone buildings, all stacked brick and slabbed roofs, ringed the edges. The doorways were open, no windows. He made sure they kept clear from those dark openings, too.

He heard stone scrape inside—and again a rattle of iron.

Once they were among the crown of pinnacles, the firelight revealed carvings on the inner surfaces of the spars: of men and women at work, tilling fields, leading beasts of burden by yoke. One spar held what appeared to be a great tangled battle with spear and ax, decorated with limbless bodies, and staked heads that were too painful a reminder of Saysh Mal. Another seemed to depict great acts of carnal passion: feasts, debauchery, rutting bodies in every pose.

He stepped between Dart and that view.

Crossing deeper, he searched around him. Here was an ancient human settlement, long before even the human kings rose, stretching to a more distant time. Here is where the human Cabalists had chosen to set up their wicked forge, believing the lies of the naethryn Cabal, to end the tyranny of the gods, to return to the majesty of human rule.

Tylar turned his eyes away, back to the ring of stone buildings. By now, he had circled to the far side of the fire. Here rose the largest of the buildings. Firelight glowed out its door. Not the green poison of this pyre, but a regular hearth.

He approached, but motioned Dart to one side of the door. He led with Rivenscryr in hand. The door was low, requiring him to duck in order to peer inside. A small pit in the room's center glowed with a few wan flames. It illuminated six stone slabs, radiating out from the fire. A single small figure lay atop each bed, draped in a gray robe, stained and ragged.

Tylar smelled the blood.

It flowed over the slabs and pooled at their feet. A few trickles dribbled toward the fire in the room. A fresh large drop rolled along one of the rivulets and extended its reach by a tiny measure.

He entered but pointed back. "Stay near the door. Watch the square."

Dart stepped within the shelter of the threshold, but she faced outward.

Tylar crossed to one of the beds. The figure was a girl, surely no more than fifteen, straight blond hair, long to the shoulder. She appeared no different than any young girl, except for two things about her neck. Under her chin, her throat bulged out, like a frog in mid-croak.

One of the songstresses.

He looked into her open eyes, such a sweet face for such a font of misery. But was she to blame? Such children were born of Dark Grace, against their will, tainted by black alchemies to become these sirens of Grace. Were they any freer than those they bound?

And then there was one last horror found at her throat.

A ragged slice drawn clean and deep. Its edges had peeled back as her lifeblood poured out. Tylar's toe nudged one of the blades, a shard of obsidian in a bronze handle. It lay near the girl's slack fingers.

She had cut her own throat.

He stepped to the next, and the next—all the same.

All the songstresses.

Dead.

He touched one cheek. Still warm. The deaths had occurred only moments before. He remembered the forlorn notes of song he had heard drifting over the lake. Maybe it hadn't truly been seersong, only one last whisper into the night, a lone child knowing what she must do.

Tylar stared across the ruin here.

"Why?" he whispered to them.

The one word encompassed two questions.

Why had they killed themselves? Were they no longer needed? Had Lord Ulf ordered them to take their lives? And if so, what did that portend for Tashijan?

But there was a larger question locked in that single whispered word. He stared across the slabs. Every face that stared up toward the roof, wide-eyed and blind in death, was the same. As with Meylan's group. All identical. But Meylan and her sisters were all Wyr-born.

Tylar's blood went cold. He knew the truth. *So were these children.* They'd been birthed in the same Wyr's forges, identical songstresses.

Why?

Dart stepped deeper into the room, a warning tone in her voice.

"Tylar—"

He turned his back on the horror here and hurried back to her side. She pointed, drawing him down so he might see better.

All around the ring, they crept out of doorways, many on hands and knees, others sliding on bellies, others hunkered into beaten postures. Had they sensed the winged guard was gone? Or was it just Tylar's trespass?

They came out of their stone dens, naked, covered in mud and their own filth. Hair caked in bile, limbs starved to bone, and many of those broken and healed crooked. But all their eyes, staring up, staring over, staring at nothing, glowed with Grace.

Here were the rogues.

What was left of gods treated brutally.

Twelve in all.

They clawed from their warrens, chained at the ankles. One began to wail at the sky, then another. One woman sat outside the doorway, tugging her hair out by the fistful. Another man rocked on his knees, digging at the stone underfoot, tearing nails and flesh in his urgency.

Though freed from the seersong, they were bound even tighter now by madness, beyond even the ability to use their Grace to break their chains.

Tylar remembered Rogger's description of tanglebriar, how if you yanked the weed, its roots only dug deeper and spread wider. How long had these been rooted with seersong? With the loss of the songstresses, something worse than raving was left behind—mindless agony and an imprisonment far worse than chain and stone, locked forever in your own horror. He had seen what such madness had wrought in Saysh Mal—not just to those around them but to the gods themselves.

He pictured Miyana stepping into fire. The same as her brother.

I want to go home.

Tylar stepped out. No one noted him. He had come to free these rogues. And so he would.

Lifting his sword, he stalked out.

"Faster!" Brant yelled.

Rogger cursed and raced the flitterskiff around another bend. The daemon had closed upon them again. They were burdened by tangle and choke. The *ghawl* had open air.

Their only advantage lay in dense cover and darting turns.

But they were rapidly losing even that slim lead.

Rogger had taken the last turn too sharply and sheered three paddles off on a shoulder of rock. The skiff jostled, and Rogger had to fight the wheel to hold them steady. And now they were heading into a familiar section of the wood, less dense with areas of open canopy.

Malthumalbaen knelt in the boat's stern, balancing one hand on the rail, holding aloft a thick branch, more a log, with the other. And Brant appreciated the giant's skill with it. They had already come close to death a few moments back. The daemon had dropped like a diving hawk at them, crashing through a sparse section of canopy.

A quick swing of that log, and he'd batted it aside. It had crashed into the muck and weed. They had cheered—but in a storm of wing and claw, it had burst up, showering filth, climbing and leaping back into the air to continue its hunt.

And it was upon them again already. It flapped above the canopy, closing the distance with a savage screech of triumph.

Rogger did his best. The flitterskiff raced but in a rattling limp compared to its effortless flight. It was over for them. Had they bought Tylar and Dart enough time? Once the beast ravaged them, it would discover the ruse and return to the island in a furious rage.

They had run out of ways to confound the daemon.

They were too few, too limited.

Too few?

An idea dawned. Maybe not.

Brant twisted back to Rogger and told him where to go.

The thief nodded. "You have a deliciously evil streak, boy. That's why I love you."

Brant faced around. He grabbed his longbow, supplied by the Wyr, and readied his arrows. The giant came next to him.

"You want me to just throw my log?"

"When I tell you." Brant worked fast, fighting the jostle as Rogger swung the boat toward the new target. It was time the daemon learned how all life in the wood was connected by a dance of predator and prey. Heartless and hard—but nonetheless perfect.

This was what Brant had been taught as a boy.

The Way.

"Here we are!" Rogger said.

And not a moment too soon.

The daemon appeared in a break in the canopy overhead, turned on a wing, ready to dive.

"Now!" Brant bellowed and arched back. He pulled hard on his bowstring. Oil dripped from his arrow's shaft to his fingers.

Malthumalbaen threw his log at the neighboring tree, then leaned down and touched Brant's arrow with a burning piece of straw.

The shaft ignited as Brant let loose the string. The arrow shot high, arcing a fiery trail up through the hole in the canopy. The daemon wraith had begun its final dive.

Brant's arrow struck true.

From the neighboring tree, woken by the giant's log crashing through the limbs of their roost, a thousand white bats took to wing, searching for the attacker. Malthumalbaen wisely threw his piece of flaming straw into the water.

The bats noted the only other flame, honed from centuries of hunting.

In their skies.

In their territory.

Impaled upon a winged trespasser.

Brant's arrow did nothing to discourage the daemon, but the thousand bats did, churning up like smoke through the hole in the canopy.

The daemon's dive tumbled as wings struck bats, and thousands upon thousands of fangs tore at skin and eyes. It twisted in midair, plagued at every turn, unable to escape the swirling white cloud. It fled higher, shedding the cloud for a moment. The rush of air fanned the impaled arrow's flame.

In that moment, the daemon hesitated, turned once on a wingtip. Then with a wail of fury, it swung away.

Back toward the island.

Rogger watched it leave. "It knows about Tylar's trespass."

Brant stood next to Rogger, shouldering his bow. "We did all that we could."

Rogger looked above. Overhead, the swirl of bats chased after the slower-flapping daemon, following its flame. A cry of rage flowed back, tinged by pain.

"And those little buggers will slow it down a bit more for us."

Malthumalbaen sank to the bench. "I could almost like those bats now. Especially fried in pepperseed oil."

Tylar stood amid the carnage.

The fire at his back had dimmed to flickers of green flame. With each rogue he slew, more fuel for the pyre died. Somehow each god's lifeforce was forged to the flames, some dread blood alchemy, forced upon them by the song. And like the chains that bound their ankles, they were unable to escape—not while they lived.

It was up to Tylar to break that curse, too.

In the only way he knew how.

Their bodies lay where they fell. He made each of their deaths swift.

He felt the tenth no less than the first—especially as he finally learned the truth of Rivenscryr.

He stepped to the eleventh rogue and lifted his sword. It was a woman of fine bone, revealed by her sunken skin. A god might not die, but they could eternally starve. She stared up at him. She did not wail. She had bitten off her tongue some time ago, and in the horror of godhood, it had yet to grow back. How many tongues had she bitten off? Had she done it to silence her cries or out of hunger?

He met her gaze and found nothing there, a burned shell, waiting to be released. Like all the others . . . or at least those who still had eyes.

Tylar heaved back his sword and swung it sharply.

Graced steel cleaved flesh and bone with hardly a shudder of the hilt.

Still, as Rivenscryr touched flesh, the last flicker of life entered the blade, drawn up the steel by Keorn's black diamond, drawing together in that exact moment all that had been sundered—flesh, naethryn, and aethryn.

And slaying all three.

That was the final truth.

No god had truly died on Myrillia in all its four thousand years since the great Sundering. Parts certainly had died. Meeryn. Chrism. But these were only a sliver of the whole. What had died before had left spirit in the naether and the aether. Like the undergod inside Tylar. Or Chrism's naethryn banished from Myrillia back to its dark underworld. They abided.

Even Miyana and Keorn.

No god died truly and wholly.

Until this night.

As the stone of Rivenscryr drew all parts together for that fleeting last spark of life, the blade cut it short, ending all.

The rogue god's head rolled toward the fire. The body slumped.

Truly and finally dead.

"Lillani," Tylar whispered.

It was the other cruelty of the sword. *What was it about a name?* As all parts joined and the raving of millennia snuffed out with each death, a name rang through the blade, full of joy. Then gone.

Tylar had learned all those names.

He stepped toward the twelfth and final.

A god who took the shape of an older boy, sixteen, seventeen. Now he was more a feral wolf than boy. He had rended his manhood to shreds with his nails, and he frothed at the mouth. One leg was broken, the one snagged in iron. He must have fought his chain with the same ferocity as he had fought seersong. But he had lost both battles. Forever trapped.

Tylar lifted Rivenscryr, hating the sword in that moment.

Across the woods, he heard a wailing screech of the daemon. He had heard it echo periodically as it hunted the forest for the flitterskiff, searching for Tylar's blood. But now it came closer. Another call followed, confirming. It swept back toward the island.

As he lifted his sword, a voice spoke behind him.

It was not Dart. She crouched by the stone house where the songstresses lay cold on their stone beds. He should not have brought her here. She sat, knees up, face buried between them.

She knew it was a mercy, too. But that didn't mean she had to watch.

The voice came from the flames.

"You are an Abomination," Lord Ulf said, whispering ice through the flames. *"Here you prove it."*

Tylar stared into the fire. "I do what must be done. Forced by malice and corruption."

"You kill all," Ulf said, with a note of confusion and wariness, plainly unsure how Tylar had accomplished this.

"I know."

"But why? When any blade can take a head from a god? Why kill all when madness has eaten only the one?"

Tylar had considered the same after slaying the first rogue, realizing how deep Rivenscryr cut. Still, he had moved on with his Godsword. He had remembered the war between Meeryn's aethryn and naethryn. Forever apart. Forever incomprehensible to the other. Such fracturing when the third was forever lost was not life. Let death be death.

Also he had remembered Miyana, when the Huntress had stepped into the molten rock. Of full mind in that moment, all three, bringing back her name. She had tried to tell him, tell everyone, knowing it was denied her even then.

I want to go home.

And there was only one way to do that.

Total release.

Tylar turned his back on Ulf and stepped to the feral boy-god.

Ulf spoke behind him. *"You are an Abomination!"*

Tylar swung the sword, cleaving madness from the boy. "Jaffin," he whispered to the night, naming him.

"ABOMINATION!" Ulf wailed.

Tylar turned to the fire. "No—just Godslayer."

With the death of the last rogue, the foul pyre expired.

But not before a thread of righteous triumph sailed clear.

"You are too late . . . Tashijan has fallen . . ."

Tylar hesitated. Was it true? Was that why the songstresses were dead? Before he could weigh the words, a screech drew him full around. It dove toward the island.

"Tylar!" Dart called out, rising and stepping toward him.

"Run!" he commanded. "Inside!"

Dart backed into the songstresses' home but stayed near the door.

Tylar gathered shadows to his cloak and shifted away from Dart's hiding place, drawing the daemon's attention by baring Rivenscryr, shining bright in the dark.

The daemon crashed to the island's center, scattering ashes of the dying hearth that had given birth to him. Wings raised as it faced Tylar. Frayed and torn, the wings bled a thick ichor. A feathered arrow, charred and black, sprouted from its ribs. With the fire gone and its font of Grace stanched, the wraithed *ghawl* had weakened.

But like a wounded she-panther, such a beast was at its most wary, its most dangerous. Its neck lowered. It hissed at him from a fanged face that bore little resemblance to Perryl. Claws dug into stone underfoot. Wings batted at the air.

It searched, as if unsure what stoked its fury. Its masters were gone, leaving it directionless, abandoned.

Then Tylar noted something beyond the wary confusion.

Pain.

And not just from its injuries.

"Perryl . . ."

The word blew the creature back like a gust of wind. It landed across the cold fire in a crouch, hissing, spitting, wings held straight up. It looked ready to take to wing and flee.

"Was that why you still came?" Tylar whispered, circling the fire, his blade ready. "The beast in you wants to run, but something holds you here."

It screeched, a note of frustration and agony, trapped in a tidal push and pull of instinct and memory.

"Perryl . . ."

An agonized whine streamed from somewhere deep inside the beast.

He knew why his friend had come back. Tylar lifted Rivenscryr. The blade's flicker ignited another hiss and snap of wing. Clawed hands ripped at him through the air, savage and raving.

Still, it held back, ending its hiss with a slight mewling cry.

Fearful on every level.

Tortured and pained.

Lost between beast and man, instinct and horror.

Tylar knew what Perryl wanted of him. He saw it in his eyes. Perryl fought the beast's instinct, to flee, to fight. But for how long? He used all the will remaining in his ilked form to hold firm, to hold steady for the blade, to beg for the same kindness Tylar had shone the rogues.

The mercy of the blade.

But Perryl could not hold out for much longer.

Tylar knew Perryl needed his help, for one last battle, one last death, one last release. Still, after so much blood on his sword, he hesitated. And that proved the cruelest act that night.

Behind Tylar, a whining and rattling erupted, the flitterskiff returning.

The noise and sudden arrival startled the beast beyond Perryl's control. With a spread of wings, it leaped with a screech of panic—ready to flee and lose itself in the hinterlands, trapping his friend forever in horror.

Tylar swept forward, but the distance was too great even for shadow.

He had failed Perryl one last time.

But another did not.

As the daemon leaped, a flaming form burst out its chest, skewering clean through, a fiery spike through the heart, gutting it.

One last screech wailed with a lick of flame from pained lips—and the daemon fell to the stones in a tumble of wing and smoking flesh.

Pupp climbed free of the debris. Steaming with black blood, shaking his spiked mane. His eyes glowed especially bright.

Dart ran up to Tylar, one hand bloody. In the other, she held one of the songstresses' obsidian knives.

Tylar sank to his knees beside his friend.

Suddenly all the grief whelmed through him, shaking up from a place deeper than where his naethryn swam. He dropped his sword and covered his face. The tears came in great racks of pain. Twelve names burnt into his heart. Or maybe it was because at least this one death did not bloody his hands.

Not this one . . .

And that was enough to save him.

Dart lowered next to him. She reached to his shoulder. "Did . . . did I do all right? I wasn't sure . . ."

He touched her arm, swallowing hard. "You did fine, Dart . . . just fine."

24

A KNIGHTING IN MIDSUMMER

SADDLED HIGH, KATHRYN SWELTERED IN A FULL CLOAK OVER rich finery. She wore polished boots to the knee. Her horse was tacked in silver, a match to her cape's clasp and warden's badge. As the retinue would be traveling through Chrismferry's main streets, she had her hood up and masklin fixed in place.

Gerrod rode up beside her. "We're just about ready to head out." Even hidden behind his armor, he appeared ill at ease, shifting in his saddle, adjusting his reins. The castellan diadem shone brightly at his throat.

Such were their new positions: Warden and Castellan.

Of Tashijan in exile.

Kathryn glanced behind her. They had made much progress over the past two moonpasses. Had it truly just been sixty days? Tylar had granted them the Blight, an empty and ruined section of Chrismferry's inner city, not all that far from his castillion, to house and rebuild Tashijan. It proved a good place to set down new roots, land that had lain fallow for a long time. Already the Blight was a jumble of rebuilding, tearing down, mucking out, and clearing. And some shape was taking form—a skeleton of rafters, stone walls, and trenched fields. Tashijan was rising again.

New land, new roots, a new foundation.

Argent had proposed the original knighting of the regent as a way to bring Chrismferry and Tashijan closer together, to unite the First Land. Now their houses were closer than ever, by both distance and determination.

A small blessing for all the blood spilled.

Beneath her, Stoneheart shuffled his hooves, restless to leave.

Kathryn patted the stallion's neck to reassure him. Atop this same horse she had led the survivors out of the rubbled ruin of Tashijan. The journey was already being heralded in song. The Great Exodus. A trail of horses, folk on foot, and wagons that stretched thirty leagues. She could have taken a flippercraft, but she had wanted to be there, *needed* to be there, among them.

Kathryn also remembered that last morning. The storm had broken at dawn. As rocks still rattled, unsettled and loose, they had found they had survived. Tylar had snuffed out Lord Ulf's font of Dark Grace, and with it went his storm and ice. But as they pushed open iron shutters and stepped out into that cold morning, all lay in ruins: toppled and gutted towers, broken-toothed walls. Even Stormwatch had been held together only by the last of Ulf's ice, and the melt of the morning sun threatened that precarious hold.

Kathryn could still picture her last view of Tashijan, from atop the rise of a hill. The once-proud citadel lay in rubble and ruin. And as she watched, Stormwatch slowly gave way, its last alchemies fading, the morning sun melting crusts of ice, and down it came, rumbling like thunder, casting up a cloud of rock dust—then gone, crushing the Masterlevels under it. So she had turned her back, left Tashijan to the haunt of wraith and daemon. Someday they might rebuild, but for now they needed a new home.

A horn sounded up ahead.

"Are you ready?" Gerrod asked.

She nodded. "We should not be late to a knighting that is long overdue."

She nudged the piebald stallion and walked Stoneheart down a lane lined by stacked planks and brick. Hammering and chiseling, shouts and laughter echoed all around.

Gerrod clopped his horse beside her. "Yet another parade of Tashijan in exile through the streets of Chrismferry."

"Another parade?"

He nodded ahead. "What with all the woodwrights and stonemasons flowing in and out our temporary gates, it's like a daily circus around here."

She offered him a small smile, but it was hidden behind her

masklin. He did not see how quickly it faded. As she led the bright retinue toward Chrismferry, she could not deny a cold worry that even the midday swelter could not melt.

"What's wrong?" Gerrod asked, shying his mount closer, ever knowing her moods. He touched her knee with his bronze fingers.

She shook her head. It was too bright a day.

"Kathryn . . ."

She sighed, glanced to him, then away again. "Did we win?"

"What do you mean?"

She lifted an arm to indicate all the rebuilding. "Or did Lord Ulf? Back at the Blackhorse, he stated what he sought through all the death and destruction he'd wrought. '*The steel of a sword is made harder by fire and hammer. It is time for Tashijan to be forged anew.*' Is that not what happened?"

He motioned for her hand. She gave it. He squeezed her fingers.

"We will be stronger. That I don't doubt. Already the other Myrillian gods unite more firmly against the Cabal, pull more strongly in support for Tylar. Did you not see the number of flippercraft in the skies over the past days? Hundreds. The knighting today is not the small affair of Argent's original design, a few Hands from the closest gods. There are retinues here from every land, from as far away as Wyrmcroft in the Ninth Land. That is proof alone."

He squeezed her hand even harder, almost painfully. "We will be stronger. Not because Ulf won, but because *you* did. He made an offer to you: to walk away, to escape with a few. But because you held fast, many more survived. And it is that victory that makes us stronger, not capitulation to the mad calculation of a cold god."

She took a shuddering deep breath and felt some of the ice inside her break apart, but still the shards hurt.

"Even Lord Ulf knew he was defeated. Did he not leave his castillion and wander into the hinterlands to the far north?"

Kathryn had heard the story of the god's last steps. Just as it was forbidden for a rogue to enter a realm, a god was equally forbidden the hinterlands. Lord Ulf's form was seen blazing like a torch as he strode north across the frozen wastes to his doom. At the end, the lord of Ice Eyrie gave himself over to the flame.

Still, Gerrod was not done. "If we are going to forge Tashijan to a harder steel, then let it be in a fire born of our own hearts. And I know no heart burns brighter than yours."

Gerrod seemed suddenly abashed at his last words. His fingers began to slip from hers. "All know this," he mumbled. "Did not every stone cast for our new warden bear your color? Not a single stone against?"

Kathryn did not let his fingers slip so easily away. She gave them a firm squeeze. "You are kind. But the casting was so clean because Argent stepped aside."

Gerrod finally freed his hand and took his reins. "How is he faring?"

"*Stubborn*—that's the word Delia used. She came by early this morning. Arrived with the dawn flippercraft from Five Forks. She says he mends well and is slowly adjusting to his new leg, but he is quick to wrath and not willing to listen to his healer's warnings."

"Little wonder there," Gerrod mumbled. "One eye, one leg. The man is slowly being whittled away."

Kathryn smiled, a rudeness perhaps, considering his maiming, but she suspected even Argent would respect it. Back in Tashijan, Argent had survived by will and alchemy—but mostly by a promise to a daughter. *Not to leave*. And as always, he stubbornly kept his word.

A commotion drew their attention to the side. A small figure ran toward her horse. "Warden Vail! Warden Vail!"

She glanced down and recognized the youth in mucked boots and muddied clothes. She reined her horse to a halt. "Mychall?"

The stableboy hurried to her stirrup. He held up a strip of black cloth. "I did it!" he shouted proudly and waved the strip. "I've been picked!"

She smiled down at him, knowing what he held, remembering when she had been chosen, given a bit of shadowcloak, picked to join the knighthood.

Mychall waved his bit of cloth and ran back down along her retinue. "I must tell my da!"

She watched him race away.

When she turned back to Gerrod, he stared at her. She knew he was smiling behind his bronze. "Still think we lost?" he asked.

She rattled her reins to get Stoneheart moving again. Inside her, the last of Lord Ulf's ice melted away.

As the last morning bell rang over the meadow field, Brant whistled sharply. They were already late, and still needed to get attired for the knighting.

Stalks of sweetgrass parted in a weaving pattern, flowing down the slight hill. The pair of wolfkits responded to his whistle, running low to the ground, a hunting posture. They burst from the field together, bounding toward the small group gathered in the shade of a wide-bowered lyrewood tree, heavy with midsummer blossoms.

Brant led the pair back to the lounging party.

To the left, the meadows rolled into the green Tigre River, its waters reflecting the castillion of Chrismferry. Four stone towers rose from each bank of the Tigre, supporting the bulk of the castillion that ran like a bridge from one side to the other. A ninth tower, taller than the rest, rose from the center of the castillion, a beacon over the river, its white quarried stone blazing in the midday sun.

Great festivities were planned for the day, but before that happened, they had all wanted a moment to enjoy the sunshine, away from the tumult.

Buried in the shade ahead, Malthumalbaen rested against the twisted trunk. He chewed the end of a churl-pipe, a gnarled piece of wood as long as the giant's arm. He puffed a trail of smoke as Brant returned with the cubbies.

Resting beside the giant, the bullhound Barrin snored, nose on the giant's knee. Malthumalbaen stirred with a crack of bone.

"Ach, are we 'bout ready to head back, Master Brant?"

He nodded.

"Good thing that. All this dogflesh is making me hungry."

The giant slowly gained his feet. Barrin groused about being disturbed, then was pounced upon by the returning cubbies. The bullhound let out an irritated grumble of reluctant tolerance.

"They're getting big," Laurelle said, packing the basket and stepping aside so Kytt could roll the blanket. "It was hard to tell when you were working them in the field."

The pair had arrived late to the gathering, returning from the adjudicator's office in lower Chrismferry, where they had gone to attend matters in regards to Liannora and her attack on Delia. They had been summoned to give testimony to what they had overheard in a hallway. Since the fall of the towers, Liannora had languished in a cell in Chrismferry, claiming her attack on Delia was all the doing of Sten, captain of the guard, insisting that in the tumult and chaos of the siege, he had misinterpreted a jest.

Unfortunately, Laurelle and Kytt could shed no more light on the foul act with certainty. They had never heard Liannora plainly order Sten to attack Delia. There were rumors she was to be set free.

But Lord Jessup had washed his hands of her. Though she might escape punishment, a god's judgment was of a higher order. She had already been banned from setting foot in Oldenbrook.

Which left Lord Jessup needing not one but *two* new Hands to fill his wing.

Brant adjusted his crimson sash, marking him a Hand of blood. But no longer for Lord Jessup. With the god's blessing, he now resided in the High Wing here, serving the regent while Delia attended her father in Five Forks. And there were rumors here, too, that she might not return at all.

"Look how they've grown!" Laurelle said. "Almost to my knee now."

The cubbies were indeed growing fast, three times their weight when Brant had found them.

"But they're still young," Dart said quietly. She bent a knee and muffed up the fur of one of the pups, the sister. The cubbie lolled on her back, tongue hanging loose, happy for the attention.

"And learning fast," Brant said. "Especially yours, Dart. She's a true little hunter."

Dart smiled up at him. He was happy to see it. Her rare smiles cheered him more deeply than he cared to admit. Since she had returned from the Eighth Land, a haunted look often shadowed her eyes. And he could not blame her. He still woke up sometimes covered with sweat, picturing moldering heads on stakes. But at least the *real* nightmare was over. Back in Saysh Mal, Harp was putting the forest in order, helped by a pair of acolytes that had descended from Takaminara. As the goddess had protected her daughter's people, she watched now over their land. They should fare well from here.

Dart straightened from her wiggling cubbie and nodded to the other, who sat straight-backed at Brant's side now.

"That boy of yours is no laggard either," Dart said. "He might let his sister run down a mouse, but it's his nose that always roots it out to begin with."

Her words lifted a proud grin to Brant's face. The whelpings had been left in his care, a burden shared with Dart. It allowed them both an excuse to escape their roles for a short time—he as a Hand of the regent, she as page to Warden Vail. Out in the fields, with the wolfkits, they could be themselves.

With everything packed up, Dart waved Laurelle on with the others. "Go on ahead. We'll catch up."

Laurelle searched between them, a ghost of a smile hovering, reading something more behind Dart's words. Laurelle had a disconcerting ability to do that, to understand what was unspoken better than any. Brant barely recognized her as the girl he'd known at school.

It seemed they were all learning fast, struggling to find where they fit in this new world.

"We'll meet you at the gates," Laurelle said. She turned, drawing Kytt along with her. If the tracker had had a tail to go along with his nose, it would have been wagging.

At least some things hadn't changed about Laurelle.

As they left, Dart lowered again to her little she-wolf. "We said that by the knighting we'd pick names for them. Have you decided on your boy?"

Brant crouched beside her in the shade, glad the others were gone. "I have."

He patted the lone blanket remaining. Dart sank to it. She seemed oddly nervous, shifting a bit too much, as if she were sitting on a root.

"What have you decided?" she asked.

The two cubbies had grown bored and taken to wrestling in the sun and trampled grass.

He nodded toward the brother. "I thought a good name would be Lorr. He was certainly wise to the wood." And he had spent his life to save theirs, so they could be sitting in the shade under blossoms with the sun shining.

She reached out and touched his knee. He glanced from the cubbies' play to her. Tears filled her eyes. "He would like that."

Brant's throat suddenly tightened. He stared at her too long, finally dropping his eyes. "What about your cubbie," he whispered. "The sister?"

"It's why I sent the others on ahead," she said softly. "I wasn't sure it was appropriate . . . not an insult . . ."

He glanced to her, sweeping back a fall of his hair, his brow crinkling.

She continued, not meeting his eye. "You mentioned what a good little hunter she was . . . what a good little *huntress*. I thought maybe . . ."

Brant knew immediately the name she picked.

"Miyana."

The god's final plea echoed in his head. *I want to go home.* Maybe in this small way, they could grant her that, a heart in which to live, to become a huntress of the forest once more.

Dart's eyes flicked to him, still moist with tears. "Is that all right?"

Brant leaned forward and brushed his lips against hers.

"More than all right," he whispered.

He stared into her eyes, their noses touching. She smiled softly, like the sun rising over Saysh Mal. It warmed completely through him.

"Thank you," he whispered again and kissed her, knowing that more than a god had found a new home this morning.

Two others had, too.

It had been a long day . . . and the night promised to stretch just as far.

Tylar stood on a small private balcony as the grand ball waged behind him, a war of pomp and finery, set to flute and drum. Dancing had already begun, and as the feast was in his honor, he would have to attend.

But first he needed a moment alone.

He stared beyond the rail of the balcony. It overlooked the Tigre River as it snaked to the east. The sun had nearly set behind the castillion, casting a great shadow across the dark green waters. A few stars shone to the east, along with the rise of a full moon.

Another Hunter's Moon.

He tried to read portent in it, but failed.

The day's knighting had left him with a heavy heart and an unsettled sense of doom. He could not shake it.

He ran a palm down the cloak that was clasped in gold at his shoulder, a new shadowcloak, and at his waist, a fine new blade. On his other hip, he carried Rivenscryr, sheathed. It did not bear its diamond as his new sword did. That was kept on a cord around Brant's neck, his new Hand of blood. Only a handful of people knew the significance of that drab, dull stone, and that was the way it would remain.

Until Tylar understood it better.

A hand drifted to the gold hilt.

A son had designed it, and a father had used it to sunder a world.

He pondered if the world might not be better if he tossed the blade into the river. Perhaps the stone, too. He wondered for the hundredth time why the stone had come again into the lives of gods and men. It had been dropped like a pebble in a still lake, and those ripples continued to spread. He feared he had not yet seen the full extent of that rippling.

He pictured again that dread island, shaped like a rocky crown.

As they had departed by flitterskiff, Takaminara had claimed the island, welling up a churn of fiery rock, no longer held off by poisonous flames. Molten fingers rose out of the boiling waters to grasp the island and drag it burning back into the waters. The fiery conflagration could be seen far across the flooded forest as they retreated. It spewed steam and great gouts of fire high into the sky as morning slowly dawned.

Finally, a creak of a door drew him around, away from that dark night.

A slender shape slid through, closing the door behind her. "I thought that was you slipping away."

"Delia?" A bit of the darkness around his heart lifted. He had known she had arrived, but commitments had pulled them both in different directions until now.

She stepped into the moonlight, dressed in a slim gown of the lightest green, a complement to her hazel eyes and dark hair. She smiled at him, shyly, as if this were the first time they met. She paused a few steps away, plainly fearful that she was intruding.

He motioned to the rail, but she remained where she was.

"Tylar . . ."

Frowning, he came forward, sensing some great consequence in her stance. "What is it?"

"I wanted a moment with you, but there's been such chaos this day. All the retinues, all the Hands from various lands."

"I know. I was hoping . . . once all the tumult died down. After the feast—"

She cut him off. "I'm leaving with the evening flippercraft."

He stared at her, stunned.

"My father," she said. "I don't like leaving him alone for too long—mostly to protect the servants from him." She offered a smile to blunt the sting of what she was saying.

"You're going so soon?"

"I must." She even backed a step to prove it.

He searched her face, her eyes, and discovered the deeper truth.

"At this moment of my life," she explained, "there's room for only one man in it. And that has to be my father. While in the past he might have shirked his responsibility to me, quite callously even, I won't do the same. I won't pay back bile with bile, or I'd be no better. He needs me. That is my place." She glanced up at him. "For now."

"Delia . . ."

She took a deep breath, and her voice somehow both softened yet held a harder edge. "I spent time with Kathryn. I've gotten to know her. Her heart and her will. She's borne much pain, now and in the past. I won't add to it."

"Delia, Kathryn and I, we've already—"

"No, you haven't, Tylar."

He wanted to protest, but she fixed him with those eyes, as hard as Argent's, as sharp as Kathryn's. He could not lie. Not to her. And in turn, he knew, perhaps it was time he stopped lying to himself.

She nodded, as if reading his thoughts. She stepped forward, kissed him on the cheek, then backed away. "I must hurry to meet my maid."

She turned, and in a shimmer of pale green she was gone.

But before the door closed, a hand shoved out and stopped it. "Now that wasn't pretty," Rogger said with a sad shake of his head as he entered. He smoked a pipe and was dressed in fine cuts, a gray cloak over black.

"Rogger, I don't—"

The thief held up a hand to silence him as he crossed the balcony, expounding his wisdom. "Young women . . . they're as fickle as they come. Pretty, I'll grant you. But I'll tell you, great-mothers and great-aunts—they have a head on their shoulders and know what to do with the rest of their bodies."

Tylar shook his head. "I see someone discovered Chrismferry's ale."

"And its cooking wine."

Tylar leaned on the balcony's rail. "I heard you met with the Black Flaggers this morning."

"Had to. Cook needed salt. A barter for the wine. And if you need salt, no better place than a pirate's ship to get it. Scrape it off their hulls."

Tylar looked at him in exasperation.

Rogger waved him off with his pipe. "I met with Krevan. That is a pirate in a sour mood. Even with that comely Calla doting on him because of his chopped arm."

"Any word on the Wyr?"

"Not a word. Like they packed everything and took off."

Tylar frowned. Here was a major source of his unease. When they had escaped back to land with the flitterskiff, they'd found the Wyr had folded up tents and vanished, leaving only Krevan and Calla. He wouldn't have been bothered by their sudden departure, except for what he had found on the island.

The six songstresses.

All identical.

Wyr-born.

Had Wyrd Bennifren left knowing what Tylar would find? Had he sold the songstresses to the Cabal? Had he fled to avoid any uncomfortable questions of collusion with the Cabal? Or were there deeper plots here?

He remembered the slain songstresses, throats cut by their own hands.

Only afterward did Tylar realize the absence of any Cabalists on the island. In fact, he had seen no real evidence of their direct involvement at all.

Only the hand of the Wyr.

But what did that portend?

Tylar's hand settled again to Rivenscryr. A cold chill crept through his bones. He wondered what hand had truly wielded this sword back on that island. And to what end it had been put. An act of mere mercy or something more dire?

Facing the Hunter's Moon, Tylar knew only one thing with certainty. In this war between Myrillian gods and naethryn, there were as many shades of gray as there were gods. And until this war was over, he would keep Rivenscryr at his side.

A knock on the balcony door announced yet another visitor.

"Regular crossroads here," Rogger mumbled.

The door opened to reveal a cloaked shadowknight. Kathryn dropped her masklin when she saw they were alone. Strands of music flowed in with her, a dance under way. "Tylar, I don't think you can hole up here much longer. Gerrod can dance with only so many Hands."

"Sounds like duty summons the weary," Rogger said and headed toward the door. "And women and wine summon the bearded."

The thief slipped past Kathryn and through the door, leaving a pall of pipe smoke behind.

Kathryn waved it from her face and stepped into the more open air of the balcony. "The feast won't be much longer."

Rogger left the door ajar when he departed.

Music flowed out to them. Kathryn joined him at the rail. Stars rose to fill the sky, reflected in the water below.

"I saw Delia heading down . . ." she began.

"She's leaving. With the evening flippercraft."

"Back to Argent?"

"Back home . . ." he said with a tired nod.

Kathryn remained silent, and they stood together at the rail. Once lovers. Now regent and warden.

"It's been a long day," he muttered.

She nodded as music flowed.

He held out a hand. "Care to dance?"

She frowned at the offered hand.

"We once knew how to dance," he said.

"That was another life."

"Still, sometimes a dance is just a dance. To prove that we still live."

He kept his hand out. She finally took it.

Stepping back, hand in hand, they spun across the balcony, two shadows in the moonlight, scribing a path for the stars to read.

That they still lived.

In Shadow . . .

THE WYR-LORD WAITED FOR THE SUN TO SLIP BENEATH THE sands of Dry Wash. Under a tent awning, Wyrd Bennifren lay nuzzled tight against the woman who carried him, his new milk mare, one hand clasped to her teat. He had already suckled his belly full, and now used the nipple to tug his watery eye up to the fold in his swaddling.

It wouldn't be long.

The screams had died a full bell ago.

From his perch, he saw that the *unkali ara* knelt in a circle around the center tent. As they had since midday. Heads bowed to the sand, waiting. They wore their traditional *haleesh* capes, brooched in silver and gold at the neck, one side knotted back to expose their family bone daggers, passed from father to son.

But all their sheaths were empty.

Each had buried his dagger to the hilt in the sand, gifting the blood to the desert. Not that the sands were thirsty, having been well slaked this past night.

Bennifren willed his milk mare to turn.

The bodies of the dead littered the sands, sprawled out in all directions, for a full league. Thousands. They were all that was left of the legion of a hinter-king who had crossed into Dry Wash, claiming dominion, as such men were wont.

Only this particular king wouldn't be wrong.

He would rule.

That is, if all went well in the center tent.

Finally, the flap lifted, and a woman stepped out, eyes

bandaged, shaven-headed, fingers stretched to an extra joint. A Wyr-witch. Few knew they existed. She bore a large tome in her hand. The *Nekralikos Arcanum*. One of the rarest texts, written on human skin and inked with alchemical bile.

The witch had overseen the long and torturous preparations within, following the rites that had been devised during the time of strife, between the Sundering and the settling, when much blood had been spilled, and all gods raved.

She had performed the *sukra lempta gall.*

The Rite of Infamy.

Even this rite had to be hidden in code within the *Nekralikos*.

Such was its great secret.

But the Wyr had always known it.

For they had devised it—they, the first to play the game of gods.

Over the past day, the hinter-king had been hollowed out—both flesh and that which lay beneath—leaving him an open vessel. Then they had baited the trap. Bennifren had hoped to use the Godslayer's seed, but other humours served just as well, especially blood.

And scent was scent.

All that remained was to discover if their prey had been woken enough, stirred enough. Their brethren had been slaughtered, twelve in all, screaming in agony. Surely those on high had stopped their ageless dreaming long enough to turn their faces down toward Myrillia. Surely they would send one of their own, drawn by the scent of the murderer.

Bennifren found it amusing that the Cabal sought to pit man against man or god against god. For the Wyr's goal, though, a larger game needed to be played, one with levels of intrigue that stretched across ages, on all sides of the field. It had required a manipulation of both shadowknight and Cabal, of ravening rogue and calculating god. Even the lives of many of the Wyr had been spent to hide the design, buried under bodies and blood, a carefully crafted game of lies and false trails—all for one reason.

To slay a god. And not just one god.

The Godslayer had proven his name so well.

A dozen rogues. A dozen deaths.

All to wake the sleepers above.

Surely those blessed with Bright Grace, undisturbed for so long, noted their brethren flickering out, torn from their midst, torn from the aether.

But had it been enough? Had they come? Had they accepted the Wyr's hollowed vessel?

The witch stepped away from the tent, holding back the flap.

A naked figure stumbled out, bronze-skinned, black-haired, and long of limb. The hinter-king. His torso had been split down the middle, from groin to collar, and burnt back together, sealing what had been captured within, a trap of flesh.

Bennifren urged his milk mare forward. He waited in the sun as the hinter-king stepped out of the shadows and into the light. The king's face lifted skyward, perhaps searching from whence he had come, perhaps merely enjoying the last rays of the sun on his face.

"Welcome to Myrillia," Bennifren said. "Do you know what you must do?"

Sky blue eyes lowered to him, shining with an azure Grace. The words issued from on high, dreadful with certainty.

"LET THEM ALL BURN . . ."

APPENDIX TO MYRILLIA

The Four Aspects of the Gods

1. Air
2. Fire
3. Water
4. Loam

The Nine Humoral Graces of the Gods

(PRIMARY QUADRICLES)

1. **BLOOD** of a god must anoint a path before the passing of Graces into a body can be fulfilled.
2. **MASCULINE SEED,** once blessed in blood, will pass the full aspect of a god's Grace to a person (until removed by a god of the same aspect).
3. **FEMININE MENSES** do the same as "seed."
4. **SWEAT** of a god lays the Grace upon *nonliving* objects until such a time the aspect is removed by a god.

(SECONDARY QUINTRANGLES)

5. **TEARS** of a god will heighten a Grace's aspect for short periods.
6. **SALIVA** will weaken the aspect.
7. **PHLEGM** will allow manifestations of the Grace beyond a body or object—useful in mixing alchemies.
8. **YELLOW BILE** (the waters passed by a god) will bless one with an aspect for a short period of time.
9. **BLACK BILE** (the solids passed by a god) will nullify a Grace.

JAMES CLEMENS

SHADOWFALL:

Book One of the Godslayer Chronicles

Four millennia have passed since the gods came to Myrillia, creating the nine lands of peace as a haven from the nightmarish, accursed Hinterlands. In all this time nothing has disturbed the harmony of the nine lands.

But now the goddess of the Summering Isles has been murdered. The only witness is Tylar de Noche, a crippled and disgraced former Shadowknight. As he holds the dying goddess, her last breath bestows a powerful blessing on him—a mark that heals his broken body. A mark that many see as proof that he killed a god. A mark that unleashes a powerful force of darkness within him.

Chased across Myrillia by enemies both human and ethereal, Tylar must uncover and face down a being powerful enough to kill an immortal—the true godslayer. For if he fails, all of Myrillia will fall into shadow.